GRAVESTONE ELITE

COMPLETE SERIES BOX SET

CAITLYN DARE

Copyright © 2021 by Caitlyn Dare

All rights reserved.

No part of this book may be reproduced in any form or by any electronic or mechanical means, including information storage and retrieval systems, without written permission from the author, except for the use of brief quotations in a book review.

Edited by Pinpoint Editing

Proofreading by Sisters Get Lit.erary

Cover by Sammi Bee Designs

SHATTERED LEGACY

GRAVESTONE ELITE BOOK ONE

PROLOGUE

Mia

"You're not ready?" My mother freezes in the doorway, her expression slipping. "But we leave in less than an hour."

"Do I have to go?" I protest. "The whole thing seems like such a waste of time when we all know he's going to be paired with Brook."

Not that I would ever want to hear my name called. But at least if there was even a shred of mystery around which girl was going to be chosen as Cade Kingsley's prosapia, it would give the evening some entertainment value.

"Mia, sweetheart," she comes up behind me and places her perfectly manicured hands on my shoulders, "the Eligere is a rite of passage, you know this."

My stomach twists. "But it's just so... so archaic. Dressing us up like virginal brides in front of all those people..."

No, thank you.

"Mia, this isn't a punishment, it's a gift." She lets out a soft sigh. "I know Cade showed preference to Brook during the courting phase, but it doesn't mean anything. Only Quinctus can decide the fate of an Electi."

God, she makes it all sound so normal, when living in a town like Gravestone is anything but.

As soon as you start high school, you hear the whispers about this place, the traditions... the strange rules. And if you're lucky enough—or unlucky enough, as the case may be—to descend from one of the founding families, you get to reign supreme over the rest of us lowly folk, forcing us to partake in these ridiculous rites of passage.

Please. What girl with even an ounce of self-respect and aspirations wants to end up tied to one of the Electi?

The Chosen.

The heirs of Quinctus.

If you ask me, it's just a smokescreen for some really messed up arranged marriage scandal.

A scandal I have no desire to be a party to.

I want to escape this town and its fucked-up traditions... but part of me can't deny I am slightly intrigued. Nobody gets to know what happens behind the doors of Gravestone Hall.

And tonight, I have an open invitation.

"Please, Mia, don't make this any more difficult than it needs to be. Your father—"

"Yes, mother," I snipe. "I'll be ready."

Because that's what you do in a place like Gravestone. You follow the rules, smile where necessary, and always respect your elders.

Of course, it isn't like that for every teenager in Gravestone. Some have the luxury of moving into the area and having zero ties with the founding families. Unlike me. Our name, Thompson, descends from the Cargill line. My great grams was a Cargill until she married a Thompson... and here I am, bound to this strange life, expected to fall in line just because of my name.

"The car leaves in,"—she checks her diamond-encrusted Rolex, an anniversary gift from my father—"forty minutes."

"I said I'll be ready." It's not like I'm trying to impress anyone. The dress code for the Eligere is written in lore. All girls of age from the founding bloodlines—or verus line, as we call it—must enter the choosing at least once.

Although they are rarely picked.

My mother leaves me alone, and I begin to dress. The white gown flows over my slender form like a waterfall. I take my time braiding my dark blonde hair into a crown across my head and then pin the remaining curls into place with golden tipped pins. Adding a dusting of blush to my cheeks, I smear a lick of kohl liner under my eyes. The girl staring back at me in the mirror looks meek and innocent. A girl on the cusp of becoming a young woman.

In mere weeks, I will start college. But tonight, I will stand in front of Cade Kingsley as a prosapia.

A trickle of trepidation races down my spine. Everybody knows Cade and the Electi, even those who don't understand what it all means. He'll be a senior at Gravestone University in the fall, but I can still remember Cade as a senior in high school. I was in ninth grade, and he was everything I wasn't. Popular. Confident. Gorgeous.

Cade Kingsley, heir to the Kingsley line and notorious playboy, is finally going to discover the identity of his future wife.

And I am one of the offerings.

GRAVESTONE HALL IS the imposing gothic building that sits at the end of Prosperous Street. The entire town has been built leading toward it, making it the beacon landmark. The huge limestone bricks give it an eerie quality as shadows dance over the frontage.

"Ready?" my father asks me, squeezing my hand.

I give him a polite nod, unable to speak over the nervous energy pinging in my stomach. It's silly, really. We all know the outcome of tonight's Eligere.

The car pulls forward outside the steps leading up to the entrance, and the door opens. "Mr. and Mrs. Thompson, welcome," a young man says, reaching in to offer my mother his hand.

She climbs out elegantly, her silk gown swishing around her body. Temperance Thompson is always the picture of refinement. She thinks a woman's worth amounts to the designers she wears. It's something I didn't inherit. I did, however, inherit her hazel eyes and soft, dark blonde curls. Usually I wear them down, hanging like a cape over my shoulders.

Tonight, however, they are intricately arranged on my head, leaving my shoulders and neck bare.

Tonight, I have no armor.

My lips curve grimly at the thought. I'm safe here. Cade didn't even attempt to court me. I know of at least four girls he took out on a date. Maisie Godiva told her friends at school that she gave him head in the cemetery. But I'm hardly surprised. Maisie gives out blowjobs like Santa gives out presents.

At first, I was relieved he didn't come for me. I have never had any interest in entering *their* world. But I'd be lying if I said it didn't sting a little. I know I'm a wallflower compared to most girls in this year's choosing. I'm pretty but not beautiful, slender but without those voluptuous curves guys seem to love so much, and I prefer lounge pants and leggings to dresses and stockings.

I have no desire to be judged on what's outside. A person can be beautiful to the eye but rotten to the core.

And a place like Gravestone… well, it's full of bad apples.

My father slides gracefully from the car and waits for me. I gather the dress in my hands and climb out, thanking the young man. His eyes skate down my body, lingering on my chest and the soft curve of my breasts. Heat rises inside me. I've never had a man look at me so brazenly before. It's both thrilling and terrifying.

Lowering my eyes, I push a loose curl from my face and offer him a small smile.

"Miss Thompson," he stutters over my name, "you look beautiful."

"Mia," my father barks, his expression displeased when I meet his eyes.

As we head inside, I feel the guy's hungry gaze follow me. Does he know why I'm here? Does he know what happens after the formal dinner ends?

The founding families—or Quinctus, as we call them—aren't stupid. They know how to cover their tracks and dress up their stupid traditions as celebrations and invite-only dinners.

Tonight is no different.

"He's watching her," I hear my father grumble.

"Relax, Garth. She looks beautiful. He'd be a fool not to look." My mother casts me a reassuring smile, but I avert my eyes.

When they talk like this, it makes me feel like I'm nothing more than a possession. A thing. It makes me feel like my life isn't my own.

I hate it.

I hate that I'm bound to these silly traditions. Suddenly, I want to run. I want to slip off my brand-new kitten heels and flee. But the minute we enter the Hall, all the fight leaves me.

"Wow," I breathe, taking in the vaulted ceiling and stained windows.

"I can still remember the first time I stepped foot in here." My mother joins me. "It's beautiful, isn't it?"

I nod, too awed to reply. Other families mingle. I spot a couple of girls from my school and we share an awkward wave. My father greets their parents, working the room like he was born to do it.

He wasn't.

It's my mother's bloodline that gives us the right to be here.

Right.

I swallow a derisive groan.

It isn't a right, it's an order.

"Come, Mia. Let's find our seats."

Of course, there's a three-course dinner to get through before the Eligere starts. I think it's just some kind of mental torture for the prosapia, but whatever.

The ballroom is a huge, elaborate room that has been dressed in white and gold. Flowers adorn the tables and huge floor-standing candelabras line the room. I pick out the other prosapia, six in total. Only Brook is missing. But she'll want to make a fashionably late entrance, no doubt. She was in my class, so we're the same age, but she's always acted superior. Probably because she's Phillip Cargill's stepdaughter. He's the town mayor *and* a Quinctus elder, one of the most powerful men in Gravestone. Brook was always full of herself, but the second her mom shacked up with Phillip, she became insufferable.

She honestly believes it's her right to be paired with Cade.

Good luck to her. Cade isn't exactly nice. Sure, he has those chiseled good looks and an arrogant charm, but there's something about him. Something dark lingering under the surface.

Something I want no part of.

As if I've summoned him from my mind, the room grows quiet and Cade and his posse make their grand entrance. Everyone—the other prosapia, the parents, even the servers handing out flutes of champagne—stops to watch them. The next generation. The Quinctus heirs... the Electi.

Cade Kingsley, Tim Davenport, Ashton Moore, Channing Rexford, and Brandon Cargill.

They move like a well-oiled machine, Cade slightly in front with Tim and Ashton flanking his sides, and Channing and Brandon coming up behind. They look ravishing in their matching black suits, although they all wear them in their own style. Channing has his collar unbuttoned, no tie. Tim looks the most clean-cut of the five, shirt tucked in and cuffs visible. Brandon's suit looks a little wrinkled, like he just rolled out of bed, or someone has been grabbing at the material. It wouldn't surprise me; rumor has it he's the biggest player of them all. It's easy to see why, though, with his easy smirk, bright blue eyes, and hair as dark as the night. Ashton has left his jacket off, draping it over his shoulder like he's in a photo shoot. And Cade... Cade looks positively breathtaking. His eyes catch mine, only for a second, and a shiver rolls down my spine. He knows who I am, but he doesn't *know* me.

Because he didn't give you a chance. I silence the little voice. I never wanted to be picked, I never wanted any of this... but I am only human, after all. An eighteen-year-old girl with dreams and desires. I press my thighs together. It's hard not to look at the Electi and imagine things... dark, sinful things.

But then a gong rings out and the spell is broken.

They are the Electi. The chosen. The future of Gravestone.

And me?

I'm no one.

DINNER IS A TOTAL BORE. I don't know what I expected, but it wasn't two hours of listening to various prominent residents of Gravestone giving speeches about the town's prosperity and bright future.

By the time Phillip Cargill steps onto the stage, I'm half asleep.

"Good evening friends." His voice echoes through the room. "Now that the formalities are out of the way, we can move onto more important things. Those of you here tonight understand the history of our great town, the importance of our heritage. Tonight, we will uphold one of our most sacred traditions: the Eligere." He takes a sip of his drink. "I now ask the prosapia and their fathers to join me in the Sanctuary for the ceremony."

My stomach flutters as my mother squeezes my hand. "Good luck, sweetheart. Remember, if you are not chosen, it doesn't reflect on you."

I barely refrain from rolling my eyes.

"Mia," my father says gruffly as he stands. I gather myself and accept his offer of help. The two flutes of champagne I drank with dinner rush to my head as the room grows small around me.

Everyone is watching, waiting with bated breath to know who Cade will emerge from the sanctuary bound to.

Of course, to anyone outside of tonight's ceremony, the engagement announcement that will follow the Eligere will be nothing out of the ordinary. Kids grow up, they attend college, date, and fall in love.

Only those with verus blood know the truth.

Everything is hazy as my father leads me out of the ballroom and down a simple stone hall. Maisie Godiva and her father are ahead of me. Her dress is slightly less demure than mine, cut low in the back and hemmed with pearls. It doesn't surprise me. Her mother is a bit of a show-off. Brook leads our quiet caravan. When she finally arrived, everyone had stopped to admire her dress. The prosapia are supposed to present themselves in a simple white gown, something pure and innocent to honor the union oath. But in true Brook fashion, her gown was something akin to a wedding dress, layered with lace and fine gold embroidery.

She is most definitely the sun, outshining the rest of us.

Eventually, we reach the Sanctuary, a place few people in Gravestone ever have the opportunity to visit.

"Ready?" my father asks me as we step inside.

"I guess," I murmur, wondering if anyone can ever be truly ready for something like this.

Candles flicker wildly in the cavernous room, bouncing shadows around the smooth limestone walls. It's simple in its decoration, nothing at all like the grand ballroom. But it only adds to the mystery and intrigue.

"Welcome to the Eligere." Phillip has slipped on a black robe that hangs to the floor. "Gentlemen, please present your daughters before the Electi."

I spot them then: Cade and his three sidekicks all standing poised and ready. Ashton isn't present because he isn't a true Electi. Of the four heirs, Tim is the only one already engaged. He and his fiancée, Fawn, were paired when he was just a freshman. But Channing and Brandon will both have to be paired eventually.

My father walks me to the line and kisses me on the cheek. "Whatever happens here tonight, I want you to know I love you, Mia."

My brows pinch, and I want to ask what he means, but he melts into the shadows.

"This is crazy," the girl beside me breathes. I've seen her around town, but she's older than me.

Phillip begins speaking again, regaling us with the history of the Eligere, the importance of unifying families and continuing to strengthen Gravestone's influence. But his voice becomes white noise to the blood roaring in my ears.

It's silly, we all know whose name is going to be pulled from the calix.

Cade and Brook are written in the stars.

"Maddoc." Phillip calls forward another robed man. I vaguely recognize him but can't place where from. My heart is pounding wildly in my chest, and the air in the Sanctuary is thick with anticipation. I can practically feel the other prosapia hold their breath as Phillip dips his hand inside the calix.

"Are you ready to meet your prosapia, Cade?"

Cade steps forward, nodding. "I am."

He's as cool as a cucumber, smug even, as if he's enjoying having eight girls lined up for his entertainment.

Asshole.

My teeth grind together behind pursed lips as I try to focus on something, *anything*, that will help distract me from the fact that this is fucking crazy.

Phillip pulls out the small slip of paper and unfolds it, keeping his eyes on the prosapia. "Tonight, one of you will be chosen. It is a great honor, a great privilege, to be bound to an Electi." His eyes flick to the note, a deep frown marring his forehead. The blood drains from his face as he looks back to us. "I-I don't understand—"

"Spit it out, old man," Cade jokes, "we have a party to get to."

Oh goodie, the after-party. I can hardly wait for that.

"Ah yes, of course." Phillip clears his throat. "Cade Kingsley, on behalf of Quinctus, please step forward and accept Miss Mia Thompson as your prosapia."

I blink, certain I must have misheard him.

"Thompson?" Cade balks at the same time as Brook shrieks, "What the fuck?"

"Mia." The girl next to me jabs my ribs. "It's you," she whispers. "You need to go up there."

"W-what?" I croak, unable to process what's happening.

But then Phillip steps forward, commanding silence. "The calix has spoken," he says more firmly this time, as if there's no confusion, no mistake. "Mia Thompson is Cade's prosapia."

Oh, fuck.

1

BEXLEY

"Come on, it's a party," Alex whines. "Our first college party."

"I'm not interested," I mutter, resting back on my bed and staring at the ceiling in the hope he gets the idea and fucks off to the party without me.

"But it's a Cade Kingsley party."

"And that's meant to persuade me? He's a prick," I say with complete honesty.

Alex and I started classes at Gravestone University on Monday, and I can't help feeling like I've pissed Kingsley off, because every time I'm anywhere near him or his little crew they throw me some serious shade.

I've never even spoken to the guy, so fuck knows what his issue is. All I do know is that he won't want me there.

"Granted, but his parties are legendary. At least, so I've heard."

"Still not making it sound appealing. I've got weed, and I've got vodka. I'm all set for the night."

"You're a boring motherfucker, you know that, right?"

I cringe at his words. I never used to hide like this. I used to be the life and soul of any party. But that was then. This is now, and things are different.

"I don't care. I just want to go to college and then get out of this weird-ass town. I don't even know why I'm here." Of all the places my parents could have sent me after... after I fucked up and shamed them in our old town, they had to send me here. I know they wanted me out of the way, but it's just bizarre here.

"You owe me one," he smirks, "in case you've forgotten."

"How'd you figure?" I ask the one and only person I've connected with since I was sent to Gravestone nine months ago.

Despite my desire to keep my head down and just get through each day, Alex, the persistent fuck, won't leave me alone. He seems to think we're friends. I just wonder what's wrong with everyone else in this godforsaken town for him to want to hang out with me.

"I went to Sterling Bay with you for that wedding."

"Yeah, although I don't remember asking you to go." Although having Alex with me to face the mistakes of my past wasn't exactly a bad thing. Not that I'll ever tell him.

"Maybe not, but I did anyway."

"Jesus," I moan, scrubbing my hand down my face and across my rough jaw. "You're not going to let this go, are you?"

"Not a chance, my friend. Not a chance."

I push from the headboard and scoot across the bed. "It had better be a really fucking good party."

"It will be. I've got no doubt."

I pull my shirt over my head and drop it into the laundry basket before dragging on a clean, black v-neck t-shirt and shoving my feet into my sneakers.

"If it's lame, I'm leaving," I warn Alex as I follow him out of my dorm room and toward the parking lot.

We walk past my BMW, and I come to a stop at the passenger side of his gunmetal grey Porsche. The second the lock beeps, I pull the door open and drop down, the new car smell assaulting my senses almost immediately.

"Where is it, anyway?" I ask as he backs out of his space and shoots down the road, leading us away from Gravestone U's campus.

"Just you wait and see."

I sit in silence as Imagine Dragons blasts through his speakers, thankfully stopping us from having a conversation. The sun is beginning to set behind the trees, casting everything in an eerie orange hue. It's about right for this town.

I always thought my hometown, Sterling Bay, was an odd place with all the money and privilege. I didn't appreciate just how normal it actually was until I was shipped here to live with my estranged uncle.

From the second I stepped foot in Gravestone, it was obvious I wasn't welcome. It almost felt like everyone already knew who I was, despite the fact that I'd never met any of them before in my life—including my uncle, Marcus.

The whole thing was crazy, but I know I only have myself to blame.

Senior year, my life was spiraling and I lost control. I thought I had it all. I thought I was untouchable. Sadly, I learned the hard way just how much of a lie that was.

With one bad decision, I lost everything.

I let out a sigh which Alex hears over Yungblud playing through the sound system, and he turns it down.

"You wanna talk about it?"

"When have I ever wanted to talk about it?"

I've been in Gravestone almost a year, and not once have I said a word about how I found myself here. I have no idea what Alex thinks about the whole thing. He knows where I came from, but that's about it. He must know I did something bad, seeing as my whole reason for attending James Jagger's wedding with Uncle Marcus a few months ago was so I could apologize to Remi Tanner, my childhood best friend.

My heart twists as I think about her. When we were kids, Remi was my everything. My best friend, the girl I thought I was destined to spend the rest of my life with. Our fathers had the money and the power, and we'd have made the perfect couple as we took the reins from our parents and their places in Sterling Bay. But much like everything else in my life, I took her for granted and fucked it all up.

I'd never met anyone else like her. Anyone who's been able to see past the mask I pull on and accept me for who I really am.

But just like my parents, I pushed her too hard as well.

I don't blame her. How I treated Remi after her life imploded was unforgivable. But this time away has taught me a lot of things. It's allowed me to see all of my mistakes, and I knew as soon as I overheard Uncle Marcus talking about James' wedding that I needed to be there to at least try to put things right.

I guess I should have been prepared for her to turn her back on me and refuse to hear anything I had to say. It's the least I deserved.

It still fucking stung, though.

My nails dig into the denim covering my thighs as my mouth waters for some alcohol, or something stronger. I shake my head. I promised myself I was done with all that shit. Vowed I was going to put the drugs, the excessive drinking, and the need to lose myself in anything or anyone I could get my hands on, behind me.

I've been offered the chance at a new life here, I need to grab onto it with both hands, not completely fuck it up like my old life. But I'm not going to lie, it isn't easy. This town freaks me the fuck out.

"What the hell is this place?" I ask as Alex pulls up to a set of massive black wrought iron gates lined with gold spears.

"This..." he says, gesturing to the vast space before us as the gates begin to open. There's a wide road disappearing over a hill in the distance, with nothing to see but trees and the ominous shadows they create with the low sun burning through them. "This is Cade Kingsley's domain."

"His parents' place?" I ask as he slowly moves forward.

"One of them, but his parents don't live here. He and the rest of the Electi do."

The Electi?

I roll my eyes. Because of course Kingsley and his merry band of fucking idiots need a weird nickname to exert their power over everyone.

"Why am I not surprised," I groan. The King of Gravestone couldn't live on campus or in a normal kind of house. "What's the deal with them, anyway? It's like they own the place," I mutter, although I'm not sure if it's to Alex or just myself.

Sure, I've heard all the rumors about this town. Apparently, there are some weird rules and rituals some of the families live by, but mostly, I think it's all bullshit. This is the twenty-first century; no one lives like that anymore. It's just school gossip, kids trying to make their lives sound more exciting than they really are.

Yes, Cade Kingsley's family and a handful of others are insanely wealthy, but part of some weird cult?

Unlikely.

The car continues forward for a few minutes. I stare out the windshield, squinting, trying to see a building, anything other than darkness.

"Are you sure this is a good idea?" I ask, my eyes locking on billowing smoke rising through the trees on the horizon.

"Yes, it's time to embark on college life, Bex. Stop being a fucking pussy."

"I'm not, I'm—"

He glances over at me, his hazel eyes narrowing on me. "Being a pussy? Everyone who is anyone is going to be here tonight. Cade probably won't even know you're here."

"I'm not scared of Cade fucking Kingsley," I mutter.

"I never said you were."

"I'd just rather stay off his radar." My shoulders lift in a dismissive shrug, and Alex chuckles.

"From the way he's been looking at you this week, I'd say you're already firmly on it."

Yeah, I was worried you might say that.

I stretch my legs out and rub my hands on my thighs, the only thing I can do to expel the pent-up energy within me and the cravings I have to grab something to make my anxiety abate.

Alex pulls off to the left and we find ourselves in what looks like a car showroom for the rich and famous.

The parking lot at Sterling Prep used to be impressive, but it's nothing compared to the rides most of the kids from Gravestone U have. It's ridiculous and just proves that many of the families in this town have more money than sense.

There are a few kids loitering around, giving us a clue—along with the smoke—as to where the party is.

"Come on, then. I need a drink, and maybe a girl or two." Alex winks at me and takes off down a track between the trees.

I jog to catch up with him, the scent of the bonfire burning in the distance filling my nose.

After a couple of minutes, the trees part and a vast clearing emerges. There are kids everywhere, some sitting on fallen trees, others surrounding trucks that have somehow made it this far into the undergrowth, and in the distance is a vast lake, its waters inky black with the twinkling stars above reflecting in the stillness.

"Here." When I look back to Alex, I find him holding a bottle of beer out for me. "Christan and Troy are over there," he says, nodding to a couple of the guys he introduced me to when I first started at Gravestone High. Much like Alex, I've kept them at arm's length, but unlike him, they've allowed me to do it.

Troy doesn't notice our arrival—he's too busy with Maisie Godiva. He's got her thigh around his waist as he grinds into her, pressing her against the tree at her back. I watch them for a little longer than I probably should as his tongue pushes into her mouth and his hand disappears under her shirt.

"Ignore him, he thinks he's God's gift to women. Ain't that right, Troy?" Christan shouts, but the only response he gets is Troy flipping him the bird over his shoulder.

The song on the huge speakers someone has set up changes to The Weeknd, and I tip the bottle to my lips, looking out around at everyone, most of whom I don't recognize. I have no idea if they're all Gravestone students, but knowing Cade and his boys, I can't imagine they allow anyone here they don't want. Not that I can see them or their little posse who follows them around like lost sheep.

I think back to my life in Sterling Prep. Captain of the football team and their star quarterback, I had one of the best throwing arms in the state. But I was no better than Cade Kingsley. I thought I was a god, that I ruled the school and everyone in it.

How little did I know.

One mistake, and I was thrown away like nothing more than a piece of trash.

As the minutes tick by, more drinks emerge, and eventually, I start to feel a bit of a buzz in my veins as I sit with Alex, Christan, Troy—who's now unattached himself from Maisie— and a few other people I've been introduced to but can't recall their names.

"I'm so fucking ready for four years of this," Troy announces, bringing his lighter up to the blunt hanging from his lips. "Booze, weed, and pussy, wet and ready for the taking."

Alex shakes his head at him.

"Told you," Christian says. "Fucking dog."

With my own blunt between my thumb and forefinger, I push from the hard ground we're sitting on and gesture toward the trees. "Going for a piss."

I stumble over some roots as I melt into the darkness, walking for longer than necessary. But the promise of a few minutes of peace is too much to deny. I want to party. I want to enjoy myself, but I'm not sure the majority of the people who are here are the people I want to do it with.

They all want to be *them*. They want the chance to be invited into Kingsley's inner circle, whereas I'm more than happy staying in the shadows and doing what I need to do until I can finally make my own decisions and embark on my own life, as far away from Sterling Bay and Gravestone as I can get.

When I'm finally alone, I take a piss against a tree before taking another hit and continuing forward when something catches my eye. Walking out from the shadows, I find I'm at the other side of the lake. I must have walked farther than I expected.

Movement at the water's edge startles me. Looking up, my breath catches when I find a girl sitting with water lapping at her feet. "Shit, I'm sorry. I was just..." I trail off, instantly forgetting my words when she turns her huge, dark eyes to me.

"It's okay," she says softly. So softly, in fact, I have to get closer just to hear her properly over the rustling of the trees behind us. "I just needed—"

"Some peace."

"Yeah. It can get a bit overwhelming. You want to..." she gestures to the ground beside her, and before I know what I'm doing, I lower myself down.

"You're in my economics class, right?" I ask her, recognizing her as the quiet girl who tries to hide at the back.

"Uh... yeah."

"Why do you sound so shocked that I would have noticed you?" The words spill out.

"Habit, I guess. I often get overlooked."

"I really doubt that..." I don't only recognize her from class, I recognize her from high school.

"Mia." She smiles, and I swear it's like being hit with lightning. "Mia Thompson."

I want to say I remember her name, but I don't. But I didn't exactly embrace senior year at a new school.

"Well, Mia. Mia Thompson." A smirk plays on my lips. "I'm Bexley. Bexley Danforth."

I hold my hand out to her, and I feel like an idiot for the move—that is, until she throws her head back and laughs. Then, everything I've been holding inside me for months—hell, for years—seems to settle. If only for a few seconds.

2
MIA

He has nice eyes.
    That's the first thing I notice about the guy who sits beside me at the edge of the lake. I vaguely recognize him from the couple of classes we've shared. Not that I've really been checked into life since the semester started.

I came to Gravestone U thinking it would be my ticket to freedom, to break free from this town. But my life is no longer my own.

I'm Cade Kingsley's prosapia.

I belong to him now, and come Monday, he and the Electi will start to sow the seeds that will mark the end of my freedom.

If I survive until then.

Brook Moore has already made it more than obvious I'm the enemy. Like everyone else at the Eligere two weeks ago, she is sworn to silence. No one talks of what happens at the ceremony outside of the verus bloodline. But it hasn't stopped her letting me know how much she hates me.

It's one of the reasons I fled to the lake. At least down here I'm not forced to endure her death stares or cruel barbs.

I snatch up the bottle of vodka I swiped off the counter before I left Cade's house and take a long pull.

"Whoa there," Bexley says. "Things must be bad if you're necking neat vodka."

"It was the first thing I grabbed."

It burns, but I swallow the urge to shudder.

"Want to talk about it?"

"I..." I let out a resigned sigh. "I really hate this place."

"Kingsley's house? Seems pretty sweet to me." He glances around.

"Not the house... Gravestone."

"Want to know a secret?" He nudges my shoulder. "I'm not a big fan either."

"You moved here last year?" I can remember him starting Gravestone High last winter. We were in the same class, but he kept himself to himself, and I didn't exactly put myself out there. "God, I miss high school," I blurt out.

"You do? Because it kind of sucked ass for me."

My eyes slide to Bexley's, and his crinkle with amusement. "At least in high school all this is a distant dream."

"All this?"

"Yeah... the big life decisions, responsibilities, the pressure... If I'd known what I know now..." I exhale a steady breath. "I would have done a lot of things differently."

"Oh yeah?" He plays along, but I can tell from his cloudy eyes that he doesn't really understand.

There's a big commotion from somewhere behind us, and I freeze.

"You okay?"

"I just don't want anyone to come down here." Especially not Cade.

He's given me my space until now, but I know come Monday that will all change.

Dread fills my chest, and I take another large gulp of vodka. "You want?" I thrust the bottle at Bexley.

It's a bad idea, sitting out here, getting drunk at the water's edge, but there's something thrilling about it too. Like I'm breaking all the rules as a giant F-you to Quinctus and their stupid traditions.

If only Mom could see me now.

The thought makes me smile.

Bexley notices, frowning. "What?"

"Just thinking... my mom would really hate the idea of me being out here alone."

"I've got to admit, you're making me a little nervous, so close to the water's edge."

"I'm fine."

"You're swaying," he points out.

I want to argue, but he's right. My body sways gently side to side as my feet swirl in the tepid water.

The noise from the party cuts through the silence again, and this time, a group of figures emerge along the water's edge.

"Crap," I murmur, not wanting to be discovered.

"It's okay," Bexley says, twisting slightly to shield me. "I don't think they can see us."

He's right. We're sheltered by some cypress trees, but it doesn't stop my heart lurching into my throat.

"Is that Kingsley?"

I don't miss the disapproval in Bexley's voice, and for some strange reason, it warms my insides knowing he isn't one of Cade's adoring fans.

"P-please, man, it was a joke, I was joking." A guy I don't recognize holds up his hands as Cade and his crew advance on him.

"Tsk, tsk, Males, you really should know better than to lie."

"I'm not, I didn't—"

Cade shoves the guy hard and he stumbles, losing his footing. Landing with a thud, he stares up at Cade. "Please, man. I'll apologize, I'll—"

"You should have thought about that before you bitched out me and my guys at my own fucking party." Cade leans down and fists the guy's Henley. "Kiss my shoes."

"What an asshole," Bexley breathes. My hand shoots out and clamps over his mouth. Cade can't know I'm down here. If he does... I don't want to think about what might happen.

"Shh," I whisper, meeting Bexley's confused stare.

"W-what, man? Come on, Cade, don't be—"

"Kiss my fucking shoes." Cade shoves the guy back and he slips, steadying himself in the muddy sand.

"He said kiss them, asshole," Ashton Moore barks.

"Come on, guys. I'm not gonna kiss his shoes."

"Fine. Guys," Cade says, and his crew swarm like bees over the defenseless guy.

"Shit, maybe we should do something," Bexley mumbles against my palm, his stubble tickling my skin.

"No, we can't," I say, hating that it has to be this way. But it's either the guy or me. And I'm not ready to be the object of Cade Kingsley's perversities just yet.

"Help, somebody help!" The guy's cries of desperation evaporate on the balmy air as they strip his clothes from his body, leaving him completely naked.

"This is bull—" Bexley tries to move away from me just as Cade kicks the guy into the water.

"Oh God," I whimper as their dark laughter drifts over to us.

"Swim, fishy, swim," Ashton calls.

"I think we'll take these." Cade bundles the clothes into his arms. "Just for safekeeping. Next time you run your mouth off about me, you won't come out of things so... intact."

A shiver runs down my spine at the threat in his words. Bexley lets out a muted grunt of disapproval beside me, but I still have my hand plastered against his mouth. As Cade and his crew slip back into the shadows, I finally pry my fingers away.

"What the fuck was that?"

"Cade's a jerk," I say.

Understatement of the century.

"I'm going to help him. Stay here." Bexley ducks out of the shadows and moves along the water's edge to offer a helping hand to the butt-naked guy as he clambers out of the water.

"What the fuck?" he growls at Bexley.

"Relax, man, I only came over here to try and help."

"Help? I don't need your help. I don't need anyone's help." He cups his junk and shoulders past Bexley, slipping into the tree line.

"That went well," I say as Bexley returns.

"I was only trying to help."

"He's embarrassed."

"If you ask me, the asshole deserved it." I bristle, and Bexley's eyes shutter. "I did not mean... fuck, that came out wrong. Obviously, I don't think he deserved it."

"I know what you mean. But Cade and his guys are... a lot."

"Yeah, what's with that?" He sits back down beside me.

"You know how every school has one group of guys who run the place? The popular kids with all the social power?"

A strange expression washes over Bexley as he nods, and I wonder what secrets he's keeping. "Yeah, I know."

"Well, Cade and his crew are like that but on steroids. Gravestone U is their territory. Has been for the last three years, since Cade was a freshman."

"You seem to know a lot about them."

My shoulders lift in a small shrug. "Everyone does."

But Bexley isn't from Gravestone. He doesn't understand what it's like.

I envy him.

"Are you going to head back to the party?" he asks me.

"Not until I have to. But you should go, I'm sure you have friends waiting on you."

"Nah, Alex will deal."

"Alex Shaw, right?" I've seen the two of them together, at classes this week and before that, at high school.

"Yeah, why?"

"No reason." I shrug again before uncapping the vodka and taking a large swallow. Everything is beginning to relax as the liquor seeps into my bloodstream, but I like the sensation. It's better than the gnawing pit of hopelessness I've felt ever since the Eligere.

That night, the night I stood beside the other prosapia and heard my name called, was a total mess.

My father was almost as dumbfounded as me. Brook looked ready to claw my eyes out. Phillip Cargill was utterly confused and slightly irritated, and I was in denial.

I still am.

Brook petitioned her stepfather, of course. My father demanded answers. And Cade seemed completely indifferent as chaos unfolded around us.

The only saving grace of that night is the fact that they couldn't decide how to proceed, so I have been afforded some time before being thrust into the Electi's world.

That time came to an end three days ago when my father got the call from Phillip Cargill that the decision was being upheld.

I am to one day become Cade's wife.

The vodka in my stomach sloshes from side to side as I let out a heavy sigh.

"Here, I'd better drink some of that before you pass out." Bexley snags the bottle from my fingers, a bolt of electricity shooting through me. We both stare at his hand, and slowly he pulls away, letting the back of his knuckles brush my arm. A shiver runs through me, but this time it isn't one full of trepidation. It feels... nice.

He uncaps the vodka and takes a long pull. I watch his throat bob as he swallows. Bexley might not be born and raised in Gravestone, but he fits right in, from his chiseled good looks and rich boy style. The Fendi polo shirt that molds to his thick biceps and broad shoulders. His eyes are a rich blue, and his dirty blond hair is styled in that casual way, as if he just rolled out of bed.

Bexley Danforth is gorgeous, and he's staring at me with hunger in his eyes.

"What?" I croak, a little light-headed. Only, I don't know if it's from all the vodka or how his intense gaze pierces me.

"I'm still trying to figure out what a girl like you is doing out here all alone."

"I... I like my own company."

"Yeah, I know that feeling," he mutters, running a hand down his face. "But we're freshmen now. Gotta make the most of college, right?"

"I guess. Where's home?" I ask.

"I hail from a place called Sterling Bay, but it hasn't been home in a while."

"Sterling Bay? I think I've heard my father talk about it. Is it nice?"

"It's not like Gravestone, that's for sure."

"Yeah, nowhere is."

Silence settles over us. Bexley seems lost to his own thoughts as he stares out at the lake. The party rages on behind us, but I have no desire to go back there. Brook will be all over Cade, begging him to fix things. Knowing him, he'll probably take her to his room and fuck her, just because he can.

God, I have so many regrets. Regrets about high school, about always being the wallflower. I'm pretty, sure, but I'm not one of those girls who turns heads wherever she goes. I didn't spend senior year embracing life and chasing after what I wanted.

And now look at me.

I'm Cade's Kingsley's virginal wife-to-be. And I can't tell a soul the truth.

Not that I have anyone to tell.

There's Annabel, but she isn't exactly a locked box. She enjoys gossip too much, so I've learned to keep my secrets from her, which kind of sucks considering she's my best friend.

"Sometimes I wish I could just leave this place," I blurt out.

"Where would you go?"

"Anywhere far, far away from here." Somewhere where I could meet a guy and fall in love. He'd treat me right and buy me flowers and chocolate and make love to me under the stars.

God, I hate this.

Tears prick the corners of my eyes, but I swallow them down. I never asked for this. I never asked to be a prosapia in that stupid ceremony.

"Hey, you okay?" Bexley touches my arms again and I feel it, I feel the connection flowing between us.

He's nice.

Warm.

He won't hurt me.

My eyes lift to his and he smiles. God, he's beautiful, and the way he looks at me with such concern, such softness, it's as if I'm the most beautiful girl he's ever seen.

It ignites a fire in my belly.

This... this is what it's supposed to feel like. Desire pulses through me as I get lost in his blue eyes.

"Make it all go away," I whisper as I lean in, erasing the distance between us.

One of his hands goes to my cheek, guiding my face to his until our lips are touching.

Heat explodes inside me as he kisses me, tentative at first but then harder, slipping his tongue past my lips and curling it around my own.

It feels amazing, like any first kiss should.

"Fuck, you taste good," he rasps against my lips before diving back in. Bexley lowers me to the ground and hovers over me, stroking his thumb along my jaw.

"Is this okay?" he asks, and I nod.

I want this.

I want to give him this so Cade can never take it from me.

Silent tears trickle down my cheeks, but I don't stop kissing him, instead pulling him closer. My body is a tight ball of nerves as I consider what this means.

Cade will expect me to be a virgin.

Fuck him.

Fuck Quinctus.

Fuck them all.

I refuse to just bow to their stupid, *stupid* rules and traditions.

"I want you," I whisper against Bexley's mouth, rubbing my body against his, desperate to feel him.

He eases back to stare at me. "We should slow down. You've been drinking, and I don't want to take advantage."

"You're not," I almost cry. "I want this, Bexley. Please, I want you."

3

BEXLEY

Mia's words are exactly what I need to hear, and I claim her mouth once again as she claws at me through my shirt.

Her addictive taste fills my mouth as I kiss her with everything I have. I haven't been with anyone since moving here. I didn't realize quite how desperate I was until she leaned toward me with her lids lowered, her eyes locked on my lips.

The length of her body presses tightly up against mine, and there's no mistaking what she does to me. My cock is trying to fight its way out of my pants to get to her.

"Fuck, Mia," I groan into her mouth as her hand slips under the hem of my shirt, her delicate touch making my abs contract.

It's been so long.

Too fucking long.

Ripping my lips from hers, I kiss down her neck, nibbling at her soft, warm skin. She damn near purrs beneath me, giving me all the encouragement I need.

"Bexley."

My name falling from her lips as nothing more than a whimper makes my cock weep for her, for the escape she can provide me with.

Climbing over her, I part Mia's knees and settle between her legs.

My hands land on her soft skin and I skim my palms up her thighs, taking her skirt with me.

Dragging my lips from her skin, I sit up and take her in. "You're so beautiful," I breathe, and even in the darkness, I see her cheeks flush.

Her lips part to argue, I can see it in her eyes, but I press my finger to her lips. "That wasn't a line, Mia. It was the truth."

"But I—"

Dropping over her, I take her lips once again in a bruising kiss as I wrap her bare legs around my waist, ensuring my solid length rubs against her lace-covered pussy.

Her hands disappear under my shirt again, my skin erupting in goose bumps as she runs her nails over me.

"Bexley, I need... I need you."

Pushing up, I place my hand in the dirt beside her head and stare down into her heated hazel eyes. They're sparkling with excitement, her cheeks still pink and her parted lips swollen from my kiss.

"Bexley, please," she begs, grinding herself against me.

"Fuck," I growl, finding her lips again, and my hand slips up her body until I squeeze her breast through the fabric of her dress and bra.

A moan vibrates up her throat as she arches her back for me.

Unable to resist, my hand descends once more, over her smooth stomach until I find the fabric of her skirt around her waist.

Her entire body trembles when my fingers gently run over her pussy. Her panties are soaked, showing me just how desperate for this she is.

Slipping the lace to one side, I push one finger inside her. She's so wet, so fucking tight.

"Oh God," Mia whimpers, her back arching once more as I thrust deeper. "Bexley." She throws her head back in pleasure as I rub at her walls, forcing me to stop kissing her.

I sit up and run my eyes down her body, focusing on where I'm touching her—not that I can see anything behind the fabric of her skirt, but I know, and it drives me fucking crazy.

Her moan of pleasure forces me to look back up at her once again, and when I do, I find her wild eyes staring up at me and realization slams into me.

I can't do this.

I glance up briefly when some noise from the party in the distance filters down to me, and it's like someone's thrown a bucket of ice water over me.

"I-I'm sorry."

"W-what?" Her voice is no more than a whisper where she's so lost to her desire.

"Y-you're drunk. I can't do this."

"I'm not that drunk. Bexley, please," she begs, but it's too late.

I pull my finger from her body and jump up. My chest heaves, my cock straining behind my jeans as I stare at her, the desire covering her face vanishing, quickly replaced by a myriad of emotions that make my chest ache. I didn't mean to hurt her.

"I'm sorry," I choke out.

"Fuck you, Bexley." She scrambles to smooth her skirt back down. "Fuck you."

Before I even have time to think up a response, Mia jumps up and takes off running into the trees, vanishing into the darkness.

"FUCK," I roar, pulling my leg back and kicking the rock beside me.

Pain ricochets up my leg, my toe burning from the connection. But it's the least I deserve for taking advantage of her like that.

She wanted it, a little voice says in my head, but I slam it down.

It would have been so easy to lose myself in her. To take what she was offering to me and forget how much she drank.

The old me would have. Hell, I'd have already been inside her if I was the same person who was exiled from Sterling Bay. I'd probably be riding her bare, with little regard for anything else but my own pleasure.

But that's not who I am anymore.

I said goodbye to that guy the moment I stepped out of line with Remi. The first crack of her boyfriend—Ace Jagger's—knuckles, and I knew everything was about to come crashing down around my feet. I knew before he ruined my future by shattering the one good thing I had in my life: my throwing arm. I was spiraling out of control thanks to my position in the school, my need for power and respect, and my crumbling home life.

It was all just too much, and I lost the person I used to be. The person Remi used to want to spend time with. The person the other kids at school used to look up to.

My need for more vodka means I don't hang around any longer than necessary. Instead, I march straight back to the party and snatch the first bottle I find.

I've got the cap in my hand and the neck halfway to my lips when I hear Alex's familiar voice behind me. "Here you are," he says. "Where did you—oh," he chuckles.

"What's so funny?" I snap, not in any kind of mood to be laughed at.

It was fucking easier when I'd ruined my conscience with drugs.

"I was going to ask where you went, but the girl that's all over your face kinda gave me my answer."

"What?" I ask, rubbing at my lips only to find dark lipstick on my thumb. Great. "Oh."

"So, who was she?" he asks with a knowing glint in his eye. He's almost as aware as I am of my lack of action since turning up at Gravestone High last winter.

"I... um... I don't know," I lie. "Just some girl I stumbled across down by the lake."

"Nice." He grins. "Any good?"

"I don't kiss and tell."

"Well, you should. It looks like you had fun."

"Whatever," I mutter, finally taking a pull from the bottle in my hand.

The vodka burns, but it's not enough. It's nowhere near enough, and for the millionth time since I arrived in Gravestone, I crave more. Crave anything that will numb the pain of my past and make me forget.

"I need to get out of here."

"But we just got here. Have a drink and chill out, man."

I look around, wondering who might have something stronger than this vodka, and that move is enough for me to know that I need to leave.

"Have a good night, yeah? I'll catch up with you tomorrow or something." Without saying another word, I take off, and by some fucking miracle he doesn't even try to call after me.

The winding driveway that seemed to take forever to get down when we first arrived is even longer on the way back. But the farther away I get from the party, the more the tension seeps from my body, and I know I'm doing the right thing.

The campus is in silence when I finally get back almost an hour later, my feet aching from the late-night walk and my bottle of vodka long empty.

I start stripping out of my clothes the second I get into my dorm and fall face-first into my bed, drowning in my regrets.

MY WEEKEND DOESN'T GET MUCH BETTER. I wake the next morning to the sound of Alex banging on my door, demanding that I get up and go for a run with him.

He's a fucking puppy that just doesn't give up.

Knowing it's the only way to get rid of him, I rip the door open and allow him inside.

"Why the fuck do you look so good? You only got in a few hours ago," I ask, turning my back on him and pulling on a pair of sweats and a clean shirt.

"Good genes?" I don't need to turn around to know he's shrugging. He's forced me to spend enough time with him over the past few months that I know his tells.

"How was the rest of the night?" I ask as I follow him out of dorms and down the stairs.

"Meh, nothing too exciting. I wasn't lucky enough to find a mystery girl in the woods to play with." He smirks. "You gonna tell me who it was yet?"

"Just some chick from college. Can't even remember her name," I lie. In reality, every time I woke up last night she was right there in front of my mind, her hungry, hazel eyes haunting me.

"You got your dick wet though, right?"

I glance over at him as we take off running through the fields out the back of campus.

"Nice, Alex. Real fucking nice."

"Jesus, Bex. When did you turn into such a prude? I know you haven't exactly been swimming in pussy since you got here, but fuck."

I scoff. "*I* haven't been swimming in pussy? At least I've had some fucking offers."

"I've had offers." He spits.

"Sure you have."

"I was chatting to that Annabel who was in my AP English lit class last night."

"She was probably taking pity on you, asshole. If she didn't suck your dick then you don't have a leg to stand on." I glance over as his lips part to respond but no words come out.

"Fuck off," he finally grumbles.

"We need to get you laid, man," I quip. "It might get you off my back then."

"Don't talk shit, you love me really."

"Sure." I roll my eyes to myself and pick up the speed, knowing that he'll be right alongside me.

I might give him shit, but the truth is, I'm jealous of him. He's the nice guy that everyone likes, he doesn't take shit too seriously, and although he might want a girl, he doesn't make a big deal about not having one. He just takes life as it comes. I wish I could be that easygoing. If I were, I might not have landed in this shithole with my tail between my legs and forced to live with a strange man I've never met before, let alone call family.

We run until our legs can't take us any farther, and then we stop for a takeout coffee and walk the distance back. We might only be on our second weekend living in dorms, but already it seems like it could become something of a tradition.

I'm not thrilled about the idea of Alex waking me up for exercise every weekend, but I need it. Now I'm not practicing every day of the week, I need to make the effort to at least keep some kind of routine in my life.

"You coming to tonight's party?" he asks as we push through the main door of our building.

"No."

"Are you going to be this boring for the next four years? If you are, just be honest with me now and I'll find a new best friend."

"When did I agree to be your best friend?"

He shrugs. "I appointed you the position a while ago, didn't you get the memo?"

"You're a fucking idiot," I mutter, letting myself into my room. "I'm done for the weekend. I've got a shit load of homework to do."

He shakes his head at me in disappointment. "I know you're scared, Bex."

My breath catches in my throat at his words. I've never said anything like that to him. "What are you—"

"I might not know the truth about how you ended up here, but I know you're scared, and I know you're trying to outrun it. But hiding in there," he glances over my shoulder to my room, "and refusing yourself the chance of enjoying it here, isn't going to help."

"You have no idea what you're talking about." I turn my back on him, ready to slam the door in his face and put an end to this conversation.

"Like fuck you don't, Bex," he snipes. "Whatever it is, you can talk about it, you know. I won't judge. I just want you to enjoy yourself. You won't get a do-over these next four years."

"Whatever, man," I grumble. "Enjoy the rest of your weekend."

EXACTLY AS I intended to do, I lock myself in my room and only emerge for our Sunday morning run—where Alex thankfully steers clear of our previous conversation—and to get food.

"So what debauchery did you get up to?" I ask him as we walk toward the Romulus Building for our first class of the day.

"Nah, nothing exciting. Troy got caught with his pants around his ankles last night, though. Some chick was giving him mixed signals, apparently."

"The only signals that asshole gets from girls is that they want to drop to their knees for him."

"Yeah, well. This one didn't. Fucking moron." He laughs as we pass other students on our way to class.

I've only been in this building once before, so I have to take note of the room numbers to make sure we stop at the right one—only before I get to the one we want, my eyes land on a girl. One I remember all too well.

"Mia." Her name falls from my lips without instruction from my brain as I take her in. She's wearing a black AC/DC shirt, a pair of ripped skinny black jeans, and, unlike Friday night where she'd been crying, her makeup is dark and sultry, flawless against her pale skin. Her hair is exactly the same, though, her dark blonde curls almost like a curtain around her in her attempt to hide. Only, I soon realize that there will be no hiding for her.

I don't know at what point I leave Alex behind, but in seconds, I'm standing before Mia, ready to apologize once again for what happened on Friday night.

It wasn't until I lay thinking about her Saturday afternoon that I realized how she might have felt with me rejecting her as I did. I need her to know that it wasn't her, that she didn't do anything wrong. It was all me and my fucked-up head and life that forced me to walk away.

The second she looks up, her breath catches as recognition dawns on her face before her eyes widen and her chin drops in shock.

"Mia, I—"

My words are cut off when a pair of tattooed hands wrap around her body, and when I look over her shoulder, I find she's been pulled back into Cade Kingsley's body.

His angry eyes lock onto mine, narrowing slighting as our stare continues. "This douchebag giving you grief, babe?" He smirks.

"What the fuck?" I glower as realization slaps me in the face. "You're with this asshole?"

4

MIA

I widen my eyes at Bexley, silently telling him to back down. Anger swirls in his baby blues, but I see the flash of hurt there.

Crap.

This is not how I wanted him to find out, but after the other night at the party, I'd assumed he didn't want anything to do with me.

I knew I shouldn't have done what I did—throwing myself at him like that, *begging* him to take me—but I wanted to be in control of when and how I lost my virginity. And deep down, I wanted to punish Cade for agreeing to this whole charade.

He's an Electi.

The Electi.

He won't go against their most sacred ceremony. It's how couplings have been decided since the beginning, back in the 1800s when Gravestone was founded.

Male heirs of Quinctus pair with a prosapia. According to my father, nobody knows exactly how Quinctus arrive at their decision or who places the name in the calix, but the decision is always final.

"Danforth, right?" Cade says with an air of arrogance, as if Bexley is beneath him. I guess in Gravestone's strange hierarchy, he is.

"Something you want to tell me, babe?" He practically smirks the words, but I feel the slight pinch in the way his fingers dig into my waist. Cade isn't pleased about Bexley singling me out, and what he says in the next two minutes could determine his entire life here at Gravestone U.

"I... uh," I stutter over the words. Cade stares at me with his soulless black eyes, and a shiver runs down my spine.

"Relax, man," Bexley says, breaking Cade's hold over me. "We're in the same econ class. I just wanted to ask Mia if she had the notes from last week."

"You're in class with this fucker?" Cade asks, and I nod.

"Look, Kingston—"

"Kingsley," Cade growls.

"That's what I meant." Bexley holds up his hands. "No hard feelings, yeah? I just wanted to ask Mia if she had the notes, that's all."

"Yeah, well, she doesn't have any. *Do you*?"

People have stopped to watch now, the air charged with tension. It isn't every day someone stands up to Cade Kingsley and lives to tell the tale, but Bexley doesn't seem in the least bit intimidated by him.

"I—" The words die on my tongue as Bexley steps toe to toe with Cade, his lip curving into a smirk all of its own. "It'll only take a second, man. I'll just borrow her and then bring her right back."

Oh God.

My heart lurches into my throat right as my stomach flutters wildly. I can't believe he just said that.

Cade's eyes slide to mine in question. It's our first day *together*. I'm his now. His girl... his property... his captive.

"I-I don't have any notes, sorry." I force myself to meet Bexley's furious gaze.

"You don't, huh?" Bexley says, but I can barely hear him over the roar of blood in my ears. "That's a shame."

Another beat passes, thick and heavy with silence. Then a tremor goes through the hall and they appear. Cade's inner circle: Ashton, Tim, Channing, Brandon, and Brandon's twin sister, Sasha. They move like a unit, slicing through the morning crowd like a sharp blade.

"What's this?" Ashton asks the second they reach us.

"Danforth was just being a conscientious student. He needs Mia's *notes*." Cade drawls the word, making it sound dirty.

"Notes, huh?" Ashton slings his arm around Bexley's shoulder and pulls him close. "I heard Mia takes the best notes, if you know what I mean."

I swallow the bile rushing up my throat.

"Ash, don't be a dick," Sasha scolds, shooting me a reassuring smile. It does nothing to ease the knot in my stomach.

I almost didn't make it in this morning. I was a bag of nerves, wondering how today would play out. I wasn't a particularly rebellious child. I worked hard at school and tried to make my parents happy, even if I couldn't readily accept Gravestone and all its secrets. But ever since hearing my name called at the Eligere, the need to rebel burns through my veins like acid, as if my soul knows it's wrong.

Cade's fingers slip under my AC/DC t-shirt—the least feminine thing I could find in my closet this morning—and begins caressing the skin there. My eyes flutter closed as I inhale a sharp breath. Most girls would pay to be in my position, having the King of Gravestone U feeling them up in the hall, but nothing feels right about his touch.

Not a damn thing.

"Get the fuck off me." Bexley shirks out of Ash's hold and runs a hand through his thick, dirty blond hair. "We're not friends," he says dryly.

"No, we're not." Cade stiffens. "Little word of advice, Danforth. You should remember that."

"I'm not scared of you, Kingsley." Bexley's eyes flicker to mine again, but this time, Cade notices.

"Don't look at her," he growls. "Don't you dare fucking look at her."

"Bex?" Alex Shaw approaches us, concern glittering in his eyes. "What's going on?"

"You'd better tell your boy to walk away, Shaw, before I make him."

"Fuck you, asshole." Bexley looks ready to lunge for Cade, but Alex grabs his arm.

"Come on, man. I'm fucking starving."

Like me, Alex has lived in Gravestone his entire life. He understands the order of things, the social hierarchy, even if he doesn't *know* everything.

Bexley glares at Cade, as if he's deciding whether to stand and fight or walk away. I want to scream, "Fight for me," but I don't.

I can't.

I belong to Cade now. If I'm going to survive this, I need to play my part and buy myself some time to figure out how I'm going to get out of it in one piece.

"Bex," Alex hisses, and he finally moves.

"Yeah, let's go." His icy gaze lingers on my face a second before he spins on his heel and takes off down the hall.

"Well, that was fun," Ashton remarks. "Think we need to be worried?"

"About Danforth?" Cade balks. "It's him who needs to watch his back."

"Mia, why don't you come with me?" Sasha says. "I was going to grab a coffee before class."

I'm about to move, but Cade tightens his hold on me. Our eyes meet, and he smirks. "Aren't you forgetting something?"

"No, I don't think I am." The words spill out before I can stop them.

His lips twist with amusement, but I don't miss the anger simmering in his eyes. Cade Kingsley doesn't appreciate insubordination.

He leans in, his warm breath caressing my cheek. "Don't play games with me, Mia. You won't like what happens when I'm pushed."

Sliding my trembling hand to his chest, I stuff down the ball of emotion in my throat and muster the best smile I can. "Have a good day, *your Highness*." My lips graze the corner of his mouth.

I start to pull away, feeling smug at my little outburst, but Cade snags me around the waist, crushing me against his chest and plunging his tongue into my mouth. Clawing at his t-shirt, I try to push him away, but he has me in a vise-like grip, his fingers digging into my hips enough to leave bruises. Cade doesn't just kiss me, he devours me. Every lick of his tongue is a dark promise of what will happen if I disobey him again.

I swallow the tears burning my throat.

"Cade, man," someone says, and I think it might be Channing.

"Just getting some sugar off my girl to get me through the day," he murmurs against my mouth, tugging my bottom lip between his teeth and biting gently. To anyone watching, we might look like two people unable to keep their hands off each other, but this isn't that.

Finally, he releases me, and I stagger back, flushed head to toe with anger.

"You—"

"Nah-ah, babe. Play nice." His eyes narrow in warning.

"Come on, Mia." A hand lands on my shoulder, and Sasha gently leads me away.

We walk in silence down the hall toward the coffee shop in the building's entrance. "Are you okay?" she asks me.

"What do you think?"

Her weak smile drops. "I think Cade is an ass."

Laughter bubbles in my chest. It's the best thing she could have said to me.

"But I thought you two were—"

"What, friends?" She shrugs. "I mean, we are. I don't really have any choice in the matter. But it doesn't mean I approve of everything he does."

"He's just so…" I don't even have words to describe how cocky and arrogant he is. He walks the halls of Gravestone U as if he owns the place, and in some ways, I guess he does. I've only been here a week, but I've known for years the power and sway Cade Kingsley holds over people.

He's the head of the Electi. The heir of the Kingsley line. With Mr. Kingsley dead and buried, the entire Kingsley legacy rests on Cade's shoulders…

And now mine.

God, I can't even stand kissing him, let alone the prospect of *being* with him.

"Mia?" Sasha says as we move down the line.

"I just can't believe this is happening. My name wasn't supposed to be in the calix. It's a mistake, it has to be."

"Q doesn't make mistakes," she whispers. "You know that."

"There's a first time for everything," I grumble as Sasha orders two lattes and a granola bar for herself.

"Is that okay?"

"Fine, thank you."

Sasha lets out a small sigh. "I tend to act without thinking. But everyone likes lattes, don't they?"

"I do."

"So tell me about yourself, Mia Thompson."

Is this really happening? Is Sasha Cargill, daughter of Phillip Cargill, really asking about me?

"What do you want to know?"

"Let's start with why Bexley Danforth was ready to throw down with Cade over you." Her brow lifts as she collects our order and guides me over to a table.

"I..." I swallow hard, wondering for a second just how much I can trust her. My gut says I can't, not when she's in Cade's inner circle. But she helped me escape that whole situation; that must count for something.

"Relax," she adds, sensing my hesitation. "I'm not interested in what or who you were doing before the Eligere." Suggestion drips from her words.

"It's not like that. Bexley is in one of my classes." I decide to glaze over the real truth.

"So, back in the hall? That was about homework?" Her brows pinch.

"Bexley... he saw something at the party."

Realization dawns in her dark green eyes. "Cade and the guys..."

"Yeah, I heard they taught Vincent Males a lesson down by the lake."

"Fuck," she breathes, smoothing a hand over her glossy auburn hair.

"I think Bexley was just surprised to see me with Cade after what happened."

"You haven't told him anything?"

"What? No! Of course I haven't." Bexley isn't from Gravestone; he doesn't know about the Eligere and Electi and Quinctus.

To know is to be sworn to secrecy, to uphold the codes of the town. It is a privilege not to be squandered.

A privilege.

I smother a bitter laugh.

Some *privilege*, being handed over to a guy like a prize cow.

"I'm not sure I can do this," I admit, hating the tremor in my voice.

Sasha leans over and lays her hand on mine, giving me a sad smile. "You have to, Mia. You don't have any choice."

5

BEXLEY

"What the fuck was that?" Alex asks when we finally come to a stop outside one of the campus coffee shops.

"Nothing."

"Fuck off was that nothing. No one with half a brain cell goes up against Cade Kingsley like that. Do you even know who he is?"

Of course I know who he is. Alex has explained more than once that he's Gravestone royalty, whatever the fuck that's meant to mean. But unlike everyone in this weird-ass town, I don't give a shit.

He's just a jumped-up prick, as far as I'm concerned.

"I don't give a fuck, Alex."

"Well, you should. You do not want to make an enemy out of Cade and his crew."

"Jesus, you make it sound like I should be running scared because he so much as looked in my direction."

"Most do."

"That's because this town is full of pussies."

"Christ, who got your panties in a twist this morning? Why were you even talking to him, anyway?"

"I wasn't, I was talking to Mia."

"Who's... ohhhh." His eyes grow big. "Mia Thompson. You know her?"

"Um..." I hesitate, not wanting to admit to Alex what almost happened on Friday night, even more so now I know that apparently she's not fucking single.

Anger swirls around me as I remember just how willing she was. Was it a joke? Did Cade set her up? Why would she tempt me like that if she's his?

"Not really, she's in my econ class. I just wanted to ask her something."

He eyes me suspiciously but doesn't say anything. Instead, he spins on his heels and pushes through the door leading inside the coffee shop.

I follow him to the counter and order myself a double espresso. I think I'm going to need it. I haven't even stepped inside a classroom and everything's already gone to shit.

"I don't even get why she was with him. No one paid her a second of attention in high school, let alone the likes of Cade Kingsley. He must have made her his new plaything for a reason. Brook's gonna be pissed."

I tune him out as we wait for our orders, not really wanting to get involved with college gossip. I just want to go to class, do my time, and get the fuck out of this place. Four years will be over in a flash, right?

"Thanks," I mutter to the barista when she hands over my order. Our fingers brush as I take the cup from her, and my eyes find hers. She's cute. Bright green eyes and short brown hair. But she doesn't stir something inside me like Mia did on Friday night. There's no connection, which is more like I'm used to.

Ripping my eyes from hers, I turn to find a table for us to sit at while Alex fills his face with his hazelnut croissant, but instead of finding an empty table, I find her hazel eyes.

"Oh, for fuck's sake. Can we at least have ten minutes before déjà vu kicks in, please?" Alex mutters. "There's a table over here."

"I'll be there in a second, I just need to—"

"She's with Sasha Cargill. It's probably best you—totally ignore me and go anyway," I hear him mutter as I walk away from him.

Her eyes follow my every move as I step up to their table and twist around the free chair, sitting down and straddling it.

I nod at the other girl before turning my attention to Mia. "Kingsley? Really?"

Mia looks between me and Sasha, panic filling her eyes. "I already told you that I don't have any notes."

"Yeah," I scratch my jaw, my eyes boring into hers, "and I think you're lying."

"That's fine. Think what you like. Will you excuse us?" She twists away from me slightly and my fingers wrap around the back of the chair a little too tightly, my knuckles turning white, something that Sasha doesn't miss.

"Okay, fine," I hiss. "Have it your way. But this isn't over."

"I think it's probably in your best interest that it is," Sasha warns as I stand, but I don't so much as look at her. I don't give a fuck what her opinion is on this situation, or what her fucking surname is. This is between me and Mia, and we are going to be talking about it.

I feel her eyes burn into me as I walk to the table Alex decided to sit at to watch the show, and just before I sit down with him, I look back over my shoulder, making sure that she knows I'm aware of her attention.

"Do you have a fucking death wish?"

I shrug. "What the fuck is he really going to do about me talking to her?"

"Do you really want the answer to that question?" Alex leans in so no one else in the coffee shop can hear his next words. "Apparently he's killed people for less."

"How fucking gullible are you?"

"Okay, fine. Don't believe me. But don't come running to me when he's ripped out your heart for touching his latest toy."

"Firstly, if I'm dead, then I'm not going to be running anywhere, asshole. And secondly..." I trail off as Mia and Sasha move from their table and walk toward the exit together. I watch them leave the building and walk in front of the windows, heading for class. I don't think she's going to look back, but right before she rounds the corner, she does, and her eyes immediately lock on mine. They widen as if she wasn't expecting to find me watching her, and I smile.

This is far from over.

"And secondly..." I smirk. "Fuck off."

CLASSES DRAG. They're only made slightly more bearable knowing that I've got economics at the end of the day and I'll hopefully have a chance to catch Mia alone afterward.

I turn up to class early in the hope she might have done the same thing, but I'm disappointed when all I find are the over-eager bookish types hovering around the classroom door. Spotting an empty bench so that I can see the students coming and going, I wait. The nerds eventually head inside once our professor arrives, probably to make sure they get prime position front seats.

There's two minutes to the start of class when I finally see her approaching, only she's not alone. She's once again being escorted by Cade fucking Kingsley.

I might have only spent a few minutes with her on Friday night and have limited knowledge of her from school, but she really doesn't seem to me like the kind of girl who'd be interested in an arrogant asshole like him.

They both look up as I stand from the bench and walk toward them. His hand tightens on her hip as I approach.

"Fancy seeing you two here," I mutter as we all come to a stop outside the classroom door.

"You seem to have forgotten your puppy dog," Cade remarks, making a show of looking around for Alex.

"And you don't seem to have lost your bullshit attitude."

Mia snorts a laugh at my comment but quickly tries to cover it up as a cough.

"I can take it from here, Mia," I gesture toward the door for her to go first.

"You need to stay well away from my girl, Danforth," Cade barks, taking a step forward and pushing Mia behind him as if she needs protecting from me.

"Or what, *Kingston?*"

His lips purse in anger as his shoulders tense and he sucks in a deep breath as if he's trying to keep himself under control.

"Don't test me." He steps right up to me, so close that our noses almost touch. "Or it won't just be your broken throwing arm you need to worry about."

My reaction falters. How the fuck does he know about that?

"Cade, that's enough. We're going to be late."

"You're with me. No one will care, babe," he purrs at Mia before he twists away from me and pulls her into his body.

"Cade, I need to get to class." She tries fighting him, but she's no match for his strength and only ends up pressed tighter to him.

"You know how much I love it when you fight back," he says, threading his fingers through her hair and slamming his lips down on hers. They're so close to me, and now blocking the door, that I have no real choice but to watch as his tongue pushes past her lips and invades her mouth.

I remember doing exactly that a few days ago, and it makes me want to rip his fucking tongue out of his mouth.

"Enjoy class, babe. I'll see you later."

"Great," she mutters, her lips curling as her palms push against his chest as if she wants him nowhere near her. The move confuses me even more.

She tears her eyes from his, glances at me, and then spins on her heels and marches into the classroom.

"I'm fucking watching you, Danforth. Keep your hands off what's mine," he seethes.

"You might want to convince her that she actually wants you first."

Before he has a chance to respond, I march through the door and swing it closed, hoping that he is standing close enough that it smashes him in the nose.

Our professor stares at me as I make my way into the room and past the nerds at the front as he waits to start his class. The seat next to Mia is empty, aside from her purse, so when I get there, I knock it off and sit my ass down.

"This is taken," she grits out.

"I don't see anyone else sitting here, do you?"

She mumbles something beneath her breath, but it rolls off me.

"What are you going to do?" I taunt. "Call your boyfriend to come and move me?"

"He's not my boyfriend," she seethes.

"Really? You might want to give him that memo, because he seems to think he owns your ass while you're—"

"Mr. Danforth, Miss Thompson, if you don't care to listen then you know where the door is," Professor Laken barks across the room.

Mia cuts me a seething look before sitting forward and pulling her notepad closer to begin taking notes.

I fucking knew she was a note taker.

Mia doesn't look at me or even register my existence throughout the whole lecture. It drives me fucking insane, because with her so close, I have no clue what the hell Laken is talking about.

I don't know what it is about her, but unlike everyone else I've met in Gravestone, she calls to me, and I'll be damned if I'm going to let that go. I've felt like an outsider, like I don't belong here, from the second I followed my uncle into town all those months ago. I hated the place then, and things haven't really gotten any better.

The second Laken looks like he's bringing things to an end, Mia slams her notepad closed and stuffs it into her bag like she's about to run.

Before she has a chance to stand, I reach out and wrap my fingers around her forearm. "Not so fast."

"Let go, Bexley." Her big, hazel eyes plead with me.

"No, not until you've heard me out."

"Not interested. You need to stay away from me." She pulls her arm free.

My need to reach for her again is almost too strong to ignore, but I refuse to be like him, dragging her around like a ragdoll. Instead, I allow her to think I've let her go before quickly collecting up my books and following her out of the classroom.

I hang well back as she makes her way across campus. She must think she's lost me, because at no point does she look back to see if I'm following her. Instead, she keeps her head down and walks as fast as her little legs will carry her. I wonder who she's running from—me, or Cade. Either could be possible.

Mia leads me straight to her dorm building, and I hang back as she lets herself in and turns toward the stairwell, leaving me just enough time to slip in unnoticed behind her.

She's still totally oblivious to me as I step up behind her, and when she pushes her door open, I press my front to her back and wrap my hand around her mouth to stop her from screaming.

"You can't escape me that easily," I breathe in her ear, and I swear she relaxes against me as I kick the door closed, cutting us off from the rest of the campus.

6

MIA

"Bexley, what the he—" My breath *whooshes* from my lungs as he spins me around and presses me up against the wall, sealing his hand completely over my mouth.

"You're with him?" he spits. "But what I can't figure out is if you were trying to use me to get back at him for something, or whether you're both trying to fuck me over."

"It isn't like that." My words are smothered by his warm palm.

"Sorry, what was that? I can't hear you." His eyes darken, anger swirling in his icy depths.

He slightly loosens his grip, and I manage to choke out, "Fuck you."

"That can be arranged." He presses his big, ripped body against the length of mine, erasing every inch of space. "After all, you were begging for it at the party. I had my fingers inside you, remember? I felt how wet you were, how much you wanted me." His hand slides to my throat, and his tongue darts out to taste my lips. "Are you wet now, Mia?"

A violent tremor rips through me. This Bexley isn't the guy I met at the lake. He's different. Angry and cruel.

And yet, I can't deny the flash of heat that pulses through me.

"You can't say that to me." I let out an indignant huff.

"Why not? Because you're *his* girl?"

"Why do you care?" I cry. "You pulled away, not me. I was there, I was right there, and you rejected me."

Tears spill from my eyes without permission, but the lock on all the anger and frustration that has been building inside me finally bursts wide open. "I was willing to give you everything," my voice shakes, "and you made your choice."

Bexley releases me like I've burned him and staggers back. "Fuck," he roars. "FUCK!"

The whole moment is bizarre. We don't know each other, not really. But I felt something at the party that night. Something real. It's still there, simmering between us, crackling in the air.

"Why?" He snarls the word, dragging his fingers through his hair. "Why play me like that?"

"I didn't... I wasn't..." Crap. I don't know what to say. It's not like I can tell him the truth.

Can I?

You know you can't.

So I go with the only truth I can admit. "I just wanted to feel something normal."

"Normal? What the fuck is that supposed to mean?" he sneers. "Doesn't Kingsley get you off or something?"

I suck in a sharp breath at his crude insinuation, and Bexley notices. His brows bunch together as he studies me.

"What aren't you telling me?" He closes the distance between us, reaching for my cheek and brushing his thumb over the soft skin there. "Is Kingsley making you do things you don't want to?"

"N-no, nothing like that. I just... he's intense."

Bexley goes rigid, his jaw clenching painfully tight. His eyes fix on mine, as if he's trying to unearth all my deepest, darkest secrets. "I don't like playing games, Mia." His words are a low whisper that sends shivers racing down my spine. "I had enough of that back in Sterling Bay, and it didn't end well... for anyone."

"It wasn't a game, I promise. It wasn't."

"But you're his?"

Silent tears drip down my cheeks as Bexley stares at me with utter disgust. He might be relatively new to Gravestone, but he already hates Kingsley. Most people do, they're just too afraid to admit it.

Not Bexley Danforth, though.

For a second, I imagine telling him. I imagine spilling every sordid detail about this town and the people who hold all the power. I imagine letting him comfort me, letting him fight my battles. But this isn't a fairy tale, and there are no happy endings here. There's only misery and pain.

His thumb strokes along my throat as he leans closer, his lips practically touching the shell of my ear. "All I can think about is finishing what we started at that party. You were so fucking wet, Mia. I wanted to make you come all over my fingers." Bexley rolls his hips against me, letting me feel exactly what I do to him.

I smother a whimper, my eyes fluttering closed as I let myself remember. "You felt so good, little mouse." My eyes fly open, and he smirks. "Small, helpless, little mouse." His grip around my throat tightens.

I know I should feel terrified; I'm completely at his mercy. But there's something else under the surface. "Fuck. You," I seethe.

"Nah." He releases me sharply, and I sag down the wall. "Something tells me you want that, and Kingsley made it pretty clear you're his. So until I find out what you're hiding, I'm not going to lay a single finger on you."

Disappointment wells in my chest.

"You should go." I can barely look at him. Bexley hovers for a second, his eyes drilling holes in the top of my head. He isn't leaving, so I say the only thing I know will get rid of him.

"If Cade finds out you're here," I finally lift my gaze to his, "he'll kill you."

Bexley bristles. His eyes narrow to dangerous slits as he backtracks to the door. But he pauses at the last second, right as he goes for the handle.

"I'd like to see him try."

BY THE TIME the next morning rolls around, the pit in my stomach is so deep, I feel a little nauseous.

Bexley was here, in my dorm room. The one I had to beg my parents to let me have.

Since Gravestone U is only a twenty-minute ride from town, nestled right on the edge of the forest, they wanted me to stay at home. Probably to keep an eye on me. My father was particularly concerned about me moving into the dorms.

But in the end, I got my own way.

Sitting on the edge of my bed, I run my fingers through my dark blonde hair. I have two hours worth of classes with Bexley today. He was so angry last night, dark, volatile energy rolling off him. But still, I didn't feel any of the fear I feel whenever I'm with Cade.

As if the universe summons him, there's a firm knock at my door, and I know, I just know, that it's him. I give myself a few seconds. Today, I'm wearing some skinny black jeans and a soft pink tank top that hangs on my body. My hair is loose and wavy around my face, which is free of makeup. I look basic, a far cry from the perfect veneers of the likes of Brook and her friends.

A shiver runs down my spine at the thought of enduring another day of Brook's death stare whenever our paths cross around campus. So far, Cade has kept her at arm's length, but I know she won't stay gone for long.

His knocks grow louder, more impatient. "Coming," I call, taking a deep breath as I move reluctantly to the door.

"Morning, babe," he drawls, pressing one hand to the doorjamb above my head. He looks good in a Fendi polo shirt, the top button undone, paired with fitted dark jeans. But then, Cade Kingsley always looks good.

"Aren't you going to invite me in?" he adds when I don't respond.

"I'm ready, we can lea—"

"Actually, there's something I need to discuss with you." He steps into my space, forcing me back into my room. Fear trickles through me as Cade looms over me like a dark prince sent to claim my soul.

"We can talk about it on the way to class."

"Actually, we can't." He kicks the door shut behind him, the sound like a gunshot to my racing heart. "This is between you and me." Cade stalks towards me as I inch back, trying to keep him at a safe distance.

Until the kiss yesterday, he's been tolerable, but something changed in the moment Bexley approached us. Maybe I'm overthinking it, but it felt like I was being placed in the middle of some brewing war.

Whatever it was, I don't want to end up in one of Cade's games. We've all heard the whispers, the cruel and barbaric things he makes his peers do just to prove a point. To exact his power over them.

For as much as I hate to admit it, I hope that being his prosapia will afford me some protection.

My back finally hits the wall, and Cade slams his hand beside my head, making me startle. "You look good this morning, babe. I like seeing your skin bare." He runs his thumb over my jaw, letting it slide down to my bottom lip and linger there. "But maybe I can put some color in your cheeks." His mouth ghosts over mine, and I'm paralyzed but to accept his kiss. It's only chaste. A quick touch. I exhale a shaky breath, and he chuckles.

"You're so nervous around me, Mia." His lip curves with dark intention. "I don't bite, you know. Well, unless you beg."

"What do you want, Cade?"

"I have something for you. A gift."

"You do?" My stomach sinks as I flatten myself against the wall.

Cade steps back, slipping his hand into his pocket, and pulls out a small box.

"No," I breathe, really hoping it isn't what I think it is.

"Relax," he chuckles. "It isn't a ring... yet. Q thinks it's too soon, and I'm inclined to agree. We need to let our relationship unfold... naturally." His eyes darken, and I hate to imagine what he might be thinking right now.

"But like it or not, Mia, you are mine now, and I want people to know it." He flips open the box, revealing a small pendant necklace. I lean in to admire the stunning filigree.

"It's beautiful." Even though it represents something I want no part of, I can't deny how stunning it is. "Is that—"

"The Electi's crest, yeah."

My eyes shutter. Cade might not be putting his ring on me, but he's stamping me with the next best thing. Most of the kids at Gravestone U don't know what it really means, but there are those of the verus bloodline that do. They'll see this for what it is. They'll see that I've been claimed by an Electi.

"I had it made specially for you."

"I... I don't know what to say."

"I have a feeling you'll be thanking me soon enough."

There it is again, the dark promise of things to come.

"Is this what you really want?" I blurt out. "To be chained to me for the rest of your life? I'm no one. You and Brook—"

"Having second thoughts?" His brows furrow, and I want to yell that I was never having first thoughts.

Me and Cade together is a disaster waiting to happen. I'm not prosapia material, cut out for a life of being arm candy and nothing more than a glorified maid.

I want more.

So much more.

"You don't want me." I lift my chin defiantly. Cade might scare me, but I refuse to show him even an ounce of fear. People like him feed off that.

"Yet here we are."

"You can make them overturn the decision, Cade. No one has to know. Choose Brook, everyone will expect—"

"Enough," he grits out, running a hand down his face. "Q's decision is final. This, me and you… it's happening Mia, whether you like it or not."

Anger boils beneath my skin. "I'm not a prize to be won, Cade."

"No, you're not. Because I don't need to win anything. You're mine, Mia. Mine." He leans back in, rubbing his nose along my jaw and letting his mouth linger over mine. "I know we have to take it slow. I know we have to wait until the Coligo before I can make you mine in all the ways that count. But that doesn't mean we can't have a little fun in the meantime." He toys with the neckline of my tank top. "We can keep it between the two of us."

I swat his hand away and slip out from between him and the wall. "We should get going," I say, swallowing the tears rushing up my throat. "We wouldn't want to be late." Grabbing my bag, I sling it over my shoulder and take off toward the door, not bothering to wait for Cade.

7

BEXLEY

I stare at Mia across the auditorium as she fiddles nervously with her pen. This is only my third psychology class, but I haven't heard a word the professor has said. My focus is entirely on her.

My fingers clench as I recall how she felt, trembling in my hold yesterday. My teeth grind as I remember feeling that pull to her again like I did on Friday night by the lake.

She's Kingsley's. Any sane guy would have walked away the second he pulled her into his body and staked his claim. Sadly, I'm not any normal guy, and that connection I feel with her... I crave it like a fucking junkie searching for his next hit.

I haven't felt that in... a really long time, and I fucking need it.

I want it.

I want *her*.

Mia is aware of my attention. She might not have looked at me since the moment she was delivered to class by *him* and glanced around to find a seat, but she knows. I *feel* it. It's why she can't stop moving. Why she keeps tapping her pen and shifting in her seat as if she's uncomfortable.

Is she wet for me again? Is she trying to push thoughts of me having my hands on her, inside her, out of her head?

I stretch my legs out before me and slump down in the seat a little more. The professor continues, but his words flow over me as a blur of incessant noise. My heart pounds steadily in my chest as I continue watching, my mind working on overdrive to try to figure this shit out.

Mia is beautiful, sexy, breathtaking, but something tells me that she's not Cade Kingsley's type. I've seen him in the past, parading girls around like they're fucking possessions, and they haven't exactly looked like Mia, always plastered in more makeup than I'm sure she owns. With their perfect smiles and flawless hair, they flaunt the assets they have. Mia... well, she's just Mia.

Classically beautiful, she doesn't need any kind of enhancement. It's the kind of beauty that Cade, the old me, never would have seen, because everything is only skin deep when you're trying to gain—or retain—that much power.

Disgust rolls through me as I cast my mind back to my past and what a douchebag I was in Sterling Bay. It's really no wonder my parents banished me here and practically forgot all about me. If I ever have a kid and he acts anything like I did, I'd want to disown them too.

A burning slap to my shoulder drags me from my thoughts, and I look to my left. "Bro, are you going to fucking listen anytime soon, or are you just going to drool over your lost love?"

"Fuck off."

Alex raises a brow at me and then shrugs. "Fine, but you're not having my notes."

"Did I fucking ask for them?"

"No, but you will. She's Kingsley's, man. You need to let it go. Let it—"

"Don't," I cut him off before he breaks into fucking song. "Something's not right there. Does she look like Kingsley's type?" I say, voicing the question I was asking myself only minutes ago.

"I guess not, but Cade isn't all that picky. He's probably running out of new girls to stick it in, to be honest."

"So the opposite issue to you then," I deadpan.

"Did I ask for your opinion?" He glowers. "No, no I fucking didn't. So pay attention and take some fucking notes, Casanova."

"ARE you actually going to tell me what happened Friday night, or am I going to have to continue making up scenarios in my head?" Alex asks me as we make our way toward our dorm building at the end of the day.

I had economics with Mia straight after our psychology class this morning, but she ensured she was late, sitting as far away from me as possible. There went another class of my college career in which I had no fucking clue what happened. I'm pretty sure I wasn't the only one, either, because much like our first class together she spent the time doodling or fiddling with her pen or necklace. At no point did she look like she was paying any attention at all.

I tried to talk to her after class, but there was a commotion at the entrance, and she managed to slip away from me before I even got a word out.

I shouldn't care. I should just let her run to Cade so they can have their happily ever after or whatever. But for some reason, I can't. Something isn't right. I just wish I could put my finger on what.

"No, no I'm not."

"Oh, come on, it's not like I don't know it was Mia that you were with."

"Says who?"

"Says me. You've never spoken to her before, and suddenly you can't drag your puppy dog eyes off her."

"It's..."

"That you got all up in her business and have now discovered that she's Kingsley's?" he quips.

"I'm going to retract your invite to dinner in a minute," I grumble.

"Feel free. I'll get my ass to your uncle's myself. His housekeeper makes the best Thai; I am not fucking missing that for shit."

"Remind me again how I ended up stuck with you?"

"Because I'm just that fucking cool."

"Oh... that's right. You had no other friends." I pull the door of my BMW open and drop into the driver's seat.

"Nah, we both know that's not true. I just took pity on the new boy."

"Are you still fucking talking?" I ask, starting the engine and flooring it out of the parking lot.

It's a thirty-minute drive to my uncle's house on the outskirts of town, in an insanely exclusive neighborhood.

His house is ridiculous. It's set behind a huge pair of gates and invisible from the road. It makes the houses I was used to in Sterling Bay look like shanty huts. I have no idea who owns the other houses, or if anyone even lives in them, because I have never seen anyone on this street.

It's creepy as fuck. Actually, everything about my uncle is creepy as fuck.

I must have watched too much trash on the TV as a kid, because I thought uncles were meant to be fun, feed you all the food your parents wouldn't allow you to have, and generally help you cause mayhem. But Uncle Marcus, he's... well, he's not any of that.

He's stern, serious, and downright weird.

He lives alone in this big old house that could easily be turned into a hotel; it's so huge. Yet he doesn't seem to work, and I haven't seen or heard any evidence of him *ever* working.

As we pull up to the gates that lead to my uncle's colossal house, they begin to open.

"It doesn't matter how many times I come here, I still can't get used to it," Alex says.

"You and me both," I mutter as we make our way down the long driveway until the gothic style building emerges before us. It looks like something out of a horror film, making a shudder run down my spine. If my uncle suddenly announced that he used the basement to imprison and torture people, I would not be surprised.

When he called before classes this morning to demand I attend dinner this evening, the last thing I wanted to do was agree. But my uncle isn't the kind of man you say no to. He might be fast approaching sixty, but his presence is still as scary as fuck.

"Let's get this over with, then," I say, shouldering the door open and climbing out.

The front door is always open, so we let ourselves in and make our way down the long entrance hall. "Uncle Marcus?" I call, not knowing which of the seemingly endless number of rooms he'll be in.

"Coming," his voice booms from somewhere upstairs.

We make our way toward the kitchen, and I pull the refrigerator open and grab us both a can of soda. "Here," I say, throwing it to Alex and watching him miss by a mile and it explodes on the tiled floor.

It's easy to forget that he's not one of the football players I spent my time with before my move here.

"Shit, sorry," he says, jumping away from the spray that's still shooting from the side of the can.

We're both on our hands and knees, trying to tidy the mess up, when my uncle joins us.

"Afternoon," he says, his voice deep and rough like always and his brow raised in question.

"I can't catch," Alex offers by way of explanation.

I'm pretty sure my uncle thinks Alex and I are in a secret relationship. He's mentioned more times than I care to count about my lack of female action since moving here, and every time I try to steer the conversation to something else, I know he's thinking that it's because I don't want to admit I'm gay.

"Leave it. Brenda can get it," he orders, and we both stand, leaving the mess on the floor.

Brenda is Uncle Marcus' long-suffering housekeeper. She's worked for him for... well, forever, I think. She hardly ever says anything, just keeps to herself while maintaining the level of cleanliness Marcus expects of his ancient looking home.

Everything about this place is old and mysterious. If I cared to look, I'd bet it's got an interesting history behind it. Hell, I'd probably find all the answers in one of the many rooms Marcus keeps locked.

Every time I've asked him about them, he just tells me that we don't need them. That the house is already too big for the two of us. I can't help but agree with him there, but it's clear he's lying. If he cares enough to lock the doors, then there is something in there that he doesn't want me to see.

"So, how's it hanging, Uncle M?" Alex asks Marcus like he's just one of the guys.

"It's good, thank you, Alexander. And how is college going?" Marcus gestures for us to join him at one end of the dining table that seats sixteen.

"It's good."

"You've both settled in okay?" He turns his eyes on me.

"Yeah, pretty well."

"Any issues with other students?"

I narrow my eyes at him. "Um... no. Nothing unusual. Why?"

"No reason. Just making sure you're happy."

"Yeah, it's good. Our dorm rooms are great. The other guys seem cool," I say, thinking of those we share a communal kitchen and living area with.

"That's good."

Awkward silence falls over the three of us, and I meet Alex's eyes over the table.

"You're a Gravestone U alumnus, right? What advice have you got to help us survive the next four years?" Alex asks, breaking the tension and reminding me why I always drag him here with me. If it's just Uncle Marcus and me, we end up eating in an uncomfortable silence. It's hell.

He nods to himself for a second as he thinks. "Enjoy these first two weeks. When the real work starts, you're going to wish you could go back in time."

"First two weeks? I thought we could have fun for at least the first two years," Alex jokes.

Marcus gives him a knowing smile before Brenda steps into the room with tonight's dinner.

Alex chats away about total bullshit as we eat, and I'm grateful for his verbal diarrhea keeping the awkwardness at bay. I hate this house. I hate the old furnishings and dark wood. I hate that the light bulbs aren't bright enough and how they leave all the corners in the dark.

This house has secrets.

Secrets I have no real interest in discovering and every intention of running away from at my first opportunity.

"Bexley," Marcus states as he lowers his cutlery after finishing his meal. "I expect you to be here no later than seven PM on Friday night."

"Friday? Why?"

"Just be here. Alex will be otherwise engaged." He glances at my friend before pushing his chair out and walking from the room.

"Is it just me," Alex lets out a low whistle, "or does that man get weirder every time I see him?"

"It's not just you," I admit quietly as the sound of Uncle Marcus' footsteps disappears in the distance.

It's not just you at all.

8

MIA

"I still can't believe it." Annabel fingers the pendant hanging around my neck. "An Electi crest pendant."

"I'm not wearing it," I scoff.

"What? You have to. You're his prosapia. If you don't—"

"Come on, Bel, you can't be serious." Pulling free of her hand, I turn to the mirror and study the pendant. It's been three days since Cade gave me the damn thing. It hangs round my neck like a noose. It might as well be a collar. A leash. Maybe that's what Cade intended. Something to degrade me and put me in my place, because God only knows he didn't do it out of kindness.

"What's it like, kissing him?"

"Seriously?" I balk at my friend in the glass mirror.

"What? I'm curious." She shrugs, running her hands over my comforter. "It's Cade freakin' Kingsley. Most girls would kill to be in your position. I'm pretty sure Brook is trying to buy someone off right now." Annabel shoots me a devious smirk.

"Ugh, don't. I thought she was going to burn actual holes into the back of my head in one of my literature classes."

"It makes you wonder though, doesn't it? Everyone thought she and Cade were a sure thing. So why didn't her name get called?"

Annabel wasn't in this year's offering. She was presented early, the summer before senior year. Her mom was sick, terminal. It was her dying wish to see her daughter at the Eligere. Since her father is good friends with Harrison Rexford, Quinctus agreed to let her enter before she turned eighteen. Of course, everyone knew she wouldn't get chosen. It was the year Tim Davenport and Fawn Bailey's relationship was officially confirmed, even though they had been promised to one another since they were just kids.

It will be Annabel's choice if she enters the Eligere again in the future, but despite her intrigue about Cade and the Electi, I don't sense she's in any rush to present herself again. That's why I like her. Annabel is intrigued about Quinctus and the Electi and Gravestone's history in the same way I am—maybe a little too starry eyed where the Electi are concerned—but she isn't brainwashed like so many of the folk in this town.

"I don't know," I whisper, fear trickling down my spine.

She's right.

I haven't stopped thinking about why my name was pulled from the calix. Someone in Quinctus wants me and Cade together...

But why?

I might be from Gravestone, but I'm not from his world. My father might work security for Phillip Cargill and the mayor's office at the town hall, but that's where the connection ends. We live in a modest house set on the edge of Gravestone Park. We're more than comfortable, but we're not rich in the same way the elite families are.

Cade could click his fingers and any number of people would come running to his aid. If I clicked my fingers there would be nothing but the sound of silence.

"Well, whatever strange magic is at work, I say enjoy it. He's the hottest guy in Gravestone U, and you, girl, get to date him."

"You do realize if everyone goes through with this, I'll be doing a whole lot more than dating him?" Bile washes in my stomach.

Annabel rolls her eyes at me. "I'm not a total idiot. Of course I know. And I approve, obviously. It's time you blew the cobwebs out of your vajayjay."

"*Never* say that word again to me."

"What? Vajayjay? Cooch, pussy, beaver, and my personal favorite… cunt."

"Oh my God, what is wrong with you?" I balk, and she explodes with laughter.

"You should see your face. You, Mia Thompson,"—she jabs her finger at me—"are a prude."

"I am not." At least, I wasn't when I was rubbing myself on Bexley at the party, begging him to fuck me. But I don't tell Annabel that. Some things are better left unsaid.

"Well, as long as you're not saving yourself for Cade. Because we all know he hasn't saved himself for his prosapia."

I wince at her words. Again, she's right. Cade is a player. Even with Brook always waiting in the sidelines, everyone knows Cade Kingsley doesn't do exclusive.

Will that change now?

Or will he continue to fuck other girls while he waits for our Coligo?

"God, I hate this," I grit out, clutching the pendant in my fist. I want to tear it off, to yank the damn chain and smash it into a thousand pieces. But I don't, because already I'm becoming docile. Everyone expects me to behave as Cade's prosapia. Anything less will be deemed unacceptable—by Cade, the Electi, and Quinctus.

At least he can't physically touch me until our unification ceremony. And after the huge shock of my name being pulled from the calix, none of the elders seemed in a hurry to announce the date of our Coligo. My father seems to think we'll have at least until the full moon after next.

"I know you're upset," Annabel soothes, "but maybe if you give him a chance—"

I make a derisive sound in my throat. "You don't give someone like Cade a chance, Bel. He chooses whether to *let* you have a chance. To walk at his side or kneel at his feet."

That's what worries me the most. I'm not submissive, not in the way some girls are. He might scare me a little, but it's not enough to make me cower… and that is a problem to someone like Cade.

I grab the nearest thing to me and launch it across the room, watching with dismay as the glass smashes into pieces and scatters across the floor.

"Better?" Annabel lifts a brow, hardly surprised by my little outburst.

My lips purse as I stare at her, my body vibrating with anger. I will be better when this nightmare is over. When Quinctus realizes they made a mistake, that I'm not the girl for Cade after all.

Because there is no other explanation.

It's a mistake.

It has to be.

THE NEXT DAY is as unbearable as the last. Cade is extra clingy, holding my hand in a vise-like grip as we move around campus. The pendant sits heavy against my chest. I almost didn't wear it, but if I want to appease him, to buy myself some time, I know I need to play ball.

"I like this." He skims the hem of my skirt, his fingers brushing the backs of my thighs.

"I didn't wear it for you," I reply.

Ashton snorts, grumbling something about 'needing to break me in.' I cast him a dark look, but he only glares back.

I like him least out of the Electi. He's too close to Cade, too much of a bad influence. Not to mention, he's Brook's older brother. I've heard the stories about Ashton Moore. The threesomes at parties, the fights, the girls running from his room with tears streaming down their faces and bruises on their bodies.

Ashton is dangerous, and he's Cade's closest friend. He's also not officially an Electi, which affords him a certain amount of freedom where his actions are concerned.

"No?" Cade whispers against the soft skin of my neck. "Then who did you wear it for?"

My spine goes rigid, but I force myself to relax. Now is not the time to be thinking about Bexley and how his piercing blue eyes follow me around campus whenever we cross paths.

After that afternoon in my dorm room, he's mostly kept his distance. But I feel him, watching. Waiting. He needs to stay away—for his benefit, and mine. But I can't deny a tiny piece of me likes feeling him there, in the shadows. Like a guardian angel watching over me.

Except… something tells me he isn't an angel at all.

A shiver zips up my spine and Cade tenses. "What is it, babe? What's wrong?" He brushes the hair from my face and grips my chin, forcing me to look at him.

We're sitting outside in the quad. Brandon and Sasha are arguing over something. Ashton is practically fucking a girl I don't recognize on the bench. And Channing is busy texting someone. I don't know where Tim is. Probably off with Fawn. I've only met her a couple of times, but she doesn't seem to like Cade either.

Maybe we could be friends. Although, she seems happy with Tim, in love. Whereas I can't ever imagine falling for a guy so conceited, arrogant, and cruel as Cade.

"Have you told her yet?" Ashton pipes up.

"Ash," Cade warns in that low growl of his.

"Oh, shit. You didn't? Shit's about to get interesting."

"Tell me what?" I glance at Ashton, narrowing my eyes, and then back at Cade.

"Nothing, babe. Just the party tonight."

"Party? You didn't say anything about a party."

"It's the new moon, Mia." Ashton grins, but it isn't friendly. It's dark and full of wicked intent. "We always party on the new moon."

"Stop being a dick, Ash," Sasha chides. "It'll be fun, Mia. We can hang out."

"*It'll be fun, Mia,*" Brandon mimics, and she claps him around the ear. "Bitch, what was that for?"

"Quit being an ass."

"I'm beginning to think they should let girls into the—" Channing presses his lips together, swallowing whatever he was about to say.

The two of them—Sasha and Channing—share a heated look, and I frown. Is something going on there? I can't imagine Cade or Brandon would appreciate Channing macking on Sasha. She's an heir, yes, but it's not the same for her as it is for her male counterparts. She'll never have a line of guys waiting to become her prosapia. Instead, she'll be matched with someone of Phillip Cargill's approval.

I heard my parents talking once, and apparently Sasha should get some say in who she settles down with, but women don't exactly hold the power in Gravestone. Men do, with their old traditions and chauvinistic ways.

"Hey Cade, guys," Brook's voice is like a bucket of ice-cold water, and I turn to meet her smug stare.

"Brookie, sister, long time no see." Ashton leans in to kiss her cheek. "I was beginning to think you didn't love me anymore."

"Oh, Ash, don't be ridiculous. You know I love you, I just didn't want Cade's latest *toy* to feel intimidated."

A ripple of tension goes through the air as Brook locks her narrowed gaze on me. Cade's hand remains firmly on my hip, but he doesn't intervene. He just sits there, waiting to see how I'll react, no doubt.

Bastard.

"Hello, Brook," I say, hoping she'll disappear back into whatever hole she crawled out of.

"Mila."

"It's Mia."

Someone snickers, Ashton probably. But I don't look, because I don't want Brook to think I'm scared of her, even if my stomach is a tight knot of nerves.

"Oops, my bad," she shoots me a saccharine smile, "I guess that's what happens when you're completely and utterly average. People forget your name. They forget *you*."

"Brook, play nice," Cade drawls, pulling me back into his chest.

"Whatever." She lets out an indignant huff. "I only came to ask if the party is still on tonight."

"You know it is." Cade stiffens, and I wonder what has him so on edge.

"It's going to be one hell of a night." Ashton whistles between his teeth. "Don't be a stranger, Sis. We should all hang out. Show Mia a good time."

The air crackles again, and I realize I'm the only person on the outside of whatever is going down tonight. The icy fingers of realization wrap around my throat.

"Where is this party?" I ask, schooling my expression.

"At the house, of course," Cade says, his dark eyes fixed right on mine. "But don't worry your pretty little head about it, babe." He presses the end of my nose with his fingertip. "I'll protect you."

His words make my heart beat harder. It isn't a promise...

It's a threat.

But something tells me there will be no escaping the party or Cade. Because I'm one of them now.

Whether I like it or not.

9

BEXLEY

The second I attempt to push Uncle Marcus' front door open and find it locked for the first time since I moved here, I know something is wrong.

The hairs on the back of my neck rise as I'm forced to ring the vintage-looking bell hanging beside the colossal double doors. A dong echoes in the silence around me, making my heartbeat increase a few notches, and I stand there wondering if anyone is going to answer for the longest time.

The sun is quickly descending in the sky, casting eerie shadows across the imposing brick building before me. When I'm starting to think that Uncle Marcus has forgotten he even invited me here and I consider returning to my car, there's a loud bang from inside the building.

There's a second bang before the doorknob twists and the door creaks open as if it's not moved in a few years. I blink a few times when my uncle appears in the doorway. The hall is completely dark behind him, making him hard to make out in head-to-toe black.

"What the hell are you wearing?" I balk when my eyes adjust, and I realize he's standing before me in a hooded black robe.

"Come in," he says in his usual creepy, low voice.

"Oookay."

I step inside and allow him to close and lock the door behind me.

"Follow me," he says cryptically.

Okay, I mouth behind him as I follow him through the darkness, noting that all the curtains are drawn and no lights are on. Instead, candles illuminate our journey.

"What's going on?" I ask the second he comes to a stop in front of a door that has been locked since the first day I stepped in here.

"All will become clear."

My brow furrows as he pushes open the door and I get my first look at the room inside. It looks like an office. A fucking creepy office at that.

Like the parts of the house I've seen this evening, this room is also only lit by candles. The walls are covered in bookcases, filled floor to ceiling with old books. I slip inside and take a seat when he instructs me to do so. He lowers himself to the wingbacked chair on the other side of the mahogany desk and drops his hood.

"This is really freaking weird. You're aware of that, right?" I muse, running a shaky hand over my face.

"Bexley," he says so seriously that it wipes the smirk off my face. "There are things you don't know about who you are, about who your family are, and tonight you're going to learn the truth."

"Uh... okay."

"Bexley, your surname is not Danforth. And I am not your uncle." My head spins with his words, making me wish I'd had a drink before I came here.

"What are you talk—"

"I'm your grandfather, Bexley, and your family name is Easton."

"Riiight. And this is meant to mean something to me?"

"How much do you know about the founding families of Gravestone, Son?"

"Um... not a lot. But their *heirs* are a bunch of douchebags, if you ask me."

"There are five founding families in Gravestone," he continues, ignoring my comments about Cade and his crew. "Kingsley, Davenport, Cargill, Rexford, and Easton."

"Easton?" I balk. "So, you're telling me *your* family is one of the founding families?"

"*Our* family, Bexley," he counters.

My lips part to question him, but no words leave my mouth as realization begins to dawn on me. I vaguely remember Alex trying to feed me all this bullshit back in high school. Stories of the town's founding families and their shady operations. But I didn't care then, and I still don't. It's just rumor and urban legend.

Isn't it?

"Tonight, you begin the journey to take your rightful place in Gravestone, Son."

My head spins, his words blurring into just noise. Blood rushes past my ears with a *whoosh*, the racing of my heart making my chest heave.

I have no idea how much time passes, but I don't come back to myself until Marcus pushes an ornately carved box toward me. There's a crest in the top, one that looks vaguely familiar, but I have no idea where I might have seen it before.

"This is for you."

Hesitantly, I reach out, running my fingertip over the smooth wood.

"Open it," he demands, and I flip the brass catch and lift the lid.

"What the—" I stare down at the contents, my brows pinching in confusion.

"They're part of your initiation—or Initium, as we call it."

"I-initiation?" My voice cracks.

What the actual fuck?

I look at him and then back to the contents: a gold ring with that same crest stamped in it, and a glass vial.

"W-what's this for?" I ask pointing to the little bottle with a gold lid.

"Your blood."

"I-I'm s-sorry, *what?*" I splutter.

"Your blood," he repeats, like it's the most obvious thing in the fucking world.

"This is a joke, right?" Sweat beads down my back. "This has to be a fucking joke."

"No, Bexley. This is your reality. You are one of the five Electi."

I slump back in the chair as I think about that word, about the guys I know who hold that title.

Fucking hell.

I scrub my hand down my face, praying that I'm fucking dreaming, that I'm going to wake up any moment and realize that none of this is real.

"I need you to strip down and put that on." He lifts his chin to a coat stand in the corner of the room behind me, where a black cape that resembles his is hanging up.

"Strip off?"

"Yes. Then we need to leave."

I look between Marcus, the box, and the cape. My lips part to question all of this, but no sooner has my mouth opened then it closes again.

I'm speechless.

Utterly fucking speechless.

Ten minutes later, I'm sitting beside Marcus in the back of a black SUV complete with blacked-out windows and driver, head-to-toe in black.

I glance over at him, my fists clenched so tightly on my lap I wouldn't be surprised to find my nails have pierced the skin of my palms when I finally uncurl them. I have no idea where we're going, and Marcus doesn't seem to want to give up the information, either.

"You need to put this on," he says after what feels like the longest silence in history.

I look at his hand to find a black blindfold between his fingers.

Why am I not fucking surprised.

Despite the fact that I want to argue, I already know it won't get me anywhere, so instead I take the fabric from him and slip it over my eyes.

With my vision gone, the rest of my senses come to life. The second the car comes to a stop and I'm encouraged to step out, I focus on the scent of pine that fills the air and the fact that it's deadly silent aside from our feet on the gravel beneath us.

Marcus—well, I assume it's Marcus—leads me forward with his hand on my shoulder until I hear a sound not unlike when he opened his front door earlier and this whole fucking nightmare began.

"Step," he whispers, stopping me from falling on my face a second before my toes connect with the concrete.

We take a few more steps forward, the chill in the air as well as all the unknowns right now making my skin erupt in goose bumps.

"You can remove the blindfold now."

Part of me doesn't want to. While I can't see, I'm in the dark—figuratively and literally—about what's happening around me. But knowing I won't be able to hide much longer, I reach out and pull the fabric from my face.

"What the hell?" I breathe, taking in the scene before me.

We're in some kind of old church. Candles line the walls, casting a warm glow throughout the vast space, and the rows of pews occupied by countless black-hooded figures.

"What is this?"

"It's the Initium. It's for you, and the new Rexford offering."

"I'm an offering?" I ask, reading between the lines.

Marcus nods, but he doesn't speak again. Instead, he wraps his fingers around my upper arm and walks me forward, down the aisle toward a cloaked figure standing at the front. "Cargill," he says once we come to a stop. "I present the Easton Electi initium. Bexley Louis Easton."

The figures turn to reveal two more men who each assess me silently.

My hands tremble at my sides under their scrutiny, and I hate that I'm intimidated by them, but there's no fucking chance I'm going to show it. I might not have a fucking clue as to what's going on right now, but there's no way I'm showing even an ounce of weakness.

I lift my chin in their direction as the door we came through only minutes ago closes behind us once again.

Footsteps head our way before two more hooded figures come to a stop beside us.

"Cargill," one of them says, just like Marcus did. "I present the Rexford Electi initium. Alexander Harrison Rexford."

Alex?

I turn to the side and find exactly what I was expecting.

Alex is standing in the same insane outfit that I am, only he doesn't look like he usually does. There's no sign of the smirk that's usually playing on his lips, and his face is white, as if all the blood drained out of it a while ago.

"Thank you," one of the men says, nodding to Marcus and the man who brought Alex in. "You may be seated."

Rustling sounds out behind us, and, finally, Alex looks over at me. His eyes widen in shock when he recognizes me. Confusion covers his face. It's a look I understand, and a huge part of me is relieved that I'm not the only one who doesn't have a fucking clue what is happening right now.

"Easton, Rexford. Thank you for your offering."

Both Marcus and Mr. Rexford take a step forward and stand either side of the two men before us.

I look at each of them standing there with their chins raised in their air like they're in charge of the fucking world and their eyes on the men —I'm assuming—behind us.

I knew Gravestone was a weird place, but this right now is going beyond anything I ever could have imagined.

"Welcome to tonight's Initium. We have two offerings for initiation tonight. Gentlemen, I present you with Bexley Easton and Alexander Rexford.

Alexander Rexford...

Did he know about all of this, or is he as clueless as I am right now?

I don't know why I'm asking myself this as we're encouraged to turn around. His wide eyes and pale face say it all.

The second I look up from the stone floor at my feet, I lock eyes with the one person I want nothing to do with.

Cade fucking Kingsley.

He stands there in the front row with his crew on either side of him, his hood over his head and a smirk playing on his lips.

He knew about this. Whatever the fuck *this* is. That motherfucker knew.

"Tonight, on the dawn of a new moon, begins the initiation process. Over the next two weeks, the initium will be tested." Phillip Cargill's voice echoes through the chamber. "The status of Electi, though a birthright, must be earned. Upon successful completion of the Initium, on the night of the full moon, you will be anointed as Electi and take up your rightful place in society.

"Initium Easton, initium Rexford, please take a step forward." Every set of eyes before us watches as we both do as we're told.

"Electi," he barks, and Cade, Tim, Channing, and Brandon stand and take a step toward us. Amusement dances in Cade's eyes, and I swallow down my apprehension and hold his stare.

"Disrobe." The voice booms from behind us, and to begin with I don't think it can possibly be directed at us. That is, until Cade's brow rises as if his patience is running out. "You heard him. Disrobe."

"Uh..." I glance over at Alex and watch in horror as he does as demanded of him. The black fabric pools on the floor at his feet, leaving him totally naked.

"Easton," someone growls quietly.

Realizing I don't have much choice, I follow orders and allow the fabric to fall from my shoulders.

I regret it the second Cade moves and the reflection of the candlelight flashes in the blade I now realize he's holding.

My stomach twists with uncertainty.

"Please stand for the blood oath."

One of the men behind us begins chanting something in another language I don't understand before the rest of the men start repeating certain words back to him.

Marcus steps up to me once more, and, when I look down, I find him holding that small glass vial that was inside the box.

Holy shit.

Blood oath.

They're not joking.

I look to my left, and my eyes collide with Alex's at exactly the same time Cade steps up to me, the point of his knife pressing against my upper thigh.

"Sanguis." The knife presses into my skin. "Imperium." He drags it across my thigh, pain burning through me. "Electi." Warmth begins to trickle down my leg before Marcus drops to his knee and collects some in the little bottle before twisting the top closed and passing it back to one of the men behind me.

Cade takes a step back, an accomplished smile on his face.

What just happened might be some kind of fucked-up ritual...

But he's going to fucking pay for that.

10

MIA

"You look pretty," Sasha says as she finishes coating her lashes with mascara.

"Thanks." I smooth the skirt down my thighs, hoping it'll grow a few inches. It's short. Really short. But when I arrived at Cade's house an hour ago with my outfit choices, Sasha took one look at them and deemed them all inappropriate. Apparently, the theme of the night is sexy slut, because she's wearing what can only be described as something that wouldn't look amiss on a professional dominatrix. Effortlessly, she pulls off all the leather and lace with her slim frame and feminine curves. I, on the other hand, am not so used to having the curve of my ass on display.

"Cade will freak when he sees you. Bexley, too."

"Bexley? He's going to be here?" My stomach flutters.

"Maybe." She winks at me through the mirror. "All set? The guys will be back soon."

"Where have they been again?" Cade's instructions for tonight had been vague. He texted me, telling me to be at the house for seven and to wait with Sasha.

"They had a meeting..."

"A meeting? Like an Electi thing?"

"Something like that." She brushes me off, grabbing her cell phone and shoving it into her back pocket. Picking up the red lip gloss off the dresser, she coats her lips in it before offering it to me.

"I'm good, thanks."

"You need a little something to take off the edge." Sasha moves over to her nightstand and opens the drawer, pulling out a small tin. "I've got E, blow, or some good old pot. Choose your poison."

"You want me to... I mean, I don't take drugs."

"Of course you don't." She rolls her eyes at me, and I feel about six inches tall. "It might make the night a little easier."

"Easier? What's that supposed to mean? It's just a party." But the second the words fly out of my mouth, I know I'm wrong.

It's not just a party.

It's a party at Cade's house—the Electi's house—on the night of the new moon. Who knows what strange things will go down. Especially after how cagey they were all acting today.

"Should I be worried?" I ask Sasha. I still don't know if I can trust her. She is one of them, after all. But she's been nothing but nice to me, and I have a gut feeling she's on my side.

"You'll be safe. Everyone who matters knows who you belong to." She eyes the pendant lying against my chest.

"Great," I mutter under my breath.

"You sure you don't want something? I think I have some Xanax in the bathroom cabinet, that might be—"

"I'm good, thanks." I plan on sticking to alcohol only.

"Suit yourself." Sasha plucks a small blue pill from the tin and pops it on her tongue.

"Do you do that a lot?" I watch her wash it down with the remainder of her soda. Although, now I'm beginning to wonder if it's more than just pop.

"Sometimes." She shrugs as if it's no big deal. "I like the buzz."

"Are the guys into all that?"

"They dabble now and again, but usually only when it's the inner circle. In case you haven't noticed, Cade doesn't like to be out of control."

The doorbell rings somewhere in the house, and Sasha gives a little shriek of excitement. "Time to get this show on the road." She fluffs her thick, auburn hair and grabs my hand, and I'm almost positive I hear her whisper, "You're going to wish you took the drugs."

CADE'S HOUSE—THE house he shares with the other Electi—is a big, sprawling place on the edge of the lake. Shrouded in trees and set on the edge of the forest nestled between Gravestone and the college campus, it's the perfect place for college kids to let loose and go wild.

Tonight is no exception.

When I followed Sasha to open the door earlier, a group of guys and girls spilled into the house and turned it into party central. There's a DJ booth set up in the corner of the huge yard, pumping out chilled beats, and girls in bikinis sit around the edge of the pool, splashing their toes in the water, while guys circle them like piranhas.

I recognize almost everyone here. They're verus, like me; kids descended from the founding families.

Annabel spots me and hurries over. "There you are." Her dress barely covers her ass, and she's got a goofy grin plastered on her face. "Are you okay?" I ask, frowning. Her pupils are blown wide, and she can hardly stand still.

"Hell yeah."

I grab her hand and pull her to the side. "What did you take?"

"Relax," she shrugs, "everyone is doing it. I feel so freakin' good." Annabel throws her arms around me and hugs me like her life depends on it. "I love you, Mia."

"Okay, happy girl." Sasha peels my friend off me. "Why don't you go hang out with Jared and his friends." She spins Annabel around and gives her a little shove.

"Will she be okay?" Dread pools in my stomach as I watch some guy I recognize from school pull Annabel into his side.

"Jared will watch out for her. Come on, let's go find the guys." Sasha takes my hand, leading me away from the crowd and down a dark path. I can see a small stone building, some kind of mausoleum. Shadows dance over the roof and walls, and a shiver runs up my spine.

"What is this place?"

"The guys come out here sometimes to get away from the craziness.

Relax..." I ground to a halt, hesitating, and she rolls her eyes. "Nothing's going to happen to you."

"Easy for you to say, you're one of them."

"Newsflash, Mia. So are you."

Just then, male laughter pierces the air and Cade and Ashton spill out of the door.

"Sasha, I see you delivered us tonight's offering." His lip curves with wicked intent.

"Knock it off, Ash." Cade moves around him and stalks toward me. "You look beautiful, babe." He runs his knuckles down my cheek, and although I want to repel his touch, I can't deny his sudden one-eighty softens something inside me.

But I know better than to fall for Cade Kingsley's attempt at seduction.

"We should get going." He flicks his eyes to Brandon and Channing, who spill out of the building. Something passes between them, and my brows furrow.

"What's going on?" I ask, the hairs on the back of my neck tingling.

"You'll see." Cade dips his head and kisses the corner of my mouth, then grabs my hand and starts leading me back toward the party.

Like a slow-building wave, people stop what they're doing as Cade and the Electi pass. I feel their stares of intrigue and glares of jealousy. Like me, the verus understand Gravestone's history, the traditions and ceremonies. We don't truly *know*, nobody does... nobody except the Electi and Quinctus, but we're aware of the town's ways.

Cade comes to a stop in front of the French doors leading back into the house. Pulling me into his side, he waits for his friends to fall into line beside him. I catch Sasha's eye as she lingers at Brandon's side, but she simply smiles.

I don't feel like smiling. I feel like the rug is about to be pulled out from beneath me.

"Who's ready to party?" Cade yells, and his voice is like a shot firing in the air. People cheer and clap, their crazed maniacal laughter rising into the night's sky.

"I said, who's ready to party?"

The noise turns to madness as the gathered crowd jostles to get closer, as if they can't resist Cade's magnetic allure. Even I sense it—his power rippling around us like a current in the air.

"Tonight is the new moon. It marks the beginning of a new cycle. Rebirth. It also marks the start of the Initium." There's a collective gasp. The Initium is one of Quinctus' most sacred ceremonies: the trials of the new Electi. All first-born male heirs must complete the Initium.

A commotion behind the crowd of people draws my attention, and I narrow my gaze to see Tim and Channing pushing two hooded figures toward us.

"What is this?" My voice wavers.

Cade grins down at me, his eyes glittering with victory. "Surprise, babe."

Before I can ask what he means, the two guys stumble before us, landing on their hands and knees. They're dressed in some kind of robes, their legs bare beneath.

Cade nods at his friends, and Tim and Channing fist the hoods and yank them off.

"Bexley?" His name dies on my tongue as I stare into his cloudy eyes.

"What the f-fuck, King... sley," he slurs the words, his head rolling on his shoulders.

"What did you do?" I breathe, trying to wiggle out of Cade's hold.

"Meet our newest initiates. Alexander Rexford and Bexley Easton."

A shock goes through the air. Excited whispers carrying on the breeze, but I'm speechless.

Completely and utterly speechless.

"What the f... uck did you give... us?" Bexley thrashes against Channing's hold, but it's futile.

"Electi isn't just handed down because of your name," Cade sneers. "It's earned. So tonight, consider this your first test. Take them to the pit."

"The pit?" I balk. I've never heard of something called the pit. But whatever it is, it doesn't sound good.

Channing and Tim haul Alex and Bexley to their feet and drag them across the yard toward the lake.

Cade is about to follow them, but I grab his arm and tug sharply. His eyes collide with mine, darkening.

"What the hell is this?"

"Turns out Bexley and Alex aren't who we thought they were." His jaw clenches. "Consider this part one of their induction into the Electi."

I have so many questions, but Cade looks one second away from storming off, so instead I ask, "What happens at the pit?"

"That depends on your boy." He eyes narrow with accusation.

"My—" I stop myself. He's baiting me, but I refuse to give him the ammunition. Nothing happened with me and Bexley, not really. And now I know he's Electi—or at least, he will be once the trials are over—whatever spark I felt with him is gone.

He's one of them.

My stomach sinks.

Whether he wants it or not, Bexley Danf—I mean, Easton—is one of them.

How did this even happen?

Maybe Sasha was right when she said I should have taken the pill, because this night is already fucked up, and I have a bad feeling it's only going to get worse.

I press my lips together in defiance. Cade's brow arches, and he looks almost impressed. He doesn't say another word as he snags my wrist and pulls me toward where everyone has disappeared to. Darkness envelops us as the trees seem to close in, making the world grow small. But then we spill into a clearing, the amber glow of flames from a nearby bonfire lighting up the night sky. Everything is quiet, hushed as Cade leads me through the human circle. He hands me off to Sasha and Channing, who each take my arms as he moves toward the center. There, Bexley and Alex wait on their knees.

"Do you know what this is?" Cade asks them.

"F-fuck you," Bexley spits, his body swaying. His tan skin glistens under the moonlight. He's burning up, his muscles quivering as Ashton grips the back of his head and forces him to look at Cade.

In this moment, I realize the whispers and rumors are true. Ashton Moore is depraved. Maybe even more depraved than his best friend. His maniacal grin twists his face, making him appear like a monster in the dark.

"Rexford... be a good boy and tell your guy what this is."

"Caedes."

"Ding, ding, ding, and the point goes to Rexford." Cade leans down and roughly grabs Alex's jaw. "You'll make Daddy Rexford proud before the night's out. That's right, everyone, Alexander Shaw is, in fact, Harrison Rexford's bastard child. But rules are rules, and the first-born son of an heir gets their shot at becoming an Electi."

Anticipation buzzes through the crowd. A lot of these kids live for the whispers and rumors that circulate Gravestone like an unrelenting breeze. But hearing it and seeing it are two very different things.

"Caedes is usually a little bloody fun. A chance for initiates to show their strength and go head-to-head with their fellow initiates. But not this year... this year, they will compete in a different gauntlet. This year, they'll take on... us." Cade yanks his t-shirt over his head and cracks his knuckles. Raucous applause fills the air, a bloodthirsty shrill that I feel all the way to the pit of my stomach.

"Did you know about this?" I ask Sasha, but her pupils are already blown and the grin splitting her face tells me she's as high as a kite.

"I told you to take the pill." She shrugs as if it's just business as usual.

It isn't business as fucking usual.

"Tell me you're not going out there?" I hiss at Channing, but he's already moving away from me, yanking his t-shirt over his head and approaching his friends. The five of them—Cade, Ashton, Tim, Brandon, and Channing—stand before Bexley and Alex like bronzed gods.

"The only way you leave here tonight," Cade says, ushering the crowd into silence once more, "is to submit."

"Oh God," I breathe. He's insane. Completely and utterly insane.

Alex looks green, like he's going to puke at any moment. But not Bexley. He looks furious, his eyes burning with contempt. Staggering to his feet, he runs a trembling hand through his hair, levelling each of the Electi with a murderous glare.

"You want carnage?" He spits the words, their venom snaking through me like barbed wire. "Come get it."

11

BEXLEY

"The only way to make a difference, to make a change, is to see this through. Everyone in this town needs you to do this." Uncle Marcus—Grandad's, I guess—words ring out in my mind as I stare Cade fucking Kinsley right in the eyes.

If he thinks he's scaring me enough to make me back down, to make me submit like he craves, then he needs to think again. Because I don't submit to anyone, especially not a jumped-up, power-hungry cunt like him.

Even without Marcus' words ringing loud in my ears and the haze from whatever they gave us back at that freaky-as-fuck chamber, there's no way I'd walk away from this fight. Even if it ends up being five against one.

It might have taken a lot of time and effort on Alex's part to scale my walls and worm his way inside my life, but he's the opposite of me, and I already know that he can't fight for shit.

They're going to take him down in less than two minutes, I'd put money on it. I, however, have every intention of making it hard work for them.

The bloodthirsty crowd chants and cheers, desperate for the fight to start as tension ripples around us.

I don't look at the other four. I don't give a fuck about them.

I'm going for the main man.

He's my target. And I think that might be the case long after tonight is done.

"Robes off, initium. Let's see what you're made of," Cade taunts.

My hands drop to the tie around my waist as my head continues to spin. I should have guessed they'd spike the drinks we were forced to down as part of whatever fucked-up ceremony we endured in that church not so long ago. But the second my vision started to blur and my muscles started to relax, I knew what they'd done.

Lucky for me, though—after all the shit I've taken over the years, I have a high tolerance for that crap, and unlike Alex, who almost passed out on the journey here, I'm still somewhat with it.

I rip the tie open and shrug the fabric from my shoulders, now grateful for the shorts they allowed us to pull on, although suspicious of them doing something as kind as that.

A smirk pulls at my lips as I wonder if it's because my cock is bigger than Cade's.

"Something funny, Easton?"

"Yeah," I spit. "You."

I crack my knuckles, the crunch settling something inside me for a second as a growl rumbles up Cade's throat.

"You're going down, motherfucker."

He flies at me, but I'm ready for him and block his first hit. That really doesn't do anything to tame the beast.

He chuckles, but there's nothing amusing about it. It's more like I imagine the devil himself might look if he were ever to laugh.

"What are you waiting for?" I taunt as Ashton steps up beside Cade.

"Nothin'," he spits, and this time when he lunges, I'm not as fast, and his knuckles connect with my jaw, snapping my head to the side as my face burns red hot and pain lances down my spine.

I barely get a chance to catch my breath before more fists rain down on me. Cade focuses on my face, because he's a twisted motherfucker and will want to be the one to claim the visible evidence of this night, while Ashton focuses on my torso, as if his main goal is to crack every single rib.

I give it everything I have, but the moment Ashton stepped up to the plate, I knew the odds weren't in my favor, and the second a massive cheer booms from the crowd, it's clear my job just got a hell of a lot harder.

Glancing to my left, I find what I feared: Alex is out cold on the muddy, wet ground at my feet, while Brandon and Tim take a step back.

"One down, one to go," Cade taunts. "And it's five against one. How are you fairing your chances, Easton?"

"Fuck. You," I spit, spraying his face in blood and spittle.

The sick cunt doesn't even bother to wipe it away as he closes the space between us. He nods his chin over my shoulder, and I sense the others move behind me until I'm in the middle of their fucked-up circle.

Silence falls around me as the crowd watches, waiting to see what's going to happen next. Movement over Cade's shoulder catches my eye, and once I manage to focus, I find Mia.

All the breath rushes from my lungs at the devastated look on her face and the tear tracks down her cheeks as she stares at me.

Fuck. Even crying, she's beautiful.

That's the last thought I manage to get in before someone's fist lands in my lower back and I fall forward onto my knees, right before Cade.

"Time to bow to your fucking king, asshole." Cade's foot lands in the center of my chest, putting enough force behind it that I have no choice but to crash to the ground, my shoulder smarting as I land on it.

"I'm not cowering to you, Kingsley." I jump back up and fly at him, my fist connecting with his nose with a loud crunch. That one sound momentarily makes the pain searing through my body worth it.

Blood pours down his face and into his mouth. He spits a load out, shaking his head at me. "Cunt," he roars before both he and Ashton strike again.

Hit after hit rains down on every inch of my body they can reach. The crowd goes wild, but after a while, all the noise and chaos surrounding me begins to quiet, probably my body's way of telling me this is coming to an end, and not in the way I hoped it would.

Two pairs of hands wrap around my upper arms, and I'm hauled back against two warm bodies, giving Cade and Ashton free shots without me fighting back.

I jolt against their hold, my quickly depleting energy is nothing compared to their strength. The darkness is starting to set in, and I know that soon, Cade is going to get exactly what he wants: me in a bloody pile on the ground at his feet.

Their fists continue as my knees start to buckle under my weight. Still I try to fight back, but it's futile.

I'd lost this fight long ago, and it's time I accept the inevitable.

The pain lessens, and I start to think it's over, but seconds later, a stronger punch snaps my head to the side. Stars flash in my vision as I rely even more on the two guys taking my weight.

Two more brutal punches land before Ashton's name being called rings through my ears. Seconds later, everything goes black.

THE PAIN IS the only thing I can focus on. It's like when I was seven and fell off my bike, breaking my leg in two places. Only this time, the pain isn't just in my leg. It's in every single inch of my body. I swear to fucking God that even my toenails hurt.

But that all seems to vanish when she touches me.

Her fingertips gently run down my cheek as she inspects me for wounds.

Mia

I want to say her name, but nothing works. I can't even part my lips.

I put everything I have into moving my arm to reach for her. To feel her warmth against my skin. To know that she's really here.

Tell me all of this is a nightmare, I want to beg.

This can't be real. I can't really be part of this fucked-up world that I know nothing about. I'm a Danforth. My dad is a Danforth, right?

But if this is real, and Marcus is my grandfather, then who is...

Something soft and warm presses against my bottom lip, and all thoughts fall from my head.

She's fixing me.

She's here.

It comes as some comfort, but the fact that I've got these wounds in the first place means that there's a chance it's real.

Fuck.

My head spins and my body remains motionless as I draw support from her tender touch. I wish she'd talk to me. That she'd explain what really happened tonight. Because the reality has to be different. It *has* to be.

I feel myself fading, and I try to claw to reality to keep me here with her. I don't want to succumb to the darkness where I'll be alone. Cold. Confused.

I want her to tell me that everything is okay, normal, and that my life as I know it isn't completely over.

That I'm not basically owned by Cade Kingsley and his asshole friends who chanted all that Latin at me earlier, watching as that fucker dragged a knife across my skin and forced me to drink out of a chalice.

It can't be real.

I awake with a start, ripping my eyes open to find that I'm shrouded in darkness and that the pain I thought I'd dreamed about is very, very real.

Blinking a few times, I allow my eyes to adjust, and when they finally do, I find a figure sitting with his back against the wall and his arms wrapped around his legs that are pulled up against his chest.

"A-Alex?" My voice is so rough, it sounds like I've been asleep for a week.

Maybe I have.

"Yeah," he replies. His own sounds hollow, broken.

"What did... Are we really... Fuck," I breathe through the pain burning every inch of me. "What the fuck was that?"

"Our worst fucking nightmare," he sighs.

"Did you know that was going to happen?" I ask. Whatever *that* was.

"Does it sound like I fucking knew?" he hisses, and I don't know if it's from the pain, frustration, or both.

"You're a Rexford? How is that even possible?"

"You tell me. I thought my dad was dead." His defeated tone speaks to me, and I fight to sit up so I can support him. My body screams as I attempt to move. After what feels like an hour, I finally manage to push from the cold, solid concrete floor beneath me so I'm on my hands and knees.

I crawl over to him, hating that Cade Kingsley has reduced me to this, before lowering my ass back to the ground beside him. "I'm sorry," I croak.

"It's not your fault."

"At least we're in this together though, eh?"

"Oh yeah," Alex lets out a strained chuckle, "that really makes it all better." He stiffens, sucking in a sharp breath. "Motherfucker..."

"What is it?"

"He wouldn't... no way..." he murmurs to himself, and for a second, I'm worried he has a head injury, because he's not making any sense.

"Alex," I bark, "will you tell me what the fuck is going on?"

"There's something you should know." His words come out strained as he meets my bleary stare.

"Go on..." My throat is dry, because somehow I know I'm not going to like whatever he says next.

"Your uncle... I mean, your grandfather... well, he... fuck." He hesitates, and I drill holes into the side of his face. "He asked me to befriend you all those months ago."

"What the actual fuck?"

"Yeah, he checks in on my mom occasionally. One day he was over for dinner and collared me. Said he had a nephew coming to live with him and that he'd need a friend—"

"He pay you or something?" I grit out, anger skittering up my spine as I try to process what he's saying.

"What? No! It wasn't like that, I swear, man."

"So what the fuck was it like?"

"He said I'd be doing him a big favor, and he's always helped me and Mom out, so I thought, why not? Besides, it only took one look at you to know you needed a friend."

"Fuck you, *Rexford*," I sneer.

Alex flinches. "Guess I deserve that. But you know it's true." The faintest of smiles tugs at his mouth. "I had no idea you were his grandson or the Easton heir, Bex, I swear. He pulled the wool over both our eyes there."

"Why, though? Why go to all those lengths?"

None of this makes any sense.

"Maybe he knew about my dad all along. Maybe he knew this day would come and wanted us to be in it together."

The fight leaves my body on a pained sigh. He's right. Somewhere deep inside, I know Alex is right. My uncle... no, my *grandfather* orchestrated this to make sure we had each other going into this thing.

But to what end?

Silence settles between us, and I rest my head back against the wall and close my eyes, willing the pain to subside. "How much do you know about... about all of this?"

"Not enough to fully understand, but enough to know that our lives have just turned to shit," Alex replies.

"This Initium thing, is it serious?"

"As far as I know, yeah. There are stories... I heard one guy died way back..."

"Fuck."

"This isn't just some rich pricks playing games, man."

"We can say no though, right?"

Alex laughs, and for a minute he sounds like his old self, but then it turns manic and I start to wonder if the drugs they plied us with are having a lasting effect on him.

"No, Bex. We can't get out of this. It's our blood right. The only way out is to... is to die."

"We could leave," I suggest.

"They'd find us. The Easton name is on the verge of extinction. Without us, they don't have a firstborn heir for our family lines."

"But Channing is a..."

"He's not a firstborn heir. Now I exist..." he trails off, clearly not ready to go there. "You're the only Easton heir. Marcus' son, your... your dad, he died..." I raise a brow, wondering how true that is, seeing as he thought his own father was dead until tonight. "It's true, man. I'm sorry."

"My dad is a Danforth," I say, more to myself than him, because I know it's a lie.

"You might need to talk to your mom about that." He lets out a weary sigh.

"Right. Fucking hell."

"We need to get out of here."

"You fucking think?" I deadpan. "First, we need to figure out where the hell we are."

He makes a nondescript noise in the back of his throat. "I think we're in Cade's basement. If you really listen, you can just about hear the music from the party."

"How long have we been down here?"

"A long time."

"And the party's still going?"

"It's the night of the new moon. They'll party until sunrise and then some."

I have no intention of hanging around and waiting for Cade and his gang of loyal followers to find us and do whatever the fuck else they've got planned for us.

"There's only one door." Alex nods toward a set of stairs. "There's no fucking way they'll allow us just to walk out through it."

"Maybe not, but we've at least got to try."

And then when we're free, I'm going straight to my uncle to get answers.

12

MIA

I wake with someone pressed up against my back. Fear steals my breath as I lie there, frozen in place. My bleary eyes strain against the light as I take in my surroundings. It's a fairly plain room, light gray walls and darker gray curtains, but there's a feminine touch in the pale gray and pink covers I'm under and the pink swirls painted around the mirror.

Glancing gingerly over my shoulder, I sigh with relief at the sight of Sasha lying there.

It's not Cade.

I'm not in Cade's room. Thank God.

I can't quite remember how I got here, but I'll take it over waking up in Cade's bed any day.

"Ugh, what time is?" Sasha croaks, squinting up at me.

"Uh, it's," I turn to check the clock on the nightstand, "a little after nine."

"I need water… and headache pills. And maybe some pancakes."

I chuckle. "Some night, huh?" The words make me bristle as I remember watching Cade and his friends beat the crap out of Bexley. When they dragged him and Alex away, the two of them a bloody, barely conscious mess, I'd tried to go after them, but Sasha and Channing had marched me to the nearest keg and made me drink. One drink turned into two, and two turned into three, and before I knew it, the pit in my stomach had gone, replaced by a warm buzz.

Flipping onto my back, shoulder to shoulder with Sasha, I let out a small sigh. "What was that last night?"

"Caedes?"

"Yeah..."

"You really haven't heard of it?"

"I've heard stuff... but I've never heard of Cade and Ashton almost beating a guy to death." Anguish snakes through me as I wonder how Bexley is this morning.

"They didn't..." She stops herself. "Bexley will live. He's going to have to survive a whole lot more than that."

"I don't understand."

"Bexley wasn't supposed to exist, Mia. He's an Easton heir." She lets out a heavy sigh. "Easton was always the dominant bloodline until Marcus' son died. Bexley's existence changes everything."

"I'm still not sure why it matters?"

"Why?" Sasha scoffs. "Because Cade doesn't like outsiders, and Bexley didn't grow up in Gravestone. He doesn't know of our ways. Cade sees him as a threat."

"Wait—you knew, didn't you? All along, you knew who he was?"

It makes sense now, the strange animosity between Cade and Bexley. I thought it was about me, but it wasn't. At least, not for Cade. I'm not sure Bexley knew any of this until yesterday. If he did, he sure did a good job of hiding it.

"Yeah, Q told us about Bexley and Alex over the summer. But we were under strict instructions not to say anything."

"And Alex is Harrison Rexford's son?"

"Yep."

"Wow. So... he's Hadley Rexford's brother." Hadley left Gravestone three years ago under mysterious circumstances. Rumors at the time were that she got into some trouble with an older guy, so her parents sent her away.

Sasha grows stiff beside me, and I ask, "What is it?"

"Nothing."

"You mean you can't tell me?"

"It's nothing, I promise. I'm sorry last night went down the way it did, but I—"

"I get it, Cade's in control. What he says goes."

"Yeah, something like that," Sasha grumbles.

"Hey, can I ask you something?" She nods. "You and Channing—"

Her hand slaps over my mouth, and she shakes her head. "Don't." I frown, and she quickly adds, "There's nothing going on with me and Channing, got it?"

I nod slowly, my eyes wide with confusion.

"Sorry," Sasha removes her hand, "if the guys overhear you asking that, they'll freak. Electi aren't free to choose who they date, and they definitely can't date each other's siblings."

"But... Channing isn't technically the Rexford heir now, is he?"

"As far as Q is concerned, he isn't. But Cade is a whole other story."

"Just exactly who is in control here?"

"Quinctus control the town, they always have. But Gravestone U is the Electi's domain. Crap, I probably shouldn't be telling you all this." Sasha sits up and runs a hand through her hair.

"I'll find out one way or another." I shuffle up, pressing my back against the headboard.

"Yeah, I guess."

I toy with my Electi pendant. "Cade is determined to see this thing through. Why?"

"Honestly, I don't know. But if there's one thing I do know, it's that Cade Kingsley doesn't do anything without a motive. Watch your back, yeah?" She climbs out of bed and stretches. "And never let your guard down. Not for a second."

I nod, my throat too thick to reply.

"Get cleaned up and then come down to the kitchen. Cade will expect to see you there."

My stomach drops. The last thing I want to do is eat breakfast with the Electi and pretend everything is okay. But I'm starting to realize that I don't have a choice.

I'm Cade Kingsley's prosapia, and for some unknown reason, he's determined to make me his.

AFTER WASHING my face and finger-brushing my teeth with some toothpaste I found in Sasha's small bathroom, I slip on the Gravestone U hoodie she left out for me and make my way downstairs. Male laughter drifts down the hall, making the hairs along my neck stand on edge.

They're all in there. Cade and his minions, eating breakfast, acting like they didn't beat Bexley and Alex to a bloody pulp.

What is this life?

I hesitate, contemplating making a run for it. But Sasha is right: the last thing I want to do is give Cade more ammunition. Steeling my spine, I inhale a shuddering breath before entering the kitchen. The room falls silent.

"Sleep well, babe?" Cade gets up and stalks toward me, a wolfish grin on his lips.

"It was fine," I say, trying to disguise the tremor to my voice. Channing catches my eye over Cade's shoulder and something crosses his expression, but then Cade is there, demanding my full attention.

He slides his finger under my jaw and lifts my face to meet his. "I missed you this morning. I had a little... actually, a very big problem you could have helped me out with."

Ashton snickers, and I shoot him a harsh look.

"Kitty's got claws," he says. "You'd better watch this one, Cade. Something tells me she won't come easily... if you get—"

"Ash!" Cade barks, his eyes not leaving mine. "Ignore him, babe. He's just jealous I get to tame you and he doesn't."

"Nah, I like my girls with a little more bite, if you know what I'm saying."

"I'm hungry." I shirk out of Cade's grip and make for the breakfast counter. "Are there pancakes?" Flipping my hair over one shoulder, I take Cade's stool, forcing him to stand.

Sasha's lips curve, and I'm sure I see a little flash of pride in her eyes. She's right. You can't show Cade and his friends even an ounce of fear, because they'll use it against you.

"So Mia," Ashton says as I load a plate with pancakes. "What did you think about the party?"

"It was okay, I guess." I shrug, barely meeting his eyes.

"Okay?" He chuckles darkly. "It was fucking epic. Did you see Alex go down? I thought he was going to cry... shit, I would have paid to see that."

A ripple goes through the room.

"I still can't believe the two of you are related." He pins Channing with a skeptic look. "I mean you're so... and he's so..."

"Knock it off, fucker. I didn't know any more than you did."

"The two of you are cousins?" I ask.

"Apparently so. Our dads are brothers." Channing sips his juice. "I guess Aunt Marissa wasn't putting out enough, so Uncle Harrison went elsewhere."

I bristle at his words. I don't know Alex's mom very well, but I know she isn't like most of the vapid, snobby women of Gravestone.

"Why do you think he waited until now to claim Alex as his son?" The words spill from my lips before I can stop them. Rexford has an Electi heir—Channing. But his father isn't the Quinctus elder. Harrison is. So although Alex is younger than Channing, he's the heir of an elder, which trumps everything.

I feel Cade's eyes drilling holes into the top of my head as he curves his body over mine and drops his chin to my shoulder. "Well, that's the million-dollar question, isn't it?"

"Probably realized Channing isn't fit for the job," Ashton says, and Channing flips him off.

"Fuck you, man. I've got more right to be here than you."

The air crackles with tension, and I get the sense that perhaps the Electi aren't as united as they make out.

"Ashton's here because I want him here," Cade says. "Q can go fuck themselves if they think a Rexford or Easton heir changes anything. Channing has Rexford blood, that's all that matters."

I catch Sasha's eye, a million and one questions running through my head. I always thought Quinctus ruled Gravestone, but Cade talks like *he* holds all the power. She shakes her head discreetly and I press my lips together, swallowing the other questions I want answers to.

"What did you do with them?" she asks. "After you beat the shit out of them."

"You're not upset over a little blood are you, Sash?" Brandon teases, and she flips him off.

"Just wondering is all."

"They're learning their place." Cade moves around me and snags a pastry from the plate. I have no idea who prepared all this food, but I can't imagine the Electi did it.

Just then, Tim comes running into the kitchen. He stops sharply when he sees me and arches a brow at Cade.

"She's with me." He pins him with a hard look. "Whatever you've got to say, spit it out."

"We've got a problem… with the… rats."

"The rats?" Ashton smirks. "What kind of problem?"

"They're gone."

"Gone?" Cade shoots upright. "What do you mean, they're gone? They were supposed to be locked up."

I wince. They're not talking about rats at all. They're talking about Bexley and Alex.

Cade scrubs a hand down his face and lets out a frustrated breath. "You two," he moves closer to Ashton and Brandon, keeping his voice low, "go with Tim…" His words become inaudible over the blood roaring in my ears.

They all glance at me, but I pretend to be eating my breakfast. Then the three of them march out of the room, taking the air with them.

"Everything okay?" I ask Cade.

"Nothing for you to worry about, babe." He winks. "But I'm going to need to take care of this. Sasha and Channing will make sure you get back to your dorm okay."

"Sure."

His eyes drop to my lips and I hold my breath, silently hoping he won't kiss me.

"Cade, man, let's go," someone yells through the house, and he backs away from me.

"I'll see you soon, Mia."

My stomach twists at his words. "Bye."

Cade runs his thumb over his lower lip before spinning on his heel and taking off after his friends.

"They had them down there?" Sasha pins Channing with a look of disbelief.

"Leave it," he warns her, and hurt etches into her expression.

"Fuck you, Chan." Sasha slides off her stool, the legs scraping against the tiles. "Fuck you." She flees the kitchen, leaving me with Channing.

"Channing, about—"

But he cuts me off, shooting up from his stool and raking a hand through his dirty blond hair. "You need to watch your back." He echoes Sasha's words from earlier. "I don't know what Kingsley's obsession with you and Easton is, but it isn't going to end well. For anyone." He stalks off without so much as a backward glance.

But his warning stays with me long after he's gone.

13

BEXLEY

My entire body screams as I stumble through Marcus' once again unlocked front door. I have no idea if he's expecting me or not, but he's about to discover I'm here.

"MARCUS," I bellow as loud as my ribs will allow. It might have been more than thirty-six hours since Cade and his friends beat the crap out of me, but they still smart.

Silence ensues.

"MARCUS."

Still, there's nothing. But he's here. I know he is. His car was out the front, and there are lights on.

Remembering my first visit to one of his hidden rooms last night, I go in that direction, staring at the grand staircase as if it's Mount Kilimanjaro. Sucking in a steeling breath, I wrap my fingers around the polished mahogany bannister and begin dragging myself up.

We might have managed to walk out of Cade's mansion way easier than we were expecting to, but I'm not foolish enough to think that's the end of it.

The streets were deserted yesterday morning as we escaped, and neither of us had our cells to call for a cab. I wanted to go straight to Marcus, but Alex insisted on dragging me back to campus and sleeping off some of the pain. Considering I slept most of yesterday, waking only to take a piss and shove more pain pills down my throat, I guess he had it right.

I suggested that Alex come with me this morning, so we could get some answers together, but he wanted to see his mom and unearth the truth about his father. I don't blame him. I've got a million and one questions for my mother, too, but Marcus is more pressing.

I need to know what the hell is going on here, and what he meant when he told me that I had to see this through. Hell knows I need a solid reason to continue with this farce.

Cade wanted to kill me last night, I could see it in his eyes. But he can't, and he knows it. If all of this is true and Alex and I are Quinctus heirs, then he can't lay a hand on us. I guess that explains why he hated me on sight, because I have no doubt he's known this little secret all along.

It takes what feels like a year to get to the door I want. I come to a stop beside it, resting my hand against the wall as I try to catch my breath, squeezing my eyes closed tight as I will the pain to subside.

This isn't my first beating—and I somehow doubt it'll be my last. I can deal with the pain, and, much like events in my past, I use it to fuel my own anger and my need for answers.

Knowing that I either need to do this or go and find my old bedroom and curl up in a ball, I take a step forward, not bothering to knock. After last night's revelations, I think we're a little past that.

I throw the door open and stumble inside. The scent of the incense he was burning in here and in the chamber last night assaults my senses, and my fists curl in frustration.

As I expected, Marcus is sitting behind his desk. He was staring at a notebook sitting atop it, but at my interruption, his eyes lift to find mine.

He gasps, pushing to stand the second he takes in my injuries. It's not hard. My face is littered with cuts and bruises, one of my eyes almost swollen shut.

"What the hell happened?"

"What do you mean *what happened*?" I ask, mocking his tone. "You sent me into that bullshit initiation with zero knowledge of what to expect. That's what fucking happened, *Gramps*."

"Take a seat," he encourages, pulling one out for me.

If it weren't for my legs being minutes away from giving out, I'd refuse, but as it is, I gratefully accept the help. Marcus walks to one of the ornately carved cabinets and pulls out a decanter of amber liquid and two glasses. Despite the time, he pours generous amounts into each before placing one on the desk before me and keeping his own in his hands.

"Caedes?" he asks, running a hand over his jaw.

"Yeah," I mutter, knocking back the whiskey. It burns all the way down, but I welcome the warmth.

"I didn't think Alex had that in him," Marcus mutters, taking a sip of his own drink.

"*Alex*? Alex didn't do this," I spit, pointing at my ruined face.

"But Caedes is meant to be the initium fighting for supremacy." His brows pull together in confusion.

"Not last night. It was Cade fucking Kingsley throwing his weight around and reigning supreme," I mutter, wishing my glass had been refilled already.

"It's worse than I thought," he says to himself.

"What was that?"

He sighs, relaxing back in his chair and staring directly into my eyes. "There's a lot I need to tell you, Son."

You fucking think?

"Before we start at the very beginning, there's one thing you need to know right now." A dark expression crosses his face.

"And that is?" I prompt, wishing he'd just spit it the fuck out.

"Cade is a threat."

"No shit."

"I don't just mean to you and Alex. I mean to Gravestone. To everything we've built here... To Quinctus."

Now it's my turn to look confused, although it literally pains me to frown.

"The Easton bloodline has always been dominant. We've reigned Quinctus for generations. But after my son, your father, died and we didn't have an heir—"

"But—"

"We didn't know about your existence then. We had to hand power over to the Kingsley line.

"Gregory Kingsley—Cade's father—wasn't the man any of us wanted in charge. Where Quinctus had started to move with the times with regard to some of our rituals and traditions, Gregory wanted to revert things to how our ancestors intended. But it was how it had to be without an Easton heir."

"Go on..." I urge.

"Gregory died seven years ago, leaving Cade the next Quinctus heir. After college, he'll go through his final initiation and become a senior member, taking his place alongside Quinctus elders."

"But now I exist," I say, filling in some of the gaps.

"Yes. Now you exist. Cade will not want to give up his power because you've suddenly appeared."

"He wants me gone." It's not a question. We both know it's a fact.

"You're not an immediate threat. The power has officially been handed to the Kingsley line. We can't just snatch it back, that's not how things work. But there are ways we can do it."

"And that's why I'm suddenly here and have been thrust into this world. Was this always the plan?"

"Yes and no," he admits.

WHEN I LEAVE Marcus almost two hours later, my head is spinning with information. Most of it makes no fucking sense, although it does help to understand this weird-ass town I've found myself in.

Thankfully, he called for a car to take me back to the dorms, and with no doubt another party somewhere on campus last night, the hallways and our communal living space are empty.

I don't bother knocking on Alex's door to see if he's back. Something tells me he'll come and find me as soon as he can so we can share intel.

Dropping my shorts to the floor, I march straight through to my bathroom and turn the shower on without looking in the mirror. Right now, I'd rather not face reality. It's all too unbelievable.

What Marcus told me is just a drop in the ocean as far as Quinctus and the Electi are concerned, but what he did explain did start to help me fill in some spaces.

Quinctus heirs—the Electi—are unable to choose the woman they're to spend the rest of their life with. Their archaic tradition is that girls descending from verus bloodline are put forward for the Eligere, and Quinctus know how they arrive at their decision.

Well, the woman who was chosen for my father wasn't my mother. But it turns out that it was too late by then because she was already pregnant with me, although my father didn't know that at the time.

She fled to Sterling Bay, met my father, and allowed him to believe that I was his in order to protect me. She was happy to lie, for me to grow up as a Danforth so that I wouldn't be subjected to all of... *this*.

But things changed. *I* changed, and things started unravelling around me.

My home life was hell back in Sterling Bay. My parents' constant arguments were one of the reasons I turned to drugs. That and the pressure they put on me, that everyone put on me.

I had a talent, I knew that. But too much was expected of me.

It was all just too much, and in the end, I cracked.

So when things got out of control and I needed a way out, up popped Marcus—who had long discovered the truth—with a plan my mother had no argument against.

So here I am.

The latest pawn in Cade Kingsley's need for power.

The water stings my tender and broken skin as I stand there with my head down and my shoulders dropped in defeat. Marcus is worried about Cade's need for control—and I must admit that part of me is too—but I'm not sure I'm the one to go head-to-head with that motherfucker in an attempt to bring him down a peg or two.

He's already shown that he means business. And he's already breaking the rules and long-written traditions in order to break me.

He wants me to walk away. And I should, I do know that.

I've got enough money sitting in a trust fund to up and leave this town—this country—and never look back.

But that's not who I am.

I'm a stubborn motherfucker, and Marcus has just laid down the challenge. I might have failed in Sterling Bay, I might have disappointed everyone, but I refuse to be that man again.

I hated Cade Kingsley on sight, and now I understand why.

If he wants a fight, then he's going to fucking well get one.

He's seen nothing yet.

SHATTERED LEGACY

I curl my fists, my knuckles splitting open and the muscles up my arms burning as I tense them. Cade might think he broke me last night, but he's about to learn that it takes a lot more than a brutal beating to take me down.

I will not submit to him.

Easton blood reigns supreme, and I intend on showing him so.

ALEX and I spend the rest of the weekend hibernating in my room while the worst of our injuries heal.

We were half expecting a visit from our new rivals after we escaped from the basement. I find it hard to believe that after everything, they'd let us walk out like that. But they've made no attempt to come to us.

By Monday morning, our cuts have scabbed over. Our bruising is as gruesome as ever, but it's time to show Gravestone that it will take more than Friday night to scare us off.

Side by side, we walk toward our first class of the day. Heads turn in our direction as we walk, and students start gossiping. Some even go to the extreme of pointing us out.

I learned from Marcus that most things about Quinctus are hidden from the wide population. Families of the verus bloodline know some things and are welcomed to some of the ceremonies. But it's only founding families who know everything.

I can't believe they're showing their faces.

I heard Cade is after blood.

Did you see the way he went down? Fucking pussy.

Look at them, walking here like they suddenly own the place. They're nothing. No one.

Alex growls beside me as the gossip filters to us as we make our way down the hallway.

"Ignore them," I whisper.

He might still have been the same Alex over the past two days, but since talking to his mom yesterday morning, I've seen a darker side to him. He's suddenly harboring anger that I don't think he's ever experienced before, and he has no idea how to deal with it.

I should know, because I've been there. Hell, I'm *still* there.

My steps falter as Cade, Ashton, Brandon, Channing, and Tim appear at the other end of the hallway.

A ripple of anticipation flows through the students lining the walls.

My heart pounds in my chest as my eyes lock with Cade's. Fury bubbles up inside me, pulling my muscles tight, and it only becomes worse when he pulls Mia into his side and places his lips to the top of her head.

"Bex," Alex warns. "Play nice. We've got a plan, remember?"

Fuck our plan. I'm going to take his fucking head off.

14

MIA

The second I see Bexley enter the room, I try to catch his eye. My stomach flutters, waiting for the moment he spots me. But the hope in my chest withers and dies when I see the anger swirling in his eyes. The hatred.

He hates me.

And I don't blame him.

But he doesn't know everything.

Steeling my spine, I lower my eyes to the empty desk beside me, but he walks right past my row and drops down in a seat a couple of rows in front.

I let out a frustrated sigh. Students are still arriving, and the professor is nowhere to be seen yet, so without overthinking it, I grab my bag and hurry down the stairs. Bexley doesn't even acknowledge me as I slide into the seat beside him. It's a risky move. Anyone here could run back to Cade and tell him what I've been up to, but I have to do this.

I have to make sure he's okay.

I tried earlier, sneaking into Bexley's building. But he wasn't there—that, or he ignored me.

My stomach sinks. Maybe this was a bad idea.

"Hi," I whisper, keeping my eyes on the front of class.

"You need to leave," he grits out, shifting away from me. It stings, his dismissiveness, but what did I really expect?

"I just wanted to make sure you were okay? I stopped by, but—"

His hand shoots out and grabs my wrist under the table, squeezing until it hurts. Bexley pulls me closer but doesn't look at me. "I said, you need to leave."

Tearing my hand away, I glower at him. "I'm not going anywhere. I came over here to ask you if you were okay. Is that such a crime?"

His eyes finally lower to mine. Blown with rage, a low growl rumbles in his chest. "I'm going to fucking destroy your boyfriend."

"He's not—" I press my lips together, swallowing my words.

The class settles down, hushed conversations growing quieter as the professor enters the room.

"I'm sorry," I whisper. "I didn't know he... he planned to do that."

Bexley's brow lifts, suspicion glittering in his blue gaze. But he doesn't say whatever is on his mind. Instead, he sneers, "Class is about to start. You should pay attention."

CLASS DRAGS. Professor Lincoln spends fifty minutes talking about our first assignment, and Bexley spends fifty minutes ignoring me. A couple of times, he shifts in his seat, his jean-clad knee brushing mine, sending a thousand volts through me. I don't know why he has such an effect on me. It's like something shifted in me that night at the lake. I wanted Bexley. I wanted him to be the one to take my precious virginity. But it was more than that.

For those few minutes or hours, I wanted to belong to someone—anyone—other than Cade Kingsley.

Whether Bexley realizes it or not, that night entangled our lives in ways I'm not sure even I understand yet. All I know is, watching Cade and his friends beat the crap out of him hurt.

It hurt me, made my heart ache in a way I didn't expect.

Professor Lincoln dismisses us, and Bexley shoves his notebook and pen into his backpack. His face is a patchwork of cuts and bruises, and before I know what I'm doing, I reach out to touch him.

"Don't."

The severity in his voice startles me, and I snatch my hand away, feeling the icy lick of rejection trickle down my spine.

"You should go, little mouse," he says so darkly, a shiver rolls through me. "You might not like what happens if you stick around."

"You don't scare me, Bexley." I tip my chin in defiance. "I know you think I screwed you over, but it isn't like that. Surely, you know that now."

The room is emptying around us, but we stand there, locked in a silent war. Eventually, he breaks the tense silence, pushing his face into mine. "What I know is that you're Kingsley's… and I don't want his sloppy seconds."

My breath hitches. I'm so stunned I do nothing as Bexley hops over the back of his chair and takes off toward the door.

I file out of the classroom with the other stragglers, surprised to find Annabel waiting for me.

"Hey, is everything okay? You didn't tell me you're in a class with Bexley Easton."

Just the very mention of his real name makes me wince.

"I didn't think it was important." We lace our arms and head out of the building.

"It wasn't, until the party Friday. Can you believe it, an Easton heir? That's some crazy shit."

"Mm-hmm," I murmur, hoping she'll drop it.

"Shame about Alex, too."

"Is it?" My head whips around to her, and I notice the slight flush to her cheeks.

"Bel?"

"Yeah, he's cute. We were talking at the party."

"And you never told me?"

"Well, I was pretty out of it." She laughs, but it's strangled.

"You need to quit taking that stuff."

"What?" Her shoulders lift in a shrug. "It makes me feel good."

"Just promise me you'll be careful."

I have never really understood the fascination with drugs. Enough people seemed to be high on Friday night, Annabel and Sasha included. But I have no desire to be that out of control and unaware of my actions. Even watching Bexley getting beaten to a pulp. I'd felt every crack of

Cade and Ashton's knuckles... every crunch of bone... every grunt of pain. It was real, though. Real and raw and messy.

And one day, it will be the ammunition I need to escape from Cade. Maybe not today, or tomorrow, or even the next day. But if he thinks for one second that I am just going to be some meek, docile prosapia willing to do his bidding, he is sorely mistaken.

"Mia?" Annabel frowns and I blink at her. "Is everything okay?"

"Sorry, I'm tired. I didn't sleep well."

"Still stressed over this thing with Cade?"

"Wouldn't you be?" It comes out harsher than intended.

"I... don't know. I mean, it's Cade." She leans in, lowering her voice. "He's practically one of the most powerful guys in Gravestone."

"I didn't take you for some shallow—"

"Mia, it's not like that, and you know it." Her tongue slips between her teeth. "All I'm saying is, is it so awful being with him?"

Yes, yes it is, I want to scream. But I swallow the words.

"I just want to carve my own path," I say. "Is that too much to ask?"

But as we approach the student union and silence settles over us, we both know the answer.

In a place like Gravestone, freedom is the worst thing you can ask for.

I MANAGE to avoid Cade and the rest of the Electi for the remainder of the day. I want to believe that luck is on my side, but by my last class, I can't help but wonder if they're even in school today. I haven't seen so much as a glimpse of them.

No text messages from Cade.

No narrowed stares from Ashton.

No remorseful smiles from Channing.

There's been nothing, which only sets alarm bells ringing.

News about the fight at the party Friday has been travelling through campus quicker than wildfire. I see the way the outsiders watch Bexley, wondering what he did to piss off Cade. Of course, no one whispers the truth: that they were forced to partake in some archaic ritual called Caedes.

A small, derisive sound crawls up my throat as I approach my dorm building. It's late, a little after six thirty, but I wanted to visit the library and get ahead on some course assignments. Something tells me if I want to survive freshman year as Cade's prosapia, I'm going to need all the distractions I can get. And since I actually want to make something with my life, studying seems like the obvious choice.

A couple of girls give me a wide berth as I reach the dorm building. They watch me like a hawk, and I can practically hear their thoughts.

What does Cade see in her?

He could have anyone, yet he chose her.

Maybe she's bribing him.

Maybe it's a game.

"I bet she doesn't know what to do with a guy like Cade. I heard he likes it rough," I hear one of them whisper, and the two of them break out in fits of giggles.

I glance over my shoulder and arch a brow. "Sorry, did you need something?"

"I... we were just—"

"Yeah, I didn't think so." Shaking my head, I shoulder the door and slip inside.

I can take their whispers and stares. I have bigger problems to deal with.

By the time I reach my room, my skin tingles with irritation. I didn't ask for this. I didn't ask for any of it. But here I am, because I was born in some fucked-up town where your name and blood means more than your own dreams and desires.

Stomping inside, I drop my bag down by my desk and kick off my pumps while I switch on the lamp. My side of the building doesn't get the sun, thanks to the huge cypress trees outside.

I begin stripping out of my tank top, but a trickle of awareness darts up my spine and I turn around, clutching the material to my chest.

"Don't stop on my account, little mouse." Bexley pushes off the wall and stalks toward me.

"W-what are you doing here?" I swallow hard, aware that I'm half naked and he's... well, his eyes are so dark with anger. Or maybe it's lust.

A bolt of desire shoots through me.

"We need to talk." He grabs my arm and yanks me over to my bed.

"Sit." He shoves me down, and my shirt slips from my fingers, fluttering to the ground. I move to snatch it up, but Bexley beats me to it.

"Really?" I sneer.

"You said you came to see me. Why?"

"I wanted to make sure you were okay." I glance away, too affected by his presence, but Bexley grips my chin, yanking my face up to his.

"You were there, weren't you?" He glares at me. "In the basement."

"I—" My throat goes dry. He isn't supposed to remember.

"You cleaned me up."

"I tried," I admit, the quiver in my voice betraying my attempt at confidence.

"What game are you playing?"

I let out an exasperated breath. "I'm not playing a game, Bexley. I'm as much a pawn as you."

"But you're his…"

I nod. He doesn't let go of my chin, and I don't want him to. Something crackles between us, the same thing I felt by the lake.

Bexley's eyes drop to my lips, his tongue darting out and tasting his own as he runs his thumb over my skin. "Would he care, do you think? If I destroyed you… his precious prosapia."

He spits the words like they're acid in his mouth, and I flinch.

"I didn't ask for any of this."

"But here we are anyway." He releases me sharply, and I instantly feel cold at the loss of his touch. Bexley glances at the wall, running a hand down his face

"What happened at the lake—"

"Don't." He pins me with a hard look. "What happened at the lake was a mistake."

On shaky legs, I stand, putting us almost chest to chest. I can feel the heat radiating from Bexley's body, see the harsh rise and fall of his chest as he tries to hold onto his control.

"It wasn't a mistake, Bexley. You felt it too," I whisper. "I know you did."

His hand snaps out and grabs the back of my neck, anchoring my face right in front of his. His eyes burn into mine, searing my very soul.

"You're his… you think I want to dip my end where that fucker has been?"

"He hasn't... I'm not..." I swallow desperately. "He can't touch me. Not yet."

"No?" That piques his interest. Bexley studies me for a second, time ticking by in a painfully slow fashion.

"So he hasn't felt you here?" His hand drops from my neck and skims down my spine to the curve of my ass. He grabs a handful and squeezes.

"No," I press my lips together, fighting the urge to moan. My heart is a runaway train in my chest as lust clouds my thoughts.

"And here?" Bexley skims his other hand up the flat of my stomach, toying with the shell of my pale pink bra.

"Never." A soft moan slips from my lips as his thumb rolls over my nipple.

"You want more?" It's a gravelly challenge.

A small nod has Bexley groaning.

"You're a bad girl, little mouse. And I'm going to have so much fun," he leans in, licking a line from my jaw to the shell of my ear, "devouring you."

"God, yes." I tilt my head to the side, giving him more access. I've never been touched or talked to like his before. I know I'm not supposed to like it... but I do.

And I want more.

I want Bexley to make me forget. To make me feel.

I want him to mark me as his own so Cade has no choice but to discard me.

Suddenly though, Bexley tears away from me.

"What's wrong?" I ask, my stomach sinking.

But then something akin to hunger flashes in his baby blues, and a wicked smirk tugs at the corner of his smile. "Get on the bed, mouse," he says darkly. "It's time to play."

15

BEXLEY

"*He can't touch me. Not yet.*"

Her words repeat in my head over and over as she follows my demands and slides herself back onto her bed.

Her pink lace bra is the only thing that's hiding her swollen breasts from me, and a pair of skinny jeans are wrapped around her hips and thighs as if they've been molded to her curves.

She might be Cade's. But right now? She's mine.

A wicked smile twitches at the corner of my mouth as I imagine being the first one to take her. To take away something that Cade is expecting to be able to claim as his.

I only know the basics about this prosapia bullshit, but her needing to be a virgin for her chosen Electi is kind of obvious. In a world of chauvinistic assholes, why wouldn't they want their chosen women to only be with them while they stick it in anything that moves?

Her chest heaves as she settles back on her elbows. She stares at me with wide, hungry eyes.

I should walk away.

I should turn around and take myself out of the middle of this situation which will probably only end with me receiving another beating like Friday night.

But that's not what I'm going to do.

I've wanted Mia since that night by the lake, and like fuck am I going to screw it up a second time, especially when I now know that it's going to fuck with Cade.

That motherfucker needs taking down. Even more so now I know some of the truth from Marcus.

And taking his girl? That's just step one in my plan to fuck him over until he has nothing left.

I'm going to take away everything he cares about. One by one, I'm going to take his power, his respect, his beloved status.

He doesn't deserve any of it.

And I'm going to start right here.

"Bex?" Mia whispers, dragging me from my thoughts and back to what I should be doing.

I run my eyes down the length of her body. The clothing she's hiding behind pisses me the fuck off, and I climb onto the end of her bed to rid it from her body.

My fingers brush the smooth skin of her stomach as I pop the button on her jeans before dragging them down her legs and discarding them on the floor behind me.

Her panties match her bra, and my fingers itch to rip the lace off her.

"You're too beautiful for that asshole, little mouse."

"Bex," she moans as I trail my fingertips from the waistband of her panties, up her flat stomach and between the valley of her breasts.

"This," I hiss, wrapping my fingers around the Quinctus crest that sits against her breastbone. The crest symbolizes that she belongs to him.

Her eyes widen as I pull on it.

"Bexley," she warns.

"This should be mine, not fucking his. You don't belong to him."

"But—" She swallows her argument, because I don't think she really has one.

She's got to toe the line, she knows that. Quinctus has spoken, and she has no choice but to follow through with it.

"You really want this? You want to be his?"

"No. No, I don't want to be his."

Her gasp of shock rings out around the room as I tug on the chain, forcing it to snap and fall away from her body. "Bexley, you can't—"

"Can't what? I can do what the fuck I want. I'm not scared of him, little mouse."

You should be.

I hear her words in my head, despite her lips never moving.

The sound of the metal hitting the wall somewhere behind me pierces through the silence before she squeaks in surprise when my hand wraps around her throat—although she looks anything but scared as her eyes turn almost black with desire and a flush creeps up her cheeks.

"I look much better around your throat, don't you think?"

I shift forward until my thighs are tucked between her legs, my cock brushing against her lace-covered core. Just that gentle touch is enough to have me weeping for her.

I drop down so my lips are next to her ear. "You want me to leave, little mouse? You want me to leave and let him take this from you?"

Her head thrashes back and forth in her refusal.

"You wanna be mine? You wanna give it all up to me?" My free hand skims up her side, cupping her breasts and squeezing hard enough to make her moan.

"Yes," she cries. "Yes, plea—"

She doesn't get a chance to finish that word, because my lips find hers and my tongue plunges into her mouth.

Her familiar taste explodes on my tongue, and I feel myself drowning in her like I did by the lake.

My fingers flex around her throat as I kiss her, consume her, ruin her.

I want her to remember this moment every time he tries to touch her, every time he tries to take anything from her that she's not willing to give.

And I want her to remember it when she finally manages to break the shackles he used to bind her to him.

My lungs burn when I finally break our kiss, and I drag in deep breaths as my head spins. Ripping my eyes from hers, I look at her nightstand and snatch up the scarf that's hanging from the handle.

"What are you—fuck, Bex," she cries in a panic, trying to squirm out of my hold. But I'm a hell of a lot stronger than her, and in less than a minute she finds herself with her hands over her head and bound to the bed.

Crawling down her body, I wrap my fingers around her ankles and tug until her restraint pulls tight.

So fucking beautiful. And all mine.

Reaching forward, I undo the clasp holding her bra together and allow it to fall to the sides, exposing her breasts and rosy pink nipples to me.

"Fuck, little mouse."

"Bexley," she squeals when I wrap my lips around one and pull it deep into my mouth.

Her back arches as I tease the bud with my tongue before sinking my teeth into her skin.

"Oh my God," she cries, fighting against her restraints.

"That hurt, little mouse?" I ask once I've released her with a pop. "Try watching that motherfucker pretend you're his."

I don't give her a chance to respond. I don't need her words, anyway. I need her gasps of pleasure and pleas for more.

I repeat my previous action on the other sides before ensuring that I pay every inch of her breasts some attention. I kiss, suck, and bite every bit of flesh until she's begging for me and her perfect tits are covered in my marks.

My lip splits open once more, and her sweetness mixes with the unmistakable copper taste of my own blood. I can't help but smile, my chest puffing out in pride when I pull back and take in my handiwork, my teeth marks, hickies, and blood covering her chest, showing Cade motherfucking Kingsley that she's not his.

"Too fucking beautiful," I muse.

Lowering myself down her body, I ignore the screaming pain that shoots through my ribs and down what used to be my prize-winning arm.

But the pain pales in significance to the woman beneath me.

I nip my way down to her panties, and the second I wrap my busted fingers around the lace, I rip them clean from her body.

"Fuck, little mouse. So fucking pretty." I run my finger over her smooth mound.

"Oh God," she murmurs, her eyes squeezing closed as her cheeks burn bright red.

"Eyes," I demand, and immediately hers fly open.

She swallows nervously as our gaze holds.

"Anyone ever—"

"No," she breathes.

"Good. You'll have no choice but to remember this, then."

I swallow down the cry of agony that wants to rip from my throat as I lie on my stomach, my face right in front of her pussy. Her scent fills my nose, and my cock aches to sink inside her tightness.

"Bexley," she moans when I blow a stream of air down her slit. "More. Please."

"Trust me, little mouse. It's going to be memorable."

I lean forward, but I don't go for her pussy. Not yet, anyway.

Instead, I latch onto the softness of her thigh and suck until I know I've broken the skin.

She thrashes about beneath me, but I don't let up. Instead, I do it over and over until her thighs look much like her breasts with my signature all over them.

"Bexley," she almost sobs, but I know it's not with pain. It's with desire; her pussy is so fucking slick for me.

"Ready?"

"Oh God, I don't—argh," she cries as I suck her clit into my mouth. "Holy shit," she screams, making me wonder if anyone is out in the communal areas listening to this.

I smile at the thought, because she's cried out my name enough for them to know it's not Kingsley dragging this much pleasure out of her.

Teasing her clit, I alternate between flicking her with the tip and gently licking over her with my tongue flattened.

Her hips lift from the bed as she seeks more, and her arms tug so hard on the scarf I've tied her with I wonder how she's still bound at all.

"More?" I growl against her, letting her feel the vibration of my voice.

"Yes, yes."

Lifting my hand, I circle her entrance with one finger, dipping inside her until my first knuckle, loving the feeling of her muscles trying to tug me deeper.

"Who do you belong to, little mouse?" I growl.

"Bexley," she cries as I sink my finger deep inside her tight pussy.

As good as hearing my name fall from her lips is, it's not the answer I quite wanted.

"Who do you belong to, Mia?"

"You, Bexley. You."

"Right fucking answer."

I go back to her clit and suck hard as I slip another finger inside her and search out her g-spot.

I know the second I find it because she cries out, her hips thrusting from the bed.

"Come for me, little mouse. Give me everything," I demand, and after two seconds she shatters.

"Bexley," she screams as she falls over the edge, her entire body quivering as pleasure surges through her.

Her juices run down my hand, and I drop lower to lap them all up, needing everything she can give me.

Fuck, this girl.

I don't release her until she's come back down, and when I sit up and look at her, I can't wipe the smile off my face.

She looks fucking perfect covered in my marks, covered in a sheen of sweat and her cheeks and neck flushed with pleasure.

My heart races and my mouth waters for more. My cock aches, straining against my zipper, desperate to sink deep inside her and make sure I brand myself on the inside as well as the out like I already have.

But as much as I might want to, today is not the day.

I have a feeling she's going to need another reminder of whom she really belongs to in the future.

"This isn't the end, little mouse," I say, crawling from the bed and taking a huge step back before I throw caution to the wind and take what I need.

"Bexley, no." She tries to sit up, but she can't with her hands bound to the headboard.

Pulling my cell from my pocket, I open the camera.

"Smile, little mouse. Make sure Kingsley knows how much you enjoyed being my little whore."

Her chin drops as tears fill her eyes.

"What?" I ask innocently, lowering my cell once more. "I thought you knew this was all a game. And guess what." She continues to stare at me in disbelief. "I'm going to fucking win."

Without a second thought, I rip my eyes away from her and pull the door open, storming through it and not giving a thought to anyone who could be outside until it's too late.

16

MIA

I barely sleep a wink. My skin burns with Bexley's marks.

He branded me.

That asshole marked me, knowing Cade would see.

And I let him.

Gah. I really shouldn't have done that. But the second he moved closer and touched me, I knew how it would end. I just hadn't anticipated him discarding me so easily.

It hurt.

It hurt a lot, but I knew he was only pissed because Cade has the one thing Bexley wants more than anything.

Me.

God, it felt so good when he went down on me, kissing and licking my pussy. I've never let anyone touch me like that, and now I know how good it can be with Bexley, I don't want to let anyone else.

Especially not Cade.

Crap, Cade.

He's on his way over right now.

After being MIA all day yesterday, he finally texted me late last night telling me he would see me this morning for breakfast.

"Dammit." I throw down the broken necklace and let out an exasperated breath.

I've been trying to fix the clasp for the last thirty minutes, but it's no use. Bexley wrenched it too hard and the dainty mechanism is beyond repair.

A loud knock at my door startles me, and I cuss Cade out under my breath. He couldn't have been late on the one morning I'm covered in love bites with my Electi pendant necklace in tatters.

Then a thought hits me. I scramble off the chair and hurry over to my dresser, rummaging through the ornate jewelry box located there.

"Bingo." I fish out an old necklace my mom gave me. The chain is slightly tarnished, but it's better than nothing. Making quick work of switching the pendants, I secure it around my neck and stuff the broken one in the box.

"Just a second," I call when Cade knocks again. I can practically sense his impatience.

King Cade waits for no one.

I open the door just as he's raising his fist to knock again.

"Are you always this impatient?" I ask.

"Only when it's you." He smirks, frowning at my turtleneck sweater. "Interesting choice."

"What?" Heat sears me inside out as I shrug. "It's cute."

It has capped sleeves and a cropped hemline, so isn't entirely inappropriate for a warm day.

He studies me for a moment, letting his dark eyes drift down my body in a lazy perusal. When they lift back to mine, his smirk is even more wolfish. "You're right, it is cute." Cade leans in and kisses my cheek. "I missed you yesterday."

Rolling my eyes, I brush him off. "Of course you did. Where were you?"

"Electi stuff," he replies cryptically. "Tomorrow is the next test."

"Oh."

"Oh? That's all you have to say? You disappoint me, babe. Especially after how concerned you seemed about Bexley the other night."

"I would have been concerned about whoever was in the pit with you." I school my expression.

"You're a terrible liar, Mia. But it doesn't matter. You're my prosapia, my girl." He steps forward, putting us chest to chest, and plucks one of my curls between his fingers. "Your pussy is mine."

"Do you speak to all your whores like this, or am I special?"

"Oh babe, you're as special as they come." He pulls sharply, sending a bolt of pain through my skull. My eyes burn but I refuse to cry, swallowing down the rush of anger.

"We should go."

"Or we could stay and fool around..."

"Cade." My throat dries. This cannot be happening. He cannot choose today of all days to try to progress our relationship. If he so much as sees even a glimpse of my chest or thighs, he'll know my secret. And he'll use it to destroy Bexley even more than he has already.

"You want to please me, don't you, Mia?" His fingers trail down my cheek and lightly grip my jaw. "I could make you feel so fucking good."

"There are rules."

"Fuck the rules. You're mine to do what I want with. And if I want to ruin your good girl image, I will." His hand slips to my throat, making my breath catch. "Scared, prosapia?"

His deadly words caress my face.

"Of you? Never." My eyes narrow, anger licking at my spine. Everything inside screams at me to fight back. To knee him in the balls and run. But I know it'll only make things worse. Besides, my father always taught me that the best defense is a good offense. I need to bide my time and figure out my play.

"Ash is right." Amusement glitters in Cade's dark gaze. "Kitty has claws."

I press my lips together, refusing to play this game with him. The back and forth. The cat and mouse chase.

Instead, I give him a taste of his own medicine. Leaning up on my tiptoes, I let my lips hover dangerously close to Cade's. He goes deathly still as I linger there. "If we want to make breakfast, we should go." I make sure my lips skate across his before turning away to grab my backpack.

But when I turn back around, his eyes are firmly on my chest. "Your necklace," he says thinly. "What happened?"

"It got tangled up in my hair, and when I tried to pull it free, the clasp broke." The lie rolls off my tongue with ease. "I found another chain to wear instead until I get it fixed."

His eyes narrow a fraction, but then his expression softens. "So long as you're wearing the pendant, it's all good."

"So Neanderthal." I roll my eyes and step to move around him, but Cade grabs my hips and shoves me up against the wall.

"Don't ever forget who you belong to, Mia." He all but growls the words. "This, me and you, it's done." He leans down, kissing the corner of my mouth. "You can keep fighting me, keep pretending that it isn't going to happen, but honestly, it only gets me hard." He snags my wrist and pushes my hand down to the bulge in his jeans. "Feel what you do to me. Every. Single. Time."

A shudder rolls through me, and it isn't a good one.

"Keep pushing, and you won't like what happens. Don't forget that." He smirks. "Now be a good girl and kiss me like you mean it."

His mouth crashes down on mine, his tongue plunging past my lips and curling around my own. I have two choices: bite him, hard, and seal my fate right here, or submit.

I will my body to go lax and open up to him. Everything about the kiss is wrong. His mouth is too eager, his tongue too forceful… and he doesn't taste like Bexley.

God, Bexley.

If he saw me like this, I wonder what he would do. Would he rip Cade off me and beat him to a bloody mess, or would he walk on by and leave me to my fate?

Cade grinds his hips into me, letting me know just how much he enjoys forcing himself on me.

Perverted asshole.

A guy who can have any girl he wants, and this is what gets him off.

But I guess to guys like Cade, there's something rare and unknown about the chase, about acquiring the untouchable—because they never experience it.

He presses me into the wall, letting his hands glide up my waist and dip under my sweater top. Warm fingers toy with my skin, trying to elicit the same desire in me as I spark in him. But he'll be trying forever.

A door slamming out in the hall startles him, and he finally breaks away.

"Fuck," he hisses, running a hand over his cock. "Taking you for the first time is going to be so fucking sweet, Mia. Tonight, there's this dinner."

"Dinner? What dinner?"

"So inquisitive," he teases. "A car will pick you up at seven. Don't be late, Mia. It's important you're there."

"I know my place, Cade." My body trembles with anger, but I manage to force a smile.

"I'm sure you do, my prosapia." He leans in, kissing my cheek. "My queen."

Another shudder rolls down my spine. "Now let's go before, I break the rules and fuck you right here."

I glare at him before shoving past him.

I don't need telling twice.

WE MEET the others for breakfast, in some secret dining room that seems far too big for the six of us. Tim is nowhere to be seen.

"What is this place?" I ask.

"Why, it's our private eating quarters," Ashton mocks.

"You're such an asshole," I retort, earning me snickers from Channing and Brandon. Sasha nudges me under the table and mouths, "Nice one."

A server is busy placing down baskets of fresh bread and pastries, and there's a hot food counter with eggs and bacon and pancakes.

The huge ornate doors swing open and Tim appears... with Fawn in toe.

"About fucking time," Cade grumbles. "I called you an hour ago."

"We were... busy." They join us at the table.

"I bet you were. Nice hickey, Fawn," Ashton smirks, and Tim leans over, smacking him around the head.

"Show some fucking respect."

"Tim," she soothes.

It's the first time I've seen her around the group. Fawn Bailey is a quiet, meek girl who seemingly keeps to herself.

"Hey, I'm Mia," I say.

"I know who you are." Sympathy glitters in her eyes. "Nice to meet you."

"Hey, Fawn."

"Sasha."

The air cools between the two girls, and I wonder what history lies there.

"Okay, everyone eat," Cade says, and mayhem breaks loose as the guys clamber over the pastries and fruits. I follow Sasha to the hot food counter.

"Do you always eat in here?"

"For breakfast, usually. Sometimes we escape here for lunch if the guys want space."

"Pancakes?"

I nod, and she loads a stack on my plate.

"Syrup?"

"I think I can manage," I say, and her cheeks flame.

"I'm doing it again, aren't I?"

"You're a good friend, Sasha."

"Oh, I don't know about that. Being Brandon's sister doesn't really afford me the luxury of friendship."

"It's hard," I glance over my shoulder to make sure none of the guys are within earshot, "being one of them?"

"Look around you. Do you really think I'm one of them? That they'll let me choose my prosapia?" She leans in closer, lowering her voice. "We are the fairer sex. The weaker sex. The submissive sex."

I can't argue with that—it's clear Cade and at least Ashton think that way. That we're property. Possessions. There to serve and please.

As if on cue, Cade calls over, "Mia, babe, bring me some bacon and eggs."

"Is he for real?" I hiss.

"Deadly." Her expression darkens. "It's a test, girl. Never forget that. Everything you do, everything you say, it's all part of his game."

She takes off toward the table, but I give myself a second to catch my breath.

I'm not ready for all *this*. The games and veiled threats. My fingers curl around the edge of the counter as I try to rein in the onslaught of emotion.

What am I doing?

I should get out of here. Run far, far away and never look back.

Nothing good can come of staying in Gravestone, of staying with Cade.

Bexley's face fills in my mind. The way he stood up to Cade at the fight. How he refuses to bow to the King of Gravestone U at every turn. Bexley won't run. He's made that clear.

"Mia, babe, the bacon..." Cade's sharp tone makes me flinch, and I look up to find Ashton looming over me.

"Better not keep Kingsley waiting," he drawls.

"Excuse me," I say, darting around him, but he grabs my arm as I pass.

"Oh, and Mia… wear something pretty tonight. It's going to be a very special dinner indeed."

17

BEXLEY

"Are they for fucking real?" I bark, staring down at my cell and the summons from the fucking king.

"Sadly," Alex mutters from behind me.

"You're okay with this?" I snap, spinning away and drilling him with a look I'm sure most would cower away from. Not Alex, though. He's too laid-back for that shit.

He drags his head up from his own cell and meets my eyes.

"No, Bex. I'm not fucking okay with this." His lips thin in frustration. I know he's had a meeting with his mom and Harrison to find out the truth about everything, but he's keeping schtum about the details.

He's hurting, I get it. But I could use whatever he knows. We need all the ammunition we can get if we're to go up against that asshole.

"What choice do we have?"

"We fucking don't," I sulk, knowing that he's right.

We might not totally understand what we're suddenly involved in, but I know that we've gotta see it through.

Marcus has told me enough to know that Cade is a threat. To Gravestone, to Quinctus' traditions and beliefs... to Mia. Kingsley is a loose cannon, one my uncle seems to think needs reining in.

"I don't fucking like it."

"I know. But we've got to do what we've got to do."

"Do we?"

"You have another option? We can't go up against them, we'll end up dead. We can't run, we'll end up—"

"Dead, yeah. I got it," I mutter, pulling my closet door open and rifling through my shirts to find a suitable one for tonight.

Thirty minutes later, we're pulling up to Cade Kingsley's mansion in my BMW. Alex is tense as fuck in my driver's seat, and I fucking get why.

The last time we were with the five of them, they damn near killed us. There's no way this is just a normal dinner to get to know us better, as the message said.

There is nothing friendly about this visit. We're initiates, after all. We've heard all about the tests we're expected to pass before we're officially welcomed into this fucked-up world.

"Ready?" I ask Alex, forcing some confidence into my voice. The reality is that my heart is racing and I'm about ten seconds from having sweat rolling down my spine. But equally, my muscles are ready for the impending fight.

My injuries have barely had a chance to heal, but there's no way I'll back away from a chance to plow my fists into that motherfucker's face.

"I'd rather be heading to my own funeral."

"That could well be what's about to happen."

"That's it, fill me with hope."

"I'm not gonna fucking lie to you, man. This has 'set-up' written all over it."

Without waiting for his response, I push the door open and make my way to the front of the oppressive building.

It seems Quinctus has a thing for gothic architecture.

Alex catches up with me right as the door opens. A young woman smiles at us and pulls the door wider for us to enter before thrusting a tray I didn't notice she was holding toward us—I was too taken aback by her outfit. Watching Cade with Mia makes my skin crawl, and I'm not sure if it's a good thing or not that he seems to be just as demeaning to all women.

"Nah, I'm good," I say, remembering all too well what happened the last time I took a drink from them.

"You will take what is offered to you," a voice booms from somewhere in the building.

The woman pushes the tray closer once more, but still I hesitate.

"Things will get much worse for you if you don't follow orders, Easton."

My eyes flick around the vast entryway before us, trying to work out where the owner of the voice is, but after a couple more seconds, I no longer need to wonder. He emerges from a doorway, and he's not alone.

My breath catches in my throat as my eyes lock onto Mia's.

She looks breathtaking in an elegant high-necked little black dress. Her hair is curled with most of it pulled into an updo. Her long-ass legs are on full display, and I can't help but smirk that she's been forced to wear something that covers her chest.

I wonder if he has any idea why that is.

"Drink," he demands, pulling Mia closer into his body and holding her neck with a painful grip, if her wince is anything to go by.

With my eyes still fixed on Mia, I reach out for the shot glass and down it in one. Whatever it is burns the second it hits the back of my throat, and I have to fight not to react to the strength of it.

I'll take the consequences of his fucking games any day, if it keeps her safe.

Alex follows my move, and when I finally look at the asshole, an accomplished smirk plays on his lips.

"Good boys," he announces patronizingly. "This way. Dinner will be served shortly. It's going to be an incredible evening, I can feel it."

Without warning, he spins Mia around. She wobbles on her heels and it takes every bit of my restraint not to reach out and steady her, to pull her into my arms where I know she'll be safe.

But I can't. I can't put her at risk like that.

What I did to her last night is bad enough.

It was reckless to leave my mark. To brand her. But fuck, I couldn't not.

My cock swells as I think back to her laid out on her bed, tied up and completely at my mercy.

"Ow," I hiss when Alex's elbow connects with my sore ribs. "What?"

"You're drooling."

"Fuck off."

Fuck knows what he was doing there, but after escaping from Mia's dorm I ran headfirst into Alex in the hallway. He took one look at me and smirked. He knew exactly what I was doing. And from the state of his hair, it didn't take a genius to work out what he was up to either. My excuse of us doing an economics assignment fell on deaf ears.

Seeing as we were both thrown into the basement while unconscious during our last visit here, we didn't get a chance to really check out the lavishness of the house, and fuck me is it something else.

Our shoes tap against the black marble tiles, and huge chandeliers hang above our heads.

It puts all the houses I thought were over the top in Sterling Bay to shame.

Huge canvases of modern art line the light grey walls along with sculptures on each of the ornate pieces of furniture. It looks nothing like I would expect from five college kids. Although they are college kids with more money and power than sense, so I guess I really shouldn't be surprised.

I didn't have Cade down as an art lover—not that I've spent all that much time thinking about him or considering him having a life that doesn't involve ruining everyone else's.

We pass multiple closed doors as we follow, my eyes taking in everything, trying to absorb any information that might come in useful one day.

"Our guests are here," Cade announces, throwing open a set of double doors and walking in with his arms held out wide.

Mia hurries around him and darts toward one of two empty chairs at the head of the table. Predictably, she doesn't go for the one that looks like a throne. I think we all know who that belongs to.

The room itself is quite plain. There's more artwork, but the most distracting thing is the floor-to-ceiling windows that look out over the forest in the distance. If it weren't for all the sets of eyes drilling into me, I might get a chance to appreciate it.

"Please, come and take your seats." Cade smirks as he gestures to the only two vacant chairs that aren't his over-the-top throne. Fucking asshole.

While everyone else is sitting in high-backed, cushioned mahogany dining chairs, the two waiting for Alex and I look like something from first grade.

Alex takes a step forward, clearly ready to accept this fate and allow this cunt to humiliate us, but before he can take another, I throw my arm out to stop him.

My ribs smart with the sudden movement, but I fight the grimace that wants to cover my face. He doesn't need to know that I'm still suffering because of him.

"Get us some decent seats and we might join you."

Cade's brows rise at the fact that I even dare to speak out of turn.

"I'm sorry, did you say something?"

"Yeah."

He takes a step toward us, tension crackling between us.

"Bexley," Alex hisses, but I ignore him.

"It would be in your best interest to do exactly as you're told, Easton."

"Why? Gonna take me back to the pit?"

His eyes drop down my body as if he can see the bruises that still mar my skin from their brutal attack on Friday night.

"No," he drawls. "I know how to make it hurt worse than that." He studies me for a few seconds as my fists clench and unclench at my sides, more than ready to take a swing for the asshole.

"Babe?" he calls, not taking his eyes from mine for even a second.

"Y-yeah?" Mia's soft voice flows through me and makes my chest ache with my need for her, my need to get her away from this cunt and to safety.

"Remind our initiates who's in charge here."

"Uh... I'm... I'm not getting involved," she stutters.

Finally, he rips his eyes from mine and looks over his shoulder, piercing her with his death stare.

"Bexley, Alex, please, just sit down," she says after a beat, clearly deciding that this isn't worth Cade's wrath.

My chest heaves as Cade's attention comes back to me.

"You heard my queen. Take your seats."

I swallow down the response that's on the tip of my tongue and nod once at him in agreement.

His lips twitch in a smirk, but I'm not doing this for him. It's for Mia. Always for Mia.

The tension is heavy as Alex and I sit like we're a couple of toddlers at the adult table.

Each of the Electi stares at us with amused smirks on their faces.

After a few silent minutes, Cade's knife taps against his glass at the head of the table. I can't help but roll my eyes at his need to command the room. It's pathetic.

"Welcome, Electi. Prosapia." He looks at Mia and smiles insincerely at her.

It makes my skin crawl that she has no choice but to be close to him, to accept whatever he throws at her. "Initium. Before your initiation tasks continue, we thought it only right to get to know you. To learn what makes you both tick." He narrows his eyes on me. "Although I think we already know one of your weaknesses." One of his hands drops beneath the table and Mia startles, a quiet gasp passing her lips.

My teeth grind as my fingers twist in the fabric of my pants.

"So, without further ado, please enjoy our food—and more importantly, our company. After all, so long as you pass and are still breathing at the end, we are all now bound to each other for life." He smiles down at me, but it does nothing to lighten the weight of the threat that was laced through his words.

This is a death sentence, regardless of whether we're still breathing at the end of it.

The doors behind me open and two young women dressed in small black and white maid's outfits, just like the one who greeted us, carry two huge trays in and begin placing plates down in front of the Electi. As they bend over, their asses are on show in their short dresses and their breasts threaten to spill out the top.

Ashton and Brandon eat it up, taking in every inch the women have to offer, while Cade watches on, seemingly unfazed, and Mia squirms uncomfortably beside him.

The scent of herbs and spices fills the air and my stomach growls in anticipation. Maybe one good thing could come out of tonight.

But before the women get down to us, they turn and leave the room, closing the door behind them.

18

MIA

This is hell.
No, it's worse than hell.
Cade lords over the entire meal like he's the king and we his lowly people. He keeps one hand on me at all times, touching my arm, my knee, sliding his fingers up my thigh, dangerously close to my panties.

It's all a game. A sick, twisted game I want no part in yet can't escape.

"Something wrong with your meal?" he asks Bexley.

"Maybe you should come try it."

While we sit and dine on a meal of filet mignon, crushed potatoes, and fine green beans, Cade had the servers bring them what can only be described as scraps from the kitchen. Alex has picked his way through some of it but Bexley hasn't touched a morsel, and I don't blame him. But Cade doesn't reward insubordination, and part of me wants to yell that he's playing right into his hands.

"There'll be no dessert if you don't finish your meal," he taunts Bexley, and Ashton snorts under his breath.

I take another gulp of wine. Cade didn't allow me to get ready with Sasha tonight, maybe because he didn't want her to warn me about whatever the night holds, because I feel it in the air. Something is coming... like a storm on the horizon.

"Aren't you hungry, baby?" Cade trails a finger along my shoulder. I feel Bexley's eyes drilling into the top of my head, but I don't meet his gaze.

I can't.

This is the worst thing that could have happened tonight. Sitting here, between them, Bexley's marks still on my skin, hidden by my high-collared dress.

Part of me wonders if Cade knows, if this is all some kind of sick punishment. If it is, we're prisoners along for the ride either way.

I'd called my father earlier and begged him to find a way around Quinctus' decision. It was no good calling my mother; she doesn't get why I wouldn't want to take my rightful place in our great town's history.

If this is greatness, I want no part of it. Cade and his friends care more about their reputations and abusing their power than they do anything else.

Cade might be able to give me a life of luxury, of money and privilege... but at what cost?

"The food is fine." I force a smile in his direction.

He leans in, brushing his lips over my cheek. "I think you'll like dessert, Mia. There's something very, *very* special on the menu."

My stomach churns violently, but I don't show my fear.

Sasha catches my eye and gives me a reassuring smile. At least she's here too. Fawn is nowhere to be seen, and I wonder why she doesn't have to endure this.

The servers—girls dressed in maid's outfits that leave very little to the imagination—keep our glasses topped up, and I find some relief in the slight buzz in my veins. I couldn't survive this stone-cold sober. It's too intense. Every look, every sigh and shift on a chair draws attention.

"So Bexley, tell us... are you looking forward to your next initiation task?"

"Whatever you throw at me, I'll complete. You know that, right? Nothing you do to me will break me."

"Is that right?" Cade sits back in his chair, loosening his collar. All the guys are dressed up in slacks and dark shirts. It only adds to the bizarre vibe of the evening so far.

Dining with the Electi in our formalwear wasn't something I ever anticipated would become a normal event in my life, but here we are.

The servers make quick work of cleaning away our plates. Bexley still hasn't touched so much as a bite of his food, earning him a scowl from Cade.

"Don't say I didn't warn you, Easton," he snarls as the servers wait for the signal to remove Bexley's plate. After a second, Cade nods and the table is finally clear.

"Why don't we move this party into the den. Dessert will be so much better in there."

Sasha's brows furrow, and I try to figure out what's going on, but then Brandon says, "You should go to your room, Sis."

"I'm coming." Her chin lifts defiantly, and relief floods me. She isn't going to leave me. Thank God. But a low growl rumbles in Cade's chest.

"Brandon is right, Sasha. Unless you want Daddy dearest to find out about your little drug habit, I suggest you go to your room."

She pushes from the table, slamming her hands down. "Fuck you. Fuck all of you." Grabbing her glass, she downs the contents before pinning me with an apologetic look. "I'm sorry," she mouths before hurrying from the room.

"What's going on?" I ask.

"This doesn't concern Sasha," Cade says, as if it's that simple.

"But she's one of you."

"Only when it suits," Channing mutters, and Cade levels him with an icy look.

"Something you want to say?"

"Nope." He glances away, his anger obvious in the tight set of his jaw.

"Come on." Cade stands, holding out his hand. Bexley's eyes burn into the side of my face as I slip my hand into Cade's and follow him through another set of double doors. This room is smaller, filled with a huge sectional and a selection of huge chairs. There's a massive fireplace with an electric fire flickering wildly, casting an amber glow around the dimly lit room. Music pumps out of hidden speakers, and there's something in the air, a scent I can't quite put my finger on.

"What is that?" I ask, my voice quivering because nothing about this feels right.

"Just a little something to help everyone relax. Here," Cade grabs a champagne flute off a nearby tray and hands it to me, "drink this."

I eye the contents suspiciously, and Cade chuckles darkly.

"Such a fighter. Trust me, you'll want to drink it for what comes next."

"What comes next?" I'm vaguely aware of the others filtering into the room behind me. The icy fingers of fear grip my throat. I'm all alone now, surrounded by five guys I know have illicit morals and two guys I barely know anything about.

"Initium," Ashton barks, "take a seat."

It's then I notice the two chairs in the center of the room.

"Drink it, Mia." Cade pushes the glass to my lips. "I won't ask again."

I knock the drink back and gulp it down. If it's anything like the last party, I don't want to be sober.

Not this time.

Ashton and Tim manhandle Alex and Bexley into the chair, securing their hands behind their backs with restraints.

"Come sit with me, babe." Cade leads me to the loveseat and pulls me down beside him. His arm slips around my waist, anchoring me into his side. We have a perfect view of Bexley, and Alex to his other side. He doesn't look at me, just stares straight ahead, ready to take whatever punishment Cade doles out.

"It might seem like being Electi affords us the opportunity to indulge. But really strength comes from knowing your limits. From being able to abstain."

Cade gives Ashton a subtle nod, and he moves over to the far wall and opens a hidden door. A stream of girls file in. They're the servers from before, except now they're naked from the waist up, their perfect breasts on display.

"Ladies. Please, make our new friends feel welcome." Cade motions to Bexley and Alex.

Bile rushes up my throat and I go to clutch my neck, but my arm feels heavy. In fact, my entire body feels strange.

"Cade, what did you do?"

"Relax." He whispers against my ear, stroking his hand along the curve of my knee. It feels good.

It's not supposed to feel good.

I don't want to watch as the girls begin to dance for Bexley and Alex, but I can't tear my eyes away from them.

Alex grins as one girl grabs his face and presses it right into her breasts. He audibly groans, shifting on the chair, no doubt trying to get his hands free to touch her.

Bexley pays the two girls making out for his pleasure little attention. One breaks away, straddling his lap, running her hands up his chest, and unbuttoning his shirt.

In the corner of the room, Ashton grabs one of the girls around the throat and pushes her up against the wall, kissing her hard.

Heat floods me.

"It's hot in here," I murmur, pulling at my collar, suddenly remembering Bexley's bite marks.

"Just relax." Cade's hand slides higher under my dress, finding the soft flesh of my thighs. "Enjoy the show."

The girls have rid Bexley and Alex of their shirts completely now, trailing their lipstick-covered mouths up and down their bare chests.

"Fuck yeah," Alex grunts, and Cade explodes with laughter.

"So fucking eager, Rexford. When was the last time you got some good pussy, huh?"

Tim watches on. He's relaxed back on the couch, his shirt open and a glass of whisky in his hands. His eyes are black with desire as he watches the show.

Moans fill the room. Ashton's hands are under the girl's skirt. Brandon saunters over to them and grabs her face. "Is she wet for it?"

"So fucking wet," he says.

Channing is over by the window, nursing a drink, staying on the fringe of the party. Not that this is any kind of party I ever wanted to find myself at.

Yet I can't help but relax into Cade's side as he continues stroking my skin. I know I should be repulsed by the moans, the number of half-naked girls in the room... but my thoughts are cloudy. As if I can't quite reach the edge of my rationality.

"Fuck, man, let me touch her. Just let me touch her," Alex begs as the girl grinds up on him, running her hands through his hair and peppering kisses all over his face.

"What was that, Rexford? I couldn't quite hear you."

The girl with Ashton and Brandon is moaning louder, her cries of pleasure sending shivers down my spine. She's caged between them, her back to Ashton's chest and her breasts smushed up against Brandon. I have no idea what they're doing to her, but it sounds like she's in the sweetest kind of agony as they make her come.

A gasp slips from my lips the second she succumbs, and Cade leans in again, kissing the corner of my mouth. "Does that get you wet, baby? Knowing that they both have their fingers deep inside her?"

"Oh God." I fight the disgust rolling through me. Disgust tinged with pleasure.

Why does it feel good?

It's not supposed to feel good.

But everything is hazy, my limbs heavy and detached.

There's an orgy going on around us, and still, Bexley doesn't flinch. His eyes remain fixed on some invisible spot ahead of him as the girl tries to seduce him.

"Easton, I don't know whether to be disappointed or impressed. Or maybe there's another girl in the room you'd prefer."

My breath hitches. Surely he doesn't mean—

"Molly, switch places with Freya. Let's see if he prefers brunettes to blondes."

The girls switch, Molly approaching Channing over by the window. He waves her off and she shrugs, going to join Ashton, Brandon and the girl currently getting on her knees for them.

"What do you say, Rexford? Should I let Calia blow you?"

"Just let me loose, please..." His voice sounds distorted and I notice how blown his eyes are.

"Channing, cut our friend free and let him enjoy his prize."

"Fuck yeah."

Channing produces a switchblade from his pocket and slices through Alex's restraints. He scoops the girl up and they stumble over to the sectional, falling down in a tangle of limbs and laughter.

"What did you give him?" I ask Cade.

"Consider it a present." He winks, curving his hand around my neck and leaning in to kiss me.

"Cade... don't—"

"No?" His brow arches. "Doesn't this feel good?" His lips trail down my jaw and along the slope of my neck. "And this..."

Bexley catches my eye, and I'm caught in his murderous gaze. I realize whatever they've taken hasn't affected him the way it has Alex.

"Cade." I run my hands up his chest, pushing gently. "Not in front of your friends," I say.

"So shy, baby. We're going to have to work on that. But first... Molly, enough." She stops and backs away from Bexley. "It would appear that our new friend has more willpower than I gave him credit for. And since this was a test of abstinence, which Rexford clearly failed..." He motions to Alex who is already fucking the girl on the couch. "The winner is Easton. Congratulations."

Bexley scoffs. "Now can I get the fuck out of here?"

"So soon? But the party is just getting started." Cade runs his hands up my leg once more. "Besides, you need to receive your prize first." His eyes flash to mine, and my heart drops.

"After all," he smirked, "you do want your reward, don't you?"

19

BEXLEY

My heart pounds wildly in my chest as I pull at the ties around my wrists holding me in place. It's not from what the girl was doing, the way she was rubbing and grinding herself against me, but from knowing Mia watched the whole thing.

There's no way I'd have given in to her with or without having Mia here, but knowing she was watching my little test made it so much worse.

Cries of pleasure and moans for more fill the room as the scent of sex mixes with whatever that motherfucker has permeated the air with. I knew the second that woman thrust drinks into our hands when we walked in that we were in for a night of it.

There's a reason I didn't eat that dinner, and it's not just because it looked like dog food. There was no way that Cade wouldn't make use of an opportunity like that and not lace it with something.

Alex clearly didn't have the same concerns—or if he did, then his fear of not eating and disobeying this cunt was stronger. Based on the fact that he's fucking that whore only a few meters away indicates that he's had a little too much of whatever, because it's not like him to be quite so open to this shit.

He might be happy to talk about his lack of action and desperation, but this isn't his MO.

Fucker is strung out on something, I'd put money on it.

Ignoring whatever the fuck he's doing behind me, I keep my eyes trained on Cade and fight not to look at where his hand has disappeared up my girl's dress.

His smirk continues to play on his lips as his previous words repeat over and over in my head. *"You do want your prize, don't you?"*

No, I really fucking don't, but I have little choice while I'm tied up here like a fucking animal and at their mercy.

My breath catches when he lifts Mia and places her on his lap, her back to his front.

She gasps. "What are you doing?"

"Giving Easton his reward and reminding him of who's in charge here."

She fights him, trying to get away, but his hold on her is too strong, and after a few moments she has no choice but to give in.

With his arm clamped around her waist, pinning one of her arms down in the process, he hooks his feet around the insides of her legs and spreads them wide.

I don't look down, refusing to play his game.

My pulse picks up and my body temperature soars as anger like I've never felt before surges through me.

I thrash against my bindings, the chair rattling beneath me, but it's no use. All I achieve is for the ties to cut deeper into my skin.

My eyes narrow on his as delight covers his face.

He's a sick motherfucker.

Marcus is right. He needs taking down.

I just fucking wish I wasn't the one who had to do it, and that Mia wasn't part of this twisted game.

She's too pure, too innocent.

"No," she cries when his fingers start trailing up the smooth skin on the inside of her thigh, over my brands. "No, Cade. Please. Don't do this."

He growls something in her ear that's too low for me to make out, but his movements don't even falter.

I'm pretty sure nothing could stop him right now.

"No, please," she whimpers again, thrashing her body about as much as she can, but it's futile. All he's doing is holding her tighter and probably hurting her in the process.

The second he cups her pussy over the fabric of her panties, I pull at my restraints so hard I feel the thin plastic slice my skin, and a few moments later, the wetness of my blood drips from my fingertips.

"Leave her out of this," I bark, kicking myself that I'm reacting.

Maybe I should have just accepted my fate with the girl.

Anything would have been less painful than this.

But then I think about him forcing her to watch as I fucked someone else and bile burns up my throat.

No, I can't do that to her.

"She's mine to do with as I wish." His voice is low and menacing as he pushes the lace aside, giving me a prime view of what I know is hiding beneath.

My cock hardens at the thought of her pussy, of how sweet she tasted. I want to smile, I want to tell him that he's too damn late and that I got her first, but I can't. I have no idea how that would end for her.

"Cade, no," she begs, her eyes drilling holes into my face, begging me to look at her, but still I refrain.

"Look at her. Tell me how pretty her cunt is."

"You're fucking sick," I spit.

"Now, now. I don't think you're in any position to start throwing around insults like that."

"I don't give a fuck, Kingsley. Let her go. Do whatever you want to me, but leave Mia out of this."

A wicked smile curls at his lips as his hand moves and Mia stiffens in his hold.

"Oh, don't worry, I will do whatever I like to you. But your reward comes first. Now. Look. At. Her."

Footsteps come closer until a shadow falls over me.

Cade nods at Channing, and I glance over briefly to see he's got his back to Kingsley and Mia, thankfully not watching the show, but the glint of his switchblade catches my eye.

"Do what the fuck he says," he barks, pressing the tip of the knife carefully against the side of my throat. "Everyone will get out of this sooner if you follow orders."

I swallow harshly, accepting my fate. Although right now, I'd seriously consider death if it would get both Mia and me out of this. Only, I don't think it's going to be that easy.

She's in that cunt's clutches, and I won't give in until he's done and she's safe.

I drop my eyes back to Cade, my jaw popping as my anger begins to boil over. My fists curl, shooting pain up my arms and forcing my blood over my hands.

"I'll fucking kill you if you hurt her."

"Hurt? No, Easton. You've got this all wrong. It's all about *pleasure*." At that final word, he spears two fingers inside her. Mia's hips lift at the intrusion and she cries out for him to stop. Which, of course, he totally ignores.

"You know it feels good, babe. Now be a good girl and let's show Easton how it's done."

I lift my eyes from where his fingers are moving against her clit, and they lock on to her dark ones.

Tears spill down her cheeks as she accepts her fate.

"I'm sorry," she mouths to me. My jaw tenses so hard I swear I'm about to crack a tooth or two.

I pull at my restraints once more. I already know they're not going to release me, but I can't not try. Although, I soon stop when Channing presses a little harder on the knife.

"Do as you're told, *initium*."

Sucking in a deep breath, I continue to hold Mia's eyes, trying to silently tell her that it's okay, that it'll be over quicker if she just complies. Even if it's all a lie.

A sob racks her body as she must read my eyes, but she begins to relax and allows Cade to do his worst. It fucking slays me, witnessing her come apart under his touch, but I've got little choice but to watch as he builds her higher.

Her nails that were clawing at his forearm to make him stop lose their ferocity as she starts to fall and her eyelids begin to drop as she succumbs to the pleasure.

I force myself back to her dorm room, to when I put that look on her face. I remember exactly how she tastes, exactly how she felt as she came apart against my face, and I distinctly remember the noises that ripped past her lips as she fell.

He murmurs something in her ear and she violently thrashes her head back and forth, but it's too late, she's too close. Not a second later does her body lock up as he pushes her over the edge.

"So fucking beautiful. I knew you wanted me, babe." He lifts his hand from her and pushes two fingers into his mouth. "And so fucking sweet. Next time I'm drinking straight from the source."

"Get the hell off me," she screams. For some reason he must comply, because she jumps from his lap and, without a second glance in my direction, flees from the room, leaving only the echo of the slamming door in her wake.

"Molly, baby. Get over here and suck my cock."

"Jesus, fuck," I mutter to myself. "Are you for real?" I ask him.

He shrugs, as if letting another woman blow you right after your chosen one has run from the room is okay.

"You're not going to get away with this."

"Watch. Me." He tears his eyes from me and widens his legs as Molly settles herself between them. She wastes no time in running her hands up his thighs and going for his waistband.

"Get them fucking out of here. I won't party with initium watching," he spits. Thankfully, Channing removes the knife from my throat and instead uses it against my wrists.

"Don't do anything fucking stupid," he warns as I pull my aching limbs around to my front and inspect the damage.

"Why? Do we leave all that to him?" I spit.

"He's in charge. We do as he says."

"He's a fucking power-hungry cunt."

Channing shrugs but neither affirms nor denies my statement.

"Alex, let's go." I storm over to where he's still fucking the whore and physically drag him off of her before gathering up his clothes and pushing him out of the room, much to his disapproval if his slurred diatribe is anything to go by.

My eyes lock on the staircase, and I wonder if that's where Mia has fled to, or if she was sensible and left the building. I know what I'd do if I were her. It's exactly what I want to do now: run and never return. But we both know we can't.

"Put some fucking clothes on, or I'm taking you back like that," I warn Alex, who thankfully has come to some kind of sense and, after stumbling around and using the wall for support, finally drags his pants up his legs.

"Let's go. You need to sleep that shit off."

UNSURPRISINGLY, Alex passed out on the drive back to campus, and I didn't have the energy to find his key and dump him in his own room so I took him back to mine and threw him into my bed.

I already knew I wouldn't be making use of it. I was wired and had too many thoughts and concerns spinning around in my head to fall asleep.

After showering, I wrapped up my wrists and pulled on a clean pair of sweats and a shirt before slumping in my desk chair to torture myself with the events of the night.

I must have managed to drift off at some point, because a voice startles me and I sit bolt upright on the chair, having had my head resting on my arms on the desk.

"Where the fuck—Bex?"

I glance over at my disorientated friend. If the situation weren't so dire, I might laugh at the look on his face. But as it is, I can't find the humor in any of it.

"Morning. How good is your memory?"

"I remember the food, it tasted like shit. And then… then nothing…"

"Jesus fucking Christ." I scrub my hand down my face, already dreading having to repeat the details.

He's going to be fucking mortified.

20

MIA

"Hey, how are you feeling?" Sasha hovers over me with a mug of coffee. "Thought you might need this."

It's the morning after the night before, and I still feel sick.

A deep shudder rolls through me as I sit up and accept the mug from her. "Thanks."

"Did you manage to get any sleep?"

"Surprisingly, yes."

"It was probably the G." She gives me a bitter smile. "I'm so sorry I didn't give you a heads up, but I thought—"

"It doesn't matter." Cade would have embarrassed me either way. He would have spiked my drink and teased me in front of Bexley... just because he can.

"I still can't believe he did that."

"It's all a game, Mia. I keep trying to tell you that. Cade is... well, he's unstable."

"Why do you all follow him so blindly?"

"It's not like we really have a choice." She shrugs, picking lint off her bed covers.

After fleeing the party, I'd run straight to Sasha's room. I didn't want to be in this godforsaken house, but I was confused and upset. Sasha welcomed me into her room as if she'd been waiting for me.

I slept here, curled up beside her.

The shame I felt last night has turned into something else this morning.

"We're Quinctus heirs, Mia. It's not something you just get to deny or walk away from. The first-born son of an heir must complete their Initium and eventually take their rightful place in Gravestone. It's the foundation of this place."

"And you?"

It's different for Sasha; she isn't a male heir. "I'll be married off to spend my days breeding new heirs." There's a wry tone to her voice, but I know there's an element of truth in her words.

"But it's so—"

"Unfair? Life isn't fair, Mia. Gravestone is one of the richest towns in the US. That kind of accolade isn't earned just off of hard work and luck. It's built into the fabric of the town. Nothing comes for free in this life... not a single thing. You'd be surprised what men are prepared to do for money and power."

"W-what do you mean?" I place my mug down, my stomach too unsettled for strong coffee.

Sasha hesitates, probably unsure whether I'm to be privy to their insider secrets. But I'm Cade's prosapia. I deserve to know this stuff—I *need* to know.

"It's okay," I say. "You can tell me. I won't tell anyone."

"This is so weird," she laughs, but it comes out all wrong. "I've never had a girl friend to share this stuff with."

Her words give me some comfort. Sasha might not always be able to warn me about Cade's devious plans, but she's a pawn like me, shackled to a life she seems to want no part of.

I wait, giving her the time and space she needs to reconcile things. Sasha wants to let me in; I see it in the small looks she gives me when we're with the guys, silent shows of support and reassurance or discreet warnings when I'm overstepping the line or about to be blindsided.

"Gravestone isn't as small-town as everyone thinks, Mia," she says cryptically.

I want to ask what she means, but there's a knock at the door.

"Sis, you awake?"

"Go away, Brandon."

The door cracks open and his face appears. "Oh, hey, Mia. Does Cade know you're still here?"

"Brandon!" Sasha shrieks. "Go away."

"Geez, relax." He slips into her room and closes the door. "If you must know, I came to make sure you're alright after last night."

"Like you care."

I avert my eyes, hardly able to look at him after what happened. I saw him with Ashton and those girls... and he saw me with Cade... Oh God, how embarrassing.

"Just because you're not looking at me, doesn't mean I can't see you, Mia." There's a hint of humor in his voice, but he also sounds apologetic.

Slowly, I lift my eyes to meet his gaze. "Hey."

"Don't cower," he says. "Not for me, not for Cade. Not for anyone."

"I—"

"Brandon, just go," Sasha rushes out. "We're fine. I'm fine. Just go, please."

Something passes between them, but eventually he concedes. "Yeah, okay. You two should think about staying in here this morning. I'll have Mulligan bring you some breakfast up."

"Mulligan?" I ask the second Brandon leaves.

"Yeah, the cook. He makes a mean omelet."

"What did Brandon mean, we should stay in here?"

"It means their sluts have overstayed their welcome."

"Oh." I frown. "Did Cade—"

"Probably. I don't need to tell you this, Mia, but Cade isn't a good guy." She keeps her voice low. "He takes what he wants, when he wants. But he can't have you, not yet. Because there are some rules not even the mighty Cade Kingsley can disobey."

"I hate this," I admit, feeling a lick of vulnerability inside me.

"Yeah." Sasha reaches for my hand and squeezes it gently. "So do I."

"We could run away." The words just spill off my tongue.

"Even if we did, they'd find us, Mia. You can't hide from Quinctus or the Electi for very long."

"But Hadley Rexford got out." She was Alex's half-sister and she'd just upped and disappeared.

"That's different." A strange expression passes over Sasha's face.

"Different how?"

"I... uh... we're not supposed to—"

"Sasha, you're going to have to trust me eventually. I'm here, aren't I?"

"She fell in love with the wrong guy," she whispers, glancing at the door as if she expects someone to burst in at any moment.

"That doesn't seem so scandalous."

"It is when the guy you love is an Electi three years your senior and promised to someone else."

"Oh my God, who was it?"

"Tim."

"Tim?" I clap my hand over my mouth, surprised at my outburst. "Sorry. But he's engaged to Fawn and they seem so... together."

She avoids the Electi like the plague, but whenever I catch glimpses of her and Tim together around campus, you can see how smitten they are.

"It was before he was officially with Fawn, but Tim's old man brokered that arrangement when Tim and Fawn were just kids. Her dad is the district attorney."

My eyes widen. "Hal Bailey?"

Sasha nods. "Anyway, when they found out about Hadley, Q went into meltdown about it."

I frown and she adds, "Female heirs shacking up with male heirs is a big no-no." Sasha stares off into space, and I can't help but wonder if it has something to do with the weird tension I've picked up on between her and Channing.

"You know," I say, testing the waters, "now Alex is initium, he'll be the rightful Rexford heir. Which means Channing will be—"

"Don't, okay?" She gives me a sad smile. "It isn't that simple."

"Sorry. I didn't mean to upset you."

"Upset me?" She scoffs. "There's no room for tears in this world, Mia. If you want my advice, wrap your heart in thorns and sharpen your claws, because in a place like Gravestone, it's a game of survival for girls like us."

Sasha excuses herself to take a shower, leaving me with my thoughts.

Everything is such a mess. The Electi are lawless in the way that only young men with too much money and power can be. Cade assaulted me last night, spiked my drink and touched me without my consent because everything is a game to him. And me and Bexley... we're pitted on different teams.

God, Bexley.

I've tried not to let my thoughts wander to him since I woke up with a feeling of dread deep in my stomach.

He resisted that half-naked girl. He sat there, stoic and unwavering, as he watched Cade make me come. Not once did he look away. I don't know whether he knows it, but his resolve gave me strength. It fueled the fire in my stomach.

The fire that still burns.

But I need time to regroup, to figure out what the hell I'm going to do, because if last night proved anything, it's that Cade is a cruel bastard.

And things are only going to get worse.

I DON'T GO to classes. After getting a ride back to campus with Sasha, I make my excuses and hurry back to my dorm room.

I need time to think. Time to process everything that's happened over the last few days.

The guys had already left by the time we surfaced this morning. Someone—I assume it was Brandon or Channing—had texted Sasha to let her know the coast was clear. Whomever it was, I was grateful to them.

Facing Brandon had been mortifying enough, but facing all of them over breakfast... yeah, no thanks.

I spend the day binge-watching *The Vampire Diaries*, wishing I was more like Rebekah Mikaelson. She wouldn't stand for Cade's bullshit, for his demeaning, cruel, chauvinistic ways.

But the bottom line is, I don't know what to do. My mother sees being Cade's prosapia as a gift, something to be cherished. She truly believes it's my birthright. And my father wouldn't dare to go against Quinctus. They're too brainwashed by Gravestone's history and traditions.

No one would believe me if I tried to accuse Cade of assault. He's Cade freaking Kingsley. Besides, Police Commissioner Walters is Phillip

Cargill's best friend. The police department protects the town's most sacred secrets.

I'd never really given it much thought, but after my conversation with Sasha, I can't help but wonder just how corrupt the town's roots are. What was it that Sasha had said? *'Gravestone isn't as small-town as everyone thinks.'*

Ugh. I grab a pillow and press it against my face, screaming with frustration. I hate this. I hate Cade and all the secrets and lies and traditions.

The ping of my cell finally makes me leave my soft, feathery sanctuary, and I read the message.

Sasha: Are you okay?

Me: I'm fine, just needed some space.

Sasha: I get that. Do what you need to do but then strap on your big girl panties. The guys are busy tonight, and I'm surplus to requirements if you want to hang?

Me: Maybe. I'll let you know.

Sasha doesn't reply. I like that about her. She doesn't push, but she's honest in a way girls like Annabel wouldn't be. I guess that comes from being on the inside.

I grab a handful of candy and stuff it into my mouth. As the hours pass, the hazy memories of last night become even more distorted. But I could still remember how turned on I'd been by it all. It was the drugs, whatever aphrodisiac Cade had pumping into the air and added to our drinks, but it felt real.

My skin grows warm as I remember watching the girl moan and writhe against Ashton as he touched her. It's so fucking messed up, but I can't stop myself, walking my fingers down my stomach.

I'd wanted it to be Bexley… when Cade had started touching me, I'd imagined it was him.

I press my thighs together, trying to tamp down the confusing sensations rushing through me.

I hate Cade. I do. But my body betrayed me last night.

Leaping off the bed, I hurry into the bathroom and splash my face with cold water.

"What the hell am I doing?" I mutter to myself, frustration bleeding from my words.

I feel like I'm losing my damn mind, all thanks to a guy who wants to hurt me and a guy who wants to hate me.

Just then, a knock at the door startles me. I didn't text Sasha back about hanging out, but maybe she decided to take matters into her own hands.

When I yank open the door, though, all air leaves my lungs. Because it isn't Sasha at all.

It's someone much, much worse.

21

BEXLEY

The last thing I wanted to do today was go to class and risk seeing that motherfucker's face. But I knew I didn't have a choice.

Skipping would make it look like I was running away. Hiding. And like fuck is that happening.

Plus, I needed to see Mia. I needed to know she was okay after last night. I needed to ensure he didn't go after her once we'd left and done... I shudder at the thought of him touching her again.

She might have enjoyed it, he might have tipped her over the edge, but it wasn't welcome. And it certainly wasn't welcome while I was witnessing it.

Anger swirls around me like a vortex as memories from last night flash through my mind.

After sending Alex back to his dorm to continue sleeping off his hangover and dying in his own mortification, I reluctantly grabbed my books and headed to class.

But Mia never showed.

They did. The King and his fucking sheep.

Thankfully they didn't talk to me. The closest we got was Ashton shouting some suggestive comments about the night before, but I walked straight past them with my head held high and my shoulders squared.

It'll take more than his big fucking mouth for me to show any shame about what went down.

I was challenged to abstain, and I passed with flying colors, so they can fuck right off.

They don't need to know how it damn near killed me to watch Cade with Mia like that. I lock the feelings down and fix my mask into place.

By the time my last class of the day lets out—a class she should have been in—I'm more concerned than I want to admit.

What if they spiked her and something happened? What if he hurt her? He's sure fucking capable.

Instead of heading for my dorm building, I head in the opposite direction across campus toward where I hope she's hiding.

Thankfully, her dorm is empty when I walk through the communal area. The last thing I need is to be seen here. I have no idea who her dorm mates are or if any of them are in the Electi's back pockets. I've been lucky so far, being able to slip in unnoticed, but I know my luck is going to run out at some point.

Sucking in a breath in the hope it'll tamper down all the emotions that are raging inside me, I lift my hand to knock, but my cell buzzes in my pocket.

Pulling it out quickly in case it's Alex, I stare down at the name, and the anger I was trying to cool surges back full force at the sight of my mom's name.

My entire body tenses, and my lips curl in disgust. I've refused to talk to her since she confessed that the man I've called Dad my entire life isn't actually the man who had a hand in making me.

Shoving it deep inside my pocket and locking any thoughts out of my head, I focus on the task at hand.

Finally, I rap my knuckles against her door and listen to her light footsteps as they head my way. My heart pounds as the handle twists and a sliver of her room becomes visible in the gap.

The second she reveals herself, my fists curl at my sides.

She looks perfect, beautiful, and I've spent all day fucking worrying about her.

Mia gasps in shock as she averts her eyes.

"Too late to be embarrassed, little mouse," I say.

Without waiting for her to invite me in, I step into her room, forcing her to back up if she doesn't want to collide with me. The door swings closed behind me, and the force of the slam makes the floor beneath us vibrate.

"B-Bexley?" she whispers, making my body burn red hot with anger.

Reaching out, I take her chin between my fingers and push her back until she bumps up against the wall.

"How could you?" I growl. "How could you let him fucking do that?" I lean right into her, our noses almost brushing.

Her lips tremble and her eyes fill with tears, but neither are enough to bring me down off the ledge. Every time I so much as blink, all I can see is him with his hands on her.

"You think... you think I l-let him?" she whispers.

"Well, you didn't fucking stop him. I know that for a fact."

"I didn't... I didn't want that," she cries.

"Then maybe you should have looked like you were enjoying it less." I step closer, the length of my body pressing hers into the wall.

"Admit it. You liked it," I taunt, my heavy breaths racing over her face. "You were so fucking wet for him."

"No. Stop," she demands, her tiny hands lifting and slamming down on my chest in an attempt to make me back up, but she's no match for my strength.

"Did he make you feel better than I did? Did you come harder for him?"

"Fuck you, Bexley." I catch her wrist before her palm connects with my cheek.

Collecting up the other one, I pin them above her head and hold them in one of my hands.

I trail my knuckles down the exposed skin of her inner arm and she shudders.

"Tell me. Was he better?" My eyes burn into her, daring her to tell me the truth no matter how much it hurts both of us.

"You really want to know?"

No. "I'm fucking asking, aren't I?"

Her lips press into a thin line, and I prepare for the barbed words that are about to fall from her lips that I already know are going to rip me in two.

But a beat before her lips part to respond, her entire body relaxes slightly. No one else would probably notice, but I do. I notice every-fucking-thing about her.

"I imagined it was you." My heart damn near stops at her confession. "W-what?"

"In my head, it was you touching me. When I fell, it was for you."

My lips are on hers before I've even registered that I've moved. My tongue plunges into her mouth, twisting with hers as I hike her leg up around my waist.

I kiss her, grinding my cock against her core until I swear I'm going to combust with my need for her.

"I need you. I need you so fucking bad," I pant into her mouth.

"This doesn't change anything, Bex. This... it—"

"Like fuck it doesn't."

"I'm still his. I can't be yours."

I hear her words, but I refuse to actually listen to them. I can't. It's too fucking painful.

"Right now you can be."

I lift her from the floor and her legs automatically wrap around my waist as I carry her to the bed.

Lowering her back to her feet, I wrap my hands around the bottom of her tank and pull the fabric up her body, revealing her bare breasts beneath.

"Fuck, you're beautiful." Stooping down, I suck one of her nipples into my mouth, tracing the marks that still linger on her chest from the last time I was here.

"Bexley," she cries out, and my chest swells. Not once did she cry his name last night.

"Again. Say it again," I demand as I switch to the other side.

"Bexley." Her fingers thread into my hair and she scratches at my scalp.

It feels so fucking good.

Wrapping my hands around the back of her thighs, I flip her back onto the bed and quickly rid her of her leggings and panties until she's laid out beneath me in nothing but her Electi crest.

I want to demand she takes it off—or better, rip it from her like I did last time—but part of me needs the reminder that this isn't how our future looks.

She's his, no matter what I take from her.

Reaching out, I take it between my fingers and her eyes widen in horror.

"N-no. Not again," she begs.

My nostrils flare with anger that she wants that piece of him.

Releasing the pendant, my fingers wrap around her throat. "I'm taking what's his, Mia. I don't give a shit about the consequences."

She swallows nervously, but after two seconds she nods. "I... I don't want to give it to him."

My heart swells to the point I fear it might just explode in my chest. "You shouldn't be giving it to me. I'm not a good person either."

"I know, but you're a saint compared to him."

Silence falls over her room as we stare at each other. The magnitude of this moment weighs down on both of us, but like fuck is it going to stop me.

Releasing her, I reach behind my head. I pull my shirt off in one move and drop it over the side of the bed before I lower my hands to my waistband and quickly shed my jeans and boxers.

Her eyes zero in on my hard cock, and she props herself up on her elbows so she can get a proper look at me.

The bruises from last weekend are still there, but they're beginning to fade now.

She watches, fascinated as I wrap my hand around my length and begin to stroke it slowly.

"Bex?" she breathes.

With my eyes locked on hers, I crawl on my knees between her legs and rub the tip of my cock against her pussy. She's so slick already, and the temptation to thrust straight into her is almost too much to deny.

Falling over her, I plant one hand on the mattress beside her head and lower my lips to hers.

"Let's get one thing clear," I growl. "I don't give a fuck about what's hanging around your neck. You don't belong to anyone other than me. You got that?"

She swallows nervously but nods.

"He can torture me, hurt me, drug me. Whatever he fucking wants. But I'm not giving you up, little mouse. You. Are. Mine."

I thrust forward on my final word, and she cries out in agony.

Slamming my lips down on hers, I swallow down her pain, wishing I could take it away and make it my own.

I kiss her like I'll die without it as I force my body to remain still.

Long minutes pass by as we devour each other before she pulls back and looks at me in horror.

"C-condom?"

"I'm clean. I haven't been with anyone in..." *A really fucking long time.* "Are you on—"

She nods. "Yeah."

I roll my hips, and her eyes shutter and her teeth grind. "It'll fade, I promise."

She reaches up and wraps her hand around the back of my neck, forcing me to close the space between us. "I don't care if it doesn't. Fuck me, Bexley. Make me remember it. Make me remember you."

"Jesus, fuck."

I claim her lips once again and give her what she's asked for.

Fuck Kingsley.

Fuck the Electi and Quinctus and all their stupid rules and traditions. Nothing is more important than this right now.

"Oh God," she cries when I slip my hand between us and pinch her clit, making her pussy contract around me.

"Fuck, you're so fucking tight, little mouse."

"Bexley," she whispers as I do it again, thrusting deep inside her and circling my hips.

Her body is covered in a sheen of sweat, her breasts marred in fresh bite marks, and her hair is a matted mess around her shoulders.

I sit up and drag her with me until we're chest to chest and her legs are wrapped around my waist. Sinking deeper into her, my eyes roll back in my head in pleasure.

In this moment, she's the only thing that exists. Exactly how it should be.

"You're mine, Mia. Nothing he does will change that."

"But he's—"

"No," I snap. "Just... no. This is us. Me and you." I thrust my hips and she cries out, slamming her lips down on mine as I bring us both to the edge.

"Come for me, little mouse. Show me you're mine." I pinch her clit and circle my hips, and she explodes around me.

"Oh my God, Bexley."

She squeezes me so fucking tight that I have no choice but to follow her over the edge, my cock jerking and spurting jets of hot cum inside her.

Mine.

Fucking mine.

Still inside her, we fall to the bed in a tangle of limbs, our bodies spent and our chests heaving.

Contentment fills me as I hold her tighter, but after two minutes of blissful silence with her, she opens her mouth and ruins everything.

"What the fuck did we just do?"

22

MIA

Bexley flinches at my words, and I immediately regret them. But this isn't a stolen kiss and a few concealable love bites.

This is so much more.

"That came out wrong," I add quickly, turning into his warm body. I want to lean in and run my nose across his chest, but he's still rigid, anger rolling off him in thick waves.

"Bexley," I say, testing the waters and laying my hand on his stomach. He doesn't reply, and I peer up at him through my lashes. "Look at me, please."

Finally, he gives me his eyes and I see the hurt there. "You think this was a mistake?"

"No, I would never... I'm just confused. Being with you was..." It was everything. I swallow the words.

"Yeah." He concedes. "Things just got a whole lot more complicated."

Bexley turns onto his side too, so we're nose to nose. I really need to go clean up, but I don't want this moment to be over. Not yet. He leans in, tracing the shape of my lips with his finger, chasing the trail with his mouth. We sink into the kiss, slow and tender. His tongue slips past my lips and curls around my own, stirring my body to life once more.

"Okay," I breathe, pressing my hands firmly to his chest. "Stop. I can't think straight when you do that." It comes out teasingly.

"I could spend all night kissing you and it still wouldn't be enough."

His words wrap around me like a warm blanket, and I know I'm getting too comfortable. This is a dream, a fantasy. It can never be more. But for tonight, I'm willing to pretend with him. Pretend that I'm just a girl falling for a boy.

"You are so fucking beautiful, little mouse." He pushes the hair from my face and leans in to kiss me again. When he pulls back, he's full-on gazing at me.

"What?" I ask, my cheeks pinking under his intense regard.

"You were a virgin."

I nod.

"Explain that to me."

My brows furrow. "I've never found anyone worth giving myself to."

"So it isn't some prosapia bullshit?"

"Historically, Electi expected their prosapia to be untouched, yes. But I didn't hold onto my virginity for the likes of Cade and his friends, if that's what you mean," I snap.

"Mia," Bexley plucks my chin between his fingers, forcing me to look at him, "that isn't what I meant. Part of me knows this is real. It knows that you fucking belong to Cade, knows that he rules Gravestone U and what he says is law. But part of me is having a real fucking hard time accepting it."

"I hate this too," I admit, pain lancing my chest as my eyes flutter closed.

"Mia, look at me," Bexley demands, but I can't do it. I can't look at him. "Give me your eyes, mouse." His arm slides down my waist and around my thigh, squeezing my ass.

My eyes fly open and he smirks. "There she is."

Silence settles between us, and Bexley closes his eyes.

I whisper, "I wish this didn't have to end."

I WAKE COCOONED in Bexley's arms. His body curls around mine so close there isn't a part of me not brushed up against a part of him.

"Hmm." A sigh of contentment slips past my lips.

After our conversation last night, Bexley had dragged me into the shower and acquainted himself with every inch of my body.

I blush just thinking about all the ways he'd made me squirm and scream.

It was risky, letting him spend the night, but I didn't tell him to go, and he hadn't asked if he should. We'd just fallen into bed together in a tangle of limbs and frantic kisses… and he'd dirtied me up all over again.

"Keep doing that and you might not like how it ends." Bexley kisses the nape of my neck, grinding his hardness right against my butt. "What time is it?"

"Early still."

"Guess we fell asleep, huh?"

"Like you ever planned to leave." A faint smile traced my lips.

"True." His gravelly laughter makes my tummy clench in the most delicious way as he pulls me even closer.

"What happened to you, Bexley?" I whisper. I know he's the Easton heir… but I don't know the whole story. In fact, I don't know much about him at all.

"When my mom found out she was pregnant, she fled Gravestone. She must have known life wouldn't be easy for her, hiding an Easton heir here."

"She wasn't your father's prosapia?"

"No."

"Wow, I had no idea." For as long as I can remember, there has been no Easton heir. I heard my father say once that their line would eventually die out.

"My uncle told me that until my father died, Easton had always been the dominant line, but when my dad died, Gregory Kingsley assumed leadership over Q."

No wonder Cade is pissed that Bexley exists.

"It just all sounds so fucking unbelievable. I'm just a guy, Mia. I had friends, a life… football…"

I turn in his arms and gaze up at him. "What happened?"

"My parents started arguing, always at each other's throats. They tried to keep it quiet, but I heard them. I even asked my mom about it once, but she told me not to worry. It was the summer before senior year and things got really bad. My dad came home drunk, got aggressive. Not with my mom or me or anything, but he was just so angry, you know?"

"I'm sorry," I whisper, leaning in to kiss his jaw.

Bexley tucks my body against his and continues. "I started drinking, partying hard on the weekends. Some guys I knew liked to dabble with pills and coke. I guess escaping reality became easier than trying to figure out what the fuck was going on with my parents. Mom was always crying behind her glasses, Dad was never home, and I had the pressure of the team on my shoulders."

"You played football?" I ask, because I remember hearing a few whispers back in high school.

"Yeah, I was one of the best quarterbacks in the state." Bexley stiffens.

"You don't have to tell me if you don't want to."

"I want to, it's just hard... I had this friend, Remi. She was my best friend growing up. I guess I always thought we'd end up together.

"But her mom and dad split up, and Remi withdrew. The kids at school were cruel, especially the girls. Sterling Bay is a lot like Gravestone. Everyone cares more about what car you drive or how big your trust fund is than the kind of person you are. We grew apart, and then she met someone else. Ace Jagger." He hisses the words as if they pain him. My brows furrow. There's something familiar about that name.

Jagger.

"He wasn't like the rest of us. He and his brothers came from the rough side of town. But he caught Remi's eye, and I just didn't get it. She'd never once returned my interests and yet she was falling over herself for a jumped-up asshole like Jagger. It was the final straw. I started losing control until I... I messed up. Really fucking messed up."

"We all make mistakes, Bexley," I offer when I see the regret shining in his eyes.

"Yeah, well that mistake cost me my entire future." He rubs at the scar along his shoulder.

"I remember, you came to Gravestone High still wearing a bandage."

He nods. "It was the worst few weeks of my life. My parents practically disowned me, shipping me off to live with an uncle I'd never met in some strange-as-fuck town..." he inhales a sharp breath. "If only I knew then what I know now."

"Would you have run?"

"You can't ask me that." His eyes shutter.

"Why not?"

"Because... fuck, Mia. I hate this. I hate Cade and all the Quinctus, Electi bullshit. But I met you..." He cups my face and lets his thumb brush my lips. "And I'm not sure I can ever be sorry for that."

"Bex..."

He kisses me, slow and sure, his tongue tangling with mine. Liquid lust floods my veins as I rub the length of my body against his.

"Mia, we should stop. I need to go before campus becomes too busy."

"We have time," I purr, hitching my leg around his waist, feeling the hard outline of his erection.

"Jesus, little mouse," he drops his lips to my collarbone, "maybe I underestimated you."

"I want you." I stare into his eyes, hoping that he can see how much I need him. "I want to pretend for a little longer."

He inhales a ragged breath, his hooded gaze dropping to my lips. And then he's on me, hard, brushing kisses that turn my knees weak and send shivers down my spine.

Bexley rolls me on top of him with a smirk. "You want to play, mouse? Let's play."

God, his words do things to me. Dark, dirty things. I whimper as his hands slide under my t-shirt and finds my breasts. He plucks my nipples, squeezing and kneading my skin in a way that has me writhing above him.

"Fuck yeah," he groans, lifting his hips to make his cock bump my clit.

"I need you inside me," I moan, lost to the sensations he's stirring within me.

Taking my hand, he grasps his length between our bodies and says, "Up you go."

I rise on my knees slightly and let him hook my panties to the side so he can slide himself through my wet folds.

"Fuuuuck," he hisses as I slowly sink down on it. It stings at first, but pain quickly gives way to pleasure and he feels so good I think I might die.

"You feel incredible." He cups the back of my neck and pulls me down to kiss him. Our teeth smash together as our tongues fight for dominance as he begins thrusting inside me. I rock back and forth, finding a steady pace. But it isn't enough. I need more... I want Bexley to imprint himself on my soul.

"Fuck, Mia, I need you to move." He grabs my hips and begins moving me in the way he likes. He looks so good, sprawled out beneath me, all tan skin and muscle.

He pushes my t-shirt up my body to lick and suck my breasts, painting my skin with his teeth and tongue.

"You're mine, Mia." He fists my hair at the nape of my neck and pulls my face to his. "Whatever happens from here on out, you're mine."

I want to believe him, I do. But I can't see a way for that to become reality. Not with Cade at every turn.

All worries melt away as pleasure rises inside me as Bexley fucks me fast and hard. His fingers grip me a little too tight and he kisses me a little too rough, but I know it's because he feels it too. Time is running out for us. All we have is this moment...

And who knows when we might get another.

23

BEXLEY

"Can't we just stay here all day? It's the weekend, no classes. We don't even have to leave your bed," I suggest as I reluctantly pull my clothes on after another shower where very little actual cleaning went on.

"We can't," Mia says sadly, being the voice of reason. "You know as well as I do, I'm not going to be able to hide forever. The fact that I wasn't summoned yesterday is a shock in itself."

I nod at her, running my hand through my wet hair as I watch her brush hers.

"This fucking blows," I groan, feeling totally out of sorts at the thought of leaving her to wait for Cade and whatever sick games he might have in store for her.

My fists curl as I watch her.

"I'll be okay, I promise." Her eyes lock with mine in the mirror, and she gives me a small smile that in no way makes me believe her words.

She might think she can hold her own, but the reality is that I don't think anyone can do that when it comes to Kingsley.

Ripping my eyes from hers, I find her cell sitting on her nightstand and I march over.

"What are you doing?"

I tap away, ignoring her question.

"If he does anything, tries anything... If you need me..." I flash her the screen with my number. "Call me. Yeah?"

She nods, but I fear it's only to appease me.

"Kitty Cat?" she asks, walking over and taking her cell off me.

"You're my little mouse, I can be your cat." I wink before a smile curls at my lips.

"You're a goof. Come here." Her tiny hands slide up my chest until her arms rest over my shoulders and she reaches up on her tiptoes so she can kiss me.

"I'll miss you," she murmurs against my lips. My cock swells once again at her closeness, and I wish I could take her away from all of this, away from him, and just keep her for myself.

"You too, little mouse."

I push my tongue past her lips and I just start to lose myself in her once more when a knock sounds out around the room like a gunshot.

She jumps away from me as if I burned her, and pain wraps around my chest at her move.

"You need to go," she hisses.

I look around the room at a loss for how that's supposed to happen while someone—probably the devil himself—is standing at the other side of the only door.

"The window." She points at it as if I don't know what one is.

Before I look over, I take her in for a second. All the color has drained from her face and her eyes are wide, like a rabbit caught in headlights.

"You're serious?"

"The fire escape is right there, you won't plummet to your death."

"Great," I mutter, shoving my feet into my sneakers and making my way over.

"Who is it?" I ask as I pull the curtains back to see she's right about the escape.

I lock that little nugget of knowledge away for later, because it's the perfect way to get to her unnoticed in the future.

She rushes over to the door and presses her eye to the peephole.

"A-Annabel."

She gestures for me to hurry up and I throw open the window, pissed off that it's come to this, although I knew it would.

I shouldn't even be here, let alone doing the walk of shame after the night before.

With one last look at her, I throw my leg out the window and climb to the small platform beside it.

Mia quickly closes the window behind me, but I don't go. Instead, I watch her reflection in the mirror in her room as she smooths down her hair and pulls the door open.

I expect to see Annabel's blonde hair flounce into the room, but instead, all the air rushes from my lungs when Kingsley steps inside, his face hard, clearly pissed off that he was made to wait.

She lied to me.

After everything that just happened between us. She lied to me.

My stomach plummets.

I know I'm only torturing myself, but I can't take my eye off them as he takes her chin in his hard grip and slams his lips down on hers.

Pain shoots from my chest as I watch the girl I'm falling for kiss another man.

No, not just another man.

Him.

My stomach churns and bile burns its way up my throat, yet I still don't move.

It's not until he walks them out of sight that I'm released from my frozen trance and am able to jump over the railing, landing on my feet on the ground below. Without looking back, I take off running across campus, but when I get to my building, I don't bother going inside.

Instead, I climb into my car and speed out of the parking lot.

I DON'T HAVE a destination in mind, I just know that I needed to get away and attempt to clear my head.

Mia has me feeling all kinds of things that I know I shouldn't, especially when she's promised to someone else.

I think of my mom and my biological father. Is this how it happened for them? Have the two of us just condemned ourselves to lives full of deceit and lies?

I slam my hand down on the wheel, the frustration getting the better of me.

She's not mine.

She can never be mine.

All we're going to do is cause each other more pain by carrying on this charade, by pretending that we can have everything we want.

I've already taken something from her that I shouldn't have. And if he finds out... I shudder at the thought. Cade is already gunning for me. I can only imagine how bad it will get if he knew I took her v-card when it should belong to him.

My fingers tighten on the wheel as I picture him sliding his tongue past her lips and claiming her.

Could he smell me on her?

Was my scent still in the room?

Does he know?

My stomach is awash with nervous energy and fear for my little mouse when I pull up to a house I haven't seen in a while.

I shouldn't really be surprised that this was where I'd end up. I like torturing myself, after all, and I've just left one car crash behind only to walk into another.

Killing the engine, I sit back, staring at the house that was my home for almost all of my life—well, until I was banished from town and cast aside as if I never existed.

I blow out a breath and push my door open. Mom's home. Her car is in its usual space, along with the housekeeper's.

My hands tremble as I try to contain the storm that's threatening to erupt within me, and I swing the front door open and step inside. The familiar scent of jasmine hits my nose, but where it once made me feel safe, content, I no longer feel anything.

"Hello?" I boom through the silent house.

Movement erupts from upstairs, and in a few seconds footsteps race toward the stairs.

"Bexley? Oh my goodness. Bexley!"

Mom flies down the stairs at the speed of light before she crashes into me, flinging her arms around my neck and squeezing me tight.

I don't return her excitement. Instead, I leave my arms by my side and wait for her to get her fill.

"I've missed you so much," she sobs against my shoulder. I refrain from pointing out that if she never sent me away like an unwanted pet then she wouldn't have to miss me, but at this point, my leaving Sterling Bay seems like the least of my issues.

Finally, after long minutes, she pulls back and wipes her tear-coated cheeks.

"Oh it's so good to... your face," she says in horror as she attempts to frown, but her Botox stops most of the movement in her face.

My bruises are mostly gone now, but there's still some evidence lingering from last weekend's fight.

"What happened?"

"*You* happened," I spit, turning my back on her and stalking toward the kitchen, my sudden need for a drink too much to deny.

I march straight to the refrigerator and pull out one of Dad's beers.

"Bexley, isn't it a little early for—"

"Really?" I spit. "Are you really going to stand there and criticize my choices after all the times you've fucked up?"

"Bexley?" she sighs, fresh tears welling in her eyes.

"No. Don't 'Bexley' me, Mom. You lied to me my entire life. No, actually, you didn't just lie to me. You lied to Dad, too. You betrayed both of us."

"It wasn't like that," she cries.

"No? So what was it like?"

"I was protecting you. Don't you see that?"

"Well, a fine job you've done of that, Mom. I've ended up right in the middle of where you apparently didn't want me. You ran, you lied, you did all of that to keep me from my rightful place as heir of that bullshit, yet at the first sniff of trouble, you send me back there. What the hell, Mom?"

Her tears finally fall, and she makes no attempt to hide them from me like she would have in the past.

"I didn't have a choice."

"You always have a choice."

"Marcus discovered that you were his blood. Before that, you were safe. *We* were safe."

"How? How did he find out?"

She throws her arms up. "I have no idea. How do Quinctus find out anything? They have eyes and ears everywhere."

"You should have been more careful."

"That's why I came here, Bexley." Her expression softens. "Sterling Bay is meant to be a safe haven. It was agreed that Sterling would be a safe haven. That we couldn't be touched here. The Jaggers made sure that we could live our lives as we wished and were able to leave our pasts behind us."

A safe haven? What the fuck does that mean?

"You're not making any sense," I grit out. "If it's so safe here, why did I have to go back?"

"It's complicated, son. There's still things I can't tell you."

"What the fuck?" I balk. This is crazy. I need answers. I need to know what the fuck is going on.

"You were a firstborn heir, Bexley. The second I discovered I was pregnant, I knew I had to get you out of there. And then when I gave birth and discovered you were a boy... I was terrified. I know what Quinctus are capable of, and I didn't want that life for my child."

"Yet look where I am. In the middle of my fucking initiation." My voice booms across the kitchen, my anger over this whole situation getting the better of me.

"I'm so sorry, Bex. I'm so sorry." She drops her head into her hands and sobs.

"Not good enough, Mom. I'll never forgive you for this. For lying to both of us for so long."

"I just wanted—" she hiccups.

"To protect me, I know."

Her eyes lift to mine, devastation and guilt shining brightly within them.

"Where's Dad?"

"A-at work."

"Tell me he hasn't forgiven you for this?"

"He—" Hiccup. "He's moved into the pool house."

"What?" I roar. "You deceive him for your entire relationship, and *he's* the one to leave the house—the house that he pays for? Unbelievable."

"We need to keep up appearances, you know that."

I sigh, my fight leaving me at the ridiculousness of this entire situation.

Of course this is all about how things look to the rest of Sterling Bay and all of their pretentious, asshole friends.

"This is a fucking joke. *You* are a fucking joke."

I blow out of the house, slamming the door so hard behind me I wonder if the glass might have cracked as I storm toward the pool house.

I didn't come here for Mom, although she might have some of the answers I so desperately need. I came for Dad. The only other person on the planet who understands how I feel right now. And who is probably as confused as I am by all this bullshit.

The space looks mostly the same as I remember, but instead of it being where I hung out with my boys, it's now a bachelor pad. Bottles of beer and whiskey cover most of the surfaces, along with work folders and notes.

I fall down on the couch and rest my head back, closing my eyes, wondering how the hell my perfect life turned to such shit.

24

MIA

"What's wrong?" Annabel asks as we walk up to my house. After spending the night—one amazing night—wrapped in Bexley's arms, and then finding Cade standing at my door this morning, I needed space.

Cade is out of town for the weekend—he wouldn't tell me why. But I'd texted Bexley straight away, asking if he wanted to do something.

He never replied, and my mood went from hopeful to despair in five minutes flat. So when Annabel called and asked if I wanted to go home with her for the weekend, I said yes. It beat sitting around all weekend, waiting for Cade to come back or wondering what Bexley was doing that was so important he didn't want to speak to me.

"Nothing." I force a smile.

"Come on, Mia. This is me. I know when my best friend is upset about something. You barely said two words at lunch." We'd visited her mom first, spending a couple of hours eating the ridiculous spread Mrs. French had laid out.

"It's just weird being back, I guess."

"Since everything?" she asks, and I nod.

"I didn't exactly leave on great terms with my parents." There had been raised voices and cussing, mostly from me. But I didn't understand how they were so okay with me being Cade's prosapia. With Mom, I got it a little. She was born into this life. But Dad? He'd always been a bit more of a free spirit.

"But they're family. You always find your way back to family."

"Thanks, Bel." I grab her hand and stop her just before we reach the front door. "I know things have been a bit strange since we started Gravestone U—"

"And you became one of them, you mean?" She smiles, and I find no malice there, only understanding.

"I'm not one of them. I'm not sure I ever will be."

"I get it. But I want you to know something, too. I'm proud of the way you've handled everything. You should be, too. Being the chosen prosapia is never easy. But look at Fawn and Tim. They're wildly in love."

I want to argue after what Sasha told me about Tim and Hadley, but I don't, because although Annabel is my only real friend at Gravestone U, she's right. Some things have changed. I'm on the inside now, or at least, I've entered their world. Annabel is still an outsider.

"Here goes nothing, I guess," I say, digging out my key and letting us into the house.

"Mom?" I call.

"Mia, sweetheart, is that you?" She rounds the hall, looking every bit her immaculate self.

"Oh, baby, it's so good to see you." Her hug is overbearing, but I let her have this moment.

"Okay, Mom." I pat her back. "We've only been gone a couple of weeks."

"Two weeks too long, if you ask me." She holds me at arm's length, inspecting my face. "Are you getting enough sleep? Eating plenty of greens? You look a little—"

"Mom! Take a breath, I'm fine."

"Hey, Mrs. Thompson," Annabel says.

"Oh, Bel, sweetheart call me Temperance, please. Mrs. Thompson sounds so formal. Come," she takes my hand, leading us into the living room, "I want to hear all about it. I still can't believe my baby is at college. College!"

I shoot Annabel a silent plea for help, but she only offers me a reassuring smile. Traitor.

"So how are classes? And the dorms? Oh, and how are things with Cade?" Her whole face lights up at the mention of my tormentor's name.

"Cade is... a bit of a jerk, Mom."

"Mia!"

"What? It's true." I shrug.

"Cade Kingsley is a fine young man, sweetheart. You're a lucky girl—"

I bristle, and Annabel finally jumps to my rescue. "I love your blouse, Mrs.—I mean, Temperance. Is it new?"

"This old thing? No, but thank you, Annabel. My motto is it never hurts to be dressed for an occasion. Who knows what the day might bring. Did you already eat? I could make—"

"Bel's mom did a whole spread for lunch. I'm stuffed," I say. "Actually, if it's okay with you, Mom, I think we're just going to hang out in my room. I'm kind of beat."

"But you just got here, and me and your father have the gala tonight."

"That's okay, we can hang out tomorrow before I leave."

Her brows pinch. "Mia, I'd really like—"

But I'm already up out of my chair and making for the door.

"I guess we'll see you later." Bel grabs her bag and follows me upstairs.

When we're in the safety of my room, she says, "That was mean."

"I know, but I couldn't stand listening to her going on about Cade as if he's this hero. He's really not, Bel."

"Did something happen?" She kicks off her sneakers, grabs a pack of Twizzlers from her bag, and dives onto my bed.

"You mean aside from him being his usual cocky, arrogant, cruel self?"

"Whoa, tell it how it really is." She chuckles.

But I'm not laughing. I'm remembering his fingers on my skin, moving inside me, and I want to vomit all over my plush carpet.

Taking a deep breath, I brace my hand against the dresser. "I know everyone thinks he's this powerful, sexy guy, but honestly, he's kind of an ass."

"But have you seen his ass?" she asks. "You can't tell me the guy isn't packing a serious hot body beneath his Fendi t-shirts and jeans."

I press my lips together, refusing to answer. I don't want to talk about Cade, let alone imagine him naked.

"Have any guys caught your eye?"

Heat creeps into her cheeks, and I know I'm onto something. "Who? Alex?" I tease. She mentioned him a while back.

"No one." She plays dumb, biting the end of the candy stick.

"Oh, come on, I saw the way you blushed. There is a guy."

"Well, there was, but now it's confusing."

I grab my beanbag and smush down on it. "How so?"

"It's Alex."

"I knew it!" I smile, but realization quickly dawns and my expression falls.

"Now you understand my predicament." Annabel lets out a resigned sigh.

"You didn't say anything?"

"Yeah well, you've been kind of occupied."

Guilt floods me. "I've been a crap friend, I'm sorry."

"It's fine. Being in their world changes things."

"Are we talking about me, or Alex?" Internally, I'm cringing because I saw Alex fucking a girl at Cade's house that fateful night. He probably can't even remember it, but I can. The image of his white ass pounding into her is imprinted on the backs of my eyelids. A shudder runs down my spine.

"Have the two of you..." My eyes widen.

"What? No! We made out a couple of times..." She blushes. "And there might have been some clothed groping, but that's it. I don't just go around sleeping with random guys, Mia."

"Sorry, I wasn't—"

"Relax." Her laughter fills the room. "I'm just messing with you. I'd totally jump Alex's bones if I had the chance. But now he's initium..." Her smile falls. "He probably won't even notice me again."

"No way, Bel. You're beautiful. He'd be a fool not to notice you."

Withholding the truth from her twists my insides, but I don't do it. I can't tell her what happened that night.

For more reasons than one.

WE SPEND the afternoon hanging out in my room. Mom appears a couple of times to provide us with snacks and drinks. I know she's hurt at the way I hurried to my room, but the truth is, I wish she was in my corner. Not Quinctus and their archaic rules. And certainly not Cade's.

"Sweetheart." There's a knock at the door, and I leap up at the sound of my father's voice.

"Dad."

"It's good to see you, kid." He pulls me into his arms. "How are you? How's college?"

My mouth twists into an uncomfortable smile.

"That good, huh?"

"I'm not cut out for this, Dad," I whisper, burying myself in his chest the way I used to as a kid.

"Sweetheart." He gently grips my shoulders and eases me back. "You are so strong, Mia. You can handle anything life throws at you, and this, Cade, being his prosapia... you can do this."

My brows knit at his strange choice of words, but before I can ask him what he means, my mom appears.

"We're heading out now. Do you girls have everything you need?"

"I think so."

"Okay, well, have fun. We won't be too late." She smiles at me and then at my dad. "I'll grab my purse and then we can go?"

"I'll be right down, love." Dad turns his eyes on me. "You sure you're good?" he asks me, and I nod.

"Have fun tonight."

"We always do. Night, girls." He walks away, but then I remember something.

"Hey, Dad?"

"Yeah, sweetheart?"

"Does the name Jagger mean anything to you?"

"Jagger?" His expression gives nothing away. "I don't recognize it. Why do you ask?"

"No reason." I smile. "See you tomorrow."

"That you will." He stalks off down the hall. Anyone else would think nothing is up, but they don't know my dad like I do.

And he's lying.

Which means he *does* know the name Jagger.

But why would he know about anyone living in Sterling Bay?

"Mia?" Annabel says, cutting through my reverie.

"Huh?"

"So I did a thing."

"You did?" I close the door behind me.

"Yeah. Pass me my bag."

I pick it up, feeling its weight. "Jesus, what is in here?"

She unzips the bag and pulls out a bottle of vodka mixer.

"What the hell is that?"

"Emergency supplies. I knew you were feeling a little worried about coming home, so I figured..." She shook the bottle. "I have glasses too."

"Oh my God, who are you and what have you done to my friend?"

"We're freshmen now, Mia. College students. We should be out partying and hooking up with hot guys. But here we are."

"So this is what, your attempt at bringing the party to us?"

"Something like that. Are you game?"

Am I?

So much has happened over the last few days, I can't deny I'm tempted.

"Oh, what the hell. Fill me up." I grab a plastic cup from her bag. "Just don't let me get too drunk."

"At least we're already in bed if we do." Annabel cackles, uncapping the bottle and pouring us both a glass.

"To a night of laughter, freedom, and bad decisions. Cheers."

AN HOUR LATER, I'm drunk. Not out of control, stomach churning wasted, but that warm and giggly drunk.

"This was a good idea," I say, draining the last of my drink. "I feel so good."

"Right? I don't think we've ever done this, you know."

"Gotten drunk?"

"Not like this, just the two of us."

"I'm not a very good friend, am I?" I chase the shadows dancing across the ceiling. Billie Eilish blasts out of the docking station, serenading us about ocean-eyed boys that are dangerous for our hearts.

My mind instantly goes to Bexley. The way he kissed me... touched me... the way he made me come so hard I saw stars.

Heat unfurls in my stomach, and I let out a heavy sigh.

"What was that for?"

"Nothing," I reply.

"You can trust me, you know. I know I don't have a great track record with gossip, but I would never betray your confidence, Mia. I hope you know that."

I glance over at her, surprised at the honesty glittering in her eyes.

"You don't believe me?" Hurt flashes across Annabel's expression.

"It's not that, Bel, I just..."

Crap. The alcohol flowing in my veins is clouding my judgement. I want to tell her, I want to share the burden.

Bexley still hasn't replied to my message. We spent an amazing night together, and then he just ghosted me... and it hurts.

Damn him, it really hurts.

"Oh, come on, babe. You're killing me over here. Is it Cade? Did you two..." Her brows waggle.

"No." God no!

"So what is it? Because I can see your secrets, Mia Thompson. They're written all over your face."

"It isn't Cade."

"So what, then..."

My breath hitches as the urge to confess overpowers me. I need to tell someone, I have to. It's killing me, holding this all in.

"You promise you won't breathe a word of it... to anyone?"

"Cross my heart, hope to die." She drags her finger over her chest.

"You can't tell a soul, Bel. I mean it."

"Whatever it is, it can't be that bad."

"Oh, it's bad," I sigh. "Me and Bexley—"

"Bexley? As in Bexley Easton?"

I nod slowly, tears rushing up my throat and burning the backs of my eyes.

"Mia, what is it?" She sits up, looking cornered.

"We…" I can't. I can't tell her. But before I know what's happening, the words are spilling out. "We slept together, Bel. I gave him my virginity."

25

BEXLEY

Dad didn't come home last night. I should have called him, told him that I was in town, but if I'd dragged him away from some important business thing I'd have felt guilty. His life is already shit enough as it is because of my existence; I don't want to make it even worse.

Besides, part of me was scared he would reject me now.

I ended up drinking until I passed out after finding Dad's stash of scotch in the small kitchenette.

When I wake, I'm on the couch with a stiff neck, a bad back, and a pounding head.

The sun streams through the floor to ceiling windows that overlook the backyard and glistening blue pool.

My limbs ache for me to dive in and ease the stiffness with the warm water, but the chance of Mom being home and coming out to try to talk to me makes it a little—or a lot—less appealing.

A groan rips from my lips as I push up until I'm sitting on the edge of the couch.

Dropping my head into my hands, I think back to the message I found sitting on my cell yesterday morning from Mia.

She wanted to know my plans because the asshole was away.

Typical that the weekend I take off is the weekend he also fucks off.

Karma really is a fucking bitch.

I want to feel bad about what happened between me and Mia. I should feel at least a little remorse, but I feel nothing.

Well, that's not true. Just thinking about her makes my chest tighten. The pain of her lying to me about who was on the other side of her dorm door is still fresh.

Why lie? What was the point?

We both knew what we were doing was wrong. It's a little late for her to worry about protecting me now.

If she were going to do that, then it should have been the night we first met.

But she didn't. She let me get close, and she allowed me to see her beauty.

I sigh, pushing from the couch and going in search of painkillers. Finding half a packet of Advil, I throw two back with some Gatorade I grabbed from the refrigerator.

I stare at the main house, wondering what the chances are of sneaking in so I can change. Hell knows I used to sneak in and out of that place like a pro back in the day.

Needing to do something other than spend any more time cooped up in here and hiding like a pussy from my mother, I swing the door open and step out into the warm morning sun.

I slip through the back door, moving as silently as I can and finding that remembering the noise spots is a little like remembering how to ride a bike. Those little creaky patches are ingrained in my brain, and I move on instinct.

I don't look around my old room. There are too many memories of a life I fucked up. I'm way too hungover to deal with those regrets right now. Instead, I rush toward my closet and pull out some workout clothes.

I shed everything I'm still wearing from two days ago and pull them on before making the journey—once again unnoticed—to the back door.

Pushing aside my hangover and the marching band that's taken up residence in my head, I take off down the driveway and out onto the sidewalk, taking the route I always used to.

As I run, I focus on the movement of my limbs and the rhythmic pounding of my feet on the sidewalk. For that small amount of time, everything else ceases to exist. I can imagine that my life is still here, that I still have football and a future that I crave. That I didn't fuck every single thing up.

I might have lost it all and been forced to move, but really, nothing changes. Because I still end up screwing everything up.

I've chased and touched the one person in that godforsaken town that I shouldn't have, and eventually, I'm going to pay the price for that. And something tells me that when that mistake catches up with me, it's going to make what Ace Jagger put me through look like child's play.

I run until my lungs burn and my muscles quiver with the need for rest. But I don't slow to a walk until I hit the beach.

My feet sink into the golden sand as I step down onto the beach I used to spend so much time at as a kid.

The tide is out, so I keep walking until the ground hardens beneath me and I get to the ocean's edge.

Slipping off my shoes and socks, I carry them in one hand as I begin walking along with the water lapping at my feet, just absorbing the familiar comforting sounds of the crashing waves and families enjoying themselves.

I'm lost in my own world, watching the waves when I sense two people in front of me.

Reluctantly, I lift my head to see who I'm about to collide with. Dread sits heavy in my stomach that I'm about to come face to face with some of my old friends that I let down and abandoned.

It took me quite a few weeks, but eventually, I did some research and discovered who took my place as captain of the Seahawks. Part of me wanted to see them crash and burn without me, but deep down, I was happy that they were thriving and went on to achieve success, despite how much it killed me.

It should have been my year. My epic win. But I wasn't even in the stadium for their final game.

I lift my eyes at the very last minute, and they land on the one and only person I'd be willing to talk to in this town right now.

Hadley Rexford.

Okay, Hadley Rexford and a shocked but angry-looking Cole Jagger, her boyfriend.

His shoulders widen as our eyes hold. He pulls Hadley into his side as if I'm an actual threat to her safety.

It should piss me off. But I get it.

I fucked up, and I need to pay the price.

"Danforth," he growls. "Thought we'd seen the back of you for a while."

Ignoring Cole, I keep my eyes fixed on Hadley's.

"We need to talk," I state as Cole's grip on her becomes borderline painful, I'm sure.

I understand. If the situation were reversed, I wouldn't want my girl anywhere near me either.

Hell, I experience the exact same thing as Cole every time Cade so much as looks at Mia, let alone anything else.

The images of them kissing, of him touching her, flicker through my mind briefly, but I force it down into its box.

This is not the time.

"Like hell you do," Cole growls, attempting to steer Hadley around me.

"Wait, please. My name..." I start, and thankfully Hadley forces Cole to slow down a little. "My name isn't Danforth. It's Easton." I hold Hadley's eyes and watch as understanding and recognition hit her.

"Holy shit," she gasps. "For real?"

I ignore Cole's death stare and act as if he's not standing there.

Taking a step toward Hadley, the one person from my past who understands my future, I suddenly feel a little lighter.

I have someone to actually talk to about all of this.

"Marcus, the guy from the wedding. He's not my uncle. He's my grandfather. And..."

"You're the only Easton heir," she finishes for me.

"Apparently so."

"Fuck." She drops to the sand and pulls her knees up to her chest for a few seconds as she thinks.

I sit down beside her, and finally Cole does the same.

"So... um... your dad d-died in a car crash, right? His wife, your—" I shake my head to stop that train of thought.

"My mom *is* my mom. She got pregnant by Richard Easton and ran before anyone found out."

Her lips part before she closes them again, having found no words.

"Mom lied to Dad and me this whole time. Somehow Marcus found out and the timing was perfect, because my parents were more than ready to pack me up and send me away.

"I did almost a year there with no idea who I was or what all of it meant.

"And then came the new moon ceremony and—" She sucks in a deep breath and covers her hand over her mouth.

"Bexley, you're Electi initium." It's not a question. It doesn't need to be.

Pulling my shorts up higher on my thigh, I show her my still red scar from the blood sacrifice they forced on me.

"What the fuck is going on here?" Cole barks, clearly not understanding anything we're saying. I get it, it took awhile for it to make any sense to me too.

I look from Cole and back to Hadley.

"Yes, Bex. Always," she assures me, answering my silent question as to whether we can trust him or not.

Hadley very quickly skims over the details of Gravestone. She misses a ton out, so I can only assume that Cole already knows some of this twisted shit.

"Bexley is now one of the most important people in the town. But don't think that's a good thing. Because in my opinion—sorry, Bex—it's a death sentence."

"Don't worry, I feel the same right now."

"He gets initiated in. Tasks are set by Quinctus and the other Electi. They can be brutal. Guys have died in the past, trying to claim their rightful place."

Cole frowns, clearly having a hard time understanding why anyone would put themselves through that. "Just walk away."

"He can't. That's an even bigger death sentence."

"Marcus wants me to take down Cade," I blurt for the first time, and it feels so good to let it out.

"Oh?" Hadley's eyes widen. "But he's..."

"King? Yeah, I got that fucking memo." I scrub my hand through my sweat-damp hair and look out to the sea. "According to Marcus and your... father," she sucks in a breath at the mention of him, "he's getting out of control. I can't help but agree with them after the shit he's put us through."

"Us?" Her eyes narrow and I chastise myself. "Is someone else initiating with you? And what's my father got to do with this?"

"I... uh... I've just had a chance to talk with him about it, that's all."

She holds my eyes, clearly sensing that I'm not telling her the whole truth. But like fuck am I going to sit here and tell her she's got a new brother. That is not my place.

"You should come back, Hads. Visit your parents. Things have... things have changed recently and—"

"Do you know why I left?" she asks, cutting me off.

I shake my head. "I've heard rumors. Nothing concrete."

"I fell in love with Tim," she admits, much to Cole's irritation if his curled fists and white knuckles are anything to go by. "He got me pregnant."

"Jesus, Hads." I scrub my hand down my face as I let this new information sink in. "But Fawn is his prosapia."

"Exactly. See my issue?"

I think of Mia, of the thoughts I had about my biological father and my mother on the drive here.

This is another thing pointing to the fact that whatever is growing between us will never work.

She's not mine, and I can't have her.

I bend my legs and drop my head to my knees. "This is such a fucking mess," I mutter as Hadley's warm hand lands on my back.

"I wanted to kill you for what went down with Remi, Bex. But this... I wouldn't wish this on my worst enemy.

"I was lucky, I guess. My father found out the truth and I was exiled. It worked out perfectly for me. But I know that things are very different for male heirs. If I were a boy and this happened then... I can only imagine what they'd have done to me. I guess it's good that I never had a brother."

I tense at her words.

She needs to know the truth.

I turn to look at her.

She looks happy. Really fucking happy.

"Shouldn't you two be at college or something?"

"We're both at Colton U. Cole is a Colt."

Of course he is. Cole Jagger is a killer running back, so it's not surprising a team like Colton picked him up for college football.

"We just came back for the weekend for James' birthday."

"About the Jaggers," I start, knowing there are some pieces of the puzzle I'm still missing. "Where do they all fit into this?"

26

MIA

By the time we get back to campus, all the relief I felt confiding in Annabel melts away, and I can't help but wonder if I did the right thing or not.

But in that split second, I needed to tell someone. All the secrets and lies are slowly killing me, and since it appears Bexley is ignoring me, I turned to the only other person I could.

Of course, I swore her to secrecy. But after my emotional breakdown as I confessed to her, I think she knows how important it is that she doesn't breathe of word of it. To anyone.

"I'll see you tomorrow?" Annabel pauses as we arrive outside my dorm.

"Yeah."

"And I'm here, Mia. If you need anything."

Her eyes say everything she doesn't, and I reach for her hand, squeezing it.

"Thank you, for everything."

"Of course."

I slip inside and close my door, breathing a sigh of relief. For as much as I've enjoyed Annabel's company, I'm glad to have some space.

Kicking off my sneakers, I flop down on the bed and grab my cell from my pocket, bringing up my messages to Bexley. They all show the little read sign, so I know he's seen them.

So why hasn't he texted me back?

The obvious reason is that he's realized I'm not worth it.

It shouldn't hurt so much, but it does. Even though I know it'll save us both a lot of inevitable heartache if we walk away now, I can't get his words out of my head.

"You're mine, Mia. Mine."

Why would he say that and then ghost me?

Tears prick the corners of my eyes, but they're ones of frustration and anger. I could go to his dorm room and demand answers, but I can't risk being seen. It's bad enough that Bexley sneaks in and out of my room.

Soon he'll no longer be initium. He'll be Electi. I can't imagine him and Alex part of Cade's group. But that's what being initiated means—it means becoming one of them. Sasha explained that once they pass the final test, they'll have to move to the Electi house on the outskirts of campus. I can't imagine Bexley ever living under the same roof as Cade. Perhaps he has a plan, an escape plan to avoid a life of being Cade's lapdog.

Who I am kidding?

You don't ever escape the Electi or Quinctus. They'd rather kill you than let you walk away. There are too many secrets, too much at stake.

Why me?

Why did my name have to be called that fateful night?

It still doesn't make sense.

I'm no one.

Cade never looked twice at me before. But now his attention is set firmly on me, and it worries me. I know I'm a game, a conquest... but I can't help but wonder what happens when he finally wins. When he finally makes me his.

I'm just about to send Bexley another text message when my cell phone pings. For a second, excitement fills my chest, thinking it's probably him, at last.

But it isn't.

I read Cade's text with a sense of dread. He wants to see me tonight. I quickly text him back that I have to study, hoping that he'll let me off the hook. But his reply is instant, and it chills me to the bone.

Cade: I've missed you, Mia. Wear something sexy. I'll pick you up at seven.

THE CIBUS IS one of Gravestone's most exclusive restaurants, reserved only for the elite families of the town and their associates. Of course, Cade breezes into the place as if he owns it, and the host almost falls over himself to accommodate us.

"We have your table waiting, sir."

I smother a chuckle. Cade is barely twenty-one. To call him sir seems so inappropriate when he's nothing more than a man-child with more money and power than sense.

The host pulls out a chair for me and I fold myself into it, placing my purse on the table. I settled on a modest navy dress for this evening. It has a collared neckline and cinches in at my waist before flaring over my hips. Most girls would have spent hours primping and preening themselves for a date with the infamous Cade Kingsley. But not me. I wield my makeup like it's armor. From the way Cade hungrily eyes me across the table, I know my efforts at demure have backfired.

"You seem nervous," he says.

"I'm not." The lie rolls off my tongue.

"Good to know." He takes it upon himself to order us a bottle of champagne.

"Are we celebrating?" I ask, impressed by how together my voice sounds.

"I guess you could call it an early celebration of sorts." He cocks a brow at me, giving me a wolfish grin. "Did you enjoy your weekend?"

"Did you?" I retort, and he chuckles.

"It's just dinner, Mia. I promise. No ulterior motives." Cade smooths a hand through his perfectly styled hair. There's no denying he looks good in the black dress shirt and charcoal slacks. People watch us discreetly over their menus and meals. News has spread across town about Cade and his new girlfriend. Those of verus bloodline understand what it means, while outsiders just think the infamous playboy has finally decided to settle down. Tonight, we're in verus territory. The Cibus is as exclusive as it comes.

I feel their stares of curiosity, their judgement. In high school I blended with the shadows. I didn't occupy the limelight or hang with the most popular kids. I was a wallflower, and I was happy being there. But now, everything is different. The light shines too brightly on me, and I feel like every flaw, every imperfection and doubt I have, is on display for all to see.

Especially Cade.

"Everyone is staring," I hiss after it's apparent we're not going to get to eat in private tonight.

"Welcome to my world." Cade winks. He actually winks. Conceited asshole. "You know, most girls would pay, maybe even kill, to be where you're sitting, Mia." His dark eyes study me, making my heart race. And not in a good way. "And yet, I can't help but feel like you want to be anywhere but here."

I grab my glass of champagne and bring it to my lips. Before all this, being in the Eligere and Bexley's initiation, I would have turned down the offer of alcohol. But now, I need it. I need something to tamp down the constant anger and betrayal I feel at my dire situation.

"It was a mistake, and you know it."

"Q don't make mistakes, Mia. Every thought, every action is carefully planned and considered. You think they didn't know exactly whose name was going to be called that night?"

"But that's not—"

"Isn't it? You verus are always so happy to believe everything we tell you. Do you really think Quinctus would leave the Eligere to mere chance?"

"Well, no. I didn't..." He's right. I guess I hadn't given it tons of thought. We're brought up to believe that the calix produces the name of the chosen prosapia. Of course we all know that someone has to physically put the name in the calix, but we don't question it. Just like we don't question any of the traditions of our town.

But maybe we should.

Brook's name should have been called that night. Everyone knows it, including Cade.

So why am I sitting here in her place?

It's the question that refuses to leave me. The question I fear I may never have an answer to.

"There's a reason they want us to be together, Mia. And I am all about giving Q what they want." He smirks, and I find nothing but sarcasm in his words.

"Where were you this weekend?" I change the subject.

"Always so inquisitive. For someone who claims not to like me, you seem to care a lot about my whereabouts."

"It's just a question," I quip. "Don't read too much into it."

"You're not the only pawn in this game, Mia." He levels me with a hard look. "Don't forget that."

"So you were on official business?"

"Something like that." He takes a big gulp of his drink. "It's the full moon next weekend. There's a lot to plan."

My stomach drops. "Already?" Of course I should know this, but it's been a crazy couple of weeks. "The Transitus," I whisper, and Cade nods.

"Our initiums' final test." Something glints in his eyes, but the server arrives to take our order.

"What do they have to do?" I try to disguise the tremor in my voice.

"If I tell you, where would the surprise in that be? Just know, it's going to be one hell of a weekend."

Oh God.

Whatever they're planning, it isn't good. But how much worse can it be than the pit?

From the wicked glint in Cade's eyes, I'm guessing a lot.

"You'll need something to wear for the dinner. I'll have Sasha take you shopping."

"I'm quite capable of choosing a dress, Cade."

He stiffens, no doubt growing tired with my defiance. But I can't do it, I can't be the meek and submissive girl he expects.

His jaw works overtime as he runs a hand down his face. "And I'm telling you to go with Sasha, and since you belong to me, you'll do what I say."

His hand grips my thigh under the table, squeezing hard. For a second, I'm so overcome with fear and surprise that I'm paralyzed. His hand slides higher, grazing the soft skin of my thighs.

Without thinking, I thrust my hand under the table and wrench his fingers back. "Don't ever touch me like that again in public," I seethe through gritted teeth.

Cade explodes with laughter, bringing his hand above the table and flexing his fingers.

"I underestimated you, Mia." He doesn't look pissed. In fact, he looks... impressed.

He curves his hand around the back of my neck and draws me closer. "You want to play hard to get, baby, just say the word." His warm breath fans my face. "But rest assured, Mia. I will have you. And when I do, you'll be screaming my name while I fuck your virginal pussy hard and fast until you know exactly who you belong to."

I suck in a harsh breath, my entire body shuddering from his threatening words. Because that's what they are—a threat.

A promise.

Cade is counting the days until he can make me his. I see it every time he looks at me. For as unnerving as his words are, I can't help but feel a lick of smug satisfaction. Because Cade will never get to take my first time from me. That belongs to Bexley.

And when Cade finds out I'm no longer his virginal prize, maybe he'll drop this charade and finally cut me loose.

At least, that's what I tell myself...

Because the alternative is simply too terrifying to consider.

27

BEXLEY

I keep my head down as I walk toward my first class Monday morning.

I arrived back in Gravestone late last night, having spent the morning discussing the place with Hadley while Cole looked on, totally bemused by the whole setup.

It was nice to see someone else's mind blown by the reality that is now my life, even if it was Cole Jagger.

I guess it could have been worse. It could have been Ace.

I'd wanted to stop by the Jagger house to see if I could talk to Remi while I was in town. I still need to apologize to her. Ace and his brothers kept her so well protected at the wedding I attended a few months ago that I couldn't even breathe near her, let alone talk to her.

I need her to know how much I regret my actions back then. I need her to know how sorry I am for ruining everything that was between us.

Students gossip as I pass them by, but I ignore them. I'm beginning to get used to being the center of attention once again, even if it is very different from my time in Sterling Prep.

I wanted it back then. I wanted to be both the king of the school and the football field. Now, I'm happy for someone else to wear the crown. Granted, it could be someone better than Cade fucking Kingsley who reigns supreme, but as long as it's not me, I guess I'll take it.

I don't talk to anyone—I don't even look at anyone—as I make my way into the empty auditorium and take my seat.

Pulling out my cell, I once again stare at Mia's messages.

I've tapped out a few replies to her since I received them, but all of them have gone unsent. This thing between us. It's a disaster waiting to happen.

My dad fell for the wrong woman and she ended up fleeing town to restart her life, while his tragically ended a few years later along with the woman who'd been promised to him.

I have no idea if he even loved her.

Then there's Hadley.

At only sixteen, she was practically banished from this place for falling for the wrong guy.

Love is meant to conquer all. I think Quinctus maybe forgot that when they decided on their stupid fucking rules.

I twist my pen around in my hand as students begin filling the space around me. The sound of chairs moving and their excited chatter about what they got up to on the weekend filters up to me where I'm hiding at the back.

I feel the burning stare of more than a few of them, but I don't give them any of my attention in return. I refuse to feed the gossip in any way.

The atmosphere changes the second she steps into the room. Maybe no one else notices it, but suddenly, the air around me becomes hard to breathe and every nerve in my body is on full alert.

I'm desperate to torture myself further and look up to see if he's delivered her to class like he seems to enjoy—any chance to lord it over everyone—but I keep my eyes glued to my desk, telling myself that I don't need to know.

What either of them do shouldn't have anything to do with me. Thoughts of them being together also shouldn't tear me up inside like this.

The seats on either side of me might be empty, but I already know Mia won't take either of them. She's not stupid and knows that even if Cade doesn't see it with his own eyes, he's got enough minions roaming Gravestone U halls to ensure all information gets straight back to him. Hell, he's probably got access to the entire campus CCTV.

When my need to see her becomes too much to bear, I lift my eyes. But before I manage to find her, a body drops into the seat beside me.

"No one's sitting here, right?" a sickly sweet voice says. One that I recognize but don't want to hear.

"It's taken," I growl, spinning to look at Brook, Cade's old plaything.

"It is now." She gets herself comfortable and pulls her books out, ready for our professor to begin his lecture.

"What do you want, Brook?" I snap, deciding that I've probably got more chance of getting rid of her if I allow her to say what she's got to say.

I have no time for anyone who's connected to any of the Electi—even Alex right now, seeing as I left the dorms without knocking for him this morning—and I certainly don't want to talk to Ashton's little sister.

"Did you hear about their little date last night?"

My teeth grind. If she's just come over here to push my buttons, then she's going to be bitterly disappointed because she's going to get nothing out of me. It doesn't matter how painfully I might be shattering on the inside; she's never going to witness it on the outside. I've got a better game face than that.

"Is there a point to this?" I grit out.

"Cade took her to the most exclusive restaurant in town, bought her the most expensive bottle of champagne they sell."

"Right? Was there also gold leaf on their dessert?"

She shrugs, completely missing my sarcasm. "Probably."

"Brook," I warn as the professor begins and every other student in the room focuses their attention on him, just like I should be doing.

"Okay, fine," she huffs as if I'm the one wasting her time. "I think... if we team up, maybe we both get what we want."

"And what is it that you think I want, Brook? Other than for you to leave me alone."

"Bexley, Bexley," she sighs. "Always so quick to judge." My lips press into a thin line as I stare at her.

Her makeup is thick and flawless, her hair styled within an inch of its life. While she's beautiful—any hot-blooded guy can see that—she doesn't hold a candle to Mia.

Mia's natural beauty brings me to my knees, and it's not just her outer beauty. What she's hiding beneath is even more breathtaking.

"Cut to the chase. I need to listen. I'm in college for a reason, and it's not just to spread my legs for Electi." I pin her with a look, but if she's shocked by my words then she doesn't show it. That, or she's just well aware of her rep and happy to own it. I don't know whether to feel sorry for her or be impressed.

"You want her." She tilts her chin in Mia's direction.

"Do I?" I ask, keeping all emotion and desire out of my voice.

"You do. You might think I'm a dumb blonde, but I see things. I've seen how you watch her, how you stare at her with longing in your eyes."

"I get it, because I watch *him* like that. Let's work together, and maybe we can both come out of it happier."

"She's his prosapia, Brook. You understand what that means, right?"

A smile curls at her lips at my comment, and I regret it instantly. I might as well have just told her I was falling for Mia faster than I can control.

"I understand more than you know, Bexley. But I'm not one to back down from a challenge, and we all know that my name should have been drawn that night."

"Yeah, about that... why wasn't it?"

"Fuck if I know. Someone screwed up. She's not the one for him. Everything about them as a couple is just wrong. She'll never be able to give him what he needs."

I open my mouth to argue, to tell her that Mia is everything, but I catch myself at the last minute and swallow down the words.

"So what do you say?" She leans forward on the desk, ensuring her tits are pushed up and right in my view.

I roll my eyes at her display. If she believes any of what she's just said to me, then she must realize that she's barking up the wrong tree, trying to convince me with her body.

"I'm not interested, Brook. I'm already in deeper with the Electi than I want. I'm not starting any games with them."

"But—" she pouts. "Don't you want her?"

Yes, more than anything. But not like this.

"No. She's Cade's."

Her chin drops, and she stares at me as if I'm about to throw my head back and laugh.

"Wait... you're serious?"

"Deadly. Now, do you mind? I actually want to pass this class."

I turn away from her, pull my notebook closer, and focus on the professor as he paces back and forth, his enthusiastic voice booming across the vast space.

Brook huffs and pouts beside me, but she doesn't say anything else, although something tells me that it won't be the last I hear from her.

She's clearly serious about getting Cade back. Fuck knows why anyone would want that conceited asshole, but she's more than welcome to him. And somehow, she's discovered my weakness. And while I might have just refused her offer to break up the not-so-happy couple, that doesn't mean I don't want to figure out a way to make it happen. I'd just rather not have to sell my soul to the female version of Cade fucking Kingsley to do it.

Thankfully, I manage to catch up with what I'd missed while Brook was spouting her crap at me, and by the time I walk out of the auditorium a couple of hours later, I've almost forgotten about the whole exchange. Almost.

Just like my journey here, I keep my head down and don't acknowledge anyone as I grab a coffee before my next class starts.

BY SOME MIRACLE, I manage to keep up my hiding in plain sight act for two whole days.

I come to the conclusion that I must be emitting some weird back-the-fuck-off aura, because even Alex gives me a wide birth, which is seriously unlike him.

It all comes crashing down, though, as I leave my economics class on Wednesday morning.

I'm the last one to pack up and leave. Even the professor has given up waiting for me and disappeared.

I'm just about to reach for the door when it swings open and I find myself locked in Mia's dark and angry hazel eyes.

She's been messaging me, trying to catch my attention in class, but I haven't so much as looked her way. If I weren't so in tune with her then I might have missed it, but if we're in the same room together then I know everything. I'm aware the second she turns her eyes on me. I feel the tether that's between us pulling tight, begging me to turn her way and to make that connection with her that we both crave.

She takes a step toward me, looking up through her lashes. Her shoulders are tense and her lips are downturned.

"You're ignoring me," she states, dropping her purse to the floor with a thud as she continues to close the space between us.

Her scent fills my nose, and my resolve to put some distance between us begins to crumble.

"Did you have a good date on Sunday night?" I snarl.

"You know I didn't. I spent the entire time I was there wishing that I was with you. But there was little chance of that, seeing as you can't even respond to my messages." Anger comes off her in waves. "You told me you wanted me, Bex. That it was me and you. And then you just ran away."

"You lied to me," I seethe, my voice laced with anger and disappointment.

"What? When?"

I suck in a deep breath, trying not to lose myself in the memory of him backing her into her room and pushing his tongue into her mouth.

"I saw him, Mia," I spit. "I know it wasn't Annabel at your door Saturday morning."

28

MIA

Bexley's words ring in my ear.
He knows.
He knows.

"Bexley, I can explain." My voice echoes around the now empty room.

"Explain how your mouth ended up on his?" he seethes.

"I'm his prosapia, I don't exactly have a choice."

"Fuck," he hisses, jamming his fingers into his hair and tugging sharply. Then his defeated gaze settles on mine. "This was a mistake. I don't think I can do this anymore."

I suck in a ragged breath, his words lashing my insides.

"Y-you don't want me?" My arms go around my waist as I try to hold myself together. I gave myself to him. I let myself believe his words.

You're mine.

And now he's throwing them back in my face like I'm nothing.

"It doesn't matter what I want," he says coldly. "Like you said, you're Kingsley's prosapia. Soon enough you'll be his fiancée. And I'll be one of his lapdogs. This," he motions between us, "us. It can never work."

"So that's it, huh?" I swallow the ball of emotion in my throat. "You're just going to walk away?"

My body begins trembling as my chest cracks wide open. I knew he might have been having second thoughts, but I didn't think he'd break my heart quite so brutally.

"I'm not the guy for you, Mia." He glances away, and I know we're done here.

Bexley is choosing—and he's choosing the coward's way out.

Well fuck him.

Fuck him and Cade and the Electi.

Fuck them all.

If Bexley won't help me figure this out, I'll do it myself. Because I refuse to stay in this situation and just let Cade ruin me. Which is exactly what I know he'll do. He's just biding his time, toying with me until the day he can finally make me his in all the ways he wants.

"You know, I really thought you were better than him. I thought you were trustworthy." I slam my hands against his chest. "I thought you'd keep my heart safe. Guess I should have known you'd fuck off as soon as you got what you wanted," I shriek, aware that if anyone passes the room they'll hear me. But I don't care. In this minute, all I care about is letting Bexley know just how deeply he's betrayed me.

I storm away, but Bexley grabs my wrist and yanks me back. My eyes snap to where he's roughly grasping me and then flick to his dark gaze.

"I suggest you get your hands off me." My voice is a low growl as I wrench myself free and stagger back.

"What did you say about me?" He sneers.

"You heard me. You're a coward. You're—"

"Not that. The bit about me being like him. I am *nothing* like that fucker." Bexley's eyes spark with contempt, sending shivers skating down my spine.

"Keep telling yourself that."

"That's rich, coming from you. Or did you forget that his fingers have been inside your pussy?"

My gasp fills the air. "That's different, and you know it." What Cade did to me was against my will. I didn't want it. I hated every second of it.

Except... I didn't.

Shame burns through me.

"You came like a good little whore, Mia. All over his fingers."

"How dare you..." I tremble as I back up, but Bexley prowls toward me like a predator tracking its prey. My heart gallops in my chest, fear flooding my veins. Bexley won't physically hurt me, my head knows that, but my heart is already bruised from his cruel words.

My back hits the wall, and there's nowhere left to go. Bexley looms over me, his breaths coming in short, sharp bursts. He's furious.

Well, that makes two of us.

He reaches around me and locks the door.

"What are you doing?" My voice wobbles.

"You really think I'm like him?"

"Do you care?"

"Mia..." he warns, and I press my lips together in defiance.

"You want me to be like Kingsley?" His hands slide into my hair and winds it around his fists, making my scalp pinch. I swallow the cry building in my throat and narrow my eyes.

"Little mouse, didn't you know you shouldn't say things you don't mean. It's mean. And mean girls get punished." He yanks me down, pushing me until I'm on my knees at his feet.

His other hand snaps his belt and frees his cock. It's hard and ready. And I know I should be pissed, I know I should lean forward and bite the goddamn thing off, but all I feel is the sweet taste of victory.

Bexley can say we're done, he can say he doesn't want me, but he does. The proof is staring me right in the eyes.

"Don't just look at it, mouse." He fists himself, pumping a couple of times. "Suck it."

The head is swollen, a bead of pre-cum glistening there. My tongue darts out, tasting him.

"Fuck," Bexley rasps, and I smile with satisfaction. He thinks he's in charge here, but I hold all the cards. And I'm going to make him kneel at my feet by the time we're done.

My hand wraps around his shaft and I suck him into my mouth, taking him as far as I can. A garbled moan flies from his lips as I swirl my tongue around the tip again. I pump him in firm strokes as I tease and lick and suck.

"Fuck yeah." He tries to force me over his length again, but I stand my ground, teasing him into complete submission. My hands gently cup his balls as I take him to the back of my throat again, swallowing down the urge to gag. Bexley's clean, salty taste is addictive, and I suck him like a popsicle.

My hands slide around his thighs and find his ass, gripping firmly. I've never gotten past second base with anyone except Bexley, but the thought of making a guy like him come undone spurs me on to experiment and do what feels good.

"Look at me," he commands, raggedly, and I stare up at him as I flatten my tongue against the underside of his cock and lick.

"I could blow my load just watching you." He reaches down and cups my face, stroking my cheek. "More," he grunts, and I go back to sucking him deep into my mouth.

I'm so turned on, I'm half-tempted to slip my hand into my panties and make myself come, but I have a mission, and I'm not about to fail.

Slipping a finger into my mouth, I make it nice and wet before sliding it against Bexley's ass. He stiffens, grabbing my hair and tilting my face to his. "What the hell are you doing, little mouse?"

"I've heard it makes you come harder." I gently push my finger deeper, feeling his tight ring of muscle.

"You think I want to come in your mouth when I can come in your pussy?" His eyes darken as he yanks me to my feet. "Playtime is over." Bexley lifts me up, forcing my legs around his waist. He pushes my skirt up. "Ready to be punished, mouse?" He nips my lips, smirking. But I see the affection in his gaze.

"Do you worst," I taunt, needing him more than I need air.

Bexley lines himself up and slams inside of me, making me cry out. He covers my mouth with his big hand as he drives into me over and over, fucking me like he hates me when we both know it's a lie.

"Fuck, I want to fuck you right out of my system."

"Liar," I cry, lost to the sensations, the sheer pleasure, coursing through my veins.

His eyes flicker with surprise and I smirk.

"What happened to punishing me?"

His hand slides to my throat and he squeezes. "Know what I think? I think you like it when I hurt you."

"I like it when you *fuck* me."

"Jesus." His mouth crashes down on mine, stealing my breath, as he continues pounding into me.

"Harder," I breathe. "More..."

"Fuck, Mia... fuck, are you close?"

I'm not, I'm too wound up. Too all up in my head.

"Tell me what you need, mouse." Bexley peppers my mouth with tender kisses, slowing his pace, grinding into me so that his pelvis hits my clit, sending bolts of pleasure rippling through me.

"Like that," I whisper, my head rolling back against the wall as I chase the wave building deep inside me.

My legs begin trembling as I hurtle toward the edge. "Close?" he asks again, and I smirk.

He cares.

Bexley cares so much he'd do anything right now to make sure I come first.

"Touch me." I grab his hand and push it between our bodies, smothering a moan when his fingers find my swollen clit. My orgasm hits like a wrecking ball, slamming into me so hard I can do nothing but ride out the wave.

Bexley follows me, jerking hot ropes of cum inside me as he kisses me with long, lazy licks of his tongue.

I press my body closer, holding onto him for dear life. "Don't ever tell me we were a mistake again." Easing back, I meet his hooded gaze. "Nothing about us is a mistake, Bexley. Not a single thing."

"This won't end well," he says, his words like a gunshot to my heart.

"I don't care," I say, whispering against the corner of his lips. "I'm yours. Say it." My fingers graze his jaw. "I need you to say it."

"You're mine, Mia. Every." Kiss. "Single." Kiss. "Piece of you."

"Good." I nod, feeling like a weight has been lifted. "Now let's get out of here before someone finds us."

AFTER BEXLEY and I snuck out of the classroom, we both went our separate ways. But he'd spent most of the day texting me, reassuring me that we would find a way through this.

I'm still smiling when there's a knock at my door a few hours later.

My stomach plummets as I expect to see Cade on the other side of the peephole. But it isn't Cade at all.

"Sasha, this is a surprise."

"I hope it's okay that I stopped by. I kind of got the impression you've been avoiding me."

"Not avoiding, just... it's been a strange weekend."

"How were the parentals?"

"Frustrating," I admit, welcoming her inside. "How was your weekend?"

"Fairly dull. The guys were... preparing."

"For the weekend?"

She nods but doesn't meet my eyes.

"Why do I get the feeling it's going to be bad?"

"It's never good where Cade and Ashton are concerned."

"What's that?" Her eyes drop to my neck, and my hand drifts there.

"What?" I walk to the mirror, and my eyes widen in horror. "I... uh, nothing."

"That's not nothing." She storms over to me and bats my hand away, pulling the neckline of my tank top down. "That's a hickey."

"No, it's not."

Her brow arches. "You're a terrible liar. The question is, though, who gave it to you? Was it Cade? Are you two—"

"What? No!" Disgust rolls through me.

"Oh my God," realization dawns in her eyes, "it was Bexley, wasn't it?"

"No, it wasn't. I don't know what you're talking about." I can't look at her, because I know there's guilt etched into my expression.

"Oh, Mia, what did you do?"

She steps around me so I have no choice but to meet her sympathetic gaze.

"I like him, Sasha. I really, really like him."

"But you're Cade's prosapia. If he finds out, and he will, what do you think he'll do?"

A violent shudder rips through me. "You can't tell him, please. I'm begging you."

"God, I would never... but you have to end it, Mia. You have to."

"I can't. I won't." I'm falling for Bexley, and I refuse to accept that we can't find a way to make it work. Even if it is stupid.

"This isn't a case of Cade getting his feelings hurt, Mia. It's a game of life or death, and if he finds out what you've done... Bexley's life won't be worth living."

Oh God.

What have I done?

29

BEXLEY

Mouse: The coast is clear

My heart begins to race as I stare down at her simple message.

We'd arranged for me to sneak into her dorm after school this evening. We pretended it was so we could work on our economics assignment, but we both knew we were lying. No homework was going to be completed once we were alone in her room.

But as if he knew, Cade decided that tonight was the perfect time for him to pitch up to Mia's dorm to complete his own homework with her.

Mia promised she'd message the second he left, but as the time ticked on, I started to wonder if he was intending on staying the night.

That thought made my blood run cold.

It's bad enough having the memory of him kissing and touching her in my mind, but knowing he's lying beside her like I did only days ago… A shudder rips through me, and my fists curl in frustration.

"What's wrong with you? Need a shit or something?" Alex asks me as I jump from his bed like my ass is on fire.

After spending those short minutes with Mia in the auditorium yesterday, I decided it was probably time to pull my head out of my ass and talk to Alex.

In typical boy style, he took one look at me standing at his dorm room door, asked me if I'd stopped sulking yet, and invited me in as if nothing ever happened.

He made everything seem so easy, and I wished I could go through each day without this oppressive weight pressing down on my shoulders.

Alex is stressed about this Electi thing, don't get me wrong, but he seems to be accepting it a hell of a lot better than me.

"I'm going for a run."

"A run? It's nearly eleven."

I glance at the time on my cell and notice that he's right.

"I'm restless. We've got some shit heading our way this weekend, and I can't settle." It's not a total lie. What Cade and his goons have in store for us for our final initiation task is never far from my mind.

He's already drugged us, beat us half to death, and forced us to act like peasants while they lord it up over us. And that's without mentioning the sluts they sent our way.

This last thing is going to be worse, so much worse. But how?

It's no secret that they all have more money than sense, and access to anything their hearts desire. And, of course, they're all twisted motherfuckers. It literally could be anything.

"I know, me too. It's gonna be brutal."

"You don't look too concerned," I point out.

"They're not gonna kill us." He shrugs—fucking shrugs, as if this is water off a duck's back. "We're firstborn heirs of bloodlines that will become extinct without us. Their lives wouldn't be worth living if they offed us."

Alex has a point, but it doesn't fill me with much confidence. So they're not gonna kill us. It still leaves it open to any other sick and twisted games they can come up with.

I collect up my books and shove them all into my bag, ready to switch it with the one I packed earlier that's waiting in my dorm.

I'm at the door, about to say goodbye, when he speaks again.

"Where are you really going?" he asks, his eyes holding mine as if he'll read the answer within them.

I pause with my hand on his doorknob, my temperature spiking.

I want to tell him. Forgetting the fact that he only searched me out on my first day at Gravestone High on the instruction of Marcus, he's been nothing but a great friend. If it weren't for him, I've no doubt I'd have spent my entire time at high school here in the shadows, but he forced me to do things I didn't want to do. He forced me to live, and while I dug my heels in at every opportunity, I really appreciate that he never gave up on me.

But I can't. This is one thing that I can't confide in him. If Cade were to find out that Alex knew... I shiver. No, I can't do that to him.

"I'm going for a run. I'm too wired to sleep. I need to burn some energy off."

"Riiight. For the record, I don't believe you, and I think you're playing with fire."

My mouth opens to respond, but I can't find any words.

I pull the door open and step through, but just before I round the corner I hear his warning loud and clear.

"I hope she's worth it."

You have no fucking idea.

I quickly change, dragging on a pair of joggers and a hoodie before swiping up my overnight bag and heading back out of my dorm.

Campus is pretty empty at this time of night. There are just a few students loitering around, but most are home, working their asses off in preparation for the weekend. I'm sure this place will look very different come tomorrow night when everyone is heading to all the different parties that will be scattered around campus.

My muscles burn as I run, reminding me that I went out first thing this morning and did double my usual distance as I tried to outrun my demons. As usual, though, I never leave them behind for long.

Mia's dorm building comes into view, and I lock my eyes on her window right as a figure emerges from the bushes to my right.

My heart jumps into my throat as the moonlight illuminates the harsh lines of his face.

"Going anywhere in particular this time of night, Easton?"

Motherfucking cunt.

"Just for a run. Gotta keep my strength up. Never know what you motherfuckers are going to throw at me next."

A smirk appears on his face, and my fists curl to wipe it off.

I'd fucking love to have a round or two with him just one-on-one. I'm sure I could fucking take him down. Actually, I'd put money on it. Without Ashton and his little gang of pussies, he's nothing.

"With a bag?" he asks suspiciously, glancing over my shoulder.

"Not that it's any of your fucking business, but I've just come from Alex's."

"But his dorm is—"

"Is this really necessary? I've got shit to be doing, Kingsley, and I'm sure you need to get home for your beauty sleep. Or your chosen whore for the night." His lips press into a thin line, and I wonder if he made use of Mia for his needs tonight.

My stomach churns at the thought of her sucking him like she did me in the auditorium yesterday.

"I guess not." He taps his forefinger to his chin as he studies me. "Just remember, Easton. I own this fucking campus. There isn't a thing that goes on here that I don't know about. I have ears and eyes everywhere."

"Great, thanks for the reminder. I'll remember to flip off every camera I pass in case you're watching."

"You know, it doesn't have to be this way."

"Oh?"

"You could just do as we say. You don't need to fight us at every turn."

I laugh at him, which only serves to piss him off further.

"You're talking bullshit and you know it, Kingsley." I take a step toward him, but he doesn't back down at all. "Whether I was a good little boy and took your shit or not wouldn't make a bit of fucking difference. I'm a threat to you. My bloodline is stronger and you know it. You might be reigning right now, Kingsley, but rest assured, all you're doing is keeping the throne warm for the real king."

His lips twist and his eyes narrow as his fists curl at his sides.

"So thanks for the warning, but I think maybe *you* should be the one watching *your* back. You can throw whatever you want at me, but I *will* win, and I *will* take my rightful place in this town. And I will rewrite all the motherfucking rules. Just. You. Watch. Me."

Even in the darkness, I see his face turn beet red with anger.

"Go on," I taunt. "Hit me. I know you're fucking gagging for my blood."

A growl rips up his throat.

"Exactly as I thought. You're nothing without your soldiers backing you up. Enjoy your night, Kingsley. I'm coming for you."

I take off before he can respond. I continue toward Mia's dorm but veer right before the path that leads toward her main entrance.

I know he's watching me. My skin prickles with his attention. I'm also aware that I just poked the beast, and I've only made it worse for myself. I have no doubt that whatever he'd planned for this weekend has just been ramped up another level.

Fine by me.

Bring it on, asshole.

It's almost forty-five minutes later when I finally climb up Mia's fire escape and tap on her window. I needed to make sure the motherfucker had gone, because the last thing I need right now is to get caught in his prosapia's dorm room.

She quickly pulls the window open and attempts to drag me inside. I let her think she's helping, but the truth of it is that I've got a foot on her in height and at least fifty pounds in weight, so she's unlikely to be able to pull me anywhere.

"I didn't think you were coming," she whispers as if someone is going to hear us, despite the fact that she's already closed and locked the window behind me.

"I got intercepted by an asshole."

"Cade?"

"Yeah. It was almost like he was waiting for me."

Mia pales at my words.

"It's okay. I took off in the other direction. He doesn't know I'm here."

"But why would he be waiting for you?"

"I didn't say he *was* waiting for me." Although it sure looked that way when he emerged from the bushes. Not that I'm going to worry Mia with that. "He probably stopped off somewhere after leaving here. He was heading toward the parking lot." Kind of.

"I really hope you're right, because if he has any idea about this then—"

"Shhh," I say pressing my fingertips to her lips and stepping into her body. "Everything's okay, mouse. Everything is going to be okay." It has to be.

She doesn't look like she believes me, and I don't blame her. Everything feels utterly impossible right now.

"You're all sweaty," she points out when she slips her hands under my hoodie and connects with my flushed skin.

"Hmm... so I am. Think you could help me out with that?"

"I have an idea or two."

"Two? I only had one in mind, and it involved getting you naked."

In minutes, we're both naked, and I've got her in my arms with her legs wrapped around my waist as I carry her into her attached bathroom and walk us straight into the shower.

"Argh, that's freezing," Mia squeals when I turn it on and we both get blasted with ice-cold water.

"Allow me to warm you up." I drop her feet to the floor and press her back against the tiled wall.

I claim her lips in a bruising kiss before descending her body, sucking her nipples into my mouth and grazing my teeth down the soft skin of her stomach before I throw one of her legs over my shoulder and dive for her pussy.

My tongue sweeps up the length of her as she squirms above me, her fingers twisting in my hair causing biting pain to race down my spine, making my cock impossibly hard for her.

"Mine," I growl against her. "This. Is. Mine."

"Yours, Bexley. Oh God," she cries as I suck her clit into my mouth before lifting my fingers up to her entrance, working her until she's screaming my name and coming all over my face.

Heaven. Fucking heaven.

It's just a shame that it's all going to come crashing down around our feet long before we're ready.

30

MIA

By the time Friday rolls around, my stomach is a tight ball of nerves. I survive morning classes but barely hear my professors due to the constant thoughts on loop in my head.

This weekend marks the full moon, and Bexley and Alex's Transitus. Cade wouldn't tell me what it will entail—he wouldn't tell me much at all when he stopped by to study the other night. It had been a total surprise, finding him at my door. But now, I can't help but wonder if he had an ulterior motive. If he knows about me and Bexley.

We've tried to be discreet. But it's Cade. He owns this campus and most of the people in it. There's no use in worrying about that now, though. Not when I have bigger things making me nervous, like tonight's party.

Sasha has invited me over to the house beforehand, to get ready and hang out. But I fear that it's just a distraction while the guys do whatever it is they plan to do to Bexley and Alex.

God, I hate this.

Class breaks for lunch, and I file out of the room with my classmates. I'm meeting Annabel, but when I reach the end of the hall, she isn't waiting for me. Sasha is.

"Hey," I say. "This is a surprise."

"I have a free period so thought we could grab some lunch."

"I'm supposed to be meeting Ann—"

My cell vibrates in my pocket and I dig it out, reading the message. "Something came up. She's busy."

Sasha smiles. "Guess I've got you all to myself then." Lacing her arm through mine, we walk to the food court, keeping conversation to safer shores. Classes. Tonight's party. Today's lunch menu. I don't ask about Cade's plans, and she doesn't ask me if I've been seeing Bexley.

It's like we've reached a stalemate and neither of us wants to surrender first. But I know the questions will come, they always do. Just as I know I'll cave and ask her to tell me anything she knows about the weekend.

We choose our lunch and find an empty table near the back of the room. But as soon as we sit down and start tucking into our food, someone approaches us.

"What do you want, Brook?" Sasha grumbles.

"Nice to see you too, sister."

Sasha bristles. "Go suck dick, we all know you're a pro at it."

"Maybe I'll see if Channing's around." The color drains from Sasha's face as she grips the edge of the table. "He loves this thing I do with my—"

"How can we help you, Brook?" I ask, cutting the tension.

"Oh, Mila. Mila, Mila, Mila." She tsks. "So much to learn."

"It's Mia."

"I'm sorry, what?" Her shoulders lift in a dismissive shrug, twirling a lock of hair around her finger.

"Did you actually need something, or did you just come over here to be a bitch?" Sasha seethes, and I wonder what happened between the two of them. Sasha claims to be my friend, but I hardly know anything about her. Although, I haven't exactly been an open book either.

"Just came to say I'll see you tonight at the party. We should all hang out. Take notes, if you know what I mean." With that, Brook saunters away.

"God, I fucking hate her."

"But I thought the two of you—"

"Are stepsisters?" Sasha balks. "Please. I have to tolerate her bullshit at home because my daddy can't stand the arguing. But there is no love lost between us."

"Is what she said about Channing true?" I whisper.

"Mia," Sasha warns.

"Oh come on, I know you like him."

"And like I told you, it doesn't matter. He's Electi, and I'm... a female heir."

"Don't you ever wish you were born somewhere else?"

"Every. Single. Day." She lets out a heavy sigh before popping a fry into her mouth.

"I know you can't tell me much about this weekend—"

"Don't, Mia. Don't put me in this position."

"I'm scared," I admit. "For Bexley."

"Shh. You can't be saying his name in public." Her eyes widen. "If anyone overheard and it gets back to Cade..."

"God, I hate this."

"Join the club," she grumbles. For a second, I think she might say something else, but she doesn't, and the moment passes.

"Look, I know you're—crap." I look up and see the source of her panic. Cade and the Electi are heading right toward us. They speed up and sit down, Cade taking the empty chair beside me.

"Mia," he drawls, leaning in to kiss my cheek. "I missed you."

Ashton snickers. "You are so fucking whipped, man. If you ask me, you need to go fuck some unsuspecting girl and get her out of your system."

"Do you always have to be such an asshole?" Channing grumbles.

"As opposed to such a pussy?" Ashton flips him off.

"There goes my appetite." Sasha pushes her tray into the center of the table, and the vultures descend, eating the remaining fries.

"Looking forward to tonight, Mia?" Ashton asks around a wolfish grin.

"Ash," Cade warns.

"What? It was just a question. The full moon party is always lit, but something tells me this weekend is going to be epic."

I let out a small sigh, reminding myself that this is nothing more than a game to Cade and his friends. But two can play at that.

"Where's Tim?" I ask.

Cade bristles, and I go on. "Is he with Fawn? The two of them are so cute together. Will she be at the party? I haven't really had a chance to hang out with her yet."

Silence falls over our corner of the seating area. Cade shifts his chair, dragging it until he's pressed right against me. "I know what you're doing, babe," he whispers, "and it won't work. You think Tim is soft? That he's the weak link just because he's wifed up? You have no fucking idea what Tim is capable of."

A shudder rolls through me at the venom in his voice.

It doesn't make any sense. Tim is the quietest of the group, the most withdrawn. I'd assumed it was because he was already engaged.

I glance around at the five of them, and Sasha catches my eye and discreetly shakes her head. *Don't push him.*

Defeated, my shoulders sag. "I think I'm done here." I shove my tray away and stand, but Cade grabs my wrist.

"We're not done here," he hisses.

"Actually," I yank my hand away and shoot him a saccharine smile, "I think we are."

THE SECOND I walked away from Cade, I texted Bexley. I needed to see him. To feel his lips on mine, his arms wrapped tight around my body. But he didn't answer. So I went to my next class and tried to let the dulcet tones of the professor distract me.

By the time class is finished, I'm more than ready to go back to my dorm and shut away the world.

But as I'm walking toward my dorm building, Sasha catches up with me.

"Hey, are you okay?"

"I guess."

"Ashton is a dick, like his sister. And Cade... well, he enjoys toying with people's lives."

She laces her arm through mine and rests her head on my shoulder. "I know you want to stand up to him, but fighting back will only make it worse."

I shirk her off and face her. "What does that even mean? Everyone is always talking in riddles, and I don't understand."

"That's kind of the point." Sasha gives me a sad smile. "He wants you to be disoriented, to drop your guard, even for a second." She glances away, only briefly, but I see the hesitation shining in her eyes.

"Sasha," I say quietly, "what is it?"

"Nothing." Her smile is too forced, her tone too peppy.

"You know something, don't you?"

"Not really, no." She tries to keep walking, but I snag her wrist and pull her back to me.

"Sasha... please." A sense of dread washes over me. "Are they going to hurt them again?" I don't think I could bear it if they are.

"I overheard them talking..." she hesitates, glancing around. The path to the dorms is quiet, but she pulls me to a nearby bench and we sit down.

"Have you ever heard of DOM?"

"DOM?" I shake my head.

"It's a psychedelic. Strong as fuck. I heard Ashton saying DOM was ready for tonight. I thought he meant a person until I realized this is Ashton Moore and Cade Kingsley we're talking about."

"They gave us something at the dinner the other week."

"DOM isn't like E or G, Mia. It's hardcore mindfuckery. If they're giving Bexley and Alex DOM, they have big plans for them."

Fear trickles down my spine. "I have to warn them." I leap up, but she grabs my hand.

"If they resist or don't show, Cade will know, and that won't end well for anyone."

"But I can't just not tell them, Sasha. What if something goes wrong? What if—" I drop back onto the bench. "At least if I warn them, they'll know what's coming. Maybe they'll be able to avoid taking it or something."

Sasha doesn't look convinced, but she doesn't stop me either when I pull out my phone and dial Bexley's number.

"It's ringing," I say. "He isn't answering."

"Perhaps he's still in class. Text him."

Relief floods me that she's on my side.

I pull up a text and type as quickly as I can.

Mouse: Hey, we need to talk... about tonight. Call me when you can.

I hit send and wait.
And wait.
But ten minutes later, he still hasn't replied.
"Maybe he's in the shower or something," Sasha says, her expression betraying her.
Because as the minutes pass and he still doesn't reply, I know what she's thinking. Because it's what I'm thinking.
Bexley isn't answering because he can't.
Because they got to him first.

31

BEXLEY

The Electi have been markedly absent all day, and while I should probably be relieved that they're not down every hallway lording it over everyone, I'm not.

They're not here for a reason, and I know it's got to do with what's coming our way.

They want us on edge. They want us to have noticed.

"There's a weird vibe in the air. Can you feel it?"

"You already on something?" I ask Alex, trying to laugh off his comment. But the truth is, I do feel it.

My entire body is on alert as we make our way out of the building after our last class.

I pull my cell from my pocket to see if I've got anything from Mia. She's been trying to dig for information to give us a heads up for what we might be about to walk into, but she's found nothing yet.

It doesn't fill me with reassurance.

We're halfway across the quad, our building in sight, when I sense movement behind me.

The hairs on the back of my neck stand on end, and I twist my head to see who it is—praying it's Mia, but already knowing it's not—when everything goes dark.

"What the fuck?" I bark as something stings my upper arm.

I spin, ready to throw my fist toward whoever just shoved a bag over my head, but my head starts to spin.

Did they just fucking inject me with something?

My arms are pinned behind my back, and I'm marched forward. Everything around me gets hazier with every step I take. The voices from behind me stop making any sense, and my legs feel like jelly.

I'm vaguely aware of being thrown into a van. I feel the vibrations of the engine as my shoulder smarts from the force I'm thrown to the floor with before everything goes black.

WHEN I COME TO, my entire body is shivering, and my fingers and toes feel numb.

Pressing my hand against the cold floor beneath me, I push myself up so I'm sitting.

Ripping the bag off my head, I throw it down, but when I look up, I find the room I'm in is pitch black. I can see no more than I could when I was bagged.

Motherfuckers.

"Hello?"

Silence.

Or there is for a few seconds, until I hear a groan beside me.

"Alex?"

"Y-yeah. Where the fuck are we, and why is it so cold?"

"No idea. And we're naked."

"W-wha—oh."

He shuffles about beside me, but even with my eyes adjusting to the light, I can't see anything other than a few shadows.

"So this is their game? Kidnap us and make us freeze to death?"

"Nah, that'd be too easy."

As if they're listening—which they probably are—a door creaks open. It sounds like one of those from a creepy horror film, and it sends a shiver of terror racing up my spine.

"Welcome to the party, boys." I have no idea who it is, because they're using something to disguise their voice.

"Here's your first gift. Open wide."

I have no idea how he can see me, but in seconds he's standing before me, waiting for me to follow orders.

Clearly, they haven't figured me out yet, because I don't do that.

"Open your fucking mouth."

I press my lips together, but, not deterred at all, whoever it is wraps his hand around my chin and physically pries my lips apart before shoving something on my tongue.

"Cunt," I spit as whatever it is instantly dissolves in my mouth.

I do not have a good feeling about this.

"What the fuck was that?" Alex asks, but the guy just laughs before the door creaks once more and he disappears.

"I've got a bad feeling about this," I admit.

"You're only just getting that now?"

I blow out a breath and rest my head back against the wall, curling my limbs into as tight a ball as I can in an attempt to warm up.

My entire body shudders violently, and it only gets worse the longer we're forced to sit in this cold and dark room, waiting for whatever is going to happen next.

I have no idea how much time passes. It could be ten minutes or ten hours.

I lost all sense of time the second they stabbed me with a fucking needle. All I know is that it's too fucking long.

"Holy fucking shit," Alex shouts.

"What?"

"Something's happening." A frantic scrambling sound hits my ears before he screams. "Get them away from me. Help me, help me." Pure fear fills his voice.

"What the fuck are you talking about? There's no one here." But the second I finish speaking, I realize what he's talking about... because whatever they slipped us starts to take its hold on me too.

"Nooo," I scream as the lights flick on and a broken and beaten Mia is revealed in the corner. "Nooo," I cry again, crawling over to her. "No, please no."

My frantic hands run all over her as the lights continue to flash on and off above and Alex continues to scream, fighting off whoever it is that's chasing him.

The lights flash once more, and I look over my shoulder, but I don't see Alex. Instead, I see Remi. She's sitting in the corner of the freezing cold room with her arms wrapped around her legs, rocking back and forth with tears streaming down her cheeks.

But then Ace Jagger appears, drags her from the floor, and wraps her in his arms.

"He's nothing, Remi. Scum of the earth. He deserves to die."

"No," I cry, as he pins her up against the wall and begins stripping her clothes off her. "No, I'm here. I'm watching. Treat her better than that, you cunt," I warn, but he continues.

I can't help but get turned on as he nails her against the wall, my cock jutting out from my body, ready for some action of my own.

But my girl is…

I spin to where Mia was in a pile on the floor, but she's gone.

In her place is my mother. Blood oozing from the deep slash across her throat and the word 'traitor' carved across her bare torso.

I back up until I hit the wall, only it's not the wall—it's the door, and it swings wide open.

The flashing above me continues, but down the dark hall, I see a light.

The way out.

With one final glance down at my mother, I find her now standing with Mia beside her. Their eyes are dark and their bodies covered in blood and bruises.

"Kill him," Mia says, both of them taking a step toward me. "Kill him. Kill him. Kill him," she chants.

"No, no. It's me. It's Bexley. I'll keep you safe. Let me look after you."

"Kill him. Kill him," Mom adds.

Holy shit.

They both pull knives from behind their backs and run at me.

I stumble on the rough ground beneath me. Glancing down, I find I'm running over rocks, but I have no time to hesitate. I can hear their chants getting louder.

I take off, scrambling over the larger rocks.

Finally, I get over to the other side, but all that greets me is a giant red lake.

I look over my shoulder, not seeing them behind me.

But I know I can't go back.

I prepare to jump, and it's then I see the bodies lying face down in the water... and I realize it's not water, it's blood.

I retch as the chant hits my ears once more, and I know that I can either jump or I let them kill me.

Or I could push them...

Standing tall, I wait for them to approach me with their knives raised, ready to plunge them into my chest.

Mom lunges first, and I manage to grab her arm and throw her over the side, into the pool of death beneath us.

"This was always how it was meant to end, Bexley. It's all a game."

Her final words echo around me.

All a game.

All a game.

The second she moves toward me, I act on instinct, and she follows Mom over the edge. But the second I realize what I've just done, I dive in after her.

Not Mia. Not my Mia.

I finally find her lying face down amongst all the other bodies, and I carry her from the lake and lay her down on a bed in a room I find.

"It's okay, little mouse. You're safe. Come back to me, please. I'm sorry."

Footsteps approach from behind me, and when I look back I find the Electi walking toward us.

"Help her, Cade, please. You can't let her die."

"You killed her. You killed my prosapia," he roars, throwing me to the floor so he can tend to her.

My head bounces off the floor, and I have to blink a few times to get my vision to focus. When I do, I find Mia alive and awake, straddling Cade's naked body as he thrusts up into her, sucking her nipples into his mouth. Ashton walks up behind her, wraps his fists around her hair and rips her head back to him as he forces his cock into her ass.

I expect her to cry out in pain, but when a scream rips from her throat, it's with pleasure.

She sucks Brandon off while wrapping her fist around Channing's cock, taking everything they give to her.

"No," I scream. "Get off her."

Cade's hooded eyes turn to me. "Mia is exactly where she belongs. And you love it, too, don't you, babe?"

"Harder," she cries, and I recognize her tells. She's close.

She's going to come for them.

"Nooo." My heart shatters in my chest as I watch her fall apart and they continue using her.

Dropping into the corner, I close my eyes and will it all away.

When I wake again, I'm in my dorm room.

Holy fuck, it was just a dream.

My chest heaves, my skin dripping with sweat, but when I look down at my hands, they're covered in blood.

What the—

A knock sounds out at the door, and I quickly go to it, hoping it's Mia and that none of that really happened.

I need to see with my own two eyes that she's okay. That I didn't kill her, that they didn't— My stomach turns over at the thought of them all taking her like that.

Swinging the door open, my heart drops into my feet, because it's Mom and Mia again... only their skin is hanging off their bodies, blood dripping everywhere, and they're still wielding their knives.

I back up into my dorm room, but I never hit the wall. Instead, I fall over the edge, and I just keep falling... until I land in a dark room with a person strapped to a chair in the center. There's a bag over their head, and their limbs are restrained to the legs.

"This is your final test, Easton. You do this, and you join us as Electi. You become a part of everything we and this town have.

"You'll be legendary and go down in history as we take over this town and show everyone how it should be run."

Cade steps up beside me and hands me a knife.

"W-what do I have to do?"

"I want her heart. I want what you have. Then, and only then will this end."

He moves, stands behind the person, and pulls the bag off.

Mia's eyes are wide as she stares at me. She's trying to scream, but she's gagged, and I can't make out what she's trying to say.

"No, I can't. I can't."

"This won't end until you do."

Others step into the room—the Electi, Mom, Dad, Alex and Remi.

"You do it, or I kill them." He raises a gun along with the rest of the Electi, and they aim them right at those I love.

It's her or them.

"What's it going to be?"

"Holy fucking shit," I pant. "Oh my God." I drop my head into my hands, feeling the tears streaming down my face.

When I finally look up, I find Alex curled in a ball in the corner of the room that's now fully illuminated, shaking and sobbing his heart out.

"Alex," I say, but he doesn't stir. "ALEX," I shout as loud as I can.

But again, no reaction.

He's still lost. Still living out his worst nightmares and being chased by his demons.

Assuming that this right now is real, and he's not about to come at me with a knife.

The creak of the door startles me, and my head snaps over to find a dark, hooded figure in the doorway. Their hood is so low that I have no way of telling who it is.

But I know it's one of them.

When he speaks, it's that weird voice again.

"You need to escape. If you don't, you die, and this is all over."

Without another word, he slams the door closed and we're plunged into darkness once more.

32

MIA

The party goes on around me, but I can't relax. I haven't been able to ever since I sent Bexley that text and he didn't reply.

Sasha insisted I attend the party, so as not to alert Cade to anything.

But I don't want to be here, smiling, pretending. It's too much. Especially when I know Bexley and Alex could be in some kind of trouble.

"You need to relax," Sasha hisses, swaying her hips to the beat. She hasn't left my side, and I'm thankful. Especially since Brook is here, working the room like she thinks she owns the place. Like she thinks she's Cade's prosapia. I want to tell her she's welcome to him. That she can take my place. But I know it doesn't work like that. Everyone likes to remind me enough.

"You should take some Xanax, it'll help you loosen up."

"No, I'll be okay."

"I get it, Mia. You don't want to break your moral code or whatever. But sometimes, to play with the devil you have to become a sinner."

"This is enough." I shake my drink at her, and Sasha rolls her eyes.

"I envy you. So fucking naïve." She slips a small tin out of her pocket and plucks a small white pill from it. "Last chance."

I shake my head.

"Suit yourself." She pops it on her tongue and chases it down with her drink. "Showtime." Her eyes go to the front door right as Cade enters the house, followed by the other Electi.

A chill goes through me, but no one else seems to feel the ripple in the air. They're too enamored with their king. Too eager to party with the Electi and live in their world. It's pathetic really, how quickly people will shed their integrity if they think it'll help their social status.

The sea of bodies part as Cade makes a beeline for us. "There you are." He wraps a hand around my waist and pulls me into his side.

"Did you miss me?" His lips graze my neck, and I force down the urge to retch.

"Looking good, Sash," Ashton says with a lazy smile. "Maybe I'll break a rule or two tonight and let you ride my dick."

"Dude, that's my sister," Brandon protests, snagging the hand of a passing blonde. He pulls her into his chest and whispers something to her.

"And what did your momma teach you, Brandy boy?" Ashton taps his face. "It's good to share your toys. What do you say, Sasha?"

"Go fuck yourself, asshole."

"Ooof, I think she likes me." He explodes with laughter.

"I'll be back," Sasha whispers to me. I want to go after her, but when I catch Channing's stare he shakes his head. He looks murderous, watching Sasha as she melts into the crowd.

"Hey Cade." Brook saunters over to us and leans in to kiss his cheek. "You're looking good."

"What can I do for you, Brook?"

"Come on, babe. Don't be like that. It's been too long since you came over and—"

In one second flat, Cade has his hand wrapped around her throat.

"What did I tell you about coming around to cause trouble? Mia is my girl now... it would serve you right to fucking remember that."

She claws at his fingers, but he lets her go, shoving her gently.

"What the fuck, Cade?"

"Like you don't love being choked."

"Yeah, when she's sucking dick," Ashton snorts.

"Nice, Ash. Real fucking nice."

"You know where my loyalties lie, Sis, and it's not with you."

Brook glowers at him. "It's all her fault." She sets her sights on me, but Cade pushes me behind him.

"Mia is off limits. I mean it, Brook. Back. The. Fuck. Down."

"But—"

Cade mouths something, but I can't make out what it is. Whatever he says has Brook spinning on her heel and disappearing down the hall.

"She's becoming a nuisance," Brandon says.

"But even pests have their uses." Ashton shrugs.

I sip my drink and pretend to be paying them no attention. Cade has me tucked into his arm, furthest away from them.

"Are you sure about this?" Channing asks. "Maybe one of us should…" The music drowns out his voice.

"You need to relax, Chan," Ashton says. "Everything is under control. For us at least. Man, I'd kill to see—"

"Ash," Cade barks, and silence falls over them.

"Where the fuck is Tim, anyway?"

"Fawn had an episode again."

"Fuck." A heavy sigh leaves his lips. He catches me watching and smirks. "Sorry, babe, are we neglecting you?" His lips graze mine, but then his tongue licks the seam of my mouth, demanding entrance.

I kiss him, hoping if he lets his guard down enough, I'll find out what they've done with Bexley and Alex.

But twenty minutes later, I know nothing… except whatever it is, it's bad.

Bad enough that Channing and Brandon both seem uneasy. Even if Brandon is dry fucking the blonde against the wall right now.

"I'm going to find Sasha," I eventually say, hoping he'll release me from his possession long enough to find her or Annabel.

"Sure, but come back to me," he teases, his eyes pinning me to the spot. "I'm not done with you yet."

I FIND Sasha kissing some guy I recognize from around campus.

"I, uh… sorry, I need to borrow her for a second." I grab her hand and tug sharply. She stumbles after me, giggling.

"He's cute."

"And you're drunk." And high.

"It makes it easier." Her eyes are glazed, her pupils blown wide. "You should try it."

"I'm really worried. It's late, and there's no sign of Bexley or Alex. And Brandon and Channing—"

She huffs at the mention of his name. "Channing... Channing can go fuck himself."

"Sasha, focus." I gently shake her shoulders. "The guys seem... worried."

"Doesn't mean they don't follow orders like the good little lapdogs they are, though."

"Think, Sasha... think... Has Cade said anything that might help me figure out what he's done to them?"

"He's obsessed with the old ways."

"The old ways?"

"Yeah... things used to get pretty crazy back then. Blood rites and all these weird initiations with hallucinogens. I heard my dad and Gregory talking once."

Fear snakes through me. "I have a bad feeling about this," I say, chewing my thumbnail.

I lead Sasha back to the party, but Brook spots us and saunters over.

"Oh look, it's the Electi's pet."

"Fuck off, Brooklyn, we don't have time for your bullshit." Sasha barges past her, but Brook grabs her arm.

"Why do you always have to be such a bitch?"

"Me? *Me!*" she shrieks, and everyone stops to take notice. "You're the queen bitch around here, acting like you're something just because your mom got with my dad. My mom's bed wasn't even cold and she just—"

Brook lunges for her, and the two of them start going at it, hands swinging and nails scratching. I don't know what to do, so I stand there, hoping someone will intervene. It takes Brandon and Channing to finally tear them apart, but neither of the girls go down without a fight, bucking and broncing.

I try to move around Brandon to get to Sasha, but someone's fist catches the corner of my face and I stumble, losing my footing.

'Mia," someone yells right as my head collides with the ground...

And everything goes black.

MUFFLED VOICES FILL MY HEAD, but I'm too confused to latch onto them.

"Maybe we should take her to the ER."

"No fucking way. Not tonight. The last thing we need is the local PD sniffing around."

"We should go get them. It was a bad fucking idea to leave them out there on DOM."

DOM? Who's DOM?

I try to move, but pain explodes in my head. God, it hurts.

"They'll be fine. Quit being a pussy."

"DOM fucks you up. They could do some serious damage," someone says. His voice is softer than the other guy's. Kinder.

Slowly, I blink, forcing my eyes open. I'm in a bedroom, lying on a huge bed cloaked in black sheets. My eyes find Cade and Channing over by the window.

"W-what happened?" I try to sit up, but the pain rattles my teeth.

"Mia, babe, thank fuck." Cade rushes to my side.

"What happened?"

"Brook—"

"She hit me."

"It was an accident," Channing says. "She was trying to get to Sasha."

"They were fighting." I remember now. Sasha was drunk and high and Brook accosted us in Cade's huge yard.

"You had quite the fall by all accounts." Cade glances up at Channing.

"Where's Sasha?" I ask.

"Sleeping off all the pills and vodka."

"I am—"

"This is my room." Cade's eyes darken. "You look good in my bed." He runs his knuckles over my cheek. "Just a shame it isn't under different circumstances."

I'm too weak and confused to fight him. I already want to close my eyes and drift off into a deep sleep.

"Whoa, Mia. You need to try and stay awake, in case you have a concussion." Channing moves closer, concern shining in his eyes.

"Stay with her," Cade orders. "I have shit take care of. Do what he says, okay?" He leans in and kisses my forehead. "I'll be up later."

Cade leaves and Channing takes his place in the chair beside the bed.

"You like to make life difficult for yourself, don't you?"

"What's that supposed to mean?"

"It means stop ruffling feathers, Mia." His brows crinkle.

"I'm not supposed to be his prosapia, Channing. You know that, right?"

"I'll admit, it's a little suspect your name got picked. But the decision is final."

"Ugh. Everyone keeps saying that, like I'm supposed to just accept it."

He studies me carefully. "You're not what I expected."

"What the hell does that mean?" I wince as pain shoots through my head.

"Here, take these." He hands me some pain pills and a glass of water.

"You promise it's just Advil?"

"I might be Electi, Mia, but it doesn't make me a monster."

"What will you do," I ask, "when Alex is inducted in?"

"You should rest. Just don't fall to sleep, okay?"

"Easier said than done," I grumble. "My brain feels like mush."

"We could watch TV."

"Or we could talk, and you could tell me where Bexley and Alex are."

"Nice try." He chuckles darkly. "But not gonna happen."

"But why? You helped me clean up Bexley that night after the pit." He'd snuck me down to the basement and then left the door open for them to escape.

Channing is a good guy. He's just in a bad situation.

"Shh," he hisses. "You can't be saying stuff like that in here."

"Is it bugged?" I glance around.

"No, but it doesn't mean there aren't spies everywhere. Just watch the TV and don't make this any harder than it has to be, okay?"

"Fine," I huff. "But tell me just one thing?"

"Go on…"

"Will Bexley and Alex be okay?"

He looks at me with a grim expression.

"I really fucking hope so."

33

BEXLEY

"Do you have any fucking clue where we are?" I ask Alex as we finally emerge through a door that has daylight on the other side of it.

The bright sun burns my eyes, making them run and my head to once again spin as I come down from whatever fucking trip that was.

Whatever it was, I know for a fact that I don't want a repeat.

I glance over to see Alex looking around as he shields his eyes from the sun.

He looks like hell. His pupils are blown and there are dark shadows circling his eyes. I have no fucking clue how long we were down there, but from how exhausted I am and how high the sun is, it's got to be damn near twenty-four hours.

"If I had to guess, I'd say the forest behind the Electi house. The graveyard is over there." He points. "But really, it could be anywhere."

"How the fuck are we meant to get back? We're fucking naked."

"Ever hot-wired a car?"

I stare at him with my brow quirked. "Do I look like the kind of kid who used to spend his weekends doing that?"

"No, but guess who did?" He winks, and I can't help snorting with laughter.

"Fuck off. Did you? You're too good."

"Am I?"

I open my mouth to respond, but I soon find that I have no words.

"You're not the only one who likes to keep the past in the past, dude."

"Okay, well, lead the way, Mr. Grand Theft Auto."

As naked as the day we were born, we start tracking through the forest.

Sticks, stones, and God knows whatever else digs into my bare feet until by some miracle Alex navigates us to a house.

"Is that—"

"Just as I suspected. Now, whose baby did you want?"

"You can steal those?"

"No, there's no fucking chance. I can barely remember how to do it to an old banger."

"I fucking believed you," I snap.

He shrugs. "Come on. We've made it this far."

"We'll get pulled over for indecent exposure. We can't walk down the fucking street like this."

"I know a back way. Come on."

He drops back into the forest and takes a wide berth around the back of the house.

By the time our dorm comes into view, my feet are a bloody mess and I'm ready to fall headfirst into my bed and sleep for a week.

Sadly, that's not what happens, because the second we push through into the communal area of our dorm—after amusing more than a few fellow students with our mortifying walk of shame—we stumble straight into an ambush. Sitting on the couch is none other than the motherfuckers who did this.

"You all owe me a hundred bucks," Ashton announces, jumping up in delight.

"Smug motherfucker," Brandon mutters, pulling a few bills out of his wallet and throwing them at Ashton.

Anger explodes in my stomach, my entire body trembling with my restrained fury.

"You were fucking betting on us?"

"All's fair in love and war, Easton. Stop getting your panties in a—oh, that's right, you're not wearing any."

"You're all fucking sick. What did you give us?"

"Just something to make sure you had fun." The smirk on Cade's face has me stepping toward him, my fists curled at my sides, ready to take a swing at him.

"You've got three hours until tonight's dinner. You'll both find suits in your rooms."

"Fuck. You. I'm not doing anything else you fucking say, you sick bastard."

"Oh, but I think you will."

My teeth grind as our eyes hold, hate crackling between us.

"You don't show and I'll make sure something very precious to you gets broken. And not just by me."

He must read the horror on my face, because an accomplished smile curls at his lips as the images from my time locked underground come back to me.

"I don't want to share her. But I will, if I need to. And I'll make sure you get a front row seat."

I fight not to react, but I fear it's pointless. He already knows.

"Fucking cunt," I mutter, knowing he's got me over a barrel.

"Make sure you're at Gravestone Hall by seven. If you're late, I can promise you, you will regret it."

"I'll probably regret it if I'm on time, too," I mutter under my breath. "Are you done throwing your weight around, *boss*?"

"Just make sure you're there. Or don't, actually. I think I might enjoy your punishment too much."

He pushes from the couch and steps toward me. If he wants me to cower to him, then he'll be bitterly disappointed.

"Don't let me down, Easton."

He breezes past me, his little minions following soon after.

Channing's eyes hold mine for a second too long, and I can't help but wonder if he's trying to tell me something, but I'm too exhausted to attempt to decipher it.

"I need sleep before the games continue," Alex announces, turning toward his room.

"I'm so fucking sick of this," I bark, watching him go.

"Tonight is the last test. It'll be over then."

"We might initiate in, but I think we both know this isn't going to stop. Not unless we kill that motherfucker."

"We'll see how it goes, eh? I'm gonna pass out now."

He damn near falls through the door before slamming it behind him.

Following his lead, my feet take me to my room before the others return—assuming they were banished the second the Electi turned up.

My chin drops the second I step into my room.

All my stuff has gone.

All that's left is the furniture and a black suit hanging on the closet door.

"What the fuck?" I mutter, looking around, but in all honesty, I don't care right now.

I fall into bed, not giving the fact that I have no alarm set for a few hours time a second thought as I pass out.

"WAKE THE FUCK UP," someone shouts as my shoulder starts to shake.

"No, it's too early."

"It's really fucking not. I suggest you shift your ass unless you want Cade to follow through on his threat."

Ripping my eyes open, I blink a couple of times as the blurry image of Channing standing over me emerges.

"Why the fuck are you in my room?"

"You should be thanking me, Easton. If he knew I was here he'd kick my ass."

"You think I give a shit? You're no better than him."

"Really? I thought you were fucking smart, Easton."

"Whatever." I wave him off and push to sit in bed, keeping the sheet over my waist, not wanting to flash him twice in one day.

"You've got thirty minutes to be at Gravestone Hall. Get your fucking ass moving. Mia needs you."

My eyes find his, and for the first time, I see genuine concern in his depths.

"Fuck, okay." I jump from the bed and make a beeline for the bathroom.

"Is Alex up?" I shout over my shoulder.

"Going there now. I'll be down in the parking lot. Be fucking fast."

I have the quickest shower of my life. It's hard fucking work, because my limbs don't want to move as fast as my head tells them to. But finally, I drag on the suit that's waiting for me and head across the living area to grab Alex before we're late.

"You ready?" I ask, shoving my head into his room without knocking. Seems fairly pointless, seeing as I've almost seen him naked more than I have myself in the past week.

"Yes, let's go."

We blow through the dorm, earning us more than a few curious looks. Alex still looks like hell, and I didn't bother looking in the mirror. I just ran some wax through my hair and hoped for the best.

"What the fuck is Channing playing at?" Alex asks when we step into the night to find his headlights illuminating the parking lot.

"I don't know, but something tells me he's helping."

"Really? You think he'd go against Cade like that?"

"Fuck knows. I feel like I don't know which way is up right now. You still tripping?" I ask.

"I thought I was showering in snakes."

"I'll take that as a yes," I laugh.

"That shit was brutal. I lost count of the number of people I killed."

"Tell me Cade was one of them," I mutter, stepping up to Channing's car.

"Sadly not. He's fucking invincible, that cunt."

"Yeah, I got that sense too."

We pull out of campus in silence, tension rippling around the small space.

"What can we expect tonight?" I ask, needing to get out of my own head.

"It's a formal meal with Q to welcome you to the fold."

"We're in?"

"You'll have to wait to find out. It's not over yet."

"Fucking great." I scrub my hand down my face.

"For what it's worth, I'm glad you're both okay. I had nothing to do with the DOM."

"The what?" Alex asks, poking his head between the front seats.

"DOM. It's what you took. A hallucinogen. A fucking strong one."

"You don't say," I mutter, staring out of the window as the town passes us by.

"Just... just watch your backs tonight. Cade is planning shit, but he hasn't even told us what it is. But historically, the after party gets a little... wild."

"More than the last event we were forced to attend?"

"You have no fucking idea. Prepare yourselves for the worst," he says, pulling into a full parking lot. It's like a showroom for the rich and famous. "Let me go in. Give it five minutes, then follow. If he finds out..." Channing trails off. He doesn't need to say the next words. We all know.

We climb out of his car and I nod at him before he takes off across the lot and toward the entrance.

"Something tells me tonight is going to be anything but fun."

"You got that message as well, huh?"

"I fucking hate this. I much preferred life when I was just Alex Shaw," he says sadly.

I want to agree with him, but I soon realize that I never really liked the man I was before being Bexley Easton either.

After our five minutes are up, we head toward the entrance.

We're welcomed by name by a couple of young men I've never seen before and directed through to the bar while everyone else seems to already be in the main ballroom.

Pushing the door open, I square my shoulders and jut out my chin when we find it occupied by only the Electi and Quinctus.

"Ah look, our initium are finally here," one of the elders says—Tim's father, I think—before every other set of eyes, including Marcus', turn on us.

"We didn't think you were going to make it," Cade pipes up.

"Sorry to disappoint you, Kingsley, but we wouldn't have missed it for the world."

He smiles at me, but it's full of venom.

They chat briefly, exchanging pleasantries with us about how our initiation is going like they don't already know what twisted games Cade is playing before someone comes to tell us that we need to make our entrance.

Yeah, our entrance.

The ten of us walk into a silent reception room that's laid out much like a wedding reception complete with a top table. It's empty bar one person waiting for us.

Mia.

Everyone in the room stands as we enter, and I barely contain a snort. It's fucking ridiculous.

We take our seats, and at Cargill's instruction, everyone in the room takes their seats once more.

The whole sight is really something to behold.

I look around the room, wondering where their wives are, and find a table at the back of the room full of females. Chauvinistic assholes.

They have every right to be up here with their husbands.

34

MIA

Nervous energy zips around my stomach as I watch the Electi and their fathers enter the room. Bexley immediately catches my eye, his widening with surprise.

I know what he's thinking. It's probably the same thing I'm thinking.

Why am I seated at their table?

The men.

When I'd arrived with Sasha earlier, I followed her to what was clearly the female's table, only to be steered away by a server and directed to the other table.

I knew immediately this was all part of Cade's game... but to what end, I still don't know.

Sasha and Channing have been warning me to be on my guard tonight, but it's not easy when I'm about to be thrown into the lion's den with Cade, the Electi, and Quinctus.

They all take their seats. Bexley and Alex at the end of the table, with the Electi in the middle and their fathers at the head of the table. Channing looks awkward as he glances between his uncle and Alex. Cade waits for everyone else to be seated before sitting down.

"You look stunning," he drawls, leaning in to kiss my cheek.

There's no denying the black bodycon layered in sequins is

beautiful, but it does little to soothe the knot in my stomach. I don't want to be here.

Phillip Cargill stands and clinks his glass, ushering the room into silence. "Friends, family, our future," his eyes rake over each and every one of us, "tonight we welcome two of our heirs into the fold. Initium Easton and initium Rexford, you have demonstrated the strength, integrity, grit, and determination to take up your rightful place as Electi. To the initiates," his eyes find mine, flickering with something I can't quite decipher, "and to Miss Thompson. Welcome."

Everyone lifts their glasses into the air and toasts them. Alex looks like a fish out of water and Bexley looks positively pissed. But he doesn't object to Phillip's speech, lifting his own glass in appreciation before taking a large gulp of champagne.

Cade snorts beside me, and I throw him a strange look. What I really want is to ask him what he's up to, but the doors burst open and servers flood the room, serving the first course of the evening.

It smells delicious, but I know I won't be able to eat much. I'm too restless. Too concerned about what comes after the formalities. There's another party at Cade's house. Something smaller, he said. Something intimate. I don't know what that means, but I know it won't be anything good.

His fingers linger on the back of my neck as he absentmindedly strokes my bare shoulder while talking to his friends and their fathers.

I gulp my wine, unsure how I'm going to survive the evening. Everyone is acting like this is normal. The wives chat happily to one another while the men sit at their own table, lording over the town. But it occurs to me this is normal for them.

"Cade," I eventually ask, curiosity getting the better of me.

He gives me his full attention, a smirk playing on his lips. "Yeah?"

"Why am I the only female at the table?"

"Would you have preferred to have sat with the wives?" His brow arches.

"Just answer the question."

"Because I wanted you here, okay?" He leans in, whispering the words. "So do us both a favor and sit pretty and behave like a good little prosapia."

SURPRISINGLY, dinner passes without drama. Quinctus are a strange bunch. Phillip Cargill is clearly the leader in the absence of Cade's father. He commands the room with gentle authority. The man I learn is Bexley's grandfather, Marcus, doesn't engage in the monotonous conversation about town growth and sustainability. Harrison Rexford and Bradley Davenport drink like it's going out of fashion, acting far too handsy with the female servers. But overall, for something as mysterious as Quinctus, they really are quite a boring bunch of men.

There's more laughter and gossip from the wives' table. I glean snippets of their conversations remarking on their husbands' latest business transactions and plans for next month's harvest ball.

Throughout the whole ordeal, I realize something. Cade isn't only playing a game with Bexley and Alex, he's also playing a game with Quinctus. Tension ripples between him and Phillip every time the other speaks, as if they're vying for power. But Cade is only Electi. Which means he's either trying to impress them and fulfil his father's shoes sooner rather than later, or he's coveting their power for himself.

"You know, Son, it really is time you took a prosapia for yourself." Phillip Cargill gives Brandon a pointed look.

"He has time, Phil," Bradley suggests. "Let the boy sow his wild oats first." His haughty laughter sets my teeth on edge.

"How are you finding everything, Mia?" Harrison Rexford finally pulls me into the conversation.

"The food? It was lovely, thank you."

"You know, it's quite curious that your name was pulled from the calix."

Heat blooms in my cheeks. "I... I certainly didn't expect it."

"No, I'm sure you didn't." Something goes through the air, but then the servers are back, cleaning away our dessert plates.

Phillip Cargill stands and clears his throat, ushering the room into silence. "And now the moment we have all been waiting for. Your Transitus." He dips his hand inside his jacket and pulls out a small wooden box.

"Initium Easton, initium Rexford, please join me at the altar."

They follow him to the small wooden altar at the head of the room. An open fire flickers behind them.

Phillip flips the lid and pulls out a small iron symbol, attaching it to a long poker and moving over to the fire. "Please kneel and unbutton your shirts," he says.

Alex and Bexley glance at one another but then take a knee, unbuttoning their shirts.

"You have successfully completed the tasks set before you. There is just one final test. Initium Easton, please repeat after me. *Sanguis. Imperium. Electi. Aeternum.*"

Phillip moves to Bexley and lowers the brand, shimmering with heat. He presses it into his skin, right above his heart. The smell of charred flesh fills the room, turning my stomach, but Bexley doesn't falter as he repeats the words back to Phillip.

He's one of them now.

An Electi.

Cade's brethren.

A little part of my heart dies with every Latin word that rolls off his tongue.

I don't want this for him. But he's imprisoned just like me.

And as I watch him accept Phillip's hand and let him pull him to his feet, I silently wish that together, we'll find a way to set each other free.

SASHA IS quiet on the ride back to the Electi house.

"Hey, are you okay?"

"Not here," she mouths. I wonder what has her so upset.

"At least Cade went ahead in the other car," I say, and Channing snorts.

"If you think that's a good thing, you're sorely mistaken."

"Will you just put me out of my misery and tell me what happens tonight?"

"No can do, Mia." He gives me a strained smile. "Not even we've been graced with his majesty's plans."

"You really don't know?" Fear creeps up my spine.

"Nope. He wouldn't tell us."

"Even Ashton?"

"Of course Moore knows. Where do you think he's been all night..."

My stomach sinks, and we ride the rest of the way in thick silence.

By the time the car pulls up outside Cade's house, I can barely breathe. I scramble out and inhale a ragged breath.

"I'd ask if you want something to take the edge off, but that fucker stole my stash." She glowers in Channing's direction. He's already walking off, probably to catch up with the rest of the Electi.

"He did?" I ask.

"Yeah, after what happened last night, he thought I needed a little break."

"Or maybe he's pissed you were kissing that guy."

"That's not it, Mia." She lets out a soft sigh. "If I disappear tonight, I'm sorry, but I really don't feel like partying."

"It's okay." It isn't. But I'm not about to beg her to stay.

"Ladies," Brandon yells from the door, "let's go."

Sasha grumbles something beneath her breath and takes off toward him, leaving me alone.

I could run now. Run and never look back. But Bexley is in there somewhere. So I inhale a deep breath, smooth my hair off my face, and head inside.

The first thing that hits me is how quiet the house is. Cade appears out of nowhere. Gone are his suit jacket and tie. He's rolled back the sleeves of his shirt and unbuttoned the collar. He looks good, but I know he's the devil in a handsome god's clothing.

"There you are." He offers me his hand, and I slide my palm against his. "Are you ready for tonight's celebrations?" Cade guides me down the long hall leading to the kitchen. But we don't stop there, leaving the house through the patio doors and walking across the perfectly tended lawns. It's the same path I took with Sasha all those nights ago, when Cade made Bexley and Alex fight in the pit.

A shiver runs through me when I spy the small building.

"What's going on?" I ask.

"Time to find out," he replies cryptically. I notice Ashton standing guard and fight a groan of disgust. Of all Cade's friends, I despise him the most. But something tells me he's the most dangerous, because he's not really Electi at all.

"Ready to play, kitty?" He smirks, and I bristle.

"Where were you tonight?" My voice is all saccharine sweetness. "Or didn't you get the invite?"

"Oh fuck." Cade explodes with laughter. I notice Ashton isn't laughing. He looks like he wants to wrap his hands around my throat and squeeze the life right out of me.

"Fucking bitc—"

"Watch it, Moore," Cade growls.

Silence falls between them and I inch closer to Cade.

"Come on," he says, breaking the tension. "Make sure no one else comes down here."

Before I have time to ask where 'down here' is, Cade guides me into the small stone room.

A dark archway leads to a black abyss, and fear grips me in a chokehold.

"W-what is that?" I croak.

"Relax, babe. I'll protect you." Cade places a hand on the small of my back and nudges me forward. Something travels on the musty air, the faint sound of laughter and music. As the darkness swallows me, candlelight flickers off the wall, revealing a staircase that sinks into the ground. The music grows louder as we move deeper.

We come to another huge stone door, and Cade moves around me to push it open. Inside is nothing like I am expecting. It's a vast room, the decor modern and sleek. A huge black crushed velvet sectional adorns one wall, and a chrome bar runs the length of the other, complete with glass shelves full of expensive liquor. Brandon is perched on a black leather stool, kissing the face off some scantily-clad girl, his fingers pushed under her skirt as she rides his hand. He sure didn't waste any time.

Channing and Tim sit in two wingback chairs, drinking from tumblers as they watch a girl contort her body around a pole. She's in an itty-bitty bikini, her breasts spilling out as she swings and bends.

"What is this place?" My voice quivers.

"It's our den."

"Where's Sasha?" I ask, hoping she'll magically appear.

"She sends her apologies. But don't worry, I'll keep you company." Cade brushes my hair off my shoulder. "So beautiful." His thumb strokes my cheek, dropping to my bottom lip. He teases the seam of my mouth, slowly forcing it past my lips.

For a second, I imagine biting down hard, but sense gets the better of me and I gently pull away. "Not in front of your friends."

His brow goes up at the suggestion in my voice.

Just then, Ashton enters the room and makes a beeline for one of the girls serving drinks behind the bar. He grabs her wrists, pins them above her head, and kisses her passionately.

Sex lingers in the air, the sultry beat thrumming deep inside of me. I don't feel the overpowering lust I felt before, at the dinner where Cade touched me. But I feel *something*.

"Aren't you going to ask?" Cade studies me.

"Ask what?" I meet his inquisitive stare with my own.

"Where your boyfriend is?"

I falter but quickly slide my stone expression back in place. "I don't have a boyfriend."

"So you aren't fucking Easton behind my back?"

My heart plummets into my toes.

He knows.

Cade knows.

"How did you find out?" I don't even bother denying it.

"Nothing happens on campus without me knowing about it, Mia. Nothing happens in this town without me knowing about it."

There's something in his dark gaze that I don't understand. He's angry about Bexley, yes, but it's more than that.

"Where are Bexley and Alex, Cade?" I manage to get the words out despite the huge pit in my stomach.

"So eager, prosapia." He spits the word as if it's something less than human. And I realize that maybe it is.

"Mia wants to start the party early," Cade announces.

Ashton tears away from the girl he has pinned against the wall and stalks toward us. "You sure, kitty? You might not like what you find." His smirk is wicked, making dread snake through me.

"Where are they?" I demand, adrenaline pounding through me. Maybe it's foolish to think I can stand up to them, but I can't just lie down and take whatever they have planned, either.

I sense Channing watching me, but I don't meet his eyes. I can't. I'm too far in to turn back.

"Take me to them," I say.

"Very well." Cade nods, and Tim gets up and moves to the closed velvet curtains. I thought they were hanging on the wall, but when he pulls a cord and they open, I realize they were concealing a huge glass window.

And on the other side is Alex and Bexley.

"W-what is this?" I demand as bile rushes up my throat.

Alex pounds mercilessly into a girl as she claws at his back. But it isn't Alex who has my attention, it's Bexley…

Bexley and the girl riding him as if her life depends on it. He thrusts up inside her, over and over, gripping her hips and whispering dirty words at her. I can't hear them, but I can see the way they form on his lips.

"N-no," I cry, clutching my throat as tears spill down my cheeks. "He wouldn't—"

"Oh, but he would." Cade's warm breath fans my face, and I swallow a fresh wave of bile.

"This was their final test, Mia. The final task standing between them and the Electi. And as you can see, they both passed with flying colors." His hand runs up my spine, cupping the back of my neck, forcing me to watch Bexley fuck the girl.

A girl who isn't me.

A girl I hate almost as much as I hate Cade.

Brook.

"What did you do to him?" I shriek, feeling despair lash my insides. He wouldn't do it.

Bexley wouldn't have sex with a bitch like Brook, task or no task.

Ashton snickers. "Your guy was gagging for it, kitty. Couldn't wait to dip his cock in her dripping pussy. They've been at it a while." He lounges against the glass, smirking at me in that vile way of his. "I jerked off to her riding his face. Looked like she was having the time of her life."

"Don't." My voice shakes with anger and betrayal as I try to turn away, but Cade forces me closer to the glass, pressing me up against the cool surface.

"Watch them. Watch him take her... does it look like he's being forced to do anything?"

"You gave him something..." I cry. "You drugged him..." Because that's the only explanation.

It has to be.

"I wish I could say we did, kitty," Ashton chuckles. "But sometimes good pussy is too hard to resist. And Brook has the kind of pussy that makes a guy see stars. Or so I've heard."

"Oh my God," I breathe. "What is wrong with you?"

They're sick, all of them.

Ashton is watching Bexley fuck his sister as if it's just another day, and Cade is hard at my ass as he watches his ex-fling fuck a guy he claims to hate more than anything.

And I stand there, my heart bleeding out on the ground, wondering what nightmare I've found myself in.

"I hate you," I seethe, my body trembling.

"No you don't, babe," he says. "You hate yourself for believing Easton was different, when all this time he was just another guy waiting for a better piece of ass to come along."

Keep reading for Tarnished Crown

TARNISHED CROWN

GRAVESTONE ELITE BOOK TWO

1

BEXLEY

I roll over in bed, the images of the night running through my mind, and my body grows hot.

Her touch. Her kiss. The softness of her skin against mine.

My hand automatically lowers until my fingers wrap around my hard length.

Fuck, she's perfect.

Our time together plays out like a movie in my head as I slowly jerk myself. I didn't think we'd get any time together. I'd expected Cade to monopolize all her attention and keep us apart.

My eyes fly open at that thought, and I bolt upright in bed.

Why *didn't* he keep us apart?

My brows pinch as I look around the unfamiliar room, but as my eyes move over each piece of furniture, I start to see all my things.

"What the—"

Throwing the covers off, I walk naked across the room to the window and look out. The forest spreads out for miles before me, and realization begins to dawn.

Glancing down at my chest, I take in the brand. It burns like it did when that asshole pressed the red-hot iron into my skin.

I'm one of them now.

I saw their matching brands that day in the pit, but I was too drugged up, too high to really put much thought into it.

I'm Electi now. Part of Quinctus.

I stumble back until I'm sitting on the edge of the bed. I'm sure this is meant to be a privilege, but, right now, it just feels like a death sentence.

What happens now?

We passed. We're in their little fucked-up gang; they've played their games. They've tried to break us.

What's next?

I want to say that we join them and do whatever it is we're meant to do. I've only heard whispers about their 'jobs' for Quinctus; I'm yet to actually know what they entail.

But the games are over... right?

I think of Mia. Of Cade's arm around her shoulders at the meal like he owned her, the pendant around her neck evidence that he actually does, and my fists curl.

She's mine.

So why did he allow last night to happen?

My head's fuzzy from the alcohol and whatever else might have found its way into my system. Cade has a way of ensuring the food I'm eating, the drinks I'm drinking—hell, even the air I breathe—is laced with something to fuck me up.

I have no reason to believe last night was any different.

Last night.

My cock swells again as I think about sinking deep inside her, watching her ride me, listening to the mewls of pleasure rumbling from the back of her throat.

I'm missing something here. I know I am, but my fucked-up head won't allow me to see it.

I fall back on the bed and squeeze my eyes tight, hoping that if I lay still and quiet it will come to me. But it remains just out of reach.

Footsteps outside the door finally get me moving once again. The last thing I need is for them to come storming in here while I'm still trying to get my head together. Stalking across the room, I twist the door that I hope leads to a bathroom and sigh with relief when I find it does.

Turning the shower on, I brush my teeth and then step under the spray. I groan as the powerful jets of water hit my shoulders. I might not want to be here, but fuck if this isn't better than the shitty shower in my dorm room.

I have no idea how long I stand there for, trying to reach the dark recess of my mind that I know is holding something back from me.

Finally, I step out, but before my hand connects with one of the white fluffy towels on the rail, a loud click sounds out from my room. My heart jumps into my throat at the possibility that it could be Mia. I throw a towel around my waist and rip the door open, but disappointment floods me as I take in the person standing in the middle of my room.

"Wow, what a welcoming look," Alex mutters. "Anyone would think you wanted someone else."

"Shut up," I bark, walking over to a chest of drawers to see if I can find some underwear.

Alex drops into the chair on the other side of the room. "Last night was fucked up, man. I don't remember what happened after leaving Gravestone Hall. Do you?"

Little warning signs fly at his words, but my mind goes straight to the gutter, thinking about her again.

A smirk curls at my lips. "Yeah, I remember a few things."

"Like?"

"They took us to their den to celebrate."

"Kinda what I was afraid of," he mutters. "What did they give us this time?"

"You don't remember any of it?"

"Nah, but I ache like a motherfucker, so something tells me I didn't just drink and pass out. Oh, and then there's this."

He unzips the front of his hoodie and shows me his neck and chest.

"Fucking hell." I snort, taking in the mass of hickeys littering his pale skin. "Looks like you had a good night."

"You know, for once I'd like to fuck a girl and actually remember it," he grumbles.

I can't help but throw my head back and bark out a laugh. This situation might be dire, but we've got to find some joy in it somewhere, right?

"This fucking sucks. I don't want to live here, pretending to be some fucking god who lords it over the rest of the college. Hell, over the rest of the town. This shit isn't me." He zips his hoodie back up and tips his head to the ceiling.

"I know," I reply. "I thought shit was meant to get easier moving here. What a fucking joke."

I feel his stare as I rest my hands on the top of the drawers and lean forward, hanging my head.

The silence continues between us as we both contemplate our new lives.

"You hungry?" he asks after the longest time.

"Yeah, although not if it comes with having to see *them*."

"We just moved into their fucking house. Everything is going to involve seeing them."

Fucking great.

There's no outrunning the devil now.

Ripping open the top drawer, I find my boxers all neatly folded. I frown, wondering who did all this while we were out of it on Friday night. Dragging a pair out, I drop my towel and Alex balks.

"Seriously, dude. I know we've seen each other naked, but that was... different. Put it away."

"Shy of a little dick, Rexford? Color me surprised." I chuckle, pulling them up my legs and going in search of some clothes.

"Fuck off," he mumbles, staring anywhere but at me.

After running some wax through my hair, I turn toward the door. "Ready?" I ask Alex.

"To run away and never return? Hell yeah."

While it sounds appealing, the thought of leaving Mia behind in this mess shuts down any possibility of it ever happening.

"This place is fucking massive," Alex murmurs as we navigate through the hallways to find the staircase. Just like downstairs, modern art lines the flawless soft gray walls. The whole thing confuses me.

Finally, we make our way down, the scent of food directing us toward what I hope is an empty kitchen, but the second we turn a corner and hear deep, rumbling voices in the distance, I know we're shit out of luck.

"You ready for this?" I whisper to Alex.

"Pretty sure I should have had more pain pills to deal with these assholes."

"Yeah," I mutter, the gentle pounding at my temples not getting better at the thought of having to look at them.

At *him*.

My stomach twists as I consider the possibility of walking into that room and seeing them together. Of him lording it over me with his arm wrapped around Mia, touching her, kissing her.

My fists curl and my muscles tense, but I know there's nothing I can do right now. Hell, there might never be anything I can do. With that depressing thought swirling around my head, I continue forward to find out what the day might hold.

The second we step into the room, all talk halts and all sets of eyes turn on us. I breathe a sigh of relief that she's not here and pinned to his lap.

All four of them assess us as we stand there. Cade's eyes are dark, but instead of the usual anger that fills them, I want to say he looks amused. Ashton doesn't even attempt to hide his delight at our arrival as a wide, menacing smile tugs at his lips. Brandon looks torn as he glances between the two of us. He knows he should follow his leader, but there's clear concern in his depths. Same with Channing. Actually, he looks downright pissed. As usual, Tim isn't around.

"Ah, look. Our new recruits decided to grace us with their presence," Cade announces. "Mulligan, could you please get our new Electi their breakfast."

A middle-aged man eagerly nods at Cade's command, and my lips part to be a little more polite, but I notice Channing shaking his head at me so I decide against it, instead pulling out the chair closest to me and sitting my ass down.

"So..." Cade starts. "What did you think of last night?"

"Want to be more specific? When you branded us like fucking cattle, or when you drugged us... again?"

He waves me off as if the last part is nothing. "We were just celebrating. Enjoying ourselves. You can't be mad about that. Alex sure isn't." He nods his chin toward my friend. "Feeling nice and... *sated* this morning, Rexford?" He smirks.

Alex growls in frustration. I can only imagine how he feels about Cade and his posse knowing the exact details when he has no memory of them. The sick motherfuckers probably watched.

"Come, eat, you must be starved." But as he says this, his eyes lock on mine.

My stomach twists, and the alcohol that's still in my system threatens to make an appearance.

Does he know?

Does he know what I did—*who* I did—last night?

Fuck.

My hands tremble. If he knows, then there's no way she's not in danger. That motherfucker is deranged, and he's staring at me as if he knows all my secrets.

My heart continues to thunder in my chest as Ashton takes one of the empty chairs beside me. "Good lay, right, Easton?"

Bile rushes up my throat.

Has he been fucking her this whole time? Was all of this a game? Has she been lying to me? Playing me?

I can barely breathe as images of my time with Mia flash through my mind.

Every confession, every touch, every promise.

Were they all lies?

"Sir, I hope you enjoy."

A plate of food is lowered to the table before me, but I can't even think about eating it.

Feeling eyes drilling into the top of my head, I look up. Cade's wearing a shit-eating grin on his face, as if he knows something I don't.

Who am I kidding? He knows a lot of shit I don't.

"How much do you remember about last night, Easton?" Ashton asks, earning himself a scowl from the devil.

"It was a great night," I say with the fakest smile I can muster while the memories of having Mia in my arms refuse to leave my head.

"Oh yeah, I've heard all good things about that one," he mutters with a smirk.

My fists curl under the table. He's lying. He knows nothing about her.

I'm the only one she's been with... right?

"Eat," Cade demands.

Alex immediately picks up his silverware, probably ravenous after his exploits with an unknown girl last night.

I do the same, but I'm hesitant to eat anything because that motherfucker has history when it comes to spiking our shit, and I'd rather keep a clear head right now—at least until I figure out what the nagging at the edges of my mind is about.

It's like when you wake up and you know there was a dream, but you can't quite grasp it.

What am I missing?

The sound of light footsteps gets louder, and everyone turns to look at the doorway. I know I should probably keep my head down and not show any interest in front of Cade, but the prospect of seeing her again after last night is too much.

I suck in a shaky breath as Sasha appears in the doorway. She looks good. Better than I feel, that's for fucking sure. She walks farther into the room before the person attached to her hand emerges.

All the air in my lungs rushes out in one go.

Mia's face is pale. Too pale. She has swollen, dark circles around her eyes, as if she's been up all night, and her hair hangs limply around her shoulders. Fury surges through me as thoughts of what that motherfucker might have done to her last night hit me.

"Mia, what's wrong? What happened?" I'm up and out of my seat, the words of concern spilling from my lips before I even registered that I've moved.

Her lips part in shock as her eyes harden in anger. "Wha—What happened? Are you fucking kidding me?" Tears fill her eyes as her lips twist. "I can't do this."

She rips her hand from Sasha's and takes off.

"Ah, she still pissed about the little show Bexley put on last night?" Cade barks through a laugh.

"Shut the fuck up, prick," Sasha spits before running after Mia.

My brows furrow as I glance around the table at everyone, zeroing in on Cade. He smirks, only fueling the anger swelling inside me.

"Will someone tell me what the fuck is going on?"

2

MIA

I run and don't look back, taking two stairs at a time as tears drip down my face.

How could he?

How could he act as if nothing happened? As if he didn't bang Brook at the party last night?

God, I'm such a fool. Cade was right—Bexley is just like the rest of them. Conceited and selfish. Callous and cruel.

A thought flickers in the back of my mind, but I'm too distraught to latch onto it as I storm into Sasha's room and slam the door. She follows me inside a second later, her expression etched with concern.

"Ready to tell me what happened last night?" Her brow arches.

"He... he fucked her." The words sour on my tongue.

"What?"

"Bexley... he was... fucking her."

"You're going to have to be a bit more spec—Brook." Realization dawns on her. "You mean Brook, don't you?"

"I saw it." I drop down on the edge of the bed. "I saw everything."

"Motherfucker," she hisses. "He knows, doesn't he?"

I nod, my heart breaking in my chest. I didn't think it was possible to cry any more tears after last night when I finally fled to Sasha's room, but they wrack my body, great big ugly sobs I feel all the way down to my soul.

"He must have done something... there's no way Bexley would—"

"Oh my God." I shoot upright. "You're right." Hurrying to the door, I heave it open and spill into the hall. I just reach the staircase when Bexley appears.

"Thank God, we need to—"

"Hey, lover boy." Brook comes sauntering down the hall. "Miss me?"

"W-what?" He stares at her blankly.

"Oh, don't tell me you've already forgotten. I can barely walk after you—"

"You bitch." I lunge for her, clawing and pulling her hair.

"Get the fuck off me," she shrieks, digging her fingernails into my arms. But I'm so angry, drowning in hatred and the need to hurt her the way she hurt me. I scratch and pinch and slap. I've got a fistful of her blonde locks when someone bands their arms around my waist and yanks me away.

"Fucking psycho," she snarls, smoothing a hand through her hair. There's a cut on her face, and I have a clump of strands in my grasp.

It isn't nearly half of what she deserves, but a sense of satisfaction washes over me.

"Will someone tell me what the fuck is going on?" Bexley says, finally releasing me. I wrap my arms around my waist and step away from him.

"Mia?" His brows knit, hurt flashing over his face.

"Well, if this isn't awkward..." Cade and Ashton join us on the stairs. The air turns thick, heavy with secrets.

"What did you do?" I grit out.

"Me?" Cade smirks. "Are you suggesting that I had a hand in what happened? Like I told you last night, Brook is *very* convincing when she wants to be."

A wicked smile curves her lips. God, I hate her. I hate her so much I feel it bubble over into a low snarl.

"Down, kitty," Ashton teases. "We're just getting to the good part."

The truth circles us like a storm closing in. I can't get the image of Bexley with Brook out of my head, their bodies writhing, moving as one.

Tears prick the corners of my eyes, but I swallow them down.

"Go on, Sis, tell him. Tell Bexy boy how he fucked *you* like a champ last night."

The blood drains from Bexley's face as he staggers back. "N-no, I didn't... I would never..." His alarmed expression finds me as the tears burst free, rolling down my cheeks.

"It's true... I saw you." The words gut me, but it's nothing compared to the expression on his face.

"No. No way." He laughs, but it comes out strangled. "This is a joke. You're joking with me. I was with you last night. We..." I see it the moment he realizes. Pure anger explodes across his face as he barrels toward Cade.

My scream fills the hall as the two of them stumble down the stairs in a flurry of fists and limbs. Bexley is like a man possessed, throwing everything he can at Cade. But eventually, Ashton steps in and the two of them manage to subdue him, Cade pinning him against the wall by his throat.

"Let's get one thing straight, Easton. Mia is my prosapia. Mine to toy with, mine to taunt, mine to fuck. It would serve you well to remember that."

"Although now she knows you've dipped your end in my sister's pussy, I'm sure she won't want your dick anywhere near her."

A violent shudder rolls through me at Ashton's crass words. I sway a little on my feet, emotionally annihilated by the revelations.

Of course Cade drugged Bexley. It makes perfect sense now, but I'd been too upset, too shocked, to see it last night.

"You fucking drugged me again and let me... fuck." Bexley dry heaves.

"Don't act like you didn't enjoy every damn second," Ashton chuckles. "We all saw you giving it to her like you couldn't get enough. I bet she has the bruises to prove it."

"And the bite marks." Brook shoots me a smug look, and I want nothing more than to gouge her eyes out.

"I can't believe I—"

"Believe it." Cade slowly relaxes his arm, the one pinned against Bexley's throat. "Can I trust that you won't come at me again?"

Bexley nods, unable to meet my eyes. It hurts. But it doesn't hurt anywhere near as much as knowing that Cade has driven a huge wedge between us.

Bexley slept with Brook. Had hot, animalistic sex with her… and I saw it all.

We can never come back from this.

Cade has played his ace, and there's nothing to do except admit defeat.

"I need some air," I say, backing away from them all slowly.

"Mia, please—"

"It's done, Bexley. We're done." My voice cracks, the words like a knife to my own heart.

His eyes drill into mine, silently pleading with me not to do this. But there's nothing more to say.

Cade knows.

He knows, and he will never let us be together. Last night was proof of that.

"I-I need to go." I push past them all and take off down the hall. I don't know where I'm going, but all I know is that I can't stay here a single second longer.

SASHA FINDS me sitting down by the lake. My feet are in the cool water, grounding me.

"Hey, can I join you?"

I shrug. Not because I don't want her here, but because I'm scared of what might spill out if I open my mouth.

"Feeling any better?"

"What do you think?"

"Honestly?" She offers me a weak smile. "I think you need to take all that anger and hatred and turn it into a weapon. Cade is unhinged, Mia. The things he does, the way he thinks… it isn't normal…"

"I don't know how to do this. I don't know how to live in your world."

"*His* world," Sasha whispers. "It's his kingdom, Mia, and we're all just pawns."

"Why doesn't someone do something? Quinctus, can't they—"

"What? Send him away? Have him killed? He's the heir to the Kingsley bloodline. They need him."

"I don't understand."

"I know, but you will. And when you do, you need to remember everything I've told you." She glances back at the house.

"You're worried they're watching us."

"Someone is always watching, Mia. Don't ever forget that."

"What happens now? Now Bexley and Alex are Electi?"

"They'll live here, run errands for Q."

"Errands?" Sasha presses her lips together and I sigh deeply. "Let me guess," I add, "you can't tell me."

"There are some things even I'm not privy to, you know that. For what it's worth, though, I am sorry."

"I hate him. I hate him so freaking much, I don't understand why anyone would think I'm the right girl for him."

Silence falls over us as the events of the last twenty-four hours play in my mind.

"Why would Brook do that? I thought she wanted Cade."

"Oh, she does. Which is exactly why she did it."

"That makes no sense."

"You're looking for answers that aren't there. Cade, Ashton, Brook... they only care about one thing. Power. You ended up in the middle of Bexley and Cade... well, she's just put your boyfriend right in the middle of her and Cade."

"He's not my boyfriend." He's not my anything now.

"He didn't know what he was doing."

"It doesn't matter. I can't keep doing this. Cade isn't going to ever give me up. Not unless I find a way out."

"What are you saying?"

"I need to find his weakness. I need something I can use against him."

"Mia," Sasha tsks, "don't start something you can't finish. Cade is... well, he's a special brand of crazy."

"So what would you have me do? Just accept that this is it for me? Because I won't do that, Sash, I won't."

Lacing her arm through mine, she pulls me close, laying her head on my shoulder. "You can't win against someone like Cade. He doesn't play by the rules, Mia. He *makes* the rules. What do you think is going to happen to Bexley now he knows the truth about the two of you?"

Oh God. Bexley.

"He won't let you forget, babe. And when you're least expecting it, he'll pull the rug out from under you."

"I can't just do nothing." The idea makes me feel nauseous.

Sasha peeks up at me and gives me a weak smile. "I know it sucks, but I don't think you have a choice."

SASHA GAVE me a ride back to my dorm after that. I might not have been able to go to war with Cade yet, but I could fight each battle. And if he thought for one second that I was going to walk back in there and act as if everything was okay, he had another thing coming.

I throw my bag down by the desk and grab my laptop, getting comfy on the middle of my bed. Sasha said I don't have any choice, but there's always a choice. I just have to find my leverage.

I open up a new search bar and type in Cade Kingsley. Everyone has secrets, and something tells me Cade's are bigger and darker than most.

I just need to find the right one.

The one that will get me out of this in one piece.

But after an hour of researching Cade and his family's name, I'm still drawing a blank. Google isn't going to give me the information I need. I need to go straight to the source: the town's archives. But they're not public records. I know, because my dad told me once.

And lucky for me, my dad just happens to work security for the building in which they're kept.

3

BEXLEY

"You're out of fucking line," I bark at Cade the second Mia disappears from the hallway.

"So? What the fuck are you going to do about it?"

"You're not going to get away with this," I warn, taking a step toward him once more.

I don't give a fuck that my shoulder smarts from where we tumbled down the stairs; I'll take this motherfucker out right now.

Ashton steps up beside his leader, and I scoff at his loyalty.

Cade leans in, a cocky smirk playing on his face. "Who's going to fucking stop me? You? Your ancestors might have been in charge, but that time has long past, Easton. Kingsleys are in charge around here now. And lucky for you, I'm right here."

A growl rumbles up my throat.

"Mia is mine. Promised to me. She was meant to be a fucking virgin, but I'll be nice and let that one slide. You got a taste of mine, after all." He tilts his chin toward where I know Brook is standing behind me.

"I hate to break it to you, but everyone has had a taste of her," I spit, disgusted that I've now joined that club.

I didn't want to believe it, but one look at the devastation on Mia's face and I knew it was true.

It wasn't Mia I was fucking last night like my skewed memories led me to believe. It was Brook.

My heart splinters in my chest again.

She watched. This fucking cunt made Mia stand there and watch me as I fucked someone else.

My nails dig into my palms as I try to restrain myself from taking his head off. But, just like the last time, it's four against one. I'm going to have to wait until I can get him alone.

A little one on one time is well overdue for us already.

"Good, right?" Ashton smirks, and I do a double take.

"That's your fucking sister," I spit in disgust. "This is fucked." I lift my arms and gesture to the house, to this situation. "All of this is fucked up, and I want nothing to do with any of it."

"Trust me, Easton. If I thought there was a way for that to happen, you'd be long gone already. This is your life now, so suck it up. Forget about the girl. We've got plenty more for you to dip your end into—most a hell of a lot hotter and more experienced than Mia. You'll be thanking me soon enough." He winks, and I see red, but before I manage to throw a punch, hands wrap around my upper arms and I'm hauled back.

"Leave it," Channing growls in my ear.

Shaking my head at the lot of them, I storm from the house. Fuck knows how, but when I walk out to the driveway, my BMW is sitting right there beside Alex's Porsche.

I don't overthink it. I just pull the key from my pocket, unlock it, and shut myself inside.

His burning hate stare makes my skin tingle, and when I look up at the house, I find him standing in the middle of the open double doors, glaring at me in warning.

Flipping him off, I floor the accelerator and speed away from what is now apparently my home.

IT'S over an hour later when I feel calm enough to talk to anyone about what went down last night, and there's only one person I need to have it out with right now.

I pull up to the huge gates of Marcus' home ten minutes later, and, after a few seconds, they open for me. The front door is open and I let myself in and walk straight down to the kitchen, starting the coffee maker.

"Sit down, boy. I can do that for you," Brenda says, walking into the room with a feather duster in hand.

"It's okay, I don't mind."

Whatever she sees on my face when I look up stops her arguing immediately. "He's up in his study if you're looking for your un—grandfather."

My eyes narrow on her, wondering just how much she knows about all of this. Seeing as she's been here since the dawn of time, I assume everything.

"You always knew, didn't you?"

"Your father was a wonderful man, Bexley. It breaks my heart that he never got to meet you. You look so much like him. He'd be so proud of you for taking your rightful place in this town."

My lips part to respond, but I soon find I have no words.

Why would any parent want this kind of life for their child?

Everyone acts as if this Electi Gravestone shit is a privilege. It's utter bullshit, if you ask me.

The fighting, the drugs, the secrets, lies, power, money. All of it is total bullshit, and I want nothing to do with it.

I just want a college degree and to get a decent job, have a decent life.

I never asked for any of this.

I shake my head at her excited smile, turn my back on her, and head upstairs.

"Bexley," Marcus greets me as I peer inside his study. "How do you feel?"

"Like shit," I answer honestly. At least I now know why my hangover is so fucking bad.

"Last night's party that good, huh? I remember the night I passed the initiation." A smile pulls at his lips as he relives his former life.

"Cade drugged me and forced me into sleeping with Brook Moore," I blurt. I'm not here to beat around the bush. I want some fucking answers.

"Sounds just like the parties I remember, although I don't ever remember it ever being forced," he mutters.

"This isn't a fucking joke. He found out that I—"

"That you're in love with Mia Thompson?" he finishes for me.

My lips open and close as I stand there in his doorway.

"Come in and sit down, Son."

I hesitate but eventually do as he requests.

"How'd you—"

"I make it my business to know things, Bexley." He leans forward on his elbows and looks me dead in the eyes.

"Well, thanks for the warning."

"I said I know things, not that I'm psychic."

"I'm done, Marcus. I'm so fucking done with this." I push to stand and begin pacing. I'm too irritable to sit still. "I'll transfer somewhere else. I don't need this fucking shit."

"You can't—"

"Because they'll find me? Kill me? Let them. I'm not fucking doing this. I'm not letting him do this, control us like this." I scrub my hand down my face. "The look on her face this morning... I've never seen hurt like that before. She fucking hates me. I get it. I hate myself. I thought it was her. I woke up this morning thinking that I had this amazing night with her, and it wasn't. It was that fucking whore." My fist connects with Marcus' office wall, my knuckles splitting with the force of the hit and pain shooting down my arm. "And she watched. She wanted me—" A sob rips up my throat, cutting off my words.

"Bexley," Marcus says softly, but I don't react. Instead, I rest my palms against the wall and hang my head, squeezing my eyes closed and picturing what I thought happened last night. Mia's flawless face flushed with pleasure as she rode me, throwing her head back as she came, my fingers gripping her hips tightly as I pistoned in and out of her.

But it wasn't fucking her.

My stomach churns, and I think I'm going to puke right here on Marcus' carpet.

"Bexley, you can't leave."

"Watch me." Pushing from the wall with blood dripping down my hand, I stalk toward the door.

But I don't get through it, because he says the one thing that will ensure I do anything he wants.

"If you love her, you need to be here to protect her."

I suck in a deep breath at his words.

"She needs you, Bexley. She needs you here, doing as you're told and protecting her from a distance."

I don't turn to look at him. Instead, I close my eyes and speak what's on my mind, no matter how much it hurts. "I can't stay here and watch her be his."

"You have to. Cade is... Cade is a liability. He—"

"You think I don't fucking know that?" I bark, spinning around and pinning him with a look that most would cower away from—only Marcus doesn't so much as flinch. "Do you know what he's done to me? To Alex? To Mia?"

"Yes."

"They locked us underground and gave us a fucking hallucinogenic..."

"The vault. I know. It's a standard initiation task."

"A standard—the fuck?" I run my hand through my hair. "This is fucking crazy. He's out of control."

"And that is exactly why you need to see this through."

I stare at him, trying to read the truths that are hiding in the depths of his eyes. "What aren't you telling me?"

His lips part but no words come out, not for long seconds. "This is bigger than you think. You need to play your part. We all do."

"I fucking hate these games, the lies... the cryptic secrets. Why can't you just tell me everything? I'm on the inside now." I drag my shirt aside, showing him my fucking brand that will forever remind me of this fucking disaster.

"I know, Son. But it's too dangerous for you to know everything. You have to trust that Q knows what they are doing. You have to take your place and do as they wish."

"And what the fuck is that? I haven't even spoken to them outside of bullshit ceremonies where someone brands me or draws my fucking blood," I seethe.

"You will. You will be invited to a meeting soon enough."

"Great," I mutter, less than excited about the prospect.

"You must play your part, Bexley. Protect her."

"She hates me. She won't let me near her ever again." I blow out a long breath as I finally fall back into the chair opposite Marcus.

"You can do it from a distance, for now."

I stare at him, waiting for him to say more, but he never does. "You want me to accept this, don't you?"

"We don't have a choice, Bexley."

"Someone needs to take his power away before he really hurts someone."

"It's not that easy. He's the only Kingsley heir. Without him—"

"Yeah, I get it. But I don't fucking like it."

"Trust me, no one does. Just... please, Bexley. Don't make this any harder than it needs to be."

"Why does everything have to be a fucking game?"

"It's life, Son. And you are the Easton heir. Life as you know it will never be the same again."

4

MIA

"Hey." I march up to Annabel. "What's up?"

"Is it true?"

"Is what true?"

Her expression morphs into a grimace. "I heard that Bexley and Brook are—"

"Don't." I bristle.

"So, it is true?" She laces her arm through mine and we walk the short distance to the humanities building. I have a psychology class first, which means I'll have to see Bexley.

The permanent knot in my stomach tightens, but I've got to get used to seeing him, to being around him. If I'm going to play the part I've been given, then our paths are going to cross.

He's Electi. One of them now.

I'm going to be over at the house, and he's going to be there.

God, how am I supposed to do this?

"Hey, are you okay?" Annabel squeezes my arm gently, pulling me back to the moment.

"Yeah, I'm fine."

"So Bexley and Brook?"

"It's none of my business." I shrug, determined not to break. Not even in front of Annabel. After what happened yesterday in the house,

I need to control myself around Cade and his lapdogs, especially Ashton.

"I'm glad you think so, because she's coming over."

Crap.

"Annabel, Mila."

"You know my name," I hiss. "Use it."

"There's no need to be so rude. It was an honest mistake." Her words are as saccharine as her smile. "Some party Saturday night, huh? I still ache." Brook flicks her long blonde hair off her shoulder, revealing little love bites all along the slope of her neck.

Bile rushes up my throat, but I swallow it down.

"Well, I just wanted to say hey. Maybe the four of us could double date sometime."

"Excuse me?" My body vibrates with anger.

"You and Cade, and me and Bex, silly."

Bex.

She called him Bex.

I want to wipe the smirk clean off her face, but I force myself to calm down. Hurting Brook again will do no good. Even if it did make me feel better for a few seconds.

"You're crazier than I thought," I say, tugging Annabel away from her.

"You know, Mia, I think given half a chance you and I could be friends." Her words roll off my shoulders, and I let them. I have no desire to make friends with the devil, because I have no doubt that girl is pure evil, and the fact that she's been with Bexley makes my heart ache.

He's mine.

At least, he was. For a little while.

Now he isn't mine, and I'm not his. What we had is tainted by what happened Saturday night.

"God, she's such a bitch," Annabel says once we're clear of Brook.

"She wants Cade," I state.

"Well, duh. But pulling Bexley into it?" She gives me a pointed look. "You can't let her get to you."

"Easier said than done."

Annabel glances away, chewing her bottom lip.

"What is it?" I ask.

"There was a party?"

"It wasn't like that."

"Electi stuff," she says, a trace of hurt in her voice.

"You know I don't want to be tangled up in all this."

"But you are, and I know it sounds really selfish, but I can't help but feel like you'll leave me for them. You and Sasha are already—"

"No. No way." I squeeze her hand. "Sasha is an ally, and I won't lie, it's nice to have her in my corner through all this. But trust me, I'd rather just be plain old Mia Thompson."

She gives me a weak smile, and I want to say something to reassure her that I'm still the same Mia. But the truth is, I'm not. And whether I like it or not, there will always be things I can't tell her.

IN PSYCHOLOGY, I choose a seat right at the back. I can't explain it, but I need to know where Bexley is. I don't want to feel his eyes on me for the entire class, begging, pleading. Because nothing is going to change the fact that he had sex with Brook. Nothing is going to erase the image of him thrusting into her, clawing at her body like he couldn't get enough.

At least he thought it was me. He doesn't have to live with the pain of knowing.

Except he does, a little voice whispers. He watched Cade touch me. He watched my body betray me, betray us both.

God, what is this nightmare I've found myself in?

I feel him before I see him. The air grows thin, as if it's being sucked from the room. Bexley finds me and hesitates, but I shake my head. He can't sit with me. If he tries, I'll have to leave. I'm not ready to face him. It's bad enough being in the same room as him.

Tears burn the backs of my eyes, but I steel myself. I can't keep letting my emotions get the better of me. If I'm going to play Cade at his own game, I need to toughen up. I need to learn to manipulate my feelings the way he manipulates everything and everyone around him.

Bexley winces, dejection flashing over his expression, but, to my relief, he seeks out an empty seat in another row.

I thought it would help, watching him instead of him watching me, but I can't focus on a word the professor says. All I can see is Bexley and her. Together. Their naked writhing bodies. My fingers curl into a fist, my nails biting into my palm. It isn't until I feel blood that I notice I've cut small crescents into my skin. Wincing, I dig some tissue out of my bag and clean my hands. The guy beside me shoots me a funny look, and I glower at him.

By the time the professor dismisses the class, my stomach is knotted so tightly I feel nauseous. I want to escape, to get far away from Bexley, but the girl at the end of my row is being so freaking slow at packing up her things. The second she leaves, I slip into the aisle, but Bexley is right there.

"We need to talk," he whispers over my shoulder as we file out in the crush together.

"No, we really don't."

"Mia, come on. Don't do this."

"If I remember correctly, I didn't do anything."

The second we reach the door, he gently grabs my elbow and steers me aside, letting the rest of the students pass us. "Please, just hear me out." Pain is etched into his expression, but I can't do it. I can't forget.

"I need to go," I say, unable to meet his heavy gaze.

"Mia, please... this is killing me." The room is empty now except for the professor, but he pays us little attention.

"You had sex with her," I hiss, the words rippling through me. "With Brook."

"I thought it was you. I didn't—"

"Don't you see it doesn't matter?" My chest heaves with the weight of my words. "Nothing we do or say is going to change the fact that Cade owns us now. Everything we do, everything we do and feel... he knows, Bexley. So this, us... it's done."

"No," the blood drains from his face, "you don't mean that."

"Yes, I do. If I want to survive this thing, I have to accept that I'm his. Now please, don't make this any harder than it needs to be." I yank my arm free and shoulder past him, hurrying from the room.

Before I do something stupid.

Before I beg him to take me far, far away from this godforsaken place and never look back.

ANNABEL DOESN'T WANT to hang out after class. I get the impression she's hurt about the party, even though I tried to explain to her that it wasn't one. Nothing about it was fun, not a damn thing. But it isn't like I can tell her the truth. Not all of it, anyway. I leave my last class of the day ready to head back to my dorm room alone, but I find Sasha waiting for me.

"This is a surprise," I say. She's almost as elusive as her brother and his Electi friends.

"I thought we could hang out."

"At the house?" Because I'm not ready to step foot back in that place. But then an idea hits me.

"No, we don't have to go there."

"It's fine." I nod. "I've got to get used to being there. Besides, we can stay in your room, right?"

"Or we could check out the pool. I have extra bathing suits."

"Maybe."

"Cool. Come on." Lacing her arm through mine, she guides me to the parking lot, and we climb into her silver Porsche Boxster.

"How were classes today?" she asks, gunning the engine.

"Okay."

"Did you see…"

"You know I did."

"And?"

"And nothing." My shoulders lift in a small shrug. "I told him it's over."

"It's for the best." She offers me a sympathetic smile.

"Did you hear the rumors about him and Brook? I don't know why she feels the need to spread that crap. I had a front row seat to the show." Pain lashes at my insides.

"I don't think that's about you."

"Cade," I say. "She's trying to make Cade jealous."

"Stranger things have happened."

"How do you do it?" I ask.

"Do what?"

"This. Be one of them. It's exhausting, and I'm not even an Electi." My head falls back against the soft leather rest.

"It's all I've ever known," Sasha replies. "For as long as I can remember, it was me, Brandon, and the guys. Girls tried to make friends with me, but they just wanted to use me to get to the guys. So eventually, I just stopped making friends."

"It sounds lonely."

"It is what it is. I accepted my fate a long time ago."

"And you and Brook… you've never seen eye to eye?"

"God no, she's a vapid bitch who takes after her mother. I didn't speak to my dad for a month when I found out he was seeing her."

"What about Brandon? What does he think about everything?" He and Tim are the two Electi I still haven't gotten a read on. Tim loves Fawn, I don't doubt that, and from afar it looks like he's one of Cade's closest friends. But there's something that doesn't quite add up.

"Brandon doesn't give a crap so long as he's drowning in beer, pot, and pussy."

I smother a snicker. From what I've seen, that sums up the Cargill heir perfectly.

"Are he and your dad close?"

"My father isn't close to anyone, Mia. I think he thinks if he lets Brandon get it all out of his system now, it'll make his transition into Q life smoother."

"So when will his Eligere be?"

"Next spring."

We finally pull up at the Electi house and my skin vibrates, my heart racing in my chest. They're all here. Their cars line the driveway like perfectly polished weapons. Including Alex's Porsche and Bexley's BMW.

Sasha reaches for my hand and squeezes gently. "You've got this, Mia," she says, and I gulp.

"Yeah." A thin smile graces my lips.

I really don't.

But if I want to find a way out of this nightmare, I know I don't have any choice.

5

BEXLEY

The house is in silence when I get back from college on Monday afternoon despite all of their cars being here.

I don't bother looking for them. Instead, I grab some food from the kitchen and head up to my room, locking the door from the inside and falling down on my bed, wishing that I was back in my dorm. Hell, wishing I was back in Sterling.

Listening to Mia tell me we were done earlier hurt. It really fucking hurt. But what can I do other than let her walk away?

Deep down, I know she's right.

There is quite possibly nothing either of us can do for us to be together.

I might be new to this world, but I already sense that you don't go back on things like the Eligere.

I blow out a long, frustrated breath.

I've successfully avoided Cade and his lapdogs since yesterday morning when the truth was revealed, but I know my time is running out.

I'm one of them now. Certain things are going to be expected of me. Although I still have no fucking clue as to what they could be.

Needing to talk to someone—someone who doesn't live under this roof and isn't controlled by Cade—I pull my cell from my pocket and find Hadley Rexford's number. I know she left a few years ago, but I need to know more about Cade and his family.

"Hey," she says with a bright smile as she answers my video call.

"Hey." My voice is much less animated than hers, and her face falls immediately.

"I was going to ask how things were, but I think your face pretty much says it all. How was the weekend?" she asks with a wince.

"Well," I say, placing my cell on the bed and quickly pulling my shirt off. "I got this," I say, showing her my new brand.

"Holy shit," she breathes, her eyes so wide it looks painful. "It's really real."

"You thought I was lying?" I hate that my voice breaks on that question. She has every right to question my words after everything that went down in Sterling Bay, but it still stings.

"No, not at all. No one knows all the things you do unless they're part of this. But seeing that, it just makes it so—"

"Real," I mutter. "Tell me about it."

"Did it hurt?"

"Not as much as what came after."

"What happened?"

"I didn't tell you everything on the beach," I admit, scrubbing my hand down my face. There is so much she still doesn't know.

"Oh?"

"Did you know Mia Thompson back in high school?"

"Err... the name is familiar, but I can't picture her."

"She'd have been in your class at Gravestone High. She's a freshman at Gravestone U and—"

"Bexley," she interrupts, "I'm actually a year older than all of you. After everything with... After all that, I retook my sophomore year here. So she'd have been in the class below."

"Right, okay." Hadley seems impressed that I just skim over that nugget of information, but really, after everything I've discovered recently, it's hardly earth-shattering. "Anyway, Mia is... Mia is Cade's prosapia and—"

"Bexley," Hadley warns, "tell me you haven't."

"I didn't know about any of this bullshit when I first met her."

"You need to walk away." She lets out a resigned sigh, her face deadly serious.

"I can't, Hads. I can't leave her with him. I don't trust him."

"Jesus." She drops her head into her hands. "Carry on and you're going to end up getting yourself killed."

"Rather me than her."

Her chin falls in shock. "Wow, she must really be something, Bex."

"She is. She's... fuck—" I hang up the second my door flies open.

"What the fuck?" I bark as Kingsley marches into my room like he owns the fucking place. "How'd you—"

His manic laugh cuts off my words. "You think I'd let you lock yourself away, Easton? Clearly you're stupider than you look."

I glance behind him to see Alex loitering in the doorway.

"Who were you talking to?"

"None of your goddamn business."

"I can find out anything that goes on under this roof. Don't forget that."

"Whatever," I mutter, staring out the window instead of looking at him, knowing it'll piss him off.

"You need to get dressed. You and Rexford have a job."

"A job?"

"Yeah, you're Q's little bitch boys now. They tell you to jump, you ask how high."

"What about you?"

He laughs again. "What about me?"

"They order you around like that too?"

He shakes his head, not even bothering to answer my question as he begins ripping drawers open. He throws a black hoodie and a pair of black sweats at me. "Black, always. Meet me downstairs in ten."

Spinning on his heels, he marches out of my room, barging through Alex who's still awkwardly standing there. It's only now I realize he's dressed as Kingsley is expecting me to.

"Look at you, doing as you're told," I mutter, nodding toward his outfit.

"What's the alternative?"

I shrug, because fuck if I know.

Making quick work of changing, I follow Alex down to where his highness is waiting.

"So, who were you talking to?" he whispers as we descend.

"Your sister."

His steps falter a little. "Hadley? Have you told her?"

"About you, no. She knows about everything else, though."

"She's good people. I'm glad you've got her."

"You should too."

"It's not my place to tell her. That's a job for Harrison, don't you think?"

"Yes, but if she's going to be able to help you then I say go for it. Something tells me we need as many people in our corner as we can get right now."

He mutters an agreement as we hit the hallway and find Cade dressed all in black. "Let's go," he barks, spinning away from us and marching out of the house.

"What about the others?" Alex asks as he climbs into Kingsley's Range Rover. Much to his irritation, I take the passenger seat, seeing as it looks like this little mission is just the three of us.

He glances over at me as he puts the car into drive, his lips pursed in frustration.

I smirk at him.

We're equal now. Unless you look at the history books, which suggests that once upon a time the Easton line reigned supreme, not Kingsley.

My chest puffs out in triumph when he focuses his attention back out the windshield. The second we pull away from the house he turns the stereo on and blasts Bring Me the Horizon loud enough to ensure we can't have a conversation.

Fine by me. I have no interest in talking to the motherfucker.

"Where are we?" I shout as we pull into an old motel parking lot on the very outskirts of Gravestone.

Reaching out, Kingsley turns the music off. "Part of being Electi means you're at Q's beck and call. That means tidying up their messes and running their errands."

"Just spit it out."

"You don't get a choice," he says. "You do what they say, when they say, and you never ask questions."

"Right." I roll my eyes. It's not like I was expecting anything different.

"Why aren't the others here? I thought you worked as a team."

"Usually we do, but Q still wants to know what you two are made of, so this is all yours." He looks at me and then catches Alex's eye in the rearview mirror. "Room one-two-nine. An associate got a little carried away with his party. Everything needs cleaning up with no evidence left behind. You think you can do that?"

"Clean a motel room?" I grumble. "Yeah, I think we've got it covered."

A wicked smirk curls at Kingsley's lips and my stomach knots. I knew this wouldn't be as simple as picking up a few bottles and stripping the bedsheets. The look in his eyes tells me that we're nowhere near ready for what we're about to walk into.

"In the trunk, you will find two bags containing everything you need. Do what you need to do. I'll be here when you're done."

"Why don't you come help?"

"Not my job."

I hesitate for a few seconds, my eyes watching a young kid kicking a ball against the end wall of the building.

"You in? Or do I have to tell Q that you're a pair of pussies?"

"Fuck off, Kingsley." Throwing the door open, I climb out. Alex quickly follows, and, after throwing the bags over our shoulders, we follow the signs to the room.

"What the hell are we about to walk into?" Alex asks as we climb the stairs.

"I wish I knew. Something tells me it's not going to be pretty."

We come to a stop in front of the door. The curtains are drawn on the dirty window, giving us no clue as to what's waiting inside.

"Ready?" I ask.

"No."

Despite his words, I reach forward and throw the door open.

"Oh my God," Alex gasps before heaving as I drag him into the dark room.

The smell... I don't even know what the smell is.

Death, I guess.

I cover my nose and mouth with my arm as we walk deeper into the room. The stench still filters through my nose, and my eyes burn.

Piss. Shit. Puke. Drugs. Blood.

It all mingles, making my stomach turn.

The bed is covered in dark red blood, and right in the middle is a woman. She's completely nude, her body battered and bruised, her arms bearing the scars of years of drug abuse.

But it's none of that which holds my attention.

It's the deep slash across her throat.

"What the fuck are we meant to do with this?" Alex manages to get out through his dry heaves.

"What's in the bag?" I ask, assuming that Cade knew exactly what was inside this room and ensured we were fully equipped.

Alex rips the bag open and shows me the contents.

"Okay," I say calmly, dragging up all the things I've watched in movies for how people deal with disposing of dead bodies. "Let's wrap her up, strip the sheets, and then start cleaning everything."

"You're not fucking serious? You want me to touch her?"

"Would you rather deal with Kingsley's wrath when we fail to do this?"

If it's possible, Alex pales even more at my words.

"Exactly."

We work in silence as we do what we need to do. We've got the poor woman bundled up and we're almost done stripping the bed so we can take the sheets and burn them when Alex suddenly stops dead.

"What's wrong?" I ask

"Listen."

I do, and, for a few seconds, I don't hear anything. But then flashing lights illuminate the darkness outside the window. My heart jumps into my throat, pounding so fucking hard I can feel it in every inch of my body.

"T-there not here because of this, are they?"

I walk over to the window and peek out. What I see makes my blood run cold.

"They're pointing up here."

"We need to get the fuck out of this room, Bex." The panic in his tone doesn't make this situation any better.

"We can't. They're right out there."

"Bathroom window?"

"Fucking hell."

We storm through to the bathroom, taking in the fucking tiny window. We're on the second floor. If I'm lucky enough to even fit through it, then I've still got to deal with the fall.

"You go first, you're smaller than me."

"But—"

"You really want to choose now as a time to argue with me?"

"But that..." He points to the murder scene behind us.

"Fuck that. Not our problem."

"Fuck my life," Alex mutters, wrenching the window wider than it's meant to go and climbing through. "This is a really fucking bad idea."

"So is getting locked up. Now fucking jump."

He does, and everything goes silent.

I follow his lead, and, just as I jump into the thick bushes below, I hear the motel door get kicked in.

6

MIA

I hide out in Sasha's room for the entire evening. Mulligan, Cade's cook, makes us tacos and delivers them to her room. It's all very five-star, but nothing surprises me where the Electi are concerned.

"I'm glad you came," Sasha says as we clear the plates away.

"Me too."

"It's nice to have a girl to hang out with here."

"Can I ask you a question?"

"Sure."

"Why do you stay here sometimes but not others?"

"Home just isn't home anymore since Ashton, Brook and their mom moved in." She shrugs. "Brandon talked Cade into letting me have a room here. Officially, I don't live here. But unofficially, I sleep here more than my room at home."

"I'm sorry."

She gives me a weak smile. "It isn't your fault. Just another thing I have to accept without question."

"It must kill Brook, knowing you have a room here and she doesn't."

"Yep. Which is why I like to rub it into her face at every opportunity."

We share a chuckle. "I really don't like that girl," I say.

"Join the club."

"We should get matching t-shirts."

"Hashtag Brook is a bitch." Sasha grins. "We could sell them around school. I'm sure we'd make a fortune. It's getting late, I should probably give you a ride back to campus."

"Okay." I climb off her bed and wedge my feet in my sneakers. "We should make this a weekly thing."

"Sounds good to me."

"Are the guys still around, do you think?"

"Beats me. They could be anywhere, but as long as they're not annoying me, it's all good." Her lips curve with amusement. "Come on."

We leave her room and make our way downstairs. The house is steeped in silence, nothing but the chime of the grandfather clock opposite the foot of the stairs disturbing it. It's a relic but looks to be in perfect working order.

We've almost reached the front door when it flies open and Bexley appears, panting for breath.

"What happened?" Sasha asks.

"Ask Kingsley," he grits out, his sharp gaze going to mine.

"Is Al—"

"Hey." Alex steps inside too, as breathless and flushed as Bexley.

"What did they have you do?"

"You don't want to know." He holds Sasha's gaze until her lips press into a disapproving smile. "Cade left us. He fucking left us there to get caught."

"He doesn't play by anyone's rules but his own, but he won't allow you to get caught. The whole thing would have been a setup—you know that, right? Just one big game to the high and mighty Cade Kingsley."

Bexley's jaw pops as his teeth grind in frustration.

"What are you all talking about?" They aren't making any sense.

"Nothing." A hard expression slams down over Bexley's face.

"Fine, forget I asked," I clip out. "Will you give me a ride now?"

Sasha nods, glancing between me and Bexley. The air has turned thick between us.

"Let me just grab a snack." Her eyes drill into Alex's face and his head whips up.

"Say what?"

"A snack... you should help me."

"Sasha, I don't—"

But it's too late, she's already taken off toward the kitchen with Alex in tow.

"Real stealthy." Bexley's lips pull into a half-smile. "How are you?" He looks like he's about to step forward but immediately changes his mind, inching back instead.

"I'm okay. Where were you two just now?" They're both dressed all in black, like they're about to commit the heist of the century.

"Electi business."

"So that's how it's going to be now?"

He lets out a thin breath. "What other choice is there? You ended things, Mia... *you* did that. We're all just pawns in Kingsley's game of life, right?"

Silence falls over us again. There are so many things I want to say. But I can't. No words will change the fact that I'm Cade's prosapia. Unless I can find some leverage to get myself out of this mess, I am his. Just as Bexley is.

"Fuck, this is so fucked." Bexley runs a hand over his head and down the back of his neck. "All I can think about is kissing you, little mouse." He finally takes a step forward, close enough that I can feel the heat radiating off his body.

"You can't... don't." I put my hand up between us, barely touching him. It's enough to make him shudder, though. "It'll get easier," I whisper as the cracks in my heart splinter wider.

The longer we're apart, the longer we bury our unresolved feelings for one another, the easier it'll be.

At least, that's what I keep telling myself.

My heart breaks all over again as I step away from Bexley and wrap my arms around my waist.

"Mia?" His voice cracks, but I don't meet his intense stare. If I look at him, I'll break. And if I break, nothing good can come from that.

"Tell Sasha I'm waiting outside," I say, slipping around him and out the front door.

To my bittersweet relief, Bexley doesn't follow me.

THE NEXT DAY AT SCHOOL, my worst nightmare comes true. Cade is waiting outside my morning class to walk me to their secret dining room. And when he ushers me inside, I find Bexley, Alex... and Brook, all sitting there.

"What is this?" I ask, swallowing the ball of emotion stuck in my throat.

"The whole gang together." He chuckles. "Easton and Rexford are Electi now. They're going to be around a lot." Cade takes my hand and tugs gently, forcing me to stop. "Is that going to be a problem?"

"Not at all." The lie rolls off my tongue. "I was referring to Brook." My lips purse.

Amusement glints in Cade's eyes. "I know you two don't see eye to eye."

"Understatement of the year," I murmur. "She wants you. That's a problem."

"Hmm, I like it when you get all possessive, babe." Cade closes the small distance between us and brushes his hand along the side of my neck. "But I'm not hers, am I?"

He's testing me.

This is a test.

And I walked right into it.

Crap.

I feel them all watching. Feel their stares of curiosity and concern and jealousy. Cade wants me to prove my loyalty in front of them. He wants me to claim him.

"No, you're not," I say without missing a beat.

"Better prove it then." He smirks.

But I almost feel relieved that I figured it out.

Wrapping my arms around his broad shoulders, I lean up on my tiptoes and brush my lips over his. Once. Twice. A third time. I can't bring myself to *really* kiss him, but I know the second he bands his arm around my waist that he's going to make this into something more.

Cade plunges his tongue past my lips as he pulls my body into his. He likes this. Dominating me. Destroying me. I feel the evidence of his arousal pressed up against my stomach as he kisses me like he's trying to devour me.

"Yo, asshole," Ashton yells. "We're trying to eat."

"Maybe I'll eat you." He murmurs against my swollen lips. "Maybe I'll lay you out on the table and feast on your traitorous little pussy. I bet Easton would love that. I know Ash would. They'd want to touch you, Mia. They'd want to taste what's mine... but you wouldn't let them, would you, babe?" His fingers close around my throat as he breathes the dirty words into me. "I'd make you come so fucking hard you forgot Easton was ever inside you."

My legs quiver slightly as my body heats at his words. I should be repulsed. I *am* repulsed. But knowing that Bexley is watching us, knowing that Cade is out of his mind with jealousy because Bexley has had me and he hasn't... well, it does things to me. Dark, twisted things.

Shame washes over me.

One of his hands skates down my spine and cups the curve of my ass.

"Cade," I warn.

"This ass is mine, Mia. And one day, I'm going to—"

"Kingsley," Channing calls. "Put the poor girl down and let her eat."

Cade inhales a ragged breath, and for a second, I think he's going to go off at Channing. But he doesn't. Instead, he grabs my hand and tugs me over to the table. "Can't help it if my girl looks good enough to eat." He shoots the table a wicked grin.

Brook huffs something under her breath but doesn't make a scene.

"Here." Sasha pats the chair beside her, and I sit down.

"Thanks."

Are you okay? her eyes ask me, and I nod. I can't explain it, but I feel strong. I feel determined to see this thing through and take back my freedom.

But I have to play my part.

I have to make Cade believe I want him.

"So what do you think of our little setup here?" Cade asks Bexley and Alex, keeping one hand firmly on mine.

"It beats eating with the masses," Alex replies, helping himself to another fry. But not a regular fry. One of those rustic, triple cooked fries.

"Easton?"

A ripple goes through the air as Bexley glares at Cade. "I think I prefer eating elsewhere." He shoots up and looks at Alex, but he doesn't follow as he storms from the room.

"You made the right choice, Rexford," Cade says. "Easton can keep fighting, but it'll only make things harder than they need to be. Brook, why don't you make sure our boy is okay?"

"Sure thing." She dabs her blood red lips with a napkin before shooting me a smug smirk. "He's probably just a little tense. I'm sure I can find a way to help him relax."

Cade and Ashton chuckle. Brandon is too busy hoovering down his lunch to notice the tension. And Sasha and Channing both watch me with pity in their eyes.

"Where's Tim?" I ask, noticing his absence.

Cade immediately stiffens, and I file that nugget of information away for another time.

"He's dealing with Fawn," Ashton says.

"Dealing with Fawn? What the hell does that mean?"

"It means don't ask questions you might not like the answer to."

Silence befalls the table, and I don't push. Tim is a sore point. Or rather, Fawn is.

"So Rexford, you ready to party with us Electi style on Friday?"

"Hell yeah." Alex puffs out his chest, and I'm surprised how readily he's accepting all this.

"Right answer." Ashton claps him on the shoulder. "Maybe we'll make an Electi of you yet. What about you, Mia?" His eyes find mine across the table. "Are you ready to party Friday?"

"Ash," Cade warns.

"What? It's just a question. Now we're one big happy family, what could go wrong?"

"I'll need a new dress," I say.

"Sasha will take you shopping. Take your friend, too... Annabel, was it?"

"Oh, I'm not sure—"

"Take her." Cade squeezes my knee under the table. "She is your friend, isn't she?"

"Yeah, but—"

"So take her. You can have a girl's trip."

"Okay. I guess." I study him, trying to figure out his angle. Because I know Cade.

And he doesn't do anything without an ulterior motive.

7

BEXLEY

Our first week in the Electi house is bullshit. After we got back from the setup, Cade denied all knowledge of who might have called the cops, but his amused smirk said otherwise.

He doesn't want me here, that much is obvious, but he's going to need to try harder if he wants to get rid of me. The gauntlet has been laid down. I'll remain right here, under his feet, reminding him at every possible moment that I hold more power than he ever has for as long as it takes for me to get what I want.

Mia.

I don't care about tradition or rituals.

She's mine.

And one way or another, I'm going to find a way around all that prosapia bullshit. I'm going to release her from Kingsley's claws even if, in the end, she doesn't want me either.

My chest aches at the prospect of that being my reality after what happened with Brook. Hell, I deserve it, even if I had no clue what I was doing.

"You all set for tonight, Bexy?" Ashton asks, throwing his arm around my shoulders as we make our way to the parking lot after class on Friday.

Fuck knows where he appeared from, but he can fuck right off back there again. I might be able to tolerate some of the guys, but Kingsley and Moore are not them. If anything, I wonder if Ashton is worse than Cade. Just the thought is terrifying.

"No. But remind me, why exactly are you always hanging around like a lost sheep? You know your blood means fuck all, right?"

His lips thin in anger. "I'm as fucking important as you are."

"Only because Kingsley thinks so. You need to know that when all this is done and I've stolen his tarnished crown, you're going to be out on your ass where you belong."

"And that's exactly why Cade is going nowhere, Bexy."

"Stop calling me that."

He smirks, telling me that my words just fell on deaf ears. "You don't have the grit, the determination, the level of ruthlessness that Cade has to see this through. You're weak, Bexy. You let a fucking chick in here." He taps harshly at my head and then my chest. "And that was a fucking mistake, let alone the fact that Mia belongs to Cade." He tuts as we continue walking.

"Are you about done?"

"We're going to end you," he warns.

"If you think forcing me to fuck your whore of a sister is going to get me to back down, then you really need to think again." He has me up against the side of my car with his fist in my shirt in the flash of an eye.

"What the fuck did you call her?" he growls in my face.

"A fucking whore. The only cock around here that hasn't been inside her is yours, but I even wonder about that at times."

He cocks his arm back to hit me but not before his name is barked across the parking lot, and, like a good little puppy dog, he lets go of me.

"That's it, Ash. Be a good little boy for your master," I taunt.

"What's going on?" Cade barks, joining us in the parking lot.

"Just having a little fun with the new boy." Ashton smirks.

"Keep your fists in check, Moore." The friends stare at each other for a few minutes as some silent conversation passes between them.

I'm just about to turn my back on them and fuck off when Cade turns his evil eyes on me. "You ready for tonight?"

"No," I deadpan, ripping my driver's door open. "And if you even try anything, I'm going to fucking end you."

He holds his hands up in defense. "We're just gonna party, man. No ulterior motive."

I raise a brow at him. Like fuck do I believe that. Motherfucker is always up to something.

"Whatever. I'm not interested." Climbing into my car, I rev the engine and gun it out of the parking lot.

The house is a hive of activity when I walk through to the kitchen as Cade's staff get it ready for tonight's party. The kitchen counters are already lined with alcohol, and, after grabbing myself a soda from the fridge, I swipe a couple of bottles of vodka so I can have myself a little party for one while the rest of them do whatever the fuck it is they want to do down here.

Swinging the door open the second I get to it, I blow into my room, slamming it behind me, wishing like fuck the lock actually worked.

Part of me wants to get the hell in my car and disappear for the weekend, but the knowledge that I'd be leaving Mia here with the devil won't let me.

"DUDE, what the fuck are you doing hiding in here?" Alex crashes through my bedroom door a few hours later. "Pity party for one, really?" he asks, taking in the bottle of vodka in my hand.

"I'm not in the mood."

"Nuh-uh. I'm not having that. The party is fucking hopping."

I stare at him as he comes closer, taking in his blown pupils. "What the hell have they given you?"

"Nah, it's not like that. Sasha gave me some pills. Everything is fucking epic, man. I feel so good. You gotta come down. The girls are fucking insane."

"I don't want girls, Alex. I'm not fucking interested."

"Wellll then," he says, falling down onto my bed and grinning up at me, "you should come down and see Mia. She's wearing this little dre—"

"Enough," I bark, not needing any more visuals than I already have floating around in my head about what could be happening downstairs.

"Come on, Easton. Don't be so fucking boring."

I narrow my eyes at him. "What's going on with you?" He's even starting to sound like one of them.

"What?" he slurs. "I'm just enjoying this shitshow we landed ourselves in. What's the alternative? Be a miserable fuck like you?"

I stare at him, my jaw popping with frustration.

"Brook's looking for you."

I can't help but laugh. If he thinks that's going to get me down there, then he really has popped too many pills.

"Apparently," he says, leaning in as if he's got a secret, "she's looking for someone to distract Mia so she can get to Cade. He must be better than you, man. She doesn't seem to be begging for your cock." He bursts out laughing.

"You need to get a grip of yourself, Alex. Haven't they already pulled enough shit on us?"

"Why do you think I'm letting go, bro?" He shrugs. "I'm just enjoying myself."

"Yeah," I mutter, dumping my bottle on the nightstand and pushing from the bed. "A little too much, by the looks of it."

Dragging my shirt over my head, I dump it into the laundry basket before pulling on a clean one and shoving my feet into my sneakers. "What the fuck are you waiting for then?" I bark at Alex when I'm at the door with my fingers wrapped around the handle and he's still pissing around on my bed.

"Knew I'd get you to come and join the fun." He leaps up, swaying a little.

Fuck. He's as high as a kite.

"Whatever," I murmur, storming from my room.

As we get closer to the stairs, the music begins to get louder and the scent of weed and whatever else is being smoked down there gets stronger. I almost change my mind, but Alex stumbles on the top step and I end up damn near carrying him down to stop him from breaking his fucking neck.

"You need to lay off whatever it is you've had."

"Chill, Bexy," he slurs, slapping my chest. "S'all good, man."

My hackles rise immediately at his little nickname for me. "You been hanging out with Moore?"

"Yeah, so? It's not like you want to hang out anymore. You just sulk in your room."

Guilt washes through me. I've been so consumed with my own bullshit life this week that I've forgotten about him. I assumed that while I was hiding in my room, he was doing the same, not that he was making fast friends with those assholes.

"Rexford, my man," Brandon shouts, stumbling into the room. "I've got these two chicks in the study. One of them really wants to meet you." He nods at me, but he looks less than excited to discover that I've finally decided to join them.

Alex disappears a few seconds later, the promise of pussy apparently enough to make him forget me.

Standing in the middle of the chaos, I wonder what the hell happened to my life. Wondering at what point my best friend decided that if you can't beat them, join them, because he's turning into one of them faster than I can cope with.

I scan the crowd of people loitering in the hallway. Most are just chatting, but there are a few dancing and there's a couple bumping up against the old grandfather clock who are about five seconds from fucking in front of everyone in the room.

"Bexley," a sickly-sweet voice says from behind me, making my skin crawl.

I take off in the hope she might get distracted, but she chases after me, her killer heels clattering against the polished marble tiles as she goes.

"What do you want, Brook?"

She darts around me, forcing me to stop. Although I must admit that mowing her down does seem like a good option. "I've been looking for you," she purrs, batting her fake lashes at me.

"Great. Well, you found me. Now, do you mind?" I forcefully move her aside and march toward the kitchen. I need more alcohol now I'm down here.

"Mia and Cade are on the dancefloor." I hate that her words make my steps falter. "Yeah, grinding it all up against each other without a care in the world."

"That's their prerogative, I guess."

"And you're happy to let that happen?"

"What the fuck do you want me to do about it, Brook? She's been promised to him. That's it. Done."

"Oh, come on, Bexy. You're not very clever, are you?"

What is it with that fucking nickname all of a sudden? My teeth grind so hard I wonder if I'm about to crack one.

"I didn't have you down as someone who gives in so easily. Let's go and have some fun, show them what they're really missing." She winks at me and runs her hand down my arm.

"I don't play games, Brook," I growl.

"No? Seems to be that your entire life is one big game right now."

She's got that fucking right.

It's one big joke as well.

"You're a boring fuck when you're not tripping, you know that?"

I stare at her, my lips parting to argue, but quite frankly, she's got a point.

"Fuck it. Lead the way."

She guides me through the kitchen so I can grab a very strong drink before we head toward the dining room which has been turned into tonight's dancefloor. I spot Mia and Cade immediately, right in the middle of the large crowd, and my stomach turns over when I take in their closeness and just how tightly he's gripping onto her ass.

If he so much as hurts a hair on her head, I'll fucking kill him.

As if she can feel my stare, Mia turns, but not before Brook presses herself up against me and latches her lips onto my neck. I feel nothing. Absolutely nothing, apart from the pain of watching my girl dance with another guy.

Ripping her eyes from mine, I see a similar agony in her depths as she watches Brook run her hands down my chest and around to my ass.

"If you'd have agreed to my offer last week," she drawls, "then all of this might not have been necessary."

8

MIA

Cade grips my waist in a vise-like hold, grinding against my ass as I roll and pop my hips. I don't want to be here, dancing intimately with him, but if I'm going to get the answers I need, I have to play the game.

"Fuck, Mia," he rasps against the side of my neck, dragging his tongue along my salty skin. It's a billion degrees in the house—that or it's the liquor coursing through my veins. I almost accepted the pill Sasha tried to give me again, but I don't want to resort to drugs. Not if I don't have to.

"The things I want to do to you." One of Cade's hand splays on my stomach, brushing the sliver of skin on display thanks to the side panels cut out of the dress Sasha gave me to wear.

Bexley glares at me, but I don't meet his eyes again. It's too hard seeing him with Brook, remembering the two of them together.

Without warning, Cade spins me around and presses his head forcefully against mine. "Come upstairs with me," he says, his voice cracking with lust.

"It's your party," I chuckle, playing up how drunk I am. "You can't abandon your own party."

"I can do whatever the fuck I want, baby. I'm Cade fucking Kingsley. These idiots would eat my shit if I told them to."

My brows knit. "You're serious."

"As a heart attack." He smirks. "There isn't anything I couldn't make these fuckers do."

"That is... I don't even know what to say."

"That's power, Mia. And power feels fucking great." His pupils are blown, and it's then I realize that Cade might not just be drunk.

He's high too.

"What did you take?" I ask, surprised he's letting his guard down.

"Just a little G. It helps me relax. But it gets me real horny." He cups my ass again.

"Cade," I hiss. "Not here."

"So come upstairs with me. I've waited long enough."

"Channing needs you in the den." Sasha comes out of nowhere.

"I'm in the middle of something," Cade growls.

She shrugs. "He said it was urgent."

"Fuck, yeah, okay. But you..." he winds his hand into the hair at the nape of my neck and brings my face to his. "I want you in my bed tonight."

When I don't answer, his eyes narrow. "Watch her," he barks at Sasha before releasing me and stalking out of the room.

"You good?"

"Oh yeah, peachy." I flash her a dry smile before glancing over to where Bexley and Brook are still dancing.

"What the hell is he doing?"

"At a guess? Trying to make me jealous." I let out a resigned sigh.

"Is it working?"

"What do you think?" I grimace.

"If it makes you feel any better, I caught some slut on her knees for Channing in the den."

"No!"

She nods. "Fucker didn't even act surprised to see me."

"Maybe he wanted you to see..."

"Maybe. It doesn't matter. I'm going to find the hottest guy I can tonight and take him up to my room and make him help me forget all about Channing asshole Rexford. But first," she grabs my hand, "let's dance."

I follow her lead, and the two of us dance like we're just two girls at a party.

Not two girls who are captive in a twisted game.

The music pumps through my body. Sasha snakes her body around mine, positioning me right in front of Bexley. Brook is vying for his attention, but he doesn't take his eyes off me. Heat burns in his gaze as he watches my every move. It's sweet torture having him watch me so brazenly, knowing that he wants me but can't have me. Part of me enjoys that I'm teasing him, taunting him.

Brook notices that she no longer has his attention and storms off. Good riddance. Bexley sinks into the shadows, leaning up against the wall. But he doesn't take his eyes off me as Sasha and I continue dancing together. I can feel him undressing me with his eyes, his intimate stare an imitation of his lips on my skin. Heat pools in my stomach, my core throbbing with need.

I want him.

I want him so freaking much.

Even after he betrayed me with Brook, I can't help the way I feel.

But it's impossible.

I force myself to turn away from him, and when I finally glance back over my shoulder, he's gone.

CADE DOESN'T RESURFACE from the den. Sasha warned me not to go in there, but I can't resist. I want to know what the guy who claims to want me so badly does when I'm not around.

I'm hardly surprised to find him fucking a girl while she sucks Ashton's cock. They have her balanced over the back of a chair, her dress bunched around her hips as Cade pounds into her so hard it makes me wince.

"You shouldn't snoop," a voice from the shadow says. "You might not like what you find." Channing steps out of the darkness and hisses under his breath when he peeks into the room. He moves around me and closes the door, forcing me to take a step back. "He wouldn't want you to see that."

"Does it matter?"

"No, but it doesn't change the fact that he still wouldn't want you to see."

"I suppose I should feel disappointed or jealous… but I only feel relief," I confess.

"He knows he can't touch you yet. Not in the way he wants." Channing gives me a dark look. "Go back to the party, Mia."

"You're not like them, are you?"

"It's complicated."

"Even more complicated now Alex is an Electi? You don't have to be one of them now he's here. You and Sasha can—"

"Don't." The word rumbles in his chest. "You should go. And Mia?" I nod. "Try to stay out of trouble."

I go back to the other side of the house to find Sasha, but when I do, she's making out with some guy, practically dry humping him against the wall. With everyone distracted, I slip out of the party and upstairs. This part of the house is off-limits unless you're Electi or one of their guests staying here. The silence is deafening, my heart crashing in my chest as I kick off my shoes and scoop them up. My dress feels nonexistent now it's just me and this big, unforgiving house.

I make it to the first floor and glance down the hall to where Sasha's room is. But I didn't come up here to sleep, not yet. Instead, I tiptoe down the hall leading to Cade's room. But a voice stops me in my tracks.

"What are you doing, little mouse?"

My eyes flutter closed at the sound of Bexley's voice. "Go away, Bexley," I sigh.

"No can do, mouse. I live here now, remember."

I turn slowly to find his eyes hooded. "You're drunk," I observe, searching his face for signs that he's more than just drunk.

He takes a step forward, taking the air with him, and my breath catches in my throat.

"Bexley, don't do this. Not here. Not now."

But he doesn't heed my warning, backing me into one of the doors lining the long hall. Pressing his hand against the wood beside my head, he leans in and inhales. "You smell so fucking good."

"Don't." I tremble. He's too close. So close I can reach out and touch him, but I don't. I can't. I need to keep my wits about me where Bexley is concerned, especially if I'm going to make Cade believe I'm acquiescing.

"You were dancing with him." His warm, liquor-scented breath fans my face as Bexley reaches out and plucks a curl between his fingers.

"I'm with him."

He hisses, his expression murderous. "You're mine, mouse, or have you forgotten? Maybe you need reminding." He presses his knee between my thighs, grazing my center.

"Don't," I rasp.

"Don't what? Don't touch what's mine?"

"You're drunk."

"And you're so fucking beautiful. I can still remember running my hands over your body that night, how you felt choking my cock, the little moans you made... I can remember all of it."

"You fucked her," I snarl. "You fucked Brook and you just want me to forg—"

His hand flies out and grabs my throat, pinning me against the door. "I thought it was you. Only ever you."

"It doesn't change anything," I say with resignation.

"Did he touch you again? Did you give it up for him?"

Bexley's pupils are blown wide open, and I wonder if he's taken something too.

"No," I whisper.

"Thank fuck." His mouth crashes down on mine as he plunges his tongue past my lips. I can barely breathe with the intrusion. The shadows cloak us, but if someone came up here, they would get a front row seat. And that wouldn't end well for anyone.

"Bexley." I grip his shirt, pulling away. "We can't."

"Like hell we can't." He leans around me and turns the door handle. It flies open behind us and we stumble inside.

Bexley doesn't give me time to think, slamming me against the wall and attacking my mouth again. My body remembers this, remembers how easy it is to get lost in Bexley Easton and his expert kisses. His hands trail a dangerous path over my body, igniting a wildfire inside me.

"Fuck, Mia. I've missed you..." His hand slides along my neck and buries deep in my hair.

"We can't," I breathe. "We can't do this."

"Yes, we can. Just open up for me, mouse. Just—"

"No." I slam my hand against his chest and push hard. Bexley staggers back, confusion glittering in his eyes.

"What the fuck?" he grunts.

"I can't do this."

"Because you're his now?" He spits the words.

"Because I'm trying to figure out a way to survive this nightmare, and if Cade thinks we're still..." I swallow the words. "I'm going to find a way out of this, Bexley. So I need for you to stop."

I move to the door, but he snags my hand. "You can't go against him, Mia. It isn't safe... it isn't—"

My chin lifts slightly, and I look him right in the eyes as I say, "Try and stop me."

THE HOUSE IS quiet when I slip out of bed. Sasha never made it back to her room. She's probably in another one of the guest rooms with her friend from last night.

I pull a Gravestone U hoodie over my tank top and shorts and make my way downstairs. Mulligan is already in the kitchen, preparing breakfast. "Ah, good morning, Miss Thompson," he says. "Coffee?"

"Please." I perch at the breakfast counter on one of the stools. All evidence from the night before is gone, and I wonder what time the housekeeper starts her shift.

"Here you go." He slides a mug across the counter to me.

"Thank you." I add sugar and creamer, stirring it together. "Am I the first one up?"

"Mr. Rexford is out jogging, but it'll be a while until the rest surface."

"Channing?"

He nods, and I'm hardly surprised. Alex was out of it last night.

"I'm going to take this up to my room," I say. "Thanks again."

"Breakfast will be served at nine."

"Thanks, Mulligan." I climb off the stool and grab the coffee mug. It's still early, a little past seven-thirty. If Mulligan is right, I have time.

Checking the hall, I wait a second, and when I hear nothing, I slip into the part of the house I've yet to explore. All three of the doors are ajar, and I discover a small library and two smaller sitting rooms, but it's the door at the end of the hall that piques my interest. It's closed unlike the others, and when I try to open it, it won't budge.

I try again, more forcefully this time, only to realize it's locked.

My brows furrow. Why would only this door be locked? I try it again, willing it to open. Now it's off-limits, my mind fills with possibilities as to why it's locked. Obviously to keep people out. People like me. Which can mean only one thing.

Whoever locked it wants to keep the secrets it holds inside.

9

BEXLEY

The sound of raised voices stops me on my way to the kitchen the morning after the party. My head is pounding from the amount I drank after Mia walked away from me. I was already well on my way to drunk just from watching her dance with that fucker, but having her rejection playing on repeat in my head sent me straight to the bottom of the bottle of vodka that was still in my room.

I slow my steps, wincing as the sound of Cade's booming voice fills my ears. My fists curl at the possibility of it being Mia his anger is aimed at. Coming to a stop in the doorway, my chin drops when I find Cade and Channing squaring up to each other in the middle of the living room.

"For fuck's sake Cade, be reasonable," Channing begs.

I only just about manage to smother my laugh. Cade reasonable. That'll be the fucking day.

"I am. This is where you belong. You're one of us," Cade grits out.

"I'm not, though. You have Alex now."

"I don't give a fuck. This is where you belong," Cade repeats, the muscles in his shoulders pulling tight with frustration. "With us."

"What if it's not where I want to be?"

"What?" Cade bellows, getting right in Channing's face, his fists clenching as if he's about to take him out.

"I don't want to fucking be here, alright? This was never meant to be my life."

I stare at Channing as he confesses, and it's like the weight of the world is lifted from his shoulders. That relief only lasts a second though, because his back slams up against the wall while Cade's forearm presses against his throat.

They're nose to nose as Cade breathes in Channing's face. Channing's eyes are wide, but he doesn't look anywhere near as scared of Cade as most would in his position, I'm sure.

"You don't have a fucking choice," Cade growls.

"You don't fucking need me."

"Hey, how's it going?" I ask, walking into the room as if nothing is amiss.

Cade's anger only increases as his dark eyes turn on me. "What the fuck do you want, Easton?" he spits at me.

"Channing and I have something to do. Right, Rexford?"

Channing looks at me, his eyes narrowing in question before turning back to Cade. "Yeah, do you mind?" He tries to shove him off.

Cade's chin drops in shock. "Since when the fuck are you two friends?"

I panic, fighting to scramble for an answer, but Channing is faster.

"We're just going for a run together," he says. "Don't get your panties in a twist."

Cade looks over at me, his eyes dropping to my gym shorts and sneakers. The last thing I want to do right now is go for a fucking run, but something tells me Channing needs an out, and let's be honest, I'm not one to pass up an opportunity to piss Cade off, hangover or no hangover.

With a growl, Cade releases Channing and marches into the middle of the room. "We're not done talking about this, Rexford."

"We've got a meeting with Q in the morning. How about we continue then?"

Cade pauses with his hand in his hair and spins toward us. "You want to talk to Q about this?"

"Yeah," Channing states.

"You actually want out?" Cade's eyes bore into Channing, disbelief filling them as if he really can't understand why everyone doesn't want this life.

"This bullshit doesn't run in all our blood, Kingsley," Channing scoffs before marching past me.

Not wanting to get stuck with Cade, I hightail it after him and out the front door. I have no idea if he was planning on going for a run, but he seems to be going anyway.

"Channing, wait," I call when he's already halfway down the driveway.

"You didn't need to do that," he mutters when I catch up with him and he begins walking again.

"I know."

Silence falls between us as we get to the end of the driveway, but before we pass through the gates, Channing takes a left and we walk along the perimeter edge.

"You really want out?"

"Don't you?"

"I never wanted in in the first place."

"I'm not the Rexford heir now Alex is here. They can let me go."

"You think it'll be that easy?"

He shrugs. "Probably not, but I want to try. I'll keep all their bullshit secrets, I just..." He trails off.

"You just?" I encourage.

Ever since he came and got us last weekend to ensure we didn't miss our own initiation ceremony, I've started to question exactly whose side Channing is actually on. This is just another thing that points toward the fact that he's not on Cade's.

"I can't have what I want while I'm part of this shit."

"What the fuck does—" Realization dawns. "You want Sasha." It's not a question. It doesn't need to be. I've seen the way he looks at her. The way he tries to protect her. "But Electi heirs aren't allowed to be with Electi siblings."

He blows out a long breath, neither confirming nor denying my assumptions, and remains silent as we approach the lake.

Fuck. That first night here with Mia feels like a lifetime ago now. Everything was so simple then. I was just a guy embarking on college and trying to figure out the rest of my life. Now, here I am, part of those I tried to stay away from and branded like fucking cattle for life.

Hadley was right when she compared this to a life sentence. But much like a life sentence, I'm starting to wonder if none of us—even Channing—will ever be able to get out of it.

We come to a stop at the water's edge and he glances over at me. "You noticed that, huh?"

His entire body sags in defeat before he drops to the ground, pulling his knees up to his chest and wrapping his arms around them. "Brandon and I have been friends forever. I used to think she was this annoying little brat that would never leave us alone. But..." He sighs. "She grew on me. Brandon and I went to summer camp one year, and when we came back and she..." He chuckles to himself as he remembers. "She was beautiful. She ran to Brandon and wrapped her arms around his shoulders, and I wanted it to be me. But all she did was tilt her chin in greeting, turn her back on me and usher him into the house. She ruined me from that moment on."

"How old were you?"

"Fourteen."

I nod in understanding. I was about the same age when I first looked at Remi like that. When I suddenly realized she wasn't just my annoying best friend who'd make me brush her hair and play with her doll, but she was turning into a beautiful young woman.

"None of it matters. We can't be together."

"What does Sasha say about all this?"

"If we lived different lives, things would be different. But we don't, so what's the point in even dreaming?"

"But if Cade lets you out..."

He scoffs. "That's not going to happen. You heard him. He's on his own little mission, and apparently that requires both me and Alex."

"What's his game?"

"Fuck if I know. I don't even think Ashton is aware of the workings of Cade Kingsley's mind. We're all just along for the ride in this unknown game he's playing.

"It's not meant to be like this. Sure, Q has always been a little corrupt. With any group of men with more power and money than sense, things are bound to get a little out of control. But times were changing. The archaic traditions were being forgotten in favor of more modern ideas, but I don't think Cade wants that. I think in his mind it means losing control. He wants the heritage, the traditions, the power. The shit he pulled with you and Alex. Fuck, none of us had it that bad."

"You didn't do the vault?"

He laughs. "Oh yeah, we did that. And Caedes. But it wasn't like what you went through. Q set out tasks, not Cade."

"You really going to bring this up at tomorrow's meeting?"

"Yeah."

"Do you think they'll overrule Cade?"

"They might. It's got to be worth a try, right?"

I think of Mia and all the things I'd be willing to do to protect her, to be able to make her mine. "Yeah, it is. And for what it's worth, I've got your back, man."

He looks at me, a silent agreement passing between us before he nods and looks back out at the lake. "That shit Cade pulled on you two the other night was bullshit," he eventually says after the long, silent minutes.

"So, it was him?"

"You thought it was someone else?" He cocks a brow at me. "When I tell you to watch your back, Bex, I really fucking mean it. He's gunning for you. The best way for both you and Mia to get through this is to do what you're told. He'll hang himself eventually."

"And if he doesn't?"

"Let's just assume he will. I'm not sure I like the alternative."

THE SECOND I descend the stairs the next morning, all eyes are on me.

Cade and his minions, and even Alex, are standing at the bottom of the stairs, dressed in head to toe black ready for our meeting with Quinctus, whereas I've just rocked up in jeans and a white shirt.

"Someone didn't get the memo about the dress code," Ashton remarks around an amused smirk.

"Like you actually have an invite to this bullshit," I retort, knowing full well he doesn't.

"Fuck you, Easton."

"Get changed. We need to leave."

My eyes find Cade standing front and center, exactly where he likes to be. "No."

His eyes widen in shock before his lips twist in anger. It must be weird, not having me immediately fall at his feet.

"I go like this, or I don't go." Lifting my hand, I brush my hair from my eyes and walk around them, out to the cars.

I can't help but laugh when I hear footfalls behind me. I have no idea if he's given approval or someone has decided that they can't be dealing with Cade's toddler tantrum right now.

Shooting a look over my shoulder, I find Alex and Channing following me with smirks playing on their lips. "You two want a ride?"

"Sure thing."

Alex pulls open my passenger door and drops down before Channing does the same to the backdoor.

"Yo, Kingsley. Might want to move. You don't want to be late." Before he responds, I climb into my car and jam my key in the ignition.

Revving the engine, I gun it out of the driveway, ensuring I shoot gravel out behind me in the hope it might hit him as he emerges from the house.

"Okay, that was fucking epic," Alex laughs in the passenger seat.

Ignoring him, I look in the mirror at Channing. "You ready for this?"

He cracks his neck as if he's about to step into the ring with Cade. "They can only say no, right?"

"What's going on?" Alex asks.

"You'll find out." I wink at him, knowing it'll drive him crazy.

The monthly Q meetings are held in the old church where we were brought the night our initiation started. Only, the meeting rooms are around the back of the building.

As predicted, we arrive before Cade, and I have no interest in waiting for the motherfucker. Hopping from the car, I waste no time in walking inside and allowing Channing to direct us to the room we need.

"It's been a while since I was here," he mutters as we make our way down the long hallway.

"I thought these meetings were monthly?"

"They are, but it's usually only Kingsley that gets the royal invite."

"So why are we all here?"

"I guess to welcome you two, but Q can be as unpredictable as Cade at times, so your guess is as good as mine."

10

MIA

Sasha finds me sitting out on the terrace, drinking my second coffee of the morning.

"They just left?" she asks me.

"Yeah."

After discovering the locked room yesterday, I'd taken a quick shower then gone to join everyone for breakfast. But Cade and Channing's raised voices had startled me, so I doubled back to her room and we'd stayed there most of the day, eating our body weight in Mulligan's cookies and watching movies. Sasha had been quiet. Too quiet. But I hadn't wanted to push her.

I hadn't wanted to stay another night in the Electi house, but when she asked, I couldn't refuse.

"I have something to tell you… but it's kind of a big deal." Sasha's eyes dart around me.

"Is it about the guy you were with all night after the party?" My brow arches. "Who was he, anyway?"

"Channing," she breathes. "I was with Channing."

"What?"

She nods, a mix of lust and confusion swirling in her eyes. "He practically dragged me off Rhett and to his room. I wanted to tell you yesterday, I just didn't know how…"

"What happened?"

"What do you think? We painted each other's nails and talked." A faint smirk traces her lips and I roll my eyes. "It was amazing. He was... oh my God, I've never come so hard before. It was like he didn't care about anything but touching me..."

"I'm happy for you, I am. But what about Cade and your brother?"

"Why do you think he told Cade he wants out?"

"Oh my God, he's leaving... for you."

She nods again, a small smile tugging at her lips. "It's crazy, right? I told him it won't work, that Cade will never let him walk away, but he wants out, Mia. He chose me over all this."

"Do you really think they'll let him walk away?"

Concern pinches her brows. "He isn't the Rexford heir. Alex is. It makes no sense for him to remain Electi."

"But he knows things, Sash... he's seen things..."

"It'll be okay. It has to be." Hope flickers across her face, but it's snuffed out as her expression falls. "I love him, Mia. I'm in love with him." Tears spring from her eyes.

"Shh." I reach over and grab her hand. "I'm sure he'll figure it out. Maybe he can be like Ashton." He isn't true Electi. The same rules don't apply to him the way they do the rest of them. "I'm sure Brandon will understand," I add.

Sasha settles, draining the rest of her coffee. "What a pair we are, both lusting after guys we can't have."

"Yeah." I swallow the ball of emotion lodged in my throat.

"You did good at the party," she adds. "You almost had me convinced."

I frown, and Sasha chuckles. "You're learning to play the game."

"Isn't that what I need to do?"

"It is. Just be careful, Mia. I don't know what you're up to but—"

"You don't need to worry about me," I say. "I'm okay."

I think back to Bexley pulling me into his room Friday night. It would have been so easy to give in to him, to my feelings for him. But I won't be so reckless again.

"What does Cade's mom think about all this?"

"Melanie Kingsley? She's still the grieving wife."

"But didn't Gregory Kingsley die years ago?"

"Yeah, but she never got over it. Spends her days over at the Kingsley Estate off her face on a cocktail of Xanax and vodka. Why do you ask?"

"Just trying to understand Cade, I guess."

She snorts. "Don't try to find reasons where there are none. Cade is a misogynistic, power hungry, depraved asshole who thrives on using people and playing games. He's sick, Mia."

"Yeah, but what does he want?"

It's the question I've been asking myself a lot. He's on a power trip, there's no doubting that. But he's still human, driven by something. He wants to see Bexley fail, to give in. But I still don't know where I fit into all of this. I was no one to him until my name was pulled from the calix.

"Where is your head right now?" Sasha eyes me with mild curiosity, but it's the concern in her expression that makes my stomach sink.

"I'm just trying to... I don't know. I just can't willingly accept that this is how it has to be."

The more I think about it, the more things don't add up.

"I know it sucks. Trust me, I know." She flashes me an apologetic smile. "But you're his prosapia. Once the Coglio takes place... you'll be his fiancée. There's no going back on that."

Like she needs to remind me.

"What exactly happens at the Coglio?" My voice cracks, betraying my nerves. It's easier to ignore what the future will bring than to overthink any of it.

"There's a dinner at Gravestone Hall. I guess you could say it's like an engagement party. And then you and Cade will... you know."

"Sex." The word is like ash on my tongue.

"Yeah."

"It's always a full moon. You know how Q likes its moon rituals." She rolls her eyes.

"It's such bullshit," I hiss. "I saw Cade at the party, fucking some girl."

"Babe, he's a manwhore of epic proportions. This whole town reeks of double standards. Gravestone is a man's world, and we're just along for the ride."

"Awful pun." I grimace. But then we share a long look and burst into laughter.

"That's the spirit, Mia. You can't overthink this stuff, it'll drive you insane."

Just then, we hear the rumble of engines.

"Looks like they're home."

"They haven't been gone long." I stand, nervous energy vibrating inside me.

All the blood has drained from Sasha's face as she sits frozen in the chair.

"It'll be okay," I say. "Whatever happens, you have me."

"It'll be fine." She shakes her head a little, snapping out of the trance she was in. "I'm sure it's all fine."

THE SECOND THE guys enter the kitchen, it's apparent that everything is *not* fine. Channing looks as pale as Sasha and refuses to meet her eyes.

Bexley, on the other hand, stares brazenly at me, willing me to look at him.

I don't.

Instead, I walk straight over to Cade and burrow into his side. "How did it go?"

"Like every other meeting with Q," he says coolly, dropping a kiss on my head. "Although Channing has some news."

A ripple goes through the room, and Channing rakes a hand through his hair. He inhales a long breath and then exhales a long sigh. "Q thinks it's better for me to stay Electi. Since Bexley and Alex are both so new to our ways, Phillip wants me around. My Eligere will be next summer." His defeated gaze finally flicks to Sasha, who has tears brimming in her eyes.

"That's... great," she chokes out. "Excuse me, I need to take a shower." Sasha all but runs from the kitchen.

"What's her problem?" Brandon scoffs.

"Dude," Ashton says. "You know she has a crush on Channing."

"Nah, she's over that shit, right, Chan?"

"Fuck if I know." He folds his arms over his chest and shrugs. His face is a stone mask. Cold and impenetrable. Our eyes lock, and I narrow mine, but he gives nothing away.

"It doesn't matter," Cade snaps. "She knows the rules. She'd be a fucking idiot to break them." The verbal warning is for Sasha, but Cade stares down Channing and I get the feeling he knows something. Which wouldn't surprise me; Cade seems to know everything.

"I should go and check on her," I say, untangling myself from Cade's arm. But he tightens his grip and bends down, kissing me hard.

I inhale a shuddering breath that could be mistaken for lust.

It isn't.

"Tell her we're having a pool party. Nothing crazy. But I expect both of you to be there."

"Okay." I smile. "We'll be there." As I turn to walk away, Cade slaps my ass, making me yelp. Male laughter rings out behind me, but I don't rise to it, keeping my head held high as I walk from the kitchen, past Brandon and Alex... and Bexley.

His jaw clenches as he watches me, tracking my every move.

"Mia." My name forms silently on his lips, but I don't respond.

I can't.

No matter how much the tether between us pulls taut.

The second I'm clear of the kitchen, I release a shaky breath and hurry to Sasha's room. My heart aches for her as I step inside and find her sobbing into her pillow.

"I should have known," she said. "I should have known it was all a lie."

"I'm so sorry." I join her on the bed, running my hand down her arm. "For what it's worth, he looked as devastated as you."

"It doesn't matter. I get it now. We're never going to be free from this life... I was fooling myself into believing it could be different. That me and Channing could—" An ugly sob tears from her lungs, and she buries her face in me.

"Shh, babe. It'll be okay."

"It hurts," she cries. "It hurts so much, Mia."

"I wish I could make it better."

"You can..." Her head whips up, her face a red puffy mess. "My tin—"

"Sasha, I'm not sure that's a good idea. There's a pool party. Cade wants us there."

"I can't go, not like this. I need something to take off the edge."

"Fine." I get up and go to her nightstand.

"The top drawer," she instructs, and I pull it open. The tin is buried under a magazine.

"I thought Channing took your stash."

"I always have an emergency supply hidden. I don't get high because I like it, Mia. I get high because sometimes it's the only way I can—" Her body trembles as she smothers another shudder.

I understand now.

Sasha has lived this life for years. Part of the Electi's inner circle but not truly one of them. She won't ever be free to choose who she loves or who she marries.

Her life is not her own.

I've been a part of this fuckery for mere weeks. Sasha has been part of it her entire life. It isn't any wonder she self-medicates.

I watch as she takes the tin from me and flips the lid, revealing small baggies of various pills. "I hate them," she says, so defeated I can feel her despair. She pops two pills on her tongue and doesn't even bother washing them down with water.

"Sometimes," she whispers as she lies back on the bed, "I think death would be better than this life. But I'm not brave enough to do it."

Her words hit me like a wrecking ball. I share her despair, share the soul-crushing pain that bleeds from her right now, but never once have I contemplated death.

I want to fight. I want to find a way out of this mess.

But what if she's right...

What if there is no way out?

What then?

11

BEXLEY

I watch Mia leave the kitchen and then glance at Channing. He looks like he's thirty seconds away from losing his shit.

"Come on, man. Let's hit the gym," I say, slamming my hand down on his shoulder and pushing him forward.

His body is rigid as he stares at Cade, the muscle in his neck pulsating.

"What?" Cade asks innocently, which we all know is fucking bullshit. Something tells me that Cade fucking Kingsley was born corrupt, and it's only gotten worse with every day that has passed. "If you're really lucky, you'll get a girl as hot as Mia as your prosapia."

I fight the urge not to react to his words, but with every barb he shoots my way, the harder it gets.

"Let's go." I push Channing forward, turning my back on Cade and his bullshit.

"The girls will be here in an hour, and they'll expect to be entertained," he calls after us.

"I'm sure you're more than capable, Kingsley," I shoot over my shoulder before heading toward the stairs to the basement.

The house sits on a hill, so one wall of the basement is a solid sheet of glass that allows us to look out over the pool beyond.

"This is bullshit," Channing spits out once the door slams behind us.

"I'm sorry, man. You kinda expected it though, right?"

"I guess." He falls down onto the weight bench and drops his head into his hands. "I fucking promised her, though. Did you see the look on her face?"

I nod despite the fact that he's not looking at me. But he really doesn't need me to confirm how devastated Sasha looked when Cade announced his news.

"I don't want anyone else," he mutters.

"Fucking know how that feels."

I'm hardly dressed to work out, but I'm not going back upstairs now and risking bumping into Kingsley. So I make do with how I am, dragging my shirt over my head and dropping it on the bench along with my cell and wallet, before stepping onto the treadmill.

The garden and pool are currently empty—well, aside from a few of Cade's staff arranging everything for his impromptu party.

It's such bullshit.

All of it.

I up the speed until the only thing I can focus on is keeping up with the belt. Music leaks through the inbuilt speakers, and when I look over my shoulder, I find Channing dropping his cell down and lying back on the bench, ready to press some weights.

I want to help, but I have no fucking idea how.

He's in just as hopeless a position as me and Mia.

Love conquers all. What bullshit.

I run until my muscles burn and sweat drips down my body. At some point, Channing climbed on the treadmill beside me and we've been running in sync for at least thirty minutes when two people walk in front of the windows and our pace falters.

"Motherfucker," he grunts, his eyes locked on Sasha.

And fuck if I can't see his issue. The bathing suit she's wearing is almost nonexistent. Not that I've paid all that much attention, seeing as Mia is walking beside her, although her body is covered in a light floral dress thing.

My fist curl, hating that despite the fact that she's tried to cover up, she's showing off way too much fucking skin for these assholes to eat up.

As if they can feel our heated stares, they both turn toward the window. Sasha is the first to find us. Her movement stops as she grabs Mia's forearm. She says something, but I can't read what it is as Mia's eyes land on mine.

Tension crackles around us despite the glass that separates us.

"Fucking hell," I mutter.

"We gotta fucking fix this." Channing slams his hand down on the stop button and his movements slow.

I do the same and glance over at him, watching him eat up his girl. His chin drops in shock, and I turn back to the window in time to see Sasha run her hand seductively down her body.

A loud growl rumbles up Channing's throat at her little display. "She's fucking taking shit again."

"Can you blame her?" I mutter, thinking how much I could use some of that shit right now. Anything to make this easier.

After a second, Channing rips his eyes from his girl and marches out of the room, slamming the door closed behind him as he goes. Disappointment washes over Sasha's face as Mia wraps her arm around her shoulders and guides her over to the loungers.

I stand there watching them, knowing full well that Mia is aware of my attention, until Cade, Ashton, and Brandon emerge, wearing black boardshorts. Ashton and Brandon immediately cannonball into the pool, sending water all over the girls. Cade uses their surprise to his advantage and wraps his arms around Mia's waist, pulling her back into his body. He drops his lips and whispers something in her ear.

Anger surges through me, pulling my muscles tight as I imagine just how she feels, how she used to shudder when we connected.

Cade buries his nose in her hair, and I inhale as if it's me.

"Motherfucker."

As if she heard me, Mia turns my way. Our eyes hold for a beat, but I can't read anything in hers, while I'm sure my anger is more than obvious in mine. She's either learning to lock down how she really feels, or she really means it when she tells me that we're over.

Either way, it's fucked up.

Shaking my head at her when Cade's fingers touch her jaw and encourage her to twist so he can kiss her, I turn my back on them and follow Channing's lead. I want to stay hidden, to refuse to attend his fucking party, but I know the longer I stay in my room the more chance I've got of being dragged out of here and made to do something I really don't want to do.

The music is now pumping through my window, and the sound of laughter and water splashing can clearly be heard, but despite how much fun they might be having, there's not a single part of me that wants to join them.

I stare at myself in the mirror before I bite the bullet and go down there. My eyes lock on the crest burned into my chest. The sight of it makes my stomach churn. I fucking hate it. It's just a permanent reminder of the life I don't want but am bound to.

Sucking in a deep breath, I rip my door open. At least if I'm down there I can somewhat protect Mia. I swipe a bottle of vodka from the kitchen as I pass through before claiming the lounger between Alex and Channing.

Almost all the girls are in the pool, flicking their hair over their shoulders and pushing their bikini-clad chests out as if it's meant to entice me. The old me would have lapped that shit up. He'd have been right in the middle, much like Ashton and Brandon are right now, taking everything they were offering.

But I'm no longer him, and the only girl I see is the one on the other side of the pool, sitting astride Cade.

Her in that position drags up images I really don't need. Scrubbing my hand down my face, I try to force them out and focus my attention elsewhere.

Sasha is sitting beside the two of them, looking about as miserable as I feel. She's sucking on a straw, quickly swallowing down whatever cocktail she has, and when I look to the table beside her, I find it full of empty glasses. She's going to regret this in the morning.

Mind you, as I twist the cap of the bottle in my hand and lift it to my lips, so might I.

As the day drags on, the drinks get stronger and the party becomes wilder. We've already been forced to witness Ashton fuck some girl in the pool, one of the many reasons I'm refusing to dive into the thing. He's now got a different girl up against the side of the house. That guy has no fucking shame.

I have no idea who all the girls are. Aside from Brook, I don't think I've ever seen most of them before. But clearly, they all know who I am, and they're more than willing to give me whatever I want.

Not fucking interested.

Watching Sasha as she gets up and stumbles away from her lounger, I sit forward.

"She's fucking wasted," Channing points out, although it's not necessary. "If any fucker touches her..." he growls.

I look to Mia, and my heart drops into my stomach. Cade has her backed up against the side of the pool. His lips are attached to her neck, and she's got her head thrown back in pleasure. Fuck knows what he's doing under the water, and frankly, I don't want to know.

"I'll go." I nod toward where Sasha is trying to get through the door and into the house and take off.

I wrap my hand around her waist when I get to her and she startles. "Sorry, wrong Electi," I say sadly. "You look like you could use some help though."

She twists to stare into my eyes. Her pupils are blown, and I crave the emptiness she's currently experiencing. Although, when she speaks, I wonder if she's actually been able to forget anything with her high.

"You know."

"Yeah, Sash. Come on, before you faceplant on the floor."

"I need... I need my room."

"Okay." Sweeping her up in my arms, I carry her up the stairs, my own legs feeling a little weak from all the vodka.

The second I put her back on her feet, she rushes to her nightstand. My brows pull together as I watch her. I was kinda expecting her to go to the bathroom.

"Don't tell him," she barks the second my eyes land on a small tin in her hands.

Walking over, I take in the contents. My mouth waters and my body aches for the high. "Make it worth my while." My eyes hold hers for a beat before she looks down, plucks two little white pills from the tin, and passes them over.

I don't bother asking her what they are as I throw them back. Right now, I don't give a shit. I just need... I need it all to go away.

She follows my action with two pills of her own before walking over to the window and staring down at the pool below. "I hate my life," she mutters.

We can't see Channing from here, but I've got a full view of the couple I don't need to watch. Only this time, it's not just the two of them. There's a topless brunette with her hands in Cade's hair. His hands are on her tits but his mouth is still on Mia's.

"Motherfucker," I growl.

"That's nothing. He's high. It makes him worse."

"He can't... I need..." Anger confuses my thoughts.

"No, you can't. You need to let her deal with this. You've got to trust that she knows what she's doing."

"How can she deal with that cunt?"

Sasha shrugs, and it does fuck all to help. "You just have to. You can't fight this for her. You've got enough on your plate now you're one of them."

"Great." We both step away from the window. Sasha drops to the edge of her bed, and I fall into the chair at her vanity unit. "For what it's worth, I'm sorry about Channing."

"I never should have gotten my hopes up. I should have known they'd never let him go."

"Don't lose faith. We can't, or all of this will be for nothing."

Sasha glances up at me, amusement dancing in her eyes. "You're not what I expected," she admits.

"Is that a good thing?"

"Yeah, it is. So, didn't fancy a taste of Brook today?" Her smirk tells me that she's joking, but the pain her words cause is still like a knife to the heart.

"No. The only good thing about that night is that the images I have are of Mia."

"That's really kinda fucked up."

I scoff. I don't need to be told.

There's a commotion outside, but neither of us stand to look. Sasha probably feels the same way I do and would rather not know. Channing's down there—I know Mia is safe. Alex too, although he's been off his head for a few hours now already.

"Channing's not one of them, you know?" Sasha says after long, silent minutes. "Brandon isn't really either. He's just easily led."

"What are you trying to say?" I ask.

"Things can change, Bex. Cade can be overruled."

"How?"

She shrugs. "I don't know the details. I'm a woman. I'm not trusted with the inner workings of Q. But your blood is stronger. You deserve his title as king. You just need to figure out a way to take it."

"Helpful, thanks," I mutter, scrubbing my hand over my jaw.

Footsteps thunder up the stairs outside the room before the door flies open.

"What the fuck?" I bark the second Channing ushers Mia into the room. Her cheek is glowing red. "Did that cunt hit you?" I ask, immediately on my feet and in front of her.

"It's nothing." She tries to turn her head to the side to hide the mark, but I'm not having any of it.

Reaching out, I turn her back to me. "Look at me, mouse," I demand, and after two seconds, she lifts her hazel eyes to mine. They're full of tears, but they're also dark with anger.

"I'm going to fucking kill him," I seethe.

"H-he's gone into the den with Ash and a handful of girls. He's... busy."

I take a step toward her, tucking a lock of hair behind her ear. "Tell me he didn't hit you." Because if he did... White hot fury licks up my spine.

I'll kill him.

I'll fucking kill him.

But then she splutters out, "H-he didn't."

"Fuck, little mouse." I drop my forehead to hers and stare into her eyes. "I need you," I admit.

"Bex, I—" I don't wait to hear what she might have to say. I slam my lips down on hers, pushing her back against the wall. She gasps in shock, giving me the opening I need. I plunge my tongue into her mouth as I lift her, her legs immediately wrapping around my waist.

I'm vaguely aware of voices behind me, but I'm too lost in my girl to care. My hands are everywhere, reminding myself of how she feels.

"Bexley," she moans when I drop my lips to her neck, shooting a look at the other couple in the room.

Channing is between Sasha's legs, his mouth attached to her now exposed chest. Heat surges through me as I turn my attention back to my girl. Slipping my hand around her ass, I tuck my fingers under the fabric of her bikini bottoms and find her slick pussy.

"Oh God, Bexley," she moans, and everything else is forgotten.

12

MIA

Bexley's fingers feel so good sliding through my wetness that I rock against his hand, desperate for more.

"Greedy little mouse," he taunts, claiming my mouth with dirty wet kisses.

The few cocktails I drank out by the pool make my head spin, but it's Bexley's touch that makes my blood boil.

Moans sound from deep inside the room, and I twist my head to find Channing on his knees, his head buried in between Sasha's legs as she rides his face. Liquid lust shoots through me as I watch my friend moan and writhe for the guy she loves.

But then Bexley pushes two fingers inside me, and all thoughts of Sasha and Channing melt away as my eyes lock on his.

"Tell me you don't feel this," he grits out. "Tell me you don't feel it, Mia."

"I feel it."

But it doesn't change anything, and this is too risky.

"Bexley." My fingers claw at his chest. "Stop, we have to stop. Cade is—"

"That fucker is downstairs with some slut bouncing on his dick. He doesn't deserve you, little mouse." He strokes my cheek, pressing me further against the wall as his fingers rub my pussy, making me shudder.

"Don't you want to get back at him? Just a little—"

My mouth slams down on Bexley's as I kiss him with all the frustration and anger I feel swirling inside me. It's like a storm, violent and unstoppable, as it tears through me. Our teeth clash, our tongues fighting for dominance as I ride his hand.

"Fuck yeah, Mia..." he rasps, adding another finger and stretching me so much it stings. But I revel in the pain. My arm loops around his neck, holding on for dear life as he keeps working me with his fingers, rolling his thumb expertly over my clit, making me moan.

"Fuck, that's hot," Channing groans, and heat creeps into my cheeks. "Maybe we should—"

"Don't be shy now, mouse." Bexley smirks, leaning in to lick his tongue along the curve of my neck. He sucks the skin there but not enough to leave a mark. I peek over at Sasha and Channing again, and he's on top of her now, fucking her. Loving her.

I want that.

God, I want that.

"Fuck me," I breathe. "Make me forget."

Bexley's head whips up, his eyes wide with surprise. "Yeah?"

"Yeah." I nod. "But not here. Not like this." He glances around quickly and hisses under his breath. Sasha and Channing are completely lost in each other now.

Bexley bands his hand around my back and carries me into Sasha's bathroom, kicking the door shut behind us. He pushes me up against the wall on the other side of the room and attacks my mouth again.

We kiss like we're at war, trying to get the other to submit. He winds his hand into my hair and yanks my face away from his.

"Bex," I whisper, "please."

His fingers sink inside me again, curling deep and hitting my g-spot. I shatter apart unexpectedly, crying his name.

"I'm so fucking hard." His voice cracks with lust. "If I don't get inside you soon, I'm gonna explode."

Bexley carries me to the marbled counter and sits me on the edge. My hands run over his impressive abs, reveling in the way his muscles contract under my touch. But it's when I ghost fingers over the barely healed brand that he shudders.

He snags my wrist, suspending my hand there. "This... it doesn't change anything, Mia. Not a damn thing." Bexley crowds me, touching his head to mine. "You own me, mouse. Always will."

His words break something inside me, and tears prick my eyes. "I need you," I breathe. "Please."

Bexley works his shorts down his hips and frees his cock, slamming it into my pussy in one smooth stroke. "Fuuuuck," he drawls, kissing the corner of my mouth. I can hardly breathe, overwhelmed by how good he feels inside me.

"It's you, Mia. Only ever you." His lips brush my ear, and he pulls out slowly and then slams back inside.

"God," I cry, "it feels... oh God." The air leaves my lungs as Bexley drives into me, hard and fast. His lips brand my skin, licking and kissing and sucking as he fucks me like he might never get to do it again.

Our moans rise above the sounds of skin slapping against skin. Bexley grabs my ass and changes his angle slightly, driving deeper, hitting my cervix until pain blends with pleasure, making me drown in sensation.

"Fuck, Mia, you feel so fucking good..."

"Don't stop," I beg. "Don't ever stop."

His hand wraps around my throat tenderly, pinning me against the wall as he licks my mouth, slowing his pace and grinding into me. "I want you to come, Mia. Come all over my cock, mouse. Give it to me. Only me. Only ever me."

An intense wave crests inside, ripping through me as I shatter around him, crying out his name.

"Fuck, Mia.... fuuuuuck," he groans, spilling inside of me.

Our chests heave, our ragged breaths filling the room. Bexley's eyes are heavy, his pupils blown with desire.

"Tell me what happened?" His thumb brushes the tender spot over my cheek.

"It doesn't matter."

"Yes, it fucking does." His voice is a rough growl.

"It was an accident. One of Cade's sluts clipped me with her elbow. Forget about it."

I sure wanted to.

"One day, Mia. One day I'm going to end that motherfucker." He seals his promise with a passionate kiss, one I feel all the way down to my soul. "I meant everything I said. You own me, Mia."

"Bex..." I sigh, slowly coming back to reality.

What have we done?

But for as much as I know we shouldn't have done it, I can't deny I feel a lick of satisfaction.

Bexley lowers me to the ground, and we clean up. I catch my reflection in the mirror. My skin is flushed, my eyes bright and brimming with lust. But what I feel for Bexley is more than that.

He comes up behind me, slipping his arms around my waist and hugging me to his warm body. "You are so fucking strong, Mia." He presses a kiss to my shoulder as he watches me in the mirror. "But I'm begging you, let me handle Kingsley."

I press my lips together, refusing to agree. I can't let this go. I won't.

"Mia..."

I'm about to answer when there's a knock at the door. "Um, guys," Sasha says, "you should really—"

"Yeah," Bexley barks, "coming."

"We should go," I say, slipping out of his hold.

"Wait." He snags my wrist and yanks me into his chest. My hands go to his shoulders as he kisses me. "Now we can go." He smirks.

I let out a small sigh of relief. I know we should probably talk about what this means, but I don't have the energy or answers to get into it right now.

When we slip back into Sasha's room, she looks upset and Channing is nowhere to be seen. "Everything okay?" I ask her.

She gives me a small shrug, wrapping her arms around herself. "Channing is waiting for you outside." Her eyes flick from Bexley to the door. "If anyone asks, I got sick and Mia is helping me deal."

"Yeah, okay." Bexley glances at me. I know he wants to say more, but he doesn't. His eyes blaze with possessiveness as he holds my gaze.

Then he leaves, and I finally inhale a deep breath. My eyes settle on Sasha and she shakes her head.

"We're screwed," she says. "So fucking screwed. But it felt good, right? Getting back at Cade?"

"Yeah." My lips curve into a devious smile. "It did."

WE STAY in Sasha's room for the rest of the afternoon. At some point, the guys return to the pool with the girls and the sound of laughter and music drifts up to us. But no one tries to come and coax us out of the room.

Sasha sleeps off her high and I lie there, next to her, replaying my time with Bexley over and over in my head.

It was so intense, the connection between us burning brighter than ever. I know I won't be able to stay away from him, not now. But Cade can never find out... he can never know.

My cell vibrates and I pluck it off the nightstand, guilt flooding me when I see Annabel's name on the screen.

Annabel: Hey… just wondered if you're ever going to return to dorms?

Mia: Hey, sorry… I'll be back later. Do you want to come over and hang out?

Annabel: Umm, do pigs fly? I'll bring snacks.

I chuckle as I type my reply.

Mia: Okay, sounds good. See you later.

Annabel: Great. You can tell me all about your weekend.

Another wave of guilt floods me. I don't want to lose Annabel as a friend, but our lives are moving in different directions, and I can't blame her for feeling left out.

Because the reality is, she is.

"Hey." Sasha stirs beside me. "What time is it?"

"A little after five."

"I didn't mean to fall asleep."

"It's okay," I say. "You needed it."

"Yeah." She sniffles. "Crazy, huh?"

I nod.

"Did anyone come up here?"

"No. Whatever Channing and Bexley told them must have worked."

"Thank God. I'm not sure I could have faced them all, not after..."

"I know. But we have to play our parts, Sasha."

She regards me, her eyes softening around the corners. "You're different. When I first met you, I thought Cade would destroy you. But you're not going to go down without a fight, are you?"

"No, I'm not."

"I'll help you," she says, pushing up on her elbows. "I'll help you find a way out."

"Yeah?" A plan forms in my head. I haven't told anyone about it yet, but maybe it's time. "My dad works at the Town Hall."

"My dad, Phillip works out of that office."

"I know. My dad works security for him. I'm going to try and get into the town's records."

"What?" Her eyes go wide.

"There has to be something, Sasha. Something I can use against Cade or Quinctus."

"I don't know... that sounds kind of dangerous."

"More dangerous than sitting by and letting Cade do whatever he wants? You said it yourself, he's unhinged. I'm not going to sit around and see how far he's willing to go."

"What do you hope to find?"

"I don't know. Something. Anything. There must be records about all of this. Official Quinctus records. If they're kept anywhere, it would be in that building."

"Okay, I'm in."

I nod, feeling adrenaline pulse through me. She's right, it is dangerous. But I need answers.

And the town archives seem like the best place to start.

13

BEXLEY

The second we emerge from the house with fresh drinks and bags of chips in hand, curious glances turn our way. But it's the moment Cade's eyes lock on mine that my previous high vanishes.

Nothing like your shitty reality to kill your buzz.

"Where the fuck have you two been?"

"Sasha's fucking out of it. I tried helping her to her room to sleep it off, but she had a meltdown halfway up and kicked off. Took both of us to get her there," I say, holding Cade's eyes steady. There is a half-truth in there, after all.

"Where's Mia?"

I swallow my nerves and say three little words that hurt more than anything. "With you, right?"

"No."

"She's with Sasha," Brandon announces, appearing from the house. "Can hear them talking."

"Right." Cade's eyes hold mine as if his evil stare will force me to spill my secrets, but he's shit out of luck with that.

No one—aside from those in the room—are going to know about what just went down.

"Come on." Channing slaps my shoulder as he passes and drops down onto the lounger.

"I'm watching you, Easton," Cade growls as I pass him.

"What's new there? I hope your whores were worth it," I quip as I march past him, hitting his shoulder for good measure. "He's a cunt," I mutter, dropping down beside Channing, "and those pills Sasha takes are shit."

"You didn't—fuck, Bex. You need to stay off that shit."

I shrug. "Because the reality is so much better?"

"No, but you need to be on guard. If he catches—"

"He won't. We're smarter than that, right?" The two of us share a knowing smirk. My body begins to heat once more as I remember him and Sasha on the bed only feet away from Mia and me.

Fuck, that was hot.

Although not as hot as sliding inside her again. God, I've missed that.

I shift on my lounger and Channing doesn't miss the move.

"Yeah," he says, answering my unspoken question. "That needs to fucking happen again."

I'm still trying to find the right answer when two more people descend on the pool.

"Wondered when you were going to show your face, motherfucker," Cade barks at Tim as he and Fawn approach.

She's as white as a sheet but dressed appropriately in a black bathing suit and pink cover-up.

"Sorry we're late."

"Don't sweat it. The party has barely started, right girls?" he asks the mostly naked girls who are once again splashing around in the pool.

Fawn looks at them and rolls her eyes, slipping from Tim's side and falling down onto one of the loungers. She looks around as if she's trying to find someone—Sasha, maybe—but when she comes up empty, she rests her head back and closes her eyes.

Tim watches her for a few seconds before taking off in Cade's direction and accepting a drink from him.

"What's their deal?" I ask Channing, more than curious about the pair—or more so the guy that had Hadley banished from town.

"Promised to each other when they were in diapers. They had their Eligere a couple years ago. They'll be married after they graduate."

"You think they're happy?" I ask, keeping my eyes on Fawn.

"Sometimes, yeah. Every now and then you'll catch them looking at each other and it makes you wonder if all of this bullshit can work. But more often than not, she's nowhere to be seen and Tim looks too exhausted to think, let alone work."

"Why?"

He shrugs. "Don't know the details, but I think she's got mental health issues. Or at least that's what I've surmised."

"What about him? He doesn't seem like them." I nod to Cade and Ashton, where the three of them are now deep in conversation.

"Oh, he is. He's Electi through and through. Fawn is just a distraction. I guess you could say she's softened him, but that's only because he doesn't live this life 24/7 anymore. But don't let him fool you with Fawn on his arm. He's just as twisted and brutal as they come."

"Devil in sheep's clothing, huh?"

"Unless you see him angry. Then he's pure fucking evil."

"Right."

I watch them for a minute or two before looking back at Fawn. If she does have mental health issues, I can't help wondering how much of it is because of this bullshit life she's been born into and the role she's now forced to play as an Electi's fiancée.

Neither Channing nor I move unless it's to get more drinks or take a piss. We don't mention what happened or either of the girls' names for fear of being overheard. We just attempt to enjoy ourselves, which is a fucking challenge when you're partying with the devil himself.

We're forced to watch him with every girl here who isn't the one he's been promised too, and with every new one he moves onto the harder my nails dig into my palms. Of course, I don't want him to be with Mia, but she at least deserves a little fucking respect.

She was fucking you not so long ago. How's that for respect?

I shake the thoughts from my head, wishing I could come up with an excuse to go back up there—mostly for Mia, but also for Sasha's little tin of goodies.

The sun is beginning to descend when she finally shows her face, no longer in her bathing suit but dressed to leave. She marches straight over to Cade, who's sandwiched between two girls. She spits a few words at him, turns, and marches through the backyard and toward the driveway.

Every muscle in my body screams for me to follow her, for her to take me with her away from his hell, but I know I can't. So instead, I remain exactly where I am, as if she hadn't just walked past and reminded me of everything I want...

And can't have.

"CANCEL YOUR PLANS, we've got a job," Cade announces at lunch the next day.

"But we've got classes," I argue. I know it's weak at best, but I refuse to just fall into line because King Cade has spoken.

"So? I'm sure you can find some chick to give you notes."

"Your chick?" I ask, knowing that Mia is in my afternoon class.

His face heats as he stares at me with pursed lips, but he doesn't respond to my question. "We need to be moving in an hour, so get your asses ready." Shoving his still mostly full plate into the center of the table, he pushes from his chair and marches from the room, quickly followed by Ashton and Tim.

"Was that necessary?" Brandon asks, turning his eyes on me.

For some reason, the girls weren't invited to have lunch with us today. It makes me wonder if Cade knew we'd be called.

"What?" I shrug. "She is in my class."

He rolls his eyes, shoves some of his lunch into his mouth and stands. "Come on then," he mumbles around his mouthful. "The king waits for no one."

Ain't that the fucking truth.

Reluctantly, I stand with Alex and Channing and we follow where the others disappeared only minutes ago.

Channing climbs into my car and Alex goes with Brandon, like we did first thing this morning. I watch Alex as he climbs inside, concern trickling through me. Not so long ago he wouldn't have gone anywhere near Brandon's car. But less than two weeks into this life and he seems to be embracing it a little too easily.

"What's the job? Any idea?"

"Nope. Literally could be anything," Channing helpfully answers as he sits back.

"Okay... well, what kind of stuff do you usually do?"

He glances over at me. "You really want the answer to that?"

My lips part to reply, but I stop myself. Do I really want to know?

"Put it this way: all of us have blood on our hands and have plenty of reasons not to sleep at night."

"Great." Exactly what I was expecting. "How do you do it?"

"Other than because we have to?"

"Yeah."

He shrugs. "I dunno. It's hard to explain, but I kinda go someplace else when all that bad shit is going down."

"You're telling me you've got multiple personalities."

"No, yeah, maybe. Fuck knows. The whole thing is fucking screwed up, and you just gotta do what you can to survive."

"Jesus," I mutter, scrubbing my hand down my face.

The second we're back at the house, we head to our rooms to dress in our 'uniform.' Ten minutes later we're standing in the entryway, all head to toe in black and looking like we're about to go rob a bank.

To be fair, we might be.

"Right, let's go."

When we step out of the house, there are two black SUVs idling out the front. Cade and his sidekicks immediately slide into the first, whereas Alex, Channing and I climb into the second.

There's a definite divide appearing in the group, and I couldn't be happier that Channing seems to have chosen my side. Brandon is hovering in the middle, although I am worried about Alex.

I glance over at him; his knee is bouncing and his hands are twisting on his lap. "You alright, man?" I ask.

"Uh... yeah." He glances over at me and his eyes are blown.

"You fucking on something?"

"What? N-no. Just the come down from yesterday," he admits with a wince.

"You need to lay off that shit."

"I know," he mutters as Channing shoots me a concerned glance.

The drive to wherever we're going is only short, and when I look out the blacked out windows, I find we're pulling up to a deserted warehouse.

Well, this isn't ominous at all.

"Out," Cade barks, pulling the door open for us.

We follow orders like good little sheep. I want to refuse, but a bigger part of me is curious about what's going to happen next.

Cade leads us to the doors and throws them open when he gets there as if he's announcing his arrival at a party. I soon realize he is. The warehouse is empty aside from a few other guys dressed the same as us, and a guy sitting in a chair in the middle of the room with a bag over his head.

Cade nods at the others and they all immediately leave without saying a word.

"Who the fuck were they?" I ask Channing.

"Q security."

"Right."

"You ready to play, boys?" Cade asks, turning to us with a manic smile across his face. His eyes land on mine before they find Alex, making dread sit heavy in my stomach.

Whatever the fuck is going to happen here is going to involve us, that much is obvious. Our initiation might be over, but we've far from passed, as far as Cade is concerned.

"This motherfucker thought he would try his hand at selling our secrets. Didn't you?" He doesn't wait for the guy to answer; instead he pulls his arm back and punches him in his covered face.

I have no clue if the man is conscious or not, but he doesn't make a noise as his head snaps back.

"Now, we all know what happens to people who try to betray us. But I'm not sure our new recruits do. Moore, wanna fill them in?"

I look at Ashton, who's got a similar blood-hungry look on his face. He really is a fucking psychopath.

He rubs his hands together. "We kill them."

Great.

Cade reaches behind him and pulls a gun from his waistband. "But we're not going to be doing it this time." He steps up to Alex, and my heart falls into my feet. There's no way Alex will pull the fucking trigger on someone. "Rexford is."

"Uh, what?" he stutters, all the blood draining from his face.

"You might wear the mark of the Electi, Rexford, but you're not a true Electi until you make your first kill. You need to prove you've got what it takes. You've already shown us you're more than capable with the women; now it's time to prove your worth with the rats."

Cade holds the gun out and Alex reluctantly takes it. It's not even raised, and his hand is trembling. With a nod of his head, Cade stalks around the person in the chair and rips the hood off. The second he does, it's obvious that the man is conscious, but his eyes are resigned, as if he's long accepted his fate.

Blood pours from his nose and into his mouth, from Cade's hit or the previous guy's, who knows. Cade steps in front of him and drops to his haunches. "Regretting it yet?" he snarls in the guy's face.

He doesn't give him an answer, just averts his gaze, but I think that pisses Cade off even more.

"Look at me when I'm talking to you, cunt." His fist connects with his eye, and his head snaps back once more. But again, no noise.

Cade points at his head, between his brows. "Right here, Rexford. You think you can hit the target?"

Alex doesn't respond, his entire body now trembling in fear.

"Come closer. Give yourself half a chance."

Alex hesitantly steps forward.

"That's it." Cade comes to stand beside him. "Now lift your arm. Aim and pull that motherfucking trigger."

His voice doesn't sound like his own. He sounds... excited.

It's just another clue to how fucked up he really is.

"O-okay." Alex does as he's told, and I suck in a sharp breath.

I really don't want this for him. Killing someone will eat him alive, I just know it.

Everyone around me gasps simultaneously, and only two seconds later, the sound of a round firing makes us all jump. But when I look, the guy is still alive, Alex is trembling violently, and the gun is hanging limply in his hand.

"What the fuck, Rexford? Do it again."

"I... I can't," Alex whimpers.

"Motherfucker." Cade slams his palm into Alex's chest. "This is why Q won't let Channing go. They know what a fucking pussy his replacement is. Kill him, or there will be repercussions for you, Rexford."

Unable to watch Alex take Cade's wrath, I take a step forward. "I'll do it. Just leave him alone. He's not ready."

Cade turns his manic eyes on me. "Fine," he smirks, almost triumphantly, "but next time, the kill is his."

Alex looks up at me, his eyes full of unshed tears, but he nods in agreement.

A smile twitches at my lips.

I owe Alex this. After everything he did for me when I first arrived—even if Marcus did set it up—he's been nothing but good to me.

I take the gun from his still trembling hand and lift it to the guy who's silently staring at the floor. Taking aim, and without putting another thought into it, I fire.

"We done here?" I ask, knowing without looking that I hit my target.

"Moore, Cargill, clean up. We'll be waiting in the cars," Cade barks and marches past me as if this is just a normal day.

I guess maybe it is for him.

I follow him out with my heart in my throat and my stomach churning.

Swallowing down the contents of my lunch, I force myself to plaster on a blank expression as if what I just did was nothing. That I'm as much a monster as Cade.

The reality is, I'm not going to forget what I just did for a long, long time.

14

MIA

"You're alive." Annabel smirks at me as I open the door wider and let her in.

"I'm so sorry."

"Relax, I've accepted my fate as an outsider."

"Bel, it isn't like that—"

"Yeah, Mia. It is." She kicks off her pumps and plops herself on my bed. "But you're my best friend, so I'm willing to overlook the fact that you're practically one of them now."

"If it's any consolation, I hate it." I sit down and nudge her shoulder with mine.

"Well, I have news." Her eyes light up. "Jared Clifton asked me out on a date."

"Jared? The guy from the party?" It had been the one at the beginning of the semester.

"Yep. He took me to that cute little diner downtown, you know the one with the jukebox, and then we went to a drive-in movie just outside town."

"Sounds nice." Jealousy snakes through me.

"It was. I'm seeing him again tomorrow."

"Good for you, Bel." I give her a thin smile.

"What about you? How's Cade?"

"As much an asshole as ever," I grumble.

"It can't be that bad... he's so freaking hot."

"Trust me, his good looks do not balance out his shitty personality."

"What did you do all weekend?"

"There was a party... it was—"

"Insiders only, got it." Dejection swirls in her eyes, and I hate it. I hate that this is causing such a rift between me and my only true friend. I mean, I like to think of Sasha as a friend too now, but she's one of them. It isn't the same. Our paths would never have crossed if it wasn't for the Eligere.

"You didn't miss much," I quickly add. "Then I hung out some with Sasha."

"And Bexley?"

"What about him?" I shrug.

"Well, what's happening there?"

"Nothing. It's over."

"But—"

"No buts, Bel. It's too risky." Memories of Bexley's hands on me, his lips tracing my skin and branding me as he fucked me on the counter fill my mind. My body heats, remembering how good it felt... how good *he* felt.

"Mia?"

I snap out of my reverie, forcing a smile. "It's done," I say, the words twisting something inside me.

We're not done, not by a long shot. But Annabel doesn't need to know that. No one does. Well, not except Sasha and Channing, but at least I know they won't be in any hurry to reveal what happened in her room.

"So Jared?" I change the subject. "Do you like him?"

"Well, yeah, I guess. I mean, he's cute, and he seems into me..."

"I sense a but there."

"There wasn't that spark." Her expression falls.

"But it was only your first date."

"Yeah, but I always imagined when I met the right guy, I'd feel... more, you know?"

I do.

Because it's exactly what I felt with Bexley down by the lake, the first night we met.

"Well, don't write him off too soon. Besides, no one says you have to marry the first guy you date." My breath catches.

Annabel won't have to marry anyone she doesn't want to... but I will.

THE NEXT DAY, I hatch my plan. I don't even know what I'll find at the Town Hall, but it seems like the best place to start. I spend the day flitting between classes. At lunch, I eat with Cade and the Electi in their private dining room. Bexley is deathly silent as he watches me with Cade, although I do catch him smirking a couple of times when my eyes meet his, and I know he's remembering the other day. But there's something else too, a dark cloud shadowing him. I want to ask him what's wrong, but I can't, not in front of everyone. So I wait until our final class together.

Cade walks me to the door, making a show of pushing me up against the wall and kissing me. His mouth is too hard and his touch too desperate. He starts grinding against me, moaning into the crook of my neck.

"Cade," I hiss, slamming my hands into his chest. "Not here." My smile is tight as I glare at him.

"You care too much what people think, babe." He plucks a strand of my hair between his fingers. "If I wanted to fuck you right here for everyone to see, I would."

"I need to get to class," I say, trying to avoid an argument. As I try to leave, he snags my wrist at the last second.

"Aren't you forgetting something?" His brow goes up.

Biting back a sigh, I lean in and kiss his cheek.

"Better. I have shit to take care of tonight, but I'll see you tomorrow."

I nod. At least he'll be distracted while I pay the town archives a visit. Nervous energy pings through my stomach, but I manage to force a smile.

"Soon, Mia. Soon I'll have you under me."

My stomach lurches. He's growing impatient. I see it every time he looks at me.

Just then, Bexley passes us.

"Kingston," he says smugly.

"Easton." Cade tenses. "Fucking asshole," he murmurs as soon as Bexley disappears into the room.

I fight a smile, keeping my expression as neutral as possible. I shouldn't encourage Bexley, but it reassures me to know he isn't going to just lie down and take whatever Cade doles out.

I ease out of Cade's grip, and this time, he lets me go. His heavy gaze stalks me until I'm all the way inside class.

Spotting Bexley in the back row, I move past him to an empty space a few seats down. His hand brushes mine as I go, sending shivers zipping up my arm. I want to meet his eyes, but I don't, forcing myself to keep looking ahead.

No one will know anything happened. But I know. His touch lingers, stays with me for the rest of the class. And although I want to be beside him, laughing with him, feeling his thigh pressed up against mine, this is enough.

For now, it's enough.

"THANKS FOR DOING THIS," I say to Annabel as she pulls up outside of the Town Hall.

"Of course. Although I still don't know what you think you'll find here that you can't find on the internet." She shrugs.

"I already told you. The professor encouraged us to go straight to the source. Everyone knows the town archives are kept here." I stare up at the big, imposing building. It's old, like Gravestone Hall, and steeped in shadows. They dance over the huge limestone bricks like monsters in the dark. But I don't let it faze me. I've been here hundreds of times with my dad. He used to bring me along when I was a little girl, and I'd spend hours nestled among the artifacts in the museum section of the building.

I haven't been here for a long time though. My dad stopped bringing me once I started middle school.

"Do you want me to wait?" Annabel asks. "I can."

"No, it's fine." I grab my backpack from between my feet. "Dad will give me a ride back if he's on shift." He usually is. He's given his life to working security for Phillip Cargill and the mayor's office.

"Okay then, if you're sure. I'm going to swing by my parents' and then see if Jared wants to hang out."

"You decided to give it another shot, after all?"

"Yeah, I think you're right. It was one date. I need to give it some time. Who knows, he could be my frog turned prince once we kiss." Her soft laughter fills the car.

"I'm happy for you, Bel. I know I haven't always been a good friend, but I'm here for you."

"I know." Something flashes over her face. "Say hi to your dad for me."

I nod before climbing out of her car. The shadows envelop me as I approach the Town Hall. It's fifty minutes before it closes to the public, but I don't plan on leaving with the other people here.

My heart crashes in my chest as I approach the steps leading to the impressive doors. The town's motto is etched into the stone arch. *Audentes fortuna iuvat.* Fortune favors the bold.

Let's hope fortune favors me tonight.

Taking a deep breath, I pull up my hood and slip into the building. A security guy is busy on his phone behind the desk, so I take a left down the hall and head for the town archives. Like most places, a section is open to the public, but it's not those I'm interested in.

I keep my head down. There's CCTV all over this building, but I think I can remember the blind spots. Hopefully.

The archive room is down a level, so I take the stairwell. The slam of the door echoes off the walls as I descend to the basement. The air is musty down here, and I hurry.

I'm hardly surprised when I enter the room to find it empty save for the archivist. She's an older woman, perched behind a curved desk tucked in one corner of the room. She glances up and I smile. "Something I can help you with dear?"

"Just here to look up some things for an assignment."

"Well, if I can help you with anything, just shout."

"Thanks." I move deeper into the room. It's a long rectangle that runs the length of the building above. One wall is lined with display cabinets, housing various artifacts and charters from the town's history.

The rest of the room is split into two sections: a lower level with rows of study desks and computers, with the records and archive stacks on a raised platform. My dad told me once that it was a precaution in case of flooding.

I disappear into the stacks, running my eyes over the various coding markers. In high school, we visited the Town Hall once for a tour, and the archivist gave us a lesson in reading the different codings. But Annabel is right; a lot of the information can be accessed online now.

Coming to stop in front of the sealed archives, my heart drops. Everything is different since I last came here. The padlock has been upgraded to a keycard mechanism. Crap. I had planned to pick the lock, but there's no way I can get inside now. Not without a security pass.

As I'm staring at the founding family records, an idea pops into my mind. My dad's pass. If I can lift my dad's pass, I can use it to get inside. But it's my dad. I don't want to get him in trouble... and I don't want him to find out what I'm doing.

Crap.

Defeated, I double back and make my way out of the archive room. The archivist gives me a small wave as I pass her. "Did you find everything you need, dear?"

"Yes, thank you," I say before slipping into the elevator.

When it pings open again, I come face to face with the security guy.

"Miss Thompson, is that you?"

"Oh hey... Bryan?"

"That's the one. Does your father know you're here?"

No.

I force a smile. "Actually, I was just going to go see him. Any idea where he is?"

"He's probably back in his office."

"Thanks, Bryan." I slip passed him.

"It's good to see you again, Miss Thompson."

Letting out a small breath, I hurry down the hall leading toward the back of the building. I've almost reached my dad's office when I hear voices.

"Not what we agreed, Phillip."

I freeze at the anger in my dad's voice.

"This is the only way, Garth." The other voice is muffled, but there's no mistaking it's Phillip Cargill. "Need her to..."

A trickle of awareness goes through me, and I creep closer.

"She is... daughter. It's not fair... Cade... dangerous..."

I can only make out every other word, but my body vibrates with fear.

Are they talking about me?

About me and Cade?

"Not a choice, Thompson." Phillip's voice is full of frustration. "We agreed. *You* agreed. Now... see this through."

My stomach drops.

See *what* through?

A bang down the hall startles me, and I hear Phillip say, "We'll finish this another time." There's a rustle and footsteps.

Heart in my throat, I take off down the hall. I don't know what I just heard, but something deep inside me tells me I don't want to be caught eavesdropping.

The women's restroom looms up ahead, so I duck inside, waiting for Phillip to leave. His heavy footsteps pass the door, and I let out a shaky breath.

This was a bad idea. A really bad idea. But I'm here now, and Bryan saw me.

Crap.

Crap. Crap. Crap.

Splashing some cold water on my face, I dry my hands and inhale a steady breath. Pulling open the door, I step back into the hall and make my way to Dad's office.

"Come in," he says.

"Hey, Dad." I peek around the door.

"Mia? This is a surprise." He leans back in his chair, studying me. There's no evidence of his tense conversation with Phillip. He looks just like my dad. Kind eyes and a warm smile that he reserves for me and Mom.

"Research for a paper," I say nonchalantly.

"You're working hard on a Monday night, sweetheart."

"Just trying to get a headstart."

"How did you get here?"

"Annabel gave me a ride into town."

"And how are you getting back?"

"I was hoping you might be able to take me?"

"Ah, I see. So this isn't a social visit..." He chuckles. "I don't get off for another couple of hours, but I'm sure Bryan will cover for me." Standing, he grabs his keys off the rack. "Come on."

"Thanks, Dad."

His eyes narrow a fraction, sadness bleeding into his expression.

"Dad?" A shiver runs down my spine.

"Come on," he says, a smile lifting his whole face. "Let's get you back to campus."

15

BEXLEY

Mouse: Hey, I need a favor.

My heart pounds as I read Mia's words. Is she for real?

Bexley: Of course. Name it and it's yours.

She starts typing immediately, but the seconds feel like hours as I wait for her words to appear.

Mouse: Can you come to my dorm?

Bexley: Is that a trick question?

Mouse: No, I need to talk to you about something.

Bexley: Talk?

My blood starts to heat, and it's not with ideas of us talking playing out in my head.

Mouse: Yes. I don't trust anyone else.

A smile twitches at my lips as my chest constricts at her words.

Bexley: On my way.

Mouse: The window will be open.

I blow out a long breath as reality slams into me. Sneaking into her dorm room because we're forbidden. Right.

I change my shirt and shove my feet into my sneakers before pulling my door open and heading down the hallway. I miss my dorm, and not just because it puts me closer to Mia at all times.

Music booms from one of the rooms down the hall—Brandon's, I think. But I don't see anyone as I descend the stairs.

"Going somewhere nice, Easton?" Cade's voice makes my steps falter.

"Out," I bark back without even looking into the room I know he's hanging out in.

"Don't do anything I wouldn't do."

"Fuck you, Kingsley." I flip him off over my shoulder, half expecting him to body slam me into the wall for my attitude, but by some miracle, he lets me leave without saying another word.

The drive to campus is quick, but I spend most of the drive looking in my rearview mirror to make sure that motherfucker hasn't followed me.

Confident the coast is clear, I park in our old dorm lot and hit the sidewalk that will take me to Mia. She's waiting for me; the second I turn the corner, her curtains twitch and she appears at the window.

My breath catches as she finds me, but when she doesn't smile as I get closer, my heart sinks.

Is this a setup?

I hate to even think it of her, but she's being controlled by Cade, so I need to be realistic. If he wants to get to me, then he knows the easiest way is through Mia.

When I'm right beneath the fire escape, she opens the window, and, without another thought, I climb up and into her room. Her floral scent hits me long before my feet meet the floor, but other than casting a quick look around to make sure she's alone, the only thing I can focus on is her.

"Fuck, you're beautiful," I whisper, taking her face in my hands and brushing my lips over hers.

"Bexley," she whispers into my kiss. "This isn't why—"

"Shhh... Let me just have a minute."

Her entire body sags, and I drop my hands to her ass and lift her. She automatically wraps her legs around my waist, and I walk us over to her bed, lying her down and continuing our kiss.

Her hands press against my chest in a pathetic attempt to get me to back off.

"Can't," I murmur against her jaw. "Addicted."

"I-I know. Me too. But I really need to talk."

I blow out a long, frustrated breath that tickles over her neck and makes her shudder. "Okay, mouse. What do you need to get off your chest?" I drop down beside her and turn her onto her side. Our bodies are only an inch apart, our noses almost touching.

She looks away from me for a beat, and I panic.

"Mia, what is it?" Wrapping my hand around her waist, I squeeze gently to get her to look back up at me.

"You can't tell anyone about this, Bex."

"Of course."

She sucks in a breath, pausing for a few minutes to collect her thoughts. "I decided to go to the Town Hall to see if I could get into the town's archives."

"Okay. Why?" I frown.

She shrugs. "I thought that maybe I could find something I could use against Cade. I don't know. It was stupid because they're all locked up, there's CCTV everywhere. I just thought..." She trails off, tears filling her eyes.

"Hey, it's okay," I soothe, wrapping my hand around the side of her neck and brushing my thumb over her cheek. "It's not stupid at all."

"My dad works there. So I went to his office when I realized it was a dead-end. But before I got there, I heard Phillip and him talking."

"Cargill?"

She nods. "I think... I think my dad might have something to do with me being Cade's prosapia."

I rear back. "W-what?"

"I didn't catch all of it, I was too far away. But I heard my name, Cade's name, and Phillip saying that my dad agreed to something and that he had to see it through."

"Shit." I sit up and let her words register in my head. "So you were never meant to be his?"

She sits up beside me, her warm hand landing on my lower back. "I don't know. It might have had nothing to do with it. But..."

"It really fucking sounded like it," I finish for her.

"Yeah."

"You need to talk to your dad."

"He's been acting weird since all of this kicked off. When I went home the other weekend, it was obvious he was hiding stuff."

"You think you can get him to talk?"

She shrugs. "He's in Phillip's pocket. If he really is involved in this, then I fear he's going to be as forthcoming with information as everyone else in this gigantic mess."

"I had a feeling you might say that." Dropping my head into my hands, I try to make sense of all of this.

Why would Mia's dad sign her up to be tied to the devil? The way she's talked about him, her childhood, he's only ever wanted the best for her.

Hasn't he?

"I'll talk to Marcus, see if he knows anything."

Although I'm not sure why I even suggest it. He's not exactly the sharing type. If he'd have let me into a few of his secrets earlier, I may not have been quite so blindsided by all this.

"You think he'll tell you anything, even if he knows something?" she asks, reading my mind.

"Honestly, no. But he keeps telling me that I need to see this through, so if he wants me to do that then he's going to need to give me some of the facts."

"I guess. Ugh," she groans, pushing from the bed in favor of pacing across the room. "I really hate this. And if I find out my dad let me be a pawn in this game, then..." She trails off, running out of words.

"I know, little mouse," I say, intercepting her and circling my arms around her waist.

She stops and lifts her eyes from my chest and up to my own. "Hey," she says shyly.

"Hey." Lifting my hand, I tuck a stray lock of her hair behind her ear.

Our eyes hold for the longest time, as if neither of us can believe we're really here. Alone. Our chests begin to heave at our closeness, and my cock begins to swell once more with her pressed against me and her scent in my nose.

"Did you have any other ideas for what we could do now you've got me here?"

She bites down on her bottom lip, and I only just about stop myself from sucking it into my own mouth and claiming it as mine.

Right now, I want her words. I want her to tell me what she wants.

"Mostly, I was freaking out and needed to tell someone. But I don't know who to trust anymore and..."

"Hey, it's okay. You can tell me anything, you know that, right?"

"I do, it's just so complicated, Bex. You shouldn't be here—" I tense, half expecting her to suddenly do a one-eighty and kick me out. "If Cade found out then... God. I don't want you on his radar any more than you already are. I just... I need... I don't even know what I—"

I slam my lips down on hers to stop her rambling. My fingers thread into her hair and I use it to move her head so I can lick deep into her mouth.

"Bexley," she moans when I kiss down her neck.

"I could really use a shower. Think you could help me out?"

"I think that could probably be arranged." Her voice is low and breathy, and it turns me the fuck on.

Walking her backward, I pull her shirt up over her head and throw it to the floor behind me. Her bra goes next, and then I set to work on her jeans, pushing them over her hips and letting her kick them off while I take care of her panties.

The rip of the lace fills the room, and she gasps. "Did you just—"

"I hope they weren't your favorites."

"Caveman."

"Yours."

I lean down to take her lips again, but she pulls back, teasing me.

"Why are you fully clothed still?"

I look down at myself and then at her naked body. "Because I just want to enjoy you."

She squeals as I lift her to the edge of the counter and push her thighs wide before dropping to my knees before her.

"Oh God, Bexley," she moans, throwing her head back as I blow a stream of air over her swollen pussy.

"Mmm, I've missed this," I whisper before licking up the length of her.

Her hands twist in my hair and she tries to close her legs as the sensation takes over her.

"I'm going to make you come all over my face, mouse. Then I'm going to take you in the shower, and then your bed. I'm going to make you come over and over to make up for us being apart."

"God, yes," she cries when I spear two fingers inside her, rubbing at her walls and pushing high until I find her g-spot. "Bexley."

"Fuck yes," I growl against her, ensuring she gets the benefits of the vibrations before sucking on her clit and pushing her over the edge.

Kissing up her body, I suck each of her nipples into my mouth before finding her lips and devouring her, knowing that she can taste herself on me.

Frantically, Mia reaches for the hem of my shirt and drags it over my head, dropping it to the floor before reaching for my waistband. The second my jeans are undone, she wastes no time in pushing her hand inside and grasping my cock.

"Fuck, mouse. Your touch... fucking addictive."

"What about my mouth?" she asks, hopping off the counter and lowering her body down the front of mine. Her lips kiss every inch as she descends before she's on her knees for me and my jeans and boxers are in her hands, ready to pull them down.

I stare at her, committing the image to memory, because something tells me that I'm going to need it to remember just how good things can be between us in the coming weeks.

The second my cock springs free, she reaches out, wraps her hand around the shaft and licks the precum from the tip. My hips thrust forward, desperately searching for more. She looks up at me, her eyes blazing with desire, and my heart tumbles.

Fuck, I'm falling harder for this girl with every second that passes.

"Mouse," I moan as she sucks me into her mouth. "Fuuuuck," I groan as she takes me deeper until I hit the back of her throat.

Just the sight has me right on the edge, and embarrassingly it's only a few minutes later when I let go and spurt hot jets of cum down her throat.

"Now I really need that shower," I admit, pulling her to her feet and crashing our lips together.

I kick off my remaining clothes and back her into the shower, blasting us both with ice-cold water, but with her touching me, I barely notice it.

We stay under the water until we can no longer bear the cold. Reluctantly, I hand her a towel and allow her to cover up her body while I do the same.

"What time do you need to be back?" she asks.

"I don't have a curfew," I say with a laugh. But Mia doesn't so much as smile.

"If he finds out—"

"He won't." I crawl over her body, forcing her back against her pillow.

"But he will. Cade knows everything."

"Then I'll take the consequences." I pin her with a dark look. "This is worth it, Mia. More than worth it."

16

MIA

"I wish you could stay," I whisper, running my nose along Bexley's jaw. Our legs are tangled together, our bodies pressed close, like two pieces of the same puzzle.

"We have time," he says, regret coating his words. But I know it's not this he regrets, it's that he has to leave.

Bexley pulls me closer, touching his head to mine and kissing me slow and deep. Our tongues slide together, building a wave of intense need inside me again.

"Bex," I moan softly, and he grinds against me.

"I can't believe I'm going to say this," he breaks the kiss, letting out a heavy sigh, "but we should stop."

"Yeah, you're probably right." My lips linger against his, and he steals one more chaste kiss.

"You're buried deep, little mouse." He grabs my hand and presses right over his chest where his heart is. "Right in here."

"I feel the same," I admit. "I tried to fight it... to tell myself I could ignore how I feel, but I can't." My hands curl into the hair at the nape of his neck.

"You're mine, Mia. No matter what."

His words wrap around me like a blanket. I want to believe him.

God, I want to believe him.

"I won't be with him, Bexley. I won't."

"It won't come to that, I promise." He kisses my head. "I'll talk to Marcus. He knows more than he's letting on, I'm sure of it. And maybe we should go and see James Jagger."

"James Jagger?" I sit up.

"You know him?" Bexley frowns.

"No, but I've heard that name."

"Your dad?" he asks, and I nod. There's a memory hovering on the periphery of my mind, but I can't quite reach it. It feels like I'm uncovering something though, the threads of this puzzle slowly untangling and revealing themselves.

"Who is he?"

"Ace Jagger's dad. They live in Sterling Bay, but the Jaggers were originally from Gravestone. But Lilly, Marcus' sister…she fled back in the day after falling in love with the wrong man."

"So you're related?"

"Yeah… James is my uncle, I think. Or my cousin? Fuck if I know, it all confuses the shit out of me."

"Oh my God," I breathe.

"Yeah, something tells me it's only the tip of the iceberg."

"Do you think you can take me to see him? James Jagger, I mean?"

"Shit, Mia. I don't know. Kingsley is watching my every move. Sneaking here is one thing. But if we just up and disappear to go to Sterling Bay…"

He has a point, but there has to be a way.

"We can ask Channing and Sasha to cover for us."

"Whoa, I'm not sure that's a good idea." Concern glitters in his eyes. "I don't want to do anything that puts you at risk."

"I'm already at risk," I implore. "Every minute I'm with Cade…"

"Fuck, don't," he grits out. "Just don't. If I could take you away from here, I would. You know that, right? We could get in my car and just go."

"You can't run from Quinctus." I give him a sad smile. "That's not how it works."

"But Hadley did. She got out."

"Wait a minute, Hadley Rexford? You know Hadley Rexford?"

"Yeah. She lives in the Bay. My mom said it's like a safe haven or something. To be honest, I was so pissed when I saw her, nothing really made sense."

"Is she okay?"

"Who, my mom?"

"No, Hadley."

"Yeah, she's good. She and her boyfriend are at Colton U now, living their best lives."

This new information has blown my mind. There are so many moving pieces, I don't know which one to latch on to first.

"We have to speak to James Jagger," I say.

"Mouse..."

"No, Bexley, this is too important. If I'm going to find a way to get out of the Coglio with Cade,"—and I have to—"then we need to figure out how all this fits together."

And why Quinctus are so set on me being his prosapia.

"Okay, okay. But you let me figure out how and when." I frown, and his brow quirks up. "I mean it, Mia. I need to know you're safe. As safe as you can be. No more taking unnecessary risks."

I press my lips together, because I'm not sure that's a promise I can keep.

"Mouse, I need to hear you say it."

I kiss him instead—hot, wet kisses that leave us both panting for more.

"You're not playing fair." Bexley rolls me underneath him and runs his hand along my jaw and down to my throat. "In fact, I'd call it cheating." He smirks, running his tongue along my neck. "And do you know what cheaters get?"

"What?" I ask breathlessly.

He rolls his hips, letting his hard cock slide against my slick pussy before slamming inside me.

"Punished."

I WAKE with a knot in my stomach. In Bexley's arms, I'd felt safe and cherished. But in the harsh light of day, I'm reminded that being with him is a fantasy. My reality is much darker.

He left after loving my body again. It had been slow and sensual and intense. I came so hard my entire body quivered beneath him.

I have fallen head over heels for Bexley Easton, and I know now it was foolish to think I could ever switch off my feelings for him. I didn't promise him I wouldn't keep searching for answers though, and he didn't ask me again.

I think, deep down, he understands I have to do this.

Pushing back the covers, I start getting ready for classes. I'm almost dressed when my cell vibrates. A smile lifts the corner of my lips at Bexley's message... but it's quickly chased away when I realize it's not Bexley at all. It's Cade.

Cade: Meet me outside in five. And wear comfy shoes.

I quickly text him back.

Mia: I have classes.

Cade: Are you telling me no?

I want to. I want to tell him I'm going nowhere with him, but a little voice in my head tells me to play the game.

Mia: Fine. I'll be right out.

Cade: Good. And wear something sexy.

I can just picture his smug smirk. Ugh. Just then, my cell vibrates again, and I dread to think what else he has to say. But this time my heart leaps.

Cat: I can still taste you.

I fight a smile as I text Bexley back. I tell him that I won't be in class and not to worry and then silence my cell phone and slip it into my bag.

Taking a deep breath, I shove my feet into my sneakers and grab a jacket and scarf and slip out of my dorm room. The last thing I want to do is spend the day with Cade, but after last night, I need to appease him.

I need to protect Bexley.

Cade is waiting for me, leaning against his car looking like he just stepped off a runway. His eyes drink me in as I approach him.

"You look... good enough to eat." His lip curves into a wolfish grin as he wraps an arm around my waist and pulls me into his strong body. My hands go to his chest, trying to keep a safe distance between us, but he forces me closer. "I missed you last night."

I tense for a second but quickly brush it off, meeting his steely gaze. "I had to study."

"You do know all this," he glances toward campus, "means nothing? Once you graduate, you'll never want for anything ever again."

"If you think for a second I'm going to be some trophy wife who sits at home all day while my husband goes out to work, you are sorely mistaken."

His brow rises. It's the first time I've referred to our future.

"I like those words on your lips. Say them again..."

I roll my eyes. "Where are we going anyway?"

"It's a surprise."

"Cade..."

"Relax, I just want to spend the day with you. Show you I'm not a complete asshole."

"You could have showed me that at the pool party, but instead you disappeared with Ashton and those girls." I level him with a disapproving look.

"Come on, baby, don't be like that." He runs a hand up my neck and cups my face. "They're no one to me."

"And I am?" I lean in slightly, letting my mouth linger close to his jaw.

"You are my prosapia, Mia. Mine." His fingers dig slightly into my waist.

"Then prove it." I allow my lips to part as if I'm going to kiss him, but then I pull away and move around him to the car door.

I'm playing with fire, I know that, but I won't just lie down and take all his games and bullshit. I'm stronger than that—I have to be.

Cade's laughter follows me as I climb into the car and wait for him. When he slips inside, his eyes drill into mine. "I like this side of you."

"And what side would that be?"

"Feisty... possessive... jealous." His brow arches.

I press my lips together and stare straight ahead, letting him think he's right.

Even if he couldn't be further from the truth.

AFTER TAKING me to some fancy restaurant for breakfast, Cade drives me into the woods. For a second, I panic, but then the lake appears, the crystal blue water shimmering in the distance.

"What is this place?" I ask Cade, noticing the lack of other people.

"I like to come here sometimes." There's a vulnerability in his voice that surprises me, but I know not to drop my guard where Cade is concerned.

"It's beautiful," I say, staring out at the serene sight.

"Come on." He shoulders the door and climbs out, coming around to my side. I quickly pull out my cell and send Sasha a text.

The door opens and Cade holds his hand out for me. I take it, letting him help me.

"I think I have a blanket back here somewhere." He pops the trunk and leads me around the back of the car. "Oh look, a basket of goodies too."

My brows pinch. "A picnic?"

"I don't know what the fuck Mulligan packed." He shrugs, and I fight a smile. This is more like the Cade I'm used to.

I grab the blanket and he picks up the hamper, and we walk down to the water's edge.

"Have you ever done this before?" I ask.

"Is that a serious question? I don't usually need to work so hard for pussy."

"Nice," I hiss.

"Shit, Mia, that's not... I'm sorry, okay? This is all new for me."

"Why bother?" I ask, sitting down on the blanket. "You're going to take what you want anyway."

"True," he smirks, "but Q suggested that maybe I need a softer approach with you."

"So this is all for Quinctus?" Disbelief coats my words.

"It's for you." He gives me a sincere look. "I just needed a push in the right direction."

"You accept everything so easily."

"This life is all I've ever known. All I'll ever know."

"Do you miss him? Your dad?"

Cade freezes, his expression darkening. But then it melts away, replaced with sadness. "Yeah, I miss him. He was my dad, you know?"

"For what it's worth, I'm sorry."

"I didn't bring you here to talk about heavy shit, Mia. I thought we could spend some time away from Q and the Electi and all that stuff. Just you and me." He stretches out on his front and leans up, cupping my jaw in his big hand. "You are so fucking beautiful." His mouth fixes over mine and I'm paralyzed, afraid to breathe. I don't want to let him kiss me, but I don't have a choice.

His tongue parts my lips, coaxing me into the kiss. I stuff down all my feelings for Bexley and detach myself. This isn't that Mia, the Mia falling for a boy she can never have.

This is the other Mia, hardened by lies and secrets.

I open up for him, letting my tongue meet his in a slow, sensual kiss. My body stirs to life despite the repulsion coursing through me. It's destabilizing.

Pressing my hands to his chest, I inhale a shaky breath. "Let's see what's in the basket."

Cade drops his head to my shoulder and lets out a frustrated breath. "You can't avoid me forever, Mia."

"Not avoiding," I say, "just hitting pause. This is a lot to digest, Cade. You're a lot."

"I'm trying here."

God, he's delusional, but I don't want to start a fight.

I unpack the hamper. It's full of baked goods and fruit, and there's sparkling water. "Mulligan did good," I say, helping myself to a cookie.

Cade watches me savor every bite before pouncing on me. He pushes me down underneath him, staring down at me with hungry eyes. "I'm growing real tired of waiting, Mia."

Fear trickles through me. Gone is the guy who was trying, replaced by the monster who takes and takes and takes.

"The Coglio—"

"Is a formality. You gave it up to that fucker Bexley, so you're already tainted. I think it's time I got a taste of the pussy I'll be tied to... forever."

My walls crumble as I tremble beneath him. "Not here," I say, desperate to hear the bleep of my cell. Something—*anything*—to distract him. "Not like this," I add.

Cade bares his teeth like a predator about to attack his prey. He leans in, running his nose along my jaw. "Tell me one good reason why I shouldn't just fuck you right here, right now." He grinds into me, showing me exactly how ready he is.

"Because despite what you say, I think tradition is important to you." I look him dead in the eye, hoping he can't see the fear there.

"Does this feel like tradition is important to me?" He claws at my skirt, pushing his hand underneath the layers and finding my panties.

"Cade—" The words die in my throat as he pushes his fingers inside me roughly.

Tears gather in the corners of my eyes, but I swallow them down.

"You're mine, Mia," he whispers darkly against the corner of my mouth. "Mine to do whatever the fuck I want with."

Our faces are pressed so close I can barely breathe. But I can see the monster in his eyes. The beast living inside him.

His fingers plunge in and out, setting a brutal rhythm that my body can't fight.

"No... God," I breathe as his thumb finds my clit, applying enough pressure to make me unravel.

"Good girl," he drawls. "Give it to me, Mia. Show me you want this as much as I do."

A rogue tear slips down my cheek as my body begins to tremble, enslaved to his touch. But suddenly, Cade stops.

"Fuck this," he mutters to himself. His hand goes to his belt and he snaps it open, undoing his buttons.

God, no.

Not here.

Not like this.

Just then, the blare of his cell phone cuts through the air like a siren.

"Maybe you should—" His hand goes to my throat and squeezes.

"This is happening, baby. Right here, right now." He works his cock free ,and I feel it against my thigh, thick and hard and ready to take something that isn't his to take.

But the ringing doesn't stop. Eventually, he rips his cell out of his pocket and glances at the screen.

"Who is it?" I ask shakily.

"Channing."

Relief floods me. Sasha got my message. She got it and she got help.

Cade narrows his eyes at me and then glances back at the screen.

It stops suddenly, but a text message follows.

"Fuck," Cade mumbles to himself as he reads it, rolling off and sitting up. "Motherfucking fuck."

"What is it?" I ask, smoothing down my skirt.

"We need to leave, now. Get your shit and let's go." He leaps up and storms off toward the car.

I grab my purse, pull out my cell phone and quickly text Sasha.

Mia: Thank you... thank you.

17

BEXLEY

I sit on a bench outside the Henderson building waiting for Channing to appear after his last class of the day, staring down at my cell.

At Mia's last message.

My grip on the phone tightens until I'm sure it's about to buckle under my fingers.

Mouse: I won't be in class today. Don't worry, everything is fine.

How can she say that and think I'm not going to worry? Especially when I learn who else isn't in class today.

What has he done with her... *to her*?

A million and one questions flash through my mind as images of him taking what's mine emerge faster than I can control, threatening to turn me into a version of myself I hate.

Red hot fury stirs in my belly as I stare at my reply. She's read it. I can see the little ticks.

But she never responded.

"Fuck," I mutter to myself, dragging my hand through my hair and tugging until it stings.

Just reply and tell me you're okay, I plead, staring at her previous words.

"Hey," a familiar voice says before feet appear in my vision. "What's wrong?"

"Kingsley's got Mia," I admit.

"I know. Sash and I have it under control. Don't worry."

"W-what?"

"She's back at the house; she's safe. Don't worry. We won't let anything happen to her."

"H-how? What did you do?"

He drops his bag to the floor then lowers himself beside me.

"He took her out to the lake. Gravestone Lake, not the one at the house. She'd text Sasha for help and I called him with some urgent Q news. He was back in a flash and left her at the house."

"He's going to know you lied."

"I didn't lie. Everything I told him was true. It just could have waited."

I sit and consider his words for a few seconds.

"Wait, how do you know Q news? I thought it went straight to Cade."

A smile twitches at his lips.

He looks at me, his eyes narrowing for the briefest moment as if he's trying to decide if he can tell me or not.

"Not even Sasha knows this," he warns.

"O-okay."

"Q... they called me back in after our meeting on Sunday. Seems there might just be a way for me to get what I want."

"Oh?"

"I can't tell you the details. I shouldn't even be telling you this, but... but I know you're on my side."

"I am," I say without missing a beat.

"If I can get them what they need, then maybe, just maybe there could be a way for Sasha and I to be together."

"They know about the two of you?"

"Yeah, I told them everything."

"Shit."

"Pretty much their response. Phillip looked about two seconds away from killing me with his bare hands, but it is what it is, and I'll stand up for Sasha in any way I can."

"She's lucky to have you, man."

"We'll see about that. There's always time for this all to go very wrong."

I don't respond. I can't. I know as well as he does how much is at stake right now.

"Come on, let's go home and see if your girl is still there."

My heart aches at his words. Even if she is, it's not like I'm going to get to spend any time with her. She'll be with him, playing her part, and I'll be forced to the sidelines, just biding my time.

"Easton," Channing says as I reluctantly stand, ready to head toward the lot.

"Yeah."

"Not a word about this to Sasha. I can't get her hopes up again."

I nod sadly. He's right; we need to start trying to protect the girls in any way we can. Neither of them deserves any of this bullshit.

"Whatever you need, man," I say, slapping him on the shoulder as he stands, and together we head for his car.

Everyone's cars are already in the driveway when we pull up, all of them having finished classes earlier than us today, and as we make our way through to the kitchen, the sound of their voices from the den carries down to us.

"I guess we'll be expected to join the party," I mutter quietly as we each grab a drink.

"Just play your part, bide your time. It's all we can do."

"And just how many people am I going to be expected to kill in that time?" I ask, bringing up a question I really don't want the answer to.

I've shoved the events of that night so far down in a little padlocked box inside that it's almost like it never happened.

Apart from I know it did. The memories are all too real.

I'd wanted to tell Mia when I went to her place. I'd wanted to confess. But then I looked into her soft eyes, saw the excitement within them about my being there, and I couldn't do it.

I hate that she already thinks I'm one of them, despite knowing I don't want to be. If I told her that, would she even have let me stay?

I'm a monster for doing what I did.

I'm no different than him.

"Those orders come from above, Bex. Whether Cade is here or not. There are some things that, no matter what we manage to achieve, will always stay the same."

Whether Cade is here or not.

"Are you trying to get rid of him?" I hiss.

"Don't," he warns a second before Ashton strolls into the kitchen behind us.

"Ladies, how's it hanging?" he drawls. "Got some banging fucking pussy in the den. Come check it out."

My mouth goes dry at his suggestion as images I don't need from previous experiences with girls in the den play on my mind.

"We'll be right there. Just grabbing some food."

"Good plan, man. You're gonna need it. They're fucking wild."

Ashton grabs his junk through his sweats and backs out of the room.

"He's a douchebag," I mutter under my breath, making Channing bark out a laugh.

"Putting it mildly. He's a motherfucking leech. Shouldn't even be here. Here, eat up. Like he said, you're probably going to need it."

"You're right. I have my suspicions that I'm not going to want to stay down long."

The music and voices get louder as we move toward the den. Channing slips inside as if it's just another day in hell for him, while I come to a stop in the doorway, my eyes briefly running over everything that's happening before me, searching her out.

I want to say that I relax when I find her, but that would be a lie because she's tucked into Cade's side. Her hand is high up on his thigh, while he has her skirt bunched up and her ass in his palm.

My stomach churns, watching him touch what's mine, and I know immediately that I made the right call with the food. There's nothing in my stomach right now, and I already feel like retching.

"Easton, come in. What do you fancy? Blonde, brunette, redhead?" He points with his chin toward the girls, and I reluctantly follow his instruction.

Ashton and Brandon are, unsurprisingly, knuckle deep in two of the six girls that are littered around the room. The girls moan loudly—fakely—as they play with them.

But it's when my eyes land back on Alex that they nearly fall out of my head.

"What have you given him?" I growl, ripping my eyes away from him and the two girls on the couch on the other side of the room.

"Me?" Cade asks as if he's totally innocent. "I haven't given him anything. All his own doing."

I take a step toward him as one of the girls, the one who's sitting on his face, falls over the edge. Her hands lift, cupping her naked breasts, tugging at her nipples like she doesn't have an entire roomful watching her while the other sucks Alex off.

"Leave him," Cade growls, making me stop my advance. "He's just enjoying himself. You really should do the same. Shelly and Grace over there are experts at making things seem that much better. Right, girls?"

Cade nods at them and they immediately start stalking toward me.

At least these two are still fucking dressed.

Mia isn't looking at me right now—she hasn't since the moment I appeared—but as the girls approach, I feel her eyes shift to me.

"Hey, big boy. You ready to play?" one of them purrs, making my lips curl in disgust.

I'm sure they're both very beautiful underneath the layers upon layers of makeup.

"I'm good right now. I really need to go shower before..." I trail off, knowing that nothing is going to happen here.

"Aw, that's okay, sweetie. You smell pretty fresh to me," the other says, leaning in and pressing her nose to my neck.

"If you'll excuse me..." I take a huge step back from them. "Maybe make use of each other if you're that desperate. Give Kingsley a nice little show."

I have no idea if they accept my challenge, and I really don't give a fuck as I march toward the door.

"Easton," Cade barks. I stop, but I don't look around. I can't. I can't see him with his hands on my girl right now.

I'm barely holding on as it is.

"You're an ungrateful sonofabitch, you know that?" he barks. "All of this is for you. You must be going crazy, not getting your dick wet now."

Shaking my head, I storm away and to the stairs.

One question rings out in my mind as I leave the disaster happening in that room behind.

If it weren't for Mia, would I have been like Alex and just caved in to temptation?

I want to say no, but there would have been nothing stopping me. It's not like I haven't had issues saying no in the past. That thought is one of the reasons I don't turn toward my own room when I get to the top of the stairs, but Sasha's.

I knock and wait for her to call out.

"Hey," I say softly, slipping into the room and closing the door behind me.

She's laid on her bed, already in pajamas, her eyes blown and her little tin sitting beside her along with discarded textbooks.

"Is it still going on down there?" she asks, although I think she already knows the answer because she doesn't allow me time to respond. "I tried to get her away, but he wasn't having any of it."

I nod at her, because I have no doubt she's telling the truth.

"Channing joining in?" she asks sadly.

"H-he... he um... he's in the room, but that was as much as I saw."

"He'll cave," she says with a confidence I'm sure she doesn't want. "He always does. *Got to impress the king,*" she mutters, attempting to mimic his deep voice.

"He doesn't want them, Sash," I say, walking into her room and dropping down on the end of the bed.

"Maybe not, but he still has them."

"I hate to break it to you, but I've seen you with a few guys that haven't been Channing as well."

"Can't beat 'em, join 'em." She blows out a long breath. "It was just to hurt him. To see if me being with others affected him as badly as seeing him with the girls did me."

"It does," I state, knowing that if he feels for Sasha even an ounce of what I do for Mia, then it rips him apart every single fucking time.

"Can I?" I nod to her tin.

"Bex," she warns.

"This isn't my first rodeo, Sash. I know what I'm doing." I think back to my darkest days in Sterling Bay, and I wonder just how true those words are.

But right now, it's either this, or I go downstairs, rip Mia away from that cunt and make sure that he never leaves the motherfucking room again. But I already know one of those can't happen, so...

I take the tin from Sasha's outstretched hand and pop it open.

"Thanks," I mutter, picking two out and throwing them back.

Let the oblivion begin.

18

MIA

The next day, Cade acts like nothing is wrong, but I note the way he suffocates me with attention. He was waiting for me outside my dorm this morning with a smirk on his face. A dark smile full of promises. He held my hand a little too tightly and insisted on walking me right to each class and making a show of kissing me goodbye.

It's like he's unravelling. Becoming more possessive and angrier.

"You can let her eat, man," Channing says, and Cade practically growls at him.

We're sitting in their private dining room, having lunch. Cade has me pulled close into his side, his arm draped over my shoulder as he eats his taco salad.

Bexley glances over but quickly averts his eyes. He's pissed. It radiates off him like a forcefield, but I don't blame him. I blew him off yesterday and gave him little to no explanation why.

God, this sucks.

I pick at my food, but my appetite is nonexistent.

"You should eat something," Sasha says as if she can hear my thoughts.

"We could always go for another picnic," Cade whispers against my ear, except he doesn't whisper at all. He says it loud enough to make sure everyone hears.

"Picnic?" Ashton snorts. "I bet the only thing on the menu was pussy sandwich."

"Pig," Sasha mutters over the guys' laughter. But Bexley isn't laughing. He looks murderous. I risk meeting his eyes, silently pleading with him not to make a scene, but he drops his glare, my stomach falling right along with it.

"We had some fun." Cade smirks at me, and I want nothing more than to stab my fork through his eye. "Right, babe?"

Just then his cell vibrates, and he drops his arm from my shoulder and digs it out of his pocket.

"I need to take this," he says, leaving the table. I let out a small breath. I've gotten good at holding my breath whenever he's around. Walking on eggshells and waiting for whatever bomb he's about to drop next.

I try to catch Bexley's eye again, to reassure him that nothing has changed between us, but he won't look at me.

A minute later, Cade slides back into his chair. "We've got a job tonight," he says to no one in particular.

"What kind of job?" Bexley sits straighter, and I notice the way he grips his silverware.

"Don't worry, Easton. You're off the hook tonight. This doesn't concern you."

"Like fuck it doesn't." He slams his hand down on the table. "I'm as much Electi as you are."

Bexley's outburst startles me.

"Well, not tonight, you're not. Q was clear about who they want involved, and your name didn't come up. Guess you've got a way to go to prove yourself." Smugness drips from Cade's voice.

Bexley leans forward a little, gritting his teeth. "That's bullshit, and you know it."

"Easton, leave it," Channing says, while Tim, Brandon, Ashton, and Alex watch the two of them stare each other down.

"You should listen to Rexford."

The air crackles with tension, but eventually Bexley concedes. Pushing back from the table, he shoots up. "I'm going to class. Alex?" He glances at his friend.

"I... uh, I'm still eating."

"Whatever." Bexley stalks off out of the room.

"Watch him," Cade says to Channing. "He seems to listen to you."

"You want me to babysit him?"

"Just keep an eye on him. We can't have him making waves."

"Too late for that, if you ask me." Ashton pins me with a dark stare, but I don't cower, glaring right back.

"Relax, Ash. Easton knows he needs to play nice." The way Cade says the words, so cockily, so full of conviction, makes me wonder what he's up to.

"You should hang out with Sasha tonight," he says to me, letting his hand drift up my thigh. Thankfully, I have shorts on, so he can't get very far.

"Actually, I was thinking of going to see my parents."

He stiffens—only for a second, but I catch it.

"What?" I ask him.

"Nothing." He gives me a thin smile. "I'm sure they'll be happy to see you. While you're there, you should talk to your mom about the Coglio. There isn't long left, and you'll need a dress."

My heart drops. He's right. It's next weekend.

"Maybe I'll do that," I force out.

The guys go back to their regular conversation. I watch Alex laugh and joke with them, and I don't know whether to be relieved or disappointed.

"Hey, you okay?" Sasha asks me, and I manage a small nod. As crazy as it is, I am okay.

But I shouldn't be.

And that's what worries me.

BEXLEY WASN'T IN ECONOMICS. I spent the entire hour deliberating whether to text him but in the end, decided against it.

Sasha meets me outside class. "All set?"

"Yeah. Listen, thanks for doing this." She offered to give me a ride to my parents' house. I wasn't lying when I told Cade I want to see them.

I just wasn't entirely honest about why I'm going home.

"Anytime. I'm going home for a few days, anyway. I think I need some space."

"From Channing?"

"From everything." She lets out a heavy sigh.

"I know that feeling." I sink back against the soft leather seat, watching the scenery roll by. It's hard to believe that less than two months ago, I was just a girl about to start college. Everything is different now.

I'm different.

And my freedom from this place seems to move further out of reach with every passing day.

We ride in comfortable silence until Sasha turns onto my street. "Nice place," she says, and I roll my eyes.

"You live in a mansion."

"Just because something's pretty doesn't mean it's good inside," she says with an air of sadness.

The more I get to know Sasha, the more I can't imagine growing up as an Electi heir but knowing you were born the wrong sex to ever inherit the power that comes with the title.

"Will you be okay getting back?" she asks me, and I nod.

"My dad will give me a ride."

"Okay. I'll see you tomorrow. Stay safe."

Her words hit deep, but I force a smile. "You too."

My dad's car is missing from the driveway, but I'm not here to see him.

Traipsing up the driveway, I test the door, only to find it locked. Digging out my keys, I slip inside. "Mom," I call. "It's me."

She isn't home. As I expected, she'll either be out for happy hour drinks or at the spa with her friends.

I drop my bag on the floor and chuck my keys on the sideboard, moving deeper into the house. This was the house I grew up in. The house where I learned to walk and fall down, the house where I was loved and nurtured. But it all feels tainted now. The memories I have of learning and growing all feel like some grooming experiment.

I never wanted to be a prosapia. I always knew I'd have to enter the Eligere... but I didn't know.

How could I?

It's hard not to feel bitter about that. It's hard not to resent my parents for just handing me over to Cade like some prize cow.

Tears burn the backs of my eyes, but I don't let them fall. I didn't come here for a trip down memory lane.

I pull out my cell phone and quickly text Mom.

Mia: Hi Mom, I came home but you're not here. I can't stay too long; will you be home soon?

A couple of minutes pass, but she texts back.

Mom: Sweetheart, why didn't you call first? You know I hang out with the girls today. I'll be home in a couple of hours. Please, stay. I'd love to see you.

Mia: I'll try. Have fun xo

Letting out a steady breath, I pocket my cell phone and make my way to the back of the house to Dad's office. He doesn't keep it locked. He doesn't need to. He trusts his family implicitly.

Maybe he shouldn't.

The thought flashes through my head, but I shake it off. Unlike the archives floor at the Town Hall, everything looks exactly the same in here.

There's a big desk pushed into one corner, with Dad's computer sitting proudly atop of it. The bookcase on the opposite wall houses an array of old books and filing boxes, labelled with things like 'house finances,' 'work,' and one that catches my eye. It isn't labelled with anything except the Quinctus crest.

A trickle of something goes through me as I approach the shelf. It's sitting right there, nestled along the rest of the filing boxes.

Hiding in plain sight.

I don't know what I expect to find inside, but my fingers tremble as I pluck the box off the shelf and sit down on the chair beside the bookcase. Pressing the catch, I lift the lid and peer inside the box. It all looks innocent enough. Paperwork with Mayor Cargill's official seal. I scan the faded text, quickly realizing it's my father's letter of employment.

No wonder it looks so old and worn—he's worked for Phillip Cargill for as long as I can remember. I pull out the stack of paper and flick through the rest, but I don't understand most of it. There's nothing here. Feeling frustrated, I straighten them into a pile and start to place them back inside when a slip of paper flutters out.

Gently edging it out, I scan the handwritten scrawl.

It's a list of names. Names I don't recognize, all except one.

Gregory Kingsley.

My spine tingles as I clutch the note, wondering what it can possibly mean. Cade's father was Quinctus. It makes sense my dad would have crossed paths with him, since he and Phillip both worked together.

But my father doesn't work for Quinctus. He works for the Mayor's office.

Pulling out my cell phone, I snap a picture of the names and carefully reorganize all the documents. I close the lid and place the box back on the shelf, making sure everything is left exactly as it was. Then I hurry upstairs to my bedroom and turn on my computer.

Once it flickers to life, I pull up Google and open the photo of the list of names. Typing the first one in, I wait for the search to populate.

My brows furrow as I scan the list of results. I've never heard of Landon Stanley, but apparently Google has. His name litters newspaper reports and online articles. But it's one specific headline that piques my interest.

"Investment banker Landon Stanley found dead after car spins on black ice and falls into a ravine." Huh.

The back of my neck prickles as I move onto the next name. Jeffery Poulter. Prosecutor for a law firm in Mercury Falls, a town not far from Gravestone. The results pull up a similar story. Jeffery was driving home from work when he lost control of his car and hit an oncoming truck. He died before the EMTs got to the hospital.

When I'm done working through the list, I sit back, trying to fit together the pieces of this unexpected puzzle. These men were all in prominent positions of society. Investment bankers. Lawyers. Government officials. And they all died in road traffic accidents.

Just like Gregory Kingsley.

What does it all mean?

And why the hell does my father have their names in a filing box marked with the Quinctus crest?

I pull out my phone and text the only person I trust with this.

Mouse: Can you talk?

My cell phone starts ringing, and I hit answer.

"Bexley," I breathe.

"What is it? What's wrong?"

"I think I found something, but I don't really understand what it all means."

"Where are you?"

"At home."

"I'm at my uncle's house. Send me the address, and I'll be there as soon as I can."

"Thank you." Relief floods me.

"Mia…" His voice cracks.

"I'm sorry about earlier. I should have told the truth."

"It's probably better you didn't." I feel the anger in his words. "I'll be there as quickly as I can."

"Okay." I hang up and stare at the list of names again.

Who were these men?

And why did they all end up dead?

19

BEXLEY

I pull up outside the house my GPS directed me to.
It looks like the perfect family home with a wraparound porch, complete with a swing seat. I might never have met Mia's parents, but I can almost picture her mom sitting there reading while her and her dad kick a ball around the yard.

It's the style of house that makes me yearn for the kind of normal upbringing I didn't have.

Yes, I have the money and everything my parents could buy for me, but none of that compares to having a real loving, caring family who actually spent more time at home than they did at work or schmoozing clients at fancy functions.

Climbing from my car, I spot movement in one of the upstairs windows and my heart starts to beat faster.

I was pissed at her for blowing me off yesterday and then being with Cade, really fucking pissed, but one look at her this morning with the dark circles under her eyes and I instantly softened. She wanted to be there just about as much as I wanted her there, but we both know that right now, there's little we can do about it.

I force the memories down and jog up the steps to her front door. I lift my hand to knock, but the door opens before I get a chance.

"Hey," Mia says almost shyly, pulling the door open and inviting me inside.

"Hey. Are your parents home?" I ask, noting the empty driveway I just pulled up beside.

"Nope."

"Good."

With my hand around her throat, I push her back against the wall, kicking the door closed behind me. All the air rushes from her lungs with the impact, but I don't give her a chance to recover. Instead, I make use of her parted lips and thrust my tongue between them.

It only takes her a second to get with the program before her hands wrap around my sides and she sucks my bottom lip into her mouth, making my cock swell, wishing it was that she was sucking on.

"Fuck, little mouse," I groan, ripping my lips from hers and kissing down her neck.

Her leg curls around my hip, and I grind into her.

"Bexley," she moans.

"Do you know how fucking mad I was last night, seeing you with him?"

"Yes," she breathes, and I pull down the neck of her tank to bite down on the swell of her breast. "I know, I'm sorry, I—"

"Don't. Don't apologize for something you have no control over."

"Oh God," she whimpers as I pull the cup of her bra down and suck her nipple into my mouth.

"I need you, mouse. I need you so fucking bad,"

"I'm right here."

Dropping to my knees, I undo the button around her waist and tug the fabric down her hips. She kicks her shorts and panties aside. Throwing one of her legs over my shoulder, I run my tongue through her folds.

"Oh God," she cries when I circle her clit.

As much as I might want to eat her for fucking hours, I'm too desperate to be inside her to give her too much time.

Pulling away, I stand, slamming my lips down on hers. She reaches out, making quick work of my pants before dipping her hand inside my boxers for my cock. "Mia," I moan when her fingers wrap around the length. "Need to be inside you right now. Turn around."

She immediately does as I say, sticking her bare ass out toward me, teasing me.

"Hands on the wall. This is gonna be quick."

"Okay."

I take two seconds to appreciate how fucking sexy she looks before I run my cock through her wetness and push inside. She's tight like always, and it damn near makes my eyes cross as I slide myself in deeper.

"Bexley," she moans, flexing her hips as she adjusts to my size.

Wrapping my hands around her hips, I pull her back to meet my thrust, hitting her deep and making her cry out in pleasure. My body heats as my release surges forward an embarrassingly short time later.

Releasing one side of her, I slip my hand around her front to pinch her clit.

"Bexley," she cries as her pussy clamps down on my cock seconds before we both fall over the edge.

I'm still inside her when the sound of a car outside has her body locking up with tension.

"Fuck. Fuck. Is that my mom?"

I step back, quickly tucking myself away as she flies toward the window, pulling the blind back a little.

Her relief is instant. "It's just the neighbors."

"Aw, I'm sure your mom would love me."

"Yeah, aside from the fact they think they're marrying me off to someone else. Someone, I should add, who she thinks is wonderful."

"Okay, so I've just gone off your mother a little," I admit, picking up her discarded clothes and passing them over to her.

"She's blinded by the glitz, glamor and money. She thinks that being Cade's prosapia is the world's biggest privilege."

"You're not selling her to me."

"I wasn't trying to. Come on, I need to show you something."

"Your bedroom," I ask, waggling my eyebrows.

"Well, yes, but it's what I've got inside that I want to show you."

"Okay, lead the way."

I follow her ass up the stairs, wishing all the way that she hadn't put her shorts back on yet. She shows me to her desk and starts explaining what she's found.

"So what do you think it means?" she asks, standing next to me with her ass perched on the desk.

"I think... I don't know what I think, aside from this all being suspicious as fuck."

"You said you were at Marcus'. Did he have anything to say?"

"No. He just kept repeating that we needed to trust that Q knows what they're doing and that I need to protect you."

"Me?"

"Yeah. Why do you look surprised? We all know that Cade is dangerous."

She lifts her hand, pushing her hair back. "I know, it's just hearing you say it like that... it makes the threat seem so real."

"It is. What happened at your picnic yesterday, mouse?"

"Nothing really." I narrow my eyes at her, sensing that she's hiding something. "He tried and, thanks to Channing, failed to get what he wanted."

"He's not going to wait until your ceremony at this rate."

"It's tradition. He has to."

I quirk a brow.

"I hope."

"What if you can't get out of it by then?"

"Then..." She blows out a long breath. "Then I have to see it through."

My body freezes with her words. There's no fucking way I'm letting him make things official in the eyes of Q. There's no fucking way I'm going to let him touch her.

"I'm sorry, Bex. But it might be the only way. We might need more time."

I know this, I do. But it doesn't stop it from hurting.

Pushing that issue aside for now, I focus back on why we're here.

"What are you doing?" she asks as I pull my cell from my pocket.

"Calling James. If Marcus won't help, I think you're right. He's the next one to ask about all this."

After a short conversation, I discover that he's thankfully in Sterling Bay right now, and he—somewhat reluctantly—agrees to meet us.

"He's going to send me an address for a diner out of town, and we're going to meet him there," I tell Mia.

"Now?"

"In an hour, yeah. It's only about thirty minutes from here though, so we've got a little time."

"Is that right?" she asks, a knowing smile pulling at her lips.

THE DINER IS DESERTED when we pull into the lot exactly an hour later. Not two seconds later does another car roll in behind us.

"Is that him?" Mia asks, staring out the window.

"Yeah. Come on then, let's see if we can find anything out."

"Bexley," he says, holding his hand out to me when we meet just before the entrance to the diner. "Good to see you, son. And this must be Mia. It's a pleasure," he says, also shaking her hand. "I've heard a lot about you, young lady."

Mia's cheeks turn bright red.

"F-from where?"

"That doesn't matter right now. Shall we?" He gestures toward the doors, and the three of us step inside.

There is only one server as we walk in, and we're quickly seated in a booth in the farthest corner of the restaurant.

"Is it always this quiet?" Mia asks, filling the silence that's descended.

"No. I booked the entire place."

"At an hour's notice?" She balks.

"Yes. I sense we might need to discuss some... sensitive topics, so I thought it for the best."

"Right. I'm sorry, but who are you exactly?" Mia asks as she stares James directly in the eyes. Pride for my girl oozes from me as she holds her own against him.

Everyone knows that James Jagger takes no prisoners, but she doesn't seem fazed in the slightest.

"I work for Q," he states. "My grandfather and grandmother fled from Gravestone after falling in love. My father was promised to someone else. Sound familiar?" he asks, looking between the two of us.

"Somewhat," I mutter, having already heard this story from my mom.

"They moved to Gravestone, and thankfully my father was in a position with Q that he could broker a deal. He agreed to work for them if they agreed to make Sterling a safe haven, that they wouldn't come after either of them or others who flee."

"What did your grandfather know or do to hold that much power over them?" Mia asks, enthralled by this story.

"That doesn't matter right now. Marcus—my great-uncle, your grandfather—stayed. His son took my father's place as heir, and everything would have continued."

"But he died."

"Died after also falling for the wrong woman. A woman who had you."

"Okay we know all this," Mia says in a rush, wanting to get to the main point of the meeting. "I was never meant to be Cade's prosapia," she states with confidence.

"Your name was in the calix, Mia."

"I know, but it threw everyone for a loop. It wasn't meant to be me. Someone planned it, and I want to know why." Her voice begins to rise with her anger. "Cade is unhinged, a complete psycho, and someone thought it would be a good idea for us to be together."

James swallows somewhat nervously as Mia's emotions begin to get the better of her.

"We found this," she says, slamming the list of names down on the desk. "I found it in my father's office after hearing him having a very suspicious conversation with Phillip Cargill. I need to know if this is all linked, if this is going to help me get myself out of this hell before Cade Kingsley kills me."

James takes the piece of paper, but he doesn't look at it long enough to really read the names. He knows exactly what it is.

"Gregory Kingsley's accident was no accident, was it?" I ask James, voicing my suspicions.

"No. It was not."

"So why? Why was he killed along with all these other men?"

"The other men don't matter. They are not linked. The only reason they are on the same piece of paper is because they met the same end."

"So Q killed Gregory Kingsley," she deadpans. "Why? And how does this involve me?"

20

MIA

"Why does my father have the list? It doesn't make any sense," I say, trying to process everything.

"That I can't tell you." James gives me an apologetic look. "But know that this knowledge is dangerous. In the wrong hands, it could be catastrophic."

"This is why Marcus didn't want me snooping around," Bexley says. "Why he's told me nothing."

"We all keep secrets, son. You know that." James levels Bexley with a strange look.

"What do you mean?" I ask, a trickle of awareness zipping up my spine.

"That's for Bexley to tell you."

My stomach dips as I search Bexley's face for answers.

"Not here," he says, squeezing my knee under the table. "Later. It feels like we're still going around in circles. If Quinctus are that worried about Cade, why can't they just... you know, get rid of him?"

His words made me flinch. Of course, I'm not immune to the whispers of dark deeds that follow Quinctus and the Electi wherever they go. But there's hearing about it and then knowing it.

"Nothing in this world is that simple, Bexley. Let's just say the

Kingsley name still holds a lot of sway with Q's associates. If Cade were to just disappear, it would create problems."

"How do you know all of this?" I ask.

"My business with Q affords me certain knowledge."

"And what exactly is it you do?"

"Mia," Bexley warns.

"It's quite alright." James smiles. "You're strong. Inquisitive. You're going to need that in the coming weeks. I'm what you might call a fixer."

"A fixer?"

"I make problems disappear. Paper trails, money trails…"

"People trails?" Bexley raises a brow, and James chuckles.

"I leave the more hands-on stuff to others. I'm fortunate; I have one foot in Gravestone business and one foot out."

"Why did you agree to meet us?"

"Because I'm far enough removed that I can tell you what I know without raising alarm bells. There's a splinter in Q. Those who believe in walking into the future and embracing new ways. And those who aren't ready to leave the past behind. Gregory Kingsley dabbled with bringing the past into the future, and it cost him his life."

James hesitates, waiting as the server brings us a fresh pot of coffee. "Thank you," he says. She leaves us and he continues.

"There are those in Q who want to see Cade succeed. To follow in his father's footsteps. And there are those outside of Q who have a vested interest in Cade's legacy."

"Let me guess," Bexley scoffs. "You can't tell us who."

"Cade's uncle. Lincoln Kingsley. After Gregory… died, he made Quinctus promise to protect Cade. To nurture him and raise him to fulfil his rightful place."

"Well, they didn't do a very good fucking job."

"This is why your presence is so important, Bexley. The Electi needs balance. It needs level headedness."

"If Q thinks my presence is going to do anything but antagonize Kingsley, then they really don't know their Electi very well at all. He's gunning for blood, James. My blood."

"It won't get that far." He lets out a long, steady breath. "Cade is just testing boundaries. But eventually he'll push too hard, and Q will push back."

"I don't like it." Bexley slips his arm around the back of my shoulder. "I don't like it at all. This isn't some... some game. This is our lives."

"I know. For that, I am sorry."

"Sorry? You get to live out your life in Sterling Bay, removed from all this. Ace, Cole, and Conner will never have to sacrifice their lives for some... cult."

James flinches. "There are still things you do not understand. Sacrifices my family made..."

"Yeah, I'm sure it was very hard, running away." Bexley shoots up. "I need some fresh air." He glances at me, regret shining there. "I'll be in the car. James, I'd say it's been nice to see you, but really, it hasn't." He stalks off, leaving me alone with James Jagger.

Silence hangs between us, and then I say, "All I want to know is how we get out of this."

His expression hardens, and then he says the two little words I've feared since this whole thing started.

"You don't."

JAMES SETTLES THE CHECK, and we walk out of the diner side by side.

"I really am sorry, Mia."

"Yeah, me too."

"I will talk to Marcus. The stubborn old fool is too blinded by the past to realize what's staring him in the face. I know it feels like you're alone in this, but I promise you that you're not."

"Thank you."

My head feels like it's going to explode from all the revelations. Except, they weren't really revelations, only more pieces of a never-ending puzzle.

"Tell Bexley I said goodbye." James gives me a stiff nod before slipping into his black SUV.

I watch him leave before going to Bexley's car and climbing in.

"Are you okay?"

"Nothing about this is okay," he grumbles, firing up the engine.

The ride to Gravestone is quiet, the air thick and heavy with our conversation with James. Bexley is on edge, a dark storm circling him.

"Bexley," I say softly, trying to coax him out of his bad mood. His fingers curl tighter around the steering wheel.

"Bexley, look at me."

His eyes flick briefly to mine, two black orbs full of so much anger it stuns me.

"We'll figure it out." Even though I know it's futile. There is no winning against Quinctus or the Electi. We are pawns in their game, and we have no choice but to follow the play.

I am Cade's prosapia.

One day, I will be his wife.

One day, I will bear his heirs.

A shudder rolls through me and I blurt out, "Stop the car."

"Mia?" Panic coats Bexley's voice.

"Stop the car," I cry.

I can't breathe. I feel like the air is being sucked from the car until my lungs burn.

Bexley swerves into a rest area and cuts the engine. "Mia?"

"I hate this." My hands collide with the window. "I hate this, I hate this, I hate this."

I inhale a ragged breath.

"Hey, hey." Bexley reaches for me, gently tugging me toward him. He touches his head to mine and sucks in a sharp breath. "You are so fucking strong, Mia. One of the strongest people I know. You can do this. You have to do this... I can't lose you. I can't ever lose you."

"I kept telling myself we'd find a way out, that I'd figure out something... but there isn't a way out, Bex. I'm his prosapia. That isn't going to change."

Bexley stiffens, the tether between us pulling taut. The air crackles, shifting and swirling around us.

Then the tether snaps.

I don't know who moves first, but we collide in a blur of tongue and teeth, hands and sighs. Bexley hauls me onto his lap and grinds into me.

"You're mine, mouse. Mine," he rasps, kissing me with big, open-mouthed kisses that trail down my jaw and along the slope of my neck.

His hand wraps around my throat and pushes me back against the steering wheel.

"He can't have you, because you're mine. Nothing he says or does will change that. I'm here, Mia." He presses his hand flat against my breastbone, over my heart. "You fucking own me."

A whimper spills from my lips as I dive for his jeans, tugging and clawing at his belt until it comes loose. Bexley lifts his hips, helping me get his jeans down enough to free his cock. I pump him a couple of times, reveling in the moans he makes in the back of his throat.

"I need you, mouse. I need inside you."

I lean up and pull my skirt up, slipping my panties aide, and sink down on him, crying out at the sudden fullness.

We don't move.

We just sit there.

Bexley hard and ready inside me.

My hand slides up his jaw, gripping him, and I stare right into his eyes. "Tell me I'll always be yours. No matter what, Bex, tell me…"

"Mine," he growls, thrusting up, making us both moan. His hand tightens around my throat as I start to roll my hips, slow and torturous strokes that build an intense wave inside me.

Bexley's other hand digs into my hip enough to leave bruises, but I welcome the pain. I want to feel it all, I want to feel everything with this man.

My hands curl into the hair at the nape of his neck, and I touch my head to his, anchoring us together. "I love you, Bexley Easton. I'm in love with you."

He blinks at me, his mouth parted on a small gasp. "Y-you love me?"

I nod, fighting a smile.

"Fuck, little mouse. Fuck!" He takes over, thrusting into me with complete abandon. It's hard and fast and sweat coats my skin as he tells me with actions, not words, that he feels the same.

My hand flies out, slamming against the window as I meet him, thrust for thrust. "God, Bex… God…"

"That's it, Mia. Take me, take all of me and show me who you belong to."

My legs begin to quiver as the pleasure drenches every inch of me, and I shatter.

"Fuck, that feels good. Squeeze me, Mia. Just like that." Bexley groans my name as he falls over the edge with me, spurting hot jets of cum inside me.

Our chests heave between us as we ride out the aftershocks. He buries a hand in my hair and cups the back of my neck, leaning in to flick his tongue over my lips. "I love you, Mia. I don't know when or how it happened, but I do. I love you so fucking much."

Contentment fills me as I collapse against him, and we sit there, basking in the moment, pretending that when we get back to Gravestone things will be different.

AFTER WE CLEANED UP, Bexley drove me home. I didn't want to leave him. I forced myself from the car and watched as he drove away. Dad still wasn't home, but Mom was back, waiting for me.

"Mia, sweetheart, where have you been?" she asked, and I fed her some lie about going for a walk.

I don't know if she believed me, but she didn't push. She's been too busy asking me questions about Cade and the Electi, about what it's like being his prosapia.

"We need to find you a dress for the Coglio," she says as we sit at the breakfast counter.

"You know, I still can't believe it. My baby, Cade Kingsley's prosapia." Pride washes over her, and it makes my stomach lurch.

She's so blinded by the town's ways. I wonder what she'd say if I told her the truth.

But I don't.

Maybe out of fear that she won't care, or maybe because I'm too ashamed to admit what Cade has done to me. Either way, I sit there, stuffing down the truth and playing the role of quiet, meek daughter.

"I'll book an appointment at Stella's." Stella owns a boutique downtown. She's verus like us.

"Sure, Mom."

"What is it, sweetheart? What's wrong?" Her brows furrow.

"Nothing, Mom."

"Oh, sweetheart." She reaches across and pats my hand. "You're feeling nervous about the union ceremony. It's completely normal, Mia. But Cade is a fine young man. You'll be in good hands."

I manage to force out some garbled reply, and her frown deepens.

"Mia, did something happen? You can tell me, sweetheart. You can tell me anything."

But the sad fact is, I can't.

And that kills a little piece of my heart.

A piece I know I'll never get back.

21

BEXLEY

The guys still aren't back when I pull up at the house with my head spinning later that evening.

I hated leaving Mia while she looked so confused by everything we'd learned tonight.

Gregory Kingsley was killed by Q.

Does Cade know this?

I shake my head at my stupid thought. Of course Cade knows. Cade knows everything.

"Fucking hell," I groan, slamming my hands down on the wheel of my BMW in frustration.

Is this all karma for the way I fucked up in Sterling Bay? I know I screwed things up with Remi, pushed her when she didn't want it, but fuck, I'm not sure what I did back then deserves me ending up here and right in the middle of this shitshow.

Sucking in a breath, I force everything to the back of my mind and swing my door open, walking toward the colossal house.

I miss the dorms.

I miss my small bedroom, my twin bed and my tiny closet and old bathroom.

This play, this luxury... it's not me.

I hated all the pretense in Sterling Bay, how my parents lorded it over everyone because they had more than almost everyone else, and I hate it even more here. Maybe because now I've had a chance to live differently, to see things from a different perspective.

Fuck, my life is a mess.

I push open the front door as Mulligan hurries down the stairs.

"Ah, Mr. Easton, would you like some dinner?"

My stomach groans right on cue.

"That would be great, thank you."

"I just delivered Mr. Rexford's up to his bedroom. Would you like—"

"I'll join him," I interrupt.

Mulligan is great. He's a fucking kick-ass chef, but I still feel weird about the fact that he waits on us hand and foot. I've lost count of the number of times I've requested he just call me Bexley since I was forced to live in his hellhole, but he still refuses. Cade's need to reign supreme and be above everyone really does know no bounds.

"Very well, sir."

"Thank you," I say sincerely.

"You're more than welcome, Mr. Easton."

I raise my brow at him, and he fights a smile. It's as if he's paid not to enjoy himself while he tends to our every need. It's just fucking weird.

Taking the stairs two at a time, I follow the sound of music until I get to Alex's door. I knock a couple of times and he immediately calls for me to enter, I assume knowing that it's me.

"Hey, man. How's it going?"

"It's... going," I mutter, falling down onto his bed while he eats at his desk.

"That good?"

The words are on the tip of my tongue to tell him what I've really been up to tonight, who I've been with, but I quickly swallow them down.

"Yeah. You know, assignments," I mutter, feeling the weight of the lie pressing down on me.

When it turned out that Cade and the guys were leaving us behind tonight, I knew it was my chance to talk to Marcus, so I made up some bullshit about needing to go to the library.

"Yup," he mutters, lifting his chin toward his open laptop.

"So, any idea where the guys have gone without us?" I ask, intrigued to find out what Cade is up to.

"No clue, but it sucks. They bang on about us being a part of them now, and then they just drop us when they feel like it." From the tone of Alex's voice, I'd say he's more annoyed about this than I am.

He's been swept away by them, and what he's saying right now doesn't stem my concerns at all.

"You're enjoying this, aren't you? Living here, being one of Cade's sheep."

"I'm just making the best of it," he says, nodding to his half-eaten steak.

"But last night..." I start, thinking back to him 'making the best of it' with one of Cade's sluts.

"I was just enjoying myself, man. You should really do the fucking same."

"You barely kissed anyone in front of me since we became friends, yet all of a sudden you're sticking your cock in any willing pussy in public."

"It wasn't in public," he argues.

"Fine, a room full of pricks."

He shrugs, clearly not seeing the issue I've got with this.

"What were you on?"

"I dunno, some pills Ash had. They were fucking good, man. Felt like a fucking king."

"Yeah, I could see that while you were getting your rocks off."

"You know, you could enjoy yourself too, if you stopped pining after Mia."

Anger surges through me at his suggestion that I could just forget about her that easily.

"That's not... She's not... Do you know what? Fuck you, Alex. You want to act up to the big boys, join their little fucking club, then be my guest. It's your fucking funeral. You just remember who had your back when it counted." I pin him with a look, and he pales as he remembers the night in the warehouse.

Yeah, I was the one who made that kill... for him. No other fucker was going to do it as he choked.

"Next time you need help, feel free to run to Cade like a good little fucking sheep."

I march across his room and have my fingers wrapped around the door handle when he speaks again.

"Bex, I'm sorry. I—"

"Don't," I bark, not ready to hear his apology.

Ripping the door open, I slam it behind me hard enough to make the walls vibrate before storming to my own room and repeating the move.

MY MOOD ISN'T any better when I wake up the next morning, and knowing that I'm going to have to sit through classes with Mia today doesn't help.

It's like I spend the majority of my time as a spectator in her life. On the edges, looking in, wanting more.

I guess it's how most of the Gravestone U students feel about the Electi. Well, they are more than welcome to come and take my fucking place. I don't want it.

I think back over last night's conversation with James once more and all the things he alluded to. I knew he wasn't going to sit there and spell it all out for us. This town has secrets for a reason. Hell, James has a job covering all of that shit up for a reason. Still, I'd hoped for more than he gave us. Something a little more concrete that we could use to help her get out of this. As it is, I feel like we're clawing after something that is totally unreachable.

Alex looks a little sheepish when I join him and the others in the kitchen where they're all eating breakfast. Unable to stomach their little gathering, I refuse Mulligan's offer of cooked food and instead grab an apple and cereal bar and excuse myself.

"Was it something we said?" Cade calls after me when I don't bother muttering a word to them and instead walk straight out of the house.

I'd rather be sitting in class early than hanging out with him.

The day passes slowly, classes even slower. Until we get to economics.

I don't walk inside like I have done since I discovered the truth about mine and Mia's lives. Instead, I sit on the bench outside and wait for her.

Sure, it'll piss Cade off, but right now, I don't really give a shit.

I want to be close to her. I *need* to be close to her.

My heart jumps and my stomach twists the second I see him escorting her to class like she's unable to be left alone for even a second, but before they approach the door, someone calls Cade's name and he stops and looks over his shoulder, pulling Mia by the hand with him and right into the path of another student.

I wince as I watch the two of them collide, and Mia lets out a shocked squeal as they crash into each other.

The guy plows into her with such speed that she goes stumbling back. Reaching out, he grabs her by the waist to stop her from falling to the floor, but while I see that as him protecting her, Cade seems to see it very differently.

"Get your fucking hands off her," he bellows, causing the entire hallway to be silenced as he forcefully rips the guy's hands from Mia.

Sure, the idea of another man touching Mia—namely Cade—makes my skin boil, but it was clear that he was only trying to help.

"I'm... I'm sorry, man. I-I didn't mean—"

Cade takes him by the throat and pins him up against the wall. I can't see his eyes, but I've got experience with just how dark and crazy they probably look right now.

The guy against the wall looks about ten seconds away from pissing his pants.

"Cade, stop it. Let him go. It was your fault," Mia begs, pulling at Cade's forearm in a futile attempt to make him stop.

"My fault?" he balks. "That guy plowed straight into you."

"Because you put me in his way."

"He fucking touched you."

Cade's grip on the guy's throat must get tighter, because his eyes widen in fear.

"Go to class, Mia."

"No, I won't let you—"

"I said go to fucking class."

"But—" she argues, clearly wanting to help the guy out, but I fear he's already in too deep.

"Go to fucking class before you end up next to this cunt," he spits in her face.

I'm up before my brain has caught up with my body.

"Let's go to class," I say to her, wrapping my hand around her upper arm.

She startles at my contact, her head twisting to look up at me, but I keep my eyes firmly on Cade and a scowl on my lips.

"Bex, we can't just—"

"Mia," I drop my voice, pleading with her just to go into the classroom.

"Fine, fine. But if you hurt him..." she warns, narrowing her eyes in Cade's direction.

"You'll what, babe? Hold out on me?" He laughs like a man possessed as the guy in his hold whimpers in fear.

"Come on," I whisper before gently pushing her toward the door.

"Bex, we can't just—"

"We can. Nothing we say will stop whatever Cade has in his head right now."

"But—"

"Mia, you can't save everyone. Especially when the devil is involved."

"This is all my fault," she cries, dropping down into a chair I direct her to and putting her head into her hands.

"No, it's Cade's. He caused it."

"Y-you were watching?"

"I was waiting for you."

"Bex, you can't—"

I raise a brow at her as our professor walks in to begin class.

Leaning in, I whisper in her ear. "You're mine, Mia. I can do what the fuck I like."

She squirms in her seat, pressing her thighs together. The sight of her fighting with her desire makes my cock hard as a fucking rock.

If it weren't for the eyes that Cade has in every inch of this college, I'd drag Mia out of class right now and show her just how much I mean what I just said, but I can't put her in danger like that.

AFTER CLASS, we walk toward the parking lot together. But instead of her getting in my car, she heads toward where Sasha is waiting for her.

I want to stop her, to demand that she gets in my car, but I know I can't. Us turning up at the house together would be suicide, even if Cade did watch me escort her into class earlier. I have no doubt he'll make me pay for that move before long.

I follow Sasha's car back to the house to find everyone else already here.

The three of us walk into the kitchen to find only Mulligan there, preparing dinner.

"Oh, Miss Cargill, Miss Thompson, Mr. Easton. Mr. Kingsley would like you to join him in the mausoleum as soon as possible."

The three of us look at each other, unease rippling through the air.

Whenever I've been down there, something really fucking bad has happened, and I have no reason to think this time is going to be any better.

"Let's go," I say, striding across the kitchen toward the doors that lead to the yard.

There's no time like the present than to see what kind of hell Cade is about to show us.

22

MIA

I don't want to be here.
 I don't want to step foot in the place where Cade revealed the true depths of his depravity. But we have been summoned.

And King Cade waits for no one.

"What do you think he wants?" I ask Sasha over the pounding of my heart.

"Your guess is as good as mine."

Bexley presses his hand against the small of my back, guiding me into the mausoleum.

"I really fucking hate this place," he grumbles.

A wave of nausea washes over me as I remember the last time we were here.

"Don't do that," Bexley whispers. "Don't let him in."

I don't want to, but as we descend the stone staircase, it's hard to keep the memories out. If Brook is down here, I'm not sure I'll be able to contain myself.

"You're shaking," Sasha says, squeezing my hand tighter.

"I'm fine." I steel myself for whatever we're about to find in the den.

Muffled voices fill the air and fear trickles down my spine.

We spill into the room, and I smother a gasp at the sight of a guy tied to a chair in the middle of the room.

"What is this?" Sasha asks, and I'm in awe of the indifference in her voice. She almost sounds bored, as if it's just another day.

Everyone is here. Ashton and Tim flank the guy while Channing, Brandon, and Alex stand off to the side, watching.

"Noah here has something to say to Mia."

"Me?" I balk.

"Yeah, don't you recognize him, babe? Come closer, get a better look."

I step forward, rounding the chair a little to face the guy head on, paling when I do.

"You."

"I-I swear, it was an accident. You were in my way."

"Cade, what is this?" I repeat Sasha's words from earlier.

"He disrespected you. Now he pays the price."

"Cade," I say more firmly, coaxing him to look at me, "this is silly. It was an accident."

"Nobody, and I mean nobody, touches my prosapia and gets away with it."

"Easton, show him what we do to guys who touch what isn't theirs."

My eyes flick to Bexley, and his jaw clenches. "I'm not going to hurt him. He didn't—"

"I said show him what we do to guys who touch what isn't theirs."

"Please, man... I swear, it was an accident. I didn't even see her until it was too late. She came out of nowhere, I didn't... oh fuck. This is crazy, come on. I'm not—"

"Ash." The second his name falls from Cade's lips, Ashton stalks forward and throws his fist right into the guy's face. His head snaps back on a pained grunt, and I wince.

"Please," his pleas fill the room.

"Your turn, Easton," Cade barks, but Bexley stands firm.

"I'm not going to do this again," he says.

Again?

I frown.

Bexley is keeping things from me. James alluded to that, and Cade just confirmed it. But is he doing it to protect me, or because it proves what I've been worried about from the start—that he's one of them now?

An Electi.

Cade's hand shoots out, grabbing my arm, and he hauls me back against his chest. "You might want to rethink that, Easton." There's a warning in his voice as he tightens his grip on me.

I cry out, unable to stop myself as his fingers dig into my skin, no doubt leaving bruises.

Bexley's eyes narrow to dangerous slits, but I shake my head. *Don't do something stupid.*

"This is stupid, man," he says, his voice calm and composed. "I'm not going to hurt—"

"Maybe you need a bigger incentive." Cade rips open my jacket and roughly palms my breasts through my thin t-shirt. I swallow the cry of pain, steeling my spine for Cade's assault.

What I really want is to scream, 'You'll have to try harder than that,' but I know a guy like Cade will only see that as a challenge he will gladly rise to.

His fingers twist into my hair, wrenching my head to the side. He licks my exposed skin, grazing his teeth along my jaw. "She tastes so fucking good," he rasps, his words meant for only one person in the room.

Bexley's eyes shutter as he inhales a deep breath.

"What's it going to be, Easton?"

"If I do this, you'll stop?"

A tremor goes through me.

"I only want to make him pay for hurting our girl."

Our girl.

My stomach drops.

"Please, man," the guy cries as Bexley stalks toward him, "I don't deserve this. I swear, I didn't—"

"Hit him," Cade orders, his hand still on my breast. "Hit him and make it hurt."

The guy is crying now, big fat tears that roll down his cheeks and onto his thigh.

"I'm sorry." I see the words form on Bexley's lips right before he cocks his arm and sends his fist flying into the guy's nose. Blood sprays into the air, splattering all over Bexley.

The guy shrieks with pain, thrashing against his restraints, and my stomach churns. "God, no... no... no..." He repeats the words over and over.

"Wanna take a shot, Rexford?" Cade taunts Alex, who freezes up. "No? Shame. Guess Easton will have to take your place. Again. Hit him."

"Cade, man," Channing interjects, but Cade's head whips around.

"Something you want to say?"

"He's done." He motions to the bloodied guy tied to the chair.

"He's done when I say he's done."

Bexley lets out a strained breath, flicking his eyes to me. I shake my head again, but I know it's futile.

"Again," he barks.

Bexley drops his head, defeat rolling off him.

"Why do you continuously push, Easton? I'll always push back ten times as hard. The sooner you realize that, the easier it will be. Mia is mine. Anyone who hurts her or disrespects her will pay. Surely you can't disagree with me on that."

"I'll do anything..." the guy splutters. Blood pours from his nose, running over his mouth and dripping from his chin. "Anything, please... just let me go..."

"Should have thought of that, Noah, before you put your hands on my fucking woman."

The venom in Cade's words shocks me. I don't think I've ever heard him sound so out of touch with reality. This poor guy didn't hurt me. He didn't mow me over or shame me in the hall. It was a simple mistake. Yet Cade is acting like he deserves to die.

Another shudder rolls through me. "Cade." I try to twist in his arms, but he has me in a vise-like hold. "You don't need to do this. I'm fine, see?" Desperate, I take his hand in mine and gently press it over my beating heart. "See?"

He tucks his body behind mine, pressing his lips to the sensitive skin beneath my ear. "This is what happens, Mia. Don't say I didn't warn you," he says darkly. "Easton, I suggest if you don't want me to fuck Mia right here in front of everyone, you do as I say, and... Make. It. Hurt."

Bexley doesn't hold back this time. It's like a switch flicks inside him as he lets it rip on the defenseless guy. Punch after punch, his fists rain down on him. The sickening sound of bone crunching against bone echoes around the room, setting my teeth on edge. At some point, Cade hands me off to Sasha, who wraps an arm around my waist as I bury my face in her shoulder until Cade declares, "Enough," and I finally peek over at Bexley. His hands are coated in blood, his head lowered as he inhales ragged breath after ragged breath. The guy is unconscious, a sticky, bloody mess. His face is completely mangled, no longer resembling the guy who bumped me in the hall. Silent tears roll down my cheeks as Channing moves Bexley out of the way so they can untie the guy and haul him out of the chair.

"You know what to do," Cade says dismissively, as if he didn't just give the order for Bexley to beat him to a pulp. "I knew you had it in you." He claps Bexley on the shoulder like they're two old friends. "You just needed a little nudge in the right direction. I'll have to remember that. You should go clean up. And try not to get blood all over the carpet." Cade smirks. He actually smirks, as if anything about this is funny.

Bexley's gaze moves past me, his skin pale and eyes blown with adrenaline.

"Come on." Alex approaches him, placing a hand on his shoulder. Bexley flinches but lets his friend lead him out of the room.

My heart is in tatters, watching him leave. Bile swishes in my stomach at the blood on the floor.

"Come on, Sis." Brandon motions for Sasha to follow him. She hesitates, silently asking me what I want.

"Go," I say. "You should go."

They leave, taking the air with them. Cade watches me as I stare at the chair.

"That was completely unnecessary."

"He disrespected you, and he paid the price."

"He bumped me in the hall because you pushed—"

He's on me in a second, his hand wrapped around my throat as he walks me backward and pins me against the wall. "Don't push me, Mia." His lip curls with dark intention. "You won't like what happens."

I refuse to look away despite the fear uncoiling in my stomach. "You can't hurt everyone who looks at me funny."

"I can do whatever the fuck I like," he grits out.

The air is charged around us, buzzing with tension. He's unstable, seduced by his own power and lies.

"I could take you right here," he snarls, "up against this wall, and no one would stop me."

I try to swallow over the lump in my throat, but my mouth is too dry.

"But Quinctus wouldn't like it." His eyes widen, and I continue. "They like tradition. What do you think they would have to say if I told them that you forced yourself on me, all because you couldn't wait a few more days?"

His eyes turn black as his hand tightens against my throat. "You wouldn't dare..."

"Are you really prepared to risk it?" I suppress a shudder, dangerously aware of his fingers wrapped around my neck. "Just so you can take me when we both know I'll be yours in less than two weeks?"

I have him. I have Cade right where I want him. He might lord over Gravestone U like a king, but he's still just an Electi. And he's scared of Quinctus finding out the truth about just how far he's willing to bend the rules.

But then his whole demeanor shifts. "Mia, Mia, Mia... You think you're so fucking clever, don't you? But you forget one thing." Grabbing a fistful of my hair, he pushes me to my knees, trapping me between the wall and his body. His other hand snaps his belt open and pushes his pants down his legs. Palming his cock, he pushes it against my face. I try desperately to turn my head and resist, but his fingers grip my head in a vise-like hold.

"Open wide, baby."

I shake my head, fear saturating my veins as my heart races in my chest. This can't happen...

"Open your fucking mouth." He presses the tip of his cock harder, forcing it past my lips and into my mouth. I gag around him, overwhelmed at the intrusion.

I manage to get my hands to his thighs, trying to push him away and let me up for air. To stop this madness. But it only encourages him to slide deeper until I'm choking around him.

"Fuck, your mouth feels good on me." Tears stream down my cheeks as he starts fucking my face. Hard and brutal, he pistons in and out, rubbing my tears all over my cheeks with his thumb as if I'm nothing more than a toy. His plaything.

"By the time I'm done with you, Mia, there'll be nothing left. And that's a fucking promise."

But it doesn't sound like a promise at all.

It sounds like a threat.

One he's going to enjoy making come true.

23

BEXLEY

"FUUUUCK," I bellow as Alex pushes me into my room. My fists fucking kill, but it's nothing like the pain in my chest from the memory of Mia's face as I followed orders.

That guy didn't deserve that.

All of this is fucking Cade's fault. If he was paying attention to what he was doing in the hallway earlier, then it never would have fucking happened.

"I need to go back for her," I seethe, turning on my heels and attempting to push Alex out of the way.

"I really don't think that's a good idea."

"Fuck you, Rexford."

"No, Bex. You need to get a fucking grip. If you walk back down there and go after him, you'll be the one needing a fucking grave digging, not that asshole."

"He didn't even do anything wrong," I shout, my arms flailing around.

"That's not for us to decide."

"Fuck me, Alex. You really are turning into his little fucking lapdog, aren't you?"

"No, I'm fucking not. What he did was wrong, but we have no

fucking chance of convincing Kingsley of that. His word is law around here, and if you want an easy life, you just follow suit."

"Oh, that's what you're doing? When you flake on pulling the trigger or even punching that guy? You following fucking orders then?" I bellow in his face.

The second he pales, I back down slightly. Alex wasn't made for this kind of life. Hell, I suspect he's never even been in a real fight before, let alone held a gun.

Thankfully—or maybe not—my pretentious parents ensured we went shooting a few times a year with all their fucking annoying friends, so at least I know one end of a gun from the other.

"You need to man the fuck up if you're going to survive this, Rexford."

There's only a breath between us as we stare at each other. I've got a few inches on Alex and a hell of a lot of muscle, although I have noticed him starting to bulk up recently thanks to the gym downstairs.

"Go on, Rexford. Try out that right hook. Hit me."

"No."

"Fucking hit me," I bark, spittle flying from my mouth.

"Bex, I'm not going to—"

My hands lift, my palms slamming down on his chest, making him stumble back. "Hit me," I demand once more.

"You're fucking crazy."

"No, Kingsley is fucking crazy. I'm just fucking angry. You wanna learn how to do this? Now's your fucking chance."

He stands to his full height in front of me, his fists clenching at his sides.

Maybe he can follow orders after all.

"Go on. Make it hurt," I say, using Cade's words. Hell knows I need the pain right now.

Cocking his arm back, he plows it into my cheekbone. "Fuck, fuck," he barks, shaking his hand out like he just hit a brick wall. "Fuck."

"Again."

"Nah, you're done," he mutters, staring down at his inflamed knuckles.

"You're a fucking pussy, Rexford." Spinning on my heels, I march through to my bathroom to clean up my own hands.

I stand over the basin and stare into the mirror. My usually blue eyes are dark with anger and frustration, my cheek is burning red from Alex's attempt at a decent punch, and my shirt and arms covered in that poor guy's blood.

Hanging my head, I clench my fists and wince as my knuckles split open.

Turning on the faucet, I place my hands under the running water and watch it turn red before it swirls down the drain. Like my life. Resting my palms on the edge of the basin, I squeeze my eyes closed, but all I see is Cade's harsh grip on Mia, and my anger resurges.

We've got to find a way to get her out of this before the Coglio. There's no way I can let her attend that thing, knowing that Cade is going to claim her in all the ways he's been waiting for.

I do the best I can with my busted knuckles and dry them off before ripping my door open and walking back into my room. I expect to find it empty, so I startle a little when I find Alex sitting in my chair with his elbows on his knees and his head hung low.

"I'm sorry," he mutters without looking up.

"Nothing to be sorry for," I reply, dragging my shirt over my head and finding a clean one.

"There's plenty. If it weren't for you then..."

"It's fine, Alex. You're my friend, I'll do whatever I can to make this easier. Hell knows it fucking sucks ass at the best of times."

"Yeah, I hate it."

I think back to him off his head and balls deep in that girl the other night, but I refrain from saying anything. He's just trying to deal with the hand life has dealt him. I get that.

A bang from outside makes me dart toward the window, and when I look out, my heart drops into my stomach. "Mia," I breathe as Sasha and Channing carry her from the mausoleum.

She looks... broken.

What the fuck did that cunt do to her?

"Oh shit," Alex says, coming to look over my shoulder. "Bex, no. Don't, please," he begs, clearly sensing where my thoughts are at.

"I'm going to fucking kill him."

"Bexley," he cries as I march across the room.

"If he's laid a fucking finger on her, forced her to... I'm going to fucking kill him."

"You can't, Bex. She needs you. She needs you alive, for fuck's sake." His hand wraps around my upper arm in a pathetic attempt to stop me, but my strength is no match for his.

"Get the fuck off, Alex," I bark, ripping the door open and marching down the hall.

Voices filter up from the stairs, and when I round the corner, I find the three of them climbing up.

Seeing Mia up close only makes it worse.

She's got tears streaked down her cheeks, her body is limp as Sasha and Channing hold her up, her shirt is ripped, and she's got angry red marks around her throat.

"Motherfucker," I grunt, the beast within me ready to take Kingsley down once and for all.

Channing says something to Sasha, and somehow, she takes Mia's weight and continues walking with her toward her bedroom while Channing and Alex come to stand in front of me.

"Get out of my fucking way."

"No can do." Channing actually fucking smirks at me. "You're not going down there."

"He needs to fucking die."

"Maybe so, but you don't need to go fucking with him. You knew this was going to happen. You promised to protect her."

"Fuck you, Rexford. Fuck you."

I take a step, ready to push past, but the pair of them overpower me and my back slams into the wall behind me, the force of the hit knocking all the air from my lungs.

"Mia will be fine. She's stronger than you think." Channing stands toe to toe with me, his forearm pressing lightly against my neck, ready to show me exactly how strong he really is.

"I know, I just..."

"Leave it," Channing growls. "You need to leave it. You go down there all guns blazing then you're playing right into his hand. That is what he wants."

"But—"

"But fucking nothing, Bexley. You need to let it go."

"But—"

He growls, pressing harder against my neck, and I relent.

He's right, and I fucking hate it.

"Mia is okay. He didn't hurt her."

"She's fucking broken."

"Bex," he sighs. "You need to get it together. Their Coglio is right around the corner. You need to figure out a way to let this happen."

I stare into his eyes as he silently begs me to find a way to get through this.

"We'll find a way to make this right, but it's not going to be fast. Things need to happen first."

I nod at him, remembering our conversation about whatever kind of deal he's struck up with Q that might just allow him to be with Sasha one day, and I know that I've got to trust him.

He's not on Cade's side. He's on mine.

He's on Mia's.

"O-okay," I concede, nodding my head slightly.

"Go get fucked up or something," he suggests before releasing me and taking a step back. "Sasha will look after her, you don't need to worry."

"Easier said than done," I mutter, turning back toward my bedroom.

Every inch of my body screams at me to walk toward Sasha's room, but something tells me that Cade is watching my every move right now, just waiting for me to fuck up.

I don't look back to see if anyone is following me, but I'm not surprised when Alex catches my door as I try to swing it closed. "Make yourself useful and grab whatever it was you'd taken the other night. I fucking need out of this hell."

"Bex, you can't—"

"Get it, Alex. I don't give a fuck about the past or what I should and shouldn't be doing right now." I may never have fully confessed to Alex about the sins of my past, he does know the basics about why I've stayed away from drugs since I moved to Gravestone.

Old habits die hard, and I'm always just one bad decision away from becoming that person once more.

When he returns, I don't even bother asking what they are before I throw the pills back, chase them down with the bottle of vodka he also helpfully brought me, and fall down onto my bed, ready to leave my nightmare behind for a few hours.

"WE NEED TO TALK," I say, dropping into the chair beside Mia in class the next day.

I once again waited for her to arrive so I could follow in after. Thankfully, her arrival was much less dramatic than yesterday, and she managed to get inside without signing anyone's death certificate.

"Bex," she warns, the defeat in her voice gutting me.

"No, don't even try to fight me on this. I need to know what happened last night." I turn my eyes on her and she gasps. I know why. I look like a fucking mess.

I have no idea what time I finally passed out last night, but I'm pretty sure the sun was already starting to rise. What I do know is that I had more pills than I've consumed in a long time, and the bottle of vodka was long empty.

It worked, though. For about twenty blissful minutes, I forgot about everything. I felt light. I felt happy. I felt... numb.

I missed my class this morning. Hell, I missed all of my alarms and Alex and Channing coming in to try to drag my ass from bed, but I knew I wasn't missing this afternoon and my chance to get close to her.

"What did you do?" she asks, narrowing her eyes at me.

"I drowned it all out. But that's not the point. After class, we're talking."

"It's not going to make any of it better," she sighs.

"Maybe not. But it'll stop my fucking imagination going wild."

Her gaze darts away, her face showing her own lack of sleep last night. When she fixes her eyes on me again, I add, "And I need you to tell me what to expect for this Coglio. I need to know exactly what's going to happen so I can be prepared for it."

Her fists clench in her lap at the mention of the upcoming ceremony, but I think we both know at this point that there's very little chance of her getting out of it, no matter how much it eats me up inside.

She's going to become Cade's.

Officially.

24

MIA

Bexley and I sneak into the woods after class. He goes first, and I follow him. Then, he guides me to a secluded opening and lays out his hoodie for me to sit on.

"Come on." He tugs me down onto it.

"Tell me what happened first," I whisper, noticing how tense he is.

It's peaceful out here, so serene, but the way my heart races in my chest is anything but calm.

"I... fuck." Bexley drags a hand down his face, over and over, and eventually, I take his hand in mine and peel it away.

"You can trust me," I say.

"Fuck, Mia, it isn't about trusting you. It's about admitting something that might change the way you look at me."

Dread snakes through me. "What did you do?"

"Cade... he... he took me and Alex to this warehouse on the edge of town. There was this guy. He wanted Alex to kill him." He sucks in a harsh breath. "Shoot him at point-blank. It was a test... but Alex totally froze. I knew he couldn't do it. He's not built for this life."

Oh God. Bile churns in my stomach as blood roars in my ears.

"Did you..."

"I had to." He finally looks at me, and what I see there guts me. "I had to do it."

"You *killed* a man?"

He nods, his eyes shuttering on another sharp intake of breath. "And I don't think it'll be the last time."

"The guy in the mausoleum?" A chill runs through me.

"I don't know. No one would tell me what happened."

"You didn't kill him," I say, refusing to believe it. "He was still breathing when they hauled him out of there." Unconscious but breathing. He's okay. He has to be okay. Bexley isn't a murderer... he isn't like Cade and the rest of them.

But the look in his eyes...

"Does it matter? I did that... I..." He jams his fingers into his hair and tugs the ends sharply. "I fucking hate this."

"James said—"

"James is just as bad as them." Bexley's head whips up. "Playing with our lives, our futures. We're just pawns, Mia. Pawns in a game I'm still not sure I understand."

Silence settles over us as we stare out at nothing. The trees are dense around us, closing in until I feel a weight on my chest. Then Bexley says six little words that make my heart shatter.

"What happened with Cade last night?"

"Don't ask me that." I let out a shaky breath.

"I'll kill him, Mia. I'll fucking kill him if he—"

"He didn't." I twist to look Bexley in the eye. "And I'm okay. That's all you need to know." He told me his truth, but I can't tell him mine.

"It isn't..." His fist clenches against his thigh and then his hand shoots out, curving around my neck. "The thought of him touching you..."

I blink, overwhelmed at the intensity in Bexley's voice. "The Coglio is soon. You need to accept that if I go through with it, I'll have to be—"

"Don't," he hisses. "Just don't." His eyes drop to the ground, and it's like he reached into my chest and ripped out my heart. I need him with me on this.

I need him.

"You need to understand what it means, Bexley. What I'll have to do. The ceremony at Gravestone Hall is only a formality... it's the union after that seals the—"

"I can't. I can't hear you talk about... *being* with him."

Pain snakes through me. "If you don't want to be with me, I understand."

"How can you even say that?" His eyes flicker to mine, full of desperation and regret. "I love you, Mia. I'm so fucking in love with you that I can't see straight. But the thought of letting him—"

"It's okay." I press my hand to his cheek and shift closer. Bexley surprises me by scooping me up and dropping me on his lap so that I'm straddling him.

"Nothing about this is okay. I'm your guy. I'm supposed to protect you. I'm supposed to be able to keep you safe." He brushes the hair off my face and gently wraps his hand around my throat again. "I would kill him for you."

"Don't say that. Don't ever—"

"It's true. If I thought it wouldn't start some kind of war, I would end him for ever looking twice at you."

"You think it'd start a war?"

"Yeah, something still doesn't add up. If Q are pulling all the strings, why leave Cade to run things with the Electi? He's a liability. They know that..."

"They need him to continue the Kingsley line." I shudder at the very thought of ever bearing his child.

"But why does it matter? Q is powerful. We know their reach is far beyond Gravestone... Unless someone else is calling the shots."

"James alluded to other players," I say, and Bexley nods.

"What if they want Cade around?"

"And Q is trying to buy some time to figure out their next steps."

He nods again. "I think we have to assume Q are not the ones holding all the power here, which means their control over Cade is shaky at best."

"I keep thinking about that list of names... why would my dad have it? It doesn't make any sense. Not unless..." The words die on my tongue, because there's no way.

"Unless he was involved," Bexley finishes for me.

A resigned sigh falls from my lips. "It doesn't make sense, though. He works security for Phillip. He's not an... an assassin for Quinctus."

Is he?

I swallow over the words that have been plaguing my mind ever since I Googled those names. "I should talk to him—"

"No, Mia. You can't even let them know we know. Not until we connect more of the dots."

"But he's my dad…"

"I know." Bexley levels me with a sympathetic look. "I wish I could take you far, far away from here, little mouse."

"You can." My hands slide up his chest as I lean in to kiss him.

"Mia, I'm not sure—"

"Shh," I soothe. "Give me this, Bexley. Make me forget."

A low growl rumbles in his chest, vibrating through me as I circle my hips above him, creating the most delicious friction. His hands slide down to my butt and to grind me on top of him.

"You're playing with fire, mouse."

"Maybe I like the burn." I ease back to smirk at him.

There's something thrilling about being out here with him, surrounded by nothing but the trees and nature. We could get caught at any second, but after everything that's happened, after the way Cade defiled me last night, I can't find it in myself to care.

This moment feels like a fuck you to Cade and Quinctus. I'll probably regret it later, when the lust-filled spell I'm under breaks, but right now, I want Bexley to fuck me like he might never get another chance.

"I need you," I purr against his mouth, kissing and sucking his bottom lip between my teeth. Bexley groans, his hand flexing over the curve of my hip.

"You want me, take me," he challenges, injecting liquid lust into my veins. Steadying myself against him, I make quick work of freeing his cock from his jeans and sliding him through my wetness.

"Fuck, mouse," he hisses as I hook my panties aside and slide down on him until he's seated inside me. "Nothing will ever feel as good as this," he rasps, burying his hand into the hair at the nape of my neck. Thrusting upward, Bexley sends little bolts of pleasure shooting through me.

"God…" I pant. "I thought I was in control?"

He chuckles, pulling me down to kiss me hard. Our tongues tangle, slow, lazy licks that have me rocking back and forth.

"Fuck, Mia. You were made for me." He breathes the words against my lips.

But it isn't enough. I need more.

I lift myself up and slam down over him, making us both cry out. It's messy and frantic, but it feels so good that I never want to stop.

"Harder," he groans, and I circle my hips faster, sinking down as far as I can go.

Bexley's hand travels up my stomach, squeezing my breasts then grabbing my throat. That combined with the tenderness in his eyes as I ride him sends me hurtling over the edge.

"Oh God," I cry, shattering around him. But Bexley isn't done. He flips me over and drives into me, hard enough that it hurts. But the pain quickly gives way to pleasure as he claws at my hips, my thighs, slamming into me over and over.

"Fuck, Mia... fuuuuck." He collapses on top of me and we lie there on the cold ground, underneath a blanket of trees.

"This... this is what matters," I whisper. "As long as we have each other, nothing Cade says or does matters." I let my fingers trail over Bexley's brow. "I love you."

I only hope it's enough to survive whatever is coming.

I DIDN'T GO BACK to the Electi house. Cade hadn't summoned me, and I didn't want to be around Bexley, not after what we'd just done.

So I headed back to the dorms.

But as I pull open the door to the building, Brook saunters out as if she owns the place.

"Oh look, it's Cade's pet," she sneers, blocking my entrance.

"This is a surprise." I lift my chin and meet her icy gaze with my own. "I didn't realize you knew anyone who lives here."

"Oh, you'd be surprised." She smirks. "I have friends everywhere. You know it's the Coglio soon. Are you really going to go through with it?"

"I don't have any choice."

"Mila, Mila, Mila... when will you learn? There is always a choice.

You just have to figure out what it is. How is Bexy, by the way? We never did get to compare notes."

The blood drains from my face.

"Now, he was a very nice surprise. Had me purring like a kitten. And that thing he does with his tongue..." She fans herself. "I wouldn't mind a little repeat of that. I came so hard I almost blacked out."

Bile rushes up my throat, but I swallow it down.

Brook leans in as if we're two girlfriends sharing a joke. "I bet it must really cut you up inside, knowing I've had his long, thick dick inside me. And what a dick it is."

My teeth grind together, my body vibrating with jealousy. It crashes over me like an unrelenting storm.

"Interesting," she drawls. "I guess you and I aren't that different. Despite his... indiscretions and weird infatuation with you, I still want Cade. And something tells me that despite watching me fuck Bexley's brains out, you still want him."

I flinch at her cruel words, and she chuckles. "Oh, Mila. So much to learn about this world." Brook taps my cheek like I'm a child. "If you need any advice about your *Coglio*, tips on how to please a guy like Cade, then you know where to find me."

She struts off like she hadn't just pulled the rug from under my feet.

I have never met someone as cruel and vindictive as Brooklyn Moore.

Instead of heading for my dorm room, I make a beeline for Annabel's room. She opens the door immediately. "Mia?" Surprise glitters in her eyes. "What are you—"

"Can I come in?" I blurt out.

"Of course." She steps aside and I slip inside. "What happened?"

"I just ran into Brook outside, and God, she makes me so crazy."

"Brook? Here?" She balks, and I nod.

"Weird, right? She was saying all this stuff... about Cade... about the *Coglio*, and I just... it's so hard, Bel." Tears spill down my cheeks.

"Hey, don't cry. I'm here, Mia. Whatever you need." She pulls me into her arms, hugging me tight.

"You're a good friend, Annabel," I whisper.

Although things might be different between us now I'm Cade's *prosapia*, she's always been there for me.

She eases back and smiles, but it doesn't quite reach her eyes. "That's what best friends are for."

25

BEXLEY

Despite wishing time would slow the fuck down to give Mia and me a chance to find out what's really going on, the days just seem to disappear.

I sit in the back of one of the Electi's SUVs as it speeds across town toward the church where this whole fucking mess started.

But tonight isn't a ceremony or even a meeting. Apparently, it's a party. A party to celebrate Cade's upcoming Coglio. Literally the last thing in the world I want to be celebrating right now, but according to the king himself, attendance is mandatory.

My stomach is in knots as we pull up to the old gothic building which already holds a host of more than forgettable memories, but I keep the blank expression on my face. The others were tight-lipped about what we could expect from tonight, but I'm more than aware that secrets never lead to anything good where Quinctus are concerned, so I'm trying to keep an open mind while preparing for the worst.

We're dressed head to toe in black—a requirement, apparently—but unlike when we went on that *job*, this time, we're wearing dress pants and button-downs.

"Right then. It's party time, boys," Cade announces, rubbing his hands together while his eyes sparkle with wicked intent. It does nothing to settle my unease about tonight.

The second we come to a stop, someone opens the door for us, and we climb out in turn before Alex and I trail behind the others toward the main entrance where two men are standing—also dressed all in black.

Cade nods at them and they greet him by name—as if he's actually someone worthy of it—before we all file inside. The hallway is deserted as usual, and I breathe a sigh of relief as we pass the ornate double doors that lead to the room where my initiation began. Instead, we continue forward, past the door we walked through for the meeting with Q and farther down into the darkness before a door opens for us by another security guard to reveal a set of stairs.

The small, enclosed space is lit with only candlelight, giving it that eerie look that Q seems to be obsessed with. Cade once again nods at the man who opened the door for us and we descend, going deeper into the darkness.

"Well, this isn't creepy at all," Alex whispers to me a second before the sound of men talking and low music hits our ears.

As we turn the corner and the room reveals itself, I can't hold in my gasp of surprise.

Laid out before us is a state-of-the-art casino, complete with every kind of game imaginable. But it's not the tables or the wealthy men sitting around them in their finest suits sipping vintage whiskey that catch my attention... because that would be the women.

I didn't need to ask to know tonight was going to be a male only event. I guess I should have guessed there would be a reason, because the women walking around are only here to serve one purpose.

With every woman I spot around the room, their outfits get smaller as they walk around with trays in their hands, delivering drinks to the men who shamelessly eat up every inch of them.

"Whoa," Alex mutters, clearly as taken aback as me by what we've walked into.

"Trust me when I say it only gets better," Ashton says with a hint of excitement. "You think these women are good? Look up."

Reluctantly, I follow orders and tip my head back to find a series of suspended ornate cages hanging from the ceiling, each containing women who are dancing to entertain the men below. There are also podiums with long poles, barely-dressed women twisting and twirling their slender bodies around them.

It's every man's fantasy, and I'm hardly surprised by any of it, seeing as Quinctus and the Electi seem to be full of depraved and twisted men.

"Right then, boys. Let's get this motherfucking party started."

Cade, Ashton, Tim and Brandon head off into the room. Cade is immediately called over by an older, important looking man at the blackjack table, and I watch as he shakes the man's hand as if they're in a business meeting.

"It's something, right?" Channing says, hanging back with Alex and me.

"It really, really is."

We stand there watching as thousands of dollars get won and lost on the tables and even more get poured into fine crystal glasses.

"Why do I get the idea that Ashton's warning is only the tip of the iceberg?"

"You're a quick learner." Channing laughs, but it sounds strained. "This place is a playground for the rich and powerful. Anything you want tonight, you can have. Literally anything. Every drink you could possibly imagine is behind the bar, and every drug you could desire is somewhere in this room. Any girl you want is yours. There are side rooms set up ready—or, as you'll soon learn, you can just make the most of the voyeurism."

Alex stands beside me with his mouth hanging open. "So Cade's little sex fests back at the house..."

"Are nothing compared to this," Channing finishes.

"Is that the commissioner?" Alex asks, nodding toward another group of men.

"Sure is. Anyone of importance in this town is right under this roof, ready to act out their wildest fantasies."

"Fucking hell," I say, scrubbing my hand down my face.

"You might want to plaster a smile on your face or find something to take your mind off whatever it's filled with right now, because you're here to enjoy yourself."

"And if I don't want to?" I ask, because this... it isn't me, and I want no part in it.

"Tough. Consider this... a rite of passage."

"As if we've not already been through enough."

"Holy shit," Alex murmurs, his attention on the other side of the room. "Is that District Attorney Hal Bailey?"

"Yeah, Fawn's father." Channing grimaces at the sight of him with his hand up one of the server's skirts as she flirts with the table of men. "Being an Electi is just a gift that keeps on giving," he deadpans.

"Here." Channing hands us both a stack of chips. "You want more, you need to reach into your pockets. Where are you starting your night, boys?" He winks before slipping into the room and heading for the poker table.

"We're here now," Alex says, "may as well embrace it." He shrugs and takes off, leaving me little choice but to follow unless I want to stand here looking like an outsider for the rest of the night.

Alex sets himself up on the roulette table and places a few of his chips down, which, predictably, he swiftly loses.

"Here," I say, handing mine over.

"Don't you want to play?" he asks, his brows knitting together.

"It's fine. Go on."

"Cheers. My luck has to change sooner or later, right?"

I smile at him, wondering if we're destined for perpetual bad luck now we're a part of all this.

"Here," Ashton says, suddenly appearing between us. "Something to take the edge off."

"Thanks, man," Alex says, taking the small square of paper from his hands without a second thought and popping it onto his tongue.

I stare at him in disbelief. After what they did to us down in that vault, how can he take that quite so easily without even questioning what it is?

"Don't be a pussy, Easton. It's not DOM." Ashton smirks.

"I don't give a fuck. I'm not taking anything from you."

"Fine. But I can promise you that you'll enjoy tonight with or without it."

I don't want to enjoy the fucking night, but I keep that thought to myself.

EXACTLY AS CHANNING WARNED, as the night goes on and the drink and drugs flow freely, things only begin to get wilder.

The dancers shed their already nonexistent outfits and the men seem to forget that they've got wives and families at home waiting for them. The whole place transforms into one big orgy, of which Cade, Ashton and Brandon are right in the middle of, having the time of their lives.

I, however, just want to leave as soon as possible.

Ignoring the chaos behind me, I head to the bathroom, hoping for a little reprieve. The shots of whiskey I've had are doing little to numb anything right now, and I'm desperate to have something stronger, but I also know that I need to keep a clear head.

If I let my guard down, even for a second, then that asshole is going to exploit it. I've seen him watch me, watching and waiting for me to do something that I'm sure he'd take great pleasure in reporting straight back to Mia, but it's not going to happen.

She's mine. And as far as I'm concerned, she's the only girl in the world. I don't care about the women out there flaunting what they've got for all to see. I am not interested in sharing them with any of those assholes.

My fists curl as I push through the men's bathroom door, but unlike I'm expecting, it doesn't close behind me. Glancing over my shoulder, I find a man has followed me inside. There's something familiar about him, but it's hard to pinpoint with the whiskey fogging my brain.

"Bexley," he commands, and my body immediately does as it's told.

"Do I know you?" I ask, turning to look at him.

"No. Not yet. But I understand that you know my daughter."

Realization dawns the second those words fall from his lips. "You're Mia's dad?"

Reaching behind him, he flips the lock on the bathroom door. But unlike most of the men on the other side of the door, he doesn't make me nervous despite the fact that he probably should, seeing as he's just followed me in here.

"I am," he confirms.

Silence falls between us as we stare at each other.

"I'm working security here tonight as Phillip was short a few men."

"O-okay," I stutter, trying to figure out what he really wants.

"Mia's Coglio is next weekend..." he starts, as if I need a fucking reminder. "And I know you're both suspicious." My brows rise. How the fuck does he know this?

Who the fuck is Mia's dad?

"But you have to let things play out as they've been planned. You have to allow it to happen."

"But—"

"Bexley, please. I know this is hard. Trust me, I do." His brows pinch, and he seems genuinely uncomfortable. "But this is bigger than you and Mia. Your time will come, I promise you that, but right now is not it."

My lips part to respond, but he continues. "I know that she's been sneaking around, poking her nose where it doesn't belong, and I need you to stop her. She's already in enough danger right now. If she pokes too deep, I'm afraid that I will no longer be able to protect her."

I scrub my hand down my face as his words start to sink in.

"You have to let this play out, and I need you to do everything you can to keep her safe."

"Jesus, Mr. Thomp—"

"It's Garth. I know you don't know me, but I know you care about my daughter, and I know we're on the same side. I promise you I will do everything I can, but I can't do it alone."

"I need you to give me more information. Why is she even in this position? Did you have something to do with it?"

He hesitates before he answers, making me think that deep down, he really wants to tell me the truth. But when he finally speaks, I realize it's going to take a little more to get the details I need.

"I've already said too much. If anyone knew we even had this conversation, then..." He trails off and I'm grateful, because I really don't need any ideas about what could happen should Q know that Mia and I have been sniffing around to find the truth.

"Please, Bexley. I'm begging you, just look after my little girl." Pain etches into his expression and dread floods me.

"I'll do my best."

"You have to trust that everything is happening for a reason."

"Even at your daughter's expense?"

He pales, guilt shining bright in his eyes and telling me everything I need to know about his involvement in this.

"You're not just Phillip's security, are you?"

"That's my main job, yes."

"But not your only one?"

"Bexley, you're going to make a great leader one day. You'll be a part of making this town great again, I have no doubt. But for now, you need to play the game. There is an end, and we all just need to pray that it comes sooner rather than later."

"For Mia's sake?"

He releases a heavy sigh, a dark look crossing his expression. "For everyone's sake. Enjoy the rest of your night." He nods at me and has disappeared back through the door before I've even registered that he's gone.

What the hell was that?

Locking myself in one of the stalls, I drop down onto the toilet and lower my head into my hands, replaying the entire conversation over in my head.

So he knows about Mia and me, and he knows we've been digging.

Why do I get the suspicion that he knows just as much as Q and James?

If not more.

Has his entire life been a lie, a cover-up for his true part in Q? And should we have been looking closer to home for the answers this whole time?

My cell burns a hole in my pocket. I desperately want to call Mia and tell her, but I can't. She's spending the night with Annabel. The last thing I want to do is ruin it... more than I'm sure it already is, knowing who I'm spending mine with.

26

MIA

"Oh, that one is stunning," Mom says as I emerge from behind the velvet curtain. "Isn't it beautiful, Annabel?"

"It's something, Mrs. Thompson."

"Oh, please, I've told you time and time again, call me Temperance."

"Sorry, Mrs. Thom—Temperance."

"How do you feel, sweetheart?"

"It doesn't scratch like the last one. But isn't it a little too... much?" The dress is a simple sweetheart neckline, but the back plunges to the bottom of my spine. Virginal from the front and sexy from behind. It would be ironic if it weren't for the fact that we're choosing a dress for me to wear for my union to the devil himself.

I suppress a shudder.

"Mia, darling?"

"I like this one." I admit defeat. If I don't pick one soon, she'll insist I try on another six, and I can't bear the thought of it. At least this one doesn't suggest I'm going to be his sweet little submissive fiancée.

Although knowing Cade, it will only encourage his wandering hands. I suppress another shudder. The thought of him anywhere near me makes my stomach churn. Especially after the other day in the mausoleum.

Inhaling a deep breath, I steel my spine and face myself in the mirror. I look beautiful. I look like a bride getting ready for her big day. My hair is braided in a crown around my head, tendrils spilling around my face. Mom insisted I try the dresses complete with shoes, so I'm at least four inches taller.

Annabel is right: the dress really is something.

But I feel nothing but dread wrapped in silk and lace.

"Are you sure? It's a big decision. Your Coglio is one of the most important events in your life. Except, of course, your wedding."

"Mom," I hiss.

"I know you're nervous, sweetheart. But this is a huge honor. I get chills every time I think about my little girl marrying a Kingsley. It really is something—"

"Why don't we go and look at jewelry, Temperance, and give Mia a second to collect her thoughts." Annabel shoots me a sympathetic smile.

"Thank you," I mouth, relief washing over me as my best friend leads my mom out of the fitting room.

The girl staring back at me no longer looks like me. She's hardened. Older. Wiser. The naïve sparkle in her eyes has been dimmed by the dark world she now inhabits. But she's also stronger. She won't go down without a fight. But time is running out, and I'm still no closer to coming up with a plan to stop the Coglio.

Cade and the Electi celebrated last night. Some kind of debauched bachelor party, I imagine. Bexley texted me this morning to reassure me that a) he was okay and b) he hadn't done anything bad. I can't deny that I wonder if he's lying. I know the kind of parties Cade throws. What he demands of his *friends*. We are but pawns in his game, and as I'm learning, the price of dissension is sometimes far greater than the price of submission.

I love Bexley and he loves me, though.

It has to be enough.

My breath catches. I want to believe it's enough, that we'll find a way through this. But once Cade makes me his... what if Bexley doesn't want me?

I wouldn't blame him.

It killed me seeing him with Brook, and that was only once.

Tears prick my eyes, but I force them down. If I'm going to survive the Coglio, then I have to turn my weakness into strength, my tears into weapons. Cade might hold all the power, but even the greatest kings fall.

And if Quinctus killed Gregory Kingsley, I have to hope they have a plan for Cade.

"Mia, sweetheart, can we come back in?" Mom's voice startles me.

"Sure, Mom."

They come back into the room and help me out of the dress. "We're meeting Sasha and Brook at the country club in thirty—"

"Sasha and Brook?" I balk.

"Well, yes." Mom stumbles over the words. "I asked Annabel who your friends from college were and she said Sasha, and I know she and Brook are stepsisters, so I thought... oh gosh, sweetheart. Did I mess up?"

"No, Mom, it's fine," I concede, because although part of me wants to refuse, she's still my mom and I'm still her daughter, and the need to give her this sits heavy in my stomach.

"I didn't know," Annabel whispers to me, and I shake my head.

"It's fine. It's just one lunch." Brook is in my life whether I like it or not. Perhaps it will do her good to be reminded that I'm not going anywhere.

"Oh good." Mom beams. "I've been so excited for today. I miss you, sweetheart. The house just isn't the same without you."

I wonder how she can be so clueless. How she can't see the pain behind my eyes. But that's Gravestone for you, and like every other verus woman, my mother is entrenched in its ways.

"I'm sure it'll be great, Mom." I grimace, pulling on my jacket.

It's not like it can get much worse.

GRAVESTONE COUNTRY CLUB is the pinnacle of the town's wealth. Maseratis, Bugattis, and Aston Martins litter the parking lot like sparkling gemstones nestled in a luscious green sea.

"Ah, Javier," Mom greets the bellhop. "So lovely to see you."

"Mrs. Thompson. Your guests are already inside."

"Thank you."

We follow Mom into the lavish reception room. Everything is coated in gold, from the door handles to the chandeliers, the vases, and even the bell on the check-in desk.

It's a rich man's paradise, and despite not possessing even a fraction of the money some of the people here do, my mom feels completely at home.

But that's Temperance Thompson. She's always enjoyed the finer things in life, seduced by the glitz and glamor of Gravestone.

"Mia," a voice calls, and we turn to find Sasha and Brook waiting for us.

"Girls, you both look beautiful. I'm Temperance, Mia's mom. I'm so happy you could join us."

"It's nice to meet you, Mrs. Thompson." Sasha smiles, but it's strained.

"Please, call me, Temperance."

"Tempie—can I call you Tempie? I just love your pant suit. It really compliments your eyes."

"Well, thank you Brook. What a lovely thing to say."

Brook catches my eyes and smirks. I roll my eyes, fighting the urge to groan.

"Mrs. Thompson." The maître d' approaches us. "Your table is ready."

"Girls, shall we?" Mom ushers us inside. Sasha casts me a bemused glance; she looks as pleased to be here as I am.

Brook takes my mom's arm and they walk into the restaurant together.

"You have got to be fucking kidding me," Sasha hisses under her breath.

"Can you try and play nice? For my mom's sake?" My expression softens.

"This is crazy, you realize that, right?"

"My mom invited her." I shrug. "I couldn't exactly send her away."

"That's exactly what you should have done."

"Let's just get through lunch. Hopefully Brook will play nice."

"This is Brook we're talking about."

"Girls?" Mom glances back at us dawdling behind. "Is everything okay?"

"Fine, Mom. Let's sit." I make sure to plant myself between Sasha and Mom. Annabel sits between Sasha and Brook, and Brook revels in being next to my mom.

"I just love the food here. It's always so well-cooked." Brook plucks her menu off the table and studies it as if this is completely normal. As if we're all just friends doing lunch.

"What do you fancy, sweetheart?" Mom asks me, and I shrug. My appetite has been missing since I woke up this morning and realized what day it was.

"Just a salad," I reply without looking at the menu.

"With the salmon?"

"Sure, Mom." I swallow over the lump in my throat.

"Have whatever you like, girls. Mia's father is kindly picking up the tab."

My stomach drops at the mention of Dad.

"Mia, darling, what is it? What's wrong?"

"Pre-Coglio jitters, I bet," Brook whispers, flashing me a conspiratorial wink as she takes a sip of her champagne.

"Of course." Mom pats my hand. "It is a big night for you." She chuckles. "I remember it well—my wedding night, of course. Your father and I were up all—"

"Okay, Mom. Nobody needs to hear yours and Dad's sex stories."

"We're all friends, Mia. And it's the most natural thing in the world."

I snatch up my crystal flute and gulp the champagne down.

"I agree, Mia," Brook drawls. "Sex is healthy. And you're Cade Kingsley's prosapia. He's like—"

The server appears, silencing Brook. Thank God. This is turning into my worst nightmare, which is something considering my life is one constant bad dream lately.

We reel off our orders, then Mom clinks her glass, smiling at me. "I would just like to say a few words. Mia, darling, I know this isn't what you wanted for your life, but to be prosapia is a blessing. May you walk into your new life with humility, grace, and poise. I just know you and Cade are going to live a long and happy life together."

She's brainwashed.

My own mother is completely and utterly brainwashed.

I don't know whether to laugh or cry, so I opt for a muted thanks and help myself to another glass of champagne. Sasha squeezes my hand under the table, but it does little to ease the knot in my stomach.

"Excuse me, I need a girl's minute." Brook excuses herself and struts across the room as if she owns the place. Men track her every move, especially her ass, and women watch with envy in their eyes.

Brook is made for this world. Cut from the heart of Gravestone. Nothing would have to be forced on her; she'd accept it all willingly with open arms.

Annabel's purse begins vibrating. She digs out her cell phone and checks the screen. "It's my mom. I'll be right back." Hurrying from the table, she exits the restaurant. A strange sensation trickles down my spine, but I can't quite put my finger on what's wrong.

I glance over at the doors again but can't see Annabel.

"What is it?" Sasha asks.

"I don't know. I'll be right back, okay?" I push from the table and stand. My mom calls after me, but I take off toward the doors Annabel left through.

I don't know what I expect to find, but when I spill into the foyer there's no sign of her. It's like the pieces of the puzzle are slotting against each other but all wrong.

What am I missing?

"Excuse me." I approach the check-in desk. "Did you see a girl come out here a second ago?"

"Yes, she just left."

I glance back to the main doors and take off, catching sight of Annabel disappearing around the side of the building. My brows furrow. What the hell is she doing?

Heart racing, I follow her but keep a safe distance. She's around the back of the country club now, near the kitchen. A door swings open and I duck behind a stack of crates. Brook appears, and my heart drops.

No.

No!

They start arguing about something, but I can't hear them over the whir of the fans. Annabel jabs her finger at Brook who cackles, a wicked glint in her eye. She shoos Annabel away and slips back inside the building.

The second Annabel reaches me, I step out into her path.

"Mia? My God, you startled me. What is it? What's wrong?"

My brow arches. "I saw you."

"S-saw me? What do you mean? I came out here to talk to my mom." She waves her cell at me.

"I saw you with Brook."

The blood drains from her face. "I-I can explain, it's not what you think."

"I don't know what I think right now. Are you two... *friends?*"

Her lip wobbles. "We've been hanging out. She knows what it's like to be... to be on the outside."

Guilt snakes through me, but nothing I've done deserves this kind of betrayal.

"It's Brook—or have you forgotten that?"

"I messed up, Mia. At first, I thought she genuinely wanted to be friends... she made me feel better about everything. But then she started asking me questions. Things about you..."

"What did you tell her?"

"N-nothing important, I swear."

"So what was that just now?"

"She threatened to tell you about everything if I didn't start telling her what she wants to know."

I let out an irritated sigh. "We should go back inside."

"You're not mad?"

"Oh, I'm mad. I'm so mad at you right now. You betrayed me, Bel."

Her expression falls, tears pooling in the corners of her eyes.

"But I don't want Brook to know that I know."

"I don't want to play games anymore," she cries. "She... she kinda scares me."

Narrowing my eyes on my best friend, the one girl I thought I could trust in all this, I smile sadly. "You should have thought about that before you sided with the devil."

27

BEXLEY

The house is remarkably quiet all weekend. I guess I shouldn't be surprised after the events of Friday night.

We didn't get out of that place until long after the sun had come up. Then Cade, Ashton and Brandon dragged a group of the girls with them and disappeared into the den the second we got back. Of course Alex followed like a good little sheep. Apparently banging one of the strippers in full view of every motherfucker in that place wasn't enough for him for one night.

I, however, had more than had my fill of debauchery.

Watching all those old and apparently well-respected and powerful men act like complete fucking animals was not my idea of fun. The way they treated the women as if they were nothing more than a piece of meat or a plaything while their wives, the women they supposedly loved, were at home turned my stomach.

I'd choose a night in with Mia over that any fucking night of the week.

The conversation with her father played on repeat for the entire weekend, and I argued with myself as to whether I should tell Mia about it or not. He didn't really give me any new information, just confirmed what we already knew. Something bigger is at play than we originally suspected, and Garth Thompson is very much involved in the whole thing. I can't help wondering what Phillip or Q as a whole have over him to make him agree to sell his daughter's soul and body to the devil. He's not a stupid man, so why would he do that to her? It's obvious he loves her, I could see it in his expression as he talked about her.

So why?

Why would he do this to her?

I roll over in bed and turn my alarm clock off. I don't want to go to class today. I don't want to sit there and stare at her, knowing that in only a few days she's going to be officially engaged to another man. No, not just a man. The fucking devil.

On Friday night, I'll be forced to watch the woman I've given my heart to tie herself to another. How the fuck am I meant to watch that, knowing what's going to happen after?

Anger stiffens my muscles and my teeth grind as I think of the way Cade treats women. Mia doesn't deserve to be touched like that. He'll fucking break her, and the worst thing about it?

That sick fuck will enjoy it.

"Jesus," I mutter, dragging myself up so I'm sitting on the edge of my bed.

I glance over at the cold space next to me. She should be laying there. Friday night should be *our* night. But it's not. And something tells me that while it's going to be the beginning of things changing for Mia and Cade, it's going to be the final nail in the coffin for the two of us.

We can keep saying things like 'it's going to be fine' or 'we'll find a way out,' but the reality is that we're just two people who are mostly naïve to the workings of Q and have no fucking clue what we're really up against.

Running my fingers through my hair, I tug until it hurts before I make my way to my bathroom to get ready for the day.

I'm the last one down to the kitchen, and every set of eyes turns my way as I step into the room.

"Ah look, it's the miserable fuck who refused to get his dick wet Friday night."

"Fuck off, Ash."

"Not all of us want the STIs that comes with fucking those whores," Channing mutters, standing up for me.

"I didn't hear you saying that while you had one on her knees," Brandon offers, making Channing's face twist in anger.

"Whatever, asshole."

"Bacon and eggs, Mr. Easton?" Mulligan asks.

I want to say no and escape instead, but my stomach growls loud enough for him to hear and I don't get a chance to argue.

The guys remain silent as he lowers a plate before me and pours me a coffee.

"So Cade, you ready for your last week as a single man?" Ashton asks, briefly glancing at me, ensuring that I'm aware that his question is purely for my benefit.

My grip on the fork in my hand becomes painful as I lift a piece of bacon to my mouth. I force it past my lips and chew, but I barely taste it as a wicked smirk curls at Cade's lips.

"I can't wait. Friday night is going to be fucking banging."

"Someone will be banging alright," Ashton barks out before laughing at his own joke.

Everyone aside from Channing and I join in. He's the only one who has any fucking clue how I feel right now, and I couldn't be more grateful for him trusting me with the truth about him and Sasha, proving that we're on the same team here.

"There are going to be people in and out of the house all week getting things ready, setting the bedroom up, all that shit. But I expect you all here Thursday night. No fucking excuses."

"Why?" I ask, dread already sitting heavy in my stomach.

"Just want to spend some time with my nearest and dearest before the big night. That okay with you, Easton?" He raises a brow as he waits for me to argue about my attendance.

"I need to get to class," I say, shoving my mostly full plate away and standing from the table.

I might have been hungry when I first walked in, but it's safe to say that my appetite has well and truly been ruined now.

"Bex, wait," a familiar voice calls before I get to the front door.

I don't bother looking over my shoulder. I don't want to see the pity on his face or the hurt when I say what I need to say. "I'm not fucking interested, Rexford." Alex gasps at my use of his surname.

I blow through the door, and I'm racing out of the driveway in a heartbeat.

If only I could keep fucking driving and never return.

If only... I laugh to myself. There's no way I could leave Mia here to do all of this alone.

I keep my head down all fucking day. I don't even bother looking up when I know she's walked into class. I know looking at her is going to be painful, and I'm already crumbling without having to see a similar look in her eyes.

She's all set for the ceremony. When we messaged briefly yesterday evening, she told me how she'd chosen the dress the day before and how she's fallen out with her friend Annabel, although she didn't go into detail, saying that it would be easier to explain in person. Of course, I want to know. If it's upsetting her then it's important to me, but I can't help thinking that we've got bigger issues right now than that.

As promised, the house is full of random people measuring things and walking around with paint samples when I get back. Not wanting to witness any of it, I drag on a pair of sweats and my sneakers and set off out the back of the house and run until my muscles scream at me to stop. But I keep going. Anything to take away from the pain in my chest and the thoughts of what Mia's going to be put through on Friday that I have no way of rescuing her from.

By the time I get back to my room, my shirt is soaked in sweat and my entire body trembles with exertion. I need to calm the fuck down and go eat something. But going to the kitchen means seeing Cade, and if I'm forced to spend too much time with him this week then there's a chance he's going to be forced to go to his precious fucking Coglio with a black eye and a broken nose.

My fists curl at the thought, my knuckles aching in the most delicious way, imagining just how fucking satisfying it'll feel to finally show the cunt how I really feel about him.

Instead of heading down for food, I find myself in Sasha's room once again, chasing a way to force it all out of my head.

With a few little white pills and a bottle of vodka I'd stashed in my closet, I manage to wipe the rest of the day away in a pilled-up daze. If only the rest of the week would disappear quite so easily.

"WHAT THE FUCK is he planning for tonight?" I ask when Channing pokes his head into my room ten minutes before we're expected downstairs for the king's little fucking pre-ceremony gathering.

"You mean aside from rubbing your face in it?" he asks, proving that every single thing both Cade and Ashton have said to me this week has been meticulously planned so they can piss me off as much as possible. It wouldn't surprise me if they had some kind of wager going on to see who can break me first.

"Yeah, aside from that."

"No fucking clue. I think he just wants to hang." Channing shrugs.

"*To hang?*" I balk. "When the fuck does he ever want to hang with me? Wait, don't answer that." I shove my feet into my sneakers and drop my cell into my pants pocket. "Lead the way."

Channing leads me to the den, the room where all those weeks ago Cade had me strapped to the chair while he forced me to watch him touch what's mine. Even now the memory makes my blood boil.

Walking inside, I find that everyone—minus Tim and Fawn—are already there. Sadly, that includes Brook, who makes a beeline for me. She thrusts her exposed cleavage at me as Mia watches her every move from the other side of the room.

We haven't spoken all week, but that's not through lack of trying on her part. I've just been too intent on drowning in darkness instead of dealing with reality. As she stares at me, I can almost feel the desperation in her eyes. Guilt tugs at me, but even still, it's not enough to make me go over there. Instead, I lift the bottle of vodka that's hanging from my fingers and tip it to my lips, swallowing down two generous shots.

Sasha winks at me when she passes me, knowing exactly how I'm going to be feeling in a few short minutes thanks to the extra supplies she gave me earlier today.

I know that losing myself isn't the answer, but fuck, it sure hurts less than being sober and knowing exactly what's coming for me.

Tim and Fawn join us not long later, and the eleven of us sit around the room, mostly on the couches, pretending that we're just some normal college kids hanging on a normal Thursday night, but we all know that's not true. We don't need the scent of whatever Cade has once again permeated the air with to tell us that.

"Where the fuck are the girls, man? The only single one here shares my blood," Ashton grumbles.

"Didn't stop you lusting after her when Easton was balls deep inside her?" Cade's evil smirk turns my way as Mia tenses in his hold.

"I might be sick, but I draw the line at fucking her."

I lift my bottle once more, nowhere near as wasted as I need to be for these kinds of conversations.

"What about Mia? You wanna share her before you make her yours? It's hardly fair that only Easton has had a pop."

My teeth grind at his suggestion.

"Keep your fucking hands off what's mine," Cade growls at Ashton. "That was a one-off, right, Easton?" he asks me.

I don't react, and it makes his jaw clench.

"He knows what'll happen if I find out he's touched her again." His grip on Mia's hip tightens as my stomach turns over.

Mia keeps her eyes on the floor, not wanting to give anything away about the two of us. But if Cade's proved anything over the past few weeks, it's that he knows exactly what's going on under his nose, so I wouldn't be surprised that he's already aware that nothing's changed between the two of us.

"Hell yes," Brook shrieks, her voice like nails across a chalkboard, as the song changes. "Turn it up, let's dance."

It seems that either Sasha is so wasted that she doesn't care or that the stepsisters have called a temporary truce, because the pair of them climb up on the coffee table and start grinding away to the beat.

"Shake that ass, Sis," Ash says, resting back on the couch, enjoying the view.

Sick fuck.

I don't pay them any attention, but I keep my eyes on Mia while Cade is distracted with Brook, the woman who he really should be with. They're a match made in hell.

I'm only aware that things are escalating when her shirt hits me in the face. Glancing up, I find them both now dancing in their underwear, but if the way Brook is going, that's not going to last much longer either.

"Oh shit," Sasha squeals before she loses her footing and tumbles from the table. Thankfully, Brandon is only a few feet away and just about manages to catch her before she faceplants the floor and breaks her nose.

"I'm taking her to bed," he says, throwing her over his shoulder, her body limp in his hold.

"I'll come help. See you later," Mia says, twisting to Cade and dropping a chaste kiss to his cheek.

Things only get more intense once they've left. Before long, the doorbell rings and we're joined by a few girls I vaguely recognize. Only, I think the last time I saw them, they were dressed as French maids.

Cade immediately makes the most of Mia's disappearance and drags one of them over to the corner while Ashton's eyes light up as two of them make a beeline for him.

"Whoa, you started the party without me?" Brandon says when he reappears, looking offended. He soon joins in with Ash, ripping one of the girls' shirts open and immediately sucking on her nipples.

Fucking dogs.

I wait for them to become fully distracted before I slip out of the room unnoticed, telling myself that I'm just going to go to bed. But with Mia here under the same roof, I know I'm only lying to myself.

I don't bother knocking when I get to Sasha's room. Instead, I just slip inside. The lights are all off, but the moon coming through the crack in the curtains is enough to show me their sleeping forms.

Ignoring Sasha, who's passed out drooling on her pillow, I slip around the other side of the bed. Cupping Mia's cheeks in my hand, I lower my lips to hers.

I need her so fucking badly.

She moans into my kiss before her entire body tenses as she wakes. "What the—*Bexley?*"

"Shh... it's just me, mouse. Relax."

"W-what are you doing?" she stutters as I slip my hand under the covers and find her braless breast under her tank. "Oh God. Y-you can't be here."

"Fucking stop me," I murmur into her mouth as I push my hand lower and into her panties, taking what's mine.

28

MIA

Bexley's fingers slide between my folds, dipping inside of me. He swallows my moan with his teeth and tongue, kissing me like he might never get another chance.

I try to fight him off, aware of Sasha passed out on the other side of the bed. But he's too forceful, too desperate.

"You're mine," he rasps, breathing the words into my mouth, forcing me to swallow them. His fingers curl deep inside me, making my body bow off the bed. It's wrong, I know it is. But I can't help but submit to him.

It's Bexley.

My Bexley.

The guy I've fallen head over heels in love with.

I'm no longer pushing him away—I'm dragging him closer, my arms tightening around his broad shoulders.

"You might be his in name, little mouse, but I own your body. I own your fucking heart." He spears his fingers inside me roughly, but it only fuels the desire rushing through me. My skin burns at the knowledge that my friend is laying right there while he touches me.

"I'm yours," I breathe, drowning in sensation.

His thumb rolls over my clit in torturous circles as he continues working his fingers inside me. Moans spill from my lips in rapid succession as he pushes me closer to the edge, but he drowns each one out with his tongue.

"Come for me, Mia. Come all over my fingers."

I shatter around him, intense waves of pleasure rolling through me. Bexley lifts himself off me slightly to bring his fingers to his mouth and suck them clean. "I'm going to fuck you so hard you'll never forget me."

His eyes are blown, wild and reckless. He's high. The realization makes my heart ache, but he's already clawing at my pajama shorts, pushing them over my hips and down my legs. My hands go to his jeans, unbuttoning them and slipping my hand inside. My fingers close around his long, hard cock, and he hisses quietly.

"Put it inside you," he demands. "Now."

I hitch my legs ever so slightly and guide him inside me. His chest rumbles as he tries to smother a groan, and my breath catches at the feel of him.

He grabs my hands in his and pins them above my head as he eases out of me and slams back inside. My lips part in a muted moan and my eyes flutter closed.

"Look at me, Mia." He leans in, running his nose along my cheek, coaxing my eyes open. "Watch me as I ruin you for that fucker." His hand flexes around my hip, holding me in place he fucks me mercilessly into the mattress.

"You feel so fucking good, choking my dick, Mia," he whispers. "Like you were made for it."

His dirty words make me gush around him.

"Fuck," he grunts. "You feel so fucking good."

Sasha murmurs and we both freeze, our eyes wide, our chests heaving between us. The covers shift and rustle, but then she settles back into her drug-induced sleep.

"Maybe we should—"

"Not a fucking chance." Bexley rocks into me, slow and deep, grinding his pelvis against mine. He isn't fucking me out of anger anymore, he's loving me out of desperation and fear. Every kiss, every touch and sigh, is recognition of the nightmare we've found ourselves in.

And although I don't want to believe it, I can't help but feel like it's a goodbye.

Panic floods me. I slip one of my hands free from his grip and cup his face. "Promise me you won't leave me." My voice cracks.

"Mia, I—"

"No, Bex. Say it. Promise me. No matter what happens… it's us."

He stares down at me, the lust and hunger in his eyes giving way to something else. Something darker. Something dangerous.

"I promise." He touches his head to mine, circling his hips faster, building the waves inside me again.

We kiss and kiss. We don't stop kissing until my pussy contracts around him and he jerks inside me.

"I love you," he whispers against my lips. "I love you so fucking much."

"I love you too," I breathe.

"I need to go." Regret glitters in his eyes.

"I know."

He climbs off me and straightens his clothes before helping me clean up. Crouching down beside the bed, he trails his finger down my cheek. "I meant what I said, Mia. He can have you in name, but you're mine in all the ways that matter."

Pressing my lips together, swallowing the emotion building inside me, I nod.

Bexley drops a kiss on my head and leaves…

Taking the final pieces of my broken, battered heart with him.

FRIDAY PASSES IN A BLUR. I skip classes to spend the afternoon with Mom and Sasha. We get pedicures and manicures. Annabel was supposed to come with us, but after her betrayal, I uninvited her. Tonight is going to be stressful enough without best friend drama.

It's tradition for prosapia to get ready at home and leave for their Coglio with their parents. In many ways, it's like your wedding day. The Coglio represents an Electi and prosapia's union. It binds them together in ritual and in body. There's a formal dinner at Gravestone Hall for the Electi, Quinctus, the prosapia and their families, followed by the Coglio ceremony. Then Cade and I will return to the Electi House to consummate our union.

My stomach recoils at the thought.

"Mia, sweetheart, are you almost done?" Mom appears around the door. "Oh my gosh, baby, you look... my little girl is all grown up."

"Thanks, Mom." I inhale a sharp breath and she frowns.

"Mia, what is it? What's wrong?"

"Can I ask you something?"

"Of course." She comes inside and perches on the edge of the bed, making sure to smooth out the skirt of her royal blue gown. She looks stunning—regal, even.

"Do you want this for me? I mean, really want this for me?"

"W-what?" Her brows pinch. "I don't understand..."

Disappointment wells inside me. "Don't you want me to be with someone I love? Someone who treats me right and cherishes me?"

"Oh sweetheart." She leans forward, brushing a curl out of my face. "Those feelings will come with time. Relationships take work and patience. You're young, Mia. You and Cade have your whole lives to grow together."

"I don't love him, Mom. I will never love him."

She rears back. "What are you saying, sweetheart?"

"I don't want this, Mom." My lip wobbles, pain lashing my insides. "I never wanted it."

With a soft sigh, Mom gathers my hands in hers. "To be a prosapia is a gift, Mia. You will have such a good life with Cade, baby. You'll never want for anything again."

"He isn't... good, Mom. He's cruel and conceited. He treats people like toys."

"Sweetheart, I don't know where all this is coming from..." She hesitates, and for a second, I think she might be losing her rose-tinted glasses. But then her frown deepens. "Cade and the Electi are young, powerful men, Mia. And it's college, baby. Time to make mistakes and discover who you are. But after tonight, once the ceremony is complete, everything will be fine. You'll see."

I stare at her dumbfounded.

She doesn't get it.

She'll *never* get it.

I realize that now. I think deep down, I've always known it. But I needed to hear the words. I needed to know, once and for all, that she isn't on my side.

And it kills something inside me.

Something I'll never get back.

"I should finish getting ready," I say, steeling my spine.

"Mia, sweetheart…"

"I'm fine, Mom," I say, coolly. "I'll be down soon."

She gives me a small nod and leaves. A shuddering breath leaves my lips.

I go through the motions, applying a thin layer of makeup and finishing my hair with gold-tipped pins. The Electi crest pendant sits heavy around my neck. But tonight, it will be replaced with something more permanent. A brand I will never be able to remove.

Most women wear their Coglio brands with pride, for that brand denotes power and wealth. It denotes belonging to the dark, corrupt world of Quinctus and the Electi.

A world I never asked to be a part of.

A world I want no part of.

Sliding open the small jewelry box Mom gave me earlier, I flip the lid and stare at the diamond encrusted hair brooch. It has been passed down our family for generations. A wedding gift from mother to daughter.

This isn't my official wedding, but the sentiment is the same.

I slide it into my hair, clipping it in on my crown. The diamonds glint in the light but do little to lift my mood.

It shouldn't be like this.

Grabbing my lace clutch purse, I reluctantly leave my room and head downstairs. Every step in my overly expensive shoes is like another step toward my doom. The pit in my stomach churns deeper and deeper until I'm sure I'll pass out. But somehow, I make it into the living room in one piece.

"Oh my… Mia… you look… doesn't she look beautiful, Garth?"

My father gives me a stiff nod. He's quiet. Too quiet.

"The car is outside," he says thickly, and I don't miss the hitch in his voice.

"Daddy?" I croak, the sudden weight of everything crashing down on me.

"It's all going to be okay, sweetheart," he says, gently taking my elbow and steering me toward the door.

As he opens the front door and ushers me outside, I'm sure I hear him whisper, "You can do this, Mia. You have to."

GRAVESTONE HALL IS as beautiful as I remember from the night of my Eligere. However, if I'd have known then what I know now about that night, I might not have been so seduced by its beauty and charm.

My father keeps his hand on the small of my back and we enter the room. Blood hums in my ears as everyone stands to welcome me. The girl of the moment.

Cade Kingsley's prosapia.

They think it's so sacred, such a coveted title. But it's all lies. A smokescreen for what really transpires in the name of tradition.

I keep my eyes low, unable to meet any of the heavy stares I feel as we walk to our table.

Once seated, I finally lift my gaze and search for the only eyes that I know will ground me to this moment. Bexley looks as handsome as ever in his black dinner jacket and dress shirt. His eyes betray his cool appearance, though, pain flickering across his expression. I offer him a weak smile before moving on to find Sasha. She looks as miserable as I feel, seated between Brandon and Channing. Tim and Fawn are with them, and Alex. But Ashton and Brook are seated at another table, and I take small satisfaction in the fact that they don't get to sit with the Electi tonight.

The other tables are filled with men and women—some I recognize, some I don't. I spot the Rexfords, Bexley's grandfather, Tim's father, and Phillip Cargill. And I spot District Attorney Bailey, and Police Commissioner Walters.

Everyone here is directly linked to Quinctus and the Electi in some way. They know what tonight means... they know, and yet they do nothing.

I accept a glass of champagne from an immaculately dressed server just as Mom touches my arm. "Isn't this lovely?" she whispers, her spellbound smile enough to make me want to gouge my eyes out.

Phillip steps up to the podium and ushers the room into silence. "Friends and family, I welcome you all here, on the birth of the new moon, for this celebration. Tonight, we shall witness two of our young enter one of our most respected traditions." His eyes find mine and a chill runs through me. "The Coglio."

29

BEXLEY

Sitting on the end of my bed, I drop my head into my hands.

This can't be happening.

But it is. In only a few short hours, Mia is going to be officially Cade's. Okay, so it may not be as official as an actual wedding ceremony, but in Q's eyes, it's as important.

She's meant to be mine.

It's meant to be us.

"ARGH," I growl, falling back on the bed and pulling at my hair until I fear I might be about to rip it out.

Memories of my time with her last night play out in my mind, swirling with the fear I have that it could have been our last time. If it was our last time, then it shouldn't have been like that. Sasha shouldn't have been passed out in the same bed while I said goodbye to the girl who owns me, who fucking holds my heart in the palm of her hands, so she can be with another man.

A soft knock sounds out on my bedroom door, but I ignore it. I don't want to see or talk to anyone despite the fact that I'm not going to have a choice in just over an hour. I'm expected to be dressed and ready to escort his highness to this fucking ceremony.

I think of the arrogant fuck and imagine him in his room right now with a satisfied smirk on his face, knowing that he's about to win. He's about to take the only thing in this world I give a fuck about and rub it in my face.

I'm going to be forced to live here with them, to see them together every single fucking day. Any other couple would get their own place, like Tim and Fawn, but not the fucking king himself. He's staying in his fucking castle so he can lord it over me.

The door pushes open despite the fact that I didn't invite whoever it was in before it quickly clicks shut again.

"Hey," a familiar voice says. I can hear the understanding in Channing's tone, but I don't look over even though his concerned eyes are boring into me. "How are you doing?"

"This is bullshit," I spit. "There's got to be a way we can stop it."

"Trust me, Bex. If there was anything, I'd have told you by now. I don't want this for either of you. I just got off the phone with Phillip though, and he's ordered me to trail them back here—"

"But we're all going to the Cargills'," I interrupt, already dreading the party that Ashton is throwing in celebration for his best friend.

"You all are. I've been instructed to make my excuses and to come back here to keep an eye on her."

"What the fuck are they expecting him to do?" I bark, pushing from the bed until I'm sitting once more.

"They don't know. That's the problem."

Running my hand through my hair to get it out of my eyes, I stare up at Channing. "What the fuck was the deal you made with them exactly?"

His lips part to respond, and I can already hear his refusal to explain in my ears like he has done every other time I've asked... but today he must take pity on me, because instead of refusing, he comes to sit next to me.

He rests his elbows on his knees and stares straight ahead. "Phillip is worried about Cade and where his head is at, and his intentions for Mia... for the future."

"Well yeah, he's a fucking psycho."

"Agreed. But I think this runs deeper than we'll ever know. Gregory Kingsley was always an advocate of the old ways... The blood rituals and ceremonies. I think Q thought with him gone, they could keep Cade on the straight and narrow, mold him into their puppet."

"Well, that was a huge fucking failure."

"Gregory has been dead for years, but Cade is just like him. Cold, cruel, callous." Channing runs a hand down his face.

"What have you and Mia got to do with all of this?"

"Mia, I've no idea. Maybe they think she can tame him or some shit. Whatever it is, it's fucked up, and she doesn't deserve it. Me? Well, I want out and they need a snitch, so..."

"You're spying on him?" I blurt.

"In not so many words. I think there's a divide in Q. Phillip wants hard proof that Cade's taking things too far before he takes it to the rest of the elders. They need him. I don't know why, but he's important. That much is obvious.

"If I help them, I get my freedom and Phillip's blessing to be with Sasha. Well, if they uphold their end of the deal. I don't trust a single word that comes out of their mouths, to be honest."

I contemplate telling Channing what I learned from James, but something stops me. Until I know exactly who all the moving pieces are, I don't want to reveal my hand too soon.

"You don't even trust your Uncle Harrison?" I ask.

"Especially him. He's proved time and time again that he's an untrustworthy cunt. Just look at what he's done to Alex and Hadley."

Fuck, Hadley.

"What's wrong?" Channing asks, clearly seeing my expression change.

"Hadley still doesn't know about Alex. I told her that she needs to come back because there are things she needs to deal with, but she refused."

"Let's get through this first, and then maybe we can all go to Sterling Bay to see her. She deserves to know that she's got a brother."

I nod at him, happy that he's not like the others and actually cares about people—family.

"You really should get dressed. Today is not the day to get on Cade's wrong side."

"I disagree. Today is the perfect day to get under his skin."

"So he can take it out on Mia later?"

My blood turns to ice. "Fuck." I'm up before I've even realized I've moved.

"Exactly. I'll see you downstairs. I promise you, Bex. I won't let anything happen to her."

His eyes hold mine for a beat, and although I see honesty shining in them, I also see trepidation. He knows as well as I do that he can't really promise that. Cade doesn't follow the rules, which means we have no chance of being one step ahead of him.

"Thank you," I mouth before he slips back out of my room, leaving me to dress in the suit that's hanging from my closet. Blowing out a long, steeling breath, I drop my sweats and get this funeral underway.

By the time I get to the bottom of the staircase a little over thirty minutes later, all the guys are already there—well, everyone minus Cade. I'm sure he just wants to make some kind of grand entrance.

Channing nods at me before Alex smiles sadly. Not wanting to stand with Brandon and Tim, I come to a stop beside Sasha, who immediately threads her arm through mine and gives my forearm a squeeze in support.

A loud crash from above is the first sign that Cade is about to appear. When he emerges from the hallway, I find he's dressed the same as the rest of us, but instead of looking a little pensive, he's got a shit-eating grin on his face.

My fists clench as he makes his way to us.

"Calm down," Sasha hisses at me. "This is only the beginning."

Sucking in a breath through my teeth, I try to follow her orders, but it's really fucking hard when the motherfucker jumps the last few steps, his eyes never leaving mine as he approaches.

"All set for the fun and games, Easton?"

My lips press into a thin line as he taunts me. The temptation to take a swing and ensure he turns up to this thing with a broken nose is strong, but I know that he'd stop me attending, and despite knowing how fucking painful it's going to be, I need to be there for Mia. She's going to need to know that I'm there and that I meant what I said to her last night.

She's mine.

Fucking mine.

I force a smile on my lips, and, finally, he looks away.

"Great. Let's do this. I've got a fucking wild night ahead of me," he announces, pushing past me and toward the front door.

"Hell yeah. You remember Tim and Fawn's Coglio? They didn't come up for air for over twenty-four hours."

My eyes shoot to Fawn, whose face burns bright red before she attempts to hide behind Tim.

"It's the drugs, man. They're the fucking shit," Tim explains, pulling Fawn from behind him and kissing the top of her head. "Best night of my life."

I stare at the two of them for a beat, trying to work them out. At times, like now, they look like a normal college couple who are head over heels in love. But then there are other times when it's like there's a dark cloud hovering over both of them, and it seems like they've been forced together much like Cade and Mia. I know Channing says Fawn's got some mental health issues, so I can only assume it's that which puts a strain on their relationship, but still, I can't help wanting to know the whole story.

There are two black SUVs waiting outside the house when we emerge, Sasha, Fawn, and a reluctant-looking Ashton climb into the second while the six of us move toward the first.

The journey is long and painful with Cade looking smug as fuck and my stomach churning as if I'm going to empty the contents of it on the car floor at any moment.

But I'm sure it's nothing compared to how Mia's feeling right now.

I don't know what's worse: being a part of this and forced to endure what's coming her way tonight, or watching from the sidelines, not really understanding everything that's about to happen.

"Right, this is it, gentleman," Cade announces as we pull up outside of Gravestone Hall. "Time for me to make an honest woman of my prosapia." His eyes flick to mine, glowering for a second. "Hell knows she's not experienced a real man yet."

My teeth grind, but he's out of the car before I can figure out a good enough comeback.

"Ignore him. He's trying to push your buttons. Do not let him win," Channing warns.

Much like the last time we were here, we're directed to a bar where we have a drink with Quinctus before one of the waitstaff comes to tell us that it's time to go through.

Every guest stands as we enter the ballroom. I glance around at the faces, most of which I don't recognize. I don't know why I bother; I already know she's not here yet. We take our seats, as do the rest of the room. The men around me chat, but I don't hear a word of it, my eyes firmly locked on the doors, wanting to be the first one to see her.

The second a voice rings out, asking us all to rise, my heart jumps into my throat.

This is happening.

It's really fucking happening.

My breath catches the second I see her. She looks like a fucking angel in her ivory dress. My heart races and my palms sweat as I imagine how I might feel if it were me she was here for right now. Like the luckiest motherfucker in the world.

But she's not here for me.

She's here for him.

My eyes find Cade as he damn near molests her with his stare alone. My stomach turns once more, thinking about him touching her later, making her his. The room starts to spin around me, making me wish I took something before we left to take the edge off a little.

Thankfully, we're encouraged to sit again, and I fall down to my chair as if my legs can no longer hold me up.

The meal passes at a snail's pace, each plate of food more pretentious than the last—not that I eat any of it. My appetite vanished a long time ago. I barely look up, too scared of what I might be able to read on Mia's face, but I do know that she's eaten about as little as me.

Phillip brings the meal part of the ceremony to a close and invites Q and the Electi to the Sanctuary for the ceremony. The second he says that word, my eyes shoot to Mia. She looks like a rabbit caught in headlights. My scared little mouse.

Her eyes narrow as we stare at each other, a final silent goodbye passing between us that damn near rips my heart right out of my chest. She stands beside Cade and allows him to take her hand and lead her from the room. Q and her father follow before the rest of us.

The hallways are dark and oppressing, much like every building that has something to do with Q, and with each step I take it feels like it's another closer to death, because I already know that everything about my life is going to be different when we emerge from this building.

There are two rows of seats that we all take as Cade and Mia stand at the front before Phillip Cargill, as if he's about to perform their wedding ceremony.

My heart thunders as I watch them. Cade stares at Mia as if he's about to eat her alive, while Mia looks like she's about to bolt for the door at any moment.

Look at me, I silently beg in the hope that I can reassure her.

I'm sure it's luck, but I like to think our connection is so strong that she can actually hear me, because after a beat, her head turns, and she immediately finds my eyes in her small congregation.

"I love you," I mouth, not giving two shits about who might be watching me.

She nods ever so slightly, her eyes telling me everything she can't right now, before Phillip begins the service.

I don't hear a word of it as I keep my eyes on Mia, praying that she can take the strength from me that she needs.

I gasp when Phillip turns and takes hold of a similar branding iron that he used for my initiation brand. Except this one is different. The circular brand splits into two irons.

A pair.

One for Mia.

One for Cade.

Fuck, I think I'm going to puke. The knowledge that he's about to brand her beautiful, flawless skin has my fingers curling around the chair beneath me to keep me in place. But unlike when he did it to me, a woman appears from the shadows and rubs some kind of ointment onto her skin, right over her heart, before Phillip raises the iron and presses it against it.

Mia flinches, but that's the only reaction she shows as it scars her for life. Internally, I scream in pain for her, knowing that her fate has just been sealed.

That's it.

It's done.

She's his.

30

MIA

Applause rings out around us as Cade slides his hand to the small of my back and presents me to the Electi and Quinctus elders.

The fresh brand over my heart is nothing more than a faint sting. But I know its effects will live on long after tonight.

"And now for the binding," Phillip Cargill says, coming around to us. He lays my hand on top of Cade's and wraps them together with a length of fine silk emblazoned with the Quinctus crest.

"Tonight marks the start of your new life together. A toast to new beginnings." He hands us each a champagne flute. I hesitate, and Cade smirks.

"Trust me, you'll want to drink it." There's a threat laced in his words that shoots fear down my spine.

I pretend to take a sip and swallow. I'll probably regret it later, when I'm lucid for everything Cade has planned, but I want to be of clear mind.

I want to remember every single thing that happens.

"To Cade and Mia. Ubi concordia, ibi victoria."

The small crowd repeats Phillip's words, and I fight the urge to laugh bitterly at their twisted words. *Where there is unity, there is victory.* What the hell is wrong with them?

I catch Bexley's eye, and the look of devastation is like a knife to my heart. But we both knew it might come to this.

"The car is waiting," Phillip confirms, unbinding our hands as if it's the most normal thing to send a young, innocent girl off with a monster.

Cade shakes hands with each member of Quinctus, a smug expression plastered on his face. My father approaches me and pulls me into a hug. "I'm sorry," he whispers, and I frown. "I had hoped... just know that I never wanted this for you, Mia. But this place... these people..."

"Mia, it is time," Phillip says, and my father releases me and glances away, as if he can't bear to watch me leave with Cade.

I want to demand answers, to demand he tell me what he means, but Cade loops his arm around my waist and gently guides me away, perhaps more gently than he has ever touched me before.

But I know it's all part of his plan to make me lower my defenses before he strikes.

"It's almost time," he whispers, making me shudder with repulsion.

I feel the weight of Bexley's stare, the desperation in his eyes as they follow me and Cade out of the chamber.

"Tonight, you're mine," Cade snarls against my hair. "Tonight, Mia, I finally get to take what's owed."

THE RIDE back to the Electi house drags on. Cade's leg is pressed against mine, his hand gripping my knee.

A shiver runs through me, and Cade chuckles. "Nervous, love?"

Nervous doesn't even begin to cover it, but I peer up at him, steeling my expression. It only makes him laugh harder.

"You should be," he says around a dark smile, loving every minute of this. "I have waited a long time for this. For a second there, I thought they might step in and ruin everything."

"What do you mean?"

He regards me for a second, dragging a finger over my lips and down the valley of my breasts. "So much to learn about this world, Mia. They think they can control me. They think they can rein me in and do their bidding." He lowers his mouth to the corner of mine and smirks. "They're wrong."

Cade kisses me hard, all teeth and tongue, taking what he wants without a second thought to what I'm willing to give. My hands press against his chest, trying to stop him, but he's unmovable. Something isn't right. I felt it earlier and I feel it now—the same chill in the air.

"I am Cade fucking Kingsley." He grips my throat and stares at me, anger and hatred turning his eyes into two soulless black orbs. "They took everything from me... *everything*... and now I'm going to show them. I'm going to fucking destroy them."

Fear washes over me, rendering me powerless against him. He isn't making any sense... and yet, there's something hovering just outside my thoughts. The final pieces of the puzzle that once slotted into place will reveal the truth.

"Mr. Kingsley," a voice comes over the speaker. "We are almost at the house."

"Saved by the bell." Cade pulls away, smoothing down his hair. The way in which he swings between calm and composed to dark and deadly is terrifying. "But don't get too comfortable, Mia. The fun hasn't even begun yet." He shoots me a dark look as I scramble to think of a way out of this.

All too quickly, the car pulls up to the house. Steeped in shadows it looks as welcoming as a dungeon. I contemplate refusing to move, but I know it will only result in Cade manhandling me inside, because no one will help. The driver wears the Quinctus crest on his jacket, so I know he won't come running to my rescue. He's paid to drive and not ask questions.

How the hell am I going to get out of this?

I tremble uncontrollably as he climbs out and opens the back door. Cade gets out first, offering me his hand. I knock it away and inhale a shuddering breath before I step out, smoothing my dress down.

"Good night, Mr. Kingsley. Miss Thompson." The driver hurries back to his car—and, just like that, we're alone.

Cade starts to undo the tie hanging around his neck. "Shall we?" He motions to the house. Nervous energy zips up and down my spine, a ball of dread swelling in my stomach.

"I can't." The words spill from my lips as I start backing away, the urge to run so strong I feel lightheaded.

I can't do this.

I shouldn't have to do this.

"Don't make this any harder than it needs to be, Mia. You're mine now. Quinctus, your father... they handed you over so easily." My brows furrow, sweat beading along my neck, but he continues. "You know, I thought they'd question it more. When your name was pulled from the calix, I thought they'd at least turn on themselves..."

"Y-you... you put my name in there." The pieces start falling into place. I can't figure out the overall picture yet, but I know I'm getting closer. I feel it in my bones. "Why?"

"I think you know why, Mia." He stalks toward me as I inch back, trying to keep a safe distance between us.

"I-I don't know what you're talking about." My pulse drums in my skull, everything happening too fast. I need time to think... I need time to find a way out of this.

"Don't you?" His brow arches. "So you haven't been sniffing around Quinctus? Around Cargill? You haven't been asking questions? Playing detective?"

"I—" The words die on my tongue as his arm snaps out and grabs me, hoisting me up against his hard chest, making my heart lurch into my throat. "I told you, babe, I know everything about this town. All of its dark and dirty secrets." His eyes pin me with a look of contempt. "I told you... and yet you still disobeyed me."

"I am not yours to obey," I screech, hammering my hands against his chest.

"Scream a little louder," he chuckles. "It only makes it sweeter."

"You're sick," I cry, unleashing all of my frustration and anger out on him. "You're nothing more than a—"

He grips my wrists in a vise-like hold until I'm sure my bones will snap under the pressure. "Run, *little mouse*," he snarls at me. "Run before the big, bad wolf catches up with you."

I flinch at his use of Bexley's name for me.

He knows.

Of course he knows. We should never have been so reckless, so careless. But being with Bexley is the only thing that made sense in this living nightmare.

A beat passes as I gawk at him, willing this to be some kind of sick nightmare. But it isn't—it's my grim reality. I shove him hard, taking off toward the woods. His dark chuckle pierces the air like gunfire. "You're going to have to run faster than that."

I kick off my heels and pump my legs faster. My heart races in my chest, the oxygen in my blood replaced with nothing but adrenaline and fear. I melt into the dense thicket, branches clawing at my skin and dress like monstrous fingers trying to claim my soul. The ground crunches beneath my feet, stabbing and cutting into my soles, leaving droplets of blood in their wake.

But I don't stop.

I run and run and run until my lungs burn and the blood roaring in my ears sounds like a storm howling all around me.

Cade's dark laughter trails behind me. "I know these woods like the back of my hand, *mouse*."

I burst through the trees and find myself in the middle of a clearing. The moon shimmers overhead, bouncing off the trees, creating eerie shadows that seem to close in around me. I don't feel so good, my mind swimming with confusing thoughts.

But I didn't drink the toast Phillip gave me. I didn't—

"Feeling okay, little mouse?"

"W-what did you do?" I rub my head, swaying gently. Fighting to stay upright, I find Cade as he steps out from darkness like the devil coming to claim me.

"Your dessert. I had it laced with a little something special." He stalks closer. "Just for you."

"B-but why?"

"Why?" he grits out. "WHY?" His hand flies out and grabs my neck, wrenching me forward. "Because your father has been a very, *very* bad man, Mia."

I suck in a sharp breath as he confirms what my mind refused to believe.

"You see, Garth Thompson isn't just head of security at the Town Hall. No, your father has a very special job for Q." He cocks his head to the side. "But then, you already knew that, didn't you?"

No.

No!

I press my lips together in defiance.

"It doesn't matter." His lip twists in mild amusement. He's enjoying this. He's enjoying every torturous second. "You're going to pay for your father's sins, Mia. And when Q finds you broken and ruined, they'll realize what a mistake they made for ever trying to control me. I am my father's son, and it's time to honor his name." He throws me to the ground and I land with a thud, pain shooting through my skull.

Cade drops to his knees, clawing at my dress, tearing it apart to get to my skin. He's like a man possessed, his eyes feral and wild as he wrestles my legs apart and rips off my cotton panties.

"So innocent," he snarls, "when we all know you're anything but." He spears two fingers inside me, pain lancing through me. I cry out but it sounds muffled, everything growing distorted around me.

Cade covers me with his big, imposing body as he keeps working his fingers inside me. "Your father is a murderer, Mia. Q's assassin. He could have taken me out any number of times to save you from this fate... yet, he didn't. He let things play out just the way Q wanted them to... and do you know why?" He stares down at me with fire in his eyes. "Because he's weak. But I'm not weak, and I'll show them. One by one, I'll show them that they picked the wrong guy to manipulate."

Tears stream down my face as I thrash beneath Cade, barely able to breathe. He backhands me out of nowhere, my head thumping against the hard ground, stars exploding in my vision.

Everything is hazy after that. I feel his hand between us, his fingers strumming that place deep inside of me. My body begins to melt at his touch, betraying me. He kisses me—hard, punishing kisses, pushing his tongue down my throat as if he wants to suffocate me. His teeth bite down on my bottom lip, drawing blood, before moving down my neck, sucking and biting, marking me as his hand squeezes my neck to the point where I can't breathe.

My hand claws at his fingers, desperately trying to loosen them. But it's no use. My limbs are heavy and drugged, the fight slowly leaving my body and turning into synthetic pleasure.

He plucks and strums my clit until I'm no longer thrashing but writhing under his touch, needy and desperate. Tears fall harder down my cheeks as I break for him, as I shatter and splinter into dirty pieces. Pieces I know will never be whole again.

Cade smirks against my cheek, "Good girl, baby. You make it so easy. Tell me, do you come so hard for Easton? Does he know how to fuck you just the right way to make you scream?"

Cade works his buttons open and pushes his slacks over his hips, pressing himself right up against me.

"Do you think he'll want you when I'm done with you? That is, if there's anything left." His fingers flex around my thighs, stretching me wide as he slams into me so hard, I cry out in agony.

He's going to kill me.

Cade Kingsley isn't just going to ruin me. He's going to kill me.

But all I can think as the edges of my consciousness begin to fray is that at least this nightmare will be over.

31

BEXLEY

The pain that rips through me as I watch Cade lead Mia from the room is like nothing I've ever felt before.

Everything that has happened in my life, all the pain and heartache from my past in Sterling Bay, pales in comparison to this moment.

Reaching out, I hold onto the back of my chair to keep me upright as my heart pounds and blood rushes past my ears so fast that I'm sure I'm about to pass out. A warm hand lands on my shoulder before Channing whispers in my ear.

"I'll keep her safe." I nod, although we both just saw the dark glint in Cade's eyes as he looked at each of us. Nothing good is going to happen tonight.

"If she needs me, fucking call me. I don't care what it is or how bad."

He nods before following Q and the rest of the Electi from the room. I hang back, and so does Mia's father. As I stare at him, my fists curl so tight my nails dig into my palms.

"If he hurts her, I hope you know that it's all your fault. If anything fucking happens to her tonight..." My voice cracks, pain shooting from my chest as if the devil himself has just pushed a stake through my chest.

"I know." His voice is barely a whisper, and I wonder if he's actually said the words. "It was never meant to be like this."

"Well, it fucking is, and what did you do to stop it?"

I don't hang around to hear whatever excuse he's thinking up. Instead, I storm out of the room which I'm sure is going to haunt me forever and run up the stairs, needing to catch up with the others.

I don't want to go to a fucking party to celebrate this shit, but I need to be somewhere with cell signal so that I can go to her if she needs me.

Channing gives me a sad smile as I climb into the back of the SUV and the driver takes off to the Cargills'.

"You reckon he's already balls deep in her by now?" Ashton asks, a smirk curling at his lips as he stares right at me.

"You motherfu—" I launch myself across the car, my fist connecting with his jaw before anyone manages to get a grip on me and pull me back.

"Easton, enough," Tim barks, his voice terrifyingly cold.

"Fuck you, Davenport. He doesn't get to fucking talk about her like that. She's not some cheap fucking whore. He wouldn't talk about Fawn like that."

Tim growls at my suggestion.

"Exactly," I spit. "Cocksucker deserves more than one hit. He's fucking sick."

Ashton's eyes continue to hold mine, his smile lighting them up and stirring my anger to all new heights.

"Enough, Moore," Tim barks, much to my surprise, and the cunt immediately wipes the joy from his face.

If I didn't already know he was a fucking psychopath, watching his emotions flip so fast like that would have proven it.

"You good?" Tim asks, testing the water by releasing his hold on my arm slightly.

"No. No, I'm not fucking good."

Silence falls around the car before we turn toward another fucking mansion behind huge, gilded gates, and Ashton pulls a small tin from his pocket and throws back two pills.

"It's party time, boys." He holds the tin out, offering it to me first.

I stare at it for a few seconds, unmoving, before I lift my eyes to his.

"Fine, your loss. Tim?"

"Hell yes, my man." He takes the tin before passing it to Brandon, Alex, and then Channing, who also refuses.

Fuck knows why he's still here. He should be trailing Mia already, but I guess he's waiting for the best time to slip out unnoticed. Whatever he's doing, he's not doing it fucking quick enough. Anything could have happened to her already.

I stare out the window as the car pulls to a stop, but I don't see anything, I'm too lost in my own head, in my own nightmare.

Climbing out with the others, I follow them toward the house. The music pounds the second the door is pulled open, and when I look up, I find people fucking everywhere.

"Fucking move, Easton," Ashton barks from behind me, giving me a solid shove so he can get around me and start the party.

Just like always, the crowd parts like the fucking Red Sea as the guys arrive. Alex stands proudly beside them, milking the attention while I just wish the ground would swallow me up.

With little other choice, I follow them in and head straight for the quietest room I can find.

Slipping into a room that thankfully has no other people inside it, I close the door behind me and drop down onto the couch before lowering my head into my hands. My cell buzzes in my pocket after a couple of minutes of losing myself in my misery, making my heart damn near beat out of my chest.

Channing: I'm on my way to the house. I suggest you get a drink.

I want to. The temptation to drown all of this out is strong. So fucking strong that my hands are trembling with my restraint. But I can't. If something goes wrong and she needs me and I'm not able to get to her, I'd never forgive myself.

Slumping back on the couch, I look around the room, surprised to find it's some kind of office. Surely Phillip Cargill isn't stupid enough not to lock his office when his kids are throwing a fucking party?

Pushing from the couch, I walk over to the floor-to-ceiling bookcase and begin looking for something, anything, that might shed some more light on this fucking nightmare.

I have no idea how much time has passed as I flick through one of the old books I found on the top shelf which contains some of the old traditions and rituals of Quinctus.

It's a beautifully ornate book with the most stunning penmanship on the inside. Part of me didn't want to touch the pages for fear of damaging them when I first opened it, but the second I discovered what it was, I pushed all that aside and sat down at the desk with it, running my fingers over the script until I found a word that made me pause.

Coglio.

It describes the ceremony we sat through only hours ago before moving onto what happens after. My stomach turns as I think about what Mia might be doing right now.

My brows pull together as I read about how the union used to happen outside, under the new moon. It must be one of the ceremonies they've updated, given how many people have been working at the Electi house, getting everything ready for tonight.

But my mind can't help drifting back to only a few days ago when I took Mia in the woods behind Gravestone U. It was so intimate, so dirty and forbidden. My stomach drops, thinking that we'll never get that again.

My cell pings again, and I rush to pull it out, hoping that it's an update from Channing that everything is okay.

I fumble with it, in too much of a hurry to read what might be there, and it tumbles to the floor. Swiping it up, I have to do a double take when I find Mouse on the screen.

I rush to open it, my hands trembling and my heart pounding. *Please tell me that you're okay. Please tell me you found a way out,* I silently beg, even though I know it's useless.

Mouse: I need you. Please come to my parents'.

I'm up and at the door in a flash. The entryway is still full of people as I push my way through while calling for a car to come and get me. I don't give a fuck if anyone sees me leave; the only thought in my head is getting to her.

If she's at her parents' already, then something is very, very wrong.

"Fuck. FUCK," I roar as I run down the long-ass driveway so I can get to the car quicker. I'm just through the gates when a black car pulls to a stop beside me.

I bark the address at him and sit with my knee bouncing and my fists clenching as he makes his way to the other side of town.

"Can't you go any faster? This is kind of an emergency."

"I'm on it," the driver says, stepping on the gas a little.

It still takes longer than I'm happy with, but not too long later, he's pulling down the street that Mia's parents live on. I've got the door open before the car's even come to a stop. My feet hit the sidewalk and I take off running.

Channing's car is out the front, next to her parents' car, and I breathe a small sigh of relief that he's with her.

A weird noise makes my steps falter, and the second I look up to see what's going on, I'm thrown back as the house explodes before me.

I land on the sidewalk with a thud. My head ricochets off the ground, making my eyes fill with water as my heart pounds. It takes a second for my head to clear before I can scramble up to see what's happening.

"Noooo," I cry, stumbling forward and running toward the red-hot flames. My face burns as I draw closer to the fire that's already getting out of control, completely engulfing the building. "Mia," I scream, trying to find a way into the house, but it's hopeless. There's no way in.

"MIA," I scream again, looking around, hoping she's going to appear from somewhere.

"No. NO. NOOOOO."

I fall to my knees, the asphalt cutting into my skin as the scent of burning fills my nose. The air around me becomes hazy with smoke as I watch in horror while her house begins to fall in on itself with her, her family, and Channing inside.

Keep reading for Fractured Reign.

FRACTURED REIGN

GRAVESTONE ELITE BOOK 3

1

MIA

Bleep. Bleep. Bleep.
    The incessant noise rings in my head.

"Hello?" I try to speak, but the word barely forms on my lips. It's dark here. Everything is dark and dismal. Pain radiates through me like wildfire.

Like I'm *on* fire.

Oh God, am I burning?

What happened?

I try to recover the memories, to dig them up from the dark recesses of my mind. But it's futile. I'm trapped in a black abyss, unable to talk or move.

Bleep. Bleep. Bleep.

It grows louder, making me wince.

What is it?

Where am I?

What the hell is going on?

Panic begins to well inside me. I can't see. When I try to peel my eyes open, it hurts.

The light hurts.

"W-where am—" My throat is dry and sore. I feel parched. My lips are cracked.

Bleep. Bleep. Bleep.

God, I wish somebody would switch off whatever is making that awful sound.

My fingers flex, curling into stiff... bedsheets?

"Mia?" a voice says from somewhere beside me. But it sounds faint, flickering on the edge of my consciousness. "Come back to me, Mia."

I cling to the agony in his voice, the sheer desperation, trying to use it as an anchor. But I start slipping again, falling straight into the fingers of fear. They wrap around me, pulling me down.

Down... down... *down.*

Until the bleeping grows quiet and his voice disappears.

And once again, I am alone.

THE NEXT TIME I WAKE, there's something different about it. The bleeping still rings in my ears, but when I peel my eyes open, everything shimmers into focus. It's like looking at the world through water, but I can see.

I can see.

Relief slams into me as I try to survey my surroundings. It's a modest room with a big window. There's a small couch against it in the corner. A television mounted to the wall. One of those clinical trash cans. A trolley table. And the bed I'm currently laying on.

The hospital.

I'm in the hospital.

Fear trickles down my spine as I lift my hand, wincing from the pinch of the IV disappearing into my pale skin. A white sheet covers my body, but when I wiggle my toes, to my relief, I feel them. My legs too. But everything hurts.

What happened?

The memories hover on the fringe of my mind. The last thing I remember was the Coglio at Gravestone Hall. There was the dinner and then the ceremony in the sanctuary. I lift a heavy arm and slip my fingers into the gown covering me, feeling the scar over my heart.

A shudder rolls through me.

Philip Cargill branded me.

He pressed a hot iron into my skin and permanently bound me to Cade.

My stomach knots at the thought of him.

My tormentor.

My fiancé.

But what happened after that?

And why the hell can't I remember?

"Ah, Mia, you're awake." A woman breezes into the room. Her kind smile instantly settles something inside me. "Let's take a look at your vitals."

"W-what happened to me?" I croak as she checks my blood pressure and oxygen levels.

"You had quite the time of it, sweetheart." She gives me a sympathetic smile. "Your visitor is down in the café. He rarely leaves the room. I'll tell him you're awake and page the doctor. Here, you'll need this." She grabs a jug of water and pours me a glass, sliding the table over toward the bed. "Take little sips."

I do as I'm told, relishing how good the cool water feels against my parched throat. She makes some notes on a chart hanging at the end of my bed and then turns to leave.

"Wait," I cry. "Please tell me what happened."

She smiles again, but it doesn't reach her eyes. "I'll fetch your friend."

"Wait—"

But she leaves, and I'm all alone again.

Friend.

Tears pool in the corners of my eyes as I begin to tremble.

What happened to me?

I know it's nothing good. I feel like I've been hit by a truck, my body fragile and weak. And there was something about the way the nurse hurried from the room without giving me any real answers. As if she *couldn't* give them to me.

A sense of dread washes over me, making the pit in my stomach grow.

I take another sip of water, my hand trembling. Exhaustion washes over me and I begin to drift.

"Mia?"

His voice grounds me, and my eyes flicker open. "Bexley."

"Thank fuck." He rushes to my side.

"Bexley," I say again, emotion welling inside me. "What happened? Why am I here? The nurse wouldn't tell me anything, and I'm scared... I'm so scared."

He cups my face and leans down, touching his head to mine. "It's okay now, you're safe. You're—" He inhales a shuddering breath. "Fuck, mouse. I thought I'd lost you. I thought..." His lips press gently against my forehead, and I sense his apprehension.

Whatever happened is bad.

Really bad.

"I can't remember anything," I admit, the words heavy on my shoulders. "After Gravestone Hall, I can't remember anything. Where is Cade? Is he—"

Bexley goes rigid, a low growl rumbling in his chest. "Don't worry about Kingsley, Mia. All that matters is that you get better." He slowly pulls away, his eyes running over my body as if he can't quite believe I'm here.

"Will you please tell me what happened?"

Before he can answer, Sasha appears at the door. "Mia, thank God." She hurries over to my bedside, tears glistening in her eyes. "I'm sorry. I'm so fucking sorry."

My brows pinch. "What do you mean?"

I glance from her to Bexley, just in time to catch him shaking his head at her.

"Oh, I..."

"Hey." Channing lingers in the doorway. I gasp at the sight of him. He looks like he just walked out of a war zone, his face littered with cuts and bruises.

"Oh my God, what happened?" I ask as he approaches.

"Don't worry about me. It's just a few scratches." He glances at Bexley, and I frown again.

"What aren't you telling me? Why can't I remember?"

They all glance at one another as if I'm some science experiment. And I hate it.

I hate that no one is telling me a damn thing.

"What—"

"Ahh, Mia, it's good to see you awake." A doctor enters the room. "I'm Doctor Henson. Let's take a little look at you, shall we? I'm going to need your friends to give you some space."

Sasha and Channing back away, waiting over by the window, but Bexley doesn't budge.

"Mr. Easton," the doctor says. "I can't do my job if you don't—"

"It's okay." I nod at Bexley, and reluctantly, he steps away.

Doctor Henson pulls out a small flashlight and shines it in my eyes. "How do you feel, generally?"

"I feel like I got hit by a truck."

"That's to be expected, given the circumstances."

"And what are the circumstances exactly?" I ask.

"Mia..." He lets out a small breath, shoving the flashlight back in his pocket. "You were in a—"

"Doc," Bexley growls. "Philip said—"

"Phillip is not my patient. Mia is." He glances over his shoulder. "And she deserves to know what happened to her."

"Just... just let me do it, okay?"

The doctor hesitates but then gives a small nod. "Let me finish my observations first."

Doctor Henson runs a few more simple tests, asking me questions about myself and the world, testing my reflexes, and enquiring about my pain levels. When he's done, I ask, "Why can't I remember anything past the... the event I was attending?"

"The mind is a fragile thing, Mia." He gives me a sympathetic smile, just like the nurse had. "When we experience trauma, it is not uncommon to lose those memories."

"T-trauma. Right."

Something hovers on the edge of my mind. A memory I can't quite grasp.

"Will they ever come back?"

"It's hard to know. Sometimes patients make a full recovery including their recent memories. Other times, they don't."

"I see." My lips thin.

"Mia, what's important right now is that you give yourself time to heal. Physically and emotionally."

"Doc..." Bexley warns again.

But I'm too focused on the shift inside of me, the thick, sludgy fear cooling around my heart.

I begin to sweat, my body trembling. My eyes flutter as I inhale a ragged breath while Bexley and the doctor argue about something in hushed voices.

"Mia?" Bexley rushes to my side as I whimper.

"I-I remember... running. I was running. It was dark... so dark, and my feet were bare, and it hurt..."

I can feel the branches sticking into me, scratching and cutting me.

"Run, little mouse." He snarls the words at me. *"Run before the big bad wolf catches up with you."*

I gasp, fisting the bedsheets as my eyes fly open. "Cade. He... he was chasing me."

An alarm goes off beside me as my heart races in my chest so hard I'm sure it might explode out of me.

"Mia." Doctor Henson leaps into action, checking the machine. "You need to try to calm down." He pages the nurse.

"Doc... talk to me," Bexley demands.

"The stress is elevating her blood pressure. Mia, try taking deep breaths."

But I can't. I'm lost to the memory. It plays out in my head like a movie: Cade chasing me through the woods, pushing me the ground and... oh God. Bile rushes up my stomach and I dry heave.

"Sick bowl," Doctor Henson yells and a nurse appears, thrusting it under my nose.

"He—he... no. *No!*" I cry as I feel his fingers on my skin, clawing and grabbing at my flesh, his big body caging me to the ground as he taunted me. Hurt me.

"No. No!" Pain lashes my insides as the memories slam into me. Cade pushing inside me, taking what was never his to have. His teeth latched onto my skin. Biting. Devouring.

Destroying.

"Help me," I cry. "You have to help me." I thrash around on the bed, trying to get Cade off me.

"Doctor," somebody yells.

"Push 5mg of midazolam."

Something cold trickles into my hand. "No, no! Don't hurt me. Don't let him hurt me."

I fight against Cade, trying to push him off me. But then he begins to flicker, the edges of his body shimmering and shifting.

"W-what is that? What are you doing to me?" I croak as the darkness begins to close in around me. "Bexley, no." My voice fades. "Please, don't let him... oh God, no..."

It's futile. The pull of the abyss is too strong, dragging me down. Down... down... *down*... My limbs become heavy and my thoughts melt away.

Until there's nothing.

2

BEXLEY

My heart shatters as I watch her fight against her memories. I only know the very basics of the events after she got back to the house with Cade. The only two people who know the truth are those who were there, and I'd really hoped that Mia wouldn't remember, because from what Channing told me about the state he found her in, and the fact that she was only wearing his shirt when she was brought into the hospital, I know it can't have been good.

I've tried to push the marks that fucker left on her body from my mind, but I can't. They're right there, along with the image of her lying on the ground around the back of her house.

As I ran toward the house after the explosion, I heard Channing's voice calling for help, and I ran faster than I think I ever have in my life. My heart was in my throat as I refused to allow myself to consider the possibility that they weren't inside when the house went up in flames.

It turned out that they'd only arrived seconds before I had, and after trying and failing to get through the front door, Channing was carrying a passed-out Mia around the back of the house to get inside.

After tracking her cell to the Electi house, he heard her scream and went searching. She demanded that he take her home, assuming it would be a safe place to go.

How wrong she'd been.

No one has confirmed our suspicions, but we're all thinking the same thing.

Cade is behind it.

We have no idea if he intended for Mia to go home and get caught up in the blast, but he clearly wanted her parents gone. Which only confirms what we already knew about her father.

Garth Thompson killed Gregory Kingsley.

All of this was one big, fucked-up revenge plan on Cade's part.

He wanted vengeance for his father's murder, and what better way for the twisted motherfucker to get it than to take it out on the murderer's daughter?

I hate to say it, but he did a fucking good job. It seems that no one had any idea what he was planning, which is both impressive and terrifying. Mostly because no one has seen him since that house blew up and we have no idea where he is.

At some point, Sasha and Channing make their excuses and head back to the house so they can shower and sleep, but I still refuse to leave her.

I've been here since the moment the ambulance brought her in, and I won't leave until she does. I don't give a shit how many times people tell me to go home and get some rest. I refuse to leave her side, even more so now I've seen how terrified she was when her memories started coming back.

With Mia's hand locked in mine, I rest back in the chair and close my eyes for what feels like the first time in a week, but the second I start to drift off, the image of him touching her fills my mind and I jolt awake once more.

"Fucking hell," I mutter, rubbing my hand across my rough jaw.

The motherfucker isn't even here, and he's still fucking tormenting me.

I stare at Mia. Her face shows the evidence of the trauma she went through on Saturday night, both at the hands of that monster and from the explosion that blew her and Channing halfway across her parents' backyard. There are cuts and grazes along her cheekbones and forehead, and her neck is covered in fading hickeys from that motherfucker. The sight makes my stomach turn over, but it's not enough to make me walk away.

Nothing will ever force me to do that. I just wish I could take her pain away.

She doesn't deserve this.

She doesn't deserve any of it.

It's hours later when she starts to stir as the drugs they pumped into her veins begins to wear off.

"Mia?" I whisper when her fingers lightly squeeze mine and her eyelids start to flicker.

Sitting closer, I make sure I'm in her eyeline so that when she does finally open her eyes, she knows she's not alone.

"Bex," she breathes. "Tell me all of this is a nightmare?"

Pain slices through my chest at the vulnerability in her voice. "I'm so sorry, mouse," I whisper.

It takes her a few more minutes before she finally drags her eyes open and I get to look at her.

"Hey."

"Hey." The slightest smile curls at her lips when she sees me, but it doesn't last anywhere near long enough.

"How are you feeling?"

"B-better," she lies. "What happened, Bex? Please, I need to know how I ended up here."

I swallow nervously, not wanting to be the one to tell her but knowing that it can't really come from anyone else. "Let's start at the beginning. What do you remember?"

She looks away from me and swallows nervously as pain twists her features. "You don't want to hear it."

I know. "You need to tell me, Mia."

She nods and closes her eyes.

When she doesn't start speaking, I pour her a fresh glass of water and hold it up for her. "Here, drink this first."

She looks down at the cup and allows me to help her. "Thank you," she whispers when she's had enough. After holding my eyes for a beat, she looks at the wall once more and sucks in a deep breath. "When we got back to the house, I told him that I couldn't do it. I refused to go into the house," she starts quietly. "He... he called me 'little mouse.' He knows, Bex. He knows we've been together again."

Reaching forward, I hold one of her hands in both of mine, hoping that I can give her some strength to tell me all of this.

"Then he told me to run. So I did. I ran so fucking fast through that forest, but I was no match for his speed. He soon caught up with m-me." She inhales a ragged breath.

"Motherfucker," I growl, the word falling from my lips without instruction from my brain.

"I can't, Bex. You don't need to know."

"Mia, baby. I already know. The doctors examined you when you first came in."

"Oh my God," she cries, covering her face with her free hand.

"It's okay," I say softly, pulling her hand away so she can't hide from me. "I'm here, and I'm not going anywhere. No matter what you tell me."

She nods, tears pooling in her eyes, but none of them fall. Not yet, anyway.

"H-he... he was crazy, Bex. His eyes, they were pure evil. He spat all this crap at me. Told me h-how... my dad had k-killed Gregory and that he wanted revenge. It was like he was possessed. It was awful, worse than I ever could have imagined. It hurt. All of it hurt so much."

Fuck. It's painful to hear this, but she needs to get it out, and part of me needs to know.

"I'm so sorry."

"It seemed to go on forever. But then, all of a sudden, he was gone, and I was alone. I remember screaming, crying... certain that no one was going to find me, wondering how I was ever going to find my way back to the house." A sob erupts from her throat, causing a lump to grow in mine with the knowledge that I wasn't there to help her.

"Then Channing was there, pulling his shirt off for me and lifting me into his arms. He had the moonlight glowing behind him and I remember thinking that he looked like my guardian angel."

"Do you remember what happened next?"

She's silent for a few seconds as she thinks. "He... he put me in his car, I think, and I asked for you. I needed you. I needed you so badly, Bex." It's those six little words that finally force her tears to drop.

The sight guts me.

Reaching out, I wipe them from her cheeks as more fall. "Anything else?" I ask softly.

She shakes her head. "I must have passed out in the car. Then the next time I woke, I was here. With you." She falls silent again, lost in thought. It's as if she has more memories but can't quite get a grasp on them.

"I'm not here just because of what Cade did, am I?" she guesses correctly.

"No, baby." I squeeze her hand tighter as I prepare for what I need to tell her next. "Channing took you to your parents, like you asked, and I got straight into a car to meet you there, but when I got there—"

A knock on the door startles us both before it opens and Phillip Cargill appears.

"Mia, it's so good to see you awake," he says, his expression neutral like always as he holds her eyes. "How are you feeling?"

"I'll be okay. W-why are you here?"

If he's offended by her blunt question, then he doesn't show it. I guess he should have expected it. He doesn't strike me as someone who's cared about her well-being before, evidenced by the situation he allowed her to get in the middle of.

"I wanted to come and offer my condolences for your parents," he says before I'm able to cut him off.

"F-for my parents." Mia's brows pull together. "What's wrong with my parents? Bexley?" She turns to me, panic filling her eyes, her already pale complexion even worse as all the blood drains from her face.

Ignoring Phillip, I continue where I left off. "When I arrived at your house, it was seconds before it... fuck," I murmur. "There was... an explosion, Mia. I'm so sorry."

"Oh my God," she gasps, her free hand covering her mouth as more tears spill down her cheeks.

"I'm so sorry."

"M-my parents were inside?"

"Yes," Phillip answers before I get a chance to say anything.

"Oh my God." Her cries get louder before sobs begin to wrack her body.

Unable to leave her in bed alone, I kick my sneakers off, lift the sheet covering her and climb in beside her so I can pull her into my arms. "I'm so sorry, mouse. I'm so sorry," I whisper into her hair as she clings to me.

My own eyes burn with emotion as she continues to cry, and I hold her as tight as I can, hoping that I'm not hurting her worse than she already is.

"It was him, wasn't it? It was Cade. He wanted them dead," she says after a long excruciating minute.

"We don't have confirmation of that but—"

"It was him," she says, her voice strong and confident. "He knows that my father killed Gregory." For the first time ever, Phillip looks unsure of himself.

"H-how do you know that, Mia?"

"It doesn't matter how," she hisses, disdain dripping from her voice. "What's important is that Cade knows, and he's not going to stop until he's brought you all down."

"We have no idea where Cade is right now."

A humorless laugh falls from Mia's lips. "I really suggest you look harder, because if you're not careful, you and everyone you love is going to end up as collateral in all of this. Cade won't stop."

Phillip swallows somewhat nervously.

"Find him," she demands. "Find him and kill him before he gets to everyone else."

Her warning rings out loud long after the words have left her lips, turning my blood cold and sending a shiver down my spine.

Cade might be gone right now.

But this is far from over.

3

MIA

My parents are gone.
    Dead.
No. *Murdered.*
Killed by Cade as part of some sick revenge plot against my family. Against Quinctus.
Pain splinters my chest as I inhale a ragged breath.
"Mia?" Sasha knocks on the bathroom door, and I startle.
"Just a second."
It's the first time I've been allowed to come in here alone. I stare at myself in the small mirror, horrified by what I see. Faded cuts and bruises mar my skin. The faint finger marks around my neck. The bite marks. It's hard to tell which injuries were caused by Cade and which by the explosion, but I look like I just survived the apocalypse.
And Phillip Cargill stood there.
He just stood there, with his indifferent expression, apologizing for the death of my parents as if it was all just business as usual. He and the rest of Quinctus sent me off with Cade knowing what he was capable of...
They...
A garbled whimper spills from my lips. *They did this.*
It all starts and ends with *them.*

From instructing my father to kill Gregory Kingsley and the other men on that list, to allowing it to stand when my name was pulled from the calix.

Anger rushes through me like wildfire as I grip the edge of the sink. They did this.

"Mia?" Sasha's voice comes through the door again.

"Yeah," I sigh, feeling the walls close in around me.

One of them has been at my side ever since I woke up yesterday.

After finding out the truth about my parents, and Phillip's visit, I had to be sedated again. I woke up this morning with Sasha curled up in the chair beside me.

I rinse my hands and dry them before gingerly walking to the door. Everything hurts. My muscles, my bones, my organs. My body aches in a way I never thought possible as I gently turn the handle.

"Thank God," Sasha breathes. "I was getting worried."

She helps me back to bed, holding my IV stand out of the way as I climb up and slide under the stiff sheets.

"I can't believe I was out of it for almost a week," I say. "Will you tell me what happened after—" The words get stuck in my throat.

"It was chaos." She gives me a sad smile. "Bexley was beside himself. At one point, I thought he was going to kill Dad." Regret simmers in her eyes, and I swallow down the urge to tell her that he should have.

"They knew, didn't they?" I say, coolly. "They knew Cade might…" Bile churns inside me, forcing me to take a deep breath. "They knew, and they sent me with him like a lamb to the slaughter."

A shudder rolls through me. Now I remember that night, I can't forget it. I almost wish my memory hadn't returned. At least then I wouldn't have to relive Cade… hurting me, over and over until I was nothing more than an empty shell of skin and bones in the cold undergrowth.

"Are you hungry?" she says. "I could ask the nurse to—"

"No." I couldn't eat if someone paid me. "Do they have any idea where Cade went?"

"None." She sucks in a thin breath. "Q have people looking, though."

"This is just the beginning," I say, my eyes shuttering. "You didn't hear him, Sasha. He was so bitter and twisted. He was like a different person."

And that's saying something.

"I still can't believe my dad and Q had his dad..."

"Murdered?" It comes out harsher than I intend. "Isn't that what Q does? How far their power stretches?" I pin her with a hard look.

"Y-yeah, but he was an elder." She says the words as if they matter.

As if anything about this dark and cruel world makes sense.

"I still can't believe they're gone." My heart breaks all over again. We might have had our recent ups and downs ever since the Eligere, but they were still my parents.

And they're gone.

I blink away the tears, bone-weary from crying.

"I think I want to sleep," I say, and Sasha nods.

"Sleep. I'll be right he—"

"Alone." My voice shakes. "I need to be alone."

"Mia, I'm not sure that's—"

"Please, Sasha."

She stands, reluctance etched into her expression. "Okay, but if you need anything..."

"I know."

I don't watch her leave. Instead, I close my eyes and let the darkness consume me.

WHEN I WAKE, it's to Bexley staring at me.

"Hey," he says around a weak smile.

"How long was I out?"

"A little over three hours. Can I get you anything?"

I shake my head. What I really want is to get out of here, but every time I think about it, I remember I have nowhere to go.

"Mia, I—"

"Don't, please... just don't."

His jaw pops as he runs a hand through his dirty blond hair. We knew the Coglio would change things once Cade finally claimed me as his. But I never predicted... this.

I turn my head away from him, wincing at the sharp breath he takes. "Tell me what to do to fix this," he whispers, his voice so full of pain it lashes my insides. I want to comfort him, the way I have so many times. But I can't.

Not this time.

"Mia, look at me." Bexley's hand touches mine, and he threads our fingers together. His touch has always settled me but I'm too numb to feel it this time. I do look at him, though, unable to fight the invisible tether binding us.

Silence stretches out before us, thick and sticky, making it hard to breathe. So much has happened.

So much pain and darkness and desperation.

But this... waking up in this hospital room to find out my parents are dead, is beyond my wildest nightmares.

"You want to help me?" My voice tremors with anger. "Then find Cade and kill him, Bexley." Silent tears roll down my cheeks. "That's all I need from you."

His eyes flash with pain. "Little mou—"

"Don't. Don't *ever* call me that again."

"Run, little mouse. Run before the big bad wolf catches up with you."

My eyes shutter as I inhale a ragged breath.

"Mia?" Bexley squeezes my hand.

"You have to find him," I cry, sobbing, unable to fight the swell of emotion dragging me under.

"Shh, Mia. I'm here, I'm right here." He shifts closer, leaning down to kiss my knuckles.

"He has to pay." I sob harder. "He has to pay."

"He will, I promise."

Just then, the door opens and Channing peers inside. Our eyes lock and he frowns. "Sorry, I can—"

"No." I sniffle. "It's okay, you can come in."

He slips inside, closing the door behind him. "I just wanted to see if you guys needed anything."

"I'm good, man, thanks." Bexley gives him a small nod, and the two of them share a long look.

"How are you feeling?" he asks me.

"Like all of this is a dream and I'll wake up any second. But then I remember it's real life, and my heart breaks all over again."

"Shit, Mia, I—"

"Don't. It isn't your fault." There's only one person to blame here.

Cade.

Well, Cade *and* Quinctus.

"Any news?" Bexley asks Channing, and he shakes his head as he pulls over a chair and sits down.

"It's a fucking mess. Q are running scared. Ashton is... well, you saw how he was, and—"

"Did Ashton know?"

"He says he didn't."

I scoff at that, my ribs smarting. "Of course he says he didn't, but he's Cade's best friend. If anyone knew, it was him. Have Quinctus tried to make him talk?"

"They've talked to him."

"Talked to him?" Disbelief coats my words. "Maybe they need to try harder. Be more persuasive. I'm sure they have the ways and means—"

"Mia, this isn't helping."

My eyes lock on Bexley's, hardly able to believe my ears. "*Not helping*? He killed them, Bexley. He planted an explosive in my house and blew them up without a second thought. So don't sit there and tell me that I'm not helping." My chest heaves with the weight of my words. "He's not going to stop. Cade is out for blood, and he isn't going to stop until—"

The door cracks open, and Sasha peeks her head inside. "Hey."

"Hey," Channing says, gently shoving his chair back. She comes inside and sits on his lap, giving me a timid smile.

"The two of you are—"

"With Cade gone, we're the least of Q's concern. Besides," Channing says, "I told them I'm done."

"Done?"

"Yeah, I didn't sign on for this, Mia. And when I found you..." He swallowed roughly. "He almost killed you."

I almost wish he had.

I don't realize I say the words out loud until it's too late.

Bexley is as white as a sheet, staring at me like he doesn't recognize me. "You don't mean that," he whispers.

"Don't I?"

"Maybe we should go," Sasha says, but I shake my head.

"No, stay."

I'm not sure I want to be alone with Bexley right now. From his grim expression, he knows it too.

"They knew," I say with little emotion. "Quinctus knew all along what Cade was capable of—"

"Mia, we don't know that." I hate that Bexley is even suggesting it, as if he's one of them now. Loyal to Quinctus and all they stand for.

"Yes, we do. We can't trust them." They've made that perfectly clear.

"Phillip said—"

"Phillip is the reason I'm laying here. What about that don't you understand?" I glare at him. "My father killed Gregory Kingsley... he killed all those men... for Quinctus. And then when my dad tried to argue about me being Cade's prosapia, Phillip forced him to be quiet about it, because *everything is a game to them*, Bexley. It's all one giant game."

And I've been on the losing side since the start.

Pain splinters through my head, and I cry out.

"Mia?" Bexley jumps up just as a nurse rushes into the room.

"You feeling okay, sweetheart?" she asks, moving around Bexley to get to the machine. "Your blood pressure is elevated. You need to rest, Mia. Your body has been through a great deal of trauma. She can't be getting worked up about anything." The nurse levels my friends with a stern look.

"I'm okay," I say.

"Well, your blood pressure says different." She scribbles on my chart and heads for the door. "Let her rest, or I'll have you all removed."

Bexley growls at that, and I shoot him an irritated look.

My feelings for him are conflicted. I love him—I love him so much. That hasn't changed. But everything is different now. The cracks in my heart have severed something between us.

"I'm sorry," he concedes. "When do you think Mia will be able to go home?"

The word makes my breath hitch. I don't have a home. Not anymore.

"The doctor wants to observe her for a couple more days, but then there's no reason why she can't go home. But she'll need plenty of rest."

He nods, his lips pressed into a thin line.

The nurse leaves, and a heaviness settles over the four of us.

"We should go." Sasha stands, pulling Channing up with her. "We'll see you back at the house," she says to Bexley.

"Actually, I think I'm going to stay here tonight." He glances at me, pleading with me, his eyes saying all the things I'm not sure I want to hear.

He's sorry.

He loves me.

He's here for me.

He'll protect me.

But I just feel numb.

"No," I say. "You should go with them."

4
BEXLEY

I stare at Mia with my chin dropped and my fists clenched in frustration.

"Can you both leave, please?" I instruct Sasha and Channing, but at no point do I take my eyes off Mia's tired ones.

The sound of their shoes squeaking against the floor soon rings in my ears before the door opens and then closes behind them.

The silence is almost deafening. The only things that can be heard are the whir of the IV machine Mia is still plugged into and our increased breathing.

"You don't mean that," I tell her.

She holds my eyes strong, the darkness within them making me wonder if I'm staring at the same person. Mia might have been apprehensive about what the future held before, terrified even. But at least she was full of fight, determination. All of that has gone. Vanished. And all because of him.

"Yes, Bexley. I do."

"No, it's just the drugs they're filling you with," I argue, beginning to feel myself getting desperate.

I can't leave her alone here.

What if... What if he comes here?

Q might not be able to find him, but something tells me he hasn't gone very far. They're just not looking fucking hard enough.

They have already been outwitted by him once; you'd think they'd be embarrassed for it to happen again, but right now, we're all just sitting ducks, waiting for him to strike.

"I need you to leave, Bex. *Please.*" Her voice is hard. Cold. It's not a tone I've ever heard her use before, and I hate it.

He did this to her. He fucking corrupted her innocence, her strength and zest for life, all because he needed revenge on something that has nothing to do with her.

Her dad? Fine. Q? Definitely. But not Mia. She's innocent in all of this.

"I'm not leaving you alone. It's not happening." I take a step toward her, and my heart shatters when she flinches away from me as if I'm going to hurt her. "Mouse?" I breathe, unable to speak through the giant lump in my throat. "I'd never hurt you."

Her eyes shutter as she inhales through her nose. "Then you can do as I ask and leave."

I never saw her hand move, but two seconds later, the door behind me opens and the nurse steps into the room once more.

"You called?" she asks Mia.

"Yes, please can you tell Bexley to leave. Get security if you have to."

My chin drops at her words.

The nurse turns to me, but I don't let her get a word out before I spin on my heels and march toward the door, swinging it open with everything I have and wincing when it slams back against the wall.

The sound of Mia's sobs rips through me, but it doesn't make me stop. Nor does Sasha and Channing calling my name as I race past them.

Now I've walked away, I need to get as far away from this place as possible.

"Bex, wait." Their voices echo down the empty corridor as I head for the exit, in desperate need of fresh air.

I burst through the doors and suck in deep lungfuls of fall air as I look around at my surroundings. Gravestone Hospital sits on a hill right on the edge of the forest, the lake sparkling in the distance making this place seem serene and peaceful. Two of the many lies that are hidden by the beauty in this town.

"What happened?" Sasha asks softly, coming to stand beside me as I stare out at the forest, taking in the changing colors of the leaves.

"She doesn't want me here."

"She doesn't know what she wants right now, Bex. Don't take it personally. She's just had her world turned upside down.

"I can't just leave her here alone. What if—"

"Q have security all over the building. No one is going to get to her."

"I'm sorry, Sash, but that doesn't fill me with any confidence. I hate to say it, but he's smarter than all of them. If he wants to get to her, then he will."

I stare at her for a beat, and I see my own fear reflected back at me in her eyes.

"Fuck this," I bark, storming past her.

"Bex, where are you—"

"I'm going to fix this," I call over my shoulder as I pass Channing, who was watching us by the exit.

"And how are you going to do that exactly?"

"I... I'll figure it out," I spit, not really having an answer to his question. "Stay here, both of you, and don't let anyone get to her."

"She's safe here, Eas—"

Spinning, I pin him with a look that will ensure he doesn't argue. "Stay the fuck with her."

"Okay, fine," he concedes, holding his hands up in surrender.

The second I drop into my car, I start the engine and wheelspin out of the parking lot, heading for the town hall.

"EXCUSE ME, sir. You can't—" The security guard's warning falls on deaf ears as I storm past him and take the stairs two at a time that lead to the office where I hope I'll find Phillip Cargill.

"Mr. Easton, you can't just—" I swing the door to his office open after ignoring his second lot of security and his assistant, who mostly just stare at me with wide eyes as I race through her office.

"Easton," Phillip says in surprise, standing from his desk as I slam the door closed.

But I soon realize that he's not the only one here, because another man stands.

"M-Marcus?" I stutter, staring at my grandfather.

"Bexley."

I stare between the two men, my eyes narrowing in suspicion. "Where is he?" I spit, taking a step toward them.

"We don't know," he says, as cool as a cucumber, as if Mia's parents weren't blown to pieces by that sick fuck. "We're still working on it."

"Not fucking good enough."

"Son, look." Marcus raises his hands in a calm down motion. "We know you're angry. Hell, we are too. We—"

"Bullshit. You don't care. You don't care about anything other than your stupid fucking Quinctus and your reputation. If you did, then you'd have fixed this, dealt with Cade years ago."

"It's not that simple."

"No, it seems not," I sneer. "What's going on here? What's *really* going on? I think it's about time you stop leaving out important things from the Electi, don't you? Like the fact that you allowed the Eligere to be fixed and turned a blind eye when you fucking knew the girl chosen was going to end up hurt." I close the space between us, rounding his desk and standing right in front of him. "You knew this was going to happen, and you allowed it. You, him—" I point at Marcus. "You set Garth up, promised him you'd protect his daughter, and then forgot all about it and let Cade do his worst. All of this is your fault. It—"

"You're wrong, Easton."

An unamused smile pulls at my lips as I shake my head. "I'm not, and you know it. What else is at play here, Phillip? I know there's more."

"There isn't—"

"I met with James," I blurt out, cutting off whatever bullshit argument was about to fall from his lips. "What about Cade's uncle? Lincoln Kingsley. Is that where he's hiding? He seems keen to protect Cade. What about your other associates who were going to benefit out of this little deal somehow?"

Phillip visibly pales before me.

"Bexley, that's enough," Marcus says.

"No, it's nowhere near e-fucking-nough. The girl I love is laying in a hospital bed, grieving her *dead* parents... she very nearly lost her own life because of this bullshit. You should have dealt with Cade. I don't give a fuck about bloodline or tradition or Quinctus and whatever else fucked-up elite organization is involved in this. You have hurt the people in the town that you're meant to protect. You're a fucking joke," I spit at Phillip, ignoring the fact that Marcus is even in the room.

Lifting his hand, Phillip straightens his tie. "You don't need to worry about anything, Easton. We have it all under control. We all have our roles to play, and yours is to maintain the status quo. Mia was in a terrible accident." He pins me with a stern look. "I am aware that you care for her, but it would do you well to remember that, for all intents and purposes, she is still Cade's prosapia."

Like hell she is. Red hot fury skitters up my spine as I take a step forward, drawing my arm back ready to make my point a different way when the door bursts open behind me and two huge security guards drag me away from Phillip.

"You need to learn your place, Easton. You're Electi. Not Quinctus. You do as we say and only as we say."

The fingers wrapped around my arms tighten as I fight to get back to him. "This is bullshit," I spit. "Innocent people died because of you. Because of this corrupt fucking cult you call an organization."

"We will find Kingsley, and he will be dealt with."

"And Mia, what the hell are you going to do to fix that situation? He r-raped her, nearly fucking killed her, and given half a chance, he'll do it again."

"He won't," Phillip says with sheer arrogance, as if he believes the bullshit spewing from his lips.

"Yes. Yes, he will."

Our eyes hold, a silent battle of wills ensuing.

I don't care that he's the elder, that he's more powerful than me. He is the one in the wrong here. He is the one to blame for all of this.

"Get him out of here," he instructs his security detail, and not a second later, I'm being manhandled from the room.

"Get the fuck off me. I can walk myself," I snap, ripping my arms from their grasp. "This isn't over, Phillip. Find him and end him, or I will. He's not getting the chance to get anywhere near Mia ever again."

Phillip nods once before the door is slammed closed.

"You need to lea—"

"I'm fucking going," I bark, storming away from the men who are now guarding the door as if I'm about to go back in there and try again.

As I march from the building, I crack my knuckles loudly, desperately needing to feel them connecting with someone's face. And with Kingsley hiding in the shadows, there's only one other person for the job.

THE HOUSE IS quiet as I pull up, but Ashton, Brandon, and Alex's cars are parked out the front, telling me that they're hanging out inside somewhere.

I storm through the front door, swinging it closed so hard the bang vibrates through the house and alerts everyone that I'm home.

Music pumps out from the direction of the den, and I head that way.

"Are you fucking kidding me?" I bark when I find the three of them in here with some girls, drinks littering the coffee table and Kingsley's signature scent permeating the air. "You're having a party while Mia is—" My words falter as I picture her out of it and helpless in that hospital bed.

I fly over the empty couch and knock away the woman who's pressed up against Ashton's chest with enough force that she stumbles to the floor before pinning Ashton against the wall with my arm against his throat.

"Tell me where the fuck he is," I bellow, getting right in his face.

"I don't know," he says, perfectly calm.

"Bullshit," I spit. "You know everything, and I'm not stopping until you fucking tell me." He's expecting me to go for his face, so he misses my fist flying into his stomach until it's too late.

He doubles over, gasping for breath as the girl he was with screams in horror.

"Where." Kick. "The fuck." Kick. "Is he?" Kick.

5

MIA

Three days later, I finally leave the hospital.

"Are you okay?" Sasha asks me as we sit in the back of the black SUV she and Channing came to get me in. There's a driver and a security guy both sitting up front. The windows are tinted, and part of me wonders if it's bulletproof. Not that I expect Cade will attack us like this, out in the open.

He's not the kind of guy to shy away from getting his hands dirty.

A shiver runs through me as I shut down the memories. Sasha notices my discomfort and lays a hand on mine. "It'll be okay," she whispers.

"We moved all of your things into the house. I know it's not ideal, but everyone thought it was safer than you—"

"It's fine," I deadpan.

"You'll have space," Channing says, giving me a sympathetic look. It's all they've done over the last three days. Look at me with pity.

Broken little Mia Thompson.

I hate it.

I hate that my life has been reduced to this. I hate that I'm being forced to move into the last place I ever want to step foot in again.

But Cade is still out there, and I know he won't stop until he's rained down hell on every single person involved in killing his father.

The gates come into view, and my heart begins to drum wildly in my chest. I suck in a ragged breath, my hand curling around the edge of the leather seat as they begin to swing open and the car glides through them.

"Okay?" Sasha asks again and I nod, pressing my lips together, not trusting myself to speak.

Memories flash through my mind of the last time I was here. Running through the trees, Cade's wicked laughter filling the night sky as he chased me.

Hunted me.

I press myself into the leather, trying to calm my racing heart. The car rolls to a stop and the security guy climbs out and opens our door. Channing goes first, helping Sasha from the car. They both wait for me, but I'm frozen in place.

"I-I can't." My voice cracks as silent tears roll down my cheeks.

"Mia, it'll be okay," Sasha says, but I barely hear her over the roar of blood in my ears. She doesn't know... she doesn't know that a piece of me died that night here with Cade. That he broke something inside me that I'll never get back.

I sob harder, lost to the tidal wave of emotion wracking my body. It isn't until Bexley appears, reaching inside the car for me, that I break free of my trance.

"I've got you, Mia," he says, cradling me against his chest. I want to fight him, to tell him to put me down and leave me be, but being in his arms, breathing in his familiar scent settles something inside me, and I relax against his chest, letting him carry me inside.

Sasha and Channing don't follow us as he takes me straight to my room. My new room.

The only place I have to call my own, now my home is gone.

Another wave of grief hits me as Bexley lays me down on the bed. Part of me wants him to leave, to let me break in solace. But the other part, the tiny sliver of the Mia I was before I woke up in that hospital bed, is relieved when he kicks off his sneakers and climbs on the bed beside me, pulling me into the hard lines of his body. "Shh, Mia. I'm here. I'm right here."

"They're gone," I whimper, clutching at his t-shirt. "They're really gone."

"I know, little mou—Mia." He lets out a resigned sigh. "I know."

Bexley cups my face, letting his thumbs wipe away the tears streaking down my cheeks. "But I'm here. I'm right here, and I'm not going anywhere. I swear." He holds me as I lose my fight to the swell of emotion battering my insides. It's like a storm, unrelenting and unstoppable. A force of nature trying to destroy me from the inside out.

I cry and cry. I cry until my eyes hurt and my lungs burn. I cry until my body slowly shuts down, depleted and weary.

Eventually, the tears subside. But the hole in my heart is bigger than ever.

"I love you, Mia," Bexley whispers against my forehead, his lips touching the skin there. "I love you so fucking much, and I need you. I need you to fight, baby. I need you to..." He trails off, tucking me closer, holding on as if he's scared that I might disappear at any second.

And I feel as if I might.

I feel as if I might disintegrate into nothing but a cloud of grief and anger.

But as I begin to drift, I realize I'm not alone.

Bexley is here.

He'll ground me.

Even if I can't see the way out of this black abyss yet, he'll be at my side, fighting for me.

WHEN I WAKE UP, I'm alone. I gingerly push up on my elbows, wincing at the lingering pain in my limbs. The doctors said that I was lucky apart from the contusion on my head and a few deep cuts and scrapes.

Lucky.

I don't feel very lucky.

I feel cursed. Trapped in a dark and twisted game I never asked to be a part of.

I lay there, still and silent, thinking about my life. About my parents, and my childhood. Everything's tainted now, tarnished by the lies and secrets.

Lies and secrets they paid the ultimate price for.

The room I'm in is unfamiliar, but it's full of my possessions from my dorm room. My makeup litters the dresser, and my hoodie is slung over the back of the chair. My small collection of books lines the bookshelf, and someone has hung my daisy chain lights on the wall, framing the mirror.

But it does little to ease the knot in my stomach.

The clock reads four-thirty, which means I've been sleeping for hours. The doctor warned me to expect to feel drowsy for a while. Something about the effects of all the medication and my injuries.

I'm to rest and give my body time to completely heal. As if time is a magical cure for a broken heart and fractured soul. A garbled sob crawls up my throat.

The faint smell of tomato sauce permeates the air, and my stomach rumbles. I touch a hand there, trying to abate the hunger. I don't want to go out there, to face them, but I know I'm going to have to do it eventually.

A small knock at my door startles me, and I croak, "Yes?"

"Mia, it's me," Sasha says. "Do you want to join us for dinner?"

"I..." No. "Yes, okay."

The door cracks open, and she slips inside. "How are you feeling?"

"Please, stop asking me that."

Her smile drops. "I'm sorry... I'm just—"

"Sasha, please. I can't stand it, the way you all keep looking at me."

"You're right." She inhales a sharp breath, moving closer to the bed. "I know it's not easy, being here—"

"It's fine. It's not like I have anywhere else to go." My heart squeezes.

"Is Ashton—"

"Bexley thought it would be better if he weren't here when we brought you back."

"Okay." I nod, tentatively standing. I feel weak on my feet, but I manage to grab the hoodie off the back of the chair.

"Here, let me help you." Sasha takes it from me, sliding it up my limp arms and gently over my head.

"Thanks."

"Ready?" She laces her arm through mine.

"I guess."

Sasha slowly guides me downstairs. I can hear the low rumbles of chatter coming from the kitchen, and my pulse begins to kick up a gear again.

"It's okay," she whispers. "You're safe here."

I want to add *now*. I'm safe here *now*. But I don't have the energy to argue or get myself worked up again.

The second we reach the kitchen, the conversation dies down and all eyes turn to me.

"Mia," Bexley breathes, shooting up from his seat. "Let me help."

"It's okay," I say. "I can manage." Stepping out of Sasha's hold, I shuffle over to a chair and sit down, exhaling a shuddering breath.

"It's good to see you up and about," Brandon says with pity in his eyes. "I'm so fucking sorry about your parents."

"Brandon's right," Tim says. "What went down..."

I tense, and Sasha notices. "Not now," she says, giving a little shake of her head.

"Yeah, of course." A sheepish expression crosses Tim's face.

But their sympathy feels disingenuous. How am I supposed to trust anything they say, knowing how blindly—and willingly—they followed Cade?

"Here you go, Miss Thompson." Mulligan gently nudges a plate of food in my direction. "If you need anything else—"

"This looks great. Thanks." My stomach growls in appreciation, but the second I start picking at the food, bile churns through me. I push the plate aside, opting for a drink of water instead.

"You've got to eat something," Sasha says quietly as the others dig into their meals.

"I can't. Not yet. Are there any updates on him?" I ask, my questioning shattering the atmosphere.

"Mia, maybe this isn't—"

My eyes lock on Bexley. "I need to know."

"Nothing," Channing says. "There's been no sign of him."

"Has Ashton—"

"Ashton doesn't know anything."

"I don't believe him," I grit out, feeling my loose threads of control slip. "He's Cade's best friend. He must know something. Anything that will—"

"He doesn't." Ashton steps into the room, taking the air with him.

"What the fuck?" Bexley barks. "I thought we told you to stay away."

"I have as much right to be here as anyone. Kingsley didn't only screw over the—"

I'm out of my seat before I know what I'm doing. Ashton doesn't stop me as I hurl myself toward him with a knife poised in my hand.

"Oh no, you don't." Bexley shoots up and grabs me, hauling me back into his chest.

"Let me go," I yell, my eyes fixed on Ashton as he watches me.

"You should let her come at me, Easton," he says, coolly. "She deserves her pound of flesh." Regret swarms his eyes, which is when I notice one of them is black and blue as if someone hit him, and I laugh bitterly.

"Don't tell me you actually feel sorry for me?"

"I swear to God, Mia, I had no idea he was planning that."

"You knew everything—"

"Not this." He runs a hand down his bruised face, letting out a small breath. "I might be a sick bastard, but I didn't think... Kingsley betrayed me, too. And for what it's worth, I am sorry—"

"Don't! Don't you dare apologize to me." I struggle against Bexley's vise-like hold on me. Channing has moved to our side, no doubt ready to intervene if I somehow manage to break free.

"I-I can't be here," I blurt out. "Let me go, I need to go. I need—"

Bexley lifts me into his arms and stalks out of the kitchen with me.

"Put me down," I demand, but he doesn't let up. "Bexley, for the love of God." I slam my palms into his chest. "Put. Me. Down."

When he finally lowers me to the ground, I realize why he can't talk. His jaw is clenched so tightly he looks ready to crack enamel.

"Bexley?" I whisper.

"Just give me a second," he grits out, "before I go back in there and kill him."

6

BEXLEY

I stare at Mia's terrified, exhausted eyes and allow them to ground me, to calm me, to stop me from walking straight back into the kitchen and ripping that motherfucker's head off.

I told him to stay the fuck away. None of us want him here. Mia doesn't need him here, yet he ignored me like the stupid fucking cunt that he is.

Everyone else has been genuinely concerned, genuinely angry at Cade's actions, that he would hurt one of our own like that without so much as a second thought. Tim and Brandon have been surprisingly supportive, seeing as they've spent almost all the time I've known them following him around like lost sheep. But it seems that even their loyalty has its limits, and Cade has just smashed through them.

Ashton, though... we already know that his morality line is so far gone it's practically nonexistent. It's why none of us believe him when he says he had no clue about any of this.

It's lies. All of it.

He's probably feeding every single thing we do back to Cade so he can use it against us.

My breath catches at the thought of him already knowing that Mia is here, what bedroom she's using. We've increased security, but this is

Cade we're talking about. I'm sure he has a way into his own house that none of us know about.

"Bexley, what's wrong?" Mia breathes.

My eyes find hers once again, and every muscle in my body tightens as I take in her lingering cuts and bruises.

"Mia, I—" My words falter, knowing that I can't possibly have the right ones to express how scared I am that I'm going to lose her. That moment her house exploded and the seconds following it were the worst of my life, thinking that she was inside...

How do I tell her that in that moment I wanted to run inside to be with her just so we could go together?

"Fuck, I missed you."

Stepping up to her, I slide my hand around the back of her neck and lower my brow to hers, breathing in her sweet floral scent and allowing it to settle me. "I missed you so fucking much, mou—Mia." Her entire body stiffens as I almost call her by the nickname I have since we first met.

It guts me that he's ruined that for us. Tainted what we had.

"I'm so fucking sorry, I'm sorry, I'm so sorry," I chant, needing to do something, to say something to make it better, to take it all away, but knowing that in reality there is nothing I can do besides be here.

"Bex?" she whispers hesitantly. The sound of her soft and unsure voice snaps something inside, and I press my lips to hers, immediately running my tongue across the seam for her to allow me entry.

But all she does is tense and keep them closed.

"Mia, please," I all but beg. "I need this. I need you."

Her body tenses and her palms press forcefully against my chest, and the little bit of hope I had inside me withers and dies. "I can't, Bex. I'm sorry." She takes a huge step back and stares down at her feet. "I'm not the same person now."

"Mia, that's not true."

"How would you know, Bexley?" Her eyes flicker to mine, and what I see there shreds me. "You might have been there at the end, stood beside me as my parents burned, but you don't know everything I went through to get there. How he killed every single bit of hope within me. He k-killed me, Bex. I might be standing here, breathing in front of you, but I am not the same person anymore."

She backs away toward the stairs, silent tears dropping onto her cheeks as she does.

"Mia, what's wrong?" Sasha asks, stepping out and looking between the two of us.

"N-nothing." With one last look at me, she turns, wraps her fingers around the banister, and uses all her strength to pull herself up. Sasha rushes after her, wrapping her arm around Mia's waist as she helps her back upstairs.

My fists clench and my jaw pops. That should be me. I should be the one supporting her right now.

I'm in the kitchen before I've registered that my legs have moved; Ashton is just as shocked when his back slams up against the wall and all the air rushes from his lungs.

"Easton," Tim growls from behind me.

Since Cade's disappearance, he's been at the house a lot more—I assumed because he's unofficially second in command, but maybe it's to play peacekeeper.

"Leave it."

"No," I bark in Ashton's face. "He knows something. He *has* to know something."

"I don't," Ashton says without missing a beat. "If I knew anything, I swear I'd tell you."

"Bullshit. Your loyalties are with Cade, not us."

"If I knew anything, I'd tell you," he repeats, but his words still hold no weight to me.

"You're not staying here. You're not Electi. You're nothing but a fucking psychopath."

"This is my home too," he argues.

"No, your home is with your whore of a mother and sister."

He pales at my words, but he doesn't argue. I've never met his mother, but I sure know Brook and Ashton, and there's no way they came from a sweet and innocent woman. Plus, she married Phillip. Anyone who willingly marries into Quinctus needs their fucking head checked.

"I'm on your side, I swear." His expression is pleading. "I never wanted Mia hurt, not like that..."

"I don't believe a fucking word that comes out of your mouth," I say, slamming him against the wall once more and turning my back on him.

"Get out of here, Moore," Tim growls, his voice holding the viciousness I've been told he's capable of but have yet to witness.

"But—"

"Get the fuck out," he bellows. "And don't come back until you've proved that we can trust you."

"You *can* fucking trust me." He throws his hands up in frustration.

"Then prove it."

The tension is heavy as Ashton lets out a string of expletives before finally marching from the house, leaving only the echo of the slamming front door in his wake.

I stare at Tim as the others stare at me. I understand why. Right now, I'm like a pot that's about to boil over. I get it—I'd be hesitant around me too. The only time I'm calm is when I'm with Mia, and she seems to be doing anything she can to keep that time as limited as possible.

"Fuck. FUCK!" I roar, my hands lifting to my head, my fingers pulling at my hair until I think I might be about to pull it clean out.

"We'll get to the bottom of it, Easton. No one hurts one of our own and gets away with it. Even if it's Kingsley."

As much as I love that they see Mia as one of their own, as someone under their protection, I can't help feeling that it's all a bit too little, too late. They didn't seem to care when he was violating her in front of them and parading her around like he owned her.

"We never thought it would come to this," he says quieter, as if he can read my thoughts. "We thought he'd have his fun and move on."

"Well, he didn't, and now look at the fucking mess he's left behind. I want him found before Q. I want to be the one to fucking end him."

With that said, I storm from the kitchen and then soon after the house.

I take off running through the woods behind the house, looking around for any evidence of where Cade might have brought Mia, but like all the previous times I've been out here since that night, I don't find anything.

I'm aware of footsteps behind me, but I don't turn around or acknowledge them. I already know who it is, and it seems he knows I'm in no mood to talk because he stays well back.

It's not until I approach the lake that I slow, allowing my muscles the relief and my burning lungs a few deep breaths.

"What if he's telling the truth?" Channing asks. "What if he really doesn't know?"

"Then we use him to lure Cade out. Although I don't believe a word that comes out of Ashton's mouth."

I blow out a frustrated breath.

"We've got his cell monitored, his bedroom at Cargill's under surveillance." A shudder rips through me at the thought. "Don't worry, we don't have to watch the footage," Channing says, clearly understanding my reaction.

"What the fuck do you think he does in there?"

"Aside from fantasizing about fucking his sister?" Channing deadpans, and I can't help but laugh. Fuck does it feel good.

"Man, I really needed that."

"If he knows anything, if Cade tries to get in touch, anything, we'll know about it, Bex. We will beat him at this game, and we will end him."

"Spoken like a true Electi."

"No, spoken like a friend. I was serious when I told Cargill that I'm done. I'll see all this through, and then I'm just going to be regular Channing Rexford again."

"And Sasha?"

"Mine. I can be her prosapia," he chuckles.

"Only if you wear a white dress."

We shoot the shit for a while longer, pushing everything else aside and just trying to be regular college kids who are actually enjoying life for a few minutes.

"We should get back," he finally says.

"Yeah, I don't want to miss anything."

"We're all going to have to go back to class soon, and shit is going to be a hell of a lot harder with us all over the place."

My heart drops into my stomach. "I know."

"Mia will have full-time security. We'll do everything we can to protect her."

But...

He doesn't say that final word out loud, but I hear it loud and clear.

"I know. We just need to pray that he fucks up and we get to him before then."

"Maybe you should get her away for a bit. Somewhere she can properly relax before the funeral."

I scrub my hand down my face. "Fuck, the funeral. I'd never considered—"

"We've got it all covered. You and Mia don't need to worry about a single thing, but it's going to be hella hard on her."

"I can't even imagine."

"No, me neither."

We slowly make our way back. I'm relieved when I see the security that are working the house all stand to attention when they hear our approach; it fills me with a little confidence that they are actually on the ball.

They relax the second we emerge and holster their guns as we walk up the driveway and to the house.

But as good as it feels to know they're here, doing their job, I think we all know that when Cade strikes it's not going to be by walking up to the house in daylight. That is not that motherfucker's style.

I don't bother stopping in the kitchen as I pass. Instead, I head straight up to my room to shower. When I get to the top of the stairs, I look toward where both Mia and Sasha's rooms are. I desperately want to go down there and check she's okay, and my heart sinks knowing that she doesn't want me to.

It's just temporary, I tell myself as I force my legs to walk in the direction of my own bedroom instead.

I shower, pulling on a clean pair of boxers and falling onto my bed as the sun descends in the sky and casts an orange hue across my room. Watching the shadows from the trees dance across my wall, I attempt once more to get inside Kingsley's head.

"What is your next move, you motherfucker?"

I don't realize that I've drifted off to sleep until my bedroom door is thrown open and someone calls my name. I sit up, blinking against the darkness, willing my heart to calm the fuck down.

"It's Mia," Channing says. "We can't wake her up. We're worried she's going to hurt herself."

I'm out the door and flying toward her room as Channing continues to talk behind me.

The second I step into her new bedroom, my heart jumps into my throat at the sight of her thrashing around on the bed, lost to her nightmares with Sasha sitting beside her.

"It's okay," I say, climbing onto the bed with her. "I'll take it from here."

7
MIA

"No, no," I cry, thrashing against Cade.

"Shh," he whispers against my cheek. "Shh."

I blink rapidly, the darkness shifting and stretching into something else. "B-Bexley?" I croak, relaxing against his body.

"Shh, I'm right here, Mia. It's me," he says thickly. "You were having a nightmare."

Instinct makes me try to recoil from his embrace, but his arms tighten around me.

"Please, let me do this. Let me be here for you." Pain laces his words. "I'm not asking for anything in return, I just… I need to be here for you."

"O-okay," I reply, shuffling back into his warm body. Silence falls over us, thick and oppressive. Cade might be gone, but he's still here in the room with us, wedged between us like a glacier.

I inhale a shuddering breath, exhaling slowly. Bexley's hand splays over my stomach, but his touch remains innocent.

I meant what I said earlier. I'm broken. Something inside me died that night in the woods. But I can give Bexley this.

I can give *myself* this.

Because if there's one place I've always felt safe, it's with him.

"I wish I could make this all better." His sincere words flutter over my cheek. "If I could take all your pain and heartache away, I'd do it. I'd do it in a heartbeat, Mia."

"I know."

But that's a fantasy. And this is reality.

"It's the funeral the day after tomorrow," he says, and I go deathly still.

"We were going to tell you earlier but—"

"Who... Quinctus." She answers her own question.

"They've handled everything, yes."

Tears trickle down my face. "I didn't even get to tell them I loved them." I'd been so angry at them both. It felt justified at the time, but now all I want to do is rewind the clock and hug them.

"They knew, Mia. You were their daughter. They knew." I release a thin breath, and Bexley hugs me tighter. "You'll get through this," he whispers.

"How can you be so sure?" Because I feel like I'm never going to be whole again.

"Because you're one of the strongest people I know. And I love you, Mia. I love you so fucking much."

The words teeter on the tip of my tongue, like an old habit you can't quite kick. My heart remembers, even if it's too damaged to care.

I love you too. I don't say it out loud.

I can't.

Because loving Bexley won't bring my parents back.

It won't change a single thing about that night.

RAIN CLOUDS LINGER in the air, dark and angry. It's fitting really for such a somber day. Sasha and Bexley flank my sides as we stand outside, listening to the priest give his internment. Only his words don't register, because I'm too lost in what this moment represents.

Goodbye.

It steals my breath every time I allow myself to look at the two matching coffins resting beside the open graves. Oddly, I can't help but think about the fact that my mother, Temperance Thompson, would have loved the service, from the flowers to the chosen hymns and intimate readings.

The church was full of Gravestone's Elite, the entire verus bloodline and their families turning out to pay their respects. Now they stand behind me in a show of support as we wait for my parents to be lowered into the ground.

"I don't think I can do this." My legs buckle as I lean on Sasha.

"You can," she whispers.

Quinctus are here, in a rare show of force. They stand slightly separated from us, in their black woolen coats and expensive shoes. Phillip tried to offer his condolences again earlier, but I swiftly walked away from him.

I have nothing to say to him.

Not a damn thing.

I stare directly at the Quinctus elders, the men who play God with people's lives. At least Bexley's grandfather and Harrison Rexford have the decency to look upset. The same can't be said for Tim's father, who looks positively bored. Then there's Phillip. Town mayor. Leader of Quinctus in Gregory Kingsley's absence. From the way Sasha talks about her father, I know he's a cold man, but I still can't figure him out. He upholds the traditions of Gravestone and Quinctus, and yet he sanctioned Gregory's murder.

Bile rushes up my throat. It's not every day you discover your father, the man you thought you could always trust, is—*was*—an assassin for a corrupt organization.

He knew.

My father knew all along that Phillip and Quinctus decided to leave me as Cade's prosapia despite the fact that my name should never have been called from the calix.

Anger ripples through me, only making my tears fall harder.

How can they stand there and act so composed—so together—when this is all their fault?

A bird caws in the distance, drawing my eye. Gravestone Cemetery is quiet except for our small gathering. Quinctus security lines the perimeter, blending with the trees. Their presence should bring me some reassurance, but it's only a stark reminder of why they're here.

I sweep the cemetery again, a chill running down my spine as something catches my attention out of the corner of my eye. A figure hovers on the edge of the cemetery, nestled between the trees. My hand shoots out, gripping Bexley's arm.

"What's wrong?" he asks.

"I saw him... Cade..." I inhale a ragged breath, pointing toward the trees.

But he's gone.

Cade is gone.

"You're sure?" Bexley's jaw pops and I nod, trembling.

"Okay. Wait here."

People are beginning to watch us instead of listening to the priest's words. Sasha wraps an arm around me as Bexley and Channing slip away. I watch them converse with the security guy nearest to us. He radios into his wrist mic and the three of them take off.

"You're sure it was him?" Sasha asks, and I frown.

It was.

Wasn't it?

"I-I think so."

He'd been standing right there.

Hadn't he?

Phillip catches my eye, his brows crinkling as he no doubts senses something is wrong. But then my parents' coffins are lowered into the ground, and I'm rooted to the spot, unable to move. This is it...

A tsunami of grief slams into me as Sasha hugs me tighter, whispering soothing words of reassurance against my hair.

My body shakes uncontrollably as I watch the wooden caskets disappear into the hole.

"I-I can't," I rush out, pulling away from her.

"Mia, you—"

"I'll wait in the car." I take off toward the row of black SUVs and Town cars. A security guard follows me, opening the car door for me. I've barely climbed inside when Sasha and Brandon appear.

"What are you—"

"Easton wouldn't want you to be alone," he says, letting his sister climb in first.

"I'm so sorry," she says, gently slipping her arm around my back.

"I just don't understand how they can all stand there and act like..." My chest heaves. "While he's out there," I grit out, feeling the frustration unravel something inside me.

"Are you sure it was Kingsley?" Brandon asks. "Because he'd have to be a fucking idiot to show up here of all places."

"Bran." Sasha shakes her head.

"I don't know. I thought it was him... but maybe..."

"Maybe what?" She takes my hand in hers, and I let out a resigned sigh.

"Maybe my mind was playing tricks on me."

"You've been through a lot. Trauma can wreak havoc on a person."

I give her a weak smile. Maybe it wasn't Cade. Brandon's right. He'd have to have a death wish to show up here, today.

But I felt it... felt the trickle of fear down my spine.

Just then, the car door opens, and a very breathless Bexley and Channing appear.

"Anything?" Brandon asks them.

"Nothing. Security searched the entire cemetery. There's nothing." Bexley's eyes lock on mine, concern shining there. "Cade wasn't here."

I glance away, unable to stand the pity in his eyes. As if it isn't bad enough that I'm grieving for my parents, for a life I'll never get back... now I'm seeing things that aren't there.

Dropping my head back against the seat, I close my eyes and drag in a weary breath.

"You guys head to the house," Bexley says. "We'll grab Alex and Tim and take the other car." He lingers, or at least the silence does, but when I refuse to meet his intense stare, the door slams and the car whirs to life.

"He loves you," Sasha whispers, squeezing my hand gently.

"I know," I murmur.

I do.

But it doesn't change anything.

BACK AT THE HOUSE, I grab a bottle of vodka from the kitchen and slip away unnoticed to my room. I can't be down there with those people while they pretend to mourn the death of my parents. I know so much more about the underbelly of Gravestone now. I know just how deep its dark and twisted roots run.

The second I'm inside my room, I start tugging and clawing at the modest dress until it's pooled at my feet like a sludgy black puddle. I grab a Gravestone U t-shirt and pull it over my head before curling up on the window seat and pressing my head to the cool glass. The vodka burns as I swallow it down in greedy, desperate gulps. But it's better to feel something than the constant gnawing emptiness I feel every time I think about what happened.

My bedroom overlooks the luscious green lawn that disappears over a slight hill and leads down to the lake. Trees line the perimeter like a natural fence. It's beautiful. Such a thing of beauty steeped in so much pain and darkness.

I take another gulp of vodka, already feeling the liquor coursing through my veins. I should have asked Sasha for a pill. Anything to take the edge off.

The trees blow gently in the breeze, back and forth, side to side. My hand splays against the glass when I spot the same figure standing there. He's too far away to see his eyes, but it's Cade.

I know it is.

A beat passes as we stare at one another.

He's watching me.

Hunting me.

Like a predator and its prey.

Relenting first, I blink... but when I open my eyes again, he's gone.

I cry out in frustration, shoving my fingers into my hair and pulling the roots. I was so certain Cade was there. But people don't just evaporate into thin air. Besides, I can already feel the effects of the vodka. My head is spinning, and my eyes feel glazed over.

I can't live like this... always looking over my shoulder, waiting for him to strike.

I need answers.

I need to know what the hell happened, and what Quinctus plan on doing about it.

None of this would've ever happened if it wasn't for them playing with people's lives like the puppet master.

But Phillip and the other elders talk in riddles, keeping their secrets close and their enemies closer.

They're not going to give me answers willingly. No. There's only one way I'm going to get the information I need.

By taking it.

8

BEXLEY

"You ready to go?" Tim asks, coming to stand in the entrance to the kitchen on Sunday morning.

After Mia left the funeral, Phillip caught up to us before we could make our escape to inform us that he expected us all to attend a Q meeting on Sunday morning. I wanted to tell him where to go as he talked as if everything was normal, as if we hadn't just buried Mia's parents... because of him. But I also couldn't argue, because a meeting might mean we get some answers, and I am all for finding out what the fuck is going on right now.

"I'm staying," Channing announces as the rest of us stand from the kitchen table.

"He said he wanted all of us there."

"Then he needs to remember that I'm out. Plus, someone needs to stay here with Mia."

I glance at Channing—his concern for my girl is almost as strong as mine. Since she thought she saw Cade at the funeral, it's like she spends all her time looking over her shoulder or out of the window as if he's going to suddenly appear.

We keep reassuring her that security have this place locked up tight, but while she might nod like she's listening and accepting that it's the truth, it doesn't stop her.

"He's not going to be happy."

"Fuck him. Unless something changes, I'm done."

"Something *is* going to change," I say with a confidence I probably shouldn't have. But with Cade gone, it's time to make the changes that need to happen.

Tim nods, and Brandon, Alex and I move toward him.

"Let's do this then."

"They'd better have some good news," Alex mutters.

"Yeah, like they've got Cade strung up by his balls somewhere never to be found." I notice Tim tense at my words. I understand—my balls want to shrivel up into my body at the thought alone.

The journey toward the church is silent as security sits beside our driver and another car trails behind us. I wish they'd just remain at the house. Something tells me that we're not Cade's target, and even if we are, I'm confident the four of us could overpower the twisted cunt.

"How's Fawn?" I ask Tim, needing to break the tension pressing down on all of us.

"All of this has scared her. She was never Cade's biggest fan anyway."

"Was anyone?"

Tim pales. I get it—they were good friends, have been for years, and although I don't know Tim all that well, something tells me that he doesn't want the same as Cade. He was just following orders like a good little Electi.

"I know what you're thinking," he says to me.

"Do you?" I quirk a brow at him.

"Things aren't as simple as they look. Cade and his plans weren't ever my biggest concern."

I nod at him, accepting his words for now but knowing that if we're going to move past this and become a team of sorts, like we're meant to be, then we're going to need to sit down and talk properly. I'm bored of the secrets and the riddles. If we're going to move forward as Electi, we're going to somehow need to start over. I refuse to keep Cade's legacy alive. His reign of terror is over. Fractured beyond belief.

A ripple of anticipation races through us all as the car pulls to a stop. No one makes a move to get out straight away, telling me that everyone is dreading what's going to happen in there as much as I am.

"Come on, we can't sit out here all day," I eventually say and move to the door.

The early fall sun warms my skin as I step out, but it does little to raise my spirits as I make my way toward the main doors.

I look around at my surroundings as I move. Part of me is desperate to catch a sight of him so I can tell Mia that she's not going crazy, but there's no sign of anyone as the sound of the guys' footsteps crunch in the gravel behind me.

I knock when we get down to the meeting room, and as soon as Phillip calls out for us to enter, I push the heavy wooden door open and step inside. Sitting on the other side of the conference table are the Quinctus elders, including Marcus, but there's another man I've never met before.

"Take your seats," Phillip instructs, barely bothering to look up at us as we enter.

Tension pulls at every one of their faces, and I can only assume that they're as apprehensive about what's going to happen next as we are.

"Rexford?" Harrison barks, making Alex tense beside me, but I know it's not him he's directing the question at.

"At the house with Mia."

"We requested all of you."

"Channing is done. And we thought it best if he stays with the girls."

"That's what we pay security for."

"It gives us all extra peace of mind."

He mutters something under his breath but doesn't say anything else on the matter.

"I would like to introduce you to Lincoln Kingsley."

My entire body jolts at the mention of the Kingsley name, and I narrow my eyes at the man in question.

Cade's uncle.

I recall the conversation Mia and I had with James in that diner. He didn't ever say what Lincoln did, but it was obvious that he had connections with Q, even if he wasn't one of them.

I nod at the man at the end of the table. Just like the other Quinctus members, he's wearing a sharp black suit, but that's where the similarities end. Where Q look sophisticated and wealthy, he looks like a gangster. He's got tattoos running up his neck and down onto his hands. His nose is crooked, having been broken more than a few times, and he's got scars over his face, the most obvious running from the tip of his eyebrow down onto his cheek.

Quite frankly, he looks terrifying, and not at all like someone I would expect Q to be associated with or Cade to be related to.

"I asked him to join us to help reassure you all."

"Reassure us?" Tim asks before I get the chance. "How is his presence meant to do that exactly?"

"I know it's likely that you think that my nephew is with me," the man says, his voice so deep and low it practically makes the furniture in the room vibrate. "But I can assure you that he is not. I haven't seen him in years. The last time was actually at my brother's funeral."

I glance between him and Phillip, trying to figure out the dynamic between them.

James said that Lincoln had a vested interest in Cade's legacy with Q, so why hasn't he seen his nephew, and why is he here now?

Seems mightily convenient.

"This little reunion, or whatever it is, is nice and all, but who are you? What do you do, and why do you care so much about Cade's well-being and future?" I blurt, much to the shock of the rest of the Electi and the elders if their wide eyes are anything to go by.

"He's my flesh and blood, of course I'm concerned." I stare at him, not believing a word of it. "Quinctus and I are... business associates," he says vaguely, steepling his fingers as he leans back in his chair.

"You had no rite of membership for yourself, so you set up elsewhere while waiting for your nephew to take over, that it?" It's a stab in the dark, but from the slight shift in Lincoln's expression I know I'm onto something. "It seems a little strange that you turn up when Cade has gone AWOL, and yet you claim to have no knowledge of his whereabouts." My eyes narrow right at him.

"You should remember your place, son," Phillip warns, but I don't look at him. I'm too busy watching Lincoln, trying to piece together the things we're obviously missing.

"The boy has questions," Lincoln says coolly. "It's to be expected."

"Your nephew murdered my..." I forcefully correct myself. "His prosapia's parents. He left her for dead, and you're sitting there like this is all business as usual." My body vibrates with rage. Pure undiluted rage. "You—"

"Easton, that's enough," Phillip barks, slamming his palms down on the desk and pinning me with a look that might make others cower. He seems to be forgetting that my girl's safety is potentially at risk right now, and I don't give a fuck about his opinion.

"You're right, it is enough," I grit out. "Enough lies and bullshit. The Electi of the past might have allowed you to fob them off with half-truths and riddles, but I won't. I want to know everything. I want to hear from your lips why you—"

My words are cut off as the door behind us flies open and Mia comes storming in.

"Where is he? Is he here? Is this where you're hiding him?" Her face is as white as a sheet as she homes in on Phillip. "You need to tell us where he is and what the hell is going on right now," she screams at him. "I want to know why you would do this to me, to my family, to all of us." She gestures to the rest of the Electi as I race toward her.

"It's okay, mou—Mia," I say, cupping her cheeks in my hands.

"No. No, it's not." She slaps my arms away and races around me. "I watched my parents get lowered into the ground only days ago because of all of you, and I want to know why. Why was I even involved in all of this? Cade told me that he was the one to put my name in the calix. Why did you let it happen? Why would you think that was a good idea when you knew the truth? You knew he wanted to hurt me."

"We didn't know that," Phillip admits, and I'm sure I hear a trace of guilt in his voice. "We had no idea Cade knew the truth about his father's death."

"So you're going to admit it now? You planned his death. You tasked my father to kill him."

Phillips's face turns hard. My eyes skim to Lincoln, and I'm hardly surprised to see the stone mask he wears still in place. If he's shocked about Mia's unexpected arrival or about anything that just happened, he isn't showing it.

"Did you really expect that he wouldn't find out, or that he wasn't as fucking twisted as his father? A man who could only be controlled by death?"

"We never intended any harm to come to you, Mia, truly. We had hoped that you would be a good influence on Cade. Help us to steer him in the correct direction."

"The only place he's heading is hell," Mia seethes. "He's twisted. The things he said—" A sob rips from her throat as the tears that were filling her eyes begin to fall. "The things he did to me."

"Okay, that's enough," I say, wrapping my arms around her.

"No, Bex. It's not. It will never be enough until they fix it. They need to find him, and they need to kill him."

"I know, baby," I whisper in her ear. "I know."

"Can you please get her out of here?" Phillip instructs. "And remember what I said, Easton."

Her entire body tenses in anger at his words, but I doubt she understands his warning.

"Come on."

"No, Bex. I want answers."

"I know, so do I, but you're not going to get them like this."

"No, I need—NO!" she cries when I throw her over my shoulder and walk out of the room with her kicking and screaming.

Footsteps sound out behind me, but I don't look back to see who has followed us. It doesn't matter who it is; I can't imagine it will help us get the answers that we so desperately need.

I place Mia on her feet and press her back against the wall out in the hallway. Her chest heaves as her tears continue to cascade down her cheeks, although her sobs have subsided. "It's okay, baby," I say softly, swiping my thumb over her cheeks to clear her tears away.

Her eyes hold mine for a beat before a shadow falls over us, and she looks over my shoulder at whoever it is.

"We should talk," a familiar voice says, and my spine straightens.

"It's a little late for that now, don't you think?"

"Bexley, trust me when I tell you—"

"Trust you?" I ask, spinning toward Marcus and holding his eyes. "Trust you? You did this. All of this is because of your lies and bullshit. I never wanted any of this, but you stuck me in the middle of it to do your dirty work. I hope you know that all this bloodshed is on your hands. You don't get to control people's lives like this."

"Just let me explain a few things."

I stare at him, trying to decide if anything he would be willing to tell me would be worth it. "Not now. I'm taking Mia home. When you're ready to tell me everything, call me."

"Bexley," he calls as I lead Mia down the hallway, but it's too late. I'm done with Quinctus.

Right now, I just want to look after my girl.

9

MIA

Bexley manhandles me out of the church. My lungs burn with fury, a deep-seated need for answers consuming every last shred of my rationality.

"I need to know..." I cry, whacking my fists against his chest, desperate for him to let me go. But his grip on me only tightens.

"Fuck, Mia," he hisses when I catch his face, dropping me to the ground.

We're outside now, surrounded by the trees and gravestones and the ominous black iron fence that marks the perimeter. I half expect Bexley to shove me toward the car. Sasha didn't want to bring me here, but I gave her no choice, lifting her keys. I told her that if she didn't drive me, I'd drive myself.

I feel her eyes on us, watching. She tried to tell me this was a bad idea, but it fell on deaf ears. I need answers.

I need to know why.

Bexley stares at me like I'm a wild animal he doesn't know how to tame as my chest heaves with every ragged breath.

I glance back at the door we just burst through. If I'm quick, I could make it back inside.

"Don't even think about it," he says, shaking his head. "I know you're hurting, Mia. I know how hard this—"

"You know nothing." I spit the words, engulfed in anger. Fiery and wild, it spreads through me, burning me from the inside out. "Somebody has to pay, somebody has to—"

Bexley lifts me up effortlessly and pulls me around the side of the building, pressing me against the wall and his hand against my mouth. My eyes widen then quickly narrow as he lets out an exasperated breath. "You cannot go on some personal revenge mission against Q, Mia. That's not—"

My words come out muffled against his palm, but Bexley refuses to move his hand.

"I am not going to let you self-destruct. Get angry. Shout. Scream. Hurt me. Hate me... I can take it. So long as you don't do anything stupid and you're safe, I can take it, Mia." He leans in and touches his head to mine, inhaling a sharp breath as he finally lowers his hand. "Let me be your punching bag."

The desperation in his voice wraps around my heart and refuses to let go. Our breaths mingle between us as his lips ghost mine. It would be so easy to kiss him, to let him carry me away to some faraway place.

"Mia..." His voice cracks as he slides his mouth over mine. For a second, everything goes quiet. The thoughts in my head, the drum of my heart against my rib cage, the blood roaring in my ears.

For a second, there's nothing but me and the guy I love suspended in time, in a single kiss I feel all the way down to my soul.

But the second he tries to part my lips with his tongue, everything slams back into me with such force. I cry out. "No," I shriek, hammering on his chest again. "No."

"Fuck," Bexley grits out. "Fuck!" He backs up, letting me slide down the wall. "Mia, I'm sor—"

"We should go." I fold my arms around my waist, averting my gaze. The adrenaline coursing through my veins is fading rapidly as I feel myself start to crash.

"Yeah." He clucks his tongue, stepping aside to let me go ahead.

I hate the distance between us, the awkward silences and words left unsaid. But everything is different now.

I don't know how to go back to being the girl I was before.

"Come on." He gently presses his hand to the small of my back and guides me toward Sasha's car. She climbs out and locks eyes on mine.

"Okay?" she asks.

"Yeah." I yank open the door and slip inside.

"Security will follow you home," Bexley says. "We'll be there as soon as we can." His eyes linger on mine, but then he's slamming the door and stepping back into the shadows.

"What happened?" Sasha asks, and I shake my head.

"I don't want to talk about it."

The car drives straight through the gates and I glance back, unsurprised to find Bexley standing there, watching.

"He's worried about you," Sasha whispers, and I meet her concerned expression. "We all are."

"YOU LOOK LIKE CRAP," Sasha says the next morning as I drag myself down to the kitchen for breakfast.

"I couldn't sleep." I just lay there, staring up at the ceiling, too afraid to close my eyes and let my dreams haunt me.

Except they're not dreams at all, because I'm living this nightmare.

I hesitate, my hands trembling as I help myself to coffee.

"Mia?" She gives me a warm smile.

"I was wondering if maybe you can... give me something. You know, to help me sleep?"

Her smile falls. "I'm not sure that's a good idea... you're hurting."

"So you were happy to give me something to make it all go away before, but now I actually have a reason you won't?" I seethe. "Thanks a lot."

"Come on, it isn't like that and you know it."

"I just need..." A deep sigh escapes my lips. "I just need it all to stop."

"Maybe you should speak to a doctor. They can—"

"Please, Sasha," I plead, not caring how desperate I sound. "I need this. Just something to take the edge off."

"Bexley will kill me," she murmurs.

"This isn't about Bexley," I argue. He's not my keeper. I'm not sure what he is anymore.

I felt it though, yesterday morning when he pushed me up against the stone wall of the church. The connection between us. It's still there, simmering. It would have been so easy to let him in.

But I couldn't do it.

When we got back to the house, I'd locked myself in my room for the rest of the day, avoiding everyone. Including Annabel, who has been calling and texting nonstop since I got out of the hospital.

I have nothing to say to her.

Not a damn thing.

"Fine," Sasha says, pulling me from my thoughts. "Xanax will help you relax, but only take it at night, okay?"

"Thank you." I nod, relief seeping into my bones.

Just then, footsteps sound on the stairs, and a second later, the guys spill into the kitchen.

"Remind me again why we told Mulligan to take this morning off?" Brandon says, making a beeline for the refrigerator.

Bexley hovers in the doorway. I peek over at him, letting my eyes run down his body. He's all sweaty and breathless, as if he just got done working out. Channing is the same. He gives Sasha a heated look, and for a second, I think he's going to go to her. But she shakes her head, glancing at Brandon.

Right. They still haven't told him. Or the rest of the Electi, for that matter.

It seems keeping secrets is all par for the course where Quinctus and the Electi are concerned.

Grabbing my coffee, I make to leave, but Bexley blocks the door. "We need to talk," he says grimly. "All of us."

Chairs scrape against the tiles as everyone gathers around the table. I sit closest to Sasha, at the end so no one can sit on the other side of me. Bexley waits, grabbing some juice from the refrigerator before joining us.

"Q wants it business as usual tomorrow. We attend class, show a united front, and tamp down any rumors." His eyes flick to mine. "If anyone asks, Cade is out of town visiting family."

A bitter laugh crawls up my throat, and everyone looks at me. "We're protecting him now?"

"No, we're not protecting him. We're—"

"There are rules for a reason, Mia," Tim says.

My brows knit together as disbelief coats my voices. "Rules? Q can go fuck their rules," I hiss, surprise registering on his face at my outburst. "Where were—"

"Mia." Bexley breathes my name like it hurts him to say it.

"Seriously?" I shoot upright. "You're on their side now?"

"I'm not… this isn't…" He lets out a frustrated breath.

"She should know," Tim says, and my eyes snap to his.

"I should know what?" There's no disguising the tremor in my words. Whatever is about to reveal itself isn't good. Trepidation snakes through me.

"After you left the meeting yesterday," Bexley says, clearing his throat, "Quinctus made a decision. We all know Cade was the leader. It made sense for that responsibility to fall to Tim since he's the eldest. But—"

"But I didn't want it," Tim says. "My plate is full enough as it is. Besides, I'm a follower, not a leader. Which is why I suggested Easton for the job."

"You?" My heart drums in my chest. "*You're* going to fill Cade's shoes?"

"It's not like that, and you know it."

"No." I shake my head. "I don't know anything anymore. I always thought you were different, that you weren't one of them…" My shoulders sag with defeat. "But maybe I was wrong."

"Mia, that's not—"

"Excuse me." I flee from the kitchen, wincing when I hear someone's fist slam down on the table.

I go straight to my bedroom, slamming the door behind me, and walk over to the window, staring out at nothing.

"Mia?" Sasha calls from the hall, her gentle knock making me bristle. I'm still standing there, staring, when she slips inside.

Something catches my eyes in the distance. A shadowy figure moving in the trees. I gasp, pressing my hand against the glass.

"Mia, what is it? What's wrong?" Sasha hurries to my side.

"Do you see him?" I shudder.

"Who?" She leans in closer. "There's nothing down there."

"I saw him, Sasha. He was there… he was right…" My eyes shutter as I inhale a ragged breath. "I'm losing my mind."

"You need to sleep," she says with a hint of sadness. "Here." She presses a small baggie at me. "One a night. Two if you're really struggling."

"Thank you. I feel like nothing makes sense anymore."

"I know." Pulling me into her arms, Sasha hugs me tightly. "You're strong, Mia. You're so fucking strong. You just need some time to come to terms with everything. Come on." She guides me over to the bed. "You should try to rest."

"You'll stay with me?"

"Of course." Sasha pulls back the covers and I slip inside. She frowns when I place the pill on my tongue and swallow it down.

"Mia, I said—"

"I know, but I just need it to stop, Sasha. I just need... I don't know how they expect me to just pretend like everything is fine," I admit, pulling the sheet up around my body.

"Because they're assholes," Sasha snorts. "I'm sure you've worked out by now that Q aren't good people. They only care about money and power. Anything else is considered a weakness."

"You know, when I first woke up and heard Cade was gone, I thought it meant I was free... I thought..." I trail off, realizing how foolish I sound. "I'll never be free, will I?"

Cade might be gone, and my parents might be dead, but the brand on my chest marks me as theirs.

Sasha's silence is all the affirmation I need. She's bound to this life through blood, and now I'm bound to it through tradition.

There's no escape for either of us.

But still, I can't help but think there has to be another way. A way we can take back some power and carve our own paths.

Because if this is all there is... maybe death would have been the easier choice.

10

BEXLEY

The next morning, exactly as we agreed with Q, we all got in our cars and headed to college. But if Phillip thinks for one second that I'm going to act like Mia is nothing to me, then he's sorely fucking mistaken.

We've missed two weeks worth of classes, so we know the rumors will be rife. The good thing about who we are, though, is that no fucker will be brave enough to say anything to our faces.

It might have only been a few weeks, but I now fully understand how it looked when I first stood up to Cade. No one ever does that. Maybe if I knew then what I know now, I might have stayed well clear of the lot of them. Not that I ever stood a chance of that being an option, seeing as I was brought here for a very good reason.

Anger swirls around me as I sit in the parking lot with Alex beside me. I think about Marcus and everything he had planned for me, all the lies and secrets he kept—is *still* keeping.

I've done my part. I've taken my place. Hell, I've taken fucking control.

I scrub my hand down my face as I remember how that went down yesterday. Obviously, we all wondered who would take over now Cade has fucked off, but I'd just assumed like everyone else that Tim would take the job. The last thing I expected was for him to turn it down. And not just turn down—I mean point-blank refuse.

Do I want to be the leader of the younger division of this fucked-up secret society I've found myself a member of? No, not really. But what's the alternative? If I'm going to make the best of this screwed-up situation, then taking charge surely is the way to do it. If I want to make changes, move Q into the fucking twenty-first century with their archaic traditions, rituals, and ceremonies, if I want to protect Mia, then I need to put myself in a position to have a say. So that's what I've done. Fuck knows I'm not getting out of this life anytime soon, so I may as well attempt to make the best of it, and if that means ensuring that Cade fucking Kingsley is no more and has zero influence over Q, the Electi and our lives, then I'm all fucking in.

"Ready to do this then, *boss?*" Alex asks with a smirk.

Relief floods me as I look over at him. Since Mia's... Since that night, I haven't seen or heard of him taking anything. I actually haven't even seen him with a drink in his hand. Maybe, just maybe, there could be a couple of good things to come out of this whole nightmare.

"Please, don't call me that," I beg.

"I still can't fucking believe you did that."

"Well, you weren't going to. Tim didn't want it, and Brandon looked like he was about to shit his pants at the prospect."

"I guess."

"It's time for change, Alex. Time to change all the bullshit and stupid rules."

"And you think you're the one to do it?"

"No, not a chance. *We're* the ones to do it. All of us."

He nods, a smile playing on his lips. "Maybe there is hope."

"Hasn't there got to be?"

There have been so many times in my life where I would never have believed that. But right now, it's the only thing I've got to hold on to. I've got to hope that Mia will get through this and come out on the other side stronger, even more incredible than she is now. I have to believe that we can put our own stamp on his town and change the things that need to be changed to make people's lives better.

My question goes unanswered as Mia and Sasha walk past us on their way toward the building for their first classes of the day.

"I'm worried about her," Alex whispers as if she'll be able to hear him.

"You're not the only one."

I watch her move, her arm linked through Sasha's for support. We might be able to lie about Cade's whereabouts, but the house explosion, the loss of her parents... that's harder to cover up when it's all the town has been talking about.

"We need to find him. She's terrified he'll get hold of her again."

"He won't," Alex says with a confidence that I really don't feel.

I want to believe Q have it under control, that the security in place watching the house and us all at any given time is enough, but I'm not sure anything will be enough against Cade. He clearly has a game plan, and he's not opposed to biding his time in order to get what he wants.

And there's something about Lincoln Kingsley's sudden appearance that doesn't sit right with me. He'd barely said a word after I returned to the meeting yesterday following Mia's outburst. I tried to ask questions, to get a better picture of how he fits into all this, but Phillip redirected the conversation every damn time. He's hiding something—I get the feeling they both are.

But right now, I've got bigger issues to deal with. Like attending classes and pretending everything is fine.

Nervously, I look around the parking lot at the students that are both loitering around and heading for class. Is he here? Watching us right now?

I shake the crazy thought from my head. Of course he's not. He's in hiding, waiting for us to forget the threat and lower our guard, and then he'll strike, right when we least expect it. He's going to want the element of surprise.

"Come on, class calls."

"She'll be okay," Alex says before we climb out of the car.

"Yeah," I agree, although my stomach twists painfully as I say the word. "I really hope so."

As expected, the gossip surrounding us spreads through the students like a poison, but no one outwardly asks us about any of it. They just whisper and nod in our directions, letting us all know that they're watching our every move.

I hate it.

Back in Sterling Bay, I loved the attention. I ate all of it right up and did everything I could to keep the spotlight on me. To put it bluntly, I was an asshole.

Now, I just want to hide in the shadows and take Mia with me.

She sits beside me in our class, but she doesn't say a word and doesn't even look at me. I'd hoped that with Cade's overbearing presence gone, things here might get easier, but with every second that passes, I can see her closing herself off from the world. From me.

I wish I could fix it, I could say some magic words that will make all her fear, her pain and her nightmares disappear. But I can't. Other than be here, reassure her and prove that I can keep her safe, there is nothing else I can do.

Reaching over, I squeeze her thigh, needing her to know that she has all my support, but, as my touch connects with her, her entire body tenses, and after a beat, she pushes my hand away.

It breaks my fucking heart.

WITH EVERY DAY THAT PASSES, I watch a little bit more of the girl I love vanish. By Friday, she's nothing more than an exhausted shell of her former self.

"You should stay here today," I say from her bedroom door.

"Stay here?" she asks as if it's the most ludicrous idea she's ever heard. "While you're all at college? No, thank you."

"Okay, well I'll stay with you."

"No," she says in a panic.

"Mia, please. I'm trying to help. You can barely keep your eyes open right now. Did you get any sleep last night?"

"A little," she admits with a wince.

A bang sounds out from somewhere in the house and she jumps a mile, her eyes going wide and the little color in her cheeks immediately draining away. In a beat, she's at the window and frantically looking around.

"He's not out there." I sigh with desperation. "Security walk the perimeter every hour now. There's been no sign of him."

"I see him, Bex. He stands out there and watches me."

I stare at her as she loses her grasp on reality. "If I let you go to class today, will you do something for me?"

"If you *let me*? You don't own me, Bexley," she snaps.

"I'm aware, but I'm concerned about you. If you sit in class, will you even hear a word from the professor?"

"Of course," she lies. "Plus..." She hesitates, and it makes my chest ache. I know what's going to come next is going to hurt me. "He's not there."

"He's not here either, baby." I take a step toward her. "It's just us, and we're all here to protect you."

She nods, but she doesn't believe a word of it.

"Can we go now, please?"

"Does that mean you'll do something for me?"

She sucks in a breath. I know she wants to say no, but it's not going to happen. She's going to follow my lead this weekend, even if it means I throw her over my shoulder and force her. She needs it. She just doesn't know she does. "Sure. What is it?"

"After class, I want you to pack a bag. We're getting out of town for the weekend."

Her eyes finally find mine. They're bloodshot, the circles beneath them darker than I've ever seen them.

"W-where?"

"You've got nothing to worry about. Security will come with us. I've got it all planned."

Her lips part as if she wants to argue, but she must realize that it's pointless, and it is. We're going this weekend, no matter what she says. She needs the break, and it's time to lay some of Q's secrets to rest at last.

"WHERE ARE WE GOING?" Mia asks from my passenger seat later that afternoon.

"To visit my sister," Alex pipes up, poking his head between the two seats.

"Hadley?"

"Yeah, unless you know of any others Q are hiding."

"Not right now, no." She manages a small chuckle, but it's strained.

"We're meeting them at a beach house on the outskirts of Sterling Bay. It's the perfect place to just chill out. You're going to love it."

She blows out a breath, not committing to anything.

Most of the drive is in silence, and I crank up the music to allow everyone to focus on their thoughts without feeling guilty. I have no fucking clue what Alex is thinking right now about going to confess to Hadley, but this was all his idea. Well, Sterling Bay was his idea. Getting Mia out of town for a few days was all me. But it's perfect. We're meeting Hadley and Cole later on this evening at the beach house they've booked for us, and Remi and Ace are joining us tomorrow.

Hopefully, by the time we leave on Sunday, Hadley and Alex will have come to terms with who they really are to each other, I'll have had time to finally give Remi the apology she deserves, and Mia will have had some rest.

I keep telling myself that it will go that smoothly, because right now I can't allow myself to even consider an alternative.

"Whoa, this place is insane," Alex says as I pull into the driveway of the beach house.

The sparkling blue ocean spreads as far as the eye can see as both Alex and Mia press their noses to the windows. It's easy to forget that they didn't grow up on the coast.

"Come on, apparently the inside is even better. There's a hot tub."

We let ourselves in and do a lap of the place before pulling beers from the refrigerator and sitting out on the deck to watch the sunset while we wait for Hadley and Cole to arrive.

"You know, this weekend would be so much more fun if I wasn't a third wheel to all you couples."

"Aw, Rexford. I'm sure you can make good use of your right hand."

"Fuck you, man," he barks, throwing an empty bottle at my head, which I easily catch. I might not play anymore, but I guess some things are just ingrained.

I think of Cole playing college ball for the Colts, and my chest grows tight. I wanted that so fucking bad in years gone by. I thought for sure the NFL was where my future was. It's crazy how much can change in only a few short years, months even.

Football is barely even on my radar anymore. I wasn't even aware that Cole was on a bye week when I called Hadley to see if we could organize something.

I shake my head and slouch down in my chair, keeping my eyes on Mia as she picks at the label on her bottle.

11

MIA

"Bexley said I'd find you out here." Hadley joins me at the edge of the water.

"I just needed a second." I pull my cardigan tighter around my body. The air is cool, the water lapping at my feet the same. But there's something so serene about being out here.

"Do you want to talk about it?"

My eyes lift to hers and I shake my head. "There's nothing to say."

"Look, Mia. I know we're not friends. I know I got out while you..." She releases a thin breath. "But I know a thing or two about Quinctus and their rules and bullshit traditions."

"Did you love him?"

Hadley winces. "Tim?" Her expression softens. "I did. Or at least, I thought I did. But he's just like the rest of them." Silence stretches out before us. Then she adds, "He found me, you know. He found me here."

"I didn't know that."

She nods. "He found out about the baby... thought that I'd done it. That I'd gotten rid of it."

"What happened?"

"He tried to hurt me, but Cole and his father saved me."

"How does James figure into all of this?" It's the one thing I keep asking myself and still don't really understand.

"Honestly, I still don't know the whole story." She offers me a weak smile. "But you can trust him, Mia. Whatever arrangement he has with Q, he's managed to keep Sterling Bay relatively safe."

God, I envy her. Although she went through something awful, Hadley got out. She escaped. And now she has a boyfriend who would do anything to protect her, and a family who looks out for her.

"Bexley's worried about you. Alex too."

"How are things there?" I ask, knowing that she spent the last hour talking to her brother and really not wanting to keep the focus on me.

"It's not every day you find out you have a brother you didn't know about."

"No, I suppose it isn't. Do you talk to them at all? Your parents?"

"My mom reached out over the summer. But there's a lot to work through. My life is in Colton now, with Cole." She glances back to the house. "He's all the family I need."

"He seems nice."

"Nice?" Hadley bursts out laughing. "Oh, he'll love that."

"What?" My brows knit.

"I don't think I've ever heard anyone call him nice before. Cole is... complicated."

"But you love him? You're happy?"

"I do, and I am. I really, really am. He was exactly what I never knew I needed."

Her words sink inside me as I glance over at the house again. The guys are sitting around a firepit, drinking beer and shooting the shit. "I don't know how to let him back in," I admit.

"Do you love him?"

I nod, swallowing over the lump in my throat. "But I'm not the same girl he fell in love with."

"You think that matters to him? I can tell you for a fact that it doesn't. I see the way he watches you, how his eyes track your every movement. Bexley wants to carry your pain as his own, Mia. He wants to be there for you."

"I want to believe you... part of me does... but it's like something inside me broke when I woke up in the hospital. And now I'm seeing him wherever I go."

"Seeing... you mean Cade?" Her lips thin in disapproval.

"They keep saying it's because I'm exhausted. I'm barely sleeping…"

"Cade is gone, Mia. You have a whole group of guys looking out for you. Not to mention security tailing your every move. You're safe. Especially here. Come on, let's go back before they come looking." Hadley laces her arm through mine. "I know it feels dark and desperate now, but things will get better, I promise. You just have to let people in. Let people help you."

We take a slow walk back to the house. It's a beautiful place right on the edge of the beach. Under different circumstances, I'd want to try out the hot tub or swimming pool. But as it is, I'm barely holding myself together. I'm on edge, every unfamiliar noise startling me. The guys fired up the grill and made burgers and steak earlier, but I couldn't eat anything, despite the hollow pit in my stomach.

I feel like I'm unraveling. Piece by piece. Day by day. The Xanax Sasha gave me helps, but it doesn't rid my mind of the fear. The suffocating trepidation that Cade is out there somewhere, watching… Waiting. Biding his time until he strikes. I see him. I see him every time I close my eyes; I see him standing in the tree line of the house.

I see him.

But no one else does.

Because my mind is the enemy now.

We reach the gate and I pause, noting how serious the conversation looks between Bexley and Cole. They're huddled close, their heads almost pressed together as Cole says something. But Hadley alerts them to our presence, perching on Cole's knee and running her hands through his dark hair.

"What are you two colluding about?"

"Just guy stuff." Cole smirks, grabbing the back of her neck and kissing her passionately. If there's one thing I've learned about Cole Jagger since we arrived, it's that he's unapologetic, and if Hadley's near, you can bet he'll be touching her, or kissing her, or stalking her every movement like he'd go to war for her.

Watching them makes my chest ache.

I miss that. I miss being close to Bexley.

"I think I'm going to—"

"Come here," Bexley says, his voice a low growl that reverberates deep inside me.

"I don't—"

His hand snags mine, tugging me toward him. A shiver runs through me as he pulls me down on his lap and wraps his arms around my waist. "Just sit with me, please." He nuzzles my neck, and I smother a whimper, overwhelmed at the confusing emotions running through my mind.

On the one hand, I want to tell him I'm not ready. That I can't sit here like this and pretend everything is okay. But the other part of me wants to soak up his attention and bathe in his light.

"Fuck, Mia." His warm breath fans my skin, sending more shivers through me. My eyes flutter as I settle back against him.

The sun is sinking into the horizon, casting a dark pinkish hue across the sky. It's beautiful, and under different circumstances, romantic.

But there's an ugly dark cloud hanging over us.

"Hey," Alex says, joining us. He sits down with a beer. "This is... cozy."

"Jealous, Rexford?" Bexley chuckles.

"Nah. I'm not ready to settle down."

I tense, but Bexley leans in and whispers, "Relax, I got you."

"It's been a day," Cole says, taking a long pull on his beer. "I didn't expect to find out I'm gaining a brother-in-law."

"Uh, did I miss the wedding announcement?" Alex frowns, and Hadley lets out a small laugh.

"Cole is just joking."

"No, I'm not. You know what that ring on your finger means, Dove." He takes her hand in his, running his fingers over the glittering engagement band. "It means you're mine, forever. And soon as you'll let me, I'll make it official."

"Cole, we're nineteen. We cannot get married yet."

"Says who?" he asks without hesitation. "I know I want to spend my life with you, might as well get it over with."

"Seriously?" She bats his chest. "Keep talking, Jagger, and you'll be sleeping alone tonight."

"Like you could keep me out." His eyes glint with something that looks a lot like a threat, but Hadley doesn't seem worried. In fact, she melts against him and kisses him.

I drop my gaze, turning into Bexley slightly.

"You want to get out of here?" he whispers, staring at me with hunger in his eyes.

"I... I can't."

Dejection washes over him.

"I'm sorry." The words form on my lips, but he's no longer looking at me.

He's looking past me.

My heart is heavy as I stand. "I'm going to lay down for a little bit."

"No, Mia, stay," Hadley says, tearing her mouth from Cole's. "We're sorry. It's... hard to stop ourselves sometimes."

"I bet it is," Alex grumbles.

"Watch it, Rexford," Cole spits. "You might be family, but it doesn't mean I won't kick your ass—"

"Cole!" Hadley rolls her eyes. "Please, stay. We can toast marshmallows and make s'mores."

"Maybe later," I say, inching away from them.

Bexley drills holes into the side of my face, but I don't meet his intense stare.

I can't.

"See you later." I hurry inside, releasing a long breath the second I'm alone.

"Get it together," I scold myself.

Bexley brought me here to get space from Gravestone, from everything that's happened... but there are some nightmares you can't outrun.

Grabbing a glass of water, I head to my room. It's right next to Bexley's. I saw the reluctance in his eyes when I asked for my own, but he respected my wishes.

Because he loves me.

I feel it every time his eyes find mine. But there's a wall between us. A wall scratched with pain and anger and fear.

Digging the small baggie out of my purse, I pop a pill, washing it down with water, then lay down on the bed and stare up at the ceiling. I know Bexley meant well, bringing me here, but there's no quick fix for the gaping hole in my heart.

Slowly, the tension leaves my body until my eyes grow heavy and the darkness edges closer...

"So innocent," he snarls. "When we all know you're anything but." He spears two fingers inside me, pain lancing through me. I cry out, but it sounds muffled, everything growing distorted around me.

Cade covers me with his big, imposing body as he keeps working his fingers inside me. "Your father is a murderer, Mia. Q's assassin. He could have taken me out any number of times to save you from this fate... yet, he didn't. He let things play out just the way Q wanted them to... and do you know why?" He stares down at me with fire in his eyes. "Because he's weak. But I'm not weak, and I'll show them. One by one, I'll show them that they picked the wrong guy to manipulate."

Tears stream down my face as I thrash beneath him. He backhands me out of nowhere, my head thumping against the hard ground, stars exploding in my vision.

"No, please... don't. God, no!" I buck wildly against him, the icy fingers of fear wrapped around my throat.

"You're mine now, little mouse," he sneers, his breath warm against my cheek.

"No, no," I cry, but it's futile. He's too strong, and I'm too out of it to fight him off.

"Mia?" a voice calls out.

"Bexley?"

"Come back to me, baby. Please, come back—"

"Bexley?" My eyes fly open, my chest heaving as I try to drag air into my lungs.

"It's okay, you're safe. You're—"

I bolt upright, shaking violently. "He's here. Cade is here."

"He's not here. It was a dream."

"It was?"

It felt so real...

"You're safe." Bexley hugs me to his chest. "I'm not going to let anything happen to you." He cups the back of my neck possessively, pressing a kiss to my hair.

"No, *no!*" I shove him away. "He was here..."

"No one knows we're here, Mia. It's just you, me, Hadley, Cole, and Alex. It's safe—"

"Stop saying that. Stop telling me it's safe when he's out there... watching, waiting."

Bexley stands, blowing out an exasperated breath. "I know this is hard... I know you're—"

"Crazy?" I sneer. "Is that what you think? That I'm losing my mind?"

Because I think I am.

Bexley drops to his knees and runs his hands up my thighs. "I think you're hurting... and your mind is playing tricks on you. Look at me, baby." He slides a finger under my chin, forcing me to look at him. "Cade is gone. And when... *if* he shows up again, we'll be ready. I will never let him hurt you again, I promise." His hand curves around the back of my neck, drawing my face down to his. "I need you, Mia. I need you so fucking much. Come back to me, baby. Please, come back to me."

The air crackles between us as he stares at me with utter desperation.

"I don't know how to be that girl anymore," I whisper around a shuddering breath. "I feel like I can't breathe, Bex... I feel like I'm drowning..."

"I'll help," he says with so much emotion I feel winded. "Just let me help you."

12

BEXLEY

As I stare into Mia's eyes, Cole's advice from earlier comes back to me.

"She needs to get out of her head. Trust yourself to know what she needs. Take control and don't stop until the only thing she can think about is you."

Tears swim in Mia's eyes as her body trembles with fear beneath my hands. I'd give anything to be able to take away everything that's stopping her sleeping, that's stopping her from being the incredible person I know she is.

Swallowing down my trepidation, I decide to follow Cole's advice and trust that I know exactly how to give her an escape.

Sliding my hands up her legs, I massage my thumbs into her soft flesh. Her lips part as I get to the juncture of her thighs.

"Bexley," she warns, her voice still weak and full of fear.

"Trust me, Mia."

"I can't, Bex. I'm not that girl anymore." The emotion in her voice breaks my already battered heart.

"You're my girl, baby. That hasn't, and won't ever change."

"But—"

"No buts. Let me help you, please." As my fingers continue to massage her, I slowly feel her start to relax. "I love you, Mia. I love you so fucking much."

Pushing from the floor, I loom over her, my eyes flicking between her lips and her eyes. "Do you trust me, baby?"

Her nod is so slight that I almost miss it, but it's there.

Leaning over her, I force her to rest back on her palms. "Let me take it away, just for a few minutes." I brush my lips over hers, half expecting her to pull away and tell me to leave, but she doesn't. Instead, she falls back on the bed, her chest heaving as I run my hand over her hip and up to her waist.

"I'm not sure I can—"

"Shh, Mia," I whisper against the corner of her mouth. "Stop thinking. Just feel." She gasps as I move my hand higher, squeezing her breast. "Just feel," I repeat, rubbing my thumb over her hard peak.

"Bexley." My name is no more than a whisper, but it's all I need to know that Cole was right—that what I'm doing is right.

Lowering my head, I pepper light kisses along her jaw and make my way down her smooth neck. I take her breast in my hand, and she arches into my touch, her breathing becoming more and more labored as I tease her.

Pushing the fabric of her tank up her stomach, I press my lips to the soft skin of her navel before licking up her ribs and sucking her nipple into my mouth. She arches off the bed once more, offering herself up to me, and the trepidation I felt about this being the right thing to do starts to slip away.

"Bexley," she moans as I sink my teeth into her sensitive skin. "Please."

I smile around her peak, so fucking relieved that she's accepting this. That she's getting out of her head enough to enjoy it.

Popping the button on her jeans, I sit up and pull them and her panties down her legs. Not wanting to give her any longer than necessary to call a stop to this, I press my palms against her thighs and push them as wide as I can before settling on my stomach before her.

Blowing a stream of air through her slick folds, I smile when I feel her shudder. "Let go, baby. Just enjoy." Closing the space between us, I flick her clit with the tip of my tongue.

She moans loudly, telling me just how much she needs this.

Sucking her clit into my mouth, I move my hand so I can tease her entrance with my fingertip. Greedily, she tries to suck me deeper, only encouraging me to do just that so I can find the spot that will take her away from everything, even if only for a few seconds.

As my tongue laps at her, my fingers bend, and she cries out when I find her G-spot. "That's it, baby," I growl against her as her hips begin to roll against my face.

Desire races through my veins. My cock has been hard since the first moment I touched her, my need for her almost too much to bear, but I push it aside. This isn't about me and my pleasure; it's purely about Mia and giving her what she needs.

"Oh God, Bexley," she moans, her fingers threading into my hair and tugging on the lengths until it stings.

"Come on my face, baby. Give me everything." I suck on her once more, grazing my teeth against her clit and thrusting that little bit deeper.

"Bexley," she cries, loud enough for her voice to carry on the breeze, letting everyone on the deck below know what's happening in here—not that I give a fuck, and I'm sure they don't either.

Her pussy clenches around my digits, pulling them deeper as her body convulses with each wave of pleasure that rolls through her.

I don't pull away until she's taken everything.

Crawling up the bed, I lay beside her and pull her into my arms. Her eyelids are heavy with her exhaustion and her body limp from the release.

"Bexley, I—"

"Shh, baby. Just sleep."

Reaching out, I grab the sheets and pull them over both of us as I shift us until she's almost completely laid on my chest, and I hold her tightly so that she knows I'm here and that she's safe.

It only takes minutes before her breathing becomes shallow and she totally relaxes in my hold. I blow out a sigh of relief that she's finally getting the rest she's so desperate for, and I can't help the very small smile that twitches at my lips, knowing that I was able to give it to her.

Maybe Cole was right. Not that I'm going to admit that to him. His head is already big enough.

I lay with her in my arms for hours, listening to her breathing and the sounds of the chatter below filtering up to me. I had no idea how Hadley was going to take the news about Alex, but she was surprisingly accepting of the revelation. I guess that's how it is when you grow up in a place like Gravestone. Living with lies and secrets galore must eventually harden you not to be surprised by anything.

In the end, my need for the bathroom forces me to roll Mia off and slip out of bed. I silently make my way out of her room and close the door behind me, hoping that she'll be able to get some more sleep without me there.

After making use of the bathroom, I head downstairs, pull a beer from the fridge, and go back out to the deck where the three of them are still sitting around the fire.

"Went well then, I assume?" Cole asks the second I emerge.

My lips part to say something, but I can tell by his knowing smirk that he's aware of what went down upstairs.

"She's asleep," I finally say, dropping into one of the spare chairs.

"She'll be okay," Hadley says softly. "And please, take all of his advice with a pinch of salt. He likes to think he knows all there is to know about women."

"Excuse me?" Cole barks, looking totally offended by his fiancée's words.

Hadley waves him off, which only infuriates him further.

"I knew exactly how to get you out of your head, didn't I?"

"Maybe so, but I'm not sure I'd give anyone advice based on our sex life."

Cole scoffs, making me even more curious about the two of them. "You love it, and you know it."

"Yes, but Mia might not."

"Every woman needs their man to take charge every now and then. Just look at Mia. Bex clearly took my advice—we heard the evidence—and now she's sleeping soundly, her nightmares long forgotten as she remembers just how good he made her feel."

"Because sex fixes everything," Hadley mutters, crossing her hands over her chest.

"Did I say that?" Cole balks.

"No, but you're thinking it. Women are way more complex than men when it comes to their emotional needs."

"Oh really?" He raises a brow, waiting for her to elaborate.

I sit back with my bottle of beer, tipping it to my lips while I watch the couple bicker away. It only takes three minutes tops before Cole hauls Hadley onto his lap, silently proving his point as he takes charge and shoves his tongue down her throat while palming her ass.

"I need to get laid," Alex mutters as we watch.

"Careful, Rexford. You're giving off Ashton vibes right now."

"Fuck off, Easton. I'm nothing like that twisted motherfucker."

"Huh, and to think… I thought he was your new BFF."

"He gave me a few pills and supplied me with some stellar pussy. He's never been my friend."

I tip the dregs of my beer into my mouth as Alex falls silent, but it's only for a few seconds.

"Do you believe that he really knew nothing about Cade's plans?"

"No," I answer without missing a beat. "I wouldn't trust that the sky was blue if he told me. Why, are you about to tell me you do?"

"I don't know. I don't want to. I know he's never proven himself to be trustworthy, but there was something about him when he turned up last weekend."

"He's a fucking good actor, that's all it is. He probably knows exactly where Cade is. Hell, he's probably hanging out in his bedroom and fucking Brook any chance he gets."

"You spoken to her?"

"No, thank fuck. She kept her distance this week."

The sound of kissing at the other side of the firepit drags my eyes over once more before Cole stands with Hadley in his arms.

"We're gonna call it a night," he states before marching into the house without a backward glance.

"Fuck's sake," Alex mutters, grabbing another beer and knocking the top off.

"Quit being a pussy. You wanted to spend time with your sister. Here we are."

"Yeah, I just didn't plan on you both getting balls deep while I sit here alone with a bottle for company."

I shake my head at him and stare out at the water. This weekend was a good idea. Exactly what Mia needed. Hopefully, after a decent night's sleep, she'll be feeling a little more like herself.

I check on her a couple of times when I slip into the house to use the bathroom or to grab more beer, and each time, she's sound asleep.

When I finally call it a night and head upstairs to bed, I forego my allocated bedroom—the one I chose in the hope that we'd be able to share it—and instead slip into her room.

Toeing off my sneakers, I strip down to my boxers and climb into bed behind her, wrapping my arm around her waist and burying my face in her hair, losing myself in her familiar floral scent. "I love you, Mia," I breathe.

She doesn't react—not that I expect her to.

One day soon, though, she will. I know we've got a long journey ahead of us to rediscover the couple we were before—if we were ever actually a couple— but I know it'll be worth the wait. If I know one thing for certain in this whole mess, then it's that she's the one for me, and we'll come out the other side. Together.

13

MIA

For the first time in what feels like forever, I sleep peacefully. The nightmares hover on the edge of my consciousness, trying to find a way in. But Bexley chases them off, his big warm body like armor.

When I wake, the sunlight is pouring in through the blinds, but I'm still not sure how I feel about last night. Bexley was right: for those few minutes, he'd distracted me. But it wasn't a permanent fix.

I lay here, listening to his soft snores. He's laying on his back with one arm tucked behind his head and one draped over my hip. Every time I woke in the night, some part of him was touching some part of me. I spent so long craving this intimacy with him, and now we have it. We have the chance to be together without the need for all the secrets and lies.

But it's tainted.

I watch him for a second longer before slipping quietly out of bed. Pulling on a hoodie, I go in search of coffee. The beach house is silent other than the gentle hum of the refrigerator and the whir of the ocean beyond the windows.

Turning on the coffee maker, I grab a mug and stare out at the beach.

"It's beautiful, right?"

I startle as Hadley enters the kitchen. "Sorry," she says. "I didn't mean to scare you."

"It's okay," I murmur. "I'm still a little jumpy after…"

"I get it."

"Coffee?"

"Sure." She perches at the breakfast counter as I set about making our drinks. "Did you manage to get some sleep?"

"Yeah, I did, actually. Bexley, he…" My cheeks heat as I remember him climbing into bed with me last night.

"He cares about you a lot."

"I know. But what happened… it really isn't about him. It's about me."

"You know, after the abortion, I was a mess. I couldn't ever imagine meeting someone who could love me. Until I met Cole." Her eyes glitter with adoration.

"He's… a lot."

Hadley chuckles at that. "He is. But his heart is in the right place. I know it feels hopeless now, but you'll get there, Mia. You'll find yourself again."

I'd felt a glimpse of her last night—the Mia I was before all… this. But I hadn't been able to hold onto her.

"Morning." Bexley stumbles into the kitchen, rubbing his eyes. "I woke up and you were gone."

"I didn't want to wake you." I smile weakly, bracing myself for his touch.

He curves his hand around the back of my neck and presses a kiss to my head. "I missed you."

"I…" The words get stuck, and I swallow, trying desperately to find a reply.

"There's coffee," Hadley says, drawing his attention, and I exhale a small breath.

If Bexley feels my hesitation, he doesn't comment. But the tension lingers between us, and I know he must sense it too.

"Thanks." He moves over to the counter, and Hadley shoots me a reassuring smile.

Cole and Alex join us, and the five of us drink coffee and eat breakfast. Cole is busy telling us about his season with the Colts, but my mind is elsewhere.

I glance out of the window, my eyes almost bugging out of my head when I spot the black figure in the distance.

He's not there, I silently scold myself. *It's just your mind playing tricks.*

But when I look back out the window, he's still there.

Fear snakes through me, making my stomach drop. Before I know what I'm doing, I get up and move for the back door.

"Mia?" Bexley says.

"I just need some fresh air." I slip outside, a shiver running through me as I creep across the decking. But when I reach the wooden railing, the figure is gone.

Tears streak down my face as I grip the rail. I really am losing my mind.

"Hey." Bexley joins me on the deck. "Are you okay?"

"No, I'm not." I sniffle, trying to rein in my emotions.

"Hey, I've got you." He comes closer, reaching for me. "I've got you, baby." I let him pull me close, melting against his chest.

"It's like he's following me," I whisper.

Bexley tenses. "It's just your mind," he whispers. "You're safe, Mia. I promise."

But it's a lie.

Because while Cade's out there, no one's safe.

Especially not me.

ON SUNDAY AFTERNOON, we head back to Gravestone. Last night, I left them all talking around the firepit and retreated to my room. Sometime later, Bexley crawled in beside me, but we didn't talk or kiss or touch... we just lay there, in silence, until he drifted to sleep. This morning we had breakfast with Hadley and Cole before they left to visit Ace and Remi. I know Bexley was hoping to speak to her, but they couldn't make it in the end.

"So how was it?" Sasha asks, slipping into my room.

"It was okay, I guess." I shrug, unpacking my small overnight bag.

"Did it help you guys... you know." A faint smile traces her lips, but it falls when I wrap my arms around myself. "Shit, Mia, I'm sorry."

"It's not your fault. We shared a bed, and I didn't freak out, but it's like there's a wall between us, and I know it's my fault, but I don't know how to—"

"Hey, hey. No one is expecting you to paste on a smile and be okay. But Bexley loves you, and he just wants to be there."

"I saw him again," I blurt out.

"Saw wh—Cade?"

I nod. "I know it wasn't him. But it's so real, Sasha. Like he's right there, watching me." I run a hand down my face, letting out a weary sigh.

"Maybe you should speak to someone. A therapist."

"No. The Xanax helps. It does. And I feel a little better after two nights of sleep."

"So Bexley helped with something then..." Her eyes twinkle, but I don't feel the same hope she does.

"Yes, Bexley helped with that. But it's not what you think." I give her a pointed look.

"I spoke to my father earlier." Her expression falls. "He wanted to remind me that it's the Harvest Ball next weekend."

"Surely they don't expect..." I twist my hands into the bedsheets.

"Of course they do."

"It's an important night for Quinctus. Business associates from all over the state attend."

"Why do I need to be there?"

"To keep up appearances. Why else?"

My eyes shutter as I inhale a ragged breath. "What will happen to me?" I ask her. "Now that Cade is..."

Sasha perches on the edge of the bed. "Honestly, I don't know. You have the prosapia brand. You're one of them now. Maybe you and Bexley can..." Sasha's lips purse. "Don't worry about all that right now. Focus on getting better." She lays her hand on mine. "We can go dress shopping, or if you prefer, you can borrow something from my collection."

"I'll borrow something, if that's okay?"

"Of course." She hesitates. "You should know that Brook will be there."

"I don't care about Brook, Sasha." She's the least of my worries right now. I managed to avoid her last week around campus, and as far as I'm concerned, I'd like it to stay that way.

"Do you want to come downstairs and watch a movie? Or we could go swimming?"

"I think I'm going to lay down. But maybe later."

Concern etches into the lines of her face. "Okay, you know where I am if you need me."

"Thank you."

Sasha leaves me alone and I finish unpacking before changing into an oversized t-shirt. I go over to the window, staring down at the tree line below. He's not there. Cade isn't there. But it doesn't stop me from feeling him.

Ugh.

I just need it to stop. I need to find a way to exorcize him from my mind. But I don't know how.

Hurrying over to the nightstand, I pluck the small baggie out and retrieve two pills. It's still early, barely five, but I just want to close my eyes and see nothing instead of his soulless gaze haunting me.

Going into the small bathroom adjoining my room, I turn on the faucet and bend to wash the pills down, avoiding my reflection in the mirror.

It takes a while for the sedative effects to kick in, but gradually I feel the tension ebb away until my limbs feel heavy, but my mind feels weightless. I close my eyes and pray I find peace.

I WAKE WITH A START, my mind cloudy and confused.

Where am I?

As I push up onto my elbows, my eyes strain against the darkness, trying to find my bearings.

The Electi house... I'm in the Electi house.

My hands curl into the soft sheets beneath me as I search my mind for answers. But everything is foggy, as if I've been drinking.

Clambering off the bed, I struggle to stay upright as I pad around the dark room, following the sliver of light into the bathroom. Sweat coats my skin as my heart races inside my chest.

It's as if I woke up from a bad dream, except I can't remember anything.

I don't flip on the main light switch, using the soft amber glow of the vanity mirror instead. It's easier on my eyes.

My reflexes are slow, sluggish, as I pee, balanced precariously on the toilet, pressing my palm against the wall to steady myself.

When I'm done, I flush and stagger to the sink. The light on the vanity flickers, and a trickle of fear rushes down my spine. Forcing myself to take a calming breath, I dry my hands.

The room plunges into darkness and I scream, but a hand wraps around my throat, yanking me backward into the shadows and shoving me against the wall. "I'd think very carefully about doing that again, little mouse," Cade seethes, his eyes glittering with dark intent.

I'm paralyzed, blood roaring in my ears as I stare into the eyes of the guy who raped me and left me for dead, and then murdered my parents.

Dark spots swim across my vision as his fingers tighten, squeezing the air from my lungs. I gasp, clawing and scratching at his hand, desperate to get him off.

"You were supposed to die out there." He spits the words as I try to scream.

"Mia?" somebody yells from inside my bedroom. "Mia?"

"Guess our time's up, mouse... for now," Cade sneers, slowly releasing me just as someone bangs on the door.

Did I lock it?

I don't remember.

"Mia?" Bexley crashes through the door.

"He's here," I cry, clutching my neck. "He's in here."

Bexley catches me right as I begin to crumple to the ground. "What happened?"

"Cade..." I tremble. "He's here." My eyes dart wildly around the bathroom, but I can barely see.

"What the fuck?" Channing and Brandon rush into the room.

"Cade, he's here," I shriek. "You have to get him. Don't let him—"

"Shh." Bexley smooths the hair from my face. "No one's here, Mia. No one is—"

"He was right here. I saw him," I cry, pain splintering me down the middle. "I felt him."

"No one's here, man," Brandon says, and I lift my face to them.

"H-he was here." My body trembles and Bexley lifts me into his arms, cradling me against his chest.

"Check the house," he says. "Get security and check the whole goddamn estate."

"Bexley, he isn't—"

"Just do it, now."

"Yeah, man, whatever you say." They take off, leaving us alone.

"Come on, let's get you out of here." Bexley stalks straight out of my room and takes me to his.

Gently, he lowers me onto his bed and sits beside me, raking a hand through his hair. "What did you take?"

"W-what?"

"Mia, what did you take?"

"Two Xanax. But they wouldn't—"

"You're stressed, fatigued... you suffered a huge fucking trauma..."

"You don't believe me." I wrap my hands around my body, trying to fold in on myself.

He twists toward me, cupping my face in his big hands. "Look at me, baby. Look at me..." Slowly, I lift my eyes to his, the blue of his grounding me. "You are safe here, Mia. You're safe here."

"But I—"

"He's not here, baby. He's not. I need you to believe me. I need you to—"

"I am not crazy, Bexley. I know what I saw. I know what I felt..." But as I say the words, I know I can't trust them, because I can't trust my mind anymore. Everything is upside down. Reality and my nightmares blur together, twisting and contorting into something I can't control.

I climb off his bed and stand up, swaying slightly.

"Whoa, Mia, what are you—"

"Go. I need to go."

"You think I'm going to let you out of my sight now? I'm not. No fucking way."

"I'm not a child. I don't need babysitting," I yell, frustration coating my words. "I just... I need for it to stop." My fingers slide into my hair, tugging the roots. "I need to feel like I'm not one second away from losing myself. He broke me, Bex. He broke me, and I'm not sure I'll ever—"

Bexley prowls toward me, and instinctively I back up until my back hits the wall. "What are you—"

"Shh." He presses his finger against my lip. "You say you're broken, so let me put you back together. This isn't you, Mia. You're stronger than this. You're so strong, baby." He presses his hand against the wall beside my head, leaning in to run his nose along my cheek. "I am so fucking sorry about your parents. I am. But you cannot let them win. You cannot let *him* win. You're mine, Mia. And I'll do whatever it takes to bring you back to me. Even if you don't like me for it." His hands slide gently to my throat, his fingers circling me there.

A tremor of fear goes through me, but it's edged with anticipation. A drug-induced haze still lingers in my mind, but I feel more grounded in this moment than I have in a while.

"You're mine, Mia." Desperation tinged with possessiveness glitters in Bexley's eyes. "And I won't fucking lose you to him. I won't."

14

BEXLEY

Reaching out, she rips my hand away from her throat.
"I'm not yours though, am I? I'm not anyone's right now. I don't know who the fuck I am or what I'm even doing here." Fear and confusion flash through her eyes.

I knew the second I looked at her that she had taken something. It wasn't just fear I could see in her eyes; they were blown in a way I've never seen before.

I knew she'd been taking Xanax from Sasha. I also knew it was a bad idea, but Mia won't listen to a fucking thing I say right now.

"He was right there, Bexley," she screams, her body trembling as she recalls what she thought happened.

"I know, baby."

"No. No, you fucking don't. You just think I'm crazy. This wasn't in my head. I'm telling you that he was there, that he touched me. Look." She points at her neck, but I see no marks, no bruising of any kind.

"There's nothing there, mou—"

"No," she cries, emotion cracking her voice. "He called me that. He called me by your name for me. He's ruining everything, Bexley. Why can't you see that he won't stop this until he's got everything he wants."

"No, Mia. He's gone. He's done his damage, and he's gone."

"Why won't you believe me?" she sags against the wall, her arms wrapping around her waist as if she's physically holding herself together.

"There's no evidence, baby. He couldn't get in here without security seeing him."

"He did, Bexley. He was here. He touched me. He—"

I take her by the throat just like she said he did, and she gasps in shock. "Security is going to sweep the entire estate, check all the CCTV. If he was here, they'll find it."

"He *was* here," she seethes, her fear giving way to anger as her arm flies out to slap me.

Sadly for her, I'm faster. I have her wrist in my grasp and her arm pinned to the wall above her head before she even registers that her slap never made contact.

"Bexley, what are you—" My fingers tighten around her throat and her eyes widen before I lower my head, slamming my lips to hers. "Bexley," she tries again, but I'm not having any of it.

"Trust me, baby," I breathe into our kiss, stepping forward to crush her body against the wall and to show her just how much her mere presence affects me. "Trust me to know what you need."

Her body relaxes ever so slightly, and I know I've got her.

I push my tongue deeper into her mouth as my fingers trail down her body until I find the hem of the shirt she was sleeping in. Lifting the fabric, I run my fingertips up the satin skin of her thighs, stopping when I hit her lace panties.

Kicking her legs wider, I cup her mound over her underwear, pressing one finger between her folds. "So wet for me, baby."

"Bexley," she moans, clearly accepting that this is happening.

I rub her until her hips begin to grind and her little whimpers tell me that she's getting close.

"What?" she cries when I pull my hand away and release her throat, but I don't go far. I wrap my fingers around the neck of her shirt and tear it straight down the front, exposing her bare breasts that are heavy and desperate for my touch.

"Bexley!" Desire drips from her words, and I rip her panties away from her in a similar fashion, dropping them on top of her ruined shirt.

She stands before me with her chest heaving, her nipples pert and begging to be sucked on and her legs parted, teasing me with what I really want.

"Turn around, place your hands on the wall, and bend over."

She hesitates, not used to me being quite so demanding.

"Do it or get out."

For a split second, I panic that she might take the second option, but I soon realize that I know my girl better than that—even now, when she's struggling to know who she is.

It's the sign I didn't realize how badly I needed that my Mia is still in there. Under all the fear and hallucinations, she's still there.

"Fuck, baby," I growl when she arches her back and offers herself up to me.

Dragging my shirt over my head, I drop to my knees. "So fucking pretty, baby," I murmur, squeezing her ass cheeks in my palms so hard my fingers leave marks in their wake.

I pull one hand back for a second before watching my palm connect once again with a loud slap.

"Bexley," Mia squeals, her entire body jolting as a mix of shock and pleasure races through her body.

Dipping my head down, I tease my tongue between her folds, finding her clit.

"Oh God," she moans as her taste explodes in my mouth, making me even more desperate for her.

Her hips roll as she rides my face, trying to get what she needs to take her away from her fear.

"Fuck, baby. You taste like heaven." I kiss and nip at her skin before sinking my teeth into the soft flesh of her ass.

She hisses in pain as I find her soaked entrance and push two fingers inside her. Mia moans, her back arching to get more. I thrust my fingers in and out of her faster and faster; she matches me move for move, her juices beginning to drip down my hand.

Dropping my other hand, I kiss across her flawless skin before I repeat my previous actions and bite into her cheek.

"Yesss," she cries as her pain and fear mixes with the pleasure.

She gushes against my fingers, her pussy clamping down hard.

"You want to come, baby?"

"Yes, Bex. Yes."

Dropping to my ass, I twist around so I'm sitting between her legs.

I find her dark, lust-filled eyes when I look up, and my cock weeps to be able to push inside her, to become one with her again.

"Bexley." My name is no more than a whispered plea as she stares down at me.

"I've got you, baby."

Bending my fingers so the tips graze her G-spot, I stretch up and suck her clit into my mouth. Her entire body trembles as she gives herself over to me, and I can't help smiling, knowing that I've given her the release she needs in more ways than one.

Right now, Cade is so far from her mind that he may as well not exist. The only thing she can think about is me and what I'm going to do to her next. It's exactly how it should be.

"Bexley. Bexley." I feel like a fucking god as she begins to chant my name, getting closer to release.

"Come for me, baby. Give me everything," I growl against her. And with one more lick of her clit and another graze of her G-spot she shatters, her knees buckling as she does.

I hold her up with one hand on her hip as she rides out wave after wave of pleasure.

Once I'm sure she's finished, I climb from beneath her and push myself up in front of her. Her cheeks are flushed and her eyes glazed. Reaching out, I cup her cheek, trying to get a read on how she's feeling. Her eyes search mine for a few seconds before she says one word that tells me everything I need to know.

"More."

Wrapping my hands around the back of her thighs, I lift her into my body and wrap her legs around my waist. Her swollen pussy aligns with my solid cock and makes her gasp.

She rolls her hips, driving me fucking wild despite the thin fabric of my boxers that's between us.

"Fuck, baby. Keep doing that and I'll go off before I'm inside you."

"I've got all night," she whispers in my ear. A small sigh escapes me. I know she's saying it more because she's too scared to go to sleep in case she sees him again than anything else, but still, I'll take all I can get right now.

The second my shin connects with the bed, I throw her onto it. She bounces in the center as I drop my boxers and crawl on with her, forcing her legs open and settling between them.

She stares up at me, her chest still heaving, her skin flushed from her release.

"I love you, Mia." I lean over her, taking her cheek in my hand and staring into her eyes. "I fucking promise you, you're safe here. You're safe with me."

"Stop please, Bex. I-I don't want to talk right now." She shifts, and her pussy grazes my length.

"Fuck. Okay. Do you have any idea how badly I need you?"

"Show me. Take me far, far away from here."

"Fuck," I groan, desperate to give her everything I can right now.

Wrapping my hand around my length, I find her entrance and push inside in one quick thrust. Mia cries out as she stretches to accommodate me after our time apart.

Her pussy ripples around me, reminding me just how fucking good we are together.

"Baby," I moan.

"No, Bexley. No words. Just fuck me."

"Jesus."

Folding over her, I wrap my hand around the back of her neck and tilt her to the perfect angle so I can claim her lips. Plunging my tongue inside, I fuck her mouth with the same intensity I do her pussy.

Her legs hook around my waist, allowing me to thrust into her with abandon as she begins to slide up my bed until her head gently hits my padded headboard with every thrust of my hips.

"Mia, fuck," I groan into our kiss, already feeling those familiar tingles at the base of my spine which indicates that this is going to be over long before I'm ready for it to be.

Finding her clit, I press my thumb down, needing her to fall over the edge with me. "I wanna feel you come, baby. I wanna feel you coming on my cock."

"Bexley," she cries, throwing her head back and arching, offering herself to me.

Dropping my head, I suck one of her pert nipples into my mouth and bite down. It's the exact pain she needs, because with a loud cry, she shatters beneath me, sucking my cock deeper and milking my own release out of me at the same time.

"Mia," I roar as pleasure consumes me and I shoot jets of cum inside her, marking her once again as mine.

The second I'm done, I drop down beside her, my heart racing and my chest heaving to drag in the air I desperately need.

She lays deadly still on her back, looking up at the ceiling.

"Mia, baby. Look at me, please."

She doesn't show any sign that she registers my words. Propping myself up on my elbow, I stare down at her.

"No," I say when I notice her closed-off expression. "No, you're not doing this now."

Wrapping my hand around her hip, I slowly slide it up over the curve of her waist until I cup her breast. "We're not done, baby," I inform her. "Not anywhere fucking near."

Flipping onto my back, I pull her with me and settle her astride my waist before sitting so we're chest to chest. Sliding my fingers into the slightly sweat-damp hair at the nape of her neck, I pull her lips toward me.

"Reality isn't allowed tonight, baby." I take her lips once more until I'm fully hard again and encourage her to sink down on me.

We both groan as I fill her even deeper in this position and she more than willingly takes over, taking just this small bit of control back over her life.

15

MIA

Despite waking up in Bexley's arms this morning, I'm on edge all day as I move from class to class. I hate the way they watch me, the pity stares and concern as they chaperone me around campus as if I'm some poor, fragile girl unable to look out for herself.

But maybe I am.

I mean, I saw Cade last night. I felt him pressed up against me, his hand wrapped around my throat. Bexley blames the Xanax and stress I'm under. I heard him and Sasha arguing about it before I finally dragged myself out of bed this morning. But maybe I really am just losing my mind.

After class, I half expect to find Sasha or Bexley waiting for me, so I inhale a sharp breath at the sight of Annabel standing there.

"Hi," she says around a sheepish smile. "Can we talk?"

"I have nothing to say to you." Moving around her, I take off down the hall, but she hurries after me.

"Look, I know I messed up, and I'm sorry. I'm so sorry, Mia. You're my best friend. I just want to be there for you." She lays a hand on my arm, and I freeze. "God, I can't even imagine what you're going through."

"Not so alluring now, is it?" I grit out, a shudder going through me.

"What?" Her expression falls.

"This is what you wanted, right? To be in their world. To be one of them."

"I don't understand..."

"Of course you don't." Because Quinctus covered up my parents' death as a tragic house fire and Cade's absence as visiting family.

"Mia, did something happen? Something besides..." She trails off, something catching her eyes over my shoulder. I glance back to find Channing and Sasha walking toward us.

"Annabel," Sasha says coolly.

"Hey, Sasha. I was just... it doesn't matter. I guess I'll see you around, Mia. Bye." Annabel takes off down the hall, a heaviness settling in my chest.

She was my one friend outside of all this. Quinctus. The Electi. Cade and Bexley. But now even that is tainted.

"You okay?" Channing eyes me carefully.

"I'm fine. I was expecting Bexley."

"He got held up in class and asked us to swing by and meet you."

"You know, I'm quite capable of getting myself to class. Besides, Q has security all over the building." I glance to the side but see no one.

They're like ghosts, blending in with the student populous, hiding in the shadows. But they're there. I feel them, watching, following my every move.

It should settle the pit in my stomach.

It doesn't.

"He's just worried."

I purse my lips, unwilling to get into it with Channing here, of all places. "Yeah, well, I'm fine. I need to get to my next class."

"We'll walk—"

"No," I snap. "I don't even need to leave the building. I've got it." Hitching my bag up my shoulder, I take off in the opposite direction in a hurried pace. They follow, but they don't try to stop me, and I'm grateful. It's stifling, being constantly chaperoned and guarded. They all keep telling me Cade isn't here, that it's my mind and not reality scaring me. So what's to be concerned about?

I reach my next class and slip inside, relieved that neither of them follow. It's only Monday afternoon, and I'm already exhausted. And with the Harvest Ball happening this weekend, I'm going to need all my strength.

If I had my way, I'd never set foot in another Gravestone ceremony or event again. But Phillip expects me to be there. Quinctus expects me to be there. They expect me to paste on a smile and keep up pretenses.

God, I hate this.

I hate all of it.

The professor walks on stage and ushers the room into silence. "Good afternoon. Today we'll be watching the first half of a documentary. I expect you to take notes. There will be a pop quiz later in the semester, and your assignment will rely heavily on the ideas presented."

Relief floods me. At least I haven't got to sit here and pretend to be engaged. And since I'm sitting at the back of the room, no one will pay me any attention.

The room plunges into darkness, and the screen flickers to life. It isn't long before my eyes grow heavy, and I rest my head back against the wall. I'm safe here.

I'm safe.

THE NEXT TWO days are much the same. Bexley, Channing, Sasha, and Brandon divide their time to chaperone me to and from class. Bexley barely lets me out of his sight. We don't talk about what happened the other night, and it doesn't happen again. But every night, I lay in his bed, unable to step foot in my bedroom.

I'm also off the Xanax, which means I'm not sleeping again. I don't tell Bexley or anyone else that. They would only freak-out. Instead, I ply myself with strong coffee and energy drinks when no one is paying attention. But by Wednesday afternoon, the cracks are beginning to show.

I'm sitting in class again, my eyes heavy and my body weary. At least being off the Xanax has prevented any more freak-outs in the middle of the night. Now I lay awake, staring at the shadows as they dance across Bexley's ceiling while he sleeps beside me. His touch, despite everything left unsaid between us, still calms me.

"I'll see you back at the house, okay?" Bexley says as we reach my next class.

"Yeah."

"Channing will meet you right here."

"I know the drill, Bex." A resigned sigh slips from my lips.

"Hey." He cups my cheek, brushing his thumb over my skin. "I know this is hard…"

"It's fine. I'm fine. Go. Play nice with Q." I almost choke over the word. He's meeting with Phillip to get an update on things, whatever that means. It's been almost three weeks since Cade disappeared. There's been no official sign of him, since no one believes me.

I'm not sure *I* believe me anymore.

The memories are hazy, the moments in time fading further and further out of reach. Maybe it was all my mind playing tricks, torturing me some more.

"Okay." He leans in, grazing his lips across my cheek. "I'll see you later." I watch Bexley walk away, unsure whether I feel relieved or disappointed. Things are different between us since Sunday night, as if we crossed a line into unexplored territory. Part of me knows we needed it—that I needed it. But now it's like neither of us knows how to act around the other.

I follow the stream of people into class and take a seat over on the left near the back. The professor doesn't waste any time launching into today's lesson. I take notes, trying to keep up with all the terminology and theories he throws at us. But halfway through the class, I get the strangest feeling of being watched. My fingers grip my pen tightly as I discreetly glance around the room, my eyes landing on a figure in the back. He's right at the end of the row on the other side of the room, concealed by the other students so much that I can only make out his black hoodie and hands resting casually on the desk.

It's not Cade.

It can't be.

Not here, in one of my classes.

And yet…

I glance back, my heart pounding in my chest, but he's gone. My brows furrow and my leg bounces up and down as I frantically consider what to do.

He was there.

He was right freaking there.

Without thinking, I stuff all my belongings into my bag and clamber over the person sitting next to me to get out of the row. They mutter under their breath at me, but I don't stop to apologize as I slip out of the classroom into the hall.

It's empty. No sign of Cade. Or anyone else for that matter. I inhale a shaky breath, running a hand through my hair. I'm losing it. It's official. I'm—

A chill goes through me and I turn my head just in time to see someone disappear around the hall. Someone dressed all in black.

Before I can talk myself out of it, I take off after him. But when I skid around the corner, there's nothing.

A guttural scream rips from my lungs as I slam my hand against the wall, pain ricocheting down my arm. Tears prick the corners of my eyes as I take off running toward the nearest restroom. I burst through the door, heaving a ragged breath. I'm unraveling, the fragile edges of reality blurring until I can no longer figure out what's real and what's not.

I don't even realize I'm sobbing until Ashton appears, his big, imposing body filling the doorway.

"What the hell?" I seethe.

"What happened?" He takes a step toward me and I jerk back.

"Why are you in here?"

"I saw you lose it out there and followed you."

"You followed me?" It's then I notice he's wearing a black hoodie.

"You..." I point at him, my lip wobbling as I try to process what this means. "Was it you? Were you in my class just now?" The words are a garbled mess as tears streak down my face.

Ashton holds up his hands, slowly inching toward me. "Whoa, I don't know what happened, Mia. But it wasn't me, I swear."

"I-I can't trust you. You're his best friend... you're his—"

"I know. Believe me, I know. But Kingsley screwed me over too." Regret glitters in his eyes. At least, I think it's regret. But this could all be part of some elaborate plan to manipulate me.

"You should go," I cry, grabbing my cell from my pocket.

"I'm not going to do that, Mia. Why don't you just calm down and tell me what happened."

"Don't tell me to calm down," I snap when the door swings open again and Brook slips inside.

"Oh my God, what happened?" She stares at me.

"Brook." Ashton moves into her line of sight, and I realize he's shielding me from her. "Now is not a good time."

But in true Brook fashion, she steps around her brother. "What is—"

"This doesn't concern you," I seethe. She's kept her distance, much to my relief. But now she's standing there, looking at me like I'm a caged animal. And I hate her.

I hate her so much.

"Get out. Get out. GET OUT!" I yell over and over, my cracked words echoing off the ceiling.

"She's a nutcase. Look at her," she scoffs. "I don't know why you're wasting your time on—"

"I swear to God, Brook, if you don't back the fuck up, I will..." Ashton heaves a deep breath, glaring at his sister. "You need to leave. Now."

"Wait a second, don't tell me you're actually siding with... with *her*." She practically spits the word.

My eyes grow to saucers as I watch Ashton grab her and shove her toward the door. "If you know what's good for you, Sister, you'll stay the fuck away from Mia."

Brook's protests are drowned out as he pushes her through the door and lets it slam closed behind him.

"I can't believe you did that," I whisper.

"I meant what I said, Mia. You can trust me." He closes the distance between us slowly, keeping his hands where I can see them. "Now why don't you tell me what happened?"

"He was there. He was right freaking there."

"Okay, okay." His hand goes to his pocket. "I'm going to call Bexley, okay? And I'll wait with you until he gets here. We can wait right here."

My eyes dart wildly to the cell in his hand and back to his eyes. He seems genuine, not like the arrogant cocky asshole I usually know him to be.

"He's... he's at a meeting with Q."

"Okay, I'll call Channing. You trust Channing, right?"

I nod, shaking as the adrenaline leaves my body.

"You don't look so good."

"I feel..." I sway as the room spins.

"Fuck, Mia." Ashton catches me before I hit the deck, pulling me into his arms.

"I-I think I'm going to—"

The room spins again, and I fall down... down... down into the black abyss.

Until nothing.

WHEN I COME TO, I'm in a bed that feels unfamiliar in a small room I don't recognize.

"Bexley?" I murmur, pushing the hair out of my face.

"He'll be here soon," a voice says from the corner of the room.

"Ashton?" Fear snakes through me as I clutch the sheet to my body.

"Relax, I'm not here to hurt you. You fainted. I didn't know what else to do, so I brought you to the campus medical center."

"Thank you."

He nods, running a hand over his jaw. "How are you feeling?"

"Like I was hit by a truck."

"The nurse said your vitals looked okay. But she'll probably want to speak to you. I asked her to give you some space, though... until Bexley gets here."

"Thanks." My voice cracks. "I saw him, Ashton. He was right there."

"Mia, I think—"

"Mia?" Bexley bursts into the room. "Thank fuck." He rushes to my bedside. "Are you okay?"

"I'm fine. I passed out, and Ashton brought me here."

Bexley goes rigid, his jaw popping with frustration. "Explain," he barks at Ashton, who flicks his eyes to mine.

"Don't look at her, look at me—"

"Bex," I whisper, reaching for his arm. "It's okay. Ashton helped me."

"Look, I should probably go." He gets up and makes for the door.

"Wait," I call out, much to Bexley's annoyance.

"It's all good," Ashton says. "I know things were messed up before... but I didn't know he'd take it that far. I didn't—"

"You should go," Bexley grits out, anger radiating from him.

"Okay, but I meant what I said earlier." He gives me a small nod. "And I'll talk to Brook. I'll tell her to stay away." Ashton disappears, closing the door behind him.

"What happened?" Bexley runs his eyes over me, the concern there overwhelming.

If I tell him the truth, he won't believe me. No one will. So I swallow it down and instead say, "I came over all funny in class. I don't know if I was too hot or hungry, but I barely managed to get to the bathroom before I fainted."

"And Ashton just happened to be there?" Suspicion coats his words.

"He saw me stagger to the bathroom and was worried."

Bexley snorts at that.

"It's a good thing he was there, Bex," I say softly. "He helped me."

Three little words I never expected to say. But can't take them back now they're between us.

"And Brook? What did Ashton mean just now?"

My eyes shutter. "She came into the bathroom and started making things worse. You know how she is. Ashton told her to leave. He stuck up for me."

Bexley's expression hardens, but then he reaches for me. "Well, I'm here now," he says, gripping my hand in his, squeezing tightly as if he expects me to slip through his fingers. "I'm here."

He is.

But I've never felt more alone.

16

BEXLEY

"This is bullshit," I spit at whoever it is who's standing in my doorway.

"I know," Channing says as he walks into my room and sits on the edge of my bed while I'm in the bathroom running some wax through my hair. "But we gotta be good little puppets and do as we're told," he mutters, sounding about as excited as I am for tonight.

The Harvest Ball.

I have no fucking interest in a masked fucking ball, and it's really the last thing Mia needs, yet even she hasn't been excused from this charade.

Grabbing the black and gold domino mask sitting on my countertop, I hold it to my face and roll my eyes. All Electi have the same design, apparently.

Shoving the thing in my jacket pocket, I walk into my room to join Channing, who's dressed exactly the same as me in a black tux. "For the record, tonight is a really bad idea," I tell him. "Mia already thinks she's seeing Cade; the last thing she needs is everyone walking around with half their faces covered."

"I know, man. But she'll have us. We won't leave her alone. She'll be safe."

"I still don't like it. You've seen what she's been like this week. Every day she's more and more paranoid, looking over her shoulder and jumping at every little noise."

"We've been over and over the CCTV footage. There's no sign of him. She needs to see someone, Bex. She can't keep this up."

"I know. I know," I say, scrubbing my hand down my face. "I hoped getting away on the weekend would've helped. I mean, it did for a bit, but then she freaked again."

"She was with people she hardly knew while she's barely holding herself together. Maybe being just the two of you would be better. Maybe she'll open up to you properly if you're away from any reminder of this place."

"Maybe. I don't know. I just... I wanna fix her. I want my Mia back."

"She'll get there. It's just going to take some time."

I blow out a breath, staring out the window at the trees, wishing I could see what she does just so she could feel a little less crazy. I want to believe her, I do so badly, but everything points to the fact that she's losing her mind, so it's gonna take some hard evidence to convince me otherwise.

"Come on," I say reluctantly. "Let's get this shitshow on the road."

Together we walk down to Sasha's room where the girls are getting ready. "When are you going to come clean to Brandon and stop sneaking around?" I ask him.

"I have no idea. I'm following Sasha's lead. I still think she believes this isn't going to happen between us, like Phillip is going to pull the plug after all this Cade bullshit is over."

I nod at him, because although I want to be confident that he wouldn't do that to his daughter, really, it's very possible. That cunt doesn't seem to give many fucks about much, and I can't imagine his daughter's love life is one thing he does care about.

Channing knocks before Sasha calls out for us to enter.

In true Electi style, both girls are dressed in stunning black gowns.

Sasha's is a little risqué with lace and straps holding the top of the dress together, whereas Mia's is much more demure and elegant.

"Mia," I breathe, moving toward her, "you look beautiful."

She looks down at the dress, but I'm not entirely sure she really even sees herself. Sasha might have done a killer job on her makeup, but I can still see the obvious signs of her exhaustion. She might have spent every night in my bed since she thought Cade was in her room, but I know she's not really sleeping. Every time I wake in the night, she's awake too. I almost want to tell her to take the Xanax again so at least she can get some peace, but we both know it wouldn't lead to that. It'll just drag up more heartache for her when she sees him again.

Holding her at arm's length, I encourage her to spin around so I can get a good look at her. The fabric of the dress shows off every sexy curve of her body and makes my mouth water with images of peeling it off her later.

Taking a step toward her, I wrap my hand around the nape of her neck and look into her tired eyes. "We'll leave as soon as we can, okay? I want to be there about as much as you do."

She nods but doesn't say a word as she looks to the door and extracts herself from my hold. Her dismissal makes my chest ache, but I know she's just trying to get through this in whatever way she can.

"We need to do something, Bex. It's getting worse," Sasha says, echoing my concern for my girl.

"She's seen him again?"

"Not that she's said, but she's barely holding it together right now. I'm worried she's about to shatter before our eyes."

"Me too," I admit. "I'll find help. Find someone Q trusts for her to talk to."

"Good luck with that," Sasha mutters.

"There must be someone, Sash. She can't be the only one who's struggled with the reality of this life."

"I'll talk to my dad, see if there's anyone he can recommend."

"I appreciate it."

The three of us take off after Mia, and when we get to the bottom of the stairs, we find her with Alex, Brandon, Tim and Fawn.

"We ready?" Tim asks, his arm firmly clamped around Fawn's waist.

"We are."

There are two limos waiting for us outside of the house. Tim, Fawn, Brandon and Alex get in the first, and Mia, Sasha, Channing and I get in the second.

I have no clue why there are two—we'd all easily fit in one—but I guess that wouldn't be a showy enough arrival for this town's beloved Electi.

The journey to Gravestone Hall is tense and uncomfortable as Mia sits picking at nothing on her dress.

"Don your masks, ladies and gents. The party is about to begin," Channing announces with a hint of sarcasm as we make our way up to the oppressive building.

Looking out the window, I see masked couples walking up the stairs and being greeted by the staff standing at the door.

Sucking in a deep breath, I turn toward Mia. "One of us will be with you all night. You have a problem, you just tell us, yeah?"

"Everything will be fine, Bex." Her lips thin, betraying her words. "Stop worrying."

"Impossible. Let me," I say when she lifts her mask.

The girls' are a more feminine and delicate version of ours, showing just who they belong to.

Taking her hand in mine, I help her from the car, and together we walk to the entrance with the others falling in line behind us. It's weird after being forced to trail Kingsley into these kinds of events to now be the one in the lead, but I guess I need to get used to it.

I'm greeted by name by the men standing at the doors, despite the fact that I have no clue who they are. We walk through the entrance hall and turn into the grand hall. It's the first time I've been here that I haven't immediately been accosted by Q for pre-event drinks. I look around for them, confused that we haven't been summoned but equally relieved, because it means I can stay beside Mia.

"Wow, it's beautiful," she breathes as we take in all the black and gold decorations. The tables are laid up with huge black floral centerpieces and gold tablecloths and chairs.

We find our table, which is set for us and Q when they arrive. I once again look around as Mia stares down at her lap. Everyone else seems to be enjoying themselves—I guess that's a standard of these events. We're all miserable while the verus who are always invited act like it's the highlight of their year.

I look at each person, trying to figure out who they are—or more so check that they're not him—but with their masks on, it's almost impossible to tell one person from another. No wonder Mia is refusing to look up.

AS ALWAYS, the meal is incredible, Phillip's speech is... dull, but at least there is alcohol. That's one of Q's rules that I can get on board with.

"Come on, let's go and dance," I say to Mia as we move through to the ballroom where there's a huge dance floor in front of a stage with a band on. I'm not sure Phillip will approve, but he can go fuck himself. I need to feel her in my arms, to be close to her.

"Can't we just leave?"

"Not yet. But the second we can, we're out of here, okay? We can go back to the house and lock ourselves in my bedroom."

"Sounds perfect," she mutters, although her voice lacks the excitement I feel racing through my veins at the thought of what could come next. I've barely touched her all week, and after Sunday night, I'm damn near desperate to have her again.

I drag her out onto the dance floor between the other couples and pull her into my body. "How about I make it worth your while?" I whisper into her ear as I slide my hands down her back to rest on the swell of her ass.

"Bexley," she warns.

"What? You know I can make you forget everything. I could lay you out on my bed and feast on you all night long."

She shudders in my hold, my dirty words affecting her like they always do.

"You want that, baby? You want me to tease you with my tongue until you come all over my face?"

"Bex, there are people," she chastises.

"No one can hear me but you, baby. No one but me knows how wet you are for me right now."

"Oh God," she moans, her body tensing as she imagines everything I'm suggesting.

Our bodies move together in time with the music, and it's the first time I realize that we've never really had a chance to do this. To party together, to dance together like we have no cares in the world and we're the only two that exist.

I cast my mind back to when she did it with Cade and I danced with Brook to make her jealous. Anger surges through me, but my need is more insistent still. I want that. I want to party at the house and to be able to show every fucker who's turned up that Mia is mine. Just like she always has been.

"You're mine, Mia. Nothing is going to change that," I promise her, rolling my hips so she can feel my hardness against her.

"Bexley, I can't—"

"Easton," a rough voice says from behind me, pausing my movements and cutting off whatever Mia was about to say. "I need to borrow you for a moment." Turning around, I find Phillip standing behind me, his lips thinned with disapproval. "I have some people I'd like to formally introduce you to."

"I'm so sorry," I whisper to Mia before gesturing to Channing, who's dancing with Sasha, Brandon, and a girl I don't know to take over from me.

"It's okay." She smiles at me as the others flank her sides, but it doesn't meet her eyes. If anything, it's sadder than I've seen all week.

"Fantastic," Phillip says. "Miss Thompson." He gives Mia a small nod before leading me away.

We come to a stop at the bar where there's a gathering of men in black suits, an array of different masks on their faces. I recognize all of the Q elders immediately based on their identical masks to Phillip's. Lincoln is with them, along with the Chief of Police who, thankfully, is fully clothed and not balls deep in a dancer like the last time I saw him.

Phillip introduces me to the others, but his words go in one ear and straight out of the other as I keep my eyes on Mia on the dance floor. I know she's with Channing and Brandon, but I don't trust anyone with her but me right now.

Lincoln maneuvers closer to me as the men around us chat about business. "She's quite something." His gaze flickers to Mia.

"She's barely holding on," I grit out, feeling the muscles in my neck tense.

"It's... unfortunate, the way things turned out."

Unfortunate?

Is this asshole for real?

"Cade killed her parents." My voice is a low growl. "He raped her and left her for dead."

"Yes, well," Lincoln barely flinches at my crass words, "it would appear my nephew is more like his father than I perhaps anticipated."

My eyes snap to his, narrowing. "What the hell is that supposed to mean?"

"I admire your passion, Bexley. Your strength. God only knows, you're going to need it to survive."

"Is that a threat?"

"More like a piece of advice." He smirks, lifting his glass and taking a sip of his scotch. "Quinctus, the organizations it works with, does business with... it takes a strong stomach to play with the big boys, son. Now, if you'll excuse me..." He turns to address two men beside him, as if he didn't just pull the rug out from under me.

Phillip sidles up to me and says, "What was all that about?"

"You tell me." My lips thin.

"I know you have concerns," he adds, gently tugging at the collar on his pristine white shirt, "but you need to let us handle Lincoln, son. You need to trust that we know what we're doing."

"Trust you?" I gawk at him, but he's not looking at me. He's watching Lincoln. And for the first time ever, I swear I see a glint of regret in Phillip Cargill's eyes.

17
MIA

I watch Bexley talking to Phillip, the other Quinctus elders, and a bunch of men I can't identify thanks to their various masks.

Part of me had hoped the masquerade ball would give me a chance to relax, but I should have known it would only elevate the fear knotted in my stomach. He could be in here somewhere, and nobody would ever know. Bexley and the Electi are easily recognizable with their gold and black eye masks, but the rest of the room is a mix of gaudy masks, exuberantly decorated and made unique, hiding the owner's identities.

Sasha stays close to my side as we dance. Tim and Fawn join us, and for the first time since meeting her, I see her smile. Maybe she likes the freedom her mask affords.

Someone brushes up against me, and my heart lurches into my throat.

"Mia, what is it?" Sasha asks over the music as I grip her hand tightly.

"Sorry," the guy yells, laughing as he twirls his dance partner away from us.

Relief slams into me, but my pulse doesn't settle. I'm on edge, my stomach hollow and my skin tingling with discomfort.

"It's okay." Sasha offers me a reassuring smile. "My dad has security all over this place."

Her words do little to placate me. Cade is one of them... or at least, he was. If he wants to stroll right into this ball and cause chaos, I don't doubt for a second he will. But Phillip and Quinctus seem to have forgotten just how much power he really holds. Or maybe they'd just prefer to believe that over the alternative.

As I watch Bexley shake hands with the group of men, my heart sinks. He looks like one of them. He looks like he belongs in their world.

"I need a drink," I announce, pulling my hand free of Sasha.

"But—"

Winding my way through the sea of bodies, I hurry to the bar. Someone will follow me; it's what they do. I'm never more than a second or two away from someone showing up to watch me. Because I'm that girl now: a girl who needs constant supervision.

My dress feels tight, as if it's slowly shrinking around my body, compressing my lungs until I can't breathe.

"A glass of wine, please," I blurt out the second the bartender greets me.

"Well, this sucks, doesn't it?" Ashton joins me at the bar. I'm not surprised he's here. He might not be welcome at the house or even part of Electi business now that Bexley is running the show, but he's still Phillip's stepson. He's still a part of this world. He knows too much to ever not be.

"Mm-hmm," I murmur, sipping my wine. "Look at them, so oblivious and carefree."

"Everyone wants a piece of the pie, Mia." Ashton takes a long pull on his beer. He isn't wearing a gold and black mask like the Electi. His is plain matte black with a silver swirl around one eye. Oddly, it suits him.

"I see Easton is taking his new role very seriously." There's a hint of sarcasm in his voice.

"What do you want, Ashton?"

"Ouch." He laughs, but it's strained.

"We're not friends."

"No, I guess we're not. I just thought you might—do you know what, forget it. Enjoy the party, Mia." He drains his beer, slams it down, and melts into the crowd.

I feel a bolt of guilt, but he doesn't deserve it. Just because he helped me once doesn't make him a hero. It doesn't even make him a good person. Grabbing my glass, I down the remainder and hold it up for the bartender to refill. I don't intend on getting drunk, but I need something to take the edge off, and since Sasha is under strict instructions not to give me any more pills, this is the next best thing.

The bartender slides another glass toward me, and I make a promise to myself not to down it in one, no matter how tempting it is.

THE PARTY DRAGS ON. Bexley has been talking to Phillip and his associates for at least forty-five minutes while I watch from our table, nursing my third glass of wine. A warm buzz runs through me, making things almost bearable as I watch Sasha and Channing dance. They look so good together, so natural as he twirls her around the dance floor. My heart aches. Bexley and I had that. We had it, and then it was ripped away from us.

Brandon is grinding on some girl I don't recognize. Their bodies are impossibly close, and I'm pretty sure he has his hand up her dress. I shake my head, a small part of me wishing I could have his attitude to everything.

A server passes with a tray of champagne, and I swipe another glass. I like the way the bubbles fizz and pop as they sluice down my throat and settle in my stomach.

"Miss Thompson," a gruff voice says, and I glance up to find Marcus Easton staring down at me. "May I?"

I motion to the empty chair beside me, and he sits, smoothing his pants down.

"How are you?"

"How do you think?"

"I know I have given you no reason to trust me or even like me, but with Cade gone—"

"Gone?" I snap, hoping he can see the anger in my eyes. "Do you really believe that? Cade isn't gone... he's just biding his time. He killed them." The words shred my insides. "He killed my parents and left me for dead, and you dare to sit there pretending..." An ugly sob crawls up my throat, but I swallow it down, taking another sip of champagne.

"Mia, we didn't know. If we had, we would never have—"

"Don't." An icy shudder runs through me. "Don't sit there and lie to my face. You handed me over like a lamb to the slaughter. You did that. And that's something you're just going to have to live with Mr. Easton. Now if you'll excuse me," I stand, draining my glass, "my friends are waiting for me."

They're not, but he doesn't need to know that as I weave around the tables to the dance floor. Another server passes, and I grab yet another glass.

How dare he? How dare Marcus pretend like he feels guilt over anything that has happened? As if they aren't the puppet masters pulling the strings here. Cade isn't gone. If they truly believe that then they're all more deluded than I first thought.

"There you are." Sasha pulls me into her arms, a sloppy grin on her face.

"You're high," I say, surprised by the flash of jealousy cinching my chest.

"High on love." She buries her face into my shoulder, smothering her laughter.

"Is she okay?" I ask Channing, and he rubs his jaw.

"I wish she'd quit that shit."

"But you love me." Sasha lifts her head and glances over at him. "You love me, Rexford."

His eyes burn into her, hot and hungry.

"Uh-oh," she whispers. "I think I'm in trouble. I'm going to pee. You'll be okay?"

"I... uh..." But she takes off, disappearing into the swarm of people dancing.

"Wait here with Brandon and Tim," Channing barks, taking off after her.

Great.

Just great.

Now I'm tipsy, irritated, and alone on a dance floor full of couples. I really didn't think this through. Downing my glass of champagne, I deposit it on a nearby shaker table and join Tim and Fawn. They're dancing but not intimately.

"I love your dress," she yells over the music.

"Thank you."

She moves around the table to stand beside me while Tim and Brandon goof around on the dance floor together.

"I don't think I've ever seen him so... animated," I remark on Tim, and Fawn chuckles.

"Get a few drinks inside him and he's quite the clown."

"How do you do it?" The words tumble from my lips.

"Do what?" Fawn frowns. I glance over to where Bexley is still talking to Phillip and their associates. When I look back at her, sympathy glitters in her eyes.

"You know, I've loved Tim for as long as I can remember. But it's not easy, living in their world." Silence settles between us, and I think back on what Hadley told me, about Tim and the baby.

"It almost broke me," Fawn says, as if she can hear my thoughts. "I've always been an anxious person. But when I found out about Hadley, it was like I lost myself. We weren't officially together then, but everyone knew I'd be Tim's prosapia."

"I'm sorry."

"We worked through it, but I always felt bad for her. She was forced out of her life, disowned by her family... no one should ever have to go through that. It ate Tim up inside. And then he found out about the baby, and he just lost it. I've seen things... heard things... but I've never seen Tim lose it like that. It almost ruined us.

"No one knows this, Mia, but I can't have children. I can't give Tim the one thing all Electi want more than anything. An heir." Sadness washes over her, and it makes my heart ache. I assumed Tim was the villain in his and Hadley's story, but sometimes there is no villain. There's just pain and heartache and a series of unfortunate events.

"You asked me how I do it?" Fawn took my hand in hers. "I love him, Mia. I will never love another the way I love Tim. And he loves me, and although it's hard and it hurts and sometimes I wonder if it's worth the fight, I remember it's enough. It has to be."

"Thank you for telling me." I squeeze her hand, something passing between us.

"What are you two talking about?" Tim joins us, looping his arm around Fawn's waist and nuzzling her neck. It's moments like these that I can see the love between them, almost taste it on my tongue.

"Dance with me." She all but drags him back to the dance floor and I watch them, unable to fight the smile tugging at the corner of my mouth.

Maybe there is hope for me and Bexley after all. At least, I think that's what she was trying to tell me.

Love is enough.

I watch them, letting the music wash over me. The beat is irresistible, and despite my bad mood, I begin to limber up, swaying my hips to the sultry beat. It's safe here. I'm safe.

The words run on repeat in my head as I push away all the negative thoughts and energy and lose myself in the moment. It's the first time in what feels like forever that I'm not dancing for somebody else, but for myself. My hands weave shapes in the air as I close my eyes. The alcohol in my bloodstream kicks in and everything grows fuzzy, but I like the sensation. When my eyes flicker open, it's a sight to behold, the elite of Gravestone dressed in their finery, wearing their masks, and letting loose on the dance floor.

Sweat beads along the back of my neck as I dance to forget. When I look up, a flash of red catches my eye, a mask styled like the devil himself. Fear roots me to the spot, but when I blink, he's gone.

"Dance with me." Brandon pulls me into his arms, twirling me around. Laughter spills from my lips, my heart racing as the alcohol floods my system. I didn't feel this drunk earlier, but the room keeps spinning as Brandon sways me gently. He doesn't speak, and I appreciate that, finding comfort in the silence. But I can't help but think that it isn't Brandon I should be dancing with. It's Bexley. The guy who claims to love me more than anything.

The guy who's currently laughing and joking with Quinctus and their associates like they're old friends.

My chest tightens as Brandon spins me again. A sudden flash startles me, and I jerk back at the sight of his ghastly mask. "B-Brandon?" Fear pumps through me as I blink rapidly.

I'm drunk. I'm just drunk, and my mind is playing tricks on me.

He throws his head back, cackling maniacally, blood dripping from the corner of his mouth. Wrenching out of his hold, I spin on my heel, but the sea of bodies, monstrous masks and devilish faces closes in around me.

"Mia, Mia, Mia," they whisper, clawing and grabbing at me. I stumble back, falling through a small hole. Crawling on my hands and knees, I escape the crowd and glance back as I clamber to my feet. No one has noticed me, too busy dancing... but when I look again, they aren't only dancing, they're fucking. Gyrating and grinding on each other, naked flesh, hands touching and teasing.

Confusion swims in my head as I take off running toward the huge ornate doors and spill into the quiet hall. Sucking in a ragged breath, I don't wait, grabbing the skirt of my dress and hurrying away from the room.

"Run, little mouse," a voice cackles, echoing off the walls.

His voice.

Cade.

No.

Not again.

The icy fingers of fear wrap around my throat, squeezing the air from my lungs as I run and run and keep running down the never-ending hall. This isn't right.

Something isn't—

I slam into a dead end, staggering back from the force.

"You can run, but you can't hide." His voice electrifies the hairs along my neck.

"W-what do you want?" I turn slowly, pressing my back against the wall.

"Oh, I think you know." He bursts from the shadows, his red and black devil's mask terrifying to look at.

"You... you're not here. This isn't real." I squeeze my eyes shut, repeating the words over and over in my head.

It's a trick.

A cruel effect of the stress and trauma and copious amounts of alcohol running through my veins.

"Isn't it?" He leans in, his lips right against my cheek. "Are you sure, Mia? Because it sure as hell feels real to me." His hand squeezes my thigh through my dress, hard enough that I yelp.

"You're not real," I cry. "You're not real."

It will all be over in a second. Somebody will find me and snap me out of it. Security will come.

Somebody will come.

"Look at me, little mouse. Open those pretty eyes and... Look. At. Me." His hand slips to my throat, squeezing gently.

My eyes fly open, and I find myself lost in two soulless black orbs.

"You're not real." I'm sobbing now, ugly, big sobs that wrack my body.

"You're so fucking pretty when you cry." He drags his tongue up my cheek, licking my tears.

It feels real.

Too real.

"Where's your boyfriend now, Mia? Where's Sasha and Channing? We're in a room full of people all hell bent on protecting you, and I don't see a single one of them coming to your rescue. Do you?" His hand flexes around my throat.

"I watched you out there, dancing. Putting on quite the show. I bet every man in the room wanted a taste of you. But they don't know how I ruined you, do they? They don't know that you're used goods now."

Bile washes in my stomach as I fight for every breath. "Please," I sob. "Please just leave me alone."

"Tsk, tsk, don't you know I can't, baby? We're bound. Our lives will be forever entwined so long as you wear my brand over your heart."

"So kill me." The words tear from my lungs in an urgent plea. "Kill me and end this. Just fucking end it."

"Shh, Mia. Shh." Cade gathers me close, running a hand down my back. He doesn't speak or taunt me, he simply holds me as if we're a pair of lovers stealing touches in the dark.

There's a loud crash down the hall, and he stiffens. "Looks like the cavalry has finally arrived." Cade eases back to look me in the eye. "But soon, Mia. Soon we'll be together again."

He starts inching away, his form shifting and simmering until the shadows swallow him whole. I step forward, blinking and blinking some more. But there's nothing. No sign Cade was ever here. I slide down the wall, silent tears streaking down my cheeks.

"Mia?" a voice calls out. But it's not the voice I yearn to hear. "Mia... fuck."

Ashton reaches me and crouches down. "What happened?"

I blink up at him, the edges of my vision blurry, and my lips twist with pain.

"I think you are all right. I think I'm losing my mind."

18

BEXLEY

"Where is she?" I bark at Brandon the second I get to him on the dance floor.

The last time I looked over, he was dancing with Mia while some guy I had no interest in talking to tried to engage me in conversation.

"Uh... bathroom?" he asks, looking around, proving that he has no fucking idea.

"You're meant to be looking after her," I shout, slamming my palms down on his chest, my anger swirling around me like a storm.

I catch Tim's attention before the three of us set off on a search mission while Fawn goes to check the ladies' room in case she's just escaped for a little peace and quiet. I couldn't really blame her if she has; this party fucking blows. I'd rather be hiding in the bathroom, that's for sure.

The ballroom shows no sign of her.

"Anything?" I ask when Fawn emerges from the hallway.

"No."

"Shit."

Lifting my hands to my face, I rip my fucking mask off, my patience with the thing long vanished. Tugging on the length of my hair, I look at the others, fear washing through me.

She could be anywhere.

"Security have this place surrounded. They wouldn't let her leave," Tim says, concern evident on his face.

"What's going on?" Sasha asks as she, Channing and Alex finally join us. "Where's Mia?"

I narrow my eyes at her, livid that she's clearly been enjoying herself popping pills while Mia is fuck knows where. "We don't know, that's what's fucking going on. You were all meant to be watching her," I snap at them.

"Let's split up. We'll find her faster," Channing suggests.

Everyone turns in a different direction, and I take off running down the hall. I have no fucking clue where I'm going. I've only ever been in one of three rooms in this colossal building. I just have to hope she's not gone far.

Each second feels like an hour as I run down endless hallways, throwing random doors open and peering inside, but it's to no avail.

Coming to a stop at a dead end, I thread my fingers through my hair, pulling until it burns. The silence around me is oppressive as I stand and stare out of the floor-to-ceiling window before me. Gravestone Forest stretches out into the darkness beyond, only the tree line visible with the bright spotlights from the building illuminating it. Just like at the house, I will myself to see him, to see what Mia believes she sees, but there's nothing.

A noise causes me to turn around, every hair on my body standing on end, and I take a step forward, straining to hear it again. After a few seconds, I hear it again. A sob.

Racing forward, I turn toward one of the hallways I haven't been down yet and run all the way to the end. "Get the fuck away from her," I bellow when I see a figure crouched down beside Mia.

"Whoa, man," Ashton says when I wrap my fingers in the fabric of his jacket and physically drag him away from my girl.

"I fucking told you to stay away from—"

"What the fuck, Easton. I heard her shouting and screaming. *I* came to fucking help."

Not having the time right now to deal with the twisted motherfucker who seems to be stalking my girl, I turn to her and drop to my knees.

She's curled into a ball in the corner with her arms wrapped around her legs and her head resting on her knees as she sobs.

"Mia, baby. It's me. I'm here."

It takes a few seconds, but, finally, she drags her head up and looks at me. She's got makeup streaked down her face, and her eyes are dark and full of fear and... "What have you taken?"

She rears back at my abrupt question, her trembling lips parting as she stares at me as if I'm not really here.

"Fuck you. Fuck you. Fuck all of you," she screams, climbing to her feet the best she can with her body trembling. "You guys are all right, okay? Is that what you want to hear? I'm losing my goddamn mind," she shrieks, spinning around on the spot.

I watch her, pain twisting my stomach. I want to help. I want to do anything I can to take it away, but I don't know how.

"I thought he was here. I thought he chased me, pinned me against the wall. But it's all fake, isn't it? And to answer your question, I haven't taken anything," she snarls at me. "You fucking cut me off, remember?"

"But your eyes. You've had something."

"You're all a bunch of fucking judgmental assholes, y-you know t-that?" Her voice cracks as her eyes fill with tears once more. "I can't do this anymore. I can't fucking do this," she screams, pulling out the pins in her hair and allowing it to cascade down her back.

"He should have killed me," she sobs. "He should have fucking k-killed m-me." Her entire body sags, and I catch her just in time.

"I've got you, baby."

"I hate this," she cries against me. "I hate everything."

"Let's get you home, and you can sleep it off."

She doesn't argue as I lift her into my arms and walk away from Ashton. I pin him with a look that cuts off anything he might want to say before I take off down the hall. I don't stop to find anyone else. Instead, I walk straight out the front doors toward the valet and wait for one of our limos to be called.

The second it pulls to a stop in front of us, the young guy standing beside me opens the back door and I climb inside with Mia as gently as I can. Her body is a deadweight in my arms as I settle us on the bench, telling me that she's already passed out.

I bark my instructions at the driver through the lowered internal window and he takes off, not even bothering to ask about the others. I slowly ease my cell from my pocket, managing it without waking her—

although if my suspicions are correct and she's taken something then I doubt much will bring her back around for a while.

Texting the others a message, I let them know that she's safe and that we're heading back before alerting security to our impending arrival. Slumping down in the seat, I hold her tight. I twist her slightly so I can see her face. Even in her slumber, she's got deep frown lines marring her brow.

"I wish I could make it all go away, baby," I whisper, rubbing my thumb over my cheek in an attempt to wipe away some of the smudged makeup. "It will get better," I promise her. "You will find yourself again, I know you will."

I'm still staring down at her beautifully tormented face when the limo finally comes to a stop outside the house. Thankfully, our security team is already expecting us, and they help me get Mia out and into the house safely.

I take her straight up to my room and lay her down in my bed. After pulling her shoes off, I cover her with the sheets and take a huge step back, just watching her. My chest aches at the sight of her sleeping peacefully, hoping that she's actually getting some rest and not just trapped in her recurring nightmares.

A commotion downstairs alerts me to the arrival of the others only a few minutes later. Pressing a kiss to her brow, I quietly slip out of the room and close the door behind me. Everyone, including fucking Ashton, is standing in the hallway when I appear at the top.

"Is she okay?" Sasha asks as I thunder down the stairs, my heart pounding in my chest and my anger surging forward faster than I can control.

"Yeah, no thanks to him. Why is he here?"

"I'm worried about her," Ashton answers, despite the fact that I'm clearly talking about him, not to him.

"Bull-fucking-shit," I snap, getting right in his face. "I keep finding you with her when she's freaking out. It's you, isn't it? You're the one who's fucking tormenting her, making her think she's seeing things, driving her fucking crazy."

"W-what? No." He pales. "I would never."

"You're a fucking liar," I bellow, slamming my palms into his chest hard enough to make him stumble back into the wall behind him.

"I'm not. I swear to God. I'm just worried about her."

"We don't need your concern. We've got it under control."

He laughs at my words. "You should have seen her tonight. She was fucking terrified."

"Of you," I bark, cocking my arm back. "Did he put you up to it?" I roar, swinging forward, my fist finally connecting with his cheek.

Fuck, it feels good after all this time.

"No," he shouts back after flexing his jaw. "I told you, I haven't seen or heard from him since he vanished. I'm as fucking clueless as you all are."

"Lies." I fly at him again, getting his eye this time, the skin of his brow splitting, spilling blood over my burning knuckles.

Shaking my hand out, I keep my eyes on him. His fists curl at his sides; he really wants to retaliate, but for some reason, he's holding back.

"Did you ever think that maybe she's not crazy? That maybe he is actually here?"

I shake my head, not believing what I'm hearing.

"You know nothing, Ashton. Fucking nothing. Who are you even? No one. You are no one."

"Good to see the power's not gone to your head," he mutters, lifting his hand to wipe away the blood that's running down his cheek.

"Just admit it, you did this, didn't you? You drugged her. You're tormenting her. This is all you and him and your twisted fucking mind games."

He moves first this time, and I find myself flying back toward the stairs with his arms around my waist. My back connects with the harsh edges as he lands on top of me, winding me.

"I haven't done any of this, motherfucker," he bellows before his fist forces my face to the side.

"Stop it," I hear someone shout as I manage to get the upper hand, rolling Ashton onto his back and going in for another hit.

My face burns with the punches he's landed and my chest heaves as I try to catch my breath, but it's not enough to stop me, and I throw another straight into his nose, causing blood to spray over both of us.

"Don't just stand there, someone stop them." Mia's voice drags my eyes from Ashton's bloody face, and when I look up, I find her standing at the top of the stairs with her arms wrapped around herself and tears once again cascading down her face.

"Get the fuck off me," Ashton barks, shoving as hard as he can and rolling me to the side. "Don't worry," he snaps as he pushes to stand, wiping his bloody nose with the back of his hand. "I'm fucking leaving. But," he adds before walking away, "if you want my advice, I'd start listening to her." He points up at a terrified-looking Mia before storming from the house.

Her sobs rip through the silence that descends around us and Sasha takes off running, taking the stairs two at a time until she pulls Mia into her arms.

"I can't do this anymore. I can't," she cries, repeating herself from the hallway earlier. "I need it to end. I need to get away, I need t-to..." Her sobs engulf her words as we watch Sasha lead her down the hallway and into her bedroom.

"You think there's any truth to what he's saying?" Brandon finally asks. "Do you really think it could be Cade?"

His words rattle around my fuzzy head for a few seconds. "There's no evidence. How could he possibly do all this without leaving a trail?"

"Because he's Cade fucking Kingsley. That's how."

19

MIA

I wake in a blanket of sweat, cocooned in Bexley's arms. My heart races in my chest, a testament to whatever nightmare haunted me in my dreams. But I can't recall anything except a black void.

After Ashton left last night and I fled to Sasha's room, she conceded and gave me two Xanax. She and Bexley got into it, arguing over me like I'm some child unable to make her own decisions.

The drugs hit quick, and the last thing I remember is Bexley carrying me to bed and whispering that everything is going to be okay.

It's not.

Not as long as Cade is still out there. Even if he isn't really here, he's like a dark cloud hanging over us. A storm on the horizon about to hit.

Gingerly sliding out from under Bexley's arm, I push back the covers and swing my legs over the bed. Everything is hazy still, my limbs heavy and my thoughts sludgy. Bexley is frowning, even in his sleep, as if he's carrying the weight of the world on his shoulders.

I guess between me and his new role within the Electi, he is.

With one more lingering look, I grab a cardigan and slip out of the room, careful not to make a sound. The house is silent as I tiptoe downstairs. My body aches, my throat dry and scratchy. Going into the kitchen, I make a beeline for the refrigerator and grab a bottle of water.

The cool liquid feels like heaven as it slides down my throat, and I lean back against the counter, my eyes instinctively going to the patio doors overlooking the lawns. It's dawn, the fall sun just breaking through the thick clouds. A chill zips up my spine as my gaze moves over the tree line... but to my relief, there's nothing.

Discarding the bottle of water, I switch on the coffee maker. Memories of last night are fuzzy. I remember dancing, watching Bexley as he schmoozed with Phillip and his associates. I remember feeling a lick of jealousy, of dejection. Then I danced with Brandon and freaked-out. But I can't quite remember what happened. It's as if someone has shrouded those memories in thick smoke. I know something bad happened. I can feel it, but I can't see it.

I thought Cade was there, that I can remember. But he's always with me, lurking on the edges of my reality.

My eyes shutter and I inhale a sharp breath. When I open them again, something flickers in the corner of my mind. Abandoning the coffee, I rush out of the kitchen and pad down the hall, urgency filling my veins. The house is still quiet, nothing but the steady beat of my heart filling my ears as I hurry toward the door at the end of the hall. I'd forgotten all about the locked room in the house... until now.

Testing the handle, I'm hardly surprised to find it locked. *Think, Mia. Think.* An idea slams into me and I take off, hurrying upstairs, careful not to make a sound. I tiptoe down the hall, my heart racing in my chest as I reach Cade's room. Twisting the handle, I slip inside and close the door behind me. Fear wraps around my throat and I force myself to take small even breaths as I fight against the urge to run.

I scan the room, shuddering when my eyes graze the bed sitting proudly in the center. But I didn't come here to reminisce. I came here to find something. *Where would I keep it?* My eyes flit from the dresser to the desk, landing on a small leather box. Too easy, I tell myself, but I make for it anyway. Bitter disappointment clings to me as I flip the lid and find nothing but an array of cufflinks. I pull out the drawer, rummaging through Cade's things, but there's nothing that resembles a key.

Dammit.

Moving over to the dresser, I open the top drawer and reach inside, feeling between Cade's clothes for any sign of... bingo. My fingers graze something smooth and I pluck out the small box. Blood roars in my ears as I flip the lid open and a small silver key stares back at me.

Leaving everything as I found it, I quietly exit Cade's room and make my way back down to the locked door. Crouching down, I jam the key into the hole and give it a little wiggle. It slides into place, the door clicks open, and I slip inside.

It's an office of some sort. A big oak desk fills one corner, matching bookshelves lining the walls. There's a leather wingback chair facing the desk and sideboard perpendicular to it. The air feels musty, as if it's been trapped inside for too long with nowhere to go.

The sun pours in through the blinds, enough that I can see without turning on the light. Old musty textbooks line the shelves much like the ones in the town hall archives and in my father's office.

Many are labelled with Roman numerals on the spines but no titles hinting at what lies inside. I pull one out, almost choking on the cloud of dust that comes with it. "The Odyssey," I say, running my hands over the embossed title. It's a collector's edition, old and worn but still beautiful. Sliding it back in its place, I choose the next one. *The Iliad*.

I can't imagine Cade has a penchant for ancient Greek poetry, but perhaps the men who came before him did. His father. And his before that.

Returning the book to its rightful place, I move onto the lower shelves. A photograph catches my eye, and I pluck the frame up, studying it.

"Gregory Kingsley," I whisper. There's no mistaking Cade's father standing with a group of young men outside Gravestone Hall. Same piercing stare and thin smile. I pick out a younger Marcus Easton and Phillip Cargill. Marcus is smiling at something someone off camera is saying. I get the impression he doesn't smile much anymore.

I wonder what happened to them, shuddering at the answer.

They became Quinctus.

And one day, Bexley, Alex, Brandon, and Tim will do the same.

A world dominated by misogyny and power. An organization full of dark deeds and depravity.

People aren't born bad. They're shaped by their environment, by their childhood and the people around them. Cade is his father's son. It's why Phillip had my father kill him. Because he was a threat to everything Quinctus wants to achieve. Because he took it too far…

Just like Cade.

I walk around the desk and sit down, staring at the room, imagining what it must be like to step into the shoes of an Electi. To be initiated and tested and broken… until you reemerge as someone new. Someone capable of exerting their power, of hurting others… of killing without thought.

I've watched the others. Brandon, Channing, Alex, even Tim. They obey, they execute their roles as instructed. But not like Cade.

He thrived on it. He lived for it.

He got off on it.

That kind of malice and cruelty isn't just there inside someone… it's ingrained, instilled and nurtured.

It's mirrored.

Something about the idea of Gregory Kingsley molding his son into a monster makes my heart ache.

I test the top drawer in the desk, surprised when it rolls open. There's nothing much of interest, until a small black bound diary catches my eye.

Retrieving it, I unlace the leather bindings and flip it open. The handwritten scrawl is difficult to decipher, but my eyes quickly pick out words.

Gravestone.

Quinctus.

Electi.

Power.

Future.

Strong.

I turn back to the first page and find an inscription in the corner. "To my son. Remember, power is not given to you. You have to take it."

The barely legible signature could easily be Gregory. Or maybe it isn't. But the dread snaking through me tells me it is.

I sink back into the chair, letting out a small breath, when something else catches my eye. It's a bigger journal, tucked at the back of the desk.

Pulling it out, I lay it on the desk and flip it open, gasping when I read the inside inscription.

Cade Kingsley.

Could it be... no. I slam it shut. Cade might be a monster, but this, reading his personal journal, still feels like a gross invasion of privacy. But before I can stop myself, I flip it open again and start reading.

When I'm done, silent tears streak down my cheeks, my heart coiled tight. Until now, I hadn't really considered anything about Cade's past, his childhood or family life. And although this doesn't change things, it does fill in some missing pieces of the puzzle...

"Mia?" Bexley appears in the doorway, his hair all messed up with sleep. "What are you doing in here?"

Quickly drying my eyes, I stutter, "I noticed it was locked a couple of weeks ago and wondered what was hiding in here."

"Find anything?" He comes inside.

"Not really." I gently slide the journals back into the drawer and close it. "Just a bunch of old musty books."

"How are you feeling?" The unspoken words hang between us.

"I'm okay."

"Do you want to talk about it?"

My lips thin as I shake my head. Talking about it is the last thing I want to do. But there is something on the tip of my tongue.

"You looked comfortable last night, with Phillip and his friends."

"Shit, Mia." He lowers his head, rubbing the back of his neck, but his eyes don't stray from mine. "It's a role, baby. Good acting."

"Is it?"

Bexley comes closer, until he's looming over me. He holds out his hand and I take it, unable to resist the magnetic pull between us. A shiver runs down my spine at his touch. My body remembers. It always remembers.

"It's all for you," he says gruffly, pulling me to my feet. "There isn't a single thing I wouldn't do to keep you safe. To make you happy. Tell me what to do to fix this." Sheer desperation coats his words, breaking something deep inside me.

"I don't know that you can," I confess. "I feel like I'm losing myself."

"It's just trauma, Mia. Things are so fucked-up, I know that. I know how hard it is—"

"Shh." I lay my head on his chest. "I don't want to do this, not now." Exhaustion rolls through me. "Make me forget, Bexley. Make it all go away."

"Yeah?" His brow arches.

"Yeah." I step into him, running my hands up his bare chest.

"Fuck." He shudders, a low grumble of pleasure emanating from his throat. "You slay me, Mia." His hand curves around the back of my neck, guiding my face right to where he wants me. Our lips meet in a soft, tender kiss. But it isn't soft I want. I need him to consume me. To fill me so deep that there isn't a sliver of room left for anything else.

"I need you," I cry, clawing at his shoulders.

"Let me get you back to our room—"

"No." My voice cracks. "Here. I want you here."

"Here?" He searches my eyes, his own filled with doubt.

I press my lips together, nodding. Inching back out of his hold, I perch on the edge of the desk, pushing my cardigan off my shoulders and leaving me in nothing but the nightshirt Bexley wrestled me into last night.

Slowly, I start unbuttoning the material until the cool air brushes my breasts.

"Jesus." He sucks in a sharp breath, running a hand over his jaw. "You're sure?"

I nod again, popping the final button and letting the material fall down my arms. "I don't want you to treat me like glass, Bexley. I need you to make me feel." I need it to hurt.

His eyes darken with liquid lust, the hunger making my core throb.

There isn't much Bexley can do to fix this... to fix us... but he can give me this.

He can give me an escape.

"And after?" He stalks toward me. "Will we pretend like it never happened again?"

"I don't want to talk about after. I need this, Bexley. Please..."

Torment glitters in his eyes. He doesn't want to do this, to let me use sex as a bargaining chip in our relationship. But it's all I have right now.

"You keep saying I'm yours. Prove it," I taunt, victory filling my veins when he shoves his big body into mine, caging me against the desk.

Bexley slides his hand to my throat, holding me there as he leans in, ghosting his lips over my jaw. "You're playing with fire, Mia."

His body vibrates, and I realize I'm not the only one holding on by a frayed thread. Bexley is cracking under the pressure too.

He needs this as much as I do.

I lift my chin in defiance and look right into his eyes. "Maybe I want to get burned."

20

BEXLEY

Mia wraps her legs against my waist, her heels pressing into my lower back and aligning our bodies, a gasp of air rushing out of both of us at the sensation.

I knew something wasn't right when I woke up and found she wasn't there. But I wasn't expecting this. Her in here. In *his* domain.

Not once have I been in this room or even seen the door open since I moved in, and I can't say I haven't been curious about what's inside. But it's exactly as I suspected: an office full of old books, just like Phillip's.

I'm desperate to discover the secrets that might be hidden in the pages of this room, but not right now.

Right now, the only thing I need is her.

"Mia," I groan when she rolls her hips against me.

"Show me I'm yours, Bexley. Show everyone. Right here, right now."

"Fuck."

My head spins as I kiss her, my hands roaming her beautiful body, unable to decide where I want to stop and unable to get enough. My lips drop down her neck as I cup her heavy breast, pinching her nipple between my fingers.

"Bexley," she sighs, her head rolling back in pleasure, her back arching, offering herself up to me.

Hungrily, I lower down and kiss and lick both of her breasts as she moans for more.

"Oh God, please," she cries when I suck a patch of sensitive skin into my mouth until I know I've left my mark behind. "Bex, please," she moans, her chest heaving, her nipples pert and begging for attention.

"Are you wet for me, Mia?" I ask, my lips brushing her sensitive peak with each word.

"Yes," she hisses, rolling her hips teasingly against me, tempting me to check for myself.

Finally, I pull her nipple into my mouth, sucking deep until her cries of pleasure echo around the room. I have no idea if anyone else is awake yet, but if they are then there's no mistaking what's going on in here.

I glance over my shoulder at the door I left open.

"W-what?"

"Nothing, baby," I say, switching sides. "Just making sure no other motherfucker can see you like this. You're mine, Mia. All mine."

Her head falls back once more, and I lick a trail all the way up to her jaw. "I love you, Mia. You're gonna get through this."

"No talking."

I nod, pushing my boxers over my hips and exposing my solid length, but before I pull her panties aside and slide straight into her addictive pussy, a thought hits me.

Brushing my lips over her cheek, I bring them to a stop at her ear. "I want you to suck me."

"Bex." Her needy moan fills the room and makes my cock weep to feel her lips around it.

She lowers her legs and slips from the edge of the desk, ready to sink to the floor.

"Not here," I instruct.

"W-w—"

Releasing her, I stalk around the large mahogany desk, spin the chair so it's facing the window, giving her enough space, and I sink down.

"Right here."

I send up a silent *fuck you* to the person this chair belongs to as I spread my thighs wide and wrap my fingers around my cock while I wait for her. She looks around before glancing at the window for a beat. But in only seconds, she floats toward me and sinks to her knees at my feet.

"I think the power might be going to your head, Bexley Easton," she warns, running her palms up my thighs, making my cock jerk at her innocent touch alone.

I stare down at her large hazel eyes, my heart thundering in my chest as I reach out and thread my fingers through her wild mess of hair. "Right now, baby, I think you love it."

Pulling her forward, I brush the tip of my cock over her lips before she parts them and allows me access. "Fuuuck, baby. So good, so fucking good." My hips lift from the chair involuntarily as the heat of her mouth surrounds me and my entire body locks up with pleasure.

My fingers tighten in her hair, reminding her that I can take over at any moment as she pulls back from my length, licks around the tip and sinks back down. "Fuck, I'm not going to last."

Her eyes find mine while her mouth is still full of me, and I see the challenge within them as she takes in even more of me.

I hit the back of her throat before she slowly pulls back once more, but she doesn't release me before she sinks back down, making my entire body tingle with my impending release.

"I'm gonna come down your throat, baby. You ready for that?" I warn her as my balls draw up.

She nods, sucks harder, andI swear to God, she grazes me with her teeth, but the thought is instantly wiped out as my release slams into me. My hips surge forward with such intensity that Mia chokes on my length, but still, she doesn't pull back. Not until I'm done.

Wasting no time, I stand, pulling her to my feet as I go, wrap my hand around the back of her neck, and slam her lips on mine, dipping my tongue inside her mouth and tasting myself on her.

With a growl, I bend and lift her so she's got no choice but to wrap her legs around me. I walk to the end of the desk and lower her ass to the edge as I continue to kiss her, showing her everything I feel for her without using the words she doesn't want to hear.

Finally, I pull back, press my hand to her chest, and encourage her to lay back on the cool wood.

"Bexley?" she breathes, her brows pulling together, but the sparkling in her eyes tells me that despite the concern in her voice, she's fully on board with my plan.

Dropping to my knees, I spread her legs wide and dive for her glistening pussy. The second my tongue connects with her sensitive skin, her taste explodes in my mouth and I eat her out as if I haven't had food in a month.

She writhes on the desk, my hands gripping her hips tightly to keep her in place as I alternate between sucking on her clit and spearing my tongue deep inside her. Her moans and cries for more get louder and louder the closer she gets to release and the grip she has on my hair burns, but it doesn't stop me. If anything, the pain only makes me hard once more.

"Come, Mia. Come all over my face. Right now," I growl against her swollen clit.

"Oh God... God. Oh my God, Bexley," she screams, her back arching from the desk as she rides out each wave of pleasure that assaults her body.

I pull back before she's finished, kick off my boxers, and run the head of my cock through her wetness before sinking inside her still-pulsating pussy.

"Oh shit, Bex," she cries as aftershocks from her release surge through her.

"So fucking good, baby," I groan as I bottom out in her.

I slam into her, sending her sliding across the desk, but I pull her back, dragging her ass over the edge to get an even better angle.

Reaching over her body, I wrap my hand around her throat. Her swallow ripples against my palms. "Mine, Mia."

"Yours," she breathes.

I fucking love this feeling. I'm obsessed with how electric it always is when we connect, and I crave it more and more, but I can't deny that there's not a part of me now concerned that she's using it as an escape. Using me to forget for a few minutes.

I want her to use me, of course, I do. I want to be her fucking everything. But I can't shift the nagging question in my head of what happens after. Things have changed between us since the explosion, and I'm terrified about what that might mean for us in the long run.

I hold her eyes as I continue to pound into her, trying to show her just how much she means to me and hoping like hell she can read what I'm silently telling her, how desperate I am for her to come back to me.

Something moving outside the window catches my eye, and my head flies up to see what it was.

Despite drowning in pleasure, Mia notices what's holding my attention. "What? What is it?" She tries to twist to look out the window, but my grip on her throat tightens.

"It's nothing. Just a bird."

Her eyes narrow on me as if she knows I'm lying, but one roll of my hips and she seems to let it go.

It wasn't a bird.

Pushing it aside, I focus back on her, on the insane feeling of her sucking me deep into her body as sweat coats our skin and our moans of pleasure fill the room.

"You're mine, Mia. Mine. Mine. *Mine*," I tell her, circling my thumb over her clit until she detonates.

"Bexley."

Two seconds later and I can't hold back any longer. My cock jerks, filling her with hot jets of cum as I fold over her and find her lips. "I love you, Mia. I love you so fucking much."

"T-thank you," she says in response, making my heart tumble in my chest. "I needed that."

Swallowing down the emotion that clogs my throat, I brush my lips over hers. "You're welcome, baby. Anytime."

"We should probably..." she trails off but looks to the still open door once I release her from our kiss.

"Hmm... we should loc—" I rub my already hardening cock against her.

"Again?"

"With you, baby, always."

She looks up at me and gives me a small smile, showing me a glimpse of the old Mia, as she whispers, "Do your worst."

WHEN we finally leave Cade's office, we've well and truly christened every surface. Each and every time I slid into her in there, I felt like I claimed a little bit more of his life.

I still don't know if I actually want it. But hell, if me having it means that he never gets to live this life again then I'm all for it.

We walk into the kitchen hand in hand, both looking thoroughly fucked with hickeys and scratches on our skin and bright red cheeks to find Channing drinking a protein shake, dressed in his workout clothes and also covered in sweat.

"You been out for a run?" I ask him as he runs his eyes over us with an amused expression on his face.

"Yeah, just got back. It's fucking cold out there this morning."

I glance to the doors behind him. "You run through the forest?"

"Don't worry, I didn't look for long." A smirk plays on his lips.

Mia turns into my side and slams her head into my chest.

"Appreciate it, man," I say, dropping my lips to the top of Mia's head.

"I'm going to shower," she whispers before slipping away and rushing from the room.

Channing watches her leave before his eyes come back to me. "How is she?"

Running my hand through my hair, I turn toward the coffee maker. "Same."

"Last night was fucked up."

I look down at my busted knuckles and can't help but agree. "What's your gut feeling about Ash?"

Channing lowers his shake and turns to lean back against the counter. "I don't know. Before I'd have said he was a lying prick. But there's something different about him. I don't know. It might all be bullshit. He's always been a twisted fuck, but he's never really been a liar."

"Yeah," I mutter, copying his stance as the coffee maker jumps into action. "We can't continue like this. Something's gotta give. Before it's Mia."

21

MIA

"You're following me. Why?" I step in front of Ashton as he pretends to be distracted by the noticeboard in the hall.

"Not following. Call it... extra security."

My brows hit my hairline. "You're trying to protect me now? You do know that we're not friends, right?"

"Mia, give a guy a break."

"I'm not doing this," I mutter, spinning on my heel and taking off in the other direction. I'm meeting Sasha at the coffee shop just inside the building. It's only a short walk, one I insisted I could make myself.

Seems Ashton has other ideas.

He falls into step beside me. "I think you're right."

"Excuse me?" My head whips up to meet his grim expression.

"I don't think you're crazy, Mia. I think Kingsley is... fuck," he breathes, glancing around. "Can we talk about this somewhere else?"

"I'm meeting Sasha for coffee."

"Can't you unmeet her?"

"I'm not going anywhere with you. For all I know, you're working—"

"I get it." His hands go up. "I'm an asshole. I get off on the power, I enjoy being at the top. But I never signed up for..." He leans in, whispering the words. "Cold-blooded murder."

"You've killed people," I deadpan. If Cade made Bexley do it, there's no way Ashton hasn't too.

A flicker of something flashes over his face. "It's not the same."

"Isn't it?" I let out a heavy sigh. "Look, I need to go—"

"I heard something. A conversation between Phillip and Lincoln Kingsley."

"Cade's uncle?"

He nods. "Ten minutes, that's all I ask."

I'm torn. On the one hand, I want to know what he knows. But on the other, I don't trust Ashton Moore in the slightest.

"Fine." Curiosity wins out. "Ten minutes. But I'm texting Sasha."

"You should. Someone should know where you are at all times." He hesitates, rubbing his jaw. "In fact, I'd have thought Easton would be here."

"He's busy." My teeth grind as I type out a quick message to Sasha and motion for Ashton to follow me down the hall.

"Q?"

"Yeah."

"Man, they've already got their hooks into him." He holds the door open for me and I slip outside. "You want to keep a close eye on your guy, Mia. If he gets in too deep..."

"What choice does he have? He's Electi. It's his birthright."

"Maybe so. But I've watched him. He isn't cut out for this life."

His words twist something inside me. I wish it were true, but there isn't any way out for me and Bexley. He was brought to Gravestone for a reason. Marcus and Phillip wanted him to take the power from Cade. They wanted this. Maybe they didn't plan for it to go down the way it did, but the goal was the same.

Finding a bench in plain sight of everyone, I sit. Ashton joins me, careful to keep a reasonable distance between us.

"What did you overhear?" I ask, getting right to it.

"What do you know about Lincoln?"

"I know that he runs things for Q in another town. That he wanted Cade protected."

"But that's just the thing. Cade barely knows the guy."

My brows furrow. "He doesn't?"

"He talked to me once, about his old man and his uncle. Said his dad never forgave Q for sending his brother away."

"Sending him away?"

"Yeah. Apparently, Lincoln didn't take too kindly to growing up in Gregory's shadow."

"What else did he say?"

"Not a lot." Ashton shrugs. "Cade isn't one to talk about the heavy stuff."

"Did he ever talk about his childhood?"

"No, why?" It's his turn to frown.

"No reason."

"What aren't you telling me?" He studies my face.

"Nothing. You were saying you overheard Phillip and Lincoln?"

"Yeah." Ashton runs a hand over his head and down the back of his neck. "It didn't sound like a friendly meeting. I didn't catch much, but they were definitely talking about Cade."

"You think Lincoln knows where he is?"

"I think we both know where he is, Mia. Cade is close by." He glances around, and my heart ratchets.

But I'm safe here.

I'm safe.

And strangely, I do feel safe with Ashton. Not that I'll ever tell him. But there's a silent truce between us. And he believes me.

There's a huge relief in that. In knowing that not everyone thinks I've lost my mind.

I can't deny that it stings that it's Ashton sitting here, though, and not Bexley.

"Yeah," I whisper. He's right, I feel it in my bones. Maybe I have been seeing him in places he doesn't exist, but it's only because I feel him here still. Cade never left.

He won't until he's fulfilled whatever vendetta he has.

"Have you tried to talk to Phillip?" I ask.

Ashton snorts. "You underestimate our relationship. My stepdad," he spits the word, "might love my mom, but his feelings are less than warm toward me."

"You're an easy person to hate," I say honestly.

But Ashton barks a laugh. "You know, in another life, I think you and me could have been friends, maybe even—"

"Don't even go there. Just because we've called this weird truce for now, doesn't mean I'll ever forget what you did to me and Bexley."

"Noted." His expression hardens, but I feel none of his usual malice.

"We're missing something," he adds. "I don't know what, but the way Lincoln was talking to Phillip... I don't like it. He sounded... scared."

"Lincoln?"

"No." Ashton's eyes meet mine, and a chill runs down my spine. "Phillip."

CHANNING AND SASHA give me a ride back to the house. Bexley is still off doing whatever it is he's doing.

The car is quiet, and I sense tension between them. "Did something happen?" I ask.

Sasha glances back at me and grimaces. "Brandon."

"He found out?"

"He knows... something. He and Channing got into it."

"We didn't get into it," he grumbles. "We just had a few words."

"But you can tell him now," I say. "Come clean and explain that you want to be together."

"You'd think?" she grumbles, pressing her head against the window.

"I'll handle Brandon." Channing squeezes her knee.

"Have you spoken to Bexley?" I change the subject.

"He's fine, don't worry about Easton."

But that's the thing, I do worry. I worry about him being at Phillip's beck and call. I worry that he'll go too far and I'll lose him.

I can't lose him.

I might not know what we are anymore, but he's still the only guy my heart has ever beat for. If I lose him too, I won't survive it.

Digging my cell phone out of my bag, I check my messages. But there's nothing. Trepidation trickles through me as I watch the scenery roll by, and I drop my head back against the headrest, closing my eyes.

My fingers automatically go to my chest, right over my heart where that hideous brand is. It's like it has roots, coiling through me and wrapping around my organs. So long as it's there, I'll always be Cade's prosapia. I'll always belong to him.

Anger surges through me like wildfire. Anger at my father and Phillip and Marcus. Anger at them for standing by and letting this happen. Maybe they didn't know what he was truly capable of, maybe they hoped I could change him, soften his sharp jagged edges, but they knew. They knew he was Gregory Kingsley's son. They knew enough to give me to him like a lamb to the slaughter and see how things played out.

A decision I will never forgive them for.

The Electi house looms in the distance, only fueling the fire inside me. I'm a prisoner here. Cade is gone, but I'm still captive.

I need to do something, anything, to take back even an ounce of control.

An idea springs to mind, and the second Channing's car rolls to a stop, I leap out and take off toward the house. The security guards greet me, but I ignore them, blowing through the house like a whirlwind. I hurry to the kitchen and retrieve everything I need before retreating to my bedroom. Not the one I've been sleeping in with Bexley. *My* room. The one they gave me to recover in.

Closing the door, I slip into the adjoining bathroom and place the knife down on the counter and then strip out of my hoodie and t-shirt.

The brand taunts me, the skin still ugly and raised. My fingers ghost over it, and a shudder runs through me. They branded me. Marked me like some possession, something less than human. How dare they?

Snatching up the knife, my hand trembles as I bring it to my chest.

"Mia?" Sasha calls from the hall. "Is everything okay?"

"I'm fine," I yell back, my voice surprisingly calm for what I'm about to do. "I'm going to take a shower."

"Okay, if you need anything just let me know."

"Thanks." I wait for her leave and inhale a shuddering breath.

The tip of the knife feels cool on my skin, sending a tremor through me. Gently I drag the sharp edge over the marred skin. It stings, but there's a burst of relief with every drag of the blade. Beads of blood pool, spilling down my chest as I scratch the brand away, cutting and carving until there's nothing left but bloody flesh. A sob crawls up my throat, the pain setting in, dousing the adrenaline coursing through my veins.

The knife clatters to the floor, silent tears rolling down my cheeks. My chest burns as I grip the edge of the counter, sucking in ragged breath after ragged breath. I've made a mess, a raw, bloody mess, but I feel freer than I have since hearing my name called at the Eligere. Quinctus might call the shots, they might pull all the strings, but they don't get to take my heart or soul.

"Mia?" Bexley's concerned voice fills the room, and I still, my eyes wide with fear.

"Just a minute." God, I need to clean myself up... I need to—

"Mia?" His eyes catch mine in the mirror. "What the fuck?"

"I-I couldn't... I had to..."

"Fuck," he rasps, coming over to me and pulling me around. "You're hurt." His eyes flick to the knife, the muscles in his jaw popping.

"I had to..." I'm weary, exhaustion hitting me hard. "I couldn't wear it for a second longer."

Bexley leans around me and grabs a towel, running it under the faucet. Then he presses it to my chest, cleaning up my jagged handiwork. "Shit, baby, this will scar."

"Better a scar than a brand," I murmur, my eyes clenching in agony as he carefully wipes the blood away.

"You didn't say anything."

"Because it wasn't something I planned until I knew."

Skin clean, Bexley places the towel down and ghosts his thumb over my gaping flesh. "You might need stitches."

"No." I shake my head. "It'll heal. Just clean it and put a dressing on it."

"I'll need to find a first aid kit." He runs a hand down his face, his features hardened.

I nod. "I'll wait."

Cupping the back of my neck, Bexley leans in and kisses me. "I'm sorry, Mia. I'm so fucking sorry."

Then he slips out of the room and I'm alone once more.

22

BEXLEY

I close Mia's bedroom door behind me and suck in a shuddering breath. The image of her bloody, cut-up chest is burned into the back of my eyes.

My heart pounds and my fists clench.

That fucking cunt is doing this and he's not even here.

My need to hurt him, my need to watch his blood seep out of his skin is becoming harder and harder to ignore. I want to put a gun to his fucking head and torture him, just like his memory is torturing my girl.

I give myself five seconds before I push from the door and make my way down to the kitchen where there's a first aid kit.

Mulligan is in the kitchen preparing our dinner at the stove when I drag open the cupboard door and drop the box onto the counter.

"Is everything okay, Mr. Easton?" he asks, concern pulling his brows together.

"Y-yes," I force out through gritted teeth as the mess Mia has made of her chest fills my mind again.

I get it. I totally get it. There have been plenty of times I've wanted to do something similar. But carving the brand from my chest won't get me out of any of this. Sadly, it runs through my blood. A brand means nothing, really.

"Mia's just cut her finger. Nothing to worry about."

Making sure I have everything I need, I leave him to whatever he's preparing for dinner and head back up.

I invite myself back into her room and find her sitting in the middle of her bed, her face pale, the tired circles around her eyes dark and her hair hanging limply around her shoulders. She looks like a ghost of her former self, and I hate it.

I want her sparkle, her zest for life, her need to fight back.

I can't cope with watching her drown, because it feels like I'm going down with her. I feel like I'm failing.

She's clutching a towel to her chest, the blood once again pooling around the wound.

"Mia," I breathe, desperately wanting to fix all of this, to make everything right but knowing I can't.

Rushing over, I open one of the wipes and start cleaning her up again. No words are said between us as I place the bandage over her chest and smooth down the tape, but I feel her pain, her desperation.

"Where were you today?" she finally whispers when I lower my hand from her body.

"With Q. They assured me that they've got this Cade situation under control."

Phillip and Harrison looked me dead in the eyes and promised me that things were in order. Now all I can do is repeat that message and hope like fuck they're telling the truth.

"They've got him?"

"They didn't give me details."

"Well, security haven't left, so I assume they're lying."

"They want us all safe, Mia."

"Pfft." She rips her eyes from mine and looks toward the window. "I've never felt so unsafe. So weak... So vulnerable."

"I'm trying here, Mia. I'm trying to be everything you need."

"Then believe me when I tell you I see him," she erupts. "Ashton does, so why don't you?"

My chin drops at her outburst. "You've spoken to Ashton again?"

Her eyes hold mine, something akin to her old determination flashing through them as her jaw pops.

"Don't even think about lying to me," I warn.

"He came to talk to me earlier."

"Motherfuc—"

"He's on our side, Bexley."

My teeth grind at her words, my muscles burning with my need to go and find him and show him exactly how I feel about him going out of his way to talk to Mia behind my back.

"Bullshit, he's on Cade's."

"He's the only one who believes me, Bexley. The only one who doesn't make me feel like I'm losing my fucking mind."

Climbing from the bed, I begin pacing back and forth, tugging at my hair until it burns. "Of course he does. He's playing you. He's getting you on side so he can hand you over to Cade."

"No, he's not," she barks, scrambling from the bed and pulling a shirt on.

"So you actually trust him now? Ashton?" My heart cracks. "Fucking unbelievable."

"You don't trust me, Bex. I tell you what I see, what I feel, and you wave it off as me going crazy. Cade has been here." She throws her arm back, pointing to her bathroom. "He's watching me, and none of you want to believe it."

"There's no evidence," I say, beginning to feel like a broken record. "I want to believe you, I want to, baby. But how can I when you say he's been inside this house? A house that has security crawling all over it? And there's been no sign of him on the CCTV."

"Because I'm telling you he was here. Fuck the evidence, Bex. I am telling you. *I'm* evidence enough, no?"

We stare at each other, our chests heaving, her eyes pleading with me to just say I believe her, but the rational part of my brain screaming that it's just not true. He can't have been here.

My lips part to say something when a soft knock sounds out on the bedroom door and Sasha's head pokes inside two seconds later.

"Dinner is ready, you guys coming?"

"We'll be right there," Mia says without breaking her stare with me.

"Okay," Sasha breathes before disappearing once more.

"If you don't believe me, don't trust me, then what exactly is this, Bex? Why are you even here?"

"Don't do that, Mia. I love you and you know I do."

"So support me."

"What the hell do you think I've been doing? Why do you think I took over Tim's position? All of this is to fucking support you, to protect you."

"I-it's not enough." Her voice cracks, making my chest grow tight.

"I will make it enough, baby. Me and you, we're it."

"We'll see," she says sadly, turning her back on me and walking toward the bedroom door.

I let her go, my shoulders sagging in defeat, disappointment flooding me.

Spinning around, I stare out of the window, running my eyes over the array of orange that's flooding the forest beyond as we get further into fall.

I once again search the tree line. Shadows dance and move, but not one of them looks like a person hiding, watching, waiting to strike.

My stomach growls and I turn once more, my eyes landing on the knife still coated in Mia's blood on the bathroom floor. I blow out a long breath, knowing that she'd rather carve her own skin off than remain in this life.

When is this going to end?

DINNER IS tense as we sit beside each other. Sasha shoots us concerned glances every few minutes, but as she sits between her brother and Channing—both of whom are wearing murderous expressions on their faces—I can't help but think she's got enough issues of her own right now to be worrying about us.

As always, Mulligan's chili is incredible, but we all—aside from Alex, who seems oblivious to the tension around him—just pick at it, our minds too consumed with this nightmare to worry about eating.

A bang from upstairs startles Mia, her fork clattering to the table. "What was that?" she asks in a panic.

"Just a door," Alex answers absentmindedly. "It's getting pretty windy out."

I look out the doors, seeing the trees swaying in the wind, and tell myself that he's right, but it doesn't help Mia relax beside me.

Reaching out, I squeeze her thigh. "Everything's okay, baby. We're all here with you," I whisper in her ear in the hope it reassures her, but she remains tense and totally forgets about eating any more food, instead pushing her plate away from her.

"Shall we hang out tonight, watch a movie or something?" I ask, trying to come up with something, aside from getting stupid drunk, that might distract everyone.

Mia scoffs beside me. "You want us all to watch a movie?" she asks, as if the mere suggestion is absurd. I guess in the current situation, it might be, but I'm coming up short with ideas right now.

"It'll be nice to do something normal," I say with a shrug.

"I've got loads of work to do. I've got papers due." She pushes her chair out and takes a step toward the door.

"Okay, well, we can do our econ assignment then, maybe."

"Yeah, whatever."

She takes off, and after moving our plates to the side, I follow.

Instead of going to my room where we've both been sleeping since the night she thought she saw Cade, I spot her disappear into her own once again.

"I'll grab my stuff and join you in here then?" I ask from the doorway.

"Whatever." Her voice is weak. She sounds exhausted and utterly defeated.

"Okay, I'll just be a minute."

I take off with the intention of grabbing my books and laptop and getting some work done. The last thing we need in all of this is to fall behind, but the second I step inside my room, a chill runs down my spine.

My window is open. I know for a fact I never left it that way.

My heart rate picks up, a weird feeling racing through me.

He was here.

Taking two more steps into the room, I get a look at my bed and my world falls out from beneath me.

The bloody knife that I saw in Mia's bathroom before we went for dinner is sitting on my bed, with her Electi pendant that she hasn't worn since the moment she woke up in the hospital sitting beside it.

Along with a piece of paper.

I'm coming.

Backing away, my entire body trembles.

He's here.

He really has been here.

Spinning on my heels, I run from my room and crash through Mia's door. She's sitting in the middle of her bed with books around her.

"What's wrong?" she asks when she looks up.

"Pack a bag," I demand, my voice not sounding like my own.

"W-what?"

"Pack a bag. Grab whatever you can. We're leaving."

"Have you lost your—"

"Pack a fucking bag, Mia. Do it right now."

I run from the room and shout for the guys, who immediately race up with stairs. Sasha goes to help Mia as I send Brandon and Alex to the security room to see if there's anything, and I take Channing with me to my room.

"What the fuck?" he barks the second he sees what's on my bed.

"I think she's been right this whole time."

"The bang?" he asks.

"I never leave my window open, and that knife was on her bathroom floor before I came down for dinner."

"Why was that—"

I shake my head at him, cutting off his question. That's not important right now.

Ripping my closet doors open, I pull down a duffle bag and start stuffing things inside.

"What the hell are you doing?"

"I'm taking her away from here. She's not safe."

"Where the hell are you—" He cuts his words off when I pin him with a look and then glance around the room.

He could be listening to everything. If he's been getting inside undetected, then the whole place could be bugged.

Throwing my bag over my shoulder, I storm from the room. "Are you ready?" I bark, standing in the doorway of Mia's room.

"She is," Sasha says, thrusting a bag at me, following orders without question.

"You need to tell me what the hell is going on."

"I will, I promise but we need to leave," I tell her, my voice not allowing any room for question.

"Okay," she breathes, wrapping her arms around Sasha, clearly sensing that we're not going to be coming back for a while. "I'll call you," she promises her before taking a step toward me.

I wrap my free arm around her shoulders and guide her out.

Alex and Brandon emerge the second we get to the bottom of the stairs.

"Anything?"

"No, nothing."

"Fuck. FUCK," I boom.

"Bexley?" Mia's shaky voice helps to calm my anger a little.

"Let's go. I need you out of here right now."

"Wait," Channing calls, forcing me to look over my shoulder.

He doesn't say any more, but I can read his unspoken thoughts.

"You're right. Come on."

I drag Mia down to the security room so we can wait until it's dark.

He's here.

He's watching.

If we leave now...

23

MIA

We leave in the middle of the night, under the cover of darkness. Bexley keeps the headlights off as we drive away from the house.

Since he burst into my room and told me to pack a bag, we haven't really talked about Cade. We haven't really talked about anything. He's in full protector mode, his brows furrowed and jaw clenched, completely aware of his surroundings. I might find it sexy if it weren't for the fact that he only now believes me.

I stare out of the window, watching the shadows roll by. I have no idea where we're heading or what the plan is, and I'm too exhausted to argue.

The second we're out of the gates, Bexley gently applies the brakes and waits.

"What are you doing?" I ask, my heart racing in my chest. "Shouldn't we—"

"We're good," he says, glancing around. "Security are watching."

"A trap. This is a trap."

"He won't fall for it. He's too clever." Bexley's tone sends a chill through me.

His cell phone starts vibrating, and he grabs it. "Yeah… okay. I want updates." Bexley hangs up and drops his cell into its holster.

"It's clear." He flicks the headlights on, and the engine rumbles beneath us as he steps on the gas.

"So where are we going?" I ask, barely meeting his dark gaze.

"Somewhere safe."

"Do Q know?"

His jaw pops. "I don't think we can trust Q."

I scoff at that, and he slides his eyes to mine.

"I'm sorry."

"Sorry for not believing me? Or sorry for trusting Q?" I barely keep the sarcasm out of my voice.

"Fuck, Mia. I know I messed up. But they said—"

"It doesn't matter." The words gut me. I needed Bexley four weeks ago. I needed him when I felt like I was losing my mind, and he chose Q over me.

"Mia, baby, I—"

"I'm tired," I whisper. "Wake me up when we're there." Slipping my hands into my hoodie, I fold them around my waist and get comfortable, hoping sleep will come easy.

WHEN I WAKE, the fall sun is peeking through the clouds and Bexley is pulling off the main road down a dirt track leading to a lake I don't recognize.

"What is this place?" I ask around a yawn.

"Somewhere off the grid."

"How did you find it?" My eyes run over the small cabin. It has a wraparound porch with a swing chair overlooking the shimmering lake and surrounded by a blanket of trees. It's beautiful. The perfect romantic hideaway.

If only things were that simple.

Bexley runs a hand down his jaw, releasing a heavy sigh. "James."

"You called James?" I balk.

"Yeah. We obviously can't trust Phillip or Q, and I didn't know what else to do."

"Did you tell him about..."

"I gave him the CliffsNotes version."

"And you trust him?"

"He got out. He made a deal with the devil to keep his family out of Q's clutches. I think we can trust him a whole lot more than anyone else right now."

"What about your grandfather?"

"What about him?" Bexley releases another steady breath. "Come on, let's go inside and take a look around."

The air is thick between us, so I'm grateful to step out of the car and inhale a deep breath. Bexley gets our bags out of the trunk and motions me to follow him to the cabin.

"There should be a key, right..." He reaches for the lock box hanging at the side of the door and punches in the code, dipping his hand inside. "Bingo." Bexley retrieves the key and unlocks the door. Dropping the bag to the floor, he rummages inside, pulling out a gun.

"What the hell?" I gasp.

"It's just for emergencies. Wait here while I check out inside." He disappears, calling my name a few seconds later.

Grabbing our bags, I enter the cabin.

"Come here," he says, and like a moth to a flame, I go to him.

I'm still angry. It vibrates inside me like a living thing. But when Bexley takes the bags from my hands and pulls me into his arms, I let him. Because despite everything, I still need him.

"I'm sorry," he breathes. "I'm so fucking sorry."

I slide my hands up his chest, fisting his hoodie. "I told you... I told you I was see—"

"Shh, Mia." He holds me tighter, crushing me to his chest and burying his face into the crook of my neck.

Silence engulfs us as we stand there, wrapped up in each other, the weight of reality pressing down on us.

"I let you down." Bexley finally lifts his remorseful gaze to mine.

"You didn't want to believe it."

"No, but I should have believed you. You're my girl, Mia. You'll always be my girl."

"I still don't know what was real and what was my mind playing tricks..."

"It doesn't matter." A shudder goes through him. "All that matters is that you're safe. You're safe, Mia, and I'll never let anything hurt you again."

"You can't promise me that, Bex. Not in this world."

His hands go to my face, and he touches his head to mine. "Yes, I can. There isn't a single thing on Earth I wouldn't do to protect you. I won't make the same mistake twice, Mia." One of his hands curves around the back of my neck, and he brushes his lips over mine.

"Bexley." My voice cracks as I gently pull away. "It's not that simple."

"I know." Regret coats his words.

"What's the plan? We can't stay here forever. What about classes? What about our friends? What about Quinctus once they find out we're gone?" *What about Cade?* His name teeters on the tip of my tongue, but I swallow the words.

He will always be the third person in our relationship. Whether Cade is alive or... I can't say the word. He'll be there. Haunting us.

"I don't know," Bexley admits. "I just needed to get you out of there. I'll speak to Phillip. We'll figure it out."

"You know this only ends one way." My voice quivers.

"Yeah, I know. But I can't lose you, Mia. I won't."

"I'm going to lay down. It's been a long night."

"Okay." He gives me a small nod. "I'll check in with Channing and the others."

I go to find the bedroom, but Bexley snags my wrist at the last second. "It's you and me, Mia."

As I walk away, I want to believe him.

But nothing makes sense anymore.

"MIA?"

Something tickles my face, and I open my eyes to find Bexley looming over me. "W-what time is it?" I smooth the hair from my eyes.

"Almost noon. You must be hungry."

My shoulders lift in a small shrug. "I'm fine."

"I made lunch. Come on. You need to eat." He stands and offers me his hand. My stomach growls, and a small smirk plays on his lips. "See."

"Traitor," I murmur to myself.

Bexley leads me back into the living area and guides me over to one of the stools at the breakfast counter. "Sit. It's nothing compared to Mulligan's cooking." He slides a grilled cheese sandwich toward me.

"It looks great, thanks."

"Did you manage to sleep? I checked in on you a couple of times and you were out cold."

"Surprisingly, I did. I think everything just caught up to me, ya know?" I take a small bite of the sandwich, moaning in appreciation when the rich cheese hits my taste buds.

"Good?" Bexley chuckles.

"Yeah, really good." I smile. "What?" I ask as he studies me while I eat.

"I wish things were different. You deserve better, Mia. You deserve so much more."

"It just hurts. That my father could do that to me... hand me over to Cade like I was nothing. I keep trying to rationalize it but—"

"He had no choice." Bexley's expression falls. "I know it doesn't make it better, but I saw the regret in his eyes that night, Mia. He truly believed there was a way out for you."

"You spoke to him?" He nods, and I add, "Why didn't you tell me?"

"Because you weren't ready to hear it. Because everything is a fucking mess." He comes around the counter and runs his hand along my arm. "Your father loved you. But this world... it gets its claws into you and..." Bexley sucks in a sharp breath. "There's no getting out."

"So let's leave," I cry. "We're already halfway there. We could just take off and..." My thoughts trail off at the torment in his eyes.

"You'd really leave Sasha? Channing? We'd have to disappear forever. Somewhere they could never find us."

"I..."

"Gravestone is my legacy, Mia." Regret coats his voice. "They need me."

"Quinctus?"

"Fuck, no, not Quinctus. Alex, Channing... even Brandon. If we leave, what do you think will happen to them, or the next initium? The next prosapias?"

"You really want this?" I gawk at him. "To be beholden to them?

"I can't explain it..." He moves away and rakes a hand through his hair. "But sometimes it's about choosing the devil you know over the devil you don't. If we leave, we'll always be looking over our shoulders, wondering... waiting. But if we stay, if we fight, maybe we have a shot at changing things from the inside."

"Cade won't stop... he'll keep coming until he's gotten what he wants."

A flash of fury lights up Bexley's eyes, a low growl rumbling in his chest. "Then let him come. I just need to buy some time to figure out how to control the outcome."

"I don't like it, Bex." I don't like it at all.

He comes back to me, gripping the nape of my neck and dropping his head to mine. "In another life, Mia, I would give you the world. Romantic dates, the big wedding, a house with a white picket fence, and two or three kids running around, but that isn't our reality."

"It sounds nice," I breathe, fisting his t-shirt.

"Our love isn't born out of nice. It's born out of blood and pain and darkness. But together, we can walk into the light. I know we can."

"You'd want that?" I ask, palming his cheek. His brows crinkle and I explain. "You'd want to... marry me?"

"One day, yeah." His mouth curves. "We're not normal, Mia. Our lives are never going to be normal. But we can reign... together."

"It's nice to pretend." A soft sigh escapes my lips.

"We don't have to pretend, baby. We just have to stay strong."

Bexley kisses the corner of my mouth, testing the waters. At first, I flinch. But then he kisses me harder, running his tongue along the seam of my lips. "Let me in, Mia." It's a low growl.

"I-I can't."

"Yes, you can. It's me and you, baby. I promise. No one can touch you here. He can't touch you." He cups my face, rubbing his thumb along my cheekbone.

"And after?" I ask. Because this is temporary. A band-aid on a festering wound.

He steals another kiss, working his hand down my body.

"We'll worry about what comes after later."

24

BEXLEY

I stand in the doorway looking out at the deck, my eyes eating up Mia, who's sitting in the last of the fall sun before it drops beneath the tree line for the evening.

For the first time since waking up in the hospital, there's a peace surrounding Mia. One that I'd almost forgotten existed. She's sitting on the swing with her legs curled up beneath her body, staring out at nothing as birdsong breaks the silence.

This place is incredible. I had no idea what James was going to come up with when I called him and said we needed somewhere right away, but I couldn't have picked somewhere better if I'd tried.

We're totally off the grid here. It's exactly what she needs—what we both need—as we try to come out of all of this stronger together.

Pain lashes at my chest as I think about the fact that Cade has been around all this time and that none of us other than Ashton believed it. Mia should hate me for not trusting her. A part of her does—I see it in her eyes every time she looks at me—but I know that she's having a hard time trusting herself right now so she does understand.

As I watch her, I take note of all the visible differences in her from when we first met. The sparkle in her eyes has dimmed, the innocence that filled them back then long gone after everything she's been through. Under her eyes are dark circles, proving just how much sleep she's been losing because of that cunt tormenting her. Her cheeks are hollower than before from how little she's eating. But it's what's not visible that's the most terrifying. The memories of her telling me that it would be easier if she died that day with her parents. The vivid image of finding her trying to carve her brand from her chest.

My fists curl as I try to even imagine the pain she's experiencing every single second because of a game she never wanted to be a part of—a game I'm sure her father never wanted to be a part of either.

She blows out a long breath, dragging my eyes back up to hers. "Are you just going to stand there staring at me with that look on your face, or are you going to come and sit down?"

"I... uh... I'm sorry."

"I know, Bex. You keep saying that."

Picking up the drinks that I'd placed on the windowsill when I stopped, I walk over and drop down beside her. "Here, it's not too strong, but it should help you relax."

"Thank you." She takes a sip and lowers the glass to her lap. "Can we stay here forever?" she asks quietly.

"It's pretty incredible."

"Shame we're not here for a different reason."

Reaching out, I lace my fingers through hers. "It doesn't mean we can't enjoy it."

"Trust me, Bex. I'm doing my best. I feel... I feel better than I have in a while, being here," she admits. "I don't... I don't feel him," she whispers, I guess just in case he is here and listening.

"James is the only one who knows where we are. We're safe here, Mia. It's just me and you. I promise."

She nods, but despite her previous words, her eyes continue to roam along the tree line, as if she's waiting for someone to jump out at any moment.

"Can you talk about it? What you saw, what he did?"

Her head lowers for a beat as all the air rushes from her lungs. "I don't know what was real and what wasn't."

"How about we just assume it was all real?" I suggest.

"I'm not sure I can cope with that being the case. That would mean he's been—" The emotion in her voice forces her to stop for a beat. "It means he's been watching us—me—this whole time."

"Motherfucker," I curse under my breath.

"He's only stood in front of me twice. In my bathroom and at the ball."

I swallow down the lump in my throat at the image that emerges in my head of him talking to her, threatening her, scaring the living shit out of her and none of us believing it was real.

"W-what did he say to you?"

"He…he… he just threatens me, although he never actually says what he wants, what he's going to do. Just that I know. He's crazy, Bex. Hell-bent on his mission to take over, or whatever it is he really wants."

"What about the other times?"

She's silent for so long that I wonder if she's going to respond.

After long agonizing minutes, her lips finally part. "He just watches me, makes sure I know he's there. In the trees at the house, around college, in… in class."

"He was in your fucking class?" I boom, instantly feeling bad when she flinches away from me. "I'm sorry. Why didn't you tell me?"

She scoffs.

"I'm—"

"Don't, Bex. Don't tell me you're sorry again. It doesn't change anything."

"I know."

"I thought I saw him in class the day I passed out. That's what I was running from when Ashton saw me. I really believe him, you know. I think he's on our side right now."

"I trust you, Mia. And if you say that, then I'll try to do the same. But if he gives me any indication that his intentions with you, with any of us, aren't pure, then I will not bat an eyelid at taking him out. If he is a threat to you in any way, then he's gone."

More than gone. I'll put a fucking bullet through his skull myself.

She nods despite the fact that all the blood drains from her face at the suggestion of me killing someone else. I don't want to—I never wanted to kill anyone, that's not who I am. But I won't blink if someone's life needs to end to protect the girl I love. I meant it when I said I would literally do anything to keep her safe, including laying down my own life.

"I think we need all the allies we can get right now."

"It shouldn't be this way," I mutter, more to myself than anything. I can't deny that what she said earlier wasn't tempting, to just leave and never come back. But I can't. I might not have wanted this life, but now it *is* my life, and I really want to believe we can be the ones to make the changes that are necessary.

Somehow, we will get rid of Cade, and together, Mia, me, and the others can move Q into the twenty-first century and turn it into something better.

I have to believe that is possible, or all of this—all this pain and loss—will have been for nothing.

As the sun dips below the trees, plunging us into their shadows, the temperature almost immediately plummets. Mia visibly shivers, placing her now empty glass on the table and wrapping her arms around herself.

"Do you trust me?" The second the question falls from my lips, I regret it because Mia has every right to say no. But I breathe a sigh of relief when she turns to look at me, because I can already see her answer in her eyes.

I hold my hand out. She hesitantly takes it and allows me to pull her inside. I lock the door behind us and make sure she sees me do it before leading her to the back of the cabin to the impressive master bathroom.

"Bexley?" she breathes as I close the door behind us.

"You looked cold. I thought I could warm you up," I say, taking a step toward her and lifting my hands to cup her face.

Her cheeks are cold, but this time when she shivers, I know it's not because of the temperature because I feel it too, the connection that's always been between us.

"I love you, Mia," I say, dropping my head to hers. "Let me be what you need right now. Let me take care of you."

She nods, her eyes quickly filling with tears.

I drop a quick kiss to her lips before pulling away, knowing that if I allow myself any more then my good intentions will fly straight out of the window and I'll end up bending her over the counter instead of giving her the relaxation she's so desperate for.

Taking a step back from her, I spin around and turn the faucet on. Popping the top of the expensive-looking bottle on the edge of the bath, I pour the creamy liquid into the powerful stream of water and watch as white foam explodes across the top of the water and the scent of vanilla fills the air around me.

"You're running me a bath?" she whispers behind me, as if it's not entirely obvious.

"No, baby. I'm running us a bath. You can't possibly get in a tub this big alone. It was made for two." I smirk.

"I think you're right." She's pulling off her clothes before she's even finished talking, and I'm still standing there, completely captivated by her beautiful body when she steps into the growing bubbles.

"D-don't get that wet." I nod to the bandage covering her wound.

"I'm sure it won't make it any worse," she mutters sadly.

"I need it to heal as soon as possible." Her eyes find mine, her brows pulled together in confusion. "I've got a plan, a surprise."

"Oh?"

"One that I'm not telling you about."

I pull my shirt over my head, and thankfully it's enough to distract her and stop her from questioning me.

The water burns my feet as I step in behind her, making me wonder just how numb she is that she didn't so much as flinch as she lowered her body into the scalding water.

Ignoring the burn, I sink down behind her and pull her back, so she's laid against me, wrapping my arms around her waist.

Silence falls around us. Only the sound of the popping bubbles can be heard as we lay together.

"This is how it should be," I finally whisper. "Just me and you."

"Umm..." she murmurs, turning her head into my chest. "I feel like we missed out on so much. We've never even been on a date."

"Maybe we'll just have to do everything backward."

"You really do want to get married, don't you?" she deadpans.

"I didn't mean that backward. When this is all over, Mia, I'm going to take you on the best date ever. It will blow everything you've ever seen in movies or read in books out of the fucking water."

Her hands run down my arms around her waist. "I don't need all of that."

"I know. But that's not why I'm going to do it. I'm going to do it because it's the least of what you deserve."

"What do you want for your future?" she asks me quietly.

"You."

"No, I mean for your life. Your job. Your... future outside of us."

I blow out a breath... I want... "I just want to be happy, baby. I've grown up with money and all the things it can buy, and I can tell you right now that it doesn't buy happiness. I don't care if we end up in a trailer park with only a few dollars to our name, as long as we've got smiles on our faces."

Water sloshes everywhere as she flips around so she can look at me.

"I love you, Bexley Easton."

Her lips press against mine and cut off anything I want to say, and by the time she pulls back and wraps her hand around my hard length, all thoughts of words really have fallen from my head.

THE BRIGHT SUNSHINE and the birds singing wake me up late the next morning, but that's not the most beautiful thing, because that's the girl fast asleep beside me.

I woke up more times than I can count in the night to check on her, and each and every time she was sleeping.

With a soft smile playing on my lips, I reach out and tuck a lock of hair behind her ear. Seeing Mia finally relax gives me the confidence I need to know that we will get through this, that Cade isn't going to torment us forever and that there is a light at the other end of the tunnel.

Once she finally wakes up, we have the most incredible morning. Mia makes us pancakes that we eat out on the deck before we argue over what to watch on the TV, and I finally end up conceding so that she can watch some chick flick, not that I really mind. How could I when she lays curled around me, feeding me popcorn every few minutes?

If it weren't for our reality always nagging on the edges of my mind, it would be the perfect day.

Mia turned her cell off the moment we got to the security room in the house the other night, but mine is sitting in the only position in this place that I've managed to find some signal just in case of emergencies. The others know not to ring unless it's a matter of life or death, so when it starts ringing not long into our second movie of the day, both of us tense.

"It's probably a sales call or something," I say as I untangle myself from Mia, although the ball of dread in my gut tells me it's anything but.

My heart jumps into my throat when I look down at the screen and see Phillip Cargill's name.

He never calls me.

Ever.

This cannot be good.

25

MIA

"What's wrong?" I take in Bexley's pale face and shocked expression as he ends the phone call.

"It's Marcus," he says quietly, as if he can't quite believe it. "There's been an accident."

"Oh my God, is he okay?"

"He's been rushed to the hospital. Phillip wanted me to know. He said he thinks I should be there... just in case..." His voice quivers and I rush to him, wrapping my arms around him.

"I'm so sorry."

"This cannot be fucking happening." He lets out a steady breath, but I feel his torment.

"What do you need?" I ask, because he's right, this is the worst possible timing. But it's his grandad. His family.

"I don't know. I can't think. Fuck," he roars, pulling away from me. "Fuck!" His fist flies out, connecting with the wall. Bexley winces but doesn't complain.

"Bex," I say, trying to comfort him again, but he keeps me at arm's length.

"I just need a minute. I need to think..." He starts tapping on his phone and brings it to his ear. "Channing," he barks. "Phillip just called..." I stand there, but Bexley walks right out of the cabin, leaving me. Dejection burns through me, but I get it.

I'd been much the same when I woke up in the hospital. Detached. Distant.

When he comes back inside a couple of minutes later, he looks like a man with a purpose. "Channing is on his way."

"He's coming here?"

"I need to go back to Gravestone. He spoke to Phillip, there was a car accident..." The words hang between us.

"A car accident? You think... you think it was Cade?"

"I don't know what the fuck I think, Mia," he snaps, and I recoil. "Shit, I'm sorry. I didn't... this caught me by surprise."

"I know." I hug myself tightly. "I'm sorry."

"Yeah, me too. Channing will be here soon, and we can figure out a plan then."

"I know he's your family, but it could be a trap."

Bexley stares at me, his eyes darkening. "I hoped we'd have more time," he sighs deeply.

"More time?"

"To come up with a better plan."

"What else did Phillip say? Does he think it was Cade?"

"If he did, he didn't voice his concerns." His jaw pops as he runs a hand down his face. "I'll kill him. I'll fucking kill him."

"Bexley, no..." I rush over to him and grip his arms. "Promise me you won't do anything reckless."

He gazes down at me with so much love it winds me. But it's laced with regret.

"Bex..." It comes out a desperate whisper.

But he doesn't promise me, he doesn't say anything, just wraps his arms around me and buries his face in my shoulder.

CHANNING MUST HAVE BROKEN every speed limit there is, because less than forty minutes later, he arrives at the cabin.

"You take precautions?" Bexley asks him as they do that guy-hug thing.

"Yeah. I circled around twice, waited, and there was nothing. We're good."

A flash of relief crosses Bexley's face. "Come in."

"Hey," I say, offering him a small wave. "How's Sasha?"

"She's okay. Back at her family's home. I thought it would be safer…" He glances at Bexley and something passes between them. "The Cargills' place is like Fort Knox. He'd be crazy to try anything there."

"Yeah, well this motherfucker is crazy."

Silence falls over us.

"Why don't you take a shower?" Bexley suggests. "Let me talk to Channing."

"You don't need to protect me, I can hand—"

"Mia, please." He releases a heavy sigh.

"Fine." My spine stiffens as I take off down the hall, but I don't go into the bathroom at all. Instead, I open and slam the door, then creep back toward the living room, pressing my back against the wall.

"How is she?" Channing says.

"Better, lighter…"

"Good, that's good. But listen, man, what's the plan here?"

"I don't know… fuck, I don't know. I thought we'd have more time, I thought—"

"Yeah, it's a fucking mess. What did Phillip say?"

"Exactly what you said. It was a car accident. The driver lost control of the SUV."

"You think it's Kingsley?"

"Don't you?" Bexley snaps.

"I mean, it looks suspicious. You're really going back there?"

"What choice do I have? He's family. He doesn't have anyone else."

"And if it's a trap?"

"Then I guess I'd better be ready."

"Maybe you can turn it to your advantage," Channing says, and my heart catapults into my throat.

"How'd you figure?"

"There's only one way this ends, man. You gotta know that."

"Yeah, I've been thinking the same thing."

"Q are dragging their asses. I don't know what Lincoln has on them, but they're stalling, trying to buy more time. Something doesn't add up."

"I think you're right."

A chill runs through me. I don't want Bexley going up against Cade. It's the last thing I want. But someone has to stop him, or at least try.

I won't just stand by and watch, I can't.

"Use me." I reveal myself.

"Mia, what the fuck?" Bexley's eyes pop open, a mask of betrayal sliding over his expression.

"You heard me. Use me."

"No, no fucking way."

"I'm the one Cade wants. If you're right and your grandad got hurt… because of me… I can't have any more blood on my hands." My body trembles.

"Bexley's right, Mia. It's too dangerous." Channing offers me a sympathetic smile.

"So what? You just expect me to stay here, hiding like some coward, while you go back to Gravestone? This is my fight too."

"Mia, baby, don't do this." Bexley stalks toward me, running his hand down my cheek. "I need you safe. I need to know you're here, out of harm's way."

Tears prick the corners of my eyes. "And I need to do this. Cade wants me. It makes sense to use me as bait. I trust you, Bexley. I know you won't let anything happen to me. But I need to do this."

Because all of this waiting around, all of this inaction and looking over my shoulder is killing me.

He glares at me, the muscle in his neck pulsating as he grinds his teeth together.

"Please," I beg. If he leaves me behind, I'll never forgive him.

"I want you to stay here with Channing. I need you to stay here, okay? Don't fight me on this, Mia."

"But—"

"I need to go." He hooks his arm around my neck and drops a kiss on my head as tears spill freely down my cheeks. "I love you, Mia."

"Don't do this," I cry, twisting my fingers into his t-shirt. "Please, I'm begging you."

Bexley nods to Channing over my shoulder, and strong arms tug me away from him.

"No," I shriek. "NO!"

"Shh, Mia, it's okay," Channing whispers in my ear, but I feel like I'm breaking in half, splintering apart at the seams. "I'll never forgive you for this," I roar, watching Bexley as he grabs his keys off the sideboard and makes for the door. "I mean it, Bexley. Walk out of here and we're done. We're done." I don't even know if I mean the words, but the agony of him leaving me—denying me the right to be a part of this—is too overwhelming.

He hesitates, his remorseful glare settling on me.

"Go," Channing says. "I've got her."

I thrash against his hold, but he's too big, too strong for a girl like me. "Go," he hisses, and Bexley gives him a sharp nod and slips out of the cabin.

Taking my broken heart with him.

I IGNORE Channing for the next couple of hours despite his attempts at engaging me in conversation. I'm too pissed at him to reply.

"You can't ignore me forever," he says, tapping at something on his cell. Part of me wants to ask if he's heard from Bexley, but the other part isn't sure I want to know.

"I'm going to lay down." Because there sure as hell isn't anything else to do here.

"Mia, wait." His voice gives me pause, and I glance back. "I know you hate me right now, but it was the right call."

"How can you say that?" I turn slowly.

"Because if it were Sasha in danger, I would have hidden her away too."

"Cade assaulted me. He raped and defiled me. He killed my parents..." My chest heaves, pain wracking through me. "He left me for dead, Channing... he did that. And he's out there, taunting us, showing us he's still the one in control. I just want it done. I want it over."

"I know." Channing gets up and inches toward me. "But it's not that simple. Q—"

"Q can go to hell for all I care. They let this happen. They stood by and—" A tsunami of tears overwhelms me, drowning out my words.

Channing closes the remaining distance between us and pulls me into his arms. "Shh. I got you. I got you, Mia."

"If anything happens to him..."

"Easton can handle himself. If Q won't step in and do what needs to be done, maybe this is the only way. And he has the guys to back him up."

"You think they'll help?"

"I know they will. Whether you want to accept it or not, Bexley is a born leader, Mia. He's one of the only people I've ever seen stand up to Cade. That kind of power affects others. Given half a chance, it can effect change. Real change. The guys will follow him because that's what they do."

"I hate this. I hate all of it."

"You're strong, Mia. You're so fucking strong. Don't forget that. He needs you. He needs to know you're safe."

Channing's words touch something deep inside of me. I don't want to believe him, but he's right. Bexley is born to lead. Whether he wants it or not, he possesses the power to command. But does he really stand a shot at changing things?

"Why don't I make us something to eat and we can watch a movie or something, try to take your mind off things?"

"Yeah, maybe." I nod, feeling the angry storm raging inside ebb away.

"You're a good friend, Channing. I'm glad Bexley has you."

"You have me too, you know?" He winks, ushering me over to the couch. "Sit, and I'll be right back."

Channing makes himself busy in the kitchen while I pluck my cell phone off the table and move around the cabin until I find a signal to send Bexley a message.

MIA: **I hope your grandad is okay... and I'm sorry about earlier. I just hate the idea that something could happen to you, all because of me. I love you, Bexley. I love you so much. And that future we talked about... I want that. I want you.**

. . .

I HIT SEND AND WAIT, silently praying to see his name flash up. But it doesn't come, and a sinking feeling spreads through me. He's probably at the hospital, dealing with doctors.

Channing brings me a sandwich and we eat in comfortable silence. He chooses some action film and we sit together, trying to distract ourselves. He checks his phone a couple of times, texting someone back.

"Bexley?" I ask, and he shakes his head.

"Brandon. Bexley is still at the hospital."

I try not to panic that he hasn't texted me back. We didn't exactly leave things in a good place.

After the film is done, Channing cleans away our plates while I pace in front of the window. A car appears in the distance, glittering through the dense trees.

Bexley's car.

My heart soars.

He's back.

He came back.

Before I know what I'm doing, I yank open the door and run to meet him.

"Mia?" Channing yells after me, but it's too late. I'm already dashing down the steps as the car rolls to a stop. Sunlight bounces off the hood, blinding me, and I throw up my arm.

The driver's door opens, and Bexley climbs out, his dark shadow bursting through the rays of sunshine.

"You're okay," I breathe, relief settling into my bones as his face comes into view. "You're—"

"Hello, little mouse."

26

BEXLEY

"I'm so sorry," Phillip says, jumping up from the chair he was sitting in as I come to a stop in the hallway beside the room the nurse at the reception directed me to.

"Shit," I bark, running my hand down my face.

"They thought they'd be able to save him with surgery, but his heart couldn't take it."

"Fuck. Fuck." I slam my hand down on the wall, Phillip startling beside me.

"I'm so sorry. I know you weren't all that close but—"

"Where is he, Phillip?"

Phillip's brows pull together as he stares at me. He quickly looks over his shoulder at the door. "I-in there. The nurse said we can—"

"Not Marcus. Cade. Where the fuck is Cade?" I seethe.

"I already told you, we have it in hand."

A bitter laugh rips from my throat. "You're a liar. We both know you don't have him under control, because if you did then he wouldn't have been at the house two days ago and Marcus wouldn't be dead right now."

"It was an accident, Bexley."

"Bullshit. Jesus, you're so naïve. You really think he's just gone, don't you?" I shake my head as I start pacing, disbelief flooding my veins.

"It's just the shock," Phillip informs me, as if that explains why I'm so fucking angry right now.

The sound of footsteps approaching cuts off the less than polite response I was about to spit back at him.

"Here, I got you—Bexley, you got here fast," Harrison Rexford says, passing Phillip a coffee and pre-packaged sandwich. "I'm so sorry for your loss. They did everything they could."

"Oh, I'm sure they did. It's what you lot have been doing that I'm more concerned about."

Harrison's brow furrows.

"Easton thinks this was Kingsley," Phillip informs him.

"We're having the car looked at as we speak to confirm that it was just an accident. I must admit the thought had crossed my mind." Harrison's eye twitches as he says this, and my fists curl.

"Don't lie to me. I'm fucking sick of it. All you do is lie and cover shit up. It needs to end. This was Cade. I'd bet my life on it."

"There's been no sign of—"

"He never fucking left," I boom, storming past both of them and toward the door Marcus lays on the other side of.

Sucking in a deep breath, I push it open and slip into the room. I've never done this before. I've never lost anyone close to me, so I don't really know what to expect as I walk toward the bed.

All the air rushes from my lungs as I take him in. He just looks like he's sleeping.

I quietly lower into the chair beside his bed. Phillip was right; we're not exactly close. I might have lived with him for almost a year, but mostly we were just strangers under the same roof. I now understand why, seeing as he was keeping almost everything about his life a secret from me.

Why didn't he just tell me? Why keep it a secret until the beginning of the initiation?

Scrubbing my hand over my face, I push my hair back as I try to figure out what the hell I should do now, what I should say when we barely said anything when he was alive.

I stare at his peaceful face and can only hope that wherever he's gone now, it's much easier than life must have been here.

He lost his wife, his son and daughter-in-law, and for almost eighteen years, his grandson too.

A lump jumps into my throat as I think about the man who made me, who I never got a chance to meet. My dad is a great man, and I couldn't have asked for more growing up, but still, knowing there was someone else involved makes me question so much of my life. The things I thought I had in common with my dad, the things I didn't... I can't help but wonder how much of me is my bio dad and how much is the man who raised me.

There's one thing I'm sure of, though. Even with him gone, and now Marcus, I'm going to do what I need to do. A few weeks ago, I might have seen this as my chance to run, to get out. But right now, the need to make a difference, to make the changes that need to happen in this town, is burning through me.

"I'll take my place, Marcus. I'll make you, my dad, this town proud. I promise."

The lump grows until I can barely breathe around it and the backs of my eyes burn, but more than anything else, determination surges through me.

This is my chance. My time.

Our time.

I stand with urgency.

"Sleep well, Marcus." With one final look at his face, I march from the room.

Both Phillip and Harrison stand when I step out.

"Son, are you—"

"This ends now," I tell them, my voice leaving no room for argument. "You've failed to look after this town, to look after the people you should be protecting. The Kingsley line is done, and things are going to change."

"Easton, I'm not sure—"

"I'm not asking for permission, Phillip," I spit. "Get your shit in order. Either get me Cade, or I'll find him myself and put an end to all of this."

Both of their mouths are hanging open when I storm away from them, flinging the double doors at the end of the hallway open with a bang.

"Bex, are you—"

"Let's go," I interrupt Brandon who was walking toward the doors I blew through. "We have shit to take care of."

I DRIVE us both back to the house where I review the security tapes from the previous two days in case us disappearing has led to him being careless. But exactly like I thought, there's still no sign of him.

"Are these tapes even real?" I mutter. "How can a person get in and out unnoticed."

"He was the one who installed the system."

"What?" I ask Brandon, who's standing behind me, staring at the same screens.

"When we first moved in, he had the whole place redone."

"He's got fucking control of this?" I bark.

"Well, no. His cell was cut off the night of the explosion. He should no longer—"

"He has though, hasn't he? He's in this fucking system. Jesus fucking Christ. What else does he know?"

"It's Kingsley," Brandon mutters. "He knows everything. He always has."

A thought slams into me so hard I stumble back. "Mia."

Pushing Brandon aside, I race from the room and soon after, the house.

"Bex, what's—" Alex calls when I pass him on his way out of the kitchen, but I don't hang around long enough to hear the end of his question as I fly toward my car and start the engine.

My heart pounds in my chest, my palms sweating against the wheel as I make my way out of town as fast as I can. I forget all about looking in my mirror in case I'm being followed. I already know I'm not.

He's played us.

He's fucking played us.

Marcus' accident was no fucking accident. It was planned down to the very second. He knew what we'd do. He knew it would get me into town. He knew I'd leave. I suck in a ragged breath, praying that I'm wrong, that he hasn't been one step ahead of us all this time.

The drive back to the cabin seems to take twice as long as the journey to Gravestone did only a couple of hours ago.

My foot anxiously taps the floor as my fingers wring the wheel. "Please be okay, please be okay."

Dragging my cell out, I hit call on Channing's number.

By the time I get to the hidden turnoff that leads toward the cabin, I'm a fucking mess.

I slow my speed as I hit the gravel track but only marginally, causing stones to fly out from beneath me, and I come to a stop with a screech of my brakes once the cabin comes into view. It looks exactly as I left it with Channing's car parked outside, but the sight does little to calm the panic that's racing through my veins.

I have no idea how I know, but I fucking do.

My legs barely keep up with my body as I fly toward the front door and crash through it.

If they're fine, I'm probably going to terrify both of them with my panic. *But they're not fine*, a little voice says in my head. *You know that everything is wrong right now. Trust your instincts.*

My heart plummets when I look around the room. It's trashed, utterly fucking trashed. If I didn't feel so helpless in those few seconds, I might feel at least a little proud that they put up a fight.

"Channing?" I call, rushing around the living space. "Mia?"

I come to a grinding halt when a sound hits my ear. Holding my breath, I hear it again and dart forward. "Fuck," I bark when I turn the corner only to be met by a puddle of blood. "Channing, fuck." I drop to my knees beside him.

"C-Cade," he whispers. "M-Mia." His eyes plead with me to do something, but I'm helpless. Totally fucking helpless.

Blood oozes from behind his hand pressed to his abdomen.

"Here," I say, dragging my shirt over my head and balling it up in the hope it will help slow the blood. "Where did they go?"

Channing shakes his head, his eyelids beginning to lower.

"Wait here, I'm calling... fuck." I don't know who I'm calling. I can't call the cops... can I? "Shit."

Racing to the spot where I know my cell will work, I call the only person I think I can trust right now.

"Easton, everything okay?" James asks.

"N-no. He found us. He's got Mia. Channing's been shot, he's bleeding out. Fuck. I don't— fuck."

"Okay, breathe, Bexley. Where is Channing?"

"H-here, at the cabin. I left and he... he fucking got her. Shit, it's all my fault." I slump against the wall as the weight of all of this comes crashing down on me.

It's not until James speaks to me again that I realize I've ended up on the floor. "I've got medics coming to you. They'll be there as soon as they can. Try to stop the blood."

"He's on the other side of the room."

"So get off the phone and help him."

"But Mia, Cade..."

"I'll start digging. But this is Cade, Bexley. He won't do anything silently or hidden. He will want you to know where he is. He will tell you exactly where Mia is. You just have to figure out a way to be smarter than him."

"I've failed this far."

"I trust you, Bexley."

"That makes one of us."

"I'm sorry about your grandfather, son. Go and look after Channing, I'll start searching for Kingsley."

My hand falls, my cell clattering to the wooden floor. "Thank you," I whisper, feeling like nothing more than a hollow shell.

She could be anywhere. He could be doing anything to her.

Pulling my knees up, I rest my head on them as I try to force myself to think like Cade. If I were him, where would I take her?

A low moan drags me back to the here and now, and I scramble back to my feet and race over to Channing.

"Help is on its way," I say, taking over the pressure on his gunshot wound. "Everything's going to be okay."

"We'll find her, Bex," he croaks, his skin pale. "We'll find her, and we'll put him in the fucking ground."

"We will, man... we will."

27

MIA

I wake to the flicker of candlelight. My eyes strain against the darkness as I search the cold tomb. It's familiar, the huge stone bricks a feature of the nightmare that started all of this.

The Eligere.

I'm in the sanctuary, the small chamber underneath Gravestone Hall.

"C-Cade?" I cry out, my throat dry and sore. But I'm met with silence.

My muscles ache, heavy like lead from whatever Cade injected me with before bundling me into the car. I didn't even think to check that the BMW I ran toward actually belonged to Bexley. I walked straight into the trap.

I knew... I knew it was a set-up. Yet he went anyway.

Damn you, Bexley Easton.

A whimper crawls up my throat as I push up on my hands and knees and try to stagger to my feet, but I can't.

A leather strap is bound around my ankle and secured to a chain pinned to the wall. Besides, even if I could escape, whatever drug lingers in my bloodstream is still too potent and I crumple back down.

"Help me," I cry, refusing to accept this is my fate. "Somebody help me."

"Don't worry, little mouse." Cade appears out of the shadows. "Lover boy will be here soon enough."

"Cade," I breathe, as if my heart can't process what my head already knows.

"We meet again," he drawls through a vicious smirk.

"You fucking bastard," I spit. "Why?"

"Why?" He storms toward me, crouching to bring us almost to eye level. "What's that saying... an eye for an eye."

"He was just following orders. Quinctus—"

"Quinctus will pay," he hisses. "When he arrives and the truth is finally unveiled, they'll pay for ever crossing the Kingsley name."

Digging his cell phone out of his pocket, he checks the screen, frowning. "Where is he?" he murmurs.

"What?"

"Nothing." He shoots me a hard look and stands, pacing back and forth as he types out a message, his fingers moving frantically across the screen.

He's on edge. Unstable and wired.

Nothing like the cool, calm, and composed Cade I'm used to.

"I need some water," I say. "Please."

He glances down at me and stalks off into the shadows again, reappearing with a bottle of water. "Here." The bottle falls at my feet, and I scramble to get the cap off, chugging it down.

"Where is he?" he mumbles again.

"Where is who, Cade?"

"You'll see." His eyes snap to mine, wild and skittish. "You'll all see."

He isn't making any sense, and he's growing increasingly irritated. I shuffle back against the wall, wincing when the leather cuff bites into my skin.

"Ugh, where is he?" he roars just as his cell phone lights up the dim chamber. "Thank fuck." His eyes scan the text message. "He's almost here."

Fear trickles down my spine, even though I have no idea who he's referring to.

Cade instantly calms, leaning against the wooden table pushed up against the cold chamber wall. He crosses his ankles, letting his dark gaze run over me.

"What?" I bark, hating his attention. Memories rush to the surface. The overgrowth beneath my feet, the sting of pain as the branches and trees cut into my skin as I tried desperately to outrun him.

"You remember," he says quietly, dragging his thumb over the pillow of his lip.

"I remember everything." I glower at him.

"So feisty," he smirks. "Maybe he'll let me keep you. I'd love to see all the ways I could make you break. Yeah," hunger glints in his eyes, "you and me could have some fun, little mouse."

I flinch involuntarily. Cade notices, his expression darkening. Marching over to me, he bends and grabs me around the throat, yanking me up onto my knees. I scramble forward, grabbing his legs for stability, allowing me to relieve the pressure around my windpipe.

I gasp for breath, staring up at Cade and silently pleading for him to release me.

"The things I want to do to you."

"Like your father did to you?" I whisper.

Confusion clouds his eyes. "What the fuck are you talking about?"

"I found it, Cade. Your journal."

"Y-you what?" His grip on me loosens but quickly becomes a choke hold as his eyes turn pitch black. My fingers claw at his skin, desperately trying to fight him off.

"I... Cade... I can't—"

"You think you know? You know nothing... nothing about my life or what I've endured. He did it to make me strong, to prepare me for this life. He helped me."

"H-he didn't... He abused you, Cade. Your father abused you."

"No. *NO!*" He backhands me so hard I see stars. Shoving me down, I hit the ground with a thud, pain exploding along my arm and into my shoulder. "Fuck. Fuuuuck!" His guttural roar echoes around the chamber, rattling my bones.

"Cade, I..."

"Say another word and I'll cut out your fucking tongue. You haven't got the first clue about my father. But you will."

My brows pinch as my gaze darts around the room. It's hopeless. I'm chained to the wall with no way out.

Footsteps sound down the hall and Cade shoots me a knowing smirk. "Time to meet your destiny, little mouse."

The tap of shoes against stone grows louder. Cade is practically bouncing on his feet, grinning like a child. But his whole demeanor shifts the second a finely dressed man stands in the doorway. The shadows obscure his face, but I can tell from Cade's expression it's not who he was expecting.

"Who the fuck are you?" he barks, pulling to his full height.

"Hello, Cade." The man steps into the soft amber glow. "I'm your uncle."

LINCOLN KINGSLEY STANDS before us like the devil dressed in a designer suit. His hair is slicked back, and he has one hand buried casually in his pocket.

"U-uncle?" Cade chokes on the word. "But my father—"

"Ah yes, about that..."

A ripple goes through the air as realization dawns on Cade's face... realization about what, I don't know.

"All this time, it was you."

"It was." Lincoln's face is a stone mask, giving nothing away. My mind is running a hundred miles a minute, trying to place the missing pieces of this puzzle.

"No. No! It can't be... why? Why the fuck would you do that?" Cade shrieks, jamming his fingers into his hair and tugging sharply. "I... I..."

"I let you believe what you wanted, Son."

"Don't call me that. Don't you dare fucking call me that. I did all this..." His eyes flick over to me. "For him. I did it for him and he's—"

"Gone, Cade. Your father is gone."

"No... NO." He grabs a nearby candelabra and launches it across the room. It crashes against the wall and clatters to the ground.

"Look," Lincoln approaches his nephew with his hands held in a non-threatening manner, "I know you're upset, but we want the same thing, Son. We want—"

Cade rips a gun out of the waistband of his jeans and presses it to Lincoln's temple.

"Easy." Surprise and fear flicker across Lincoln's face. "You don't want to do something you'll regret. I helped you, remember? I fed you the information you needed."

"You played me," Cade grits out, staring at his uncle with fiery anger.

"No, I didn't. Think about it... did I lie? Did I ever say I was Gregory?" Cade falters for a second, but Lincoln remains eerily calm. "I didn't play you, Cade. I just withheld certain facts because I needed Q to believe you were acting alone. I needed them to turn to me in their hour of need. I needed you, Son."

"Y-you did?" The raw vulnerability in Cade's voice doesn't surprise me. He's a kid again. A kid molded by cruel words and physical abuse. A kid in desperate need of his father's validation.

"You don't want to do this." Lincoln slides his hand over Cade's and gently eases the gun away. "You truly are your father's son." A flicker of emotion crosses his expression. "And together we can be strong. Powerful. We can make them pay."

"He's lying," I cry. "Think about it, Cade. He doesn't want to help you, he wants to use you. He didn't kill my father, you did... *you did*."

Cade's eyes snap to mine, narrowing with suspicion.

"Think about it. Your father has been dead for years. Where was your uncle then, huh? He doesn't care about you, he doesn't—"

"Shut her up, Son. Now."

He blows toward me like a storm, dark and unforgiving. My eyes home in on the gun, my breath lodged in my throat.

"Cade, you don't want to do this." Tears streak down my cheeks. "He's using you... just like your father did. You're not him, Cade. You are not your father." My chest heaves as his hand shoots out and grabs a fistful of my hair. A pained cry spills from my cheeks as he wrenches me up, and my ankle smarts from the pressure.

"Cade, please..." He clicks off the safety, pressing the barrel of the gun against my temple. I feel like I'm drowning, my lungs burning and gasping for breath.

"Do it, Son," Lincoln orders. "Before they get here."

A tiny seed of hope blossoms in my chest. Quinctus are coming, they have to be. Bexley will come... he'll come and save me.

"Do it," Lincoln snaps.

"Cade, please." I clutch his hoodie, staring right into his eyes. "You don't want to do this. I am not my father, just like you're not yours. I didn't ask for this. I didn't ask for any of this. Please…"

His eyes flash with something as he hesitates, glancing between me and his uncle and back again.

"You can't trust him." My voice cracks as Cade's grip on my hair doesn't falter. I may not understand Lincoln Kingsley's motivation, but I understand these men. Powerful men driven by greed and money and dark deeds. I don't trust Quinctus, and I definitely don't trust Lincoln.

"I know Q had your father killed… but this isn't the way, Cade… this isn't—"

"Lincoln." Phillip Cargill steps into the chamber, his hard glare immediately flitting to me and Cade. "What is this?"

"This, old friend," Lincoln drawls, "is your reckoning."

Cade pulls me back into the shadows a little, leaving the two men to face off against each other. I sense his hesitation, his confusion at the revelations. It bleeds from him like sticky black tar.

"Cade, let me go," I whisper. "You have to let me—"

"Shut up." He smashes the gun against my temple, making me wince in agony as my body slumps further against him.

"You said you didn't know Cade's whereabouts," Phillip says coolly.

"I know everything. I know that you sent me away and made me into a monster. I know you had Gregory killed when he started taking too much power for himself. I know you want to extinguish the Kingsley line."

"That's not—"

"Silence," Lincoln booms. "I'm talking now. I told you, Cargill, I fucking told you that Q's days were numbered. With Cade by my side, we'll be unstoppable."

"You're deluded, Linc. There are rules—"

"Rules? *Rules?*" He growls the words, getting in Phillip's face. But Phillip remains deathly still.

"Gregory was a liability to everything we've built here. Our associates appreciate our discretion and levelheadedness. Your brother became too obsessed with the old ways. Ways that draw attention, that make people talk."

"My brother was a good man who deserved more."

"Your brother was a bloodthirsty sociopath who abused his son."

A tremor goes through Cade.

"You knew?" Disbelief coats his words as his grip on me loosens enough that I crumple to the ground.

"We had suspicions," Phillip addresses him, "yes. We thought Mia would soften you, give you something to—"

"Stop, just stop!" Cade runs a hand over his face. "You played me. You all fucking played me. But I'm done playing. I'm done being everyone's pawn." He aims the gun at Phillip.

"Fuck you, Cargill. And fuck Quinctus."

I brace myself for the gunshot, muffling the whimper that crawls up my throat as it pierces the air.

Only it isn't Phillip who falls to the ground.

It's Lincoln.

28

BEXLEY

I'm still pressing my sopping wet shirt to Channing's stomach when the sound of tires on gravel out the front of the cabin hits my ears.

"They're here," I tell him despite the fact that he lost the fight to keep his eyes open at least ten minutes ago.

He's still breathing. I keep checking every few seconds, but it's dangerously shallow.

"Over here," I call when the door swings open and footsteps thunder into the building.

I don't look up. I figure that if it's Cade then he can just take us both out right here and put an end to all of it. He'd never leave Mia now he's got his hands on her, so if he's alone it means... a giant lump forms in my throat at even the thought of him harming her. Of stripping more of her fight away from her. Of breaking her more than he already has.

When feet appear before me and a bag clatters to the wooden floorboards beside me, I know it's help.

With a sigh of relief, I finally release the pressure I'm putting on Channing's gunshot wound and scoot back. "He's been shot in the stomach. It's been at least an hour, I think. He was talking b-but—" I blow out a breath trying to keep it together. "About ten minutes ago he lost consciousness."

"Okay, you've done a great job. What's his name?"

"C-Channing Rexford."

"Okay, we've got it from here."

Standing to my feet, I back away as they begin working on Channing, cutting his shirt away and injecting him with pain relief. I don't stop until I crash against the wall behind me.

I've never felt so helpless.

There's nothing I can do to fix him, and I have no fucking clue where Mia is. I don't even know where to start trying to find her.

Would he take her to the house? The church?

This is Cade we're talking about. He doesn't think like normal people.

I hear James' words in my head once more. *"He won't do anything silently or hidden. He will want you to know where he is. He will tell you exactly where Mia is."*

"When, James? When will he tell me?" I ask myself as the medics continue working.

Please be okay. Please, I silently beg. Channing and Sasha don't deserve this.

Hell, none of us fucking deserve this.

Turning into the door beside me, I swipe up a shirt I'd discarded on the floor from the day before and pull it over my head.

The sound of my cell ringing wherever I left it in the cabin has me running out of the room in search of it. I find it on the floor, vaguely remembering it falling there after my panicked call to James not all that long ago.

My hands tremble as I turn it over to see who it might be.

For the first time ever, I pray I'm going to find Cade's name staring back at me, inviting me to whatever fucking game he's playing.

My heart drops, disappointment flooding me when I do get a look at the screen and find Ashton's name there. "What?" I bark, lifting it to my ear.

"They're at the sanctuary. We're on our way now."

"Fuck. FUCK," I bellow.

Hanging up, I look over my shoulder at the medics.

"Do what you need to do," one of them says, looking up from Channing. "We're taking him to Gravestone Hospital once we've stabilized his condition."

"Okay," I cry as I run out of the house, finding my car door still wide open from where I ran from it when I got here, and I wheelspin away from the cabin and back toward Gravestone.

THERE IS an array of cars parked haphazardly outside Gravestone Hall when I pull up. It doesn't make me feel better about what I'm going to find inside at all. They might all be here to protect her from her living nightmare, but I have no doubt that he planned for it. Cunt plans for everything.

Anger surges through me that we've been on the back foot with him all this time. I still have no fucking clue what his endgame is.

Q—or more so Mia's dad—killed his. He's got his revenge. He killed Garth and Temperance. There's no need for any of this, for hurting Mia. For making an innocent girl his target.

Before I've even registered that I've moved, I'm pushing the heavy doors open and slipping inside the silent, eerie building.

They're expecting me—*he's* expecting me—so I have no chance of a surprise arrival, but still, my need to attempt to assess the situation I'm about to walk into makes me creep toward the door that leads to the sanctuary slower than I'd like.

The walk down the dark, ominous hallway to the room where my girl was officially handed over to that monster seems never-ending as I strain to hear voices, anything that might give me a clue as to what's happening in the underground room in the distance. But there's nothing.

It's like they're not even here.

Sucking in a breath, I turn the corner.

My heart jumps into my throat when the first thing I see is Cade's hands on Mia, a gun down by his side.

"Oh look, here he is at last. My replacement."

I narrow my eyes on Cade as I take a step past Tim, Brandon, Alex and Ashton. There's something different in Cade's tone, but I can't put my finger on what it is.

My eyes meet Phillip's before dropping to a body on the floor. Lincoln Kingsley. And Cade is the only one who's obviously packing.

"You shot your uncle?"

"Bex," Mia whimpers, her voice shaking with fear.

"It's okay, baby."

"Aw, you two always were too cute for me." Cade lifts his arm, pointing the barrel of his gun right at my head.

"Cade, please. No."

"Don't fucking move," he growls at her, his arms tightening around her waist. Keeping his eyes on me but his lips close to Mia's ear, he booms. "Everyone out. This is between me and *little mouse*."

"I don't fucking think so," I bark. "I'm not leaving you with her."

"Then she dies," he says, moving the gun to her temple.

Mia's eyes fill with tears as my heart begins to beat so wildly I can feel it in every inch of my body.

"Do as he says, please," she begs.

I hear footsteps behind me as people move, but I don't look back to see if they're doing as they're told or standing with me. I really fucking hope it's the latter.

"Bunch of fucking traitors," Cade spits, giving me my answer.

"You killed innocent people, Cade. You hurt people we care about. What did you expect?" My chin damn near hits the floor when I register Ashton's voice.

"I should burn this place to the ground with you all inside."

"Go on then," Tim taunts. "Light it up. Put an end to all of it."

"You'd love that, wouldn't you? Put an end to all the bullshit you've been forced to deal with thanks to your little *prosapia*."

"Leave her out of it," Tim growls.

"That's it, pretend like you love her."

"I do fucking love her."

"She's sick, Davenport."

"Takes one to know one."

Cade's lips twist in frustration.

"Please, just do as he says."

"I'm not leaving you with him, Mia. It's not going to happen."

Quicker than I can comprehend, Cade moves his arm, and the bang of a gunshot vibrates through me before Phillip cries out in pain as he crumples to the ground.

"Lincoln is dead, my own flesh and blood. Channing is probably dead," Mia sobs while the others gasp behind me, totally unaware of the state Channing is in right now," and Phillip can be next, before I move on to each and every one of you. Or you can run away like the good little sheep you are and allow Mia and I to finish this together."

Her eyes plead with us to do as he says.

"If you're lucky, I might not even hurt her. Well, not more than I already have." His fingers thread into her hair and he pulls hard, forcing her head back before running his nose up her exposed neck. "Hmm... you always did smell so sweet."

She visibly trembles but no noise comes from her as she stands her ground against the sociopath. "Leave. All of you," she demands after another second. "Please." Her eyes hold mine as I battle with what to do.

The gun tucked into the back of my pants feels heavier than ever, but I know I don't have the time to get it out and use it. Cade's faster than me, and I can't guarantee that I'm the one he'd turn to fire on.

I can't risk Mia.

"Okay, fine," I concede, taking a hesitant step back. "Get Phillip," I demand of the others behind me. He's alive but in bad shape, blood soaking his shirt.

Brandon and Ashton rush over, lifting him and carrying him out of the room while Tim and Alex stand beside me.

"Cade, you don't need to do this," Tim says softly.

"You don't know fuck all about what I need to do," he spits, staring at Tim like he's nothing more than a piece of shit on his shoe. So much for the loyalty I thought there was between them.

"Just let her go. Walk away. Enough blood has been shed."

"Get. Out," he seethes.

"Do as he says," I say after the longest two seconds of my life.

A small smile of achievement twitches at Cade's lips as the three of us take a step back.

I hold his eyes until I'm at the door, when I look at Mia. My heart splits in two at the tear tracks down her cheeks, the dark bruising on one side of her face and the fear in her eyes, but her fight is back. I can see her need to see this through and be the one to come out on top, and I need to trust that she can do it.

She needs this. She needs to be the one to end this however she sees fit.

"I love you," I mouth, making Cade scoff. "Hurt her and I'll kill you. I don't care how long it will take me to find you, but I will put a bullet through your fucking head and bury you myself." My warning falls on deaf ears. If anything, he looks bored by the whole situation.

"What the fuck?" Alex barks the second the door closes behind me. "You're just going to leave her in there with him?"

"Alex," I sigh, keeping my shoulder pressed to the door in an attempt to hear what's happening inside. "Mia can handle this. She's as capable as any of us at dealing with him. Better, probably."

"But he might—" Alex swallows his words when I cut him a look. I don't need anyone telling me what Cade is capable of doing.

"Get him to a fucking hospital," I bark, nodding to Brandon, who's attempting to stem his father's bleeding.

"You sure?"

"Yes, I don't need more blood on my hands."

"Channing?" Tim asks.

"On his way to the hospital. Cade shot him in the stomach."

Thankfully, they drag Phillip down the corridor and out, leaving the space around us silent so Tim, Alex and I can attempt to listen to what's happening inside.

"I'd be happier if they were shouting at each other," Tim admits.

I don't say anything, but I can't help but agree.

I have no idea how much time passes before a gunshot echoes off the stone walls around us and we bolt to the door.

My heart is in my throat as I storm into the room, terrified of what I might find.

"Mia," I cry. I stumble toward her. She's in a heap on the floor, and I frantically check her body for blood. "What happened?"

"It's over," she breathes, her voice cracking with emotion.

"Kingsley?" My eyes sweep the room, landing back on Mia's face, confusion tugging at my brows.

"Gone, Bex. He's gone."

29

MIA

Bexley hesitates, clearly not wanting to leave me with Cade.
"Brave, if not a little stupid," Cade remarks, pulling me further into the shadows, the gun still pressed firmly against my head.

"You don't want to hurt me, Cade," I say calmly.

Bitter laughter spills from his lips as he whirls me around to face him. "And how the fuck would you know what I want?"

"Because I read your journal... I know what your father did to you. I know that he broke you and then left you."

"He didn't leave me though, did he? He was murdered by... Your. Fucking. Father."

"And you got your vengeance. He's gone, Cade. My father is gone." I'm surprised at how calm my voice sounds, but something clicked inside me earlier, and it's like I know what I have to do now.

There's been too much bloodshed. Too much pain and anger and chaos. Gravestone is a man's world, but sometimes it takes a woman's touch to smooth out the cracks.

I won't spend my life living in fear.

It. Ends. Today.

Courage rushes through my veins as I stare Cade down. He has the gun, the power. He holds all the cards... but I have something he doesn't.

Love.

My heart is full of it. Love for Bexley. For Sasha and Channing. For myself. I have been beaten, bruised, and broken. Raped and left for dead. But I'm still here. I'm still standing. And Bexley's right; I have too much to live for. Too much to fight for.

Cade's eyes flicker with confusion. He expects me to cower, to cry and beg for my life. But I'm not the same girl who stood before him the night of the Eligere.

It might only have been a few months ago, but it feels like a lifetime. My heart is broken and my soul is scarred, but I'm still here.

I inhale a deep breath, letting it settle the nervous energy zipping through me. "What do you want, Cade?"

"W-what?" he stutters, staring at me through wild eyes.

"You heard me. What do you want?"

"I want revenge. I want those bastards to pay."

"So why am I here and not Phillip? Why did you send them away?"

His brows furrow, and he rubs the back of his hand across his forehead. "I... you're the weak link."

"Am I? Or am I everything you've wanted but never felt you deserved?"

"What the fuck are you talking about?"

"Your dad was an abusive asshole and your mom stood by and let him mold you, break you into... *this*."

"That's not—"

"Isn't it? You hate me, I know that. You want to hurt me. To break me the way your father broke you. But deep down, I think you want something else."

"No... no, that's not—" He tugs his hair furiously, pacing back and forth. Unraveling. If I push him too hard, he might crack, which won't end well for either of us. But if I push him just enough...

"I think you want something else, something better... you just don't know how to ask for it."

"Shut up. Shut the fuck up." He marches toward me and jams the gun toward me. "You don't have any fucking idea what you're talking about."

"Don't I? Admit it, Cade. You look at me and Bexley and you want that... you want someone who loves you, someone who *gets* you."

"Love?" He scoffs. "Love makes you weak."

"You're wrong. Love doesn't make you weak, it makes you strong. You can do it. You can pull the trigger and kill me and then go after Phillip and Bexley and the rest of Q. But you'll be killing the last shred of your humanity. You'll be giving up any shot you have at redemption."

The gun vibrates against my forehead as his hand trembles, my words hitting their intended target. "Or," I continue, bringing my hand slowly to his and wrapping my fingers around it, gently starting to lower the gun away from my face, "you can do the right thing. For once in your life, you can choose to be better."

My heart is a runaway train in my chest, beating so hard I feel lightheaded. The gun hangs between us, still too close for comfort. But I see the moment Cade decides. I see the second I reach him.

"I... I... Fuck. Fuck." His roar echoes through me, making my hairs stand on end. It's so full of pain and regret and slams into me. My natural instinct is to comfort him, but he doesn't deserve my comfort. The gun clatters to the floor as he backs away from me, burying his face in his hands.

I crouch down and snatch it up, grasping it in trembling fingers. It would be so easy to end him. To rid the Earth of a messed-up guy like Cade Kingsley.

But that's how we got here.

Vengeance. Blood thirst. Secrets and betrayals.

If we want to be better, we have to do better.

Still, I lift the gun, pointing it right at him.

"Mia?" It's a cracked whisper. "What are you—"

"It would be so easy to kill you. To end you." My voice quivers. "But I'm not you. I'll never be you, Cade. Even in this fucked-up town with its dark secrets and despicable traditions, I will always choose forgiveness... I will always choose love."

I take a step forward, and the chain connected to my ankle rattles. Cade stands as still as a statue, inhaling a ragged breath. "Do it," he barks. "Do it and put me out of my fucking misery."

He means it. Resignation swirls in his eyes mixed with blistering defeat. He wants death.

And he wants me to be the one to deliver it.

My stomach twists as my finger gently tightens around the trigger. It would be so easy...

"Do it. Just fucking do—"

The gunshot cracks around us, making me flinch. Cade cusses under his breath, but he's still standing, clutching his shoulder.

"You missed," he sneers, inspecting his blood-smeared hand. Pain contorts his face as he stares at me with a strange mix of fear and respect.

"No," I say softly. "I didn't."

Voices outside the door startle me, and I quickly add, "You should go."

"Go?" His brows crinkle.

"Go." My eyes flick to the stone door behind me. "Go, and never come back here. Because next time, I won't miss."

"You're letting me go, just like that? Why?"

"Because I might be a part of this world now, but I will never lose myself to the darkness. Now go, get out of here. Before I change my mind."

Cade dashes to the door, grunting in agony as he holds his bleeding shoulder, but he hesitates at the last second. Our eyes lock, something passing between us.

I'll never forgive Cade for what he's done, but part of me does understand.

"Go," I urge.

He gives me a sharp nod and pushes the stone door open, disappearing into the black abyss. I slump against the wall, falling to the cold floor beneath me, the adrenaline leaving my body just as Bexley and the others burst into the room.

"Mia?" he cries, rushing to my side. "What happened?"

"It's over," I breathe.

"Kingsley?" His eyes sweep the room, landing back on my face, confusion glittering there.

"Gone, Bex. He's gone."

BEXLEY IS quiet on the ride back to the Electi house. He grips my hand so tightly my circulation is cut off. His hard stare searches the darkness for Cade.

But he won't find him.

Cade is long gone, and something tells me he won't ever return.

Something changed between us in the chamber. By sparing his life, I showed him that things can be different. I showed him that he can choose a different path. It will never undo everything he's done, but I have to believe he'll spend his life trying to redeem himself.

It's better than the alternative.

More bloodshed and death.

"You're quiet," I whisper.

"You let him get away, Mia." He blows out a heavy breath. "I don't understand—"

"Hey, look at me." I slide my hand along Bexley's jaw, coaxing him to me. "Two wrongs don't make a right, Bex."

"And if he comes back?"

"He won't."

"How can you be so sure?"

"Call it a woman's intuition."

His eyes crinkle. "You're being so calm about all this."

"It's over. I just want to go home, take a long shower, and wash off the events of the night. And then I want to sleep for a week."

"You're incredible, you know that, right?" His eyes light up with awe.

"I'm just me, Bexley." Just a girl in love with a guy. "Any word about Phillip and Channing?"

"Phillip will live." His face contorts. "Channing is out of the woods, but he lost a lot of blood."

A shudder goes through me, and for a second, I wonder if I made the wrong call, letting Cade escape. But I truly believe it was the right thing to do. He's been a pawn just like the rest of us. Only his puppet master was a man full of hatred and dark deeds. Gregory Kingsley groomed Cade, and then Quinctus and Lincoln sealed his fate.

"I've been thinking about what you said." I say, burying myself into his side. "About changing things from the inside. And I think you're right."

"Don't worry about that now," Bexley replies, dropping a kiss on my head. "I'm just so fucking relieved you're safe. For a second, I thought I'd lost you." A shiver rolls through him as he tightens his hold on me.

"I'm here, Bex. I'm not going anywhere, I promise." My hand slides up his chest. "I love you."

"I love you too, so fucking much." Bexley leans down and brushes his lips over mine. "And I'm going to spend my life showing you."

"Your life, huh? Sounds kind of permanent."

"Damn right," he chuckles, and it's like music to my ears. "As soon as this is all over," he lifts my hand and splays my fingers, "I'm going to put a ring on it."

"As your prosapia?" I ask around a smile.

"No." Something flashes in his eyes. "As my wife."

"What about Q and all their rules?"

"Like you said, it's time for a change. And I'm thinking it's time for the Easton line to take back the power. But all kings need a queen." He smirks, stealing another kiss. "So what do you say, Mia. Will you be my queen?"

"You're such a goofball."

"But I'm your goofball." He nuzzles my neck, licking and kissing the sensitive skin there.

"Are we almost at the house?" I pant, my stomach coiled so tightly I feel like I might explode.

"Almost, why?"

"Because I need you, Bexley." I gaze at him. "I really, *really* need you."

"Driver," he yells.

"Yes, sir?"

Bexley winks at me and says, "Drive faster."

30

BEXLEY

The sound of a gunshot jolts my entire body as I fly toward the door at the sanctuary and throw it open with my heart in my throat.

"Mia," I cry, taking in the blood already oozing from her chest. "Mia."

I drop to my knees beside her, dropping my head to hers. She manages to lift her arm and wrap her warm hand around the back of my neck, but it doesn't reassure me at all.

"I can't lose you," I sob. "I can't. Mia, please."

Her hand tightens around my neck, the grip too tight for someone who's fighting for her life. "Bexley. Bexley, it's okay. Wake up. I'm right here."

Confusion fogs my brain as her soft voice fills my ears.

Ripping my eyes open, I find the most beautiful sight. Mia's mesmerizing hazel eyes.

"Hey," she says softly, a wide smile spreading across her lips. "You were having a nightmare." I stare at her as the image that seemed so vivid in my mind only a few seconds ago begins to disappear.

My chest heaves as I stare up at her, memories from yesterday flickering through my mind.

"It's over, Bex. It's over."

It takes a couple of seconds for her words to sink in, but when they do, I expel a huge sigh of relief.

She squeals as I flip her over so she's the one on her back. I brush my nose against hers, running my hand down the length of her body, enjoying the feel of her beside me without the oppressive weight that's been pressing down on us for the past few weeks.

"Me and you, Mia. It's our time."

A smile curls at her lips, but I don't get to see the result of it because I slam my lips down on hers and kiss her until we're both panting for breath.

After assuring everyone that we were okay when we got back last night, we had a quick shower together before falling into bed, but despite Mia's words before we got out of the car, her exhaustion took over and she crashed not long after, leaving me to hold her tight and tell myself over and over that this was it. We were finally going to get what we've craved for months.

We were going to get to be us. Openly, honestly and most importantly, publicly—because no matter what happens next with Q, we're going to be doing it side by side.

Hooking her leg up around my waist, I walk my fingers down her thigh until I find the burning heat of her pussy.

"Bexley," she moans, ripping her lips from mine as I dip a finger into her wetness.

Latching on to the soft skin of her neck, I shift myself between her legs and push another digit inside her. Her hips roll as I find her G-spot.

"Oh God."

Sliding her hands up my arms, she grips onto my shoulders as I up my pace. Her nails dig into my skin, the biting pain shooting straight for my aching cock.

Just before she's about to fall, I drag my fingers from her and replace them with my length. Both of us groan as I sink inside her, our eyes locked as a million promises pass between us.

"I love you, Mia. I love you so fucking much," I tell her, wrapping my hand around the side of her neck and rolling my hips.

"Bexley," she moans, her back arching before she lifts her head, searching out my lips once more.

I move slowly, needing to take my time with her, to remind myself that it can be like this. That we don't need to be consumed by fear, secrets and lies. That we can just be us—two people giving their hearts to each other as they embark on planning their future. Together.

Releasing her neck, I gently run my fingertips over the scabs that cover where her brand used to be. My heart aches knowing that she went to such extremes to rid it from her body, but as much as we both might hate that mark, it's forever going to be a huge part of our history, of what made us the people we are right now. We're not going to let it rip us apart, but we can use it to make us stronger.

He's gone, and he no longer holds any kind of power over us. The power is all ours.

Easton.

Easton is about to regain the power, and Mia Easton is going to be right there beside me as we take over this motherfucking town.

"Bexley, I need—"

"Shhh, baby. I know what you need. Me."

"God, I love you," she moans. "Only ever you."

Despite her pleas and the pain of her nails scratching at my back in her attempt to make me lose control, I don't. Not this time.

"I'll fuck you later, baby. Right now, I want to love you."

"Oh God." Her pussy ripples around my length, making my release emerge way faster than I'm ready for.

When she finally comes, her entire body trembles with the powerful orgasm and she clings on to me as she rides out every single wave before I follow her over the edge.

We lay side by side, locked in each other's arms for the longest time as we get control of our breathing.

"Can we stay like this forever?" she whispers after long, silent minutes, but as if someone's listening. Before I get to respond, there's a soft knock on the door.

"Bex, the hospital just rang," Alex calls through.

"Reality calls." Regretfully unwrapping myself from Mia, I swing my legs from the bed and pad over to the door. I crack it open enough to see Alex but stay hidden. "Is he okay?"

"Yeah. It smells like sex in there." His nose wrinkles.

"Jealous?" I ask, quirking a brow.

"Fuck yeah. It's been..."

"Whatever," I say with a laugh, cutting off his thinking. "We'll be done in a bit. Gather the others. We need to start planning."

"Planning what?" he asks hesitantly.

"We're taking over this fucking town, man. You ready for a wild ride?"

"Um..."

"Glad you're on board." I push the door closed and turn to Mia, who's sitting in bed with the sheets pulled up to her neck.

"Shower?" I ask, holding my hand out for her.

"Thought you'd never ask."

"ABOUT TIME, *BOSS*," Alex announces when Mia and I walk hand in hand into the kitchen almost an hour later with satisfied smirks on our faces.

Flipping him off, I pull a chair out for my girl before dropping down beside her.

"What's the news on Channing?" she asks.

"He's good. Still medicated, but they're gonna start bringing him around later."

"Phillip?" I ask with just a little less concern than Mia did for Channing.

"He'll live," Brandon shrugs.

"Got Mom chasing around after him like he's the fucking king," Ashton mutters, placing mugs of coffee on the table for both of us.

"Thank you," Mia says, smiling up at him.

I can't lie, I still don't trust the motherfucker, but my girl is fighting for him, so I agreed that he could come back here with us all last night and that we'd see how it goes.

"He's called us all in for a meeting at the house this afternoon," Brandon says. "He wants to debrief after yesterday."

"Great. Well, I've got a few things I want to say as well. Can you call Sasha and see if she'll peel herself away from Channing's side long enough to be there?"

"Pfft," Brandon scoffs. "You'll be lucky."

"This is her future just as much as it is ours. I really want her there."

"I'll see what I can do."

"So what the fuck was going on with Lincoln Kingsley?" Tim blurts out, addressing the elephant in the room.

"Baby," I say, resting my arm across the back of her chair and allowing her to tell her side of yesterday's events.

"Gregory groomed Cade... Abused him. Made him into his image. After he died, Cade got a letter. He thought it was his dad. It told Cade what Q had done and began prepping him to take over, to get revenge. But it wasn't Gregory. It was Lincoln."

"Why? What's Lincoln got to do with anything? He's got his own chapter. He was happy doing his own thing."

"He wasn't." She shakes her head. "He wanted power. He wanted Q. Everything." They all stare at her as she explains the whole story that she laid out for me last night." Cade's been abused, brainwashed and corrupted almost since the day he was born by men who should have been caring for him. He—"

"That's why you let him go?" Ashton asks, looking more shocked than anyone that she did what she did.

"Partly. There are a lot of reasons why I let him walk out. Ones I'm not sure anyone else will ever understand."

"He didn't deserve to be spared," Tim barks, startling Fawn, who's sitting beside him. When I sent out my request for this impromptu meeting after Mia fell asleep last night, I made it abundantly clear that it was to involve all of us. I was done with leaving the girls out of all the decision making.

"Maybe not. But in that moment, I made a decision, and I stand by it."

I pull her into my side and drop a kiss to the top of her head. I'm so fucking proud of her and utterly in awe of her strength.

"So what's next?" Brandon asks.

"I've got some plans. But I guess the biggest question is..." A ripple of anticipation rolls through the room. "Are you guys with us?"

"Us?"

I thread my fingers through Mia's and lift our joined hands. "Us. Things are changing, boys. You ready to drag Q properly into the twenty-first century?"

"Hell yes," Brandon and Tim say simultaneously as the others also agree.

"Okay, so this is what I'm taking to Phillip."

I lay out my plans for how I see the future of both Q, the Electi and Gravestone while Mulligan appears from out of nowhere to make us all breakfast.

After we're done, we climb into our cars, all swinging by the hospital to visit a still-sleeping Channing on the way to the Cargill's house.

Sasha put up one hell of a fight about leaving Channing's side, just as we suspected, but eventually, and with Ashton promising not to move from the chair beside him, she finally conceded and followed us out.

"You sure about this?" Tim asks as we follow the girls out of the hospital.

"Hell yeah, I am. Aren't you?"

"To stop hiding Fawn like she's something to be ashamed of, fuck yeah. I just have no idea how you're going to get Phillip onside."

"We're the future, Tim. He doesn't have a lot of choice. Plus, I've still got a gun in my pants. Pretty sure I could do a better job on him than Kingsley," I deadpan, only half serious.

"Let's hope it doesn't come to that."

"It won't," I say confidently.

Silence falls between us as we make our way to the cars.

"Are you ready to change the future?" Mia asks me, draping her arms over my shoulders.

"I'm so ready, baby."

"Ready to take over the world?"

"With you by my side," I wink at her, "hell yeah."

31

MIA

We're greeted by Phillip's security men and ushered inside. The Cargill's house is a huge gated property, equipped with state-of-the-art security cameras that follow us as we approach the front door.

"Mr. Cargill will see you in the study," an older lady with a round face and graying hair says, motioning for us to follow her.

"She does know you live here, right?" I whisper to Sasha, who chuckles.

"Don't mind Hannah. She likes to treat everyone like a guest."

"She's your housekeeper?"

Sasha nods. "Practically raised me and Brandon."

"This place is insane." I burrow into Bexley's side as we move down the long hall lined with framed paintings, and portraits that are a mismatch of designs but oddly work together.

I thought the Electi house was something, but this is in a league of its own.

Hannah reaches a door at the end of the hall and stops. "Mr. Cargill is waiting." She flicks her head to the door. "I'll bring you refreshments."

"Thanks, Han." Brandon shoots her a megawatt smile as he disappears inside. Bexley glances at me and mouths, "Ready?"

I nod, my throat clogged with emotion.

A few weeks ago, I would have trembled at the thought of meeting with a Quinctus elder. But not today. Today, I feel strong. Something shifted in me last night, and I know that they no longer hold all the power.

We do.

Quinctus needs us. They need the Electi and their prosapias to ensure the future of the traditions. But with Lincoln and Cade gone, and Marcus too, it's time for a new chapter.

A new way of doing things.

The room is big and sprawling with a huge sectional on one end and a long table and bookshelves at the other. Sunlight pours in through a row of sash windows, casting an ethereal glow over everything.

"I see you brought everyone," Phillip Cargill says from his position on the couch. He's stretched out with a blanket over his legs and his arm in a sling. According to the doctors, he was lucky the bullet grazed him rather than hitting an organ.

"Well, this concerns everyone, does it not?" Bexley steps forward.

"Very well." Phillip nods. "Come, sit."

We all take a seat. Sasha perches at the end with her father, Brandon on her other side. Bexley takes one of the armchairs, pulling me down on his lap while Tim and Fawn sit on the love seat, and Alex takes the other chair.

"Any word on Channing?" Phillip asks.

"He's out of the woods," Bexley says. "No thanks to you."

"Bexley, you have to understand—"

"What I understand, Phillip, is that you and the rest of the elders failed to protect your legacies, more concerned with pacifying Lincoln than finding Cade."

"Things weren't that simple," he goes on. "Lincoln has been a thorn in our side for years, but we rely—*relied*," he corrects himself, "on his connections. A lot of our associates will only do business with Lincoln."

"Guess they're going to have to get used to doing business with someone else." Bexley shrugs.

"Gregory Kingsley abused Cade for years. He groomed him into a monster... and Quinctus did nothing," I say. "*You* did nothing."

"It was between a father and son—"

"Dad!" Sasha gasps.

"Sweetheart, please understand that we have rules, traditions—"

"Spare us that bullshit," Bexley scoffs. "You talk about rules and traditions, yet look at what happened last night. My grandfather is dead, Lincoln too. Channing is laying in a hospital bed with a bullet hole in his stomach, and you—"

"Got off lightly," Brandon hisses. His outburst surprises me. He's always been so indifferent to everything, so carefree. But I see the disappointment glittering in his eyes as he watches his father.

"I didn't ask you here to insult me," Phillip snaps, flinching in agony. "I asked you here to discuss how we move forward."

"Actually," Bexley squeezes my hand, "we have a few ideas about that."

"Bexley, I'm not sure—"

"You're going to need someone to take Lincoln's place, get a handle on that situation."

"Now hang on, boy." Phillip's face flames as he narrows his eyes at Bexley. "You can't just come in here and take over. You are Electi. There are ru—"

"Yeah, about that, Dad." Brandon runs a hand over his jaw. "We're done with your rules. It's time for a new era. Time to take Gravestone into the twenty-first century."

"W-what the hell are you talking about?" He glances at his son and to Bexley and back again.

"You got to make all the calls, dishing out your orders and carrying out all your ceremonies..." Bexley inhales a shaky breath. "You got to play puppet master over our lives, but we're done taking orders."

"Now just you hang on a minute, Easton—"

"Bexley is right," Tim interjects. "The way we've been doing things, it doesn't work. Quinctus is two members short. The Kingsley line is extinct. Things are changing, Phillip."

He studies each of us, his eyes wide and clouded with confusion. Whatever Phillip was expecting before we arrived, it wasn't this.

"What exactly are you proposing?" He regards Bexley with a hard look.

"You give me a seat at the table. My grandfather is gone." He swallows, and I squeeze his hand in comfort. "I want to take his place."

"That doesn't seem too unreasonable. I'll need to consult the other eld—"

"There's more," Bexley says.

"More?"

"Yeah, you might need to write this down."

"CHANNING." I rush over to his side and take his hand in mine. "Thank God."

"It's good to see you too," he chuckles, wincing a little.

"Oh God, I'm sorry. I didn't—"

"Relax, it's fine. I'm fine."

"Really?" I stare down at him, my eyes brimming with regret.

"Really. Now get in here and tell me what happened with Phillip."

Bexley and Sasha move deeper into the room. Sasha climbs onto the end and tucks herself into his side while Bexley sits down, dragging me with him.

"You're looking at the newest Quinctus elder," Bexley says with a hint of sadness.

"For real? He bought it?"

"What choice did he have?" Bexley shrugs. "I laid it all out for him. Told him if he wanted to continue the legacy, things had to change. Starting with the prosapia bullshit."

"Fuck." He runs a hand over his jaw. "I bet he was fuming."

"Deep down, I think he knows it's the right call. Quinctus needs to move with the times."

"Does that mean I have to call you sir now?" Channing smirks.

"Fuck you, man. I'm doing this for all of us. If I had my way, we'd be long gone and—"

"Yeah, I know." Silence falls over the four of us.

"It means we can be together, for real." Sasha grins up at her guy. "I told them both."

"You did, huh?"

"Yeah, I'm done keeping secrets."

"That isn't all..." I add, shooting Sasha a knowing look.

"What? What happened?" Channing glances between the two of us.

"Sasha has something to tell you."

"So uh, how do you feel about dating an... Electi?"

"The fuck?"

She nods around a weak smile. "They're going to initiate me, if I want it."

"No fucking way."

"You should have seen my dad's face when Bexley told him that things needed to change. It was priceless. But they agreed. Female heirs can be initium."

"Wow, I don't even know what to say to that." Channing shakes his head. "And do you?"

"Do I what?" Sasha asks, her brows knitted.

"Do you want it?"

"If it means I get to choose who I spend the rest of my life with? Then hell yeah I want it." She leans up and kisses him softly, but Channing snags her around the neck and pulls her down, deepening the kiss.

"Maybe we should go," I whisper to Bexley.

"Yeah." He chuckles. "We'll catch you guys later."

They don't even come up for air as we slip out of Channing's room, closing the door behind us.

"I'm glad he's okay," I say.

"Yeah, me too. Come on." Bexley takes my hand and leads me down the hall. We step into the elevator, and the second the doors close, he pushes me up against the wall.

"Bex," I gasp.

"Need to kiss you, Mia." His fingers thread into my hair as he tilts my face and slides his mouth over mine.

I whimper when he presses the length of his body against mine, strong and possessive. His hips roll into me and I feel the hard outline of his cock.

"Is it wrong if I fuck you right here?"

"Bex, we can't..." A soft moan slips from my lips.

"Yeah, I know." He drops his head to mine, letting out a heavy sigh. "Besides, we have plans."

"We do?"

"Yeah. Come on."

The doors ping open, and Bexley grabs my hand like an excited kid. There's a sparkle in his eyes I've never seen before.

And as he leads me toward the parking lot, I realize what it is.

Hope.

BEXLEY DRIVES us back to Electi house. A shiver runs up my spine as we pull up outside the imposing building. I'm not sure I'll ever feel comfortable here after everything that's happened.

Coming around to open my door, Bexley holds out his hand and helps me out. "Hi," he says, gazing at me with nothing but love.

"Hi."

My brows pinch when he doesn't head for the front door but instead leads me around the back of the house, toward the lake. "Remember that night, when I found you down here?"

"I do." It feels like a lifetime ago.

"I knew that night, you know. Knew you were supposed to be mine."

"You did not." I swat his arm.

"Did too. I felt this tug in my chest, like the universe giving me a sign that you were the one."

"Bex..." It comes out breathy.

We follow the path down to the lake. It shimmers before us like a blanket of diamonds.

Bexley pulls me around to face him and loops his arms around my waist.

"I know what this place means to you now... so I talked to the guys, and they agree that we should move."

"M-move?" I gawk at him.

"Yeah. If you want to."

"I want to." I want nothing more. "But what about Phillip and Q? This place is—"

"Just a house. A house full of bad memories. We're taking things into a new chapter, so I figured a fresh start will be good. For all of us."

"They all agreed?"

Bexley nods. "Tim and Fawn are going to keep their own place, but they'll have a room in the new place."

"Ashton?"

His eyes flash with annoyance. "Yeah, I guess Moore can come."

"Yes. Yes, I want to move." I fling my arms around his shoulders and he chuckles.

"That's not all, Mia." Bexley gently eases me away and dips his hand into his pocket.

"Bex..." My voice quivers as the air crackles around us. He drops to one knee, gazing up at me, and I freeze.

"What are you doing?" My voice cracks.

His lips curve into a full smile. "Finally making you mine."

32

BEXLEY

"Oh my God," Mia whimpers as I pull out the small black velvet box that's been burning a hole in my jacket pocket since I dropped it in there earlier.

"The first moment I saw you here, I knew you were the one for me. Your beauty, your innocence, your zest for life blew me away... and despite the hell we've lived through these past few months, none of that has changed. I'm in awe of your strength, of your ability to forgive, your kindness, your pure heart."

Tears pool in her eyes and her bottom lip begins to tremble as she stares down at me, my outstretched hand shaking with nerves.

I know this is soon, that it's utterly crazy. We've basically just started college and got the rest of our lives to worry about marriage and commitment, but there is no doubt that Mia is it for me.

She stole my heart that night down here by the lake, and I know that no matter what happens, she's never going to give it back.

"You're mine, Mia. You've always been mine, and it's time to make it official. Will you marry me?"

"Yes," she cries, dropping to her knees before me, her tears finally spilling over. "Yes, Bexley."

She falls into me, knocking the ring box from my hand as she wraps her arms around my shoulders, holding me tight and sobbing into my shoulder.

"Hey, what's wrong?" I ask after a few seconds when her tears don't subside.

With my fingers twisted in her hair, I gently pull her away from the crook of my neck and look into her eyes.

She drags in a shaky breath and shakes her head gently. "T-there were so many times that I didn't think you'd want me anymore."

"Baby," I breathe, cupping her face in my hands and wiping her tears from her cheeks. "Never. I see you, baby. I see what's in here." I drop one hand to cover her heart, her ruined brand, the evidence of the nightmare we've endured together. "Our past is our past. I want to focus on our future."

She sniffles and nods, the beginnings of a smile twitching at her lips. "Me too. I want us, Bex. Just us."

Leaning forward, I brush my lips over hers. She eagerly returns my kiss, and in only seconds I'm drowning in her. For the first time since our very first kiss, when we had no idea who each other were, it's just us. We're not hiding, not running, not keeping secrets.

I lean her back and she falls onto her ass, and with my hand holding the back of her head, I lay her down, deepening our kiss as I settle between her thighs.

"B-Bex," she forces out through her heaving breaths when I release her lips in favor of her neck.

"Yeah, baby?"

She holds up the forgotten jewelry box. "Did you want to give me this?"

"You make me lose my mind, Mia Thompson." I laugh as I take it from her and open the lid.

She gasps when she takes in the simple princess cut diamond with a slim platinum band. "Bex, it's beautiful."

"Just like its owner."

Her tears return as I pull the ring from its velvet cushion and lift her hand from where it was resting on my thigh.

We're both silent as I slide it up her finger. My heart beats wildly in my chest as I stare at it in place.

This is it.

Finally.

"Mia Easton has a nice ring to it, don't you think?"

"I think it's perfect." I fall over her once more, my palms planted on the ground beside her head. "But I should warn you..." Her eyes widen in curiosity. "The traditions might be done, but I fully intend on branding you, Mrs. Easton."

Her eyes hold mine, the hazel darkening as she takes in the seriousness in my stare. "I wouldn't expect it any other way."

"Fuck," I bark, dropping lower and claiming her lips.

A moan rumbles up her throat when I drop my hand down her body and slide it under her shirt. "Bexley."

"What do you need, baby?" I growl against her throat.

"You. Always you."

"I'm gonna take you right here, just like I should have that first night," I whisper, pushing my hand higher until I cup her breast, making her gasp.

"Yes. Make me yours."

I know exactly what she means, and it makes me still for a beat as I think about what she endured at that monster's hand in the trees behind us.

But that's over. I know it'll continue to haunt her for the rest of her life, but just like her decision to let him walk away, that's something she's going to have to come to terms with in her own way. I just need to follow her lead and hold her hand through it all. Something I'm more than willing to do.

"Do you have any idea how much I regretted not having you that night?"

"Hmm..." she moans as I drag her shirt over her head and drop it to the ground beside us. "I have an idea."

My shirt soon follows before I drag her skirt down her legs, leaving her in just her underwear. The scars on her chest are still healing, and I can't wait for them to, because I'm desperate to put my plan into place the second I can.

"Fuck, you're beautiful." Dropping my lips to her chest, I kiss over the swell of her breasts until my lips hit the lace and I tuck my finger beneath to expose her nipple.

"Bexley," she cries, her fingers threading through my hair as I suck her into my mouth.

"Louder, baby. Make sure everyone knows you're mine. I want the fucking world to know."

"Oh God," she whimpers when I switch to the other side.

She writhes beneath me as I tease her, my name a plea on her lips. Slipping my hand behind her, I unhook her bra and pull it away from her body, fully exposing her to me. The cool breeze around us makes her nipples even harder, and she moans in pleasure even without me touching her.

Reaching out, I drag her panties down her legs, my mouth watering when my eyes drop to her slick pussy. Dropping to my front, I press my hands against her thighs and spread her wide.

"Bexley," she cries when I blow a stream of air across her swollen clit.

"Fuck, I need you." Surging forward, I run my tongue up her before focusing on her clit. I suck, lick, and nip at her as she twists her fingers in my hair and continues to cry out my name into the solitude around us.

"I want you to come all over my face, Mia," I growl against her, allowing her to get the benefit of the vibrations of my voice. "Only then will I fuck you."

"Oh God," she whimpers as I spear two fingers inside her and bend them just so.

In only seconds she shatters beneath me.

The moment she's come down, I wipe my face with the back of my hand and rip open my pants, shoving them far enough down to release my cock.

She stares at me hungrily as I work myself for a few seconds. "Bex," she whispers, reaching for me. "I need you."

"Not as much as I need you, baby."

Dropping one hand beside her head, I lower my head, capturing her lips as I run my cock through her wetness and push inside her.

She gasps, sucking the air from me when I fill her in one thrust. "Mine," I growl into our kiss.

"Yours."

I move my hips slowly, allowing myself to be swept away by the feeling of her beneath me, surrounding me, consuming me.

"I love you. I love you so fucking much."

"I love you too, Bexley."

With the cool fall air surrounding us and only the sound of our moans mixing with the rustling trees and the afternoon birdsong, we embark on our future. A future where we can be together and can openly fight our battles, side by side.

IT'S WELL over two hours later when we finally make our way back to the house. Mia is shivering despite the fact that she's wrapped in my jacket. We spent a little too long rolling around naked after the sun dropped below the tree line, and both of us are covered in grass stains and smeared in mud, but we don't care about any of it. As we push through the front door, both of us are wearing wide smiles on our faces, and more importantly, Mia's wearing my ring.

"What the hell happened to you two?" Brandon asks with his brows raised when we stop by the kitchen for a drink. Everyone else turns our way with amused expressions on their faces.

"Oh... uh..." Mia looks back at me, her cheeks burning bright red with embarrassment.

"She said yes," I say, lifting her hand to show them her new jewelry.

"Fuck. You proposed?" Alex barks, his eyes wide with shock.

"Sure did. Every king needs a queen, don't you think?"

"Fuck man, you're certifiable, you know that, right?" Tim asks with a laugh while Fawn rushes over to congratulate Mia and inspect the ring.

"I'm pretty sure we can all claim that title. Shit's gonna get easier from here on out. It's time to decide what you really want for your futures."

"Dinner will be in thirty minutes," Mulligan informs us, emerging from the pantry.

"We'll be back," I say, pulling Mia into my arms and leading her from the kitchen so we can shower.

"It's really going to be okay, isn't it?" she asks once we're both naked again and standing under the spray of the shower.

"Yes, baby. It is."

Wrapping my hand around the back of her neck, I push her up against the cold tiles and claim her lips.

Safe to say, we're a little late for dinner.

"HERE HE IS," I say lifting my beer into the air just over a week later as Sasha helps a still-healing Channing into our den. Despite his insistence that he's totally fine, she attempts to support him as he drops onto the couch opposite us.

"It's so fucking good to be home," he sighs as he sinks into the cushions.

"Good to have you back, man." I hand him a beer, earning myself a scowl from Sasha.

"He can't have that. He's still on medication."

"Since when do you care about mixing meds with alcohol?" Channing deadpans.

Her face pales a little, because really, she doesn't have a leg to stand on but still she manages to find an argument. "Since you've been shot and nearly died."

"I can have one. The pain meds aren't even that strong."

Sasha fumes as he makes a show of twisting the top off and tipping it to his lips.

Laughing at the two of them, I pull Mia tighter into my side and drop a kiss to the top of her head as Channing cuts off Sasha's complaints by shoving his tongue in her mouth.

"Ugh, I'm not sure I'm ever going to be okay with seeing that," Brandon mutters as he emerges with Ashton and Alex.

"But it's okay for me to have to see you with your cock down some whore's throat?" she barks, pulling back from Channing.

"You love it," he says, flipping her off.

"Fuck off. The only one here who gets off on watching his sibling going at it is Ashton."

Mia tenses before me as the memory of what Sasha is talking about slams into her, but she soon relaxes. All of that is long over, and thankfully, Brook actually does have a brain cell or two because she's kept well away from all of us since Cade's disappearance.

"Hey," he complains, his brows pulling together. "Sex is sex. I can imagine someone else's head on her body."

"It's still really fucking wrong, man," I tell him.

He rolls his eyes at me. "You don't have a hot sister—"

"Thank fuck," I mutter.

"You wouldn't get it."

"I've got a—" Brandon looks at Sasha. "Okay-ish looking sister, and it's still fucking wrong."

"Wow, okay-ish. That was almost a compliment, Bran."

Thankfully, Tim and Fawn appear, putting an end to another sibling argument. Tim lowers another six-pack to the table between us, and the pair of them drop onto the other end of the couch from Mia and me.

"So what have I missed, other than Easton taking over the world?" Channing asks, desperate to get caught up on real life after his stint in the hospital.

Conversation erupts around the room, and I sit back and watch them all with wide smiles on their faces.

Yeah, everything is going to be okay here.

We've still got a lot of work to do, a lot of changes to implement. But together, as a team, we've got it all under control.

I never thought I'd say it, but I trust every motherfucker under this roof right now with my life. And as long as Kingsley does as Mia assures me he will and stays away, I think the Electi might just have a bright future in Gravestone.

Mia notices my silence and twists to look back at me. "You okay?" she mouths.

"Never better, baby."

"I love you."

"I love you too," *my brave little mouse.*

EPILOGUE
MIA

One month later...

"How are you feeling?" Sasha slips into my room with Annabel.

"Oh my God, Mia. You look amazing."

"Thanks, Bel."

After everything that happened, I finally decided to offer her an olive branch. She's one of my best friends, and I know her betrayal came from a place of self-preservation and hurt, not malice. It wasn't easy at first, letting her back into my life, but if I want to move forward, I have to lay the past to rest.

I have to let go.

At least, that's what my therapist keeps telling me.

It was Bexley's idea that I talk to someone. Of course, there are some things I can't share, but they know enough to help me come to terms with things, and it's working. I feel stronger than I have in a long time.

We moved into the new house two weeks ago. It's a huge sprawling place near campus. In some ways it's very similar to the Electi house, but this one is a fresh canvas for us to make new memories and start over. The bedroom I share with Bexley overlooks the luscious vivid green lawns and pool. Channing and Sasha have a room across the hall, and the guys stay on the other side of the house. I've had enough up close and personal interactions with Brandon, Ashton, and Alex to last me a lifetime. We have new rules now: no sex in public. Of course, they have a man cave in the basement for when they want some privacy.

I guess some things will never change.

Life is good.

Classes are going well, Channing is almost completely healed, and Bexley and I are engaged. We've decided not to get married until after we graduated. Besides, we'll be joined in other ways.

"Here, let me zip you up." Sasha slides the zipper up and over my shoulders, smiling at me in the mirror. "He's going to die when he sees you."

"You think?"

"Oh yeah, it's going to give him serious wedding day vibes. Right, Bel?"

"Mm-hmm," she murmurs around a grin.

"I still can't believe they agreed," I say, inhaling a shuddering breath.

When Bexley announced he wanted to disband the tradition of the Eligere, the remaining members of Q weren't happy, especially Tim's dad. After a lot of back and forth, they finally conceded, agreeing that future heirs can choose their own partner—of course with some provisos: the person must be vetted, and the Coglio must be upheld.

So here we are. The first couple paving the way for a new chapter in Gravestone's legacy.

It's my second Coglio, but this time I'll be walking out of the sanctuary bound to a man I love.

A man I plan on spending the rest of my life with.

The girls give me some space to stand and begin fluffing out my dress. It has a ruffled tulle skirt that falls over my body like a waterfall. It could easily be a wedding dress, but I wanted to make an effort because, in a way, this does mark the start of our life together.

"Oh, I almost forgot." Sasha retrieves her purse and digs out a small pouch.

"What is that?"

"Just a little sparkle." She pulls out the diamond-encrusted hair brooch and slides it into place, at the crown of my curly ponytail.

"It's beautiful, thank you."

"I almost got you a tiara but thought that might be a little too much."

"I'm glad you didn't."

Sasha chuckles. My new nickname between our friends is Queenie, since Bexley made the fatal error of calling me his queen once around them. Ashton loves to give me crap about it. He and I have struck up an odd friendship over the last month, but it gives me a strange satisfaction knowing that he's with us, and Cade is out there somewhere alone.

I don't let my mind go there a lot, but sometimes his name creeps into my thoughts, reminding me how close I came to losing everything and everyone I care about.

It's why I'm determined to stand at Bexley's side, to make sure Quinctus don't ever allow something like that to happen again.

"Ready?" Sasha asks, and I take a small breath, glancing back at the mirror one last time.

Only mere months ago, I was getting ready for the Eligere. A naïve girl who didn't understand the world she was about to inhabit. I'd been starry-eyed that night, seduced by the opulence and refinery.

I'm not that girl anymore.

I'm a fighter.

A survivor.

I brush a stray curl from my face, taking one last lingering look at myself. I was a girl the night of my Eligere. A scared, meek little girl. But tonight, I enter Gravestone Hall, a woman. Tonight, I will walk among the men who run this town and hold my head up high.

I settle my eyes on Sasha and Annabel and smile.

"As I'll ever be."

Bexley

"DUDE, will you stop smiling? It's freaking me the fuck out," Alex laughs as we stand in the bar at Gravestone Hall, waiting for Mia and the girls to arrive.

"I can't help it."

"Aw, he's just excited to finally make an honest woman out of her," Channing says, jabbing me in the ribs.

"Who doesn't want a wedding night before their actual wedding night? You're just jealous," I point out to Alex, whose action has seriously trailed off since the loss of Cade and Ashton's whores.

"Tying down one woman for the rest of my life?" he asks, a fake horrified look on his face. "Couldn't think of anything worse."

"You're a shit liar, Rexford." Ignoring him, I turn to his cousin. "You ready for all this?"

He briefly glances over my shoulder, I assume at Phillip and Brandon.

"Hell yeah, I am."

Channing and Sasha will have their Coglio in a couple of months. Sasha is adamant that she wants to be initiated first so they can make history together as an Electi couple. Channing seems to be less bothered about that and more interested in finally being able to call her his.

The door opens behind him, and one of the waitstaff walks in.

"Gentlemen, please could you come and take your seats. Your ladies will be arriving shortly."

A bolt of excitement races through me at the thought of seeing Mia.

Breakfast first thing this morning at the house seems like a million years ago. The second we'd finished eating, the girls whisked her off upstairs to start getting ready. I have no idea what could possibly take so long, but I'm excited to see the outcome.

It's surreal walking into Gravestone Hall's ballroom, the place where some of the worst events of my life have happened. But this time, everything is different.

I'm going to walk out of this building in a few hours with my girl officially by my side, and unknowingly to her, without being branded like a fucking cow once more. Because scrapping the unions of Quinctus heirs isn't the only thing I've changed.

We're welcomed into the room, but it looks different from all the other times, because the top table isn't empty, waiting for the men to take their seats. It's already half-full with women. The wives of the elders are no longer banished to a table like the rest of the guests. They're up here standing beside their men, acting as their equals, exactly as they should be. The only women who are missing are our Electi girls, but that won't be for long.

"Could you all please stand?" someone says from behind me, and I rush over to join the others, standing beside Mrs. Cargill and an empty seat.

Sasha, Annabel and Fawn all walk in first, Annabel slipping into the room while Sasha and Fawn walk toward our table to take their rightful places.

I stare at the doorway, waiting for her to appear, but nothing could have prepared me for the vision that appears before me.

"Mia," I breathe when she all but floats to a stop.

She looks... fuck.

Her ivory gown is incredible and hugs her curves as if it's been made personally for her.

Her eyes meet mine, and I swear a current of electricity crackles between us before her lips curl into a soft smile and she walks toward me.

I can't take my eyes off her as she comes to a stop in front of me, her floral perfume filling my nose, and my mouth waters to lean forward and capture her red lips.

"You look beautiful," I breathe, barely able to force the words out through the lump in my throat.

"You're looking pretty handsome yourself, Mr. Easton."

"Less of the formalities please, Queen."

She chuckles as I wrap my hand around the back of her neck and pull her into my body. "I love you, Queen" I whisper in her ear.

"I love you too. Shall we do this?"

"Hell, yes," I say, pulling back to look at her.

Threading my fingers through hers, we sit down at the table and everyone else follows our lead.

"How does it feel, my king?" she asks, amusement sparking in her eyes as she notices everyone watching me.

"It feels... bizarre. How is this my life?"

"No idea. I've been asking myself something similar for a few months."

Phillip taps his knife against his glass, cutting off my response. I hate talking about what's passed. I know that Mia still struggles with it, but no matter what, everything we've been through has made us who we are now, and I can't really speak for myself, but Mia is fucking incredible. She still amazes me every day, and I know that isn't going to cease any time soon.

"Welcome, ladies and gentlemen, to tonight's Coglio ceremony. Today marks the dawn of a new era for Gravestone. Not only are we celebrating the love and union of two of our own, but we're also celebrating Bexley Easton taking his seat at the Quinctus table, and my very own Sasha is soon to become our first female Electi."

A few gasps and murmurs sound out around the room from those who haven't already heard the gossip.

"I'm sure many of you will agree that it was time to update some of our traditions and rituals, but don't worry—everything you love about our incredible town will not change. Starting with tonight's meal. So please, sit back and enjoy while we celebrate a new dawn."

"Wow," Mia whispers as the room erupts into applause. "He almost sounded like he believed that."

"Part of him does. He wanted change, unlike Gregory."

"Maybe, but I'm pretty sure we're pushing harder than he expected."

"Fuck it. This town is our future now. He's had his time."

Waiters emerge from the doors around the room, carrying huge silver trays as they start delivering the first of tonight's courses.

As always, the food is incredible, and for the first time ever, I'm actually able to stomach it and enjoy it. Even Mia clears her plate, which is something I've never seen at one of these ceremonies, I guess the threat of having everything you touch spiked with something can do that.

Despite the fact that I know what's about to happen, I can't help the nerves that race through me as we make our way down to the sanctuary once the meal is over, Quinctus before us and the Electi behind.

I wanted to have this ceremony elsewhere, but Phillip drew the line there. This is where the Eligere and the Coglio have been held for generations, and apparently that wasn't changing yet.

The room is decorated just like it was the last time we were here for this ceremony, only unlike that night, I don't find a seat with the others, but I stand at the front with my girl and listen to the same speech from Phillip as I did that night.

Most of it passes me by—my Latin is still pretty shit despite the fact that I'm expected to learn it, but more than that, I find I'm too lost in Mia's sparkling eyes to even register that we're not in the room alone.

She stares at me with such happiness on her face that it damn near brings me to my knees. Only a few months ago, I never would have thought that I'd be standing here promising to spend my life with a woman, but right now I couldn't imagine anything else.

This is it for me. Mia and Gravestone.

Who'd have thought that Sterling Bay Prep's star quarterback would have ended up with this life? Not me, that's for sure.

Phillip turns away from us to grab something, and I watch as Mia stiffens. She thinks she's about to be branded again, chewing on her bottom lip nervously before Phillip turns back to us with a black box in his hand.

"W-what's that?" Mia whispers.

"We're changing things up a little," I confess.

"No brand?"

"Yes and no."

She narrows her eyes at me before Phillip starts talking again.

"Mia and Bexley. Ubi concordia, ibi victoria." He lifts the lid of the box and Mia gasps when she sees two rings sitting on the cushion.

"Eternity rings," I tell her. "We'll just do things a little backward."

"Sounds perfect for us," she laughs as I pick up her diamond-encrusted band and hold it out for her.

I slide it up her finger just like I did with her engagement ring down by the lake a month ago, and just like that day, her hand trembles in mine before she turns to Phillip and takes my ring from him, repeating my actions.

The loud round of applause and cheers from our small crowd is almost deafening as I wrap my hand around the back of her neck and pull her to me.

"Are you ready for what comes next? I ask suggestively.

"More than ready."

Lacing my fingers through hers, I turn her toward our small gathering, but I don't really see any of them; I'm too excited for the surprise I've organized.

"Where are we going?" Mia asks as our car sails past our new home, heading for the other side of town. "I thought we had a date with our bed."

"Oh, we do. Just a little later than you're expecting."

"O-okay. Is this a new tradition?"

"Nah, it's an optional thing."

"Riiight."

She stares out of the window as we make our way through the center of Gravestone before the Town car pulls to a stop on the street.

"What the hell?" she asks, looking at the various businesses that line the street.

"Come on." Jumping out of the car, I reach back in to take her hand, aware of just how big her dress is.

The street is mostly empty, but the little group of young women outside one of the restaurants immediately turn to look at us.

"They think you're my wife," I tell her when their eyes remain on us as we get a little closer to them.

"Good. It'll stop them trying to take what's mine."

A growl rumbles up my throat. "Getting possessive, Queen."

"Too right. You're mine, Bexley Easton. This town might think they own you, but the truth is, you only belong to me."

"And I wouldn't have it any other way," I say, turning her and forcing her back into a doorway.

"Bexley," she says with a laugh, pressing her palms against my cheek to stop me from molesting her in the street, or whatever it is she thinks I'm about to do.

It soon becomes very apparent that the last thing she's expecting is for me to reach out and open the door I've backed her into and guide her into the building.

"Bexley?" she asks suspiciously.

"Good evening. I hear we're celebrating," a young, almost fully inked-up man says when he emerges from a back room to greet us.

"Um... t-thank you. W-why are we in a tattoo studio?"

"It's time to get our new brands, baby."

Her chin drops. Her lips twitch, but she doesn't say anything. Lifting my hand, I run my fingertips over the scarred brand over her heart.

"It's time to replace this, to make it ours and part of our future, not our past."

"Bex," she sighs, her eyes filling with tears.

"Follow me, and you can see what your boy's been working on," Jet says, gesturing for us to go ahead of him.

I've been here a couple of times over the past few weeks as he's helped me with our design.

"Take a seat please, Miss," Jet says once we're at his section, and I help Mia up before unzipping the back of her dress and allowing her to free her arm.

"Do I get to see what you're going to do?" she asks somewhat nervously.

I shake my head at Jet—not that it's necessary; he already knows what he needs to do.

"Nope. Not until you're done."

"Okay," she states, making my chest swell. She doesn't hesitate for a second as she rests back and allows Jet to prep her skin for the ink, her new brand.

I'm fascinated as Jet turns the design we've worked on together into a reality on Mia's skin. It's unbelievable and so much more than I could even imagine from looking at it on paper.

All too soon, the buzzing of Jet's machine ceases and Mia lifts her head from the seat.

"Can I look now?"

I nod once at Jet, unable to wait any longer to see her reaction.

He brings over a mirror and holds it in front of Mia. "Oh my God," she gasps as she takes in the floral design that now adorns her chest and completely covers the old brand that bound her to another. "It's incredible."

Tears spill from her eyes as she stares at her sore skin, at the roses and thorns that symbolize our lives, our past and our future. The beauty and the pain, the hope and the hell. The pure and the evil.

"You approve?" I ask, sitting forward in my seat.

"I love it."

"Good," I say, pushing to stand, "because you're going to be looking at it a lot."

Shrugging off my jacket, I undo my tie, pop the top few buttons of my shirt, and pull it over my head. "My turn."

"What?" she asks with a laugh.

"It wouldn't be an official brand if we didn't match, baby."

"But your Electi brand..."

"It's time for change, Mia. Who we are doesn't need to be branded into our skin. Who we are is inside. It runs through our veins. It's in our every breath."

She smiles at me. "Can I watch?"

"I wouldn't have it any other way. Time to carve out our future, Mrs. Easton."

"Bring it on, my king." A smirk plays on her lips. "Bring. It. On."

Did you first meet Bexley in the Rebels at Sterling Prep series?
Go back to where it all began with **TAUNT HER**

CAITLYN DARE
DELICIOUSLY DARK ROMANCE

Two angsty romance lovers writing dark heroes and the feisty girls who bring them to their knees.

SIGN UP NOW
To receive news of our releases straight to your inbox.

Want to hang out with us?
Come and join CAITLYN'S DAREDEVILS group on Facebook.

ALSO BY CAITLYN DARE

Rebels at Sterling Prep
Taunt Her

Tame Him

Taint Her

Trust Him

Torment Her

Temper Him

Gravestone Elite
Shattered Legacy

Tarnished Crown

Fractured Reign

Savage Falls Sinners MC
Savage

Sacrifice

Sacred

Sever

Red Ridge Sinners MC
Crank

Ruin

Reap

Rule

Defy

Heirs of All Hallows'
Wicked Heinous Heirs

Filthy Jealous Heir: Part One

Filthy Jealous Heir: Part Two
Cruel Devious Heir : Part One
Cruel Devious Heir : Part Two
Brutal Callous Heir : Part One
Brutal Callous Heir : Part Two
Savage Vicious Heir : Part One
Savage Vicious Heir : Part Two

Boxsets
Ace
Cole
Conner
Savage Falls Sinners MC
Red Ridge Sinners MC

Printed in Great Britain
by Amazon